"COMPELLING"
Chicago Tribune Book World

"A BRILLIANT NOVEL . . .
It will not only captivate you; it will break your heart."

Detroit News

"SPRAWLING, VASTLY ENTERTAINING"
Chattanooga Times

"The glow of nostalgia . . . An appealing forth-rightness and sincerity . . . The fortunes of two brothers who are as different as good and bad."
The New York Times Book Review

"THE ACTION IS FAST,
THE STORY ABSORBING . . .
It's bestseller time once again for Anton Myrer, who richly deserves the honor."
Houston Chronicle

MAIN SELECTION OF
THE LITERARY GUILD
and
READER'S DIGEST CONDENSED BOOKS

A GREEN DESIRE

ANTON MYRER

AVON
PUBLISHERS OF BARD, CAMELOT, DISCUS AND FLARE BOOKS

The author wishes to express appreciation for permission to quote from the following songs:

"If I Had You," by Ted Shapiro, Jimmy Campbell and Reg Connelly, Copyright 1928, renewed 1956 Campbell, Connelly & Co., Ltd. All rights for the United States and Canada controlled by Robbins Music Corporation. All rights reserved. Used by permission.

"Yesterdays," words by Otto Harbach, music by Jerome Kern, Copyright 1933 T. B. Harms Company (c/o The Welk Music Group, Santa Monica, CA 90401). Copyright renewed. International Copyright secured. All rights reserved. Used by permission.

AVON BOOKS
A division of
The Hearst Corporation
959 Eighth Avenue
New York, New York 10019

Copyright © 1981 by Anton Myrer
Published by arrangement with G. P. Putnam's Sons
Library of Congress Catalog Card Number: 81-15690
ISBN: 0-380-61580-0

The G. P. Putnam's Sons edition contains the following Library of Congress Cataloging in Publication Data:

Myrer, Anton.
  A green desire.
  I. Title.
PS3563.Y74G7   1981   813´.54   81-15690
                                           AACR2
First Avon Printing, February, 1983

For my father
and for
ROBIN

Green, green, I want you green.
Green the wind; and green the bough . . .
                              —Federico Garcia Lorca

He walked through the cool October night, his shoes sinking in the sand at the water's edge; he looked out of place in the gray business suit and white shirt, the carefully knotted tie. His pace was purposeful, but it was the purposefulness of long habit—anyone watching would have said he had lost his way, or was searching for something.

Lights from the marina across the channel floated on the tide like low, pale moons, casting a score of moonglades that shimmered with the passage of some small vessel, and then grew still. Far out in the harbor a bell buoy capped with an emerald light uttered a mournful *clang-dang,* the memory of the two strokes quivering on the night air long after the sound had ceased.

—Always that edge of danger about her. That hunger for forbidden shores . . .

He stopped, listening for the bell. His eyes had become accustomed to the dark now, and at the top of the bluff he could make out the silhouette of one house, grander than the other summer places, the railed widow's walk crowning its gabled roof. That house was dark.

—"Don't you tempt me, now!" Unable to resist it, daring it. Don't you tempt me—

The bell buoy struck again: one plangent note.

Here is where it all began. The sun-drenched possibilities, the world hanging there like ripe golden fruit for whoever could leap high enough to take it. And the temptation. That began here, too. So long ago . . .

A GREEN DESIRE

I

THE HOOK

1

They moved hurriedly down Church Street in the
late afternoon chill. Chapin swung their strapped
books like a pendulum against his legs; Tipton was
carrying the samples box carefully under one arm. In
the long field across from Horace Crowell's store Mr.
Hunnacutt and the hired man were bucking up an apple tree that had gone down in the big wind storm
that September. The blue blade of the two-man crosscut whined in a harsh rhythm, thin and trivial
against the hollow roar of the falls. The saw seemed
to control their lunging figures, as though it were animate and the men its obedient machines. Behind
them the orchard rose steeply to two wooded hills
capped by Macomah Mountain; black with firs, it
blocked out everything but the depthless gray wall of
sky.

Chapin kicked at a piece of ice and sent it skittering ahead of them. The mud ruts of the road—the
deep one in the center where the horses' hooves broke
it down, the narrower grooves on each side where the
carriage wheels cut their way—were stamped in
waves and ridges by the cold.

"Going to snow before morning," Chapin said. He
scowled up at the mountain. Both boys had the high-
bridged Ames nose and narrow, wedge-shaped jaw;
but there the resemblance ended. Chapin was slender
and good-looking, but there was a hint of uncertainty,

3

of vexed impatience in his curiously pale eyes. Tipton's face was bonier, rougher; there was a stubborn buoyancy in the way he moved. They wore corduroy knickers and pea jackets. Tipton's cap sat jauntily on the back of his head; Chapin had pulled the visor of his down over his eyes against the wind.

"—I hate winter," Chapin said with sudden low violence, and kicked at another piece of ice; the breath burst from his mouth in small jets of steam.

Tipton glanced at his older brother mildly. "It's not so bad."

"Ice and snow, ice and snow—cold and more cold . . . Who'd ever live here if he didn't have to?"

"Well, just kiss it so long, then," Tipton answered —and was instantly sorry he'd said it. Chapin's eyes flashed at him hotly, his face turned sullen. You and your big mouth, Tipton told himself.

"Well, you can always try Tonga," he rambled on. "Live on coconuts and mango juice. *They don't have any ice*. Imagine if you could figure out a way to ship ice to the South Pacific—you could name your price!"

"Well, you can't."

"Somebody will, Chay. You'll see . . . Here's Mrs. Gilman's. I want to try her again."

Chapin looked at the Federal house set back from its dun patch of lawn. "Mother told us to be back by four. Aunt Serena's coming out on the Boston train."

"We've got time."

"We better be getting on home."

"Come on, Chay—you're always backing away from it."

"No, I'm not."

"Yes, you are. Mrs. Gilman's a first-rate customer. Come on, now."

Without waiting for Chapin he unlatched the picket gate and started up the brick walk. The Gilmans' dog, a powerful Newfoundland, rose from his place by the stoop with a low growl and advanced toward them; one step, then another.

4

"Tip, *wait*—" Chapin was whispering from the gate. But there wasn't that shuddered wrinkling in the muzzle, the stiff legs, the lowering of the head that meant trouble. Tip had learned the ominous signs long ago. The big dog was simply waiting to see what his move would be. Prince would do the same thing in their own yard.

"He's all right," Tip said, going forward again, slowly, dropping his voice to a gentle sing-song. "Aren't you, boy? You know me. Of course you know me . . ." The animal barked once—a short, sharp signal, greeting and warning both; then his tail began to swing ponderously. Tip patted him on the head and ruffled his ears, turned again to Chapin, who was easing up the walk now, on the far side. "Come on, Chay. It's your turn."

Chapin swung back the storm door and slowly twisted the flat key of the iron doorbell. There was no answer.

"Guess there's nobody home," he said quickly. "Why don't we—"

"No—now, wait. Give her time to finish up what she's doing. Now. Ring again."

The door opened. A strange face, angular, hair bound up in a wild turban of yellow muslin, chamois cloth in one hand. What kind of woman would be house-cleaning at three-thirty in the afternoon? Piercing blue eyes flaring behind steel-rimmed glasses, jaw you could hang a lantern on. A perfect stranger.

"Mrs. Gilman?" Chapin asked almost inaudibly.

"No—I'm her sister. Staying with her. Who are you?"

"I—we're Chapin and Tip Ames." Chapin glanced apprehensively at his brother, and then the dog. "Could we—speak to Mrs. Gilman?"

"She's upstreet visiting, I don't know when she'll be back. What is it you boys want?"

"Well, we're—the thing is we're, uh, going around taking some orders . . ."

5

The woman's eyes narrowed still further, she was scowling now. All wrong. Chay was going about it all wrong. As usual. Couldn't he see? You had to make it attractive, exciting, a kind of adventure—you had to make a prospect feel she was taking part in a ceremony, a voyage of discovery soon to be filled with visions and wonders. It was like the ceiling of that church in Ravenna in Miss Abbot's stereopticon—all those little colored pieces winking and flashing, making up the whole design . . . They were going to lose a sale; it was as plain as the nose on your face.

"Orders?" the woman was saying impatiently; she was feeling the cold now. "Orders for what?"

"Well, you see it's—for soap. A kind of soap." Chapin faltered again. "But if this is a poor time for you—"

"Actually we're not representing any ordinary soap, Ma'am," Tip broke in. "We're representing *Shalimar* Soap. It's a unique opportunity because it's truly a wonderful soap, so different from the run-of-the-mill brands you see on the market. And the *reason* it's superior to other soaps, Ma'am, is because Shalimar Soap is made from oil of palm, the celebrated oil of the Spice Islands—an oil that works its way right into the very pores of the skin, softens it, restores it . . ."

He had the sample box open now, was holding out one of the smooth oval golden bars with its lotus design traced in low relief. "Just *feel* that, if you will, Ma'am. Isn't it the softest, creamiest texture you ever held in your hand? Just smell that tropical fragrance. That's *palm* oil, Ma'am, and nothing can match it . . ." The words seemed to flow without effort, exciting him with the very ease of their passage, like a Fourth of July sparkler glowing and fading, glowing and fading; it was as though a celestial magician had slipped into his skin and all he needed to do was listen to him, let him release his rainbow showers of persuasion . . . He felt utterly certain of everything in this world.

"Folks here in Holcomb Falls, all over the Berkshires in fact, are taking to Shalimar Soap because they've learned it's the most softening, fragrant soap money can buy. Because Shalimar lasts half again as long as other soaps. And in times like these that's important, I'm sure you'll agree." He looked up at her then, smiling expectantly.

"Bless my soul," Mrs. Gilman's sister said. Her eyes kept darting from his face to the cake of soap she still held in her hand. She'd forgotten all about how cold she was. "You sound as though you really mean it . . ."

"I certainly do, Ma'am. I won't sell a product I don't believe in, a product that would make a liar out of me, and that's the truth. Our mother swears by it—you'll find Mrs. Gilman uses it, and most of the other ladies in town. And for the man of the house, Shalimar is famous for working grime and grit out of the hands—that's the unique quality of oil of palm, straight from the Spice Islands."

"It certainly has a pretty odor . . ." She raised it to her nose again; her thumb traced the lotus design lightly.

Now. Close.

"Doesn't it? Now we have a special offer this season, a carton of twelve bars . . ."

The woman bought two cartons of Shalimar Soap.

"Perhaps while we're talking, Ma'am, you'd be interested in this new style of ring for the Gibson Girl collar," Tip went on smoothly. "It's made by the Standish people—see, it fastens both above *and* below. Guaranteed to hold any collar perfectly in place . . ."

The woman bought a packet of a dozen. Tip was writing up the orders when Florence Gilman came through the gate; she burst into laughter.

"Hello, Addie! See something you liked?" She was a heavy, good-natured woman with a round, cheerful face. "Hello, Tip."

"Well," her sister said, "it does seem like a wonderful soap, Flo."

Mrs. Gilman laughed again; reaching down she caught Tip to her gently and tousled his hair. "Don't you feel too bad, Addie—I can't *ever* turn him down! Neither can anyone else in town. He can charm the tail off a brass elephant! You can always tell when he's coming—whistling like a perfect wood thrush, that boy . . ."

Her deep, rich laughter followed them out the gate. They moved on downstreet toward the sound of the falls.

"—I don't know how you do it," Chapin said querulously. "I'm damned if I do . . ."

Tip pursed his lips. "You can't ask them if it's a poor time, Chay. You're practically *daring* them to agree, and close the door on you."

"But you could tell we were interrupting her—"

"Of course we were! Every time is a poor time. But that's the time you're *there*—you have to make it count."

"She wasn't interested in soap, anyway."

"Then you *make* her interested." He paused. "You've got to be more confident, more sure of yourself."

"But I don't *feel* confident!"

"Then you've got to act as if you are."

Chapin gazed down at Holcomb's Paper Mill, looming now like an impregnable brick fortress behind its screen of maples; the sullen growling of its beaters and pulpers mingled with the roar of the falls.

"I just can't *do* it, Tip. I'm standing there and they look at me—as if I'm trying to sneak into the parlor and steal something—and everything goes right out of my head. I can't *remember* what you told me . . ."

"You remember well enough in school."

"That's different. In class we're all studying the same subject. Here I just—can't think of what to say."

"Well, you've *got* to. If I can do it, you can! I can't do it all by myself."

"Maybe—maybe I can get a job."

8

"Doing what? You aren't even fifteen . . . We have to help Mother," Tip said with sudden sharp force. "She needs every cent we can make. We *have* to do it!"

Chapin dropped his head and they walked in silence for a time. In a low, fretful voice he said: "I wish Dad would come home."

"Well, he won't."

Chapin stopped. "How do you know that?"

"Mother said so. He isn't coming home, ever again, and you'd better get that through your head . . . He doesn't care about us."

"He does care! He loves us—he told me so himself . . ." For a moment he stared at Tip, his pale eyes dark with anger. "You hate him. You've hated him ever since last Christmas."

Tip thrust out his lower lip. "Maybe I do at that."

"—Well, you can take that back," Chapin shouted. "I mean it!"

Tip watched his brother. Chapin was fifteen months older, half a head taller, and weighed almost twenty pounds more. They'd had four fist fights over the past two years, and they all had ended the same way. But he couldn't go back on what he felt. Not about this.

"No," he said, and shook his head.

Chapin flung their books on the road and rushed at him. Tip dodged neatly, set down the box of samples with care, and turned to face him. Chapin came in flailing both hands; Tip blocked one blow, took one high on his temple, another on the side of his neck that almost snapped his head off; he grabbed his brother's jacket and hung on, teeth gritted. Chapin finally flung him off—suddenly wheeled around and kicked the box of samples with all his might; the side of the carton burst open.

"There!" he snarled. "That takes care of that—!"

Tip went for him, then. He was conscious of nothing but rage—a cold, measuring fury he'd never felt before. Chapin caught him on the forehead and again in the neck but it didn't matter—nothing mattered but that samples box. He hit Chapin full in the face, a blow he felt all the way to his shoulder, and the older boy backed away with a cry.

"You ever touch that box again I'll kill you," he said in a careful, quiet voice, not his own. "You hear me?"

They stood glaring at each other, panting. Chapin's eyes were filled with tears; he kept dabbing at his nose although it wasn't bleeding. Tip could see him trying to summon up courage for another rush. He waited, his rage draining away. His whole head hurt.

Just then the mill whistle blew—a high, piercing blast, like a runaway freight train, that touched off half a dozen neighborhood dogs in a howling chorus. A few seconds later the bell in the town hall tower on Main Street struck the hour; four even stately strokes, the notes bowling on and on through the thin November air till they came against Macomah Mountain and sent back one last dying echo, faint as memory. Chapin looked away then, dropped one hand to his side and felt his nose with the other; and Tip went over and picked up the box of samples.

"We've got no time for this, Chay," he said. "Let's get on home, now."

"No!" Chapin answered, but in a different tone. "You've got to take that back. About Dad . . ."

Tip looked at him steadily for a long moment. "All right," he said. "I take it back. Now, let's go."

"—Why, they're beautiful!" Aunt Serena Aldridge exclaimed. She was sitting in the kitchen in the platform rocker, the one their father had always used, near the window that looked down to the river. Months ago the Ames family had moved into the rear of the old house; the parlor had been made over for Miss Abbot, who was small and doughty and taught grades four through six. Miss Pierce, who wore a bright orange wig and whom Chapin had nicknamed the Poison Parakeet to the delight of the ninth grade, occupied their parents' old bedroom.

"Very—elegant—indeed," Aunt Serena repeated; you could see she was impressed. Chapin had brought out his stone collection and she was examining it with interest, her forefinger tracing the different samples nestled in their square compartments of black velveteen. Aunt Serena had a long, straight nose and clear blue eyes which she was in the habit of dilating extravagantly at crucial moments. In the muted yellow light of the lamp she looked formidable and handsome —like those grand French countesses just before the Revolution, or the Greek goddesses Miss Abbot talked about who were always swooping down on mortals and transforming their lives. Her rich chestnut hair was piled high in a pompadour; she wore a twill traveling suit of hunter's green with silk lapels. Aunt Serena always traveled in style—whether it was a year's tour of Europe or a quick trip by rail such as this one—with an awesome array of valises and hatboxes and jewelry cases; she said she liked the feeling of having her things around her wherever she might find herself. She had never married—through choice, Tip had heard his mother say once, tersely.

"Tip, take care of the fire, please," his mother said. She was standing at the stove now, making gravy. He went over and knelt on one knee, inserted the crank and shook down the ashes smartly, then slipped two small pieces of oak into the firebox.

"This one's remarkable," Aunt Serena was saying to Chapin. "Do you know what it is?"

"That's citrine quartz," he answered promptly. "It's also called false topaz."

"False topaz," she mused, holding the nugget to the light, turning it slowly. "Where did you find it?"

"Above the falls. The side facing Mount Greylock. I found this there, too." He picked up another sample. The mica winked in the lamplight, threw a pale saffron ray across his face.

"You want to become a geologist, then?"

He glanced at her uncertainly. "I don't know—perhaps." Then, with quick enthusiasm: "I like to collect things . . ."

"So do I," she murmured. "So do I." Her eyes rested on Chapin a moment longer, then she set the piece of quartz back in its proper place. "Well, it's certainly rocky country! The ride over from Pittsfield was the roughest I've had in a dog's age."

"The roads *are* terrible," Charlotte Ames answered. "Especially this time of year."

"I think I might get a Peerless. Or a Packard Landaulet. They say they make for a vastly more comfortable ride."

Charlotte Ames's jaw dropped. "An *automobile*—?"

"Why not? It's 1911, Lottie. One ought to keep abreast of the times."

"Mr. Russell has a Maxwell," Tip volunteered. "Pretty soon everyone will have an auto, he says. Everybody'll be driving everywhere—even clear across the country . . ."

"Well, not *everyone*, I think." His aunt's eyes had fastened on the ponderous golden oak chair where he was sitting. "What a curious piece, Lottie. How did you come by it?"

His mother turned from the stove, her drawn face flushed with the heat. "Tip got it for us."

"Tip?" Aunt Serena's gaze swung back to him. "And where did *you* get it, may I ask?"

"The company," Tip answered promptly.

"What company?"

"Shalimar Soap Company. They give away merchandise—furniture, dishes, things like that—with every ten-dollar order you place."

"I see. Well, it's hardly Chippendale but I daresay it'll serve. You must be quite the salesman. Is that how you got that clock?"

Tip looked up at the Seth Thomas wall clock

framed in walnut, its brass pendulum swinging gently behind the glass. "No—I swapped for that."

"*Swapped?* Swapped what for it?"

"Well, I found this smashed-up bicycle on the dump and got it running again with some spare parts I had, and then I traded with Henry Cutler up at the livery stables for a set of brass andirons. And then I swapped *them* with Mr. Prowse for the clock."

"Did you indeed? Well, well," Aunt Serena murmured, a faint smile on her thin lips; Tip couldn't tell if she was amused or displeased. "But didn't you want the bicycle for yourself?"

He nodded simply. "We needed a good clock, Aunt Serena. There's no sense swapping for what you *don't* need . . ."

The two women laughed then, and his mother said: "Honestly, Serena, doesn't he remind you of Papa?"

"A little." Aunt Serena was still smiling, but her fine blue eyes rested on him, steady as a beacon. "You know, we don't do that, Tipton," she said.

"Don't do what, Aunt Serena?"

"Go around scavenging on dumps, trading things. We're not the kind of people who do things like that."

"But—a perfectly good bicycle, going to waste . . . it's only turning something to account." He watched her, confused. What was wrong with what he'd done? It was just making good use of things, wasn't it?

"We did need the clock, Serena," his mother said; her voice was steady, but there was a defensive edge in it that troubled him. "We need a lot of things. Tip's been a tremendous help all around."

"I'm sure he has, Lottie." Serena Aldridge arched her back and smoothed down her jacket with a firm, pressing motion. "And how are you boys doing in school?"

"Chapin gets nothing but As and Bs," his mother said. "Last report card—seven As. Isn't that remarkable?"

"Aldridges have always had brains. And how about Tip?"

"—He just doesn't study enough," Chapin put in quickly, then bit his lip. He'd meant it in his brother's defense, Tip could see that; but when it came out it sounded like just the opposite—it sounded as though Tip were some special kind of loafer.

"And why is that?" Aunt Serena wanted to know.

"I'm out selling," he answered for himself.

"But your studies are important, Tipton. They'll determine your future position, you know. You're old enough to see that."

He listened to her stolidly, his eyes fixed on the emerald brooch pinned in the silk at her throat; it inspected him like a third eye, flickering brilliantly now and then, staring him down. Aunt Serena was rich. Grandpapa had been furious with Mother when she'd married Dad, and had made only a "nominal settlement," it was called. And then when the old man died, Aunt Serena had inherited the whole kit and kaboodle, from half a century in the China trade.

Now, stung by the memory, he said: "We need the money. We're poor."

"All right, Tip," Charlotte Ames said with a touch of reproof, "things aren't as bad as all that."

"But you *said*—"

His mother shot him a glance of intense irritation and he fell silent. Now why was that? Only the other night she'd been crying, sitting on the edge of his bed telling him they were destitute, she didn't know how they'd make ends meet, get through the winter—her tears falling on his wrist . . . and here she was making light of it, pretending things weren't so bad after all. It was because of Aunt Serena, then: you put your best front to the world—even if it was your own family. No matter what.

The silence seemed to deepen around them. The fire in the stove snapped and creaked, the clock stroked

14

its even, measured rhythm, driving time. Prince, sprawled behind the stove, sighed ponderously once.

"Boys," Aunt Serena said, "how'd you like to come live with me? in Grandpapa's house in Boston?"

Tip looked instinctively at his mother. She was staring at Aunt Serena, her mouth partly open, as though she wanted to speak; her face was white as milk—she looked as though someone had slapped her, hard. Then slowly a deep russet began to flow back into her cheeks and throat.

". . . Serena!" she said finally. "What are you thinking of?"

"Is it so outlandish an idea?"

"But you—"

"Why should they be penalized for life, Lottie. Because you were bound and determined to marry a charming drifter with sand in his shoes and not one ounce of moral responsibility—"

"Serena!" Charlotte burst out. "I won't have Lyman spoken of that way in this house!" She gripped her apron fiercely, released it. "I married for love, Serena. For love!" She nodded rapidly, staring full at her sister; the flush had nearly ebbed from her face now.

"Yes. I suppose you did. I'm sure you did." Serena Aldridge smoothed the lapels of her jacket. "Well, that's all over the dam. Now you're marooned in a Godforsaken mill town on the Housatonic, with no dependable source of income and two young boys to worry about. Do you want them to go along like this— peddling soap from door to door, *swapping* things? I'll see they're decently educated, go abroad summers— bring them up the way Papa would've wanted. You can see that, can't you?"

"Yes, I can see that," Charlotte said in a strained voice, "I can see—" She broke off, holding her hand to her mouth—all at once burst out weeping and sank into a chair.

Tip went over to her swiftly and put his arm

15

around her. "Mother," he murmured. "It's all right. Mother . . ."

She hugged him to her, rocking a little. "Oh dear," she said, her voice thick with weeping, "oh, dear me," and the awkwardness of the plaintive phrase troubled him more than anything else she could have said.

"All right," Aunt Serena was saying. "Have your cry, if it helps any. But it won't solve the problem, Lottie." She was sitting perfectly still, impassive, her fine hands folded in her lap. Watching the tiniest glint behind those intensely blue eyes, Tip thought: She's getting her own back, somehow. But over what he couldn't imagine. He only knew it was so. Chapin was hugging one knee and watching them all in that inconsolable, resentful way he'd fallen into ever since Dad had left for good; he hadn't even stirred in his chair. At that moment Tip hated him more than he ever had in his life.

His mother thrust him away then, almost rudely, and groped for a handkerchief. "—I don't know what's the matter with me. It's—it just doesn't seem . . ." her voice trailed off.

"You know how they'll end up, Lottie," Serena went on quietly. "Backtender on one of the machines over at the mill, or clerking in Luther Finch's bank. Or rubbing down horses at the livery stables. Or worse, a good deal worse . . . Do you want to stand in their way?"

"Of course not! It's not that, it's . . ." Her voice had become supplicating. "They're so *young* . . ."

"Chapin's in high school. Tipton's in eighth grade. You know how crucial these next years are. How about it, boys? Wouldn't you like to come live with me in Boston? You'd go off to preparatory school, play on the academy teams, then on to Harvard, with rooms of your own and young people of our sort . . ."

She ran on, looking so elegant and grand in the meager room, her voice light yet compelling, painting a vivid world of matches and cotillions, of summer

16

voyages to Europe—those stereopticon glories of Miss Abbot's!—the Arc de Triomphe and Michelangelo's David, spinning intimations of even lordlier adventures—the pyramids and the Parthenon, even the Taj Mahal; all the things that went to make a man a gentleman, a person of substance, worthy of leadership in whatever field he might choose . . .

It was a sales pitch—a dazzling one. He knew it for what it was. And yet there was a difference: she was so certain of herself, of the glittering world she offered, that there was no need for persuasion. Troubled, half mesmerized, he watched her—stole a glance at his brother; Chapin's eyes were wide, his face rapt . . . This was the real power of money, then: it could whisk you away from hand-me-downs, from paper routes and sacks of cannel coal, snatch you up and set you down in marble halls and green pastures, place the world in your hand as easily as the bestowal of one roseate pearl. It could turn some people certain, turn others afraid . . . Money.

"Can we go, Mother?" Chapin was saying eagerly. "Can we?"

Charlotte Ames looked down at her hands, and after a moment nodded. "Your aunt is being—it's a very generous offer. The chance of a lifetime . . . It's only right that you should go."

"Good!" Aunt Serena rose, brushing at her skirts. "That's settled. All right, boys—pack up now. The driver'll be back in twenty minutes."

"Oh," her sister said, "can't you stay, Serena? Even for supper?"

"No—we'll be taking the morning train. I've reserved rooms at the inn—and I want to get over there before the snow flies."

"Aunt Serena," Tip heard himself say.

"Yes? What is it, Tipton?"

He got up and stood beside the golden oak chair, gripping its back. "Aunt Serena—I'm going to stay here."

17

She stopped abruptly, and turned; her eyebrows rose. He heard his mother make a low, inarticulate protest. His heart was thumping, washing the blood thickly to the front of his head.

"Of course you're coming—it's decided. Don't you appreciate what I've been telling you?"

"Yes, Aunt Serena. I'm grateful to you for—for so generous an opportunity. But I'm going to stay here. With Mother."

His aunt gave a snort—part laughter, part irritation—threw open her hands. "But your mother *wants* you to come. She agrees it's the best way out of a bad situation." To Charlotte she said: "He's too young, he doesn't realize what's at stake . . ."

"No, Ma'am," he answered. "I'm old enough."

Words. They were so important, magic globes that lighted the way to so many things—but they were only as good as the man who spoke them. Words could pretend to be anything, paint any landscape, promise any kingdom; but what about the speaker? It was people that mattered. Aunt Serena had flung up all these visions of gondolas and grottos and minarets, but what mattered was Mother, sewing late, squinting into the lamplight, leaning forward talking to Mr. Finch about the mortgage payments, or asking Horace Crowell about another month's extension on the grocery bill . . .

His Aunt Serena was coming toward him slowly; she put her hands on his shoulders. Her eyes, dilated in that curious way, held him like a beacon.

"Come now, Tipton. *Why* won't you come?"

They were all watching him in silence. He shrugged, feeling miserable, overborne; but he never wavered. "I don't want to. I just—feel I should stay, that's all."

"I should think you'd want more out of life than—this." Her lip curled faintly. "Do you intend to run around selling soap all your life?"

He said: "I might be selling more than that."

"Tipton!" his mother reproved him sharply.

"No—let him go on. Such as what?"

"I don't know yet." After his burst of defiance he felt troubled again, hedged about. "What's wrong with selling?"

"Nothing, I suppose. It has its place in the scheme of things. Only you could go far, far beyond that. If you chose."

He was being baited. He couldn't have said why or to what end, but he knew it without question, and it angered him.

"—I can sell anything," he declared.

"Could you?"

"I know I can." He watched her carefully, feeling apprehensive and certain all at once; he had never spoken to *any* adult like this before, let alone Aúnt Serena. He said: "There's no limit to the things I can do."

She laughed, then—a single sharp note, and shook her head. To her sister she murmured, "Just like Papa. You're right, Lottie. And that old fool Comstock prating about how it's all environment, that heredity doesn't count any more . . ." She turned to the boy again. "You'll see your mother now and again. You're not too young to face the world. Grandpapa used to say: Opportunity once forsaken is opportunity lost forever. Your mother can't do anything for you now—can't you see that? What do you want?"

He didn't mean to say it: he felt beleaguered, played with. Stung by her last assumption he burst out: "You could give Mother her share—!"

Serena Aldridge started. "What share?"

"*Her* share! Of Grandpapa's money . . ."

"Tipton!" his mother said.

". . . What a curious thing to say," Aunt Serena remarked in a cool, musing tone. "Wherever did he get that notion?"

"I'm sure I don't know, Serena," his mother answered, and now her voice was bitter, "I can tell you he never heard it from *me*."

Yet she was frightened, too; he could tell. Why was that? She was angry with *him* for saying that—yet it was no more than the truth.

"We do not discuss money in our family, Tipton," his aunt said.

No, he thought, angry all over again, his heart thumping. No, only what it can do. And can't.

"When you're older—a good deal older—you'll learn why things happen as they do. I can see I've misjudged you, Tipton. That's a pity."

She was angry with him, too, but not for the same reasons. She wanted him to come live with her, *more* than she did Chapin. The pitch had been for him—and he wasn't buying. Her gaze was cold now, cold as a northern sky; but this time he did not drop his eyes from hers.

Abruptly she turned away, her skirts rustling dryly in the still room. "Well. Skip up to your room, Chapin, and pick out what you want to take with you. Never mind too many clothes—I'll outfit you soon as we get home." She went quickly through the back pantry to the privy.

"Chapin," Charlotte Ames said, "you go on. I'll be up in a minute."

Chapin paused uncertainly, glanced at Tip. His left cheek where Tip had hit him was faintly swollen. He started to say something, then left the kitchen.

"Tipton. Listen to me." His mother came up to him. "Don't—do something rash . . . Tell her you'll go."

"No, Mother."

"Why are you so stubborn? It can be your *life* . . ."

"I can't help that."

"Tipton, I grew up with her, I know what she's like —once you turn her down she never forgives you. Never." Her hand was moving nervously through her hair. "From this day on she'll never raise a finger for you. I know it."

"I can't help that," he repeated doggedly, though he felt obscurely fearful. "I'm going to stay with you, Mama."

"Tip, I'll be all right."

"I know." She wouldn't, though. She wouldn't be able to manage without him. He would have to take care of her, and he would. It was that simple. "I know," he said again. "I'll be here with you."

"Oh, Tip . . ." She sobbed once, a sudden impulsive catch in her throat, and hugged him to her; an embrace that drove the air out of his lungs. "Oh Tip, you're such a comfort! But I'm afraid you're making an awful mistake . . ."

They had Chapin packed in ten minutes, and went out into the sharp cold where the horses were stamping restively in the shafts; the liveryman stowed the suitcases and boxes in the back of the old black Brougham.

"Goodbye, Tipton," Aunt Serena said crisply; she pressed her cheek against his once. "Perhaps you'll come visit us some summer at Turk's Head. On the Cape. Will you?"

"Thank you, Aunt Serena. I'd like to very much."

"Good." She embraced her sister. Climbing into the carriage she settled herself in and began working the heavy buffalo robe around her hips and feet, issuing orders to the driver.

"Tip . . ." Chapin was standing in front of him; he looked unnaturally excited and unhappy.

"Yes?"

"Tip, I wish you were coming—it'd be so much fun, going off to school together."

"Well," he said, and his voice was sharper than he meant it to sound, "I'm not."

"I know. Tip—"

"Come along, Chapin," their aunt called from the carriage, "don't stand there like a cigar store Indian!" She gave a high exultant laugh, and waved to her sister. Chapin hung there a moment longer.

21

"Tip?"

"Yes?"

"Tip, I'm sorry—about the samples box."

"It's all right. I can get another."

"I wish—"

"Come *along*, Chapin!"

They shook hands once; then Chapin ducked into the carriage, and the driver clucked to his horses. When Chapin leaned out of the window Tip could see his eyes were filled with tears.

2

"—Then Captain Howland put me on the whale again, and this time I got both irons in, clear to the hitches," Manuel Gaspa said. "I always liked the close chance." He teetered back precariously in the black walnut captain's chair, powerful shoulders slumped, great gnarled hands hooked in green-and-orange suspenders. His face was like flayed leather, and his eyes, almost hidden under their deep folds of skin, kept searching the harbor restlessly.

"But this old bull was like no whale *I* ever see. He upped flukes and stood on his beam ends, come up under Mr. Bannister's boat and sent it fifty feet in the air, men and gear flying like buckshot. He took us on a sleighride round and round the ship till we couldn't see a thing for the waterspouts and millrace gales. Then he backwatered a while and watched us with that great pale blue eye of his, thinking up more devilment . . ." He drew a hand back and forth below his sweeping silver mustachios, shifted his quid with care to the other cheek.

"Then what, Grampa?" Jophy cried. She was squirming in her seat with excitement, her eyes flashing. "Then what happened?"

"Another carefree day in the whaleboats," Annabella Gaspa said, and tapped the base of the heavy clothes iron with the wetted tip of her finger.

23

"Is that when your leg got bent crooked?" Jophy asked him.

"No-no, Josefína—that's when I got this!" Staring balefully at his granddaughter he raised his woolen shirtsleeve, exposing the terrible scar that ran in a jagged white furrow from his wrist all the way to the armpit. Jophy laughed and nodded; she'd seen it many times before.

"Menin Jesu', forgive us our sins," Grama said.

"Next he went for Joe Diaz' boat and stove in the bows with one blow of his flukes. Then he made for the ship, and pitchpoled himself clean over the bowsprit, fouling the dolphin striker and martingale. Then he caught sight of me. He took to lobtailing, smashed my boat to kindling. First thing I saw when I broke surface was that old bull, circling me like a gray sea tiger, watching me all the time with that pale blue eye. Then he come for me, head-to-head, and dropped that long lower jaw of his—all rows and rows of gleaming teeth. Know what went through my mind at that moment?"

"*What,* Grampa?"

"Why, I thought he'd try out to eighty-five barrels, at the least." He rolled an eye at her and grinned his lean, roguish grin.

"Aw, Grampa!" Her laughter burst around them like spring rain. "You're ragging me!"

"Now, why do you tell these foolish tales?" Grama demanded crossly. "She won't know half whether to believe you or not. I don't myself."

He smiled, watching the harbor again. "Won't do no harm . . ."

"It was dangerous enough without you turning it into some sly Yankee joke." She was a heavy-set woman with a stern, handsome face; her hair was still a rich jet black. "Sometimes I listen to you and I think I ought to go out and find myself another man."

"You'd be sorry you did, Bella." He watched her a moment, and laughed softly. "Wouldn't you, Bella?"

24

"Go chase yourself," she answered; but she flashed him a sudden, radiant smile that instantly transformed her into a younger, far more beautiful woman.

"Josefina knows when I'm joking." Reaching out he drew her to him, ran his rough hands through her silky black hair. "A minha menina encantadora . . ."

"Enough," Grama said. "Don't go turning the girl's head."

"Bella—she's only twelve . . ."

"I don't want her to grow up reeling with romantic nonsense, like all you Gaspas."

She's a Gaspa."

"Like Joe. Walking down Dock Street with that damn-my-eyes tilt to his hat, thinking every girl who should happen to look at him was dead gone."

Manuel Gaspa laughed. "I was like that. Remember?"

"And is that a matter for pride?"

"If it's true."

"A-ha! But if it isn't—? What then? Then you are stripped naked in your foolishness before the world—and the world will laugh you to scorn . . ."

Jophy smiled, listening. They pretended to quarrel, but they never did. It was their way. They were the only parents she'd ever had. Her mother had died when she was born, her father had been lost at sea when she was five. Of her mother all she had were snips and scraps. Her mother had been too self-effacing; she hadn't fought hard enough against what Grama called the land sharks of the world. Was that why she died? she'd asked once, and Grama had set down what she was doing and turned to face her.

"No, criança—she died for no other reason than that she was a woman." And her face had darkened, her eyes had flashed with the biting irony for which she was renowned throughout the Lower Cape. "It is one privilege men are not too anxious to share . . ."

Of her father what Jophy remembered was a sense of violent movement—Joseph Gaspa was always in motion: he burst into a room, swept her up in his arms with a shout, rushed out again; doors banged open or crashed shut, his flaring, furled-down sea boots thundered along the hallway—his passage was as headlong as his own schooner *Sea Eagle,* carrying on every stitch of sail, lee rail awash . . . Of all the Grand Banks captains he had been the most impetuous, the most fearless—

"Jophy." Grampa had slipped something out of his shirt pocket, was cutting it in two deftly with his jackknife. "Here you go."

She put the piece of secalhal in her mouth and began working it soft, her mouth flooded with the rich, dense taste of codfish and salt. It was better than hoarhound or gumballs, better even than Baker's chocolate; better than anything except Canton ginger.

"Teddy Roosevelt," Grampa was saying, his voice furry with tobacco juice. "Going big game hunting in Africa." He laughed—the single, deep, explosive bark. "Big game! Like to see him draw up on a proud old sperm bull in half a gale, with darkness coming and the ship five miles astern . . . Lot of good that elephant gun would do him then!"

Chewing on the morsel of flaked cod, Jophy watched him; his eyes still scanned the harbor below the windows, but they had turned opaque. He would call up some wild and wonderful adventure in a few moments; she could feel that fierce tremor of anticipation deep inside her. More than anything on earth she loved to listen to him. He'd told her of volcanoes soaring out of thunderheads dark as night, of tropic beaches white as sugar against dazzling turquoise and emerald lagoons, waterspouts like swaying pillars of death, sunrises like the breathtaking birth of the earth itself. At the age of fifteen, to escape eight years' servitude in the army, he had swum out to a whaleship anchored off his home island of Fayal in the Azores, and signed on as cabin boy; and in sixty years he had made the whole mysterious world his

26

own. He'd seen Fiji warriors with ferociously painted faces and bone rods driven through their nostrils, Madagascan sultans with jewel-encrusted scimitars, proud naked Corromantee women sold into slavery, Papuan divers hunting gold-lip deep in the coral forests of Torres Straits . . . a sweeping diorama that had inflamed her dreams. Listening through the long winter evenings with the wind booming around the house like great sails backed and filled, like cannonades, she was seized with a longing so fierce she thought her heart would burst out of sheer need . . .

"Sail-o," he murmured now. She followed his gaze, watched the schooner round the point, floating effortlessly on the southwest breeze, a dream of motion on the fretted blue plate of the harbor. "What ship, Jophy?"

"*Cormorant*," she answered promptly. "Captain Cardosa."

"What carrying?"

"Jib, jumbo, fores'l, mains'l, main topmast stays'l. Dousing fores'l now," she added.

"What sails furled?"

"Fore and main gaff tops'ls, flying jib," she chanted, and the old man laughed and nodded.

"Why make her learn such nonsense, Manny?" Grama said.

"Want her to be a good sailor." He hugged her to him again with sudden soft ferocity. "A minha marinheira activa, my Josinha . . ."

"She will never be a sailor. She is a woman, she needs to learn other things. I want her to be a part of *this* country, as it grows."

"The sea is our country," Manuel Gaspa said.

"Ridiculous!" Grama set down the iron like a scepter. "The sea is no country at all—the sea is a great, watery beast waiting to swallow you down alive . . ."

"No." He shook his head. He was still holding Jophy with the great scarred arm. "We are Portu-

27

guese, Bella. We give ourselves to the sea. And in return it gives us our power."

"*What* power, in the name of God? Power to freeze to death in Bering Straits, to perish of thirst on the Line—power to be run down in a Banks fog by some Cunarder making twenty-five knots that can't be bothered to use its foghorn because it might spoil the beauty sleep of the money-bags passengers? Such *unique* powers, *Captain* Gaspa!"

Grampa winked at Jophy—dropping one eyelid so quick only she could have caught it—and looked away to the harbor again, where the *Cormorant,* her remaining canvas rippling like silk, was luffing up to her mooring. Grama was a pastmistress of irony—Jophy had heard Judge Trench call her that one afternoon. Grama had taught herself (she'd had no education beyond the fifth grade), could recite passages from Shakespeare or Luis de Camões if the mood was on her; her memory was formidable; her wit biting. She had fallen into the habit of appearing regularly at the Barnstable Courthouse where, in the guise of offering to translate for the benefit of the court the testimony of a Portuguese woman who had little or no English, she would move with infinite subtlety into an impassioned plea for the defendant. Her most recent triumph had been interceding over a threatened foreclosure.

"—and how could this lady, so recently widowed, with four children to care for and one of them a child at breast—your Honor, how could this grieving lady have realized, burdened with the struggle to keep body and soul together as she is, that her landlord is in the employ of both Andicott Fisheries *and* the Great Atlantic and Pacific Tea Company? How could she have foreseen that the plaintiff would choose this very moment—with her husband believed dead in one of the worst Grand Banks gales in forty years—to present this bill of foreclosure? Truly a wonderfully accurate word, your Honor, this word *foreclosure*—since it

28

seeks to throw upon the streets a bereft woman *before* she can avail herself of the very means to satisfy its demands! Is the plaintiff by any chance *unaware* of the fact—as I know your Honor is not—that were it not for men like Antone Gonsalves, or your Honor's own brothers, there would *be* no Andicott Fisheries to hire *individuals* such as the plaintiff—that there would in fact be no *Great* Atlantic and Pacific Tea Company at *all*—?"

The courtroom had burst into an uproar—it was her finest hour. When she arose to "translate" some weeks afterward, Judge Trench's frosty, forbidding Yankee mouth quirked at the corners as he said: "Shall we now hear the opinion of the Portuguese Lawyer?" In the laughter Grama had nodded and said: "Sir, it is a title I will wear with honor! . . ."

"Now, Bella," Grampa was saying, "you know that's not what I meant. Why did they always want a Portuguese at the masthead? Because we raised the most whales . . ."

"And why not? They could make more money out of you, while *you* stared yourselves blind over fifty thousand miles of ocean!"

"—We know where the cod is running, the bonita. We have the nose for fish. The nose for weather, too . . ."

"Oh, we have powers all right, wonderful powers—to line *their* pockets, build *their* grand houses for them, send *their* sons to the Harvards and Yales! And what did you ever get out of it, beyond scars that would make a Turk cross himself in terror? Sixty-seven dollars for a three-years' voyage!"

"Hard-luck cruise," he murmured.

"Com certeza!"

"What about that third voyage, in the *Amelia Snow?* We took seven whales in one day, we traded for empty casks with any ship we spoke, we had barrels stowed in the main cabin—we filled everything

29

but the cook's pots! I nailed the broom to the foretopmast myself . . . What about *that* cruise?"

"Yes, and what did you get out of it, beyond a sprained back and a few hundred dollars? No! They were *all* hard-luck cruises—except for Old Man Wetherbee and his pack of vultures and sea-lawyers—*they* showed a profit every time! Giving themselves airs . . ." She raised the iron and shook it like a lance. "Never trust a Yankee, Jophy—never! He'll pick you clean as a tinker mackerel—and all the while sniveling like an undertaker, till you're ready to make a dozen novenas for the poor devil . . ."

"Now, Bella. They were good men too, plenty of them. The Yankees. Good sailors, good whalemen. Took their chances along with everyone else."

"Madmen," she said implacably. "It is madness to attack a whale in a twenty-eight-foot canoa with a piece of bent iron. You were all mad. And you paid the price for it."

"By the great Jesus, we did." He laughed softly, and brushed his mustaches again. "Well, it's all over and gone."

"Yes, and good riddance. If I could destroy every whale the world over—every last monster of them!—by raising this hand, I'd raise it."

"No—don't say that, Bella . . ." Grampa was looking at her with a kind of heavy alarm. "They are great creatures, the fish of God. No—they were glory days. Days like no others—"

"Yes, I know," she muttered, "you always say that. What was so glorious about living in fear of your liver-and-lights for years on end?"

The old man shook his head. "I can't tell you, querida minha. You would have had to be there, in the boat. All of you pulling together, pulling your hearts out, like one man, watching Captain Howland back on the sweep, and waiting for the word . . ."

Above them on the wall the ship's chronometer struck its own hour: *ting-ting, ting-ting*—the bells sweet and infinitely piercing, the final note holding firm in the silence.

"Grampa," Jophy said suddenly, "tell about the *Cassandra*. When you were cabin boy."

"Paciencia," Grama sighed. "Now why do you want to hear that hideous tale still again?"

"It's *not* hideous . . ."

Manuel Gaspa said: "You already know it by heart, criança."

She grinned at him and tossed her head, made no answer. It was true; but she could never hear it enough. Nothing so terrible and wonderful, so burning with treachery and terror and wild courage, had ever happened to anybody in all the history of the seven seas. She knew it! The man named Harriss limping aboard at Moapora with the bandaged leg and his hard-luck story and the three Islanders in tow, wanting to sign on for the remainder of the cruise; Harriss, handsome and blond and charming, who astonished the *Cassandra's* officers with his proficiency in seamanship, who could hold the entire crew spellbound evenings with his guitar and his ballads, his tales of high adventure and sexual prowess. Captain Cheever, short-handed, was delighted with him—he decided to make the four new arrivals shipkeepers until Harriss' leg had healed and the Kanakas had learned how to row in the whaleboats. Captain Cheever had a face like a peach-pit and beady bird's eyes; he had stubbornly refused to promote João Huerta, the first harpooner, to mate, or to make Grampa a foremast hand; he said Portagees were too emotional, too unstable to take charge the way a "white" man could . . .

. . . And then came the lazy, somnolent afternoon somewhere south of the Line, when the crew had lowered for a whale. Grampa, as cabin boy, was checking the gear in the spare boat in case it should be needed, when Harriss abruptly left the helm and killed Tuttle the cook with a hand ax while the natives fell upon

31

old Feuermann the cooper with cutting spades. Without thought young Manuel Gaspa snatched up one of the lances in the whaleboat and dropped to the deck; and when Harriss came running forward—not a trace of a limp now—he darted the iron once, surely, and ran him through. At the age of sixteen. He dodged a boarding knife thrown at him by the tall, arrogant Makonga and scrambled aloft, higher and higher, broke out all the ship's signal flags in a gaudy riot of confusion and made his way aft, hand-over-hand along the stays and braces, slashing and severing halyards with his sheath knife, bringing down staysail, main and spanker, robbing the vessel of steerage way.

And for the next three hours he perched high in the topgallant crosstrees keeping a forlorn lookout, while Makonga tried to persuade him in pidgin to come down and help them sail the ship to Wokai where his father was a chief, promising him an island of his own, and women and wine. The boy, gripping the iron hoop, feigned indifference, fighting down his hollow fear that the boats had been towed out of sight of the ship by a whale, that the Islanders would think of the pistols in the captain's cabin; that he would, with time, become weak for lack of food and water—

. . . And finally, miraculously—graças a Santelmo!—he saw the boats beating swiftly up out of the south. João Huerta had seen the mystifying signal flags; and from the maintop the cabin boy directed the assault, calling instructions to the boats and flinging down marlinspikes to confuse the Kanakas until João wounded Makonga with a lance and the crews boarded in a rush over the main chains and killed the mutineers. He came down from aloft then, and they crowded around him, shouting at him, touching him, profane and hilarious with relief; and even Mr. Howland gripped his hand and praised him. And it was then that young Manuel Gaspa walked up to Cheever and said: "Captain, I want to serve in a boat. I want a foremast hand's lay"; and in the sudden, stunned silence looked full and fearlessly into the pinched, prune face, the beady little eyes, stared into them until finally the captain nodded curtly and vanished into his cabin. The crew swarmed up and around him again, jubilant, and João clapped him on the shoulder, grinning, and said: "O marinheiro, ah? O mestre de barco," and he smiled and answered, "Sim, arpãoneiro. Sim . . ."

Reaching now into the tall glass cabinet at the end of the room, Jophy lifted out the knife and drew it from its worn leather sheath. The blade was long, and narrowed from countless whetting; but the point was still perfect. The pommel was flattened so it could be used as a hammer. The knife that Grampa had bid for and bought when Araujo, the Cape de Verd' man, had died of fever off Diego Garcia. The crew had laughed at him—then—and that Yankee skinflint captain had told him it came under the heading of slop chest stores and charged him a ridiculous two dollars against his lay; but Grampa said he didn't care, he'd wanted that knife more than anything.

"Spanish steel," Manuel Gaspa said to himself, nodding. "Tempered in ice, Araujo said."

The original pieces of horn on the haft had worn out and Grampa had replaced them with whalebone, held by silver rivets made from a British shilling. Jophy turned the knife over in her hands. The blade was still so sharp it prickled along the ball of her thumb.

This knife had saved the ship.

Raising it high she slashed at the air around her, cried: "Evil old Makonga—you die plentyfella quick!"

"Josefina," Grama said sharply, "stop dancing around like a wild Indian and put that knife away!"

She glanced at Grampa, but he was not smiling. "Mind your Grama," he said. "Never unsheathe a knife unless you intend to use it. You hear me?"

"Yes, Grampa."

Reluctantly she slid it back into its sheath, and began to pass her fingers over whalebone fids, ivory combs and jagging wheels, a brass compass on a lanyard. On the shelf below were pieces of coral as intricate as lace mantillas, cat's-eyes from Ponape, cowries from Halmahera, conchs from the Antilles—sea shells like tops and turbans and ancient armor. Below them lay a ceremonial mask with slanted oval eyes, a sword of shark's teeth from Manokela, a spear-shaped Fiji paddle carved with vines and dragons, and amulets to pagan island gods.

She whirled around and said: "Grampa, what if João hadn't seen the signal flags? What would you have done?"

He thrust out his lower jaw and bit at the edge of his mustaches. "Waited till night, then gone down on deck and sneaked into the steerage. I had to have food and water. And then next day, when they didn't see me aloft, they would think I'd fallen overboard, and they would become careless."

"Wouldn't they have seen you coming down the shrouds?"

"Maybe. It was a chance I would have had to take . . . They had no discipline, Josinha. They were savages—they lived each man for himself. They would have gone wandering through the ship, hunting for trinkets, other such foolishness . . . and then I would have tried to kill them. One by one."

"Wouldn't you have got the pistols?"

He shook his head. "I didn't know how to load them. And anyway, the steel is always surer. And it is silent."

"But—they wanted you to join them, help them, those Kanakas. They needed you. Why not sail to Wokai with them? Isn't that better than hiding there in the dark, waiting to be killed and thrown overboard?"

"No! *Never!*"

She looked up, startled. His seamed face was hard with reproof, unforgivingly stern.

"*No*," he repeated. "Come here, Josefina." A bit frightened, she moved over to where he sat. Even Grama had set down the iron and was watching them in silence.

"Now," Captain Manuel Gaspa said. "You listen." He took both her hands in one of his, holding her with his deep-set black eyes. "The ship is your whole world, criança. Everyone with his place, his rank, his duties—which must be carried out fair weather or foul, for the ship to survive. That is why mutiny is the great sin—o pecado mortal. Because it wants to destroy the world of the ship. That is why it is always punishable by death."

"But Grampa, if a captain is stingy and unfair, like Captain Cheever—or like that Captain Ferrick who beat that Negro to death, and put those other two men ashore on that island—"

"Then it is a hard cruise. And many a good man has jumped ship with good cause. But unjust or not, brutal or not, dangerous or not, it *is* order, it is the world of duty, of trust. Sim, of *trust*. And to mutiny is to destroy the world and throw everything back to the beginning, with one savage's hand raised against another. It leads to nothing. The mutineer is a traitor to life." His eyes bored into hers, solemn and fierce. "That is why it is better to die than give way to it. Sempre e para sempre. Do you understand me, Josefina?"

She would never forget this moment: the silence in the room, the stern pressure of her grandfather's gnarled hand; it would lie at the very core of what she would always believe.

"Sim, Grampa," she said.

3

It was an utterly different kind of land. In Holcomb Falls the shadows of the mountains pressed you close. Here on Cape Cod the moors rolled in tawny waves toward the sea, which opened away with a rush to the horizon—a fine, deep blue over which the sun threw a million winking points of light. Here there were no barriers; the very sea was a highway.

Tip Ames walked slowly along the wharves by the harbor at Turk's Head where it turned into a broad channel. He watched a winch-fed line plummet out of sight beyond a cutting shed, and a moment later a purselike net swollen with fish rise out of a boat's hold and swing high and away, raining water in a seething silver shower. A ship lay canted on its side like a dying beast and two men crouched under its belly, their caulking mallets moving in *tock-tock, tock-tock* rhythms. There were men driving hoops down on barrels or mending nets with long, slender wooden needles; in a shipyard a schooner under construction was poised on its ways, stem piece and ribs thrusting naked to the air—a skeletal ghost of the ship to be, already quick with grace . . .

A fisherman was coming toward him, his heavy seaboots folded down below the knee like a buccaneer from the Spanish Main, two fingers hooked in the gills of a great, gray fish that swung ponderously against his leg.

"Morning," Tip said.

"Bo' dia." The fisherman nodded once, his face copper like an Indian's, and moved on, his boots clashing against each other.

Tip sat on a bollard, well out of anyone's way; assaulted by a riot of foreign smells—tar and seaweed and fish and rotting wood. Gulls wheeled above his head or perched on nearby pilings, craning their heads at him like crabbed old accountants. The harbor was alive with sail: stubby catboats and rakish cutters, pinkies and brigs and knockabouts—and far, far out on the edge of the world rose a still, ghostly tower of sail, bound for Rio, or Mombasa, or Hong Kong. The world—the whole teeming, beckoning world was out there, and they were racing to it, past a hundred forbidding headlands, to make their fortunes . . .

He slapped his hand on his thigh, whistling "On the Road to Mandalay." Everything around him was beguiling and strange—a feeling that hadn't left him since he'd boarded the train at Pittsfield. There had been the Connecticut River, and Mount Tom like a shaggy green whale's head; the train's wheels rocked in a driving rhythm, *hurry-it-on, hurry-it-on,* towns and hamlets swept by, carriages and even automobiles waited for them at the level crossings as though drawn up for a triumphant procession. Boston was vast and bustling and venerable. There was a delay before his Old Colony train left, and so he set off along Atlantic Avenue, where the ships were unloading their cargoes in an uproar of stevedores and cargo nets and drays. Up on Federal Street the pace was every bit as purposeful; salesmen in straw boaters greeted one another with high enthusiasm, bankers in narrow dark suits walked straight ahead, mouths pursed, eyes veiled with privy knowledge. I'm going to be here some day, he promised himself, marveling, right here on this street, busting through those high bronze doors; some day soon . . . He almost missed his train.

Somewhere below Plymouth the sea swept into view, deep indigo in the August haze, and his heart leaped. Except for three trips to Pittsfield it was the first time he'd been away from home.

When he stepped off the train at Turk's Head a mournful-faced man introduced himself as Hynes and took his suitcase. Aunt Serena Aldridge was standing in the shade of an elm beside the automobile she'd bought the year before, a dove gray Packard touring car. She looked even grander than he'd remembered, wearing a big leghorn hat secured with a scarf and a summer frock of larkspur blue lawn with an eyelet collar. She was holding a matching blue parasol.

"Tipton," she said. Taking his hands she pressed his cheek with hers, then leaned back and looked at him; he was taller than his aunt now. "Well—you've grown up! And then some. How long has it been?"

"Three years," he answered. "In November."

"Time goes entirely too fast."

He followed her into the automobile, which smelled densely of leather and brass polish, rocking majestically along the sand ruts of the road.

"Chapin isn't back," his aunt was saying. "Mr. Langford was taken ill in London and they missed their sailing."

"Oh—I'm sorry."

"Couldn't be helped. He'll be home in another two weeks or so."

"I'll be sorry to miss him."

Aunt Serena looked at him. "You can stay on, can't you?"

"No, I'm afraid I can't, Aunt Serena. I wish I could."

"Well, we'll talk about it at dinner." Her kingfisher blue eyes rested on him a moment. "I guess you'll have to amuse yourself. Turk's Head isn't the place it once was—the glory has departed, as Papa would say. But it's still a good, honest fishing town, struggling to make ends meet."

The house—it had been known locally for over a

century as the Bluffs—was awesome. It sat on a height overlooking the harbor, gray and imposing behind its fine stretch of lawn and flanked by a high barberry hedge. It had a railed widow's walk and a long verandah framed with seven-sisters rambler roses. Inside the rooms were cool and still; the sea wind soughed through the screens. Hynes, who doubled as butler and chauffeur, served a rib roast and broccoli in a golden sauce Tip had never tasted before. The bayberry candles in their blunt pewter sticks flickered and flared in the southerly breeze.

"Now tell me why you can't stay on," Aunt Serena said.

"I promised Mr. Crowell I'd be back by the twenty-eighth. For Labor Day weekend business. He's counting on me."

"Oh yes, the store. Do you like working there?"

"Well, I can't say I wouldn't rather be doing something else. But it pays well." He added: "Mr. Crowell let me run the store when he went out to St. Louis last spring."

"Did he? But you're so young, Tipton—how did you know enough to run an entire store? Didn't the drummers try to take advantage of you?"

"I was worried about that. So when the first salesman came in I said, 'I don't know the wholesale prices, but I'm going to keep a record. I'll check with Mr. Crowell. And if I find you've cheated me, I'll switch to another man.'"

"And what did he say to that?"

Tip thrust out his lower lip. "He said I sure had nerve for a kid my age."

Serena Aldridge burst out laughing. "Tipton, you are the limit!"

"It worked, though. Not one of them tried to cheat me."

"I believe you . . . And how are you doing in school?"

"Fair to middling," he said cautiously.

She laughed again, but differently. "Chapin was an honors student, valedictorian of his class."

"I know—he wrote me."

"And he won letters in fencing and crew." She watched him a moment; her eyes dilated in that funny way he remembered. "Sorry you didn't come live with us?" she asked softly.

"No," he said. "I made my choice."

She laughed her high, short laugh and patted his hand. "Good! I'd have been furious with you if you'd said yes. I *hate* second-guessers. Your grandfather used to lump them with petty thieves and confidence men." She picked up the tiny silver bell beside her water glass and shook it briskly—a clear, tingling peal that pierced the warm night. "I had Margaret make fresh peach ice cream. Just for you."

Lying in the strange bed upstairs later, hands clasped behind his head, too restless to sleep, watching the drifting lights of the harbor, he had thought of Chapin in London, in Paris, going off to Harvard in September; and he had had plenty of second thoughts . . .

He got up now from the bollard and walked along Dock Street. The sun was much stronger here—he felt laved in its fierce light. On his right nets hung from poles in gauzy black shrouds, their glass floats gleaming blue and amber and pale ruby through the mesh. Beyond them, what looked like thousands of pieces of yellowed parchment were lying on a web of lattice-like racks. Curious, he moved closer—recognized the fish, split and salted, drying in the summer heat. At the store he'd unpacked them from barrels, the salt sifting densely through his fingers. This was how they did it, then. Salt cod. He touched one of the flakes, put his fingers to his mouth. Salt permeated this world—its water, its air, its food; spice and preservative, arouser of thirst, sustainer of life—briny deep, salt of the earth; the first savor, breaker of friendship, forge of trust . . .

He had started to turn back toward the Bluffs when he caught sight of the solitary mast, rising stark and bare above a ridge as if a ship had been victimized by black magic, snared deep in land. Piqued, he went on. The road degenerated into sandy ruts, following the narrowed channel. Clearing some abandoned buildings he saw the old schooner then, moored to a bleached and rotting wharf. Her foremast ended in a shattered stump about five feet above the deck, her bow was smashed into a jagged hole, the bowsprit lashed against her rail. The tide, at flood now, licked and lapped at her gray hull. The sign on her counter read *Albatroz, Turk's Head*. Broken, a derelict, her remaining rigging frayed and ratty, she still looked breathtakingly beautiful.

". . . Oh," he heard himself murmur in the drowsy quiet. It was the first time in his life he could remember feeling sorrow over an inanimate thing.

A figure popped up on her deck, out of nowhere, a boy in a straw hat and striped singlet and shorts; raced across the deck and scrambled up the mainmast rigging with astonishing agility, reached the masthead and peered off down the channel—pointed seaward once, again, then began gesticulating wildly, as though giving orders. But without a sound. Standing deep in the shadow of an abandoned sail loft, Tip smiled. The kid was playing some game, acting out some bold deed. He'd rarely had time for such pastimes himself, but he recognized it instantly.

The boy, engrossed in his shipboard pantomime, scurried down the ratlines and ran into the bows, disappeared again. Quickly Tip crossed the old wharf, watching for gaps in the planking, jumped up on the ship's rail and dropped to the deck, which was littered with blocks and coils of cable. A battered derelict, ready for the boneyard. Yet—it was strange—there was a curious feeling, standing there on her hard, bleached deck: the faintest tremor of excitement, a sense of limitless horizons, bold adventures; a power to *discover* things . . .

The boy burst out of the forecastle companionway running aft, dodging through a tangle of windlass machinery—all at once caught sight of Tip, leaped back and cried, "Oh!" The hat fell off, hair spilled out in a rich silky black mass; and with a pleasurable shock Tip saw it was a girl.

She recovered instantly. She straightened, said: "What are you doing on my ship?"

He grinned. *"Your* ship?"

"Well—my grandfather's. Captain Manuel Gaspa." Her face was slender with strange high cheekbones; her eyes were large and jet black—they flashed at him like precious stones. He had never seen a girl so beautiful—not even in pictures, not even in dreams. "My grandfather's schooner," she repeated in that light, prideful voice. "Who are you?"

He didn't answer; he was still bound in a storm of emotions he had never felt before. "I was just—wondering what it was doing. Way up here, away from the harbor."

"She was hurt. Badly hurt. Off Georges North Shoal." She might have been talking of a relative, some loved one. She gestured toward the foremast with a slender brown arm. She seemed to be in perpetual movement—bold, elusive, uncapturable. It was in the way she stood there with one slim bare foot planted on the other, balanced precariously yet surely, as if poised for flight. He guessed she was about his age. She didn't seem to be the least bit embarrassed at exposing her legs, which were wonderfully long and brown and slender. He tried to keep his eyes off them, could not.

"I'm going to captain her," the girl was saying. "Take her up to the Banks again. When I'm older."

Again he couldn't keep from grinning at her. *"You* are?"

"You don't think a woman can sail a ship?" She

43

flung her long hair back furiously; like her skin it caught warm, coppery lights where the sun touched it. So shining . . . "You're just like every Yankee—'She's a girl and so of course she can't be any good at sea.'"

"Well, you've got to admit—"

"Ever hear of Hester Banning? No, *you* wouldn't have. Disguised herself and sailed on a whaler as a foremast hand. She was a first-class seaman—even saved the ship in a bad gale off the Horn. She let go the foretops'l halyards—they were crusted with ice, too—while the men stood there paralyzed in terror . . ."

"A woman?" he faltered. "In a *whaler*—?"

Her eyes flashed at him hotly, she swung on one foot like a sloop coming up into the wind. "I told you: it is a—true—story! My grandfather knew a man who sailed with her. The crew only found out months later, when she was ill with fever, and one of her shipmates discovered it . . ."

"But . . . how did she manage to—?" He broke off, embarrassed.

She stared at him a moment, then she laughed—running laughter that was like the sunlight spangles on the sea. "Well, she did! Hung from the chains like everyone else, I suppose." She was still smiling, without a trace of awkwardness. "Maybe she waited till dark. I used to wonder about that, too . . ."

He felt even more embarrassed, looked down at her naked legs again. He had never seen such legs, sweeping long and elegant from the almost fragile tendon of the ankle to the tapering calf, then curving to the smooth fullness of thigh above the knee—so *smooth* and golden . . .

As if to stop himself he said harshly: "It's a hard life, on a whaler. Why did she sign on?"

Her face changed utterly. "A man betrayed her. Promised to marry her, and then left her high and dry, alone in a strange city. She was of good family, too, and pretty. She discovered he'd shipped out on a whaler. So she did, too—she actually thought she could find him." The girl's eyes had turned inward now, depthless. "She didn't realize she might never even see him in a whole lifetime of voyages . . ."

He hooked his thumbs in his pockets. "I wonder what she planned to do if she did catch up with him."

"The mate asked her that." Her lovely, slender face set like stone, implacable. "She said she would kill him. She would have, too—don't think she wouldn't!"

He smiled—this girl could vault from merriment to rage in the twinkling of an eye; it was impossible to follow her.

"I see. You don't believe me."

"Sure, I do. Only when you talk about sailing a ship: steering it, furling the sails, climbing out on the—"

"All right!" She whirled in that swift, impulsive way of hers and running over to the rail started to climb the rigging again, calling: "Well, come on, now! What are you waiting for?"

He looked up at the mast, which soared off into the silken blue vault of the sky. It must be forty, fifty feet at least; maybe more. He tore his eyes away and walked steadily over to the starboard chains and started up. There were only three shrouds, he'd always thought there were more, somehow—and the old ratlines sagged and swayed treacherously when he put his weight on them. He slipped twice, put his whole foot through once, finally managed a shaky kind of rhythm and followed the girl on up. She had already reached the masthead and was standing precariously poised on the crosstrees with one hand over her head, holding on to the single shroud that ran to the very top. She was gazing out at the bay, her hair streaming back from her face, which was glowing golden in the afternoon sun.

"Perfect," he heard her say. "A perfect time."

Her gaze met his for an instant; her eyes were

sparkling—mischievous and wild. The realization hit him then, like a blow under the heart: She isn't going to—she isn't actually going to try to jump from this—

"—No!" he cried softly.

Before he could do anything else she let go the stay, poised with the most delicate grace on her toes and leaped outward, back arched, arms flung wide; held it for one incredibly long, terrifying, exultant moment, as though to embrace everything in the whole sun-dazzled, watery world—then dropped her arms neatly over her head and entered the water in a clean flurry of foam. He could see her break her descent, tumble over once, her legs drawn up, then stroke her way upward, her eyes wide and staring; a second later she broke the surface in a playful rush of froth.

"All right," she called. "Your turn!"

". . . You're kidding," he murmured. "I've never been up this high in my life—"

"I can't hear you!"

"I said, I hardly even know how to *swim* . . ."

He peered down again. The girl looked ridiculously small down there, treading water easily, her face still rapt in that exultant smile; the deck of the schooner was a grim light-year away. On the sandy bottom he could make out what looked like a waterlogged spar, or maybe an iron bar, pocked with barnacles and hoary with swaying emerald tentacles of seaweed.

"You're not by any chance afraid, are you, Yankee?" she sang out. "To do something a weak, incompetent woman just did . . . ?"

Her laughter decided him. It wasn't simply derisive—though it was certainly edged with mockery; it was the note of sheer, irrepressible jubilation he could hear in it—as though it were the most rapturous thing in the world to leap from the mastheads of crippled vessels into shallow water.

Very deliberately he took off his shoes, laced them together and slung them over one of the ratlines, while she continued to chatter at him; took off his socks and shirt and folded them carefully over the crosstrees. He was trembling now, his legs were shaking badly.

"All right, you've put it off long enough—the tide'll be *out* in another five hours. Come on! If you *are* going to do it, I mean . . ."

He looked down again—wrenched his eyes away. Up here, high above the chandlers' roofs and the tops of the maples and locust trees, he could see all the way out to the bay and that pale cloud of sail on the hard blue line of the horizon. The sight steadied him. Without giving himself another second to think he pulled himself up on the crosstree, straightened convulsively and gripped the shroud as though it were the last line in the universe, stepped forward and threw himself out into still, empty space. He was seized with a terrifying picture of his body smashing itself to pieces, doll-like, on that hard, hard deck below, an image just as instantly gone, and in a silent and steadily expanding dream he swooped down and down, held in a light-sick, fevered rapture—was swallowed in a boiling bright rush of water. His heels hit bottom with a soft, jarring impact; he thrust himself away in a spasm and clawed toward the light in a gathering panic that he didn't have enough air in his lungs, he would drown now, *now* that he was safe— burst into air and sunlight and reality. The girl, several feet away, was pointing at him accusingly.

"You jumped! You didn't dive at all!"

"—Damn right," he panted. "I may be a simpleton—but I'm not a lunatic."

"You looked *so* funny—you should have seen your face! You looked like a man about to walk the plank for mutiny . . ."

He laughed, too, kicking water in a tiny silver maelstrom all around him. He felt exhilarated, freed from all constraint and circumspection—as though he'd just come hurtling down through the heavens,

47

clinging to the tail of Halley's Comet. He looked up at the masthead again.

"It was fun," he said.

"You did pretty well. Even if you *were* scared blue."

"Sure, I was scared. I've never even jumped off a front porch before . . ."

"Really? I like that. I love anyone who'll take a dare."

"Well, you've come to the right party, then."

" . . . My name's Jophy," she said in a suddenly different voice. "Josefina Gaspa."

"Tip Ames." He watched her gliding around him—a seal, a lovely sleek brown seal. Her long black hair swirled around her like a Botticelli painting Miss Abbot had showed him once, the striped top clung to her slender body, defined her small round breasts, the budlike boss of their nipples. He was filled with a sudden astonishing longing to hold her, press her to him, kiss her wildly.

She gazed back at him for a long moment, an expression he couldn't read, her eyes terribly dark—abruptly doubled over and plunged out of sight, her legs sliding beneath the surface with a golden elegance that made his throat ache. He peered down, couldn't find her anywhere; the moments grew, he became fearful. He started for the ship—heard a light splash and a laugh behind him.

"Now don't do that!" he said, turning.

"What's the matter?"

"What a good swimmer you are," he said, to hide his concern.

"I belong to the sea. We all do."

"Who's we?"

"We Portuguese." It was as if she were referring to some legendary, aqueous royalty. They climbed out then and sat on the schooner's rail while their clothes dried, and watched the seaweed swaying like wild sea nymphs' hair on the ebb tide, the crabs scuttling in the shadows.

"Is your father a fisherman?" he asked her.

"My father's dead."

He listened in silence while she told him about it, picturing the liner rushing out of the Grand Banks fog like a vast white wall, a falling tower, and the sickening, splintering crash, the whole world toppling crazily, the sea pouring in, the cries, the cold, the black, strangling terror; and then the silence . . .

"Well, that gives us something else in common," he said after a pause. "I don't have a father, either. He left home six years ago."

Her eyes flashed up at him. "That's different . . ."

"Yes," he agreed somberly. "It's worse."

She cried, "How can you say that?"

"Because your father died doing his work. In line of duty. You can respect him. My father betrayed us. Deserted us. And I have to carry that around with me."

"I see." She nodded, her chin resting on one bare knee. "There's nothing worse than that. Grampa says that. He says it destroys the world."

Destroys the world. Listening, watching her, swept with this rush of new and turbulent emotions, he saw his father's back again, leaving, the front door closing. The chill, boundless loss. To his consternation his eyes filled, and he looked down into the crystal clear channel. Then her hand touched his bare shoulder.

"Não importa, Tip," she murmured. "Life goes along, Grama says. In spite of everything. That's what matters." And gripping his hands together hard, his head bowed, he felt her lips brush his cheek.

4

"—Well, they fussed and they fussed over that machine for five hours," Archie Fiske said. He watched the other men sitting in a tight circle around the big-bellied Glenwood Oak stove in the center of the store, his eyes snapping with pleasure, his face flushed a deep red from the heat.

"And there wasn't *anybody* could get it started, they were going crazy. And finally they gave up and sent over to Greenfield for this fella someone said was a real whizzbang with machinery, and he got there next morning first thing. Well, he walked all around the brute, and he looked at it here and studied it there, didn't say a word. Then he picked up an eight-pound sledge leaning against the wall, set himself and gave the flywheel a good smart wallop—and up she started, slick as a whistle." Archie Fiske nodded at them, grinning. He'd taken off his shoes, and his stockinged feet, resting on the stove's apron, were steaming faintly. "Yep. She'd got caught on dead center, and that little love tap did the trick. Old Man Prouty was blubbering with gratitude, shook his hand and offered him a cigar, asked what he owed him. And the fella said one hundred dollars."

"A hundred dollars!" Dan Loughran cried.

Archie Fiske laughed. "That's about the way Prouty took it. You'd have thought the fella had pulled a derringer on him and started to clean out the cash drawer. When he finally found his voice again he asked him if he thought that was fair, three minutes' inspection and one blow of a hammer. And the fella said yes, he did. And Prouty says crossly, 'May I ask how you arrive at that figure?' And the fella squints up at the skylight and says: 'All right. Two dollars for labor. Three dollars for transportation. And ninety-five dollars for knowing how!' "

The salesmen's laughter boomed in the store. Tip, listening, smiling too, tipped the sack and poured the dusty beans down the throat of a cast iron hopper, slid the cover in place and began to crank the wheel with a brisk, even rhythm; and the dense odor of coffee flooded the air around him. Dan Loughran, who carried the Domino line, had started another story, but Tip only half listened. Archie Fiske always had the best stories. He was like the spices he sold—compact and pungent, surprising his listener with a hundred different scents and savors. Like most drummers he sported a pinchback suit, a derby and a high celluloid collar. He carried a case, but his pockets always bulged with gaily-colored tins and packets; you never knew what he was going to pull out of them. *Ninety-five dollars for knowing how . . .*

Packing up flour orders in cloth sacks at the counter beside him, Horace Crowell said: "Don't forget the lemon extract."

"Mrs. Beemis? I filled that in her order last week."

"Yes. Well, repeat it."

Tip stopped turning the crank. "How on earth does she manage to run through so much lemon extract?"

The storekeeper gave him a pitying look over his steel rims and said slowly: "It's 90 percent alcohol, Tipton."

"Oh. But it's a lot more expensive than—than liquor."

"Now be reasonable, Tip. How is Evelyn Beemis going to waltz down to Tim Rafferty's saloon, put her

52

foot up on the rail and ask for a bottle of Old Potentate? Can you see her doing that?"

Grinning, Tip shook his head. "No, I can't."

"Ah, there's a price for every vice," Horace intoned. "Don't you forget it." He was a tall, bony man who wore red sleeve garters that matched his galluses; tart and choleric, he saw himself as an unsung philosopher. He said: "You want to put up the butter? I'm going to make delivery early today. All this snow."

"Right." Tip cleaned out the square wooden tray under the coffee mill and went quickly through the back of the store to the unheated shed that served as storeroom and ice chest. The winter air burst in gray plumes from his mouth. He lifted the butter firkin on to the work table, released the clamps and raised the top section from the mold, and picking up the cutter with its thin wire blade he cut a perfect horizontal section an inch and a half from the top; then he traced six pie-shaped divisions, and carefully made the cuts, slipped them on to brown paper and carried them one by one to the scales. Five were exactly two pounds, one a fraction high. Horace always asked him to cut the butter—he never had the patience to make the cuts exact, and the housewives didn't like it if you had to make up the weight with bits and slivers. Then for a moment he stood there in spite of the cold, touching the last section; all smooth and golden, it held the intoxicating warmth of summer and sunlight . . .

He stepped over to the pickle barrel and lifted the lid, bent down and inhaled the harsh salt smell—plunged his arm into the chill liquor and ran the back of his hand across his mouth; tasting the brine, remembering . . .

He had seen Jophy Gaspa every day after that first afternoon. She took him sailing in her boat ("*Really* my own boat," she'd told him, laughing "—not glory fancies!"), a narrow-beamed, wicked-looking cutter that seemed to carry far too much sail for its size and heeled over alarmingly in the stiff southwest breeze. They seemed in perpetual danger of capsizing, but after a while he learned to handle the jib sheets with some competence, and by the day's end was perched beside Jophy, braced well out over the windward rail while the cutter slapped and slammed its giddy way along, both of them soaked to the bone and shouting and laughing at each other. She wore a bathing suit this time, the skirt below her knees, but she flatly refused to wear bathing stockings; her legs and her brown feet were bare. Her hair, caught in one shining braid as thick as his arm, hung way below her waist.

The day after that it rained, and she brought him to her grandparents' house. It was on the opposite side of the harbor from the Bluffs, a crazy old place with fanciful curlicued moldings and a second-story verandah supported on pillars that had once been ships' spars. The walk was laid with blackfish vertebrae—huge, porous, bleached medallions—edged with heather and rugosa; two whale's ribs met in an awesome arch above the front gate.

Her grandfather was badly crippled; his leg had been smashed up by a whale and a mate had set it incorrectly—Jophy had told him about it. Even now, hobbling around with a cane whose ivory head was carved in the shape of a seahorse, you could see in the broad shoulders and powerful hands the man he'd once been. He remembered Tip's Granduncle Jeremiah Aldridge, with whom he'd once sailed, and this set him on a tide of reminiscence. While the rain slipped its silvery curtain off the verandah roof and the foghorn beyond the point moaned like some lost soul in torment, Manuel Gaspa told them tales of derelicts and rogue whales and savage shores. The old man's voice seemed to echo the sea which had formed it, ebbing and surging. Jophy leaned forward eagerly, nodding now and then at Tip, or throwing him a quick, excited glance. There was no limit to the things Captain Gaspa had seen . . .

His wife was something else again. Annabella Gaspa came bustling into the room encased in gleaming yellow oilskins, her sou'wester pulled down over her brows like a helmet. When Jophy introduced them, she scowled at him hard.

"Ames? You're not the Ames boy. I've seen him around town."

"That's Chapin," he answered. "I'm his brother."

"His *brother—?*"

"Yes, Ma'am."

She inspected him from head to foot then, grimly, as if certain he were an impostor, or worse. Much worse. Then her mood changed. "Summer visitor," she pronounced silkily, with a forbidding smile. "Vacationing at the sea shore, among the natives . . . Well. And how are things among the rich and favored?"

"Grama—"

Tip looked back at her grandmother steadily, thrust out his lower lip. "I wouldn't know, Mrs. Gaspa. I've worked hard for a living since I was ten years old."

"Hard?" Her eyebrows rose, but the mocking smile remained. "How hard is that?"

"Hard enough for me."

"De verdade?" She reached out and took his hand so quickly he started—turned it palm up and peered at it, running the ball of her thumb over the calluses. "Ah! I see." She released him; her face turned stern and confused, then broke into an open, radiant smile. "Well! Then—you *do* know something about the world . . ."

"Yes, Ma'am," he answered. "I do."

"Good!" She nodded, squeezed his upper arm once, hard. "Never forget it, no matter what happens to you. There are those who pull at the seine in all weather—and those who sit back in paneled rooms and count the gold. And they never speak the same language. Never!—Bem vindo a nossa casa. You are welcome." And before he could say anything in reply

55

she had hurried off to the kitchen, her oilskins crackling.

He caught Jophy's eye; his expression must have been stunned because she was laughing at him silently, her eyes bold. "You see? There are two kinds of people."

"Cowardly Yankees and brave Portagees, you mean?" he asked her with a grin.

"Worse! People Grama likes and people she doesn't. Come on."

She led him to the tall cabinet in the front room, and he admired the scrimshaw and sea shells, and the knife that had foiled the mutiny on the *Cassandra*; and then to a sea chest awash in maps and nautical charts. Sitting on the floor side by side, their heads together, they ran their fingers over capes and bays and coral atolls, murmuring the wild, exotic names like incantations: Manokela, Bengkulu, Wokai, Pangutaran . . . And the neatly penned mariners' notations: *Shoals reported. Submerged coral reefs. Extensive changes in depth. Dangerous passage.* And then a large, blank area where there were no coastlines, no depth figures, only the single sprawled word: *Unexplored.*

". . . Unexplored," Jophy breathed, and her eyes shone. "What do you suppose it's like there? Oh, I'd give anything to find it. Anything!"

He knew how she felt. He said so. Those blank spaces—their pull was irresistible and profound. To sail there, to land on hidden, barbaric coasts, lie on their golden sands, discover silks and spices and precious jewels no one had ever seen before—to bring all that back in triumph . . . Gently he reached out and touched the rich, dark mantle of her hair, feeling as if he had just discovered *her,* brought her back from some immense and hazardous voyage. Her eyes shone so! So brilliantly . . .

"No," she was saying, "it's just to find it—just to know what's *there* . . ."

56

"But it's the trader who always opens up the territory, Jophy. Look at Marco Polo, Columbus—"

"No!" She shook her head violently. "Magellan, Vasco da Gama—they sailed for the pure joy of discovery! We were the greatest explorers of them all—we Portuguese . . ."

Unfurling the great Mercator map, her fingers pointing here and there, she called the roll of seafaring glory: Diogo Cão carving the coat-of-arms of the House of Aviz high on the cliff face at the mouth of the Congo ("he thought it was the Nile"), Dias rounding the fearsome Cape of Good Hope ("Cabo Tormentoso, he called it—isn't that a wonderful name?"), the incomparable Da Gama sailing over the very rim of the earth to the magic, dreamed-of coast of India ("four thousand miles without a single landfall—can you imagine what that *means?* No one had ever done anything like it before") . . .

Through typhoons and tropic atolls, cannibals and bejeweled rajahs, there was clearly no end to what these Portuguese had done: the great Magellan himself was Portuguese; Columbus had got his idea of a westward passage from Portuguese pilots—Pedro Cabral had already discovered Brazil. Did he know about Dighton Rock in the river below Taunton? with its cross of Santa Isabella and a date in Roman numerals? Miguel Cortereal had been there and gone—in *1502.* Lost at sea . . .

He sat perfectly still, watching her—her eyes flashing like scimitars, her slender face animate with passion. What a firebrand she was! So free . . . The girls he'd known giggled furtively behind their hands. Jophy threw back her head and laughed in heedless merriment—and then turned fierce at some remembered act of treachery or betrayal.

"You're like the south wind, Jo," he heard himself murmur. "Taking me where I've never been. You're always looking over the horizon, like your grandpa—you crazy girl . . ." And again he reached out and ran his fingers along the glowing copper hollow of her cheek, the sweet shell of her ear. He half-expected the touch of her skin to burn him.

The evening before his departure was soft and clear; they walked by the harbor together, saying nothing, watching the night tide, the night sky.

"I'll write you," he said finally, breaking the silence; then: "I wish we lived nearer each other."

"When will you be back?" she said softly.

"I don't know. Maybe next summer." Next summer. It suddenly seemed like a great, gray eternity of time, one he could never hope to traverse with his sanity intact.

They were almost at the Gaspa house. He reached down and took her hand.

"I'll miss you, Jophy."

"Yes. So will I."

He wanted to kiss her, terribly. Her face looked unutterably beautiful—night shadows caught the hollows of her cheeks, the high cheekbones, lay deep along the sides of her throat; her eyes were huge and dark.

". . . Jophy," he murmured.

Before he could say another word she brought her face up to his. Her lips, slightly parted, trembling, met his; her fingers stroked the back of his neck. He was conscious of the south wind on his cheek, the call of a bell buoy far out across the water; then of nothing but the pressure of her lips, her breasts and thighs, and the wild, wild beating of his heart . . .

She broke away from him then with a soft gasp and they stood watching each other.

"Jophy—I love you," he murmured.

He knew it was true, beyond question; the bell buoy's tolling had sealed it. She was the only girl he would ever love, he would never love anyone else, ever. He wanted only her. She had swum into his life like one of the sirens painted in the blank spaces on those ancient maps, had bewitched him and led him

58

down to her dreamy coral kingdom; he would never again look at any other woman with desire . . .

"I do love you," he repeated. She had drawn back now, and it troubled him. "I mean it—I *know* I do . . ." He caught her to him again, held her close—realized she was trembling in her whole body; she was trembling more than he was.

"Do you love me?"

She made no reply. He saw her look off toward the harbor, where a ship was moving, her running light sparkling like an emerald hung in space. The bell buoy again struck its mournful, hollow chime. Her tensed silence drew him; he had never wanted to hear anything so much as her reply.

"Don't you?" he pressed.

". . . I don't know." Her face was all at once deadly grave, her eyes jet brilliants. "Maybe."

"Maybe—!" he echoed blankly. It was inconceivable to him that she could use that word. "But don't you even—"

She whirled away from him, ran under the ghostly whale-rib arch, up the bone path; stopped again. "Yes—maybe," she called. "I trust you, anyhow." And now she laughed—her own sweet wild laughter. "I will, if you learn to dive—you can't trade with *everybody,* you know!" And before he could say anything she had vanished inside the screen door, leaving him standing there in the warm, still night . . .

In Horace Crowell's store now the voices around the stove were louder; they were arguing about the Clayton Anti-Trust Act. Archie Fiske's voice overrode the others.

"—telling American business what it can and can't do, they're going to strangle free enterprise right in its cradle . . . Coddling the unions like that—I tell you boys, this country's turning radical right before our eyes! Damned bureaucrats—next thing they'll be telling us we can't even compete for markets fair and square, dictating how much we can sell."

"Now come on, Archie," Frank Delahant said in his clear, incisive voice, "you can't have it both ways. Are they tyrants, or bomb-throwing anarchists?"

Someone snorted once, and the room quieted. Frank Delahant was far and away the most personable of the salesmen who came through Holcomb Falls. His suits always fitted him perfectly; his detachable collars smoothly encased his neck, his sleeves were exactly the right length, his trousers held a perfect crease—it was a kind of trademark.

"He's nine cuts above your every-day drummer," Horace always said. Delahant would have seemed entirely out of place with the other salesmen if it weren't for his geniality and easy wit. He represented Hampton Court biscuits and cookies, a luxury item which came packaged as handsomely as he did, in tins beautifully painted with English hunting scenes which housewives prized as sewing boxes. He was tall, with a drawn, fine-featured face, and he had a warm smile beneath that perfectly trimmed mustache. Only now and then Tip had thought he caught a flicker, a shadow of something else in his eyes—was it remorse?—anyhow, something infinitely sad . . . Then Delahant would adjust his cuffs, smile that well-bred, easy smile, and you weren't sure you'd seen anything there at all.

"They're eating away at the fundamental nature of competition," Archie Fiske was shouting. "Prohibiting rebates—how in Tophet do they think the railroads are going to make a decent profit?"

"I wouldn't worry too much about the fate of the railroads, Archie." Frank was smiling, but his voice held that quiet edge that always caught your attention. "Or your big corporations, either. You know as well as I do the minute they get big enough they all get together in one of those fancy boardrooms and fix prices—where's your open market there? Don't you see the irony? They holler for free enterprise until *they're* in the saddle. Then they join forces, freeze out the smaller competitors and burn the consumer. Hell, the government's trying to get *back* to free enterprise—"

"Sure, and let every bohunk millhand go out on strike whenever he gets the notion, so he can swill the suds all day and tell himself he's Big Jim Hill!"

There were a few chuckles, but the room was still silent, attentive. They laughed at Archie Fiske; but they listened to Frank Delahant.

"The labor of a human being is not a commodity or an article of commerce," Frank Delahant quoted, his voice soft, almost mocking. "You don't want *your* life being treated like a commodity, now do you, Archie." He ran his fingers along the dark gold fob chain. "The country's changing, boys. More than any of us can foresee. Your beer-swilling millhand isn't going to be locked out anymore, fired without cause. He wants more and he's going to get more.

"Their heads have been turned by these agitators— I've seen 'em," Dan Loughran said. "I worked twelve-hour days at Troy Foundry when I was seventeen. They don't know what work is."

"Yes, they do. They know what work is. And now they want their fair slice of the great American pie."

Tip leaned over the counter. "I guess that'll mean people will be able to afford things they never could before. Thousands of people. A whole new market."

"Sure, lad," Archie Fiske said, "they'll be able to send the old lady down to the corner saloon for two buckets of suds instead of one!"

But Frank Delahant didn't laugh with the others. He was looking at Tip, a half-smile at the corner of his mouth. "You know, you might be right about that, son," he said. "You just might be right about that."

Tip went out back again and began to load the individual orders in the wagon. The snow swirled around him, exploded like powder against the shed wall, swept away in a rolling silver mantle. Beyond, Mount Macomah was completely obscured in the whirling gray silence. He wondered if it was snowing down at Turk's Head, covering the flakeyard, the battered old *Albatroz* with a fine white shroud. What was she doing? Was she skating at Trumbull's Pond, face glowing, body arched the way it was in one of her marvelous dives? the slender, golden legs covered up now in wool stockings, but her hair flowing behind her in a glossy black skein—oh, God, what was she *doing!* Right now, this moment. To be with her, there beside her . . . Again and again at school, at the store, moving around town with his samples, she would sweep into his mind with the force of a lighthouse beacon. Studying or reading late at night, or lying in bed, he would feel again her body against his, trembling, and would groan aloud with the need, with the dense throb of sheer desire. He was consumed with longing.

But he had not mentioned her to a single soul.

"I'm sorry this visit has been such a failure for you, Tipton," Aunt Serena had said on the way to the train.

"Oh no, it hasn't been," he'd protested, a touch too quickly. "I've had a fine time. Really."

Her eyes had swung around to his. "Did you meet any young people your age?"

"A few," he said. "It's such a different world . . ."

"Yes. Isn't it."

She had said no more than that, but Tip could feel her glance pass over him now and then; he wondered how much he had given away. Or she had heard. She was cross with him, he knew, for going home before Chapin returned; did that mean she wouldn't invite him down again? His mother, harassed as always with boarders and bills, knew nothing more than that he wrote to someone on Cape Cod regularly; he wanted it that way.

When Tip came back inside, the group around the stove was breaking up, joking about the war over in

62

Europe. Archie wanted to bet anyone two dollars the Germans would be in Paris by June 1st; there were no takers. One by one they buckled on overshoes, and went out to their pungs or upstreet to the Exchange Hotel. Only Frank Delahant hadn't moved; he sat slumped deep in the chair watching absently as Tip shook down the stove and fed it.

"Horace tells me you won that Foyne's Cocoa contest," he said after a pause. "Is that correct?"

Tip looked up. "Yes sir, I did."

"I hear you've got a corner on Shalimar here in the valley."

"Almost."

"But not quite, eh?" Frank Delahant laughed. "How old are you, son?"

"Going on seventeen."

"You like selling?"

"Yes, I do." Tip stood up. "Fact is, I'm good at it."

"So I see. Ever think of going into it full time?"

"Yes, sir. Soon as I finish school, in June."

Delahant nodded, fingering the gold key on his watch chain. "I like you, Tip. You've got a head on your shoulders. You'd be surprised at how many people in this world don't *think* at all. How'd you like to come work with me? New England territory?"

"Why—I'd like to. Hampton Court?"

"No, this would be something different." He smiled the quick, engaging smile. "Can you keep a little secret?"

"Yes, I can."

"Good. Ever hear of Alexander Hamilton Institute?" Tip shook his head. "Man named Webster down in Hartford's got me all steamed up about it. It's a brand new concept in selling, in self-education. The world's changing, son. It's moving on, faster and faster. People in this country are reaching out for more, they're tired of sitting back and letting things happen to them; they want to improve themselves, gain competence . . . Ever try to listen to a lawyer? Sounded like Greek, didn't it? All those hifalutin terms . . . But it was only because you didn't understand them. You'd go to college if you could, wouldn't you?"

"I certainly would, sir."

"Sure, you would. Well, Alec Ham is the answer." Tip could see he was all cranked up with the idea, selling himself now. "Their way, anyone—right in his own home—can do it. Why should the lawyers and bankers hold all the cards?"

It was a two-year course: twenty-four books, handsomely bound, each one written by a leading expert in his field. The client mastered one book each month, took an exam, received a certificate of excellence at the end. Delahant's voice ran on, incisive and eager. And Tip could suddenly *see* all those clerks and millhands and farmers out there, learning about business management, marketing, accounting, even law—everyone burning the midnight oil, pulling himself up by his bootstrap . . . What a wizard of an idea!

"Cookies, apple corers, gloves—any run-of-the-mill drummer can sell those, Tip. Even heavy machinery. But facts, skills—*ideas!* Ideas are dreams, Tip— dreams become action, reality. For dreams you've got to reach into a man's heart, fire his imagination, his sense of horizons opening up, if he will only seize his opportunity. Follow me?"

"Yes—I do, sir."

Frank Delahant started to buckle on his overshoes. "Think about it, son. You've got the stuff. I can feel it—I'm never wrong about a salesman." Then he smiled, and that shadow of sadness darkened his eyes. "Well, almost never . . . We'll just keep this between you and me for the time. You finish up school and then we'll talk".

He nodded his courtly little nod, and set off upstreet toward the Exchange Hotel, looking slim and distinguished in the nicely tailored overcoat with its fur collar, the Homburg set at exactly the correct angle; and the whirling snow gathered him in.

Tip took the stove ashes out back, whistling softly to himself, looked across the long field—all at once cupped his hands and shouted: "Go!" And from the far curtain of pines the echo came drifting back. He felt an excitement so deep he didn't think he could hold it in, pounded his mittened hands and stamped his feet. He could do it; he could do it! There they were, all of them, out there beyond Mount Macomah, waiting for something that would give them a chance, something to free them from the grip of the college-bred lawyers and money-men. It was what America ought to be. And he could do it, he could do it better than anyone else. Frank Delahant would see—he'd be amazed at how Tip Ames could sell . . .

Pounding his gloved hands together he shouted again at the invisible mountain.

5

"No-no, Josinha," Manuel Gaspa said. "First you marry your ends."

"Marry!" she exclaimed; she laughed hilariously. "Now, Grampa—is that really the word they use?"

He grunted, watching—gave her that quick, complicit flicker of one eyelid. "You are growing up, criança."

"You're wrong—I've *grown* up!"

"Maybe so. Sim, that is the word they use. Look, now." His big, scarred hand closed over one of hers and turned it gently so that the unlayed strands of the two rope ends formed an opposed, double Y, one above the other; and slid them into each other's embrace. "See how they marry?"

"Grampa, honestly—"

"Now, open up along here with your fid; here and here. That's it. Now, take your first strand, like this, and move over and under, from right to left. No—right to left . . ."

"Like that?"

"Mais ou menos. Go ahead."

Sitting crosslegged on the old schooner's deck she went on making the short splice, tucking and tapering deftly, humming to herself. Now and then she glanced at her grandfather, who was slumped on the cabin trunk, his head back, his eyes closed. The tide, on the ebb, gave up a dense odor of brine and brack and rot and iodine; the sun was hot on her neck and arms. The mid-June days were the fairest, the longest, the ones alive with promise. It was the time of year she loved best. The May easterlies were past; the summer—the sun-washed, captivating summer—stretched out ahead like a golden channel to the open sea.

"Warm," the old man murmured, and his lips curled in a slow smile. "Like Fayal. Tenho saudades da minha ilha." Homesick, he began to reminisce about his native Azores, volcanic peaks soaring above torn snatches of rain cloud, tall curved palms, houses gaily painted in pink or cerulean or Nile green facing the blue sea, praças festive with bougainvillea; the harsh lava slopes tumbling like frozen cataracts through a riot of hibiscus and mallow and hydrangea and somber giant heather down to the boil and spindrift of the surf. And then, inevitably, of the Festa dos Baleeiros.

"—walking slowly, Josinha, very slowly down the caminho from Nossa Senhora da Guia. Some of the men are walking barefoot, as a sign of gratitude; some with staffs, to show humility. We children at the rear, carrying lighted candles; the little girls with soft white veils over their heads. Dom Fernão Machado carrying high the image of the saint as is his right, Padre Luiz bearing the gold crown of Espirito Santo. The whaleboats are drawn up on the beach, all freshly painted—white hulls, yellow strakes, red gunwales, our Fayal colors—with the line tubs uncovered and the lances laid out fanwise in the bows. When they reach the first boat Dom Fernão places the Saint on the stern sheets forward of the loggerhead; the boat-header, wearing white paramentos over his suit, lifts the line from the aft tub, takes a turn around the loggerhead, doubles it, passes it over the shoulders of the Saint and makes a French bowline—only leaving it loose—kisses the garment, and steps back three paces; then Padre Luiz walks forward to the bow; and the boat is blessed . . ."

He fell silent after that. She waited a few moments, then said: "There," and handed him the spliced rope. "How's that, Grampa?"

He started—it was almost as if he'd dozed off—took the line and gave it a brisk yank, turned it over in his hands, nodding. "Good. A good start." Picking up the smooth ivory fid he swiftly opened the strands again, released the ends and handed them back to her.

"Outra vez."

"That's mean!" she protested. "Didn't I do it right?"

"Sim." He nodded, smiled his broad, roguish smile. "But doing it over and over is how you learn so you won't forget. You know that. Next time I'll teach you the long splice—that's the *real* test of the good seaman." Gripping the seahorse cane he thrust himself to his feet—staggered suddenly and nearly fell to the deck.

"Grampa—!" She leaped up and caught him around the waist.

"No-no." He brushed her away crossly, shaking his head.

"You all right, Grampa?"

"Yes. Going on home," he muttered.

"Why? Stay here . . ."

"Going to cloud up."

"Clouds?—I don't see any."

"You will, criança." He threw her his hooded wink and moved away across the rotting wharf with that dragging gait, the smashed leg bowed, his body lurching and swaying with the effort.

Concerned, she gazed after him until he was out of sight; then turned back to the splice, thinking of Grampa as a boy, barefoot, his eyes wide with wonder, carrying a lighted candle, watching Father Luiz bless those frail, graceful craft, one by one . . . Grampa still went to early Mass; Grama hadn't once entered St. Anthony's since Jophy's father had been lost—she wouldn't even go down to Cunningham's Wharf for the blessing of the Grand Banks fleet in May. Grama didn't believe in God; her position was fierce and unequivocal.

". . . If there *is* a God, if there *is* this precious gallery of patron saints, they are remarkable by their absence! Where was Our Saviour when that whale crushed your leg and killed the others? where was He when Joey was run down in the fog that morning?"

Grampa had shaken his head doggedly. "What has God to do with the suffering or the sins of men? Should He answer for it?"

"Yes! If only to respond to our agony—if not our devotion. Is that so much to ask of the All-Powerful?"

"But—we cannot hope to know the ways of God, Bella."

"Ah—*mystery*," she breathed, drawing the word out contemptuously. "Yes. Well. 'Where mystery begins, justice ends,'" she quoted, nodding at him grimly.

"Who said that? One of your smooth-tongued sea lawyers?"

"A good man said that, a great man who fought all his life for dignity, for justice . . ."

"Bella, there *is* no justice in this world."

"And so the answer is to throw up your hands and fall on your knees!" she cried, her voice hot with scorn. "Wallow in your perfect, unshakable faith, dreaming of harps and paradise—while the misery and bondage goes on and on around us, and the saints themselves roar with laughter . . ."

Grampa said softly: "You used to have faith, querida."

"Oh, I have faith, all right! Oh, yes! In *us*—" she tapped her breast "—in what we fight for, secure for ourselves, right here, right now! No mystery there! No, *you* go on, pray till your kneecaps burst—but don't expect everyone else to strike that fool's bargain . . ."

"*Bella*—"

"I mean it! Sempre e para sempre!"

It was the only time Jophy had ever heard them quarrel in earnest. The occasion was to have been her confirmation, five years before; Grampa wanted her to be confirmed, Grama was unalterably opposed.

"No—I say no, Manny! Let her make up her mind when she is old enough. Then she can turn into a perfect Santa Teresa de Avila, for all I care—but let her at least make her own voyage. Faith! Reason! What can she know of them? I am not going to seize her up in *any* rigging . . ."

Grampa had given way in the end; Grama could be formidable. He no longer asked Jophy to go to Mass with him, though he himself went regularly, and to confession as well. Once, remembering that bitter torrent of argument, she had said without thinking:

"*Why* does Grampa go to church? After all the hardships and beatings, all the things that happened to him—why does he believe without question?"

To her surprise her grandmother's face had turned tender. "He *must* believe. In that pitiful pea pod of a boat, rowing over a hundred thousand miles of ocean, fighting the most powerful animal of them all—and in its own element at that—where could he look for comfort? All the gods and saints man has invented since the jungle beginning of time wouldn't be enough to pray to, when those terrible flukes rise up above your head like the black, forked hand of death . . . Don't judge him, Josefina—never! Not for that. You would do the same thing yourself."

Sitting in the hot, safe sunlight she shivered when she thought of the cataclysmic impact of that vast body, the shock—spinning through space in a murderous shower of lances and oars and spars and line; fighting for air in a boiling chaos of shattered planking and dying men . . . Grampa once said maybe God allowed disaster to happen because it tested us, made us better, but later Tip Ames had stuck out his lower lip in that funny way and said No, with all due re-

71

spect to her grandfather, that just didn't make any sense—how could you *be* a better person if you were battered to death? or if you were starving because you'd been thrown out of a job? Tip said it was up to you to make what you could of *yourself*—she remembered the fire in his eyes when he said there was no limit to how far anyone could go if he was willing to buckle down and apply himself.

His last letter had been bristling with plans; he was working with a man he thought the world of named Frank Delahant, selling a new, different kind of correspondence course. He said Grama would love it—it was going to enable everyone to become his own lawyer accountant, half a dozen other things: the whole world could free itself of her land sharks and money-men. When Jophy told her, Grama had laughed her wintry laugh and said she wished him luck, that *her* course had taught her there were too many chowderheads who couldn't see the road to freedom if it was lighted with a beacon every fifty feet; they were simply too lazy. Some fools would always actually *want* to put their heads right in the mouth of the shark; and what did he propose to do about *them?*

Still, Tip was going to do what he said he would; she would bet on it. She could picture him riding along the sleepy country roads, whistling some tune— that incredibly sweet, melodious trill of his, haunting and cheerful. "Where'd you *ever* learn to whistle like that?" she'd asked him, and he'd grinned and said: "Nowhere. Just picked it up. A man can't be a sourpuss if he can whistle . . ." He was so confident—he had so much determination, so much *energy*. If energy alone would do it, he was going to catch the world by the tail . . .

She finished the splice for the fifth time, yanked at it, thumped it on the schooner's deck. She felt supremely happy. The sun licked softly at her flesh, gulls rocked and soared high above Brewster's Wharf, the blood pumped warm and quick from the very core of her. She burst into a chantey, her voice high and ringing.

> *"Oh, the Cape Cod girls, they have no combs—*
> *Heave away! Heave away!*
> *They comb their hair with codfish bones—*
> *Heave away! Heave away!*
> *Heave away, my brown boys, heave away!*
>   *Heave away!*
> *Heave away—and don't-you-make-a-noise,*
> *For we're bound for—Aus-tralia! . . .*

The solitary applause, so near, made her start. A slender figure in crew shirt and flannels, leaning indolently against a bollard, clapping. She had no idea how long he'd been there, watching her.

"*Very* good!" he said, and bounded up to her. At a glance she took in a slim, handsome face, mild blue eyes, a shock of smooth, chestnut hair. "Very impressive. Not quite Melba, of course. But nicely sustained tessitura, *good* chest tone—and lovely mezzo timbre."
· He smiled then, and she recognized him as one of the occupants of a beautiful red-hulled sloop she'd found herself racing the day before. There'd been a smart southeast wind, a good 18 to 20 knots and building, and she could tell they didn't know how to handle her. With all that sail they'd overhauled her slowly, two boys and two girls, and there was much laughter and waving; then they realized they weren't going to make the Number Three buoy on that reach, and decided at the last second to jibe inside it—and very nearly capsized. That had scared them badly, and they'd hung luffing in the wind, grappling with the sheets and trying to gaff something they'd lost overboard, while she tore on past them, in high glee.

"Who is Melba?" she asked.

"You don't know the prima diva?" But he was not patronizing her; his mouth had a way of curving down charmingly at the corners. He looked eighteen or nineteen. "I'll have to play you some of my Red Seal records—she's nothing short of magnificent."

She said impersonally: "I'd like to hear them."

She had busied herself with the splice again, and he was standing with one foot on the cabin trunk, forearms loosely crossed on his knee, watching her.

"It isn't often you find a young lady splicing rope," he observed. "Especially such a beautiful young lady."

She raised her head and looked straight at him then. "It isn't often you find a brand new Marconi-rigged sloop beaten hollow by a dinky fourteen-foot cutter."

He stared at her—threw back his head in delight. "—You!" he exclaimed, and slapped his knee. "Touché."

"What?"

"Your point. Miss . . .?" He looked at her inquiringly.

"Gaspa," she answered.

"Gaspa . . . Gaspa—" he snapped his fingers, "—where have I heard that name?"

"Anywhere on Cape Cod. There are Gaspas in Provincetown, in Falmouth. My grandfather was a Grand Banks captain. So was my father."

"No—it was in some other connection. Can't remember." When he frowned he looked even more handsome. The thin, high-ridged nose and chiseled lips gave his face a faintly hawklike cast. His pale blue eyes sparkled with good humor. "No, I meant it's odd to see a girl doing—well, man's work. So to speak."

"You mean I ought to be mending sails?" she inquired sweetly. "Women's work. So to speak. I can do that too."

"Well—it might be more in your line."

"I see. And yours would be hammering out a cap iron over at the forge?"

"Cap iron. Where does that go?"

"Right—up—there." She pointed above her head to

74

where the main and topmast joined, watching his face as he squinted aloft, shading his eyes.

"That *is* high up, isn't it?"

"Not so very."

"Too high for me!" He straightened again, shoved his hands in his pockets. "I can see I've come upon a foursquare, dyed-in-the-wool blue-water sailor—where I least expected to. Would you take me sailing some afternoon, Miss Gaspa?" There was a quality of amusement in his smile that she didn't like; but there was something else—a kind of assured indifference, a leisured grace, that piqued her, drew her.

"The fact is," he was saying, "I really don't know too awfully much about sailing."

"É muito patente," she murmured.

"I beg your pardon?"

"That is *my* foreign language," she said, and her eyes began to sparkle.

"Of course! Touché again." He seemed obscurely pleased. He peered up at the masthead, but in a different way. "We passed a Portuguese schooner the second day out of Cherbourg. She was going to the Grand Banks—at least the purser said she was. There was quite a storm—well, not for you, perhaps, but storm enough for me—and that schooner was riding so low in the water. At times she'd sink right out of sight, all you could see were the tops of her sails."

"Oh, that's nothing," she said airily. "My grandfather knew a man who sailed two thousand miles in a whaleboat."

"Really? In an open boat—that's amazing."

"Not only that, but they made landfall less than two degrees south of Paita, where they were headed."

But the word *Cherbourg* had penetrated, and curiosity swept away all the cool reticence she'd striven for. "You've been to Europe?" she couldn't refrain from asking.

"Oh, yes." He might have been referring to a drive

to Barnstable. "Twice. The last time with some fellows from school."

"It sounds—exciting."

"It was great fun. We went just about everywhere." A shadow of resentment crossed his face. "I've been keen to go back—but of course that's out now. With the war."

"Yes, it's terrible. All those men killed at Verdun. Do you think it might be over soon?"

He shook his head. "Professor Hoadley says the forces are too evenly divided. Unless of course Russia sues for peace. Or we get into it."

She stared at him. "Oh, but *we* won't. Will we?"

"We could. If the Germans don't stop this new submarine campaign. If our access to foreign markets is cut off we'll have to fight—we can't allow that."

He scowled then, his face turned sterner, quite plain—and with a quick, delighted shock she knew who he was.

"What's the matter?"

"—You're Chapin Ames," she said, before she'd thought. "Tip's brother."

His eyes flickered at her—an expression she couldn't fathom. "That's right," he said. "How do you know Tip?"

"Oh, he was here one summer . . ." She stopped; his eyes had deepened curiously, gray-blue rings on rings; or perhaps it was only the heavy bank of clouds that had just begun to beat up out of the south.

"Oh, sure," he finished for her. "That summer I was in Europe. When our sailing was delayed. Of course!" His manner seemed suddenly more intent—he was leaning toward her now, his eyes moving over her face and figure in a way that made her oddly nervous.

"Where did you go in Europe?" she asked.

"Everywhere. Well, almost everywhere." His voice light with that bemused assurance he talked about the lords and ladies at Ascot, the smoky glow of Montparnasse at twilight, Montreux and Florence and the Escorial, the luxuriance of the tropic gardens in the Parque Edouardo VII—

"Lisbon?" she broke in on him. "You were in Lisbon?"

"Oh, sure. Have you been there?"

"No—no. I haven't."

"You must—it would mean so much to you." While the rain clouds swept low overhead, turning the air still and cool, he told her about the broad avenues with their festive mosaics of black-and-white tiles; and the lordly Belém Tower, with the Tagus washing against its pink stone, half-covering the marble stairs with fine sand; and above all the Church of São Jeronimo, its mighty pillars still tilted from the great earthquake, and the tombs of Da Gama and Camões, seafarer and poet, on each side of the portal . . .

"Da Gama!" she heard herself say.

He laughed, watching her out of the sides of his eyes, bounded over the cabin house, leaped to the wheel, cried: "On to the Indies! There'll be no talk of turning back. Go below, I tell you—all of you!" His chestnut hair ruffling in the sudden wind, shirt rippling at his waist, his pale eyes dancing with fun and self-mockery, he looked impossibly romantic and handsome. Laughing herself, twisting absently the bright strands of rope, feeling the first spatter of rain on her cheek, she was conscious of a tight, almost painful catch of the heart . . .

They ran back through the rain to her house. Her grandmother was in court at Barnstable, but Grampa was sitting in his captain's chair on the verandah, carving. Chapin talked with him about Lisbon, the vessels in the Tagus with their canoe-shaped prows like inverted parrots' beaks and painted heavy-lidded eyes of blue and green and red, the exotic lateen rig that made them look like corsair vessels on a daring raid . . .

When the rain let up he asked her over to his aunt's house—he wanted to show her his collection. There were snuff boxes and pill boxes and cases for sewing and writing and for nothing at all, made of tortoise, of silver, of ebony and teak and mother-of-pearl. Her hand paused on one small chest—it was of some strange dark wood, oriental or perhaps African, with ivory inlay, scrimshaw unmistakably. On the cover was a whaleship—she could tell from the tryworks, the whaleboats slung above her rails—setting off down a channel, leaving behind the pointed spire of a church rising out of a cluster of roofs.

"Why, it's beautiful!" she cried. "Wherever did you find it?"

"An antique shop over in New Bedford." His eyes moved from hers to the box and back again. "I almost missed it—it was hidden under a tray with a lot of junk . . ."

She picked it up and looked at it closely now. The front showed an outrigger drawn up on a white beach with lazily curving palms under which a girl was standing, bare-breasted, wearing a lava-lava, her arms raised. On the left side a whale was swimming peacefully, his great domed head gleaming, the jet from his blowhole like an ostrich plume; the right side showed a whaleboat, oarsmen pulling hard, harpooner standing with his thigh against the clumsy cleat, iron in his hands, mate leaning back on the sweep, urgently gesturing. Jophy quickly turned the box around. But on the back face there was only the sea, empty and immeasurable, a few seabirds circling above—what? There was nothing. Whatever had been in that vast expanse of ocean had vanished forever.

She bit her lip, set the box down on the marble-topped table with care.

"What's the matter?"

"Nothing. Nothing. It's—very beautiful."

"Isn't it? Isn't it? The man was a Cellini. Imagine a talent like that wasted in a fo'c'sle!"

"Yes—imagine." She looked up; his gaze was concentrated on the tiny chest with a fervor that was almost painful. It was—it was almost as though that box were a living creature, some actual flesh-and-blood person . . . Obscurely troubled she turned away—and looked right into the gaze of an older woman standing perfectly motionless in the doorway: her features were finer than Chapin's, more aquiline, her hair was a dull silver and piled high; her eyes were the deepest, coolest blue, and flat now with a steady appraisal. It was Chapin's Aunt Serena, she knew. She drew in her breath in surprise.

"—How do you do," she said aloud.

Chapin turned then, said: "Oh hello, Auntie. I've been boasting about my acquisitions."

"So I see." Her eyes still on Jophy she said, "I don't believe I've had the pleasure of meeting your companion."

"Oh—I'm sorry!" he said with his easy, indifferent laugh. "May I present Miss Josefina Gaspa. My aunt, Miss Serena Aldridge."

"Ma'am." Jophy made a quick half-curtsy, as Grama had taught her to do with older persons. Miss Aldridge smiled, and nodded.

"Ah, yes. Captain Gaspa's granddaughter."

"Yes. And daughter."

"Of course. And daughter. I'm told you're quite an intrepid sailor in your own right. Is that true?"

She smiled and said: "I like to sail."

"She is," Chapin broke in, "—Gus Lawring and I were out with the girls the other day and she beat us all hollow. She knew what we were going to do before we'd even thought of it—it was uncanny." He looked at Jophy with the amused, teasing smile. "Do you consult with occult powers?"

"Only sea gods," she laughed.

"Perhaps it's an inherited skill," Serena Aldridge

said. "Do you believe in inherited characteristics, Miss Gaspa?"

It was a smile that was not a smile. These Yankees! With a trace of spirit she said formally: "Yes—I believe in racial gifts."

"So do I, Miss Gaspa. I'm gratified that you share that view."

"Of course"—and now Jophy looked straight into those cool blue eyes—"they aren't always favorable. Are they?"

Serena Aldridge's brows rose, her eyes dilated in a curious way and then narrowed again in the shrewd suggestion of a smile. "Perhaps you'll stay and have tea. Would you care to, Miss Gaspa?"

Later, walking home with Chapin, crossing the rickety foot bridge over the Upper Channel, Jophy was caught up in an irrepressible hilarity. She felt as though she had just been through some unclassifiable examination and passed it with flying colors—she was both elated and furious with herself for being elated, for thinking of it that way. It had just—been tea at the Bluffs; hadn't it? What was so infernally special about that? Chapin, too, seemed off-balance, exuberant and reticent by turns, watching her askance while she did an imitation of Miss Cincepaugh, her Yankee schoolmarm, and chattered away like a monkey in a palm tree. When he gave her his hand outside the whalebone archway she squeezed it involuntarily, feeling tense and silly, almost out of control.

"You *will* teach me how to sail?" he asked eagerly.

"How *can* I?—you haven't a drop of Portuguese blood!" She laughed once, withdrew her hand quickly; her body had turned warm and moist, which frightened her a little.

"Perhaps you can give me an infusion."

"I can try!"

His eyes were ringed with gray, and flecked with tiny points of amber; she wanted to touch the hard line of his jaw and throat at the open-necked shirt. Just touch it with her fingers.

"I'm serious," he was saying.

"So am I!"

She tore her eyes away and said yes, she'd go sailing with him next day. If the weather was good.

6

"Rye whisky, rye whisky, rye whisky, I cry," Jack Darcey sang softly. Holding his shot glass like a chalice he raised it toward the tungsten bulb in the new electric chandelier hanging above the bar, and turned it with admiring care; the beveled edges glittered. "Now isn't that the most enchanting sight you've ever beheld?"

"Nope," Tip Ames answered promptly.

"Of course it is. Just look at the soothing, golden glow . . ."

"False topaz," Tip murmured, gazing at it.

"What the hell's that?"

"Oh—an old New England term."

"And a roaring misnomer, if I ever heard one." Jack Darcey downed the drink with a flourish, and gave Tip his most infectious grin, his green eyes sparkling. Jack had a sharp nose and a fine shock of red hair which he always kept perfectly trimmed. He favored high collars and snappy bow ties, and he had a ready answer for any situation. He was twenty-three. "No, Tip my lad—whisky's the one, true-blue friend in a faithless and uncertain world." Motioning toward the bartender he said, "You'll join me in another round, of course?"

Tip shook his head. "This one'll hold me."

"Ah—the Yankee discipline. I admire it, really I do. But we've earned it, Tip. Look at it that way—look at

83

the business we've done! We've set the old north woods afire . . ."

The roads, bricked or cobbled or corduroyed with logs or just plain pounded dirt, were the strands; the towns that lay between them were their jewels, glowing with infinite promise, with more flamboyant possibilities than the Arabian Nights. The two young men would stand in front of the gloomy Vermont Central depot, gazing down Main Street: bank and dry goods emporium were on one side, hardware and grain stores and mill offices on the other. Tip would take the half dollar out of his watch pocket and spin it high in the air, a blurred silver sphere in the crisp fall light.

"Tails," Jack Darcey would say.

"Tails it is."

"I'll take the mill side. You can have the bank— when Silas Pelletier gets his hands on a dollar it retires from circulation." Jack's head went back in silent laughter. "You'll never sell him in a million years."

"We'll see about that."

At five-thirty they'd meet back at the hotel. The trick was to reach Canada without spending a single dime of your own—to make it on your commissions, all the way up the long valley. They had fallen into the game one evening as the result of some good-natured banter, and now it was their pattern. Tip loved it—it was the craziest kind of rivalry he could ever have imagined.

People were the fascinating part. People were defensive, boastful, wary, stubborn, sly, cantankerous, skeptical, bitter—people were more complicated than you'd ever have believed. You learned to watch for personal mannerisms—the pulling of an earlobe, the apologetic cough, the eyelid-flicker of suspicion, most of all the movement of hands—the personal memento that served as a paperweight, the family photo, the print decorating the rear wall: often they told you more than anything else. Some prospects closed the door and wanted to hear the latest one about the traveling salesman and the farmer's daughter; or they sent out for a couple of bottles of birch beer and wanted to know what they were saying down in Springfield about this new federal land bank, whether it was going to ease the money squeeze on the small farmer; or they cocked their feet up on the desk and wondered if Hughes had a really good chance to beat Wilson. Some men hung onto you like the Ancient Mariner and wanted to tell you their life stories, others sat back behind bony, vaulted fingertips, tightlipped and forbidding; some even baited you, taunting, *daring* you to ignite their interest— and they were the most intoxicating challenge of all. And there were those who simply couldn't believe it when you called on them again.

"But I told you, young fellow—I'm just not interested . . ."

"I appreciate that, sir. But times change, attitudes—I know my own have, often enough! [A disarming opener his youth made all the more palatable.] Anyway, it occurred to me, now you've moved up in the firm [a little praise never hurt, the man didn't live who wasn't hungry for simple recognition of his worth in the scheme of things], and I remembered how interested you were in some of the new advertising techniques they've come up with down in Hartford, when I was by in August [it didn't hurt to let them know *you* remembered, either] . . . The thing is, I've seen so many businesses expanded, so many people's *lives* actually transformed by Alexander Hamilton Institute, I'm so completely sold on its tremendous possibilities myself, that I wanted to stop by again and share it with you . . ."

And of course it was more than that, too, It showed people you remembered, you thought about them; that you *cared*. And he did care: people were what mattered—he'd never stopped believing that. He dressed soberly and neatly, he kept customer files in two stacks of three-by-five cards, studded with keys and symbols he could decipher at a glance, as Beau Frank Delahant, now sales manager over in Boston, had taught him. He'd memorized everything about Alec Ham until he could recite it backwards and forwards; but it was the things about people he remembered—the chronic asthma, the partner who'd absconded with the funds, the woodworking hobby, the son off to college—that no one ever had to teach him, and that made the difference. And above and in and around it all lay that Independence Day rocket-shower of images, the sun-burst certainty that he could persuade anyone of anything, sell refrigeration to the Eskimos, as they said, or hot-air-furnaces in the Sudan. He had found his true vocation beyond any doubt, as he'd known all along he would . . .

"I don't know about you, Tip my lad," Jack Darcey was saying, "but I've got a case of the royal megrims. You ever come down with them?"

"Constantly."

"Good." Jack slapped the stained mahogany bull-nose of the bar. "Let's go pay our humble respects to the Countess."

"Who's the Countess?"

"You're standing at the rail of Fortrain's Bar in Ste. Hélène and you haven't met the Countess? Come with me, bucko—you're in for the experience of your young life."

Tip grinned slowly, watching the other man. "I'll see you back at the hotel."

"Now *why* won't you come? Give me three sound reasons why."

"I'm—just not in the mood. You go ahead."

Jack gazed at him in hurt amazement. "You mean you'd let me go there *alone*?"

"That's the idea."

"But you can't *do* that."

"Watch me."

"I don't believe what I'm hearing." Jack's face had gone slack with shocked indignation. "You're my business associate, aren't you? Fellow salesman, aren't you? That means you're responsible."

"Responsible! For what?"

"For my safety and well-being. What else?"

"The hell it does."

"Of course it does. You're my friend, my comrade-in-arms in a hostile land beset with pitfalls. Can you actually contemplate letting me go down to the Countess' and get rolled?"

"Yep."

"Ah—I see." Jack's green eyes took on a bright, madcap gleam. "I get it. You're *hoping* I'll get rolled. They'll steal my pants while I'm otherwise occupied and there I'll be, stranded and busted, and *you'll* be home free—you won't have the ghost of a worry about beating me out this time. I'm one up on you right now—I don't imagine you've forgotten that little item. Have you, Tip-O?"

Tip laughed, and wagged his head. "You've got more arguments than a dog has fleas."

"Flexibility of approach, isn't it? Imaginative enterprise, seeking out every persuasive sales angle—isn't that what Beau Frank says?"

"That's what he says. I should have known better than to let you get rolling . . . All right—I'll go down there with you. But that's it."

"Who could ask for more? I knew I could count on a colleague and pal . . ."

Ste. Hélène was noisy and tough. Lumberjacks in plaid shirts and highlaced leather boots stalked its sidewalks, their iron cleats scoring triangular scars in the broad planking. Bargemen in watch caps and pea jackets rolled down the middle of the street singing boisterously, trappers in fur caps glided by like ghosts with great wolves silent at their heels. The sense of frontier was in the air here, dense with liquor and hemlock and woodsmoke. Wide-open, the salesmen called it; a wide-open burg. Ste. Hélène caught the trade down from Montreal to New York City, or from Watertown east to St. Johnsbury. It passed along fur and lumber and apples in return for farm machinery and mouthwash and gingham and other such blessings of civilization, and threw in various forms of recreation to the weary traveler passing through. The law, cynical and harassed, did what the law so often did: it looked the other way.

The house was at the far end of the main street, where the arc lights were dim; ahead the lake glittered blackly. It was a rambling structure with a Georgian portico and a formidable Mansard roof. Tip guessed it must once have been a lakeside resort. From the street it looked dark and deserted—the curtains in the long front windows were drawn.

"—not one of your common land-office floozie parlors," Jack Darcey was saying, walking rapidly in the chill dark. "Here's-your-hat-where's-your-hurry. You know what I mean. No, the Countess runs an *establishment*, I want to tell you. The Countess has class . . ."

His voice ran half a note higher in key, and Tip, responding to its intonation rather than the words, was conscious of a low hum of excitement, of pleasurably guilty anticipation. He had never been to what the drummers winkingly referred to as a bawdy house. There weren't any in Holcomb Falls—or none that he'd ever heard about. Of course his fancies had flamed sometimes with visions of half-naked women sprawled wantonly over satin chaises or writhing in some tantalizing dance; but running from job to job, bolting his meals, scanning books he'd have liked to read with slow care, clawing incessantly for time, he'd beaten down his need . . . and since he'd met Jophy Gaspa, she had become that need. The thought of her flashing thighs, the lustrous dark sheen of hair, the coral swell of her lower lip could make him physically tremble—he wanted desperately to kiss that hollow crescent cupped between her throat and shoulder. She was all he longed for now; her wild, breath-caught passion, that secret smouldering at the core of her. He asked for nothing more than to be making enough money to ask her to marry him . . .

Jack knocked smartly once, then three times, then once again; winked at Tip. There was a soft click, and what looked like an ornamental section of moulding in the upper rail slid back; and in the sudden slot of light two eyes glittered, and vanished. The door opened, and an enormous black man in frock coat and flowing cravat said in booming, genial tones;

"Good evening, Mr. Darcey."

"And a lively good evening to you, Jethro! I want you to meet my friend and business associate, Tip Ames."

"How do you do," Tip said. He felt his extended hand enclosed in a grip he knew could crush it easily.

"Mr. Ames. New to the territory, are you?"

"More or less."

For an instant the big man's eyes held on his piercingly, marking him; then he nodded and stepped back with a slow, stately gesture.

"If you gentlemen would pass on into the parlor, please."

Entering the room Tip felt a vast sense of disappointment. Couples sat on velvet Victorian sofas or at rose-marble tables talking quietly or sipping at their drinks; girls in low-necked but hardly indecent gowns gracefully descended the long stairway and greeted clients they knew, or stood chatting easily with one another. A walnut gramophone in one corner was playing a Strauss waltz. Tip recognized a fellow named Grantham who sold farm machinery, and there was another man with a bushy mustache and imperial he'd seen somewhere on the road. There was nothing very daring down here. Except for the liquor and the intimate atmosphere the soft light reflected on the wine-red velour draperies, it could have been a church social. To cover his awkwardness he murmured:

"Well-behaved little gathering."

"It better be." Jack chuckled. "You saw Jethro, didn't you? You don't want to do anything rash, son. They say he once had Jim Jeffries on the canvas. He's part Seneca. He carries a Smith and Wesson .44, and they say he's never once had to use it."

An older woman came up to them briskly then and said in a pretty French accent, "Mr. Darcey! Quel plaisir . . ."

"Why, good evening, Countess." He took her hand gallantly in both of his.

"I don't believe I've had the honor of meeting your friend."

"No, you haven't—this is Tipton Ames."

"Ah. Mr. Ames." She was very tall, with a fine, full figure; she wore her blond hair in a feathery halo about her face. A single strand of pearls lay snug around her throat. "I am Antoinette Bouchard."

"But we all call her the Countess," Jack interjected.

"A fancy that has grown into fact." She smiled without revealing her teeth. "No country adores nobility quite so much as a solid, grass-roots democracy. Isn't that curious?"

"Maybe it's because we want a great man," Tip said.

"Maybe." Her eyes were a light brown and very clear—her glance was searching, but not suspicious. There was something deeply attractive about her. "But maybe it is another kind of dream altogether."

"Countess," Jack asked her, "is Terry around?"

She shook her head. "Thérèse is not here. Her mother has fallen ill, she has gone home. But"—and she gestured toward two girls sitting on a nearby seat who rose together and came forward—"may I present Clare and Suzanne . . ." She made the introductions like a court function, excused herself with the easy, charming smile, and moved off into another room.

Clare had a sweet face but a pouting mouth that turned down a bit at the corners. Suzanne was small and dark—a sultry little pepper-pot. Smiling at them, ill at ease, Tip thought at once of Jophy and dismissed them both. Pretty enough, but . . . to walk up those stairs, whip off your clothes and climb into bed with them, just like that—without any confidences, without that pulsing thrum of sheer need, that fierce catch high under the heart . . .

Jack however was taken with Suzanne—he was already making his pitch, teasing her, had slipped his arm under hers; with a swift, surreptitious wink at Tip he led her off up the long, curving stairway. His arm had stolen around her waist now, his flaming red head was pressed close to hers—

"Maybe you'd like a drink," Clare was saying to him in a low, husky voice. "Would you like a drink?" Underneath the pale powder she looked tired; her eyes drooped a little at the corners, like her mouth.

"No thanks," he answered. "You go ahead . . ." He gestured vaguely about the room. "Don't mind me. I don't want to—to impose on your time."

She frowned, perplexed. "My time . . .?"

"I mean—I just came along with Jack. To keep him company." That sounded even worse; he could feel his face getting warm.

"What's the matter? Are you sick?"

"Sick?—no, not at all. It's just that I'm not—interested in—"

Her hands went to her hips, she looked sullen and angry. "Well now look, if you don't think I'm good enough—"

"No, no," he protested, feeling like a complete and utter idiot, "it's not that at all, I find you very attractive, really very attractive . . ."

"Well then, give me a chance, can't you?"

"It's not that . . ." He felt baffled, amused at how ridiculous he sounded, standing here, and at the same time chagrined at letting himself in for this. "Please

91

understand," he plodded lamely on, "it's no reflection on you, on your attractiveness, I mean—it's my fault, really, I—"

But she wasn't listening; she was looking past his shoulder, her face alive with expectation—she looked like a much younger, prettier girl.

"Harry!" she called softly, and waved two fingers. Tip turned to see a stocky man with a square, weather-beaten face. "Long time no see . . ." She glanced at Tip. "I'm sorry, it's just that I've known this gentleman—"

"It's quite all right," he broke in. "You go ahead."

"You're sure?" Now she looked troubled—a hostess faced with conflicting demands; he had an enormous desire to burst out laughing.

"Absolutely," he answered. "You go right ahead. It's fine. Fine."

"Well, all right . . ." She broke away with a faint, apologetic smile and crossed over to the new arrival. Relieved, Tip wandered into an alcove off the second parlor. It was empty. He sat down on a couch, pulled out of his breast pocket the letter he'd been carrying with him for the past three weeks, and started reading at the uppermost page.

right out of the southeast, the hurricane quarter, the surf was terrifying, I've never seen anything like it. Capt. Cardosa, who's gone to the Banks for 32 years, said it was the worst Line gale he'd ever seen. The Coast Guard tried to launch four times, and each time they got swamped or capsized. Every once in a while you could see someone moving on the deck of the schooner, and then the seas would boil over her and you couldn't see anyone at all. It was terrible! Finally they got the gun in position and fired a line across her decks and rigged the breeches buoy (you can imagine what THAT took!) and started running people in. It was scary—the person lashed into the breeches buoy would creep along inch by inch, and then one of those monster breakers would sweep right over him, and then up he'd come again. Several of the men were hurt badly, you could see the bone of one man's leg sticking right out through the flesh and tendons. Maria Silva fainted dead away right there on the beach. But I was all right, all the way through it. Dr. Glover thanked me afterward, told me he couldn't have coped as well without my help. What do you think of that!!! He's such a good man, so thin, with that droopy mustache and those tired, tired eyes. His wife died the year after they were married, all those years ago and he never remarried, never even looked at another woman, they say, just buried himself in his work. Isn't that sad?

Anyway, I have GREAT NEWS!!! I got so excited by my heroic day there on the Back Beach that I'm tearing a page out of your book—I'm taking a correspondence course: in nursing! Glorified first aid is all it is really, but it's better than nothing. Maybe I'll go up to Boston and enroll at Mass. General; they say there's a great need for competent nurses in the war. I want to DO something crucial—

Northeaster moving in here. Grampa's leg is the best glass in the world. The waves are churning in out beyond Blackfish Point—the sea looks absolutely black under the white foam. Another dreary winter coming. I wish I had your steadiness, Tip. Golly, how I envy you, out on your own, traveling to New Haven and Burlington and MONTREAL!!! I wish I could fly. No, seriously. Just spread my wings like one of Grampa's albatross and soar away and away to one of his glorious islands: maybe Manokela, where they ride those thin wooden sleds right along the leading edge of the breakers—can't you imagine what sheer, dizzy FUN that must be?!?!

Oh well. Here I am. Dreaming as usual. When what I REALLY want is to be like the woman in Traviata. "Sempre libera." What courage—my God! If I could only be like her. Chapin was down from Harvard weekend before last, looking very grand—wearing a blue blazer and flannels and has taken to smoking a

Meerschaum pipe. He thinks we're going to be in the war soon, no matter what President Wilson's been promising the country on the stump. A classmate's joined the Lafayette Escadrille and Chapin said for two cents he'd join up, too—he says the only way he'll get over to Europe again is get the blasted war over with. Your Aunt Serena told him not to talk nonsense, he was going to do no such thing. And he gave her that amused, sidelong look, you know the one, and said

Tip closed the letter on his thumb and stared hard at the fringed lampshade. On the phonograph in the parlor a man's voice sang softly:

> *"Pale hands I loved—*
> *Beside the Shalima-ar . . ."*

—It wasn't enough he'd been handed St. Marks and Harvard and Europe and sailboats and expensive clothes and all the rest of it—no, by God, that wasn't enough. He'd had to move in on Jophy into the bargain . . . He struck his fist against his thigh—looked down ruefully at the crushed sheets of paper and began to smooth them with care. He had to get down there. He had to! It had been a shock when he'd learned Jophy and Chapin had met, were seeing each other. His heart had turned over in anger, in alarm. He'd tried to tell himself he was being absurd—they were after all in the same small town all summer long, it would have been only a question of time—but the chill uneasiness, the deep, hot resentment remained. If he could be there, on the ground, it would be different, he'd take his chances against anyone—let alone his brother; but here, on the road for weeks at a stretch, separated from her by the whole rocky breadth of New England, he was seized in frustration. It was too unequal a contest . . .

He'd managed to get over to the Cape on Memorial Day weekend, but everything had gone wrong. The weather was cold and blustery, her grandfather was ill, everything seemed off-balance, awry. Jophy was even more beautiful than he'd remembered her; she seemed strangely abstracted, tense and frivolous by turns. He crushed her to him; they kissed until roofs and masts and treetops whirled and dipped around their heads like sea birds, like swallows. Her eyes glowed, her cheeks glistened bronze in the rain wind. The long year's absence had been torture—he was half-crazy with wanting her, and told her so; but she hesitated when he pressed her further, and it drove him frantic.

"Engagement! Tip, that's crazy . . ."

"Why? *Why* is it crazy?"

"It's just—we're too young for that, too young—"

"I'm old enough to be on the road, earning a living . . ."

"Oh, that's not what I mean!" She made a fierce little gesture of distress. "We've got all our *lives* ahead of us."

"There's no life for me without you, Jo."

"That's ridiculous! How can you say that?"

"Because it's true. There never will be."

"You can't know that—nobody can know something like that . . ."

"*I* can."

"Well, I can't!"

Goaded by dread he said: "Is it Chapin? Is that it?"

"Chapin—?"

"All right—he's got the education, the money, all the rest of it. But damn it, Jo, *I've* got the heart—and he doesn't!"

"Chapin—I know Chapin!" Her eyes flashed at him once. "Chapin tries to shut everyone out. He wants to own the Louvre . . ."

He looked at her, hard. "But you're tempted, just the same. Aren't you?"

But she'd only laughed then, and shaken her head at him as if he'd lost his marbles.

He knew he wasn't reaching her, somehow. He'd pressed on, the wind whipping the words away from his mouth, summoning up all his persuasiveness, all his tenacity and ardor, and she'd gazed back at him wordlessly, her eyes troubled and unreadable . . . He *had* to get down there—! The need, the sheer desolate ache for her deep in his vitals was overpowering. Just to be near her, in her presence—if he could only *be* with her he could persuade her of this, he knew he could, he'd never failed to convince anybody of anything once he'd set his mind to it, it was just a question of—

"And was there no one of my young ladies who pleased you?"

He turned guiltily now, slipped the letter back into his pocket. Antoinette Bouchard was standing in the doorway. The other rooms were quiet; there was only a low murmur from the main parlor.

"No, not at all," he began, "they're very attractive, very—"

"Your wife *does* understand you, alors."

He smiled with her. "No—I'm not married."

"Ah—then you are in love." She came up and sat down beside him on the couch, her back very straight. "Deeply and irrevocably in love."

He grinned ruefully. "It's that plain?"

To his surprise she reached out and ran her fingers gently under his chin. "And so young . . ."

"Not as young as all that."

"Oh yes, you are. That is *my* business. Ages, aging. Love, no love . . ." She tossed her head, looked away. "You wonderful, impossible Americans! You are supposed to be materialistic and calculating, so cold— nothing but dollar signs in your eyes. It's not true at all. You are the supreme romantics in the entire history of the human race. You are unbeatable! *You* are the ones who should have pursued the Holy Grail— not the British. The British act as though they've already found it, anyway . . ."

He laughed, watching her—he felt utterly at his ease. This proud, handsome woman tossed thoughts here and there at random, like an empress scattering pearls before some ecstatic multitude; but the thoughts all moved in one way, toward one end. It was *her* pitch—a very subtle one; one he couldn't follow quite yet. He listened, delighted and intrigued.

"You will conquer the world," she was saying. "They are right, your politicians, your hommes d'affaires: it is the American Century."

"But we're not conquerors," he protested, "not like—" he stopped.

"Like Napoleon?" She smiled her secret smile, eyeing him; it *had* been what he was going to say. "No. You are not. But it won't matter, you see. Another two years, three, and Europe will lie empty and broken. Oh, yes." She stared at him levelly, nodding. "It is dying now. The letters I have received, the letters—you wouldn't believe it, what has happened. Half a million dead," she said, in a voice like stone. "God knows what the German losses are. Or the British. And for three forts around Verdun, a few miles of mud and barbed wire . . . A generation of young men has been blown to pieces. Europe—and that means the world—will never be the same. You will inherit all that grandeur—and then you will throw it away."

"Throw it away? Never! Why would we do that?"

"Your romantic dreams." She smiled sadly. "Europe will be too tired, too hard, too cynical for you—it will not be enough like the Grail to satisfy your dreams. You will turn from it all in disgust. And that will be the real tragedy of the American Century."

". . . Amazing." He looked down in confusion. The thought jarred him; he needed time to think about it.

"No. Just common sense. Let me see your hand."

He extended it, palm up, thinking of that rainy Cape Cod afternoon and Annabella Gaspa's dark, intense eyes boring into his. *Ah, then you* do *know something about the world!* It wasn't true—he hadn't begun to scratch the surface; but he would, in time.

"What a fine heart line!" she exclaimed. "And the head line too, here—see, how deep and firm it is? Yes, you are a constant one . . ." She caught his eye. "You don't believe in palmistry?" He shook his head. "You ought to—you're romantic enough . . ." Still studying his hand she said softly: "What *do* you believe in?"

"In us," he answered. "In people. In all the things we can do, if we only put our minds to it." Watching the lamplight on her cheek, he thought, If I hadn't fallen in love with Jophy Gaspa I'd want to make love to this woman—right here, right now—and was pleasurably shocked at the realization.

She must have felt it through his hand; he hadn't moved a muscle. Raising her head she looked at him—a long, level, intimate gaze—bent again over his palm.

"The Mount of Jupiter is very strong, very bold. So much ambition! I can't read the Mount of Apollo—it is all callus, so is Saturn. You've worked hard."

"Yes. In a country store, in a paper mill."

"And now you wear a suit and tie. Now you are a gentleman—a young gentleman."

"Well, I—"

"When the Commune fell and Gallifet's troops entered Paris, they lined everyone up—and every man who had calluses on his hands or wore a working-man's cap they shot. And their families."

"Their *families?*"

"Yes. Oh, yes. Women, and little children. You don't think men are capable of that? They are. Oh, they are. I was a little baby then, I don't remember any of it. But my sister did. She saw my father and mother led off down the Rue Mouffetard, she heard the volleys. My uncle saved us—he was a clerk in a railway office, he told them we were his children and he got us out of there. Away from these brave defenders of the state. He was a timid little man, afraid of his wife, afraid of losing his job, afraid of everything; but he risked his life for us that day, and saved us."

The music swelled up then from the lily-trumpet throat of the phonograph, and at the opening bars the Countess called softly: "Thank you, Jethro.—He knows it's my favorite. Listen to her."

The violins paused, tremulous and fearful, and a voice soared out of their midst—a voice more beautiful than any he'd ever heard; clear, velvet tones. And pure. So pure! Haunted perhaps by love, by memory . . .

"What is it?" he whispered.

"An aria, from an opera. 'Un bel di,' it is called. One fine day. A Japanese girl is telling herself that her American lover is coming back to her, that he *must* come back—listen . . . She is so certain that he will come back—do you hear it? There . . . there! And yet it has been three years, and the child of their love is a little boy, and she has heard nothing from him; and the possibility that he might *not* return, that he can actually have stopped loving her, is more than she can bear . . . Do you hear it? There: listen . . ."

The voice soared aloft, held one golden note with absolute purity, ringing—fell away into the violins again, fear bleeding through the trust; and the silence returned.

"What happened to her?" he had to ask.

"Oh, he comes back—but not quite in the way he has promised. There is now an American wife he wants to show her. And when he finds out about the child he wants to take the child home with him, too . . ."

"What does she do?"

The Countess shrugged; she seemed suddenly weary, worn down—as though the aria had sapped her of hope. "What choices does she have? She has cut off all ties to her own people, she has staked everything, absolutely everything, on her love . . . She kills herself."

"—Oh," he murmured.

She looked at him solemnly, her eyes flat and quite hard. "Can you imagine that? A love like that?"

"Yes," he said. "Oh, yes. I can."

For a moment she searched his face, shook her head in slow wonder. "Yes. I think you can. You are a singular young man . . . What do you do?"

"I'm a salesman."

"Oh yes—like Mr. Darcey. What do you sell?"

"Confidence," he said.

"Confidence?"

"Yes. All the possibilities open to everyone. Right here, right now. How anyone can take hold of his affairs. Gain the knowledge he needs to control his own life . . ."

"What a curious commodity . . . And what do you do about the other half?"

"What other half?"

"The—the subordonnés, the victims?"

"Help them to become free, too—right along with everyone else."

The Countess burst out laughing for the first time. "Of course, of course! Oh, that is priceless! And what will you do about me—at the mercy of the banks, the tax collector, the law? not to mention those very proper ladies up on Livingston Street—some of whose husbands are my most devoted clients—who *really* run this town?"

"Well," he hesitated, "I can't answer for them—"

"I should think not!"

"—but if it's a question of the law, or taxes, or loans—that's right up my alley. Here's where you don't need to give ground to anybody—you can ask exactly the right questions and answer them yourself, you don't have to defer to the lawyers or the bankers. You learn the principles yourself, you see—exactly how the system works. And that knowledge can make you its master . . ."

And now the magician had taken over, as he always did, and the words came as if wished on him, as

100

if directed from some celestial source, certain in their easy cadences, persuasive, inevitable; borne on the wings of his green conviction . . . The Countess' mischievous smile had vanished, replaced by a troubled frown, which hardened after a while into cautious resolve. By the time he broke off she was gazing at him in frank wonder, her eyes wide.

"You have such hope, such energy!" she exclaimed. "So much *hope* . . . Do you really think this would be of help to me?"

"Countess, I wouldn't be sitting here taking the time of a beautiful, intelligent woman if I didn't."

"—No," she laughed again, "I don't imagine you would!"

"A-ha! There you are," Jack Darcey said from the doorway; his flaming red hair was a bit disheveled, but otherwise he looked every bit as dapper as before. "I knew I could count on a true-blue friend to keep—"

Then his eyes fell on the contract in the Countess' hand, and his jaw fell.

"You're not—he didn't . . ." His eyes shot from Tip to the Countess and back again. "You mean you—he actually got you to—"

"Indeed I did," Antoinette Bouchard declared with some spirit. "Mr. Ames has convinced me of the need to broaden my expertise. Et voilà!"

Jack turned to Tip with the expression of a betrayed martyr. "—And you mean you—while I was— you were sitting down here and *selling the Countess on Alex Ham—?*" His voice had risen half an octave. "I don't believe this . . . For Christ sake, I *brought* you here!"

"You were here on another errand." Tip grinned at him. " 'Flexibility, initiative, imagination,' " he quoted lightly. " 'You must be alert to *every* sales opportunity.' Isn't that what Beau Frank says?"

Jack Darcey smiled hollowly. "Yeah. That's what he says."

"And now we're even for the trip. In sales."

"I know." Jack glanced around aimlessly—threw out his arms, flopped them at his sides. "I'm not even going to *try* to tell anyone this story. Because if I did, they'd hand me a jacket with no sleeves in it. Where's my hat? I'm going back to the hotel. Unless of course you plan to go upstairs and start selling from room to room."

Tip shook his head, still smiling. "I know enough to quit while I'm ahead."

7

Serena Aldridge remembered the house vividly—
which was odd, because she had almost never been on
this side of the channel. One afternoon when she was
young she and Charlotte had come here soliciting con-
tributions for some good works or other; the proper
young woman's proper pastime. She had been wool-
gathering, thinking about a carriage she wanted as
she looked out at the harbor from this strangely different vista—she'd neither seen nor heard the young
man burst out at her from under the great whale's
ribs. They had collided, lightly. Serena had recoiled
and cried "Oh!" The young man had checked his
movement, swerved aside with a cat's quickness. His
hair was black and rich and tousled, his face bronzed
from a thousand different kinds of weather; his eyes
were bold and dark and very intense. He'd laughed,
then—a pleasurable catch of his breath. His arms
were bare, the muscles of his chest outlined by the
snugly fitting, striped jersey. She had raised a hand
to her face. He was smiling at her—a broad, open
smile, full of merriment—but instead of putting her
at ease it only made her feel tense, pulled off-balance.
There was something in the line of the muscle that
ran smoothly down the side of his neck into his shoulder that disturbed her unduly. Beside her Lottie was
giggling, her teeth on her lower lip; and that vexed
her even more.

"Can't you even see where you're *going?*" she had demanded in her mother's clipped, clear voice.

His laughter died instantly, his face turned a higher bronze, like metal in a forge; his eyes narrowed, snapping at her. For the barest fragment of a second he looked as if he were going to hit her, and she felt real fear. He started to say something—then the broad, full lip went slack with derision and he swung off down the street, his shoulders swaying in an easy rhythm. He didn't once look back.

"Serena!" Lottie was looking at her with reproach. "Why did you have to say something like that? In that tone?"

"Clumsy lout." She fussed at the front of her gown; she felt curiously disheveled, as though he had actually pulled at her clothing, spun her around violently, pushed her into a—

"He didn't mean anything."

"Of course he did! Didn't you *see* him?"

Her sister leaned back and looked at her, then—a very steady, penetrating glance that made her furious. "He *is* quite handsome," she said.

"Don't be ridiculous!"

"I'm not, Serena." Charlotte was still watching her with that steady, bemused expression. "I'm not the one who's ridiculous . . ."

Joseph Gaspa. She'd learned his name afterward. She had seen him on only two other occasions, the Grand Banks fishing season being what it was—once at a Fourth of July band concert on the little green in front of the town hall, looking stiff and ill at ease, sweating in a dark suit; and much later coming out of Newcombe's Marine Supply store with a length of light line coiled over one shoulder. He had touched the visor of his cap and nodded to her gravely—she was riding in the buckboard with her father—but his eyes had glinted with contemptuous amusement—and something else: what was it, what else *was* it in that glance?—that had made her clench her fists in her lap and shut her eyes tightly with rage. By then of course he'd been known throughout the Cape, and in Gloucester and Nova Scotia as well—the youngest of the Banks captains, holder of the record from Cape Sable to T Wharf, renowned for his unerring nose for fish, for his generosity, his hot temper, his sheer irrepressible audacity (it was said he refused to lower his top course in the very wildest weather) . . . A year later he was gone—he and that beautiful, dancing blackhulled schooner, the entire crew . . . All her anger had been wasted, then. She smiled at herself grimly. All for nothing. He had vanished as though he'd never been.

Well. Not entirely.

The great whale's ribs threw their arching shadow over her, released her as swiftly. The blackfish vertebrae, too, she remembered; they felt strangely light, almost resilient as she traversed them. The nasturtium beds bordering the walk assailed her with a wild profusion of color, a rich scent in the midsummer heat. Serena rapped on the door smartly, twice.

After a short pause it opened. She recognized Annabella Gaspa at once—she had encountered her here and there in town, and at the big hearing in Barnstable that May when Congressman Shalott had urged the fishermen to continue going to the Banks in spite of the war—that America needed the fish they caught, it was up to them to show themselves every bit as patriotic as those boys who were enlisting by the tens of thousands—

"And how patriotic is our *Navy* prepared to be?"

Serena Aldridge had turned with the others. Senhora Annabella Gaspa had been standing at the rear of the hall, very erect, looking up at the platform. She wore a short bolero jacket and had a white kerchief over her head.

The Congressman had blinked at her, frowning. "I don't believe I understand your question, Madam."

"Forgive me, sir—I will try to be clearer." Her voice

was deep, carrying in the silence. "Will the Navy send destroyers to the Grand Banks—will they patrol while our men are out laying trawl in sixteen-foot dories?"

Congressman Shalott smiled tightly. "Well, I certainly think we can place confidence in our fleet. The Secretary has assured me that the Navy fully intends to protect our coastal shipping."

"In the same way the Union Navy protected our whaling fleet from the Confederate raider *Shenandoah*, you mean."

There was a murmur of laughter in the hall. The Congressman, getting red in the face, said: "The situation is hardly analogous, Madam. I don't believe any point will be served in bandying words with you further. I think the *gentlemen* here will have a clearer idea of what is involved."

"Have you ever been out of sight of land in a dory, Congressman?" Annabella Gaspa pursued in her best forensic voice. Again there was soft laughter.

"What? No, it so happens I have not. Now, I am trying—"

"*I have*, sir. These men must do it day after day, in all weather."

"Then let them speak. If they have any—any reservations, I want to hear them . . ."

Annabella Gaspa smiled her broad, forbidding smile. "Ah, but you see, Congressman, you have used that word. *Patriotic*. Men have always been silenced by it—they always will be. And so, because I am a woman and therefore unfitted to throw the lance or fire the gun—because I am a woman I can admit that I am afraid. Afraid *for* these men, who must go up to those cold, lonely waters with nothing but the word *patriotic* for ballast . . ."

"Madam, I *must* ask you—"

"No!" Annabella Gaspa cried. "I must ask *you*—what would *you* do if you were at the wheel of an un-armed schooner two hundred miles from Cape Race, and your dories were all out, and a German submarine broached half a cable length away and gave you five minutes to abandon ship? How much comfort would you take from the word *patriotic* then?"

She had given way after that and seated herself—but curiously she had carried the day: after some noisy debate the Banks captains demanded a written assurance from the Secretary that the Navy would protect them at least as far north as the Virgin Rocks and Banquereau.

Now, standing in the open doorway, Senhora Gaspa seemed less formidable: a heavy-set, moderately handsome woman, if a bit on the swarthy side.

"Mrs. Gaspa?"

"Yes."

"I am Serena Forbes Aldridge."

"Of course." Softly Annabella Gaspa repeated the name, with a curious little emphasis on the *Forbes*. Why had she used it? Foolish—a foolish indulgence. "Bom dia, Senhora."

"Good day, Madam . . . I hope you don't mind my stopping by like this. But I wonder if we might talk for a bit."

"Certainly. Please come in."

The interior was cool and quiet. A huge gray tom cat slung along the window ledge opened one cold citrine eye, satisfied himself about the intruder, closed it again. The Portuguese woman led the way into the parlor, stiff with horsehair sofa and high-backed chairs. Centered against the interior wall stood the tall glass cabinet with the extraordinary collection Chapin had talked about. Bits of ebony and ivory and steel glinted there. On the wall between the seaward-facing windows hung a very good engraving of a whaleship bowling along under full sail. She recognized the vessel at once.

"The *Amelia Snow*, isn't she?"

"—Why, yes," Annabella Gaspa glanced at her in surprise.

"I thought so—old Thomas Staynforth had those false ports painted on her. And I remember the figurehead. They say it was Jenny Nickerson who served as the model, not Amelia Snow."

"I remember."

"My Uncle Jeremiah sailed on her as third officer. I heard him say once if we were as lucky as that ship we'd all get to heaven." She laughed encouragingly, but Senhora Gaspa only smiled.

"Something more than luck, I think. Will you take a glass of wine?"

"Oh no, thank you."

"Ah. Of course." And Senhora Gaspa nodded, her lips compressed.

Serena frowned. It had been an instinctive response —she'd never cared for spirits, and it was after all only three o'clock in the afternoon—now she regretted her reply. What would it have mattered? But the other woman had turned away and seated herself in a massive mahogany armchair.

Serena Aldridge said: "And how is Captain Gaspa?"

"Well. As well as can be expected." His wife made a quick demurring gesture with one hand. "I'm sorry he's not here—he's down at the Upper Channel, on the beached *Albatroz*. Sometimes he likes to take a nap there, in his old cabin." She smiled a slow, sad smile. "Dreaming of other days. When there was nothing he couldn't do . . ."

"Those interminable cruises!" Serena shook her head. "Uncle Jeremiah used to talk about the boredom, the heat."

"Not to mention the wretched food. And the danger."

"Yes . . . Well," she laughed genially, "those days are gone forever, thank heaven."

"For some, yes."

Serena Aldridge suppressed a sigh and smoothed her hands against her skirt. There seemed to be no way to get on a congenial footing with this woman.

"I've had the pleasure of meeting your granddaughter," she plunged in lightly. "A very lively young lady, charming, quite pretty really, and a—"

"No." The word stopped her dead—not the word so much as the tone of voice in which it was delivered; as though it were the most incontrovertible fact, like the moon and its pull of the tides. "She is not. She is beautiful." The dark, liquid eyes searched hers clearly. "You and I"—again Annabella Gaspa made that swift, dismissing gesture—"may have been pretty. Josefina is beautiful. There is an ocean of difference." The Portuguese woman's eyes held the faintest hint of amusement. "Wouldn't you agree?"

"All right, then," she heard herself answer, a touch more sharply than she intended. "If you say so. In any event I was going on to say that she's turned into a well-behaved, self-possessed young lady. A real credit to you."

"Thank you, Madam."

"It must have been hard for you."

"One does what one must."

"Of course. I've had something of the same burden, as you may know—one of my sister's boys, Chapin. And of course his brother Tipton visits us often. Tipton tells me he's spent so many pleasant hours at your home, here. In point of fact there are times when he doesn't seem able to talk about anything else." She paused; Senhora Gaspa sat impassively, waiting. "And while I'm delighted to hear that he's been entertained so—so generously on his infrequent holidays, I think we ought to be mindful of the fact that occasionally these summer attachments, casual though they may seem—"

"—might become winter bonds?"

Serena smiled in return. "I think we should be aware of certain eventualities. Young people are hasty—so often they rush into relationships whose consequences they can't remotely foresee. Emotions—

events can create their own momentum, their own logic. Do you agree?"

"Yes." Annabella Gaspa studied the portrait of the *Amelia Snow*. "I like Tip. He is a fine young man. Too romantic at heart, perhaps, too stubborn—but it is a good heart; and stubbornness can be a very valuable trait." Slowly she lowered her eyes to her visitor. "How is it you haven't spoken to Jophy about this?"

"Why, she's a mere child—"

"No—she's a grown woman . . . A moment before, you were telling me what a self-possessed young woman she is—now you say she is a mere child. Which is it to be, Senhora?"

Serena uttered her high, short laugh. "Well—they certainly don't call you the Portuguese Lawyer for nothing!"

"I have earned the title." Mrs. Gaspa nodded without a trace of arrogance. "But of course Tip has been seeing Jophy for some years—as I'm sure you know. Why do you come to visit me now?" The amused sparkle in her eyes was unmistakable. "Perhaps it is not Tip, but the other nephew, the one you have taken under your wing all these years, and who has been seeing Jophy recently—perhaps that is what has prompted your visit. Would that be the case?"

Serena Aldridge drew a deep breath and arched her back. "All right, then, yes. I'll be perfectly frank with you. It does concern Chapin. I'm afraid he is becoming —involved, to a certain degree. He told me he intends to take her to the Grand Banks Ball next month."

"He has already invited her. And I believe she has accepted." Annabella Gaspa threw open her hands. "But what is that, Senhora? Costumes, a few dances, the chamariz, prizes, a moment of—"

"That's not the point. He's become—captivated by her, I am sure of it. It's made him—well, restless, uncertain. And now, with the country at war . . . who knows what might happen?"

"Yes. The war." Annabella Gaspa nodded, watching her steadily. "But then, I remember another war, when there were men who went to it—and other men who paid money for those first ones to go in their places."

Serena said sharply: "This is a very different kind of war, you'll find."

"No. I'm afraid not. All wars are the same, essentially. There are those who are ordered to lower for the whale, and those who sit in their counting houses and go over the ledgers. That will never change."

"Yes, well, *I* remember a war, too, another one . . ." Stung by a hurtful, long-buried memory she burst out, "What *I* remember is that it causes people to do foolish, disastrous things they wouldn't *dream* of doing in normal circumstances . . . Do I make myself sufficiently clear?"

"Perfeitamente, Senhora." The woman sat quite still; she hadn't lost a jot of her composure. But why should she?—what did she stand to lose?

"—It's no longer a question of childhood playmates." She could hear the strident note in her voice now, and it distressed her. "Sailing around the harbor, sodas at Birchall's Drugstore . . . I had hoped we would see eye-to-eye in this matter."

"Perhaps we do. I am not sure. In any event, Jophy is eighteen—you should speak with her. She is training as a nurse, you can find her—"

"What possible good could that do? She is an impressionable girl, highly emotional, weaned on dreams and fancies—what can she possibly know of the world?"

Annabella Gaspa shook her head from side to side. "Oh, she knows. Senhora, you haven't understood her at all—you haven't the faintest idea of what she wants."

"Then you must tell me."

Again Annabella Gaspa shook her head. "I don't

know, myself. Who ever knows what's gnawing at the vitals of someone else? And if I did know I would not tell you. That is her affair."

Serena said tightly: "You've encouraged her in this, then—led her to believe something could come of this sailing romance or whatever you care to call it . . .?"

Annabella Gaspa set one fist on her thigh. "I will be direct with you, Dona Serena. I am every bit as opposed to intermarriage between Portuguese and Yankees as you are."

"You see the danger, then!"

"Oh, yes—though perhaps from a different compass point. But that is for *me* to say—not Jophy. In point of fact I have neither encouraged her nor discouraged her. I have let her find her own way—as every woman must in this deceptive and violent world. As every man must, too."

Serena Aldridge patted her throat with her handkerchief. Gazing into those dark eyes, where the barest suspicion of derisive amusement lurked, she thought again of Captain Joseph Gaspa standing at the entrance to Newcombe's Marine Supply, blue chambray shirt open at the throat, his visored officer's cap set at a cocky angle, watching her—and her heart began to beat thickly. With the sting of Atlantic sleet she saw that, for all her social position, the Gaspa woman was harder than she, and steadier, and the realization enraged her beyond all bounds.

"It happens," she heard herself say hotly, in a mounting ferocity that amazed her, "it so happens I have plans for Chapin, certain plans—and they most emphatically do *not* include involvement with a lovestruck, mooning, adventurous girl who's decided to use her looks and her—her other charms to carry her into worlds she wouldn't dare enter, otherwise—where in fact she has no business to be!"

The glint of amusement in Annabella Gaspa's eyes had vanished; she became quite still—her handsome, broad face darkened, suffused with blood. The knuckles of her fist were dead white against her skirt. Serena Aldridge, breathing heavily, was brushed with a sharp thrill of remembered panic.

"You have nothing to fear, Senhora," the Portuguese woman said in a low, stern tone that was somehow quite threatening. "Nothing! Jophy would not throw her life away on a—on a person such as *Master* Chapin Ames . . ." And now the burgeoning contempt in her voice had bled through. "She has far more self-respect than that."

"Oh, come off your high horse!" Serena cried. "Who are you to patronize me?—what have you ever known but poverty and squalor—!"

Annabella Gaspa stood up. She was holding her arms at her sides, her nostrils were flared. "Poverty, yes," she said in a voice like a river of ice. "And I am proud of it. I would not have wealth, knowing how it is acquired in this world . . . But squalor—no. I bid you good day, *Doña* Serena.

Serena had risen, too—it was almost as though the other woman had drawn her to her feet. Her loss of control made her frantic; she cast about for something wounding to say, something that would crush this swarthy woman whose eyes were fixed on her with infinite scorn—could find nothing.

"—We have nothing to say to each other!" she stammered.

"Com toda a certeza, Senhora."

She moved out of the room in a little rush; she felt dizzy with rage and humiliation, her arms and legs burned as though deprived of blood—for an instant she was afraid she would fall. As she passed down the hall the ship's chronometer began its delicate, spinet-like double stroke. The sound made her jump—it seemed abnormally loud, ready to pierce into her very brain. She whirled and cried:

"You will regret this day, Annabella Gaspa! I promise you!"

"Oh, no." And Captain Gaspa's wife gave a short, mirthless laugh. "It is *you* who will regret it. Garanto-lhe!"

As Serena Aldridge swung open the door the ship's clock finished striking the change of watch.

8

The ball had turned out to be fun—Chapin Ames hadn't expected to enjoy himself and he was, hugely. The building overlooked the Lower Channel. The great double doors of the rigger's loft had been swung back, and the dancers drifted out onto the wharf's worn planking as the mood suited them. Nets had been slung from their wet poles in black, gauzelike festoons, and lights fitted cleverly in glass net floats bathed the celebrants in soft ruby and amber and indigo hues. The entire scene seemed to be floating on the still, inky water of the harbor. The band, a rambunctious group that called itself the Cape Corsairs, played with more enthusiasm than skill, but the couples, jouncing or dipping or gliding, were determined to have a good time—for this was the Grand Banks Ball, the climactic event of the Lower Cape's social season.

Nautical motifs inevitably predominated. There were patch-eyed pirates galore, there were Jack Tars and naval gunners of 1861 and Revolutionary captains in tricorn hats. There were mermaids and sirens and Viking maidens in gleaming breastplates and flowing blond hair—there was even a Cleopatra, outrageously décolleté, with mascaraed eyes and a golden headdress. Chapin, feeling lordly as an admiral of the Grand Armada, complete with plumed hat and basket-hilted rapier—he'd rented the costume from the Perkins emporium up in Boston—spotted a Venetian gondolier in sash and flowing shirt, and a King Neptune, draped in a horrendous mantle of seaweed. One madcap spirit had actually managed to squirm his way into a seal costume; he clapped his flippers and uttered sharp, hoarse barks now and then throughout the evening.

There were other costumes in evidence this summer of 1917. Dancing with Jophy, Chapin picked out several apprentice seamen and boatswain's mates, and a few men from the newly formed Coast Guard. At the center of the floor, moving sedately with a Portuguese queen, was a Navy commodore dazzling in dress whites; here and there were privates home on leave from Camp Devens. There would be more, many more, in the months to come . . .

"I love this tune," Jophy was saying. "What's its name?"

" 'Hindustan.' "

" 'Hindustan!' " She laughed happily, her head back. She looked stunning. She was a Turkish princess, in a scarlet vest adorned with golden spangles and loose, diaphanous trousers gathered at the ankles. There were gold bracelets at her wrists and ankles, and a chain of tiny gold coins circled her brows. She was wearing her hair long—it shone in the pastel light from the net floats; she looked older, mysterious, beguiling. Yes, daring. She moved with a sensuous ease that amazed him.

"Where did you learn to dance like this?" he demanded.

"Never had to learn!" Her eyes sparkled with mischief. "We never do."

"Another inherited characteristic, you mean."

"Of course! Actually, I'm descended from a long line of Moorish princesses," she teased.

"Moorish—!"

"Why not? Don't look so stunned—the Moors were

all over Southern Europe for centuries. Improved things no end. Othello was a Moor, you know—"

"So I've heard."

"—and Desdemona was wildly in love with him. Wildly!"

"Until he started to strangle her, I imagine."

"Even after that. *Nobody* can strangle the way a Moor can."

"But Moors—!" he bantered. "Why do you want to take after them? Sneaky people, falling down on their knees, wailing to Mecca every evening—I've seen them . . . and the way they treat their women!"

"Oh, that's only in the daytime."

He laughed, watching her out of the sides of his eyes. "But they're so grubby—that's no one to take after . . ."

"And what are you? Danish pirate with horns growing out of your helmet—"

"Oh, well—if you go back *far* enough."

"That's just what I want to do!" she cried. "Go back and back—to the first man and woman on the first South Sea island. Discovering everything for the first time—all wild and new . . ."

Smiling he drew her closer to him and spun her round and round until they were both dizzy. He never knew what she was going to say, not remotely—it intrigued him and made him uneasy at the same time; and that very uneasiness was part of her fascination. The girls he'd met at the Assemblies and the Vincent dances bored him stiff. He attended them—Aunt Serena expected him to go and he played his role, that was part of the bargain—but he despised the girls he saw there. They talked about their watercolor classes or who was going down to New London for the crew races or whether the fleet would put in at Bar Harbor this season. They stared at you blankly when something was funny—and then they giggled like children when something was serious. When you danced with them their left arms were rigid, holding you in place, measuring the distance.

Of course there was Shirley, the chorus girl at the Old Howard, whose buttocks were wide and smooth and white—he loved to press his body into them, thrust all of himself into her ripe, soft fullness, invade her and then withdraw with a calculated stealth while she moaned and clutched at the pillow, her eyes rolling. And there was a girl named Carol in a house out on Columbus Avenue who flung herself on him like a raging black Amazon, thrashing and panting until he felt whipped to pieces, soaked in sweat, his genitals aching and his mouth dry. There were other girls, in other pinched and squalid rooms; but they were boring, too—though in a vastly different way— from the Brahmin maidens . . .

"You're a wild one," he murmured in Jophy's ear.

"I know! A dead whale or a stove boat. That's why I'm going to win."

"What do you want to win?"

She tossed her head; her silky black hair whipped densely about her shoulders. "Oh—everything! I told you—a dead whale or—"

"No—really. What do you want most? Most of all?"

A jolly French sailor with a bright red pompom on his hat—Chapin knew it was Gus Lawring—cut in on him just then, and he surrendered Jophy to him.

"Remember, now," he called. "You've got to tell me . . ."

"Oh no, I don't!" she answered, and swept away into the crowd.

Chapin had a glass of punch; they'd used a siphon to pep it up a bit, but it wasn't spiked. He strolled out to the wharf. Tip, in a hastily assembled costume of bandanna, burnt cork mustache, sash and boots, with their grandfather's old cavalry saber dangling from his waist, was leaning against a bollard, gazing out at the channel. He looked curiously forlorn against the shimmering lights of the harbor, the soft night sky,

and Chapin laughed and chanted: " 'Would'st thou'—
so the helmsman answered, 'Learn the secret of the
sea?' "

Tip said: "Hello, Chay."

"Why aren't you in there, tripping the light fantastic?"

"I never was much of a dancer."

The two brothers watched the harbor in silence. At
the end of Blackfish Point the lighthouse flared into a
fierce garnet eye, died away again; the flickering yellow light of some ship slipped along in the velvet dark
like the first voyage to unknown lands. Behind them
the orchestra was playing "The Bells Are Ringing for
Me and My Gal."

Chapin drew a silver flask out of his jacket, took
several swallows and extended it to Tip, who said,
"No thanks."

"It's first-rate Scotch."

"I don't doubt it."

"Oh hell, don't be such a bluenose. It's a *party*, for
God's sake."

"So I gather . . . Been seeing much of Jophy?" Tip
asked after a little pause.

Chapin looked at him. "Now and then. Why?"

"Just wondered."

Chapin shrugged, and looked away again. So that's
what it was. Tip had only come down from Boston the
night before; Chapin had slept late, as he usually did,
and there had been no opportunity to talk before
they'd started to dress for the evening. He'd been surprised when their aunt had invited Tip down for the
ball, only the week before; surprised and strangely irritated.

"What on earth for?" he'd demanded.

"He likes it on the Cape." Serena Aldridge had
helped herself to sugar from a Georgian silver bowl,
and stirred her coffee. "The only vacations he's ever
had have been down here."

"But—he'll just be out of it. He doesn't know any of our crowd . . ."

She smiled at him brightly. "Then you must introduce him!"

"I see." He watched her closely for a moment. "I can't possibly rustle up a girl for him on this short notice."

"Then you can both escort Miss Gaspa. That's still done, isn't it? Especially among such young sophisticates." Aunt Serena smiled. "She looks lively enough for both of you!"

"Do you feel that?"

"Oh, come on, Chapin, don't be such a dog in the manger. He's been hoping to be invited down for months. We owe him that much . . ."

"Such solicitude," he couldn't help retorting.

"I don't know what you mean by that, I'm sure. You're turning into a very cynical young man, Chapin. It's not a terribly endearing trait."

"Merely realistic, I'd say."

His aunt set down her coffee cup with a sharp little click. "In any event, I've invited him. And I trust you'll prove a gracious host. And an affectionate brother—which is more to the point. And now, with the war on, who knows when there'll be another occasion?"

"Who indeed." They glanced at each other—a quick, searching glance; then Chapin set down his napkin. So sensitive to each other's responses had they become over a thousand dinner tables that nothing more needed to be said. "Yours to command, Auntie," he murmured; he kissed her lightly on the brow before he left the room.

"Look," he said now to Tip, "I invited Jophy to this shindig two months ago—I didn't even know you'd be here, for God's sake . . ."

"That's all right."

"*Of course* it's all right! Why shouldn't it be?" He

120

felt angry out of all proportion to the situation. "What are you so worked up about?"

"I'm not worked up about anything. You are."

"She didn't have to come with me if she didn't want to—there are dozens of men who would have invited her."

"Are there?"

"Of course there are! Do you think they're all blind? Or castrated?" Being with his brother invariably turned Chapin irascible. He'd gone back to Holcomb Falls over the past Christmas—his mother had begged him to come, and Aunt Serena had urged him to go out there, if only for the day. The old house, barricaded in snow, looked shabby; pinched and faded. His mother seemed smaller—as though the intervening years had actually eaten away at her flesh and bones. She'd made steamed chocolate pudding, his favorite dessert—she was pathetic in her eagerness to please him, to hear about life in Boston. Did Mr. Papanti still run the dancing classes on Tremont Street, where the flexible floor sprang up and down? Did they still hire the Cleopatra's Barge for sleighrides out to Brookline, or hold the skating parties in Back Bay? Who had he met at the latest cotillion? Feeling guilty and resentful, he told her what he felt she wanted to hear, gilding matters a bit along the way. Tip, sitting in their father's chair by the window, watched him in silence; his eyes passed over Chapin's Brooks Brothers Harris tweed jacket, the club tie. Tip was wearing a ready-made woolen suit, a touch high-key, though it wasn't one of those brash, race-track-tout horrors most drummers wore; who had guided him in matters of taste?

"Couldn't you invite Tip to one of the football games, the dances?" his mother had asked; her eyes held an edge of fearful entreaty that repelled him. "I know he'd love to go . . ."

"Why, sure," he answered, thinking rapidly ahead, wondering how he might forestall things, "there's the

Lancers Ball in February. Or why not one of the spring regattas? There's a—"

Tip said quickly: "Chapin has his own life there, Mother. His own circle. And I have mine."

"Oh, but Tip—"

"And besides," his voice was even and very flat, "I can't spare the time. Thanks very much, though."

Watching him, Chapin had the disquieting thought that their roles had somehow been reversed—that he wasn't the older brother any more, Tip was; how had that happened?

Now, irritated by the memory, he said: "Jophy's a very popular girl. In case you haven't noticed. You have some objection to my taking her out?"

Tip turned then and faced him, looking foolish in the bandanna headdress, the smudged charcoal mustache.

"That depends," he said quietly.

"Depends on what?"

"On you."

Chapin laughed. "Oh me? Why on me?"

"Because I don't know if you're serious. I don't know what your intentions are."

"Intentions—!" Chapin stared at him; he could feel the old antagonism rising between them like ground fog. "Look now, I don't owe you any explanations . . ."

"Yes, you do."

"The devil I do! I'm just one more portrait in a long gallery of admirers—what's wrong with that?" He saw a muscle flex once in Tip's cheek, and it gave him a curious, subtle thrill of pleasure. Couples were moving around them, laughing and calling to one another. The band was playing "Smiles."

"All right," he said in a bantering tone, *"why* do I owe you an explanation?"

"Because I am."

"You're what?"

"Serious. About her." Tip's lower lip was thrust out in that funny, stubborn way. "Are *you?*"

"Well, that's news—that's headline news," Chapin ran on, ignoring the last query. "I had no idea . . . Only of course the question remains: Is she serious about *you?*"

". . . I don't know." For the first time Tip looked troubled, deeply uncertain; and this pleased Chapin even more.

"Well, hadn't you better ask the lady?" he pursued, grinning. "Find out if she does harbor tender sentiments toward you, as the saying goes? I mean, if you're—"

"—Just don't go too far, Chay, You got me?"

The words were spoken quietly enough—they were barely audible over the band, the clatter of talk and laughter around them; but there was a sudden tough force behind them and a look in Tip's face he'd never seen before. The feeling he'd had at Christmas came back, redoubled. Tip was *out there*—in that unpredictable, often menacing world of cigar stores and pool halls and back alleys, of blatant vulgarity and casual violence, where a drink too many, a word too many could spill over into broken glass and smashed noses . . .

"What the hell are you talking about?" he demanded.

"You know damned well what I'm talking about." Tip nodded, his eyes flat and unreadable. "Just watch yourself, that's all."

"—Is that some kind of threat?"

"No. Just fair warning."

"Well, now . . . is it to be boyhood fisticuffs again, out behind the old barn?"

"If that's the way you want it."

Chapin snorted. "Oh, come off it, Tipton! Act your bloody age . . ."

The band had quit, other figures were on the stand now. They could hear voices calling for some new performance. Chapin took advantage of the general commotion to break off this ridiculous row with Tip and moved in the direction of the bandstand, where a huge man wearing the striped stocking cap and jersey of an Azores fisherman had begun to sing in Portuguese, accompanying himself on a guitar.

Near the bandstand Chapin found Jophy standing with a good-looking man in full cowboy costume. Jophy introduced him as Frank Furtado, a doryman with the schooner *Dauntless,* and Chapin remembered seeing him once or twice at the Gaspa house. Couples were still dancing, but most were listening, swaying to the driving rhythm of the ballad.

"What's he singing about?" Chapin asked Jophy.

"He says, marrying a girl without a dowry is worse than rowing against the tide—but arousing a woman's vengeance is worse than being cast adrift in a Line gale . . ."

The singer's expression had turned sly now, his eyes roamed over the crowd. He sang a few verses, answered himself in the chorus. The crowd began laughing, now and then joining in the refrain.

"What is it?"

"Canções de escárneo—he's taking off different people in town, making up rhymes about them. Improvising, as he sees someone."

The laughter came in bursts now, like sudden gusts of wind; individual men and women on the floor turned resentful or rueful as neighbors poked fun at them, and then waited for the next pasquinade.

"Amazing," Chapin said. "How did it—"

But just then Jophy's face tightened, was flooded with that fierce and merry defiance, and he knew she'd been singled out. Heads turned toward her, toward them both. Furtado, grinning, started to say something in Portuguese and she cut him off with flustered impatience.

"Your turn, is it?" Chapin asked her. "What was that all about?"

"He says," Furtado broke in, "a certain bold nurse must be more careful about rescuing shipwrecked mariners—" his eyes met Chapin's, glittering with hostile amusement "—there are some Yankee sailors who are strangely ungrateful—who might even ask for payment!"

"Deixa!" Jophy hissed, though she was laughing. "Stop it! It's all nonsense, everything he sings is nonsense . . ."

The song ended in a thunderous crash of guitar chords and wild applause. The band came back. Chapin took Jophy away from Furtado, lost her to Tip, to another fisherman dressed like a riverboat gambler, again to Gus Lawring. Everyone wanted to dance with her. Chapin drank some more Scotch, avoided Tip adroitly, and felt more pleased than ever with the evening. When he finally recaptured Jophy half a dozen numbers later the orchestra was playing "There's a Long, Long Trail A-Winding."

"It's simply not fair," he protested. "I bring you to this grand affair at enormous personal-inconvenience-and-expense, and I can't take three steps with you without some swarthy blackguard whisking you away."

"Does that trouble you?"

"Bien sûr." He pressed the small of her back with his hand. "I'm used to getting my own way—you know that."

"Oh, but you can be generous, can't you?" Her face was flushed, her eyes merry. "After all, for you this is just another dance. While for some of us it has to last a whole dreary winter . . ."

"Perhaps for me, too," he said somberly.

"What do you mean?"

"I'm going to join the flying corps."

"Oh, no . . ." Her face stiffened—she looked shaken and fearful and even lovelier than before. It delighted him obscurely.

"What's the matter?"

"It's so dangerous—flying . . ."

"War is dangerous. Or hadn't you heard?"

125

"Yes. But you—you don't have to enlist. Couldn't you—well, be deferred for some reason?"

"That wouldn't be very sporting, would it?"

"Oh—*sporting* . . ." Her voice was heavy with scorn. "Those stupid words . . ."

"Words we live by, all the same."

Actually he planned to do just that: secure a deferment and ride it out. He'd seen the photographs, read the accounts in the Sunday sections. He had no intention of becoming still another chunk of cannon fodder served up on some gray, wet morning in France. Or the giddy, glamorous aviation side of it, either. He'd felt a brief twinge of envy when Charlie Hilliard had left to join the Lafayette Escadrille—the feeling had been strong enough to torment his Aunt Serena with now and then; but it hadn't lasted long. Let the romantic firebrands play the dulce-et-decorum theme, rush off to the slaughter; he had vastly better things to do with his life.

The band had switched to "Till We Meet Again"; a simple tinny tune, sad with war and loss. Watching Jophy's face, feeling her arm tighten faintly at the base of his neck, he was swept with the laughable drama in the situation. How fascinating human emotions were! How inscrutable and filled with ironies . . . He threw out half a dozen words, like a silken seine, and this girl had swum into them in deadly earnest: they were *reality* to her . . .

And yet, gliding with this strange, entrancing girl under the glass moons of light, holding her tenderly, watching her dark, entreating gaze, her parted lips, he thought in distant amazement, *She's afraid for me, she cares about me—she really does!*—and he felt something thrust against the underside of his heart for the first time since that long-ago winter afternoon, terrible with clashing voices, slammed doors and more terrible silences—and a pair of legs he ran against with all his might and clung to.

"It's all right, son. Let go, now. Let go."

"Dad, please don't go—you can't go—!"

The strong arms had swung him up and held him. That face, slender and fine-featured, that face he loved more than any other; the gray eyes troubled now, uncertain.

"I'll see you soon."

But soon became never.

He leaned down, whispered in Jophy's ear, "Let's go—let's leave."

Her eyes flashed up at him like mirrors. "You mean—"

"Yes. Come with me. Let's leave. Now."

Her face tightened—a sudden, fierce decision. "All right," she said. "I will."

The night was cool and clear, the stars looked close enough to shake down, like bobbing, glowing fruit. Directly above their heads a shooting star brushed a swift, bright arc, vanished forever.

"Did you see it?" Jophy cried.

"No."

"There!" She pointed upward. "There's another one—*there* . . ."

They were sitting in Chapin's car, a Buick phaeton his aunt had given him for his birthday the year before, parked on a deserted little bluff overlooking the bay. Here, far from the harbor, they were invaded by silence.

"I love it with the top down," she said, lying back against the rich dense leather. "It makes it more like a sloop—throws you open to things . . ."

All her nerves were quivering near the surface. Tip's sudden arrival, the dance, Miguel Santos' sly allusion in the chamariz, Chapin's talk of going to war—events were moving too fast for her; a rip tide spinning her around, drawing her swiftly out to sea. Chapin's presence here in the night disturbed her most of all. He seemed subdued, ill at ease; he was staring ahead at the water, gleaming darkly under the drifting, dusty canopy of stars. She began talking rapidly about her work at the hospital, about her plans for restoring the old *Albatroz* and sending her to sea again, setting her free—knowing she sounded loony, and not caring. The very tips of her fingers burned.

"—sometimes I think that old schooner is me. Lashed to that rotting wharf, only one stick, no sails—the sea right out there at the end of the channel and she can't get there, to spread her wings and run free, off for Manokela and Palawan . . ." She thought then of a hot, sultry afternoon three years ago, treading water and watching a figure high in the mainmast crosstree, gazing seaward. She said:

"Tip looked so funny in that mustache. Didn't he realize it would smear, with the heat and everything?"

"The hell with Tip," Chapin said sharply. "I don't want to talk about Tip."

"Why? What's the matter?"

"Nothing's the matter. I just don't want to talk about him, that's all." Abruptly he drew a silver flask out of his breast pocket and said: "Drink?"

"No, thanks."

"Oh, come on. Just a sip."

She watched him a moment, gravely. "I don't need it, Chay. Let's not play that."

"Play what?"

"The ply-the-girl-with-liquor game. You don't have to play that game with me."

His head went back in silent laughter; he gazed at her wonderingly. "You are one extraordinary girl," he said. "Do you know that? You're magnificent."

"Yes," she said simply. "I know that."

His arm went around her then, his face blurred against the night, swept inside her scan of vision. As always with him, that sweet, warm suffusion began deep inside her, frightening and thrilling her. His lips were firm and warm, his fingers moved with tender stealth at her throat, her breast. She was trembling now, bound in trembling; she wanted to raise sail and run free—toward that undiscovered—

"Oh, take me, Chay," she murmured. "Take me now. . . ."

"You sweet."

His hand had reached her very core—she had never known such delight, such surging need. Yes, it was true—this was the voyage of voyages, as she'd suspected, the majestic rocking of sea and stars; there would never be anything remotely like it . . .

"I love you, Chay," she murmured, reaching out for him. "Oh, I love you so . . ."

She felt him stiffen; the hand drew away. He seemed to have stopped breathing. Something was wrong. She did not know what it could be.

"—I love you," she repeated urgently. "Don't you love me?"

"*Love—!*" The word seemed to cut into him like a knife blade. He wrenched away from her and gripped the steering wheel with both hands. "*Love*—look now, if you're going to start *that* . . ."

"Start?" she faltered. "Start?"

"I've never told you I loved you, I've never said that."

"I've never asked you."

"Then don't ask me now!"

The violence in his voice frightened her. What had happened? What had gone wrong?

". . . But you do, don't you?" she ventured softly. "You've seemed—the times we've been together—"

"Yes, of course—that." His chin was pressed against his chest, he was fighting for some kind of precarious balance. "Sure—affection, fondness—sure I do, of course I do, there's—"

129

"No," she said. "I mean *love*. There's only one word. Only one word for it, Chay."

She drew back, searching his face. The stars were so bright, so luminous she could read the confusion in his eyes, the evasion, the covert fear. Yes. Fear. She got it, then—all in a rush. None of this meant anything to him; he was toying with her, using her—it was a shadow play, a game, some kind of dirty, empty game . . . A game—! Rage gripped her—a rage greater than any she had ever known before. She struck him in the face with all her might—before he could react had flung open the door and leaped out.

"You—bastard!" she cried, in a black turmoil of fury and mortification. "You ever try this again I'll kill you—you understand? Yes! By Jesus, I'll make you pay for this—!"

"No, wait," he was stammering, "you don't understand—don't you see, I—"

"Oh, I understand, don't you worry about that—I understand all right!"

Afraid—he was afraid. All the good looks and wit and easy charm were nothing because he was afraid to act, to follow without fear the only thing that mattered on this earth. He was a shell of a man—a charming poster-shell. A fraud. And cruel. It was cruel to play with anyone this way . . .

"You filthy Yankee coward!" she shouted at him. She cursed him in English, in Portuguese—words she didn't even know she knew, spat them at him with all the scorn she possessed while he turned his face away in grim, sullen withdrawal, his hands still gripping the steering wheel. "Go on," she cried, beside herself with raging shame, "*go* into the war, get yourself killed—you might as well, you're dead anyway, afraid of everything in *life*—!"

He looked at her then, and she could see the hatred glittering in his eyes. She whirled around and walked away along the packed sand ruts of the road, sobbing dryly, muttering to herself; she thought her heart would burst. The odor of bayberry and beach plum rose dense and acrid around her. From the shoal water at the end of Blackfish Point the bell buoy sounded: *clang-ding: clang*—its message pitiless and remote on the cool night air.

9

The carnival was going full tilt by the time they got there; the tinkle of a hurdy-gurdy clashed with the compressed-air blasts of the calliope behind the merry-go-round, homely and festive. It had been set up in a cleared field between the Lower Channel and Blackfish Point known as the Hollow. Walking between Jophy and her grandmother, Tip felt his spirits lift. Everything was in motion. Performers in tights and spangles hurried from tent to tent, animals prowled in ominous rhythms behind slender black bars, clowns were cutting capers, kids ran here and there shrieking at one another in a frenzied ritual of anticipation. The whole town had turned out, strolling amiably along the crooked little midway under the tinsel strings of multicolored light bulbs. In the background, like a ponderous symbol, a small Ferris Wheel, its gondolas gleaming darkly, rose and held, rose again.

"I love carnivals!" Jophy cried. "All the strange and fabulous things you're going to see—like golden prizes . . ."

"First one you went to, you wouldn't leave—you yowled and howled and refused to come home," Annabella Gaspa said. She was very grand in a black dress with a white lace shawl around her shoulders; a tortoise-shell comb rode high in her rich black hair.

"I was right, too! I wish I'd run away with one. All

the different towns, the adventures . . . Maybe I still will!"

She gave Tip that quick mirror-flash of a glance that always stirred him. He watched her in silence. All evening she had struck him as unusually volatile, tense, on edge—a vessel carrying far too much sail.

"It isn't all parades and thrills," her grandmother said. "It's hard work and long hours, living out of a trunk from year to year . . ."

"Goodness, Grama, *I* know what it's like." As though ashamed of the angry note in her voice she laughed and said: "Weren't you ever tempted, Grama?"

"Your grandfather's been my circus." Annabella Gaspa smiled softly to herself. "Strong man, lion tamer, acrobat all in one. I didn't need to run away . . ."

"Didn't you want to, Tip?"

"Sure, I did. Plenty.—Look at that."

He pointed off into the night shadows. A pile of tarpaulins near the edge of the fence stirred magically, as if it too were part of the show, stirred again—and two thin arms and a small face appeared under the canvas edge; the eyes stared upward, round with wonder, jeweled in the lights.

Jophy laughed her high, open laugh. "How on earth did you happen to notice that?"

"Knew where to look. I used to do the same thing at the Berkshire County Fair. There was a platform for unloading cattle that made the best place . . . Look out, now—don't let him know you've seen him."

The boy had rolled clear and scrambled to his feet like a puppy—now sat on the edge of the tarp with studied nonchalance.

"Now he'll stand lookout for a friend . . . There. See?"

Another face came into view; the seated boy waited, watching for a propitious moment.

"Little hellions," Grama Gaspa said. "Got in without paying."

"They're putting one over on your land sharks, Mrs. Gaspa," he chided her. "Battling the powers that be—isn't that what you want?"

"Little devils!" But she was grinning. "And you're another."

"I only had twenty-five cents, and I was cussed if I was going to spend it on the price of admission."

"Where is Chapin?" Annabella Gaspa asked suddenly.

"He'll be along—he said he'd meet us here. Said there were some things he had to attend to first."

He watched Jophy as he spoke. She looked away, studying a fortune-teller's booth intently. It struck him as curious that she hadn't asked him that question. She and Chapin had left the dance early—he'd missed them soon after the chamariz—and he'd walked back to the Bluffs alone, cross with Chapin, feeling silly in his makeshift pirate costume; but when he'd reached the house the Buick was still gone. Around two, lying wide awake in bed, he'd heard the car, and after that Chapin crept up the stairs in his stocking feet and along the hall to his room. What had happened? Had Chapin driven Jophy off somewhere, had they been together all that time? He burned with the old hot resentment and dread.

At lunch Chapin had been silent and morose, answering Aunt Serena's queries in monosyllables, if at all. He was hung over—Tip had learned to recognize the signs by now—but there was something more; what in hell had happened? He was wild to find out, he was frightened at what he might learn. He'd suggested they go to the beach for a swim, but Chapin had demurred, and gone up to his room again. He hadn't come down for dinner at all.

They had reached the entrance to the main tent now, and paused, listening. On a platform made from barrels and wharf planking a barker in a straw boater and bright red vest was making his pitch, introducing a cadaverous juggler in top hat and tails, a handsome woman bareback rider, a fat Japanese acrobat in black pajamas whose two lady assistants looked like exquisitely fired porcelain figurines.

"—and now, as the climax, the grand finale of this evening's stellar entertainment!—let me present to you the Great Konomaku, emperor of that legendary kingdom *beneath* the seven seas, who will perform before your very eyes the terrifying Dive of Death! Ladies and gentlemen, I give you the Great Konomaku—the only man in the history of the world who has been head-and-shoulders *inside the mouth* of a great white shark—and lived to tell the tale! . . ."

There was a murmur of amused disbelief from the crowd around the platform. A big man with a smooth olive face and wearing an emerald robe adorned with dragons flung back the tent flap and stepped forward, watching the crowd out of sleepy, oval eyes.

"Do I hear sounds of skepticism?" the barker was saying, staring down at them wide-eyed. "Do I see doubters among you seafarers? All right, Kono—show them! Give them proof!—positive and unalloyed . . ."

In one quick, almost savage gesture the big man snapped the robe down to his waist; there was a low, fearful murmur from the onlookers, almost a moan. Beside him Tip heard Grama Gaspa mutter, "Santa Mãe de Deus! . . ." and some woman—or perhaps it was a child—gave a shrill squeal of fright. Running in a lazy semicircle from his shoulders deep into his massive chest were two perfect rows of huge triangular scars, pale against his dark skin. Slowly Konomaku turned; his broad back held the same terrible pattern.

"Yes, *sir!*" The barker was briskly tapping the scars with a brightly varnished baton. "There you are, you doubting Thomases! There's no thimble-rigging bluff-and-bunko hocus-pocus about *this* show! . . . Now, you're fishermen, sailors—you *know* what the dread white shark can do. Picture it—that ruthless killer spotting Kono deep in the crystalline waters of Bora

Bora, diving for pearls—and then rushing upon him with that cavernous mouth gasping wide—and then *snap!*—ready to bite Kono in two!—and at that precise instant Kono, obeying some ancient ancestral instinct, reached out and jabbed both thumbs right into the monster's *eyes!* And that demon of the deep spat him out in amazement, and swam away . . . Now, let's have a hand for this master diver, this living miracle of the seven seas!"

The clapping was tentative and ragged—it was almost as if the onlookers were too impressed to applaud. Tip, excited by the barker's pitch, was clapping away enthusiastically, looking at the islander's mutilated chest. Those fabulous tales of old Gaspa's—of savages and shipwrecks and mutinies—suddenly seemed very near. He started to say something to Annabella Gaspa—saw with surprise that she was standing still as a figurehead, scowling into the lights.

"And now," the barker was calling, "as the breathtaking heart-stopping climax of this stupendous show: the Great Konomaku, armed with nothing but a knife and his tremendous courage, will before your very eyes attempt to retrieve his gold crown from that other terror of the deep, the—giant—octopus!"

The islander was standing perfectly motionless again, gazing out over the crowd, which was now milling around, buzzing and joking, torn between fascination and incredulity.

"A giant *octopus*—?" Tip wondered aloud.

"Why not?" Jophy laughed. "Look at those scars—aren't *they* real?"

"That's God's truth," Annabella Gaspa muttered in her deep voice.

"What's the matter, Grama?"

". . . I'm going home." Her face was heavy, her lips compressed; she looked sullen and fearful. "You two stay and watch it. I'm going home. It's a sign—a Jonah."

"What?—the scars?" Jophy protested. "Oh, come on—*you're* not turning superstitious?"

"I have reason to be. And so do you."

"But that's crazy—look, it's a coincidence, a—just a coincidence!" Jophy looked almost as distraught as her grandmother, her eyes huge. Then, to Tip's amazement, her face changed as swiftly as it had darkened. "Look—you don't want me to run away with them, do you? I'll run away if you don't stay . . ."

"Tolinha," her grandmother murmured, with a slight smile.

"Come on, Grama—it'll be fun! Do you want to miss the acrobats? You know how you love acrobats!"

"All right," Annabella Gaspa said with a sigh. "For a little while."

Chapin paused at the edge of the scrub pines. The night was unbelievably dark—even after ten minutes' walking he could barely make out the wobbly footbridge that crossed the Upper Channel: a pale, meandering thread against the depthless black of the incoming tide. Toward the west, there was a ruddy, aurora-like glow from the carnival; and as though night-sight had sharpened his other senses he could hear now a dense, low hum of many voices mixed with music. The sheer unreality of his crouching here above the bridge, sweating in the navy blue sweater and black slacks, carrying the gasoline tin, swept over him again. Ridiculous! He could be over there tossing hoops at spindles, or reaching out for ring after golden ring . . . Was he, Chapin Aldridge Ames, really standing here in the close dark like some sneaky second-story man? What was he *doing*—?

Then his eyes made out the solitary mast rising above the abandoned sail loft like a skeletal, admonitory finger, and the rage came back full force.

"—Nobody calls me that," he muttered aloud. "*Nobody! . . .*" His voice, incredibly loud in the stillness, made his skin prickle; he bit down on his lip. It was true: no one could say those words to him and get away with it—least of all some Portagee tart! All day long he'd lain in his room motionless, staring at nothing, while the moment, as it always did, played and replayed itself in his head—Jophy standing by the open car door, her face white and wild, her mouth spilling that torrent of insults, scathing, derisive—*she* was scornful of *him!*—while his whole body shook with raging mortification and his mind kept fashioning replies of easy disdain, enjoying her shock, he was telling her what a silly romantic fool she was, caught in her peasant persuasions, prating of love—*that* game for innocents and fools!—he was sneering his unbounded contempt for her, he had lurched across the seat now and struck her, again, again, he had forced her to the ground and torn those tantalizing gauze pajamas from her thighs, pinioned her arms and thrust his way savagely into her, deeper, deeper still; she had started to scream—now *she* felt fear, felt pain—his hands had closed around that lovely, slender throat, he could watch her mouth gasping, soundless, her eyes frozen with terror even as he increased the pressure surely, steadily, almost tenderly while he kept plunging deep within—

With a tremor he drove the images away still again. He was sweating, trembling a little, his mouth dry; he was throbbing in full erection. The sensation was utterly pleasurable, voluptuous and furtive—like the time he'd picked up that little slut down on lower Washington Street and slipped her up the back stairs to his old room and fucked her for the rest of the night, with his aunt asleep there, right down the hall. He'd taken her three times, four, five, he'd been inexhaustible, he hadn't been able to believe it himself; the girl—her name was, characteristically, Grace— had finally, almost tearfully, begged him to stop and he'd half-bribed, half-threatened her into silence, had entered her and come again, and still again, all his senses inflamed, honed to a fine edge, alert to the slightest sound from the master bedroom down the hall. It had been better than that brothel in Naples where the women were stark naked inside their long brocade gowns and vaulted on top of you like crazed Tartar horsemen, or the night he and Gus had got drunk on champagne at the Folies and picked up the mulatto tart on the Rue Bréa. She had incredibly pointed breasts and her buttocks flared tightly against the purple silk. She'd been indignant when he'd made the suggestion, hands on her hips, eyes snapping. "Pour quoi me prenez-vous, hein? Je suis putain honnête, moi—pas abâtardie!" Gus had offered rather nervously to withdraw then but Chapin wouldn't hear of it—the poule's anger had made him want her even more. To Gus's horror he had offered her a thousand francs, and she had capitulated with a speed that amused him . . .

Abruptly he picked up the gasoline can and walked swiftly and silently across the swaying footbridge and into the narrow passageway between the ghostly, empty buildings. He was on the point of stepping out onto the old wharf when somewhere behind him he heard a cough followed by the rattling guttural of someone clearing his throat, then the explosive sound as the man spat. Chapin froze back into the shadows. The skin crawled slowly forward on his scalp; he could hear his heart thumping now, solidly. Yet this too was acutely pleasurable. The footsteps—uneven, lurching, the steps of someone drunk—moved away toward the harbor. After a moment the breeze stirred in the locusts; and now, windborne, the commotion of the carnival was wafted back in a subtle compound of music and laughter and cries of intense pleasure. She was there, now, riding the merry-go-round, her head back laughing, her eyes glittering in the whirl of lights . . . He groaned and clenched his free hand into a fist. It was what happened—it was always what came of allowing yourself to care, to open your heart. What in Christ's name had come over him? He knew—he *knew,* beyond question!—and yet he'd let himself forget. Seven years ago he'd lain on the cold gray rock in that cave above the falls, that secret place he'd found, his head in his arms, and vowed he would never open that door to his heart again. Never! And he never had, except for that afternoon in Rodney Muir's room at St. Marks, listening to Carlo and the wounded Alvaro singing the "Solenne in quest' ora" from *La Forza del Destino,* thinking of the casket with its fateful portrait, watching the sunlight raining golden coins through the elm leaves; gazing then at Rodney's face, the yearning, almost fearful eyes. Thinking how fortunate he had been to have found Rodney, how rare a discovery; and he could feel the old sweet need gliding over him like honey . . . He had leaped to his feet with some incoherent excuse and half-run from the room. He'd never gone back. He'd taken up with Gus Lawring and Brad Elwell after that. There was the hurt, baffled look in Rodney's eyes to endure for two long years, but it was nothing, *nothing* to the boundless misery of ruptured affection. He'd slammed the lid on it quickly enough then, he'd remembered in time . . .

And now, see? Here, unbelievably, he'd done it again—and this was where it led, this was where it *always* led, any sick, stupid fool could see that; the rending anguish and loss. And the humiliation! . . . Insufferable little bitch, giving herself airs, entertaining big ideas just because he'd taken her to a party or two—actually standing there accusing *him,* calling him a—

Enough. Now we'd see—we'd see how she liked what happened to the rotting shrine of her Portuguese pride! She'd see . . .

He began to curse under his breath—a string of violent obscenities; picked up the gasoline can again.

"—only one chance, folks," the barker—now in the role of ringmaster—was calling. "Kono will have only *one* razor-thin chance to slip past this scourge of the deep, seize his crown and get away before those deadly tentacles seize him in a grip from which there is *no escape—!*"

Inside the tent the air was dense with alien smells; a conspiratorial, festive atmosphere. Tip had bought a candied apple for Mrs. Gaspa and a spun sugar stick for Jophy. Sitting on the broad, sagging planks they had watched the flaxenhaired girl pirouetting on the cantering piebald horse and the clowns joining her, riding in tandem, pinwheeling and pratfalling while the audience screamed its delight. The fat Japanese had waddled up on a platform and stepped out on the low wire—and suddenly turned into a marvel of agility with parasols and Indian clubs, and wound up balancing himself on his head while the unreal porcelain maidens handed him hoops he spun at his ankles, plates he twirled at the end of slender bamboo rods, and finally an entire tea service from which he poured and drank a cup, still imperturbably upside down.

And now with a swaggering flourish the ringmaster jerked on a lanyard and the curtains swept back, to reveal a huge tank floored with white sand and laced with long green scarves of seaweed; and again the crowd broke into that low, premonitory murmur. In the dead center of the tank the big creature squatted, its eerie knoblike head sunk into its body, the canopy at the base of its tentacles undulating with a sinister, velvety motion. Behind it, in a far corner, lay a shiny golden coronet, looking ridiculously out of place in the sea-deep murk. Gazing from the octopus to the crown Tip felt excited in some deep, mysterious way he couldn't explain.

"He certainly is a big boy."

"Monstro," Annabella Gaspa muttered, and shook her head. "The things men will do to amuse each other."

"Bread and circuses!" Jophy said airily.

"I don't want to watch this."

"Oh, *Grama!* Now I suppose you're going to start in on Miguel Cabral and his loony visions."

"Yes, well, they turned out to be true. What about the time he dreamed they'd run aground?"

"Coincidence, *coincidence!*—you said so yourself . . ."

"When? When did I ever say that?"

"You certainly did! Or the time he saw those ghosts of drowned men up in the bows, baiting trawl—are you trying to tell me you *believe* that rubbish?"

They were glaring at each other, gesticulating—they had exchanged roles in some weird way: Grama Gaspa, the hard-headed skeptic, was thundering on about events beyond mortal reason and his wild, romantic Jophy inveighing hotly against these crazy medieval sorceries, lunatic witchcraft . . . Tip watched them in frank amazement. Everything was topsy-turvy, this bewitched weekend. When they finally ran down he said:

"Well, he certainly isn't going to kill it—they'll have an awful time finding a replacement octopus in Cape Cod Bay . . ."

This sent Jophy into a burst of wild laughter, and even her grandmother chuckled and smoothed her skirt. Tip, pleased with the unexpected effect, watched the ringmaster, who was pointing with the varnished baton.

"—and here he comes, the Emperor of that dread kingdom beneath the sea, the Great Konomaku—in the Dive of Death! . . .

The band burst into fierce fanfare, and Konomaku climbed onto a small platform at the opposite end of the tank from where the crown lay, while the ringmaster led the applause. Unlike the other performers Kono neither bowed low nor smiled; he gave only a curt nod and then slipped out of the emerald robe, again exposing the fearsome double necklace of the scars.

"As you can see, ladies and gentlemen, he has no protection except that dagger strapped to the calf of his leg. The little figurine around his neck is the amulet of the Tahitian god Oro—and let me tell *you*, folks, Mr. Oro is going to have to be working overtime this evening!"

The islander ignored this and began adjusting what looked like small bone plates over his nose and ears.

"What's he doing now?" Tip wondered.

"Grampa says pearl divers have to wear them," Jophy answered. "Because of the pressure."

"But it's only a tank—it's only ten feet deep."

"Well—maybe it's to hold the air in. How should I know? Oh, I *wish* Grampa could see this!"

"Well, I'm glad he won't," Annabella Gaspa said.

"—Are you ready, Kono?" the ringmaster called. The big man nodded. "Yes, he says he's ready . . ."

The snare drum started a low, ominous roll, building. Kono perched on the platform, toes gripping the rough edge of the plank, inhaling powerfully, belly swelling and caving. Tip noticed that the octopus had come alert, suspended with uncanny delicacy above the sand; a tentacle now and then uncoiled and withdrew, feline, anticipatory. The drum roll was thunderous now. Kono took one final, deep breath—dropped straight down the side of the tank with scarcely a ripple, doubled up, set his heels against the glass and thrust outward with powerful, froglike strokes, passed just over the creature's head and curved down to the sand. Tip saw him hook one arm through the crown, spin around in a tight ball, his feet against the tank wall, and push off—then one of the tentacles flicked out like a great, swollen whip and at the same instant a dense cloud of ink suffused the green water. There was a cry of bewilderment and fear, and the crowd began to stand, straining to see.

"—that's his protective ink, folks! He's a big squid really, all devilfish use it to confuse their victims—

but Kono's on to that maneuver, he knows what he's doing—"

There was a violent commotion in the sooty murk. Tip thought he saw the Tahitian rolling and writhing in the grip of a tentacle, and in the next second he wasn't sure he'd seen anything at all.

Then he did see a tentacle coiling spastically, there was another churning upheaval of water, and a few seconds later the islander shot to the surface, vaulted up on the platform with one clean, upward thrust of his powerful arms and, still unsmiling, raised the golden crown above his head to a bedlam of whistles and applause. Tip realized he was on his feet; the whole crowd was standing.

"—and he's done it!" the ringmaster-barker was shouting, his face brick red and sweaty; he flung his arms wide, scaled his straw boater off into the audience. "He has cheated death one—more—time, and before your very eyes! He has retained his crown! A big hand, folks, a *great* big hand now for the Great Konomaku, Emperor of the Deep—!"

The islander had picked up his robe; as he slipped it on Tip caught sight of several circular red welts, like blood blisters, on one thigh.

"He did get him, then. Dat Kanaka he plenty-fella brave," he said suddenly.

Jophy stopped clapping in abrupt surprise, gave him a playful shove. "You're a sneaky Yankee, Tipton Ames!—Well, he *is* . . . how'd you like to try it?"

"Not me."

"Madness," Grama Gaspa said crisply. "Imagine doing that for a living."

"But he did it!" Jophy's eyes were dancing with delight. "Don't you see?—he *won* . . ."

The tide was full, or nearly. Through the soles of his sneakers Chapin could feel the old ship strain gently at her moorings. He crept past tubs, rotted rope, and dunnage to the companionway, felt his way down the ladder. The gasoline tin clanked once against the railing and he cursed. Too dark. He should have brought a light—he couldn't see anything at all.

There was a doorway to the left, an open space of some kind. The air was heavy with fish and tar and paint. He had no idea where he was, and this too excited him. He advanced into the pitch darkness, worked his way along a cavernous area—stumbled all at once against something big and soft and almost went to his knees. Net, a mass of net. Christ, what a junk shop! There was a faint scrabbling sound and something scurried away forward. He started violently. Rats. Leaving the sinking ship. And why not? Who wouldn't? He had an almost ungovernable urge to roar with laughter, pound his fists against the worn wood of the hull. The stench of fish gurry and tar and brackish water was terrific, made him retch; he was bathed in sweat, and trembling again. This was far enough—if he kept on wandering around he'd lose his way and that would never do. The schooner gave a low, groaning creak, swaying infinitesimally. It was a wonder she hadn't sunk, sitting here all these years. Well, she'd sink now, all right. Oh, yes! . . .

He unscrewed the top to the can, tilted it and moved cautiously back toward the companionway; the smell of raw gas filled his lungs, drove out the stink of rot and fish. When the can was empty he set it down by his feet. There was no label on the tin, nothing to trace. There would be nothing to trace anyway, in a few minutes. He thought he heard something, then—a sigh, a grunt—and strained, listening, the blood washing hard in his temples. No, nothing. He was getting spooked. He felt his way to the ladder, climbed several steps, drew a few matches out of his pocket and struck them on the wood above his head; they flared into life. He tossed them down and behind him.

The blast of flame—the huge, compressed roar of it,

explosive, terrible—made him gasp out loud. He leaped up the companionway and practically fell on the deck, while that followed him in thick waves, borne on a subterranean roaring like a typhoon deep in hell. For one crazy instant he thought he was on fire and grabbed frantically at his trousers. No. He was all right. Of course he was all right—what the hell was the matter with him? Flames were licking up the companionway, pouring out of a hatchway forward, flames were roaring away everywhere, smoke in swirling black clouds; a giant furnace gone mad. So *fast*—how could it spread so fast? Get out of here, he'd better—

There was a cry—hoarse, shrill. A voice crying. Below him. *Someone*. But that was impossible. Frozen in a dream of boundless dread he crouched at the companionway, hand before his face—saw a figure lurch blackly into the rectangle of blinding light. A series of cries that turned to screams. A hand clawed at the rail, at space—a hand encased in fire, clothed in fire. Oh God. Oh no. Oh no God. Old Gaspa. He'd been down there—in the cabin, all along. Not possible—

Gaspa—

Chapin started back down, arms in front of his face. Heat swallowed him in one vast cone, beat at him, seared and half-blinded him. He drew back, gasping. The old man had fallen now, was rolling back and forth in the whirling cone of fire, all ablaze—his jacket, his hair, his hands. His mouth was moving, but no voice was audible in the dense, seething roar; then smoke swept over him again. Chapin shrank back against the worn wood; the heat stripped him of sight, of breath, of all resolve. He gazed down at the still, blackened body in a white eternity of panic—then broke for the deck and gazed around him blankly. Smoke was rolling toward him low along the deck, plumes of flame danced and capered around the great splintered stump of the foremast. Somewhere behind the sail loft he heard a shout, piercing as a command.

Without thought he leaped to the rail and slipped over the side. The water took him in a swift, soothing embrace. Cool, healing water; dark. Dark and cool. He swam powerfully, steadily until his lungs burned—surfaced in a dancing mirror-floor of flickering crazy light spouting misshapen gouts of fire. When he dove once more something deep inside him half hoped he'd never come up again.

"You see, Grama? There was nothing to worry about after all," Jophy said. The show had let out and the three of them were moving indolently with the crowd past the booths and concessions. "So much for your gloomy forebodings."

"One day the monster will get him," her grandmother answered. "One day soon.—Did you see his leg?" she demanded of Tip, who nodded at her in surprise; he hadn't thought she'd noticed. "They will pull his body from that silly tank, and bury him ten thousand miles from his native land. And what will he have proved? that there are creatures on this earth more powerful than he? that age saps all strength? that ultimately we fail at everything we try?" She grunted, patting at her forehead with a handkerchief.

"Anything worth having is worth risking for," Jophy went on in that strangely blithe, airy tone. She had prevailed on Tip to buy her another spun-sugar cone and was twirling it deftly, curling her tongue around it. A fleck had caught on the tip of her nose, which made her look more appealing than ever—Tip had a sudden desire to lean over and lick it away.

"That is a risk without purpose, without dignity. Let him make an honest living, fishing. Like his fathers."

"He wasn't fishing, he was diving for pearls. For strands and strands of glorious, pink-white, glowing pearls!" Jophy flung her arms wide to the night sky. Instead of releasing her, Konomaku's exploit had made her even more excited and perverse. She seemed

148

to be baiting her grandmother but Tip couldn't be sure. "Isn't that what Grampa did? Went up against the whale, time after time? All of us Gaspas take dares."

"Your grandfather risked his life to kill the whale for its oil and bone, to make a living—not in a foolish spectacle."

"But Konomaku did it, he *won*—he's Emperor of the Deep!"

"Yes, well, there is an old Portuguese saying: 'When the game is over, the king and the pawn go into the same box.'"

"But that's the whole point! It's when the game is *on*—who cares when it's over?"

"All right, Jophy," Tip rebuked her.

She looked up at him in the way she had from under her arched brows. "Now don't *you* start in! He wanted adventure, to see the wonders of the world—there aren't any golden crowns on Bora Bora . . ."

"Chapin says there's a palace room in Vienna that's filled with crowns, with jewels in them the size of your thumb," Tip said.

Jophy fell silent and swung away impatiently.

"Yes, and a river of blood was spilled for every one of them," Annabella Gaspa said.

"Do you think so?"

She smiled her grim, forbidding smile. "They used to say in the whale fishery: one drop of blood for every gallon of sperm oil. How much more, then, for all those emeralds and sapphires?"

She broke off. The bell in the town hall steeple on Main Street burst into sudden tolling, clanging and banging frantically, drowning out the reedy, tinkling music of the fair. There was a brief, attentive stillness, and then people began running through the crowd.

"Fire," Jophy said.

"Come. Hurry." Her grandmother moved forward with purpose, her face stern.

They passed through the gates quickly and began to climb the hill toward High Street, half impelled by the crowd. Men were running hard down Winthrop and Nickerson streets toward the harbor. Above the trees now they could see a deep crimson glow.

"It's the Upper Channel," Jophy said with sudden urgency. "Near Ryder's Wharf . . . near—"

The crowd was walking faster, as if drawn toward the lurid red flames, now capped by sparks and mounting skyward. Above the wild tolling of the bell from the Town Hall they could hear the high *nang!- nang!-nang!* of fire engines, and down in the Lower Channel some ship's horn kept hooting fiercely. In the next moment they had reached the edge of the bluff on High Street. Between the elms Tip could make out a long, low form bathed in flame; its reflection shimmered and swam on the water of the channel, and huge shadows capered and wavered in monstrous writhing shapes. It seemed to be right in the water— almost as though the tide itself were on fire . . .

"—Oh my God," Jophy breathed. "It's the *Albatroz* . . . !"

She was gone, racing down the street through the crowd, twisting and turning, holding her skirt high against her thighs, her sandaled feet flashing in the flaring light.

"No—wait! Jophy . . ." He started after her, remembered her grandmother and stopped again, whirled around. Annabella Gaspa was glaring at him, her face like thunder.

"No! she cried hoarsely, pointing. "Vai, vai! Depressa! Go on! . . ."

He turned and ran after Jophy through the running crowd.

. . . It was a shore where she had never been; intensely tropical and barbarous, with outlandish mango trees that glowed scarlet in the light sky, and a wind like the breath of a god. The bonfire leaped

150

hungrily, flinging anvil showers of sparks, and the men lying around it drank a dangerous Carib potion from silver goblets, laughing and singing snatches of ribald song; swarthy men with bronzed faces and pointed beards, who wore large gold rings in their ears. Buccaneers clearly, freebooters in wanton revolt against all proper authority, and she had fallen into their power through absolutely no fault of her own. It was quite clear that one of them was going to claim her as part of some unexplained ransom; the prospect was both odious and yet somehow deeply pleasurable . . .

It was their blithe masculine indifference to her that was enraging, and she was on the point of saying something crushing, to remind them of her own lofty position when, to her great irritation, a bell sounded somewhere, a ship's bell perhaps; and the men came alert, poised catlike on their feet, staring seaward. Now she could get away, *now,* if she wanted to—but their ringleader was coming toward her, the curly black hair on his chest gleaming disturbingly in the firelight. She wanted to press the palm of her hand against the hard swell of muscle, and the desire angered and excited her. He was much, much too handsome. She recognized him vaguely from some other place and time, but for some reason was afraid to ask him.

He had stopped directly in front of her, his eyes glinting, his lips curled in derisive amusement; then without warning he held out his hand expectantly. Some kind of offer, then, a challenge—she understood, and a decision was clearly necessary, for the seaborne bells had risen in pitch, jangling away with menacing insistence. Nothing in the world seemed more desirable than to place the palm of her hand on his naked chest. Standing quite still she extended her hand, watching his eyes. Very well, then. *Now.* The tips of her fingers touched that smooth, hard flesh with a thrilling electrical shock, and Serena Aldridge awoke instantly and fully, her heart pounding . . .

There was a sound. In the hallway downstairs, or perhaps the back pantry. She had only half-heard it but she knew, the way one suddenly completes the forgotten line from a poem. And now, farther away, there came the sound of a fire engine in full cry, its bell slamming crazily, and beyond that other sounds of upheaval, an almost festive clamor, like children on some distant beach . . .

The sound downstairs came again. At the rear of the house now, in the kitchen; muffled, abrupt. She looked at the Florentine marble clock on her bedside table. One-fifteen. It could be Margaret, of course, but Margaret never went back downstairs after she'd finished up in the kitchen. And Hynes lived above the garage, and slept like a log until his alarm went off at six.

It was Chapin, then; or Tip, or both of them. But why such curious *stealth?* No: something was unquestionably wrong; she could not say why, but she knew.

She slipped out of bed, drew on her robe and slippers, went quickly along the hall and descended the stairs. She could hear water running now, a soft high murmur in the pipes behind the wall. There were no voices. A thin bar of light came from under the pantry door into the kitchen. She paused a moment, then pushed it open; it swung back soundlessly and held on its catch.

Chapin was bent over the sink, his arms moving feverishly. For an instant, in the pale light from the cat's-eye night bulb over the stove, Serena thought he was naked, then realized he was wearing a pair of blue underdrawers. He was washing himself, scrubbing hard, sniffing constantly as he worked, and plunging his head under the tap as if he wanted to dissolve himself in water. Bells from other fire apparatus rose in discordant medley, carried on the night wind.

"What's the matter?" she said.

He started violently, his head snapped around. His face looked furtive and wild, strangely white in the bulb's febrile glow. He was wringing wet, his hair matted to his skull, his body slick and streaming; water stood in a large puddle around his bare feet, glinting on the linoleum.

"Nothing, I-I'm just washing . . ."

"I thought you went to the carnival."

"What?"

"The *carnival*," she prompted him with growing alarm, "—you said you were going with Tip and the others . . ."

"No. I didn't go—I . . ."

He broke off, shaking his head, his eyes squeezed tightly shut—and she saw he was too agitated even to speak. And then she saw the heap of sodden clothes behind him on the floor and at the same moment smelled the odor of raw gasoline and burning tar. Dread took hold of her. Connection. There was a connection, then—something very bad had happened. The wail of bells rose in a pealing crescendo. Glancing around distractedly she saw through the dining room windows the dull orange glow lying over the Upper Channel.

She came up to him. "Chapin," she said quietly. "What has happened?"

He started to say something, made a low, incoherent sound and again ducked his head under the tap. She put her hand on his shoulder. He was shaking violently, his whole body caught in a spasm of trembling, and this frightened her more deeply than anything else.

"Chapin," she repeated. "You must tell me. *What is the matter?*"

He straightened then and gazed at her fully for the first time—and she realized why his face had looked so pale; his eyebrows had been scorched away. His eyes were hollow with panic.

". . . he was *in* there!" he cried softly. "In there, all the time! . . ."

"Who was in where?"

"—I did it," he gasped, gesturing toward the dining room windows, the words coming more rapidly now. "Set fire—to the boat. The schooner . . ."

"You did *what*—?"

"That old wreck of the Gaspas'. At the dock . . . and he was *there,* in the cabin . . . and I couldn't reach him, I couldn't!—and by that time it was—"

He broke down, gripping the edge of the sink like a man about to be swept to his death; he was retching now, his head sunk in his shoulders. Absently she began to massage the back of his neck.

"Who?" she whispered. "Who was in there?"

"Old Gaspa."

". . . Are you sure?"

"*Yes,* I'm sure! He must have been asleep back there. I don't know . . ." He gazed up at her again, his eyes desperate, imploring. "But I didn't know it—I swear I didn't know he was there!"

She dropped her arm to her side. "What possessed you? To do a thing like that?"

"Oh, what does it *matter*—!" His voice broke again, turned thick with grief and rage. "I've ruined everything—destroyed my whole life because of that rotten little Portagee bitch! I'm done for! . . ."

The girl. Of course. Some people meant nothing but trouble. She'd seen it that first afternoon—the way the girl had turned toward her with that quick, defiant glance. Some things never changed.

Chapin was ranting now, out of control, going over it all again—as if another recital could alter it somehow, render it unreal.

"Be quiet, Chapin," she said.

"—out of nothing—how *could* he have been down there—!"

"Be still!" she ordered him. He fell silent then, his mouth working, still wiping and wiping at his body with a kitchen towel. She sat down in one of the straight-backed chairs. She must be calm. She must think very carefully.

"Did anyone see you?" she asked.

"No. No one."

"You're quite sure?"

"Yes. I slipped over the side and swam underwater—I came up through the pine grove and around behind the ball field. There was no one . . ."

The uproar from the Upper Channel was a bedlam now—commands, bells, whistles, and a deep muttered roaring she couldn't place. But the glow in the night sky seemed duller, less angry. She heard footsteps in the downstairs hallway, and then Margaret's voice:

"Miss Aldridge? Is everything all right?"

She threw Chapin a swift, threatful glance, put her finger to her lips, turned and went out through the pantry, closing the door behind her.

"Yes, perfectly all right," she answered pleasantly. "That infernal racket's waked everybody up."

Margaret, her hair loose around her shoulders, was holding her nightgown close at her throat as if it were cold. "I heard the engines. And then I heard voices, and I wondered—"

"No, it's nothing. Just a wharf fire. You go on back to bed."

She watched Margaret climb the stairs, and then returned to the kitchen and again sat down and tried to compose herself. The fire engines' clamor, Chapin's nearly naked body, that distressing dream all wound themselves together in a curiously distracting way, wrenching her thoughts this way and that. No, she told herself fiercely, it is *not* going to be for nothing—not after all these years, not after all my plans . . .

But there wasn't much time.

"I think," she said in a low, calm voice, "you had better go and enlist."

He stared at her. "In the Army?"

She nodded. "You're always talking about it."

"Yes, but—"

"No buts. It's too late for those now." She nodded again, more to herself than to her nephew. "You must drive up to Boston. Right now."

He frowned. "The Buick's low on gas."

"—Then take some from the Packard!" she snapped in a low, savage voice. "Siphon it out! You seem to have become clever enough with gasoline . . ." She fixed him with her eyes, hard. "Listen to me, Chapin. Are you listening to me?"

"Yes, Auntie."

"Take the Old Burial Ground Road until you get to Orleans. Drive straight to the house. No speeding, no stops for coffee or drinks or anything else. At eight o'clock sharp go right down to State Street and enlist. Waive any deferments or enlistment leaves—tell them you want to get right into uniform and off to camp. Tell them anything you think will serve, but persuade them to *take you immediately*. Do you understand? I'll talk to Coolidge and old Lodge and see what I can do. Perhaps they can wangle some staff job. If anything goes wrong you must call me at once. But be discreet—you know what these party lines are like. Under no circumstances are you to come down here again. Now go on upstairs and get into some clothes. I'll get rid of this."

Still he stood there staring at her, troubled, uncertain, his mouth slack; he was rubbing at the side of his nose—that gesture that never failed to remind her of his father. He said: "Do you—think I ought to?"

She struck at her thigh and rose. "So you want to stand trial for murder? You fool!—don't you understand what you've done?"

"But I—I didn't know," he stammered, "it was an accident . . ."

"Do you think *they'll* take that sweet, charitable view?" She held her voice low, but her tone was hard with scorn. "Those people over there have sat around for years and hoped for a chance like this—prayed for it! And the mother practically a fixture at Barnstable courthouse—"

"The mother?" he echoed.

"The *grand*mother, the old dragon—what in God's name is the matter with you!" She could have struck him. "She's got Silas Trench in her hip pocket—she'll turn this into a perfect crusade. Hang the Cruel Yankee . . . *Listen* to me! You'll spend the rest of your life in a cage. Do you want that? Do you? Now throw some clothes on and get out of here quietly, before Tip gets back. You must stay clear of him—if he even lays *eyes* on you it's all up with you. Do you understand that?"

He nodded, licking his lips. "All right." He started for the door.

"One last thing. Are you—involved with the Gaspa girl?"

He turned, his eyes flickered at her—that wary, sideways glance—and her heart sank. "I don't quite know what you mean, Auntie. I mean, we've gone to some of the—"

She spat out: "I *mean,* have you had sexual intercourse with her?"

He looked shocked; for an instant his eyes flared with rage, and something else—some vengeful ferocity she could only guess at, that frightened her even in her anger; he started to shout something, ground it down, and shook his head rapidly.

"No," he said. "I haven't."

"You're not lying to me. It's very, very important."

"I told you—no! It's the truth . . ."

"Good," she said, watching his drawn, anguished face. "That's good. Now, hurry . . ."

10

The pony—it looked to Tip like some kind of patchwork buckskin—anchored itself on all fours, stifflegged and quivering, its overlarge ears laid back, its eyes rolling white and wild; its head was shaped exactly like a driving maul.

"You trying to tell me that's a carriage horse?" Jack Darcey demanded.

"Course it's a horse," the liveryman answered; he was jerking the animal's head upward and back.

"It's one of those Cheyenne broncos, isn't it?" Jack shook his head at Tip. "I've run into them. These two cowpokes brought a whole freight-car load from Montana or some Godforsaken place and auctioned them off for whatever they could get. Look at the brute."

"Maybe it's a zebra they stole out of the Forest Park Zoo and painted yellow," Tip said.

"He's a good, smart trotter." The liveryman had forced the little mustang into the shafts virtually by main strength, his hands flying over the straps and buckles, cinching up hard on the bellyband. The buggy, an ancient affair with a splintered dashboard and a long tear in the top, rocked and groaned.

"Come on, now," Tip protested. "Can't you do better than this?"

"Sorry, gentlemen. It's all I've got. This isn't New York City, you know." He stepped back, never once taking his eyes off the animal, which was watching him speculatively. "There you go. Five dollars if you're back before sundown. That's for the whole rig, of course."

"That's ridiculous," Tip told him crossly. "I'll give you two bucks, and that's final."

"Agreed," the liveryman said with a speed that was dismaying, and vanished into the barn. The second horse plodded out docilely, eyes half closed—without any warning drove his head at the liveryman's shoulder, his teeth bared. The liveryman slammed against the stable door, dodged another plunge of the hammerhead with amazing agility, cursed once, snatched up a pick handle leaning against the wall and whacked the pony full on the nose with it. The animal grunted; its crazy walleyes seemed to glaze over briefly, and then its head went meekly down.

"You misbegotten son of a bitch," the liveryman said. Rubbing his shoulder he took hold of the bridle again. "Now, *mind*."

"Jesus God Almighty," Jack Darcey said.

"Just a little persuasion. They're smart, spirited animals, is all."

"Spirited," Tip said.

"Of course you've got to show them who's boss now and again." The liveryman turned and looked at him. Tip noticed he still kept a good grip on the snaffle ring, his knuckles white. "You can handle a horse, can't you?"

"Sure, I can. But I'm not Ben Hur."

The liveryman laughed, sweating lightly. "Hey, that's a good one. I got to remember that one."

"Oh, he's a hot sketch." Jack Darcey cleared his throat hollowly, and spat on the dry earth. He looked pale, and his eyes were narrowed to slits. He'd been in a bad mood for days, and this morning he had a ferocious hangover. The war was on his mind all the time. He eyed the two beasts, the cursing liveryman with active distaste. "Of all the hare-brained notions.

Where are we going to find anyone in this rock-filled wilderness who can even read, let alone take a course in self-improvement? I got two orders yesterday in Freemantle: one prospect ordered me to get out, and the other one ordered me to stay out."

"Side-splitting."

The second buggy was in even worse shape. One wheel was out of line, there was a decided list to port, and it had no top at all.

"What do I do if it rains?" Tip demanded.

"Can't rain, beautiful fall day like this."

"Sure.—Take your pick," he said to Jack. "There's no sense in flipping a coin—whoever wins this one loses, anyway."

"Why Christ Almighty, neither one of these pieces of junk will hold together for three miles." Jack waved one arm at the liveryman. "You want me to die out there in the tundra?" He clambered into the first buggy, which rocked and squealed on its worn-out springs. "Meet you back here at five," he muttered.

"Suit yourself."

"I'll be in the bar. If I haven't been clawed to death by a God damned snow leopard. Or maybe I'll go over to Montpelier and join the Army. Hell, all that can happen to you in France is you get shot in the ass . . ."

Tip watched him depart, sitting very erect, shoulders hunched, derby hat aslant, the dust a gray-gold powder under the wheels. Then he gingerly boarded his own relic, and reached for the reins.

"Here you go."

He looked down. The liveryman was handing up the pick handle. "Straight-grained rock marble. Might come in handy." Solemnly he nodded at Tip, his flat little gray eyes unreadable. "He's a good little trotter, but a touch unpredictable."

"Do tell." Tip took the bludgeon and set it at his feet. "What's his name?"

The liveryman hesitated just a second. "We call him Primrose."

"Oh, come on . . "

"No—that's his name. It's a might queer, I know."

Tip started to say something and closed his mouth; he got a viselike grip on the reins, braced his feet against the scarred dashboard and clucked the hammerhead into action. To his astonishment the little horse started off at an amiable trot. Perhaps the blow on the head had put it in a temporary state of shock; perhaps it was dreaming of its palmy days among the chaparral. Primrose. He glanced back over his shoulder; the liveryman was still standing there watching him, thumbs hooked high in his overalls.

This whole junket had been a disaster; it was getting harder and harder to drum up business. The war had taken over—people were worried about the Administration's price-fixing policies, they were hopping mad over the new income tax hikes, they were working up a death-hate for anything German—beer, music, God knew what else. It was as if the war had freed people from the need to think anything through, they'd been given permission to run on their emotions for the duration. Like a fever. Well. Everything had gone wrong since that damned Grand Banks Ball; and the fire . . .

He'd sent Frank Delahant a wire and stayed on for the funeral. The whole town had turned out; the vessels swung idly at their moorings, the wharves and lofts were deserted. The burial was in the old cemetery on the hill behind the town. A few white-haired whaling men had even come over from New Bedford or Nantucket, and the great Banker captains, the Highliners, were there in force. From Provincetown had come Manuel Santos, whose boast was that no schooner lived that could beat him in a haul by the wind; and Johnny-Bull Silva, loquacious and devil-may-care, who had set the all-time record from Turk Island to Boston Harbor; and Marion Perry, gaunt and taciturn, who had beaten them all in the great race off Minot's Ledge—even after his foretopmast had been carried away. From Gloucester came the legendary Ben Pine and saturnine Clayton Morrissey, who had ridden out the Portland Gale of '98 on the dread Georges North Shoal, and Simon MacKinnon, who had been blown all the way from Banquereau to the Azores and lived to tell of it . . .

They stood at the grave's edge in their black suits, holding their bowlers or cloth caps in their great hands, the tan line like a brand across their foreheads, their hair ruffling in the onshore breeze; warriors of a thousand mortal combats. They had looked death full in the eye—some of them had even descended into the black heart of the maelstrom and returned. They knew who they were; there was nothing anyone on this earth could tell them about this life—about triumph or courage or terror or despair. Now, the old rivalries set aside, they stood in proud gravity, paying tribute to a man they acknowledged as their forerunner and their peer.

Across the fresh, deep trench, watching their faces, only half-listening to the priest's sonorous cadences in the ancient nautical eulogy, Tip had a sense of greatness passing. There would be brave men, skilled mariners—but never again would there be men quite like these . . .

A bell was tolling down in the town: St. Anthony's, its deep bass notes thrumming on the autumn air, dying away before the next stroke, as though reluctant to speak. It was joined by another in the Congregational Church steeple—a flatter, drier tone—and finally the town hall bell itself gave voice; a rude and stately threnody. Beside him Jophy had begun to tremble uncontrollably, swaying; he slipped a firm arm around her shoulders while in perfect silence she wept her heart out. Beyond her Annabella Gaspa stood like a rock, her dark face set and stern. Her eyes glistened, but she did not break down even when each of the captains in turn took the shovel and the soft, sandy earth began to spatter on the hollow wood.

It was only much later, after the old whalers and captains and dorymen and their wives had come up to Annabella Gaspa and murmured their brief condolences and passed out through the whale-rib arches; much later, when the two of them were finally alone, walking along the wagon road behind the town that Jophy broke her silence.

"He *never* was careless, Tip. Or forgetful. Never! He never even smoked . . . How could it happen?"

"I don't know." He held her hand in his, watching her fine, clean profile, the long straight nose, the high arch of brow. Now, here, swept with anguish, she seemed more beautiful to him than she ever had.

"*Why* did it have to happen to him? *Why*—? A simple old man, his body smashed up, dreaming of the old voyages . . . God, I hate life!"

"Don't say that, Jo . . ."

"Why not? Why shouldn't I say it—it's true!"

He fell silent himself then, troubled, his thoughts caught in a crossrip of confusion. He'd stayed with Jophy throughout most of that terrible night. She had been desperate at the fire, beside herself. He'd caught up with her near the loft; she'd broken away from him and tried to force her way past the firemen playing great streams of water over the old wharf, which was itself on fire by then—it was almost as though she'd known her grandfather was trapped in that searing cauldron. Tip had caught her again and held her, but it had taken all his strength to contain this alien, raging woman while sparks showered crazily around them and the channel tide glowed like lava. When they'd finally discovered Manuel Gaspa was not at home, wasn't anywhere in the town, when the charred old hull had heeled over to port and settled in the channel bed, and a fireman had found the old man's body at the foot of the companionway, unlike nearly everyone else Jophy had been neither shocked nor shaken but only grim, black with implacable rage.

The Bluffs, gaunt and withdrawn in first light, had

looked curiously remote to him. He'd washed and changed his clothes, and was sitting at the kitchen table talking with Margaret when his aunt came down.

"Oh, no!" she murmured, when he told her. "Old Captain Gaspa—what a terrible, tragic thing . . . What are they saying caused it?"

He stopped stirring his coffee and looked at her. "They aren't saying anything, Aunt. They haven't any idea."

She glanced away toward Blackfish Point and the bay, pressing her napkin hard against her thigh, her back arched. "Well. It's terrible, a terrible thing. These old ships and wharves—they ought to be more careful . . ."

He got to his feet then, quickly.

"What's the matter, Tipton?"

"I'm going to wake up Chay. He better hear about this, beauty sleep or no beauty sleep."

"Chapin's gone."

He stopped stock-still and turned. "Gone? Gone where?"

"Up to Boston. He's gone into the Army."

"The Army? But—he said . . . he said he wasn't—"

"In point of fact he enlisted last week. He had to report today."

He was filled with amazement. "But he never said a thing about it. Not a solitary word, all evening."

"You're not close, you two—surely you're aware of that, Tipton." Her eyes dilated once, that curious beacon-flash he remembered, then narrowed again. "He rarely confides in others. Especially over the important things. I only found out about it a few days ago myself."

He sat down carefully in his chair. "That's too bad," he said quietly. "I'd have liked to say goodbye to him. Where's he been assigned?"

"Assigned?"

"Yes—for training. I'd like to write him."

She shook her head. "I haven't the faintest idea,

Tipton. I don't believe he does, either. I imagine he'll send me a note when he gets there."

"Of course."

Coincidences—life was full of them; unrelated events happening simultaneously, in hot pursuit of one another. And people acted unpredictably, even absurdly—he'd been around enough to know that. Yet this wasn't just that—there was something more here, something he couldn't put his finger on; something strained and false, all—wrong. It *felt* wrong. Chay would have stunted him with it at the ball, wouldn't he? The sheer fun of springing his enlistment on his brother would have been just too much to resist. And yet Chay loved to be mysterious, too . . . Down in the harbor a bell began to clang crazily, as if someone were pulling on the lanyard for dear life, and a schooner's siren answered once, fiercely.

Tip said aloud: "You're taking it very well, Aunt."

Her eyes flared at him. "Taking what?"

Steadily he watched her. "Chay's going off to war."

"Did you expect me to throw a conniption fit? He knows how I feel—he knows I've been opposed to his enlisting." Her lips compressed, she wiped at the corners of her mouth with her napkin. "He has to live his own life."

"That's true."

"Will you be taking the morning train?"

He hesitated. "I'd like to stay on for a day or two if I may, Aunt Serena. I'm staying for the funeral."

"The funeral—I see. Can you take time off from your business for something like that?"

Now it was his turn to stare. "For Jophy Gaspa's grandfather?" he said. "I certainly intended to."

"I see. I didn't realize you were so—involved . . ."

"Well," he said simply, "I am."

Now, two days later, holding Jophy in his arms, listening to the soft clamor of her despair, he thought of his Aunt's cool blue eyes and was troubled all over again.

"I'm sorry Chapin couldn't be here," he said carefully. "He wasn't here, you know—he left for the Army that same morning."

"Oh." She nodded vaguely. "He wasn't teasing me, then."

"About what?"

"The night of the—the ball." She frowned, looking like a child awakened in the middle of the night. "Something about war being dangerous, about becoming a pilot. You know how he is. That's what he meant, then."

So it was true. He'd told *her*, of course—the romantic flier off for the wars. *Smile the while I bid you sad adieu* . . . Perhaps he himself was getting just too suspicious—it wasn't his nature. Anyway, Jophy wouldn't be wrong about something like that.

She'd forgotten all about Chapin, she was back on her grandfather, the fire, the utter impossibility of it, her voice tremulous and high. Holding her gently, his mouth pressed against the deep, rich scent of her hair, he had the old guilty thought, I am here, alive, for whatever unknowable reason, the blood pumping in my veins—and glad of it; grateful and glad.

"He used to sleep there often, in the cabin. He would dream of old gales, old hunts."

"Jophy, listen—"

" 'Stern all!' I heard him say once. 'Stern all! He's lobtailing—now look out for yourselves!' And then a little later, with a laugh: 'How's *that* for a dirty Portagee—?' Oh, you can't imagine all the things he went through . . ."

"I know. Jo . . ." He held her closer, rocking her against him. "Jo, listen to me. Jo, will you marry me?"

"—For God's sake, Tip!" She threw him a look of wild reproach. "Oh, how can you talk about that *now?*"

"Because I love you. Because I'm what you need,

Jo." He lifted her chin firmly and kissed her eyelids. "Because I've got to leave in a few hours . . ."

"All right, leave then—*leave!*" Her eyes filled. "I'm sorry. I didn't mean that."

"It's all right."

"I just—can't think about anything else. Can't you see?"

"Yes," he said, though in all truth he couldn't. "I want you, honey. More than anything else in the world. I've loved you from the moment I saw you. Don't you know that? Don't you know that yet?"

"Tip, I *can't*—"

"And you need me every bit as much—you just don't know it, yet, that's all."

"You believe that . . ." She looked up at him in searching wonder, her eyes dark and shimmering and indescribably beautiful. "You really believe it."

"Of course I do—I wouldn't have said it if I didn't . . ." He would have liked to be sophisticated and masterful and debonair—and he couldn't be; he could only say what was deepest in his heart. Holding her, the old trembling urgency caught at him again. He had to make her see this; he had to! Now, while he was here. There was simply no *sense* to life if he couldn't.

"Jo," he hurried on, "I love you more than anyone else ever will—all the rest of your life. I know it! What's more important than that?"

"Oh, Tip," she cried softly, "what am I going to do with you?"

"That's easy," he came back. "Look, we've only *got* one life—we've wasted half of it already . . ."

For another hour he held her, comforted and cajoled her—then ran for his train, calling that he'd write, he'd write every day, he wasn't a whizz-bang high-pressure salesman for nothing . . . At least Chay was out of the picture for a while; that gave him some breathing room. For the rest, he'd just have to contain himself, and wait.

* * *

The whole morning went badly. The storekeeper at Danforth, a tart Scotsman named MacChesney heard him out, shaking his head forbiddingly at every pause; the lumbermill superintendent had gone to Montpelier; the postmaster, a gnomelike man with a goatee, burst into a cackle of laughter, waved in Tip's face the steamed-open mail he'd been avidly reading, and cried: "Education! You want to talk about education? I got all I'll ever want, right here. Listen to this . . ."

Clouds piled on clouds, black as old iron, heavy as granite; the wind picked up out of the northeast, a chill winter wind promising trouble. On one occasion the piebald mustang absolutely refused to start for several minutes, and the next it tore off into a shocked cornfield before Tip could get it back under control. He reached Germetz' flour mill in the early afternoon, hungry and cross, whistling variations on "You Belong to Me" to keep his spirits up. The house looked run-down and so did the mill, but the water rushed cool below the falls, skirling white over the smooth rock. Thinking of home he tied the bronco securely to the hitching post and knocked at the kitchen door.

"Yes?"

The girl was small and slender, with straight fair hair.

"Is this the Germetz mill?" he asked. She bobbed her head once shyly. "Is your father home?"

"My father?"

At the same instant he saw the baby in the wash basket near the stove, waving its tiny hands. He grinned. "I'm sorry—I guess I mean your husband."

"Oh, he—he's coming in for dinner. In a few minutes." Her eyes were almost too large for her pale little face. She had not smiled.

"Can you give me dinner? I left Cromwell this morning at seven."

"That's a long way."

"Not so bad. I mean, when you think of Honolulu, or Hong Kong . . ."

The girl looked at him solemnly, uncomprehending —then gestured toward a chair at the big trestle table, and turned back to the stove. Fragile, Tip thought, watching her stirring one of the iron pots; too delicate for this Godforsaken wilderness. Ten years of this would break her in pieces.

From the outside they heard a burst of high, harsh laughter, almost falsetto. The girl's eyes shot to the door—a glance of real fear—then to the baby in its basket, then to the stove. Ah, Tip thought, so that's it.

Armand Germetz came in, followed by his helper; Tip rose and offered his hand. The miller didn't take it, turned instead to his wife with a blank, inquiring look.

"This gentleman came to see you on business," she said in a low voice. "He asked for dinner."

"Ah—did he? Dinner . . ."

"I'll pay you for it, of course," Tip said. "I've driven up from Cromwell, and when I smelled that chicken pie my defenses broke down . . ." He stopped smiling. "But if it's any inconvenience . . ."

"No-no," Germetz waved one of his heavy hands. "Why should it be? Eh?" He was a big man, run to fat but with powerful shoulders. His hair was cropped in a short bristle; an unkempt mustache hid his mouth. He spoke with an accent—it sounded more German than French. Alsatian, maybe. The moment Tip laid eyes on him he knew he was no prospect, but he offered a brief summary of the Institute's purpose while the woman served them. The chicken pie was superb —the meat moist and tender, the dumplings light as air.

"You want me to go to school?" Germetz asked him in that high voice.

"No, nothing like that. You could keep up with it in your spare time. Evenings and Sundays."

"Ah, but I have other things to do with my spare

time. Better things." He grinned suddenly, and Tip saw he had a harelip which the mustache was designed to hide. "No-no, Mister, I don't need any courses, any schools. You see, they all come to me. They *have* to come to me, I have the only mill in forty miles. So I have what you call a monopoly, eh?" When he smiled, his cunning small eyes became wet at the corners. "Nobody can get out of our valley. Our happy little valley." He ate tirelessly, with steady voracity, the fork dipping deftly in under the harelip and out again. The girl had not sat down to eat with them; she was still moving quietly above the stove.

There was a jolly miller, lived by the River Dee—

"Now you take Lawrence, here." With a fat thumb Germetz indicated his helper, a round-shouldered boy with a diffident manner. "Now he might want to go to your school. He has nothing better to do with his nights, his Sundays. Ain't that right, Lawrence?"

"That's right, Mr. Germetz."

"Sure. He has to hunt up his own pleasures. Satisfy himself. Eh, Lawrence?"

The boy looked down at his plate. Tip shot a glance at the girl. She was bent forward intently, frowning, cutting into a deep-dish apple pie.

"Now, what Lawrence wants is a tender, delicious girl like Claudine, here. Perhaps your night school will do that for him. You think so?" The girl was serving them dessert. As she moved past Germetz he reached out and slapped her on the buttock, gripped it securely in his broad hand. She made no move to twist away. When he released her she served the boy; her face was expressionless, but her eyes flickered in the gray light.

He worked and sang from morn till night, no lark so blithe as he . . .

"He's wishing that right now. A juicy girl like Claudine. Ain't you Lawrence?"

"No, Mr. Germetz." The boy had blushed a deep red into the roots of his hair.

171

"Ha! Of course you are! And you are right—she *is* a *soft,* tender morsel . . . But you wouldn't do that, would you?"

"Of course not, Mr. Germetz."

And this the burden of his song forever used to be

"No-no, of course not." The little eyes turned watery, spilling tears at their corners. "But you would like to, wouldn't you? Now wouldn't you? Put your hand on one of those soft, round—"

A pot fell to the floor with a crash. The girl crouched over, mopping spilled water. Germetz wrenched his bulk around in his chair.

"What is the trouble, my dear? Are you nervous? Eh?"

I care for nobody, no, not I—and nobody cares for me . . .

The girl still said nothing, her face averted; Tip could see she was trembling.

"—Clumsy slut!" Germetz said with sudden savagery. "Answer me!"

Tip flung down his napkin and got up. Germetz was watching him, his eyes narrowed again.

"What's the matter, Mister? No coffee?"

"No. No coffee."

"Why such hurry? Tell me more about your night school . . ."

"I think not." He turned to the girl and gave her a dollar bill. "Thank you for the dinner, Mrs. Germetz. It was a humdinger."

She looked up at him then—her large eyes wide with hopeless appeal. She thrust the dollar into the pocket of her apron.

"What a shame," Germetz was saying, "here you have come all the way up our little valley, and no success, eh? Ah, that's how it is with you city fellows with your fine clothes, your grand ways. What you need is—"

Tip said to the miller: "I was raised in a valley in the Berkshires, Mr. Germetz. With a mountain at my back. But I know good manners when I see them. And when I don't."

Picking up his hat he went out into the gray, windy day. There were several buckets beside the pump, and he filled the poorest-looking one and gingerly watered the bronco. The miller came out, and shied a hand at him.

"So Virgil Leach fobbed one of those fourfooted devils off on you," he called. "Watch out for them—they bite!" He uttered his grating soprano laugh and went off down the path toward the privy, unlimbering his suspenders. Tip checked the breastcollar and bellyband, being careful to stay clear of the animal's head. What a stupid trip. That was the trouble with the home office—they had these maps with pins in them, they were forever looking at *territories* without taking into account what *kind* of territories they were. This one was the Jolly Miller's. Well, live and learn. But he'd like to give that—

"Mister—"

He turned. The girl was standing there. She had put on her coat and held the baby in her arms, wrapped in a blanket.

"Mister, will you take me with you?"

He stared at her. "Take you? Where?"

"Anywhere. Please. Anywhere."

He frowned. "Now, look. I can't do that—your husband's—"

"He's not my husband. We were never married. Please, Mister—just anywhere, away from *here* . . ."

Her eyes clung to his almost blindly. She looked so *fragile*, so helpless—

"All right," he said quickly. "Get in the buggy."

"Hey!" Germetz was hurrying toward them, his great belly heaving. "You whore!" he roared. "You cunt! Get away from there, before I whale the ass off you!"

The girl, in the act of climbing aboard, paused in terror now, uncertain what to do.

"Get in the buggy," Tip repeated and turned to face the miller, who now had reached them, his face purple with fury.

"What you think you're doing?"

Tip thrust out his lip. "The lady says she wants to leave."

"Why, you scummy sneakthief drummer—!"

The miller cursed violently, opened his great arms, bearlike, and came at him in a lumbering rush. Tip sidestepped neatly and using the big man's momentum slammed him against the buggy, reached in and snatched the pick handle from behind the seat. In the tail of his eye he could see the girl struggling frantically to untie the reins. Germetz had wheeled around, facing him. Tip swung the pick handle like a ball bat and caught Germetz flush on the side of the head. The miller grunted and blinked, then came on. Jesus Christ Almighty, Tip thought, I can't hit him any harder than that. Behind Germetz' bulk the girl had leaped into the shay, holding the reins in one hand. Tip ran around to the other side in time to see Germetz reaching up, snatching at the bridle, roaring curses. The mustang all at once reared in the traces, struck out with its front hoofs like a cat—one, two, three—the miller bellowed with pain and fell backward, his hands clapped to his head. Tip vaulted into the buggy in one bound, the horse came down stiff-legged on all fours, Tip grabbed the reins out of the girl's hands, the bronco plunged ahead as if his tail were on fire, and they were off, in a wild, swaying, jolting rush, the dust swirling around them in choking clouds.

"Hang on!" he roared. "I can't begin to hold him . . ."

They swept on down the road, the old buggy swaying and slewing crazily, the pony bucking in the traces, ears laid back, walleyes rolling.

"Just pray this chariot holds together!"

"Yes!"

He stole a glance at the girl, saw that she had the baby clutched close to her breasts; she was smiling, her head rocking with the buggy's swaying motion.

"Thank God he's headed for Cromwell—I'd never turn him around . . ."

He burst into laughter then, for no earthly reason he could see, and so did the girl; both of them laughing uproariously, coughing in the churning storm of dust, glancing now and then at each other while the sun burst through the slate towers of clouds and the world flashed by in a gold-and-scarlet millrace of sundrenched maples and birch and sumac. His hat was gone, he had no idea where or how he'd lost it, and that too seemed indescribably funny. In the open door of a barn two men, pitchforks in hand, glared at them in amazement as they shot by.

By the time they reached the river road the bronco had worked off most of the demon that possessed him, and subsided to a rolling canter which Tip was able to snub down to a brisk trot; and in Cromwell reality returned. The girl had fallen silent, gazing fearfully ahead. Tip himself felt filled with doubts. What in hell had he got himself into? By using all the strength he owned he managed to turn the mad little beast into the road that ran from Main Street down to the railroad station, and by the depot he got it to stop, and lashed its hammerhead tightly to the hitching post ring. He ducked into the station, checked the schedules and came out again. The girl was standing at the pump washing dust off the baby's little round face. The child was gurgling, its fat arms still waving.

"You're in luck," he told her. "The Brattleboro train will be in in ten minutes."

"Brattleboro?" she asked timidly.

"Well, southbound. Where do you want to go?"

"I don't know . . ."

"You haven't any place? anybody to go to?"

She shook her head; her eyes, close to tears, hung

on his as if he were the last hope in the western world.

"Well, you can't stay here—this is the first place he'll look. Is there anywhere you *want* to go?"

Again she shook her head. "—Away from *him*," she said finally, and for the first time her voice broke.

"All right. Look. Have you any money?"

"Three dollars and sixty cents," she murmured without hesitation. "And the dollar you gave me."

"All right. Here's ten dollars." He handed her the bill, watched her fold it inside her bodice. "I'd give you more, but it's all I've got."

"Thank you. I'll pay you back—I promise."

"Don't worry about it." He could hear the train whistle now, high and desolate. He pulled a pad out of his coat pocket and wrote on it rapidly, tore out the page. "Get off at North Grantham. It's just before you get to Rutland—ask the conductor. Go to the Montague House and ask for Mr. Coates. They need a cook. Give him this note. It's the best I can do."

They could hear the train barking down the long grade from Kingsfield. The baby had begun to fret and she stroked its round head with her slender, delicate hands.

"Oh, thank you . . ."

"Don't thank me—you've got a long row to hoe." He smiled at her. "But if you can cook everything like that chicken pie, you'll be all right. Come on, now, you don't want to miss it."

The train came in, clanging, belching gouts of white steam. She went aboard and waved down to him through the soot-streaked window, smiling at him, very frightened, very brave, the baby's head bobbing in the blue blanket. He waved back, watched the train sway on south, to North Grantham, to Brattleboro, to Springfield, and New Haven, and New York . . .

He was hurrying out to his rig when the voice said: "Mr. Ames?"

He turned. A tall man in a green felt hat was walking toward him; an even, unhurried stride. A toothpick was working at one corner of his mouth. When he was directly in front of Tip he said:

"You just put a young lady on the Brattleboro train."

"That's right. I did. And who are you?"

"Name's Purdy. Constable, Cromwell Township." Flipping back his shirt collar he disclosed a tarnished metal badge. "I'd be obliged if you'd tell me where the young lady's headed."

Tip said: "I couldn't say."

"I fancy you could. Especially as you handed her that slip of paper." Tip made no answer. "Thing is, she happens to be Armand Germetz' wife, over in Danforth."

"She says they're not married. Never were . . ."

"Suppose you tell me how you happened to be escorting Mrs. Germetz to the station. You object to that?"

"Not at all." Tip gave him an abbreviated version of the circumstances surrounding their departure. "The man's a monster. If you ask me she's well rid of him."

"Only I didn't ask you. Did I?" Prudy played the toothpick back and forth over his lower lip. "Thing is, the law's pretty clear on this point."

Tip's head came up. "Is it, now? *That'll* be a surprise—usually it's so murky you can read it five ways from Sunday . . ."

"It's clear enough here. She's had a child by him."

"Maybe so, maybe not. Do you know *that* for certain?"

The constable suppressed a smile. "You're quick, Ames. I'll give you that." The deep blue eyes roved over Tip's face. "Drummer, aren't you? That correspondence course."

"That's right." Tip lowered his voice. "Look, can't you give her a break? How'd you like to be in the clutches of that baboon?"

"The law's the law, son. Now I'll ask you once more: where's the young lady headed?"

Tip thrust out his lower lip and shoved his hands in his pockets. He said: "I don't remember."

The deep blue eyes became flat and hard. "You sure you want it this way, son? Maybe we'd better take a little walk down to the lock-up and you can cool your heels until your memory improves."

"On what charge?"

"Obstructing justice, for starters—"

"*Justice—!*"

"—and then there's improper solicitation, abduction, adultery . . ."

Tip burst out: "I get it—I'm a salesman and so I'm only after one thing—well, God damn it, we'll see about that. It so happens I'm—I'm engaged to a girl over on Cape Cod, a wonderful girl, and you can take that back!"

"You'd better come along with me, Ames."

"All right, fine! But I'll tell you this—I've got twelve hundred dollars soaked away in the First Merchants and Farmers Bank in Holcomb Falls, Massachusetts. And the first thing I'm going to do is put in a call to Wilbur Bartow of Warner, Bartow in Rutland. And we'll get it *all* out in the open—you put that foul-tongued bully Germetz on the stand and see how far you get! That German! You want that?" A couple of loafers slumped in the settee at the back of the station were listening eagerly, and the clerk was staring at them open-mouthed but he didn't care now; he was hopping mad. "And after that, Mister, I'll use the rest of that twelve hundred to bring *you* up on charges of false arrest!"

The two men glared at each other in silence. They could hear a horse drinking at the trough on the far side of the lot.

Then Purdy nodded shortly and looked down. "You've got nerve, Ames," he muttered.

"You bet." Tip wheeled around and stomped off toward his rig. "You picked on the wrong huckleberry this time. I know a little something about the law myself! Germetz may have this county by the tail, but I very much doubt if he can wrap up the whole state . . ."

The constable still hadn't moved, was staring after him in stony silence; he hadn't put the toothpick back in his mouth. Tip untied the reins and climbed into the buggy. "I'll be at the Cromwell House till the morning train," he called. "If you want to reach me. Room Fourteen . . . You're quick enough to look the other way when some leading citizen gets his feet wet," he couldn't refrain from shouting, "—why can't you do it when a poor girl's life is at stake?"

He flicked the reins and clucked to the bronco, who broke into a smart, obedient trot.

"—Adultery," Tip muttered aloud. "Abduction—the son of a bitch! He thinks I'm going to stand there and take that kind of talk from a peace officer he's got another thought on the way. Adultery!"

They had just turned on to River Street when there came a mounting, piercing shriek that seemed to come from behind his right ear. He had just time to think, *sawmill whistle, must be four-thirty,* when the mustang had reared, pawing air, its eyes rolling in mad terror, and burst into a crazy, plunging gallop, its hooves flashing in the silvered light.

"Whoa, you buzzard—now *whoa!*" he roared. Arching his back he hauled in on the reins with all his might. It had no effect at all. They tore up River Street, narrowly missing a delivery wagon and a parked Ford, gathering speed. A maple limb dipped down, golden and shivering, like a swung beam and he cringed—swept under it untouched; two small boys were hooting at them and pointing, a figure dashed in front in a yellow dress, skirts clutched up to the thighs, white ruffled petticoat flaring. The bronco, now rearing and plunging like a trapped deer, swung

179

onto Main Street; the buggy's right wheel struck the granite curb, the rig tipped wildly, hung there for one long sickening instant, the wheel snapped with a report like a pistol and the buggy fell away, flung him pinwheeling in air. A store front—Tip had a swift, indelible image of the word NOTIONS in black spencerian script—there was a terrific crash of splintered wood and shattered glass. Then there was perfect silence.

He opened his eyes. He was on his back, one arm bent behind him somewhere. A face was peering at him—a sweet face framed in white hair.

All right? the lips said, inquiring, the eyes wide. *All right?*

He nodded instinctively, raised his head. Other hands were behind him now, helping him up. Slowly he got to his feet, feeling various parts of his body gingerly; his neck hurt, and his shoulder and hip. He was all right; he hadn't broken anything.

"God Almighty!" the voice was saying aloud now. "He came flying through the new display—right through the new display . . ."

"You've got a nasty cut on the back of your head, young fella," a man's voice was saying. "Glass cut you, coming through."

He nodded, looked around him with fragile care. Dry goods. Dry goods store. Sweaters and corsets spilled against the counters, the floor was awash with bolts of calico and dimity and rep. A big-busted dressmaker's form lay at his feet like a fallen goddess, legless and beheaded.

"Sit down, son," the man said. He was wearing steel-rimmed spectacles which had been badly mended at the nose-piece. Tip sat down weakly while they fussed over him. The woman was bathing the cut in his head. "The yard goods broke your fall," she told him amiably. "That's what 'twas. Now aren't you lucky?"

"I'm always lucky."

"Good thing it wasn't the hardware store." The man laughed, his glasses flashing like huge pale coins. "Scratchy Sproul's got a two-man crosscut in his window, and I don't know what-all. You picked the right display."

"I'll pay you for that window," Tip said.

"Don't worry about it. Haven't had this much fun around here since Nero burned Rome. You know, you were actually doing a swan dive—your arms were out like a fancy swan dive!"

"Where's the rig?" Tip asked suddenly.

"Gone to buggy heaven, I'll tell you. That shay just plain exploded into matchwork."

"It was one of those wild ponies, wasn't it?" the woman demanded indignantly. "They ought to put Virgil Leach in jail for palming those wicked beasts off on perfect strangers."

"I can't tell you how sorry I am. Busting up your store this way."

"Maybe it's for the best." The proprietor pulled down the corners of his broad mouth. "Haven't been making a go of it anyway. I hurt my leg logging and they said a store was the answer. But hell's fire, it's no answer at all, it's a snare and a delusion if you aren't equipped to handle it. I don't know what I'm doing half the time. Never had any real education." He said to his wife: "What we'd ought to do is go back to Ed's farm and help out, Emma."

"Hold on, now." Tip said. "Maybe this was providential—maybe I'm the answer to your prayers."

The storekeeper's eyes glinted shrewdly. "You a drummer?"

"Yep."

"Whatever it is, we don't need it."

"You need *my* line, believe me." Tip leaned forward. "Within a few short months you'll know all you need to know about running this store and making a fair

181

profit into the bargain—I guarantee it. Now, let me tell you just a bit about Alexander Hamilton Institute. It's a course designed especially for folks like you . . ."

11

"Hello, Tip. Good to see you." Frank Delahant came toward him, his hand out. "Come on in and sit down." Leaning through the doorway he said to Miss Benson, "No more calls, Madeleine," closed the office door. Tip was conscious of the older man's gaze passing over him automatically, checking him out—suit nicely pressed, fresh shirt, hair trimmed, shoes just shined— noting all of it with swift, indifferent approval.

"Well," he said, "and how are things up in the tall timber?"

"Like squeezing sap from a stone," Tip answered. "It's not the most rewarding territory in the world."

"I know—I've worked it myself. Yet you've led the whole crowd in spite of it. You've done one whale of a job, Tip. You surprised even me. And I don't surprise easily."

Tip said quickly: "Give me Connecticut, or a slice of the Boston area, here, and watch my smoke! I mean it."

Frank Delahant laughed, rocked back in his swivel chair until his ties barely touched the floor. He never put his feet up on his desk—a public confession of indolence, he called it; Tip had once heard him severely reprimand Randy Hughes for doing that.

"I hear you've even managed a few adventures along the way . . ."

Tip grinned back at him. "Nothing I couldn't handle."

"So they tell me. Well, it gives some spice to the gingerbread. God knows we all need it. Heard from Jack?"

"Yes—he's at Upton. Says all they do in the Army is salute and peel spuds. Not what he had in mind."

"We'll miss him." Frank clasped his hands behind his head. "I suppose you're wondering why I've called you in."

"As a matter of fact I am."

"Well, for one thing, they're transferring me to the New York office. National headquarters."

Tip exclaimed: "Say—congratulations! Though I'll be sorry not to be working with you." He hesitated. "It's meant a lot to me, Frank. Not just because you got me started. It was knowing you were back here, on top of things. Setting the pace for us all . . . Whenever I was stumped I'd say to myself: 'How would Beau Frank handle this?' And it'd steady me down."

"Thank you, Tip."

"I mean it."

"I know you do." The remorseful shadow had flooded into his eyes vanished as quickly. "There's nothing I'd rather hear." Tapping a desk leg with his toe he swung himself around so that he was gazing out at the harbor. "For another thing, Walter Dabney's retiring as of next week. Which leaves us without a sales manager for the New England territory." He swung around again and threw himself forward in his chair, facing Tip. "I may be making a big mistake. Ruining a crack salesman to get a lousy sales manager. But you've led the force for eight straight months, now. I've got to offer it to you."

It was like a gulp of pure oxygen. Sales manager! It would mean a salary, an overridage on commissions—the chance to show what he could do. He thought instantly of Jophy. He could make it come true now.

"Tip, I hope you won't misinterpret what I'm going

to say. You know how much I think of you . . . I'm forced to hope you'll turn it down."

Tip stared at him. "Why, for God's sake?"

Delahant frowned at his nails. "George Maynard thinks you're far too young."

"What do you think?"

The sales manager's eyes rose to his again. "You *are* pretty young, son."

"You didn't think I was too young when you sent me up the valley with Darcey."

"Oh, sales, sure— I always knew you were a born salesman. There are those who master the techniques, but they're never as good as the naturals. You're a natural. I knew it the first moment I laid eyes on you. This is a very different jug of molasses. You'd be out front-and-center. You'd be giving the orders . . ."

"I realize that."

Frank sighed. "And I'm sure you also realize a lot of noses will be out of joint around here."

Tip thrust out his lip. "You mean Maury Zimmerman."

"Well, yes, Maury, a few others . . . He's more or less expecting me to move him into the slot."

"—Let him beat me out for sales, then . . ."

"Tip, it isn't just sales any more. Field manager's a whole different ball game. You've got to use applied psychology—kick some, kiss others—and God help you if you mix up your formula. Now, look at it from their point of view. Maury's been with the firm for—"

"No," Tip burst out, "—let him look at it from *mine* . . ."

Frank Delahant glanced at him, said sharply: "What's eating you? Has there been trouble between you and Maury?"

"Not at all. I like him a lot."

"Then why in hell are you so fired-up about this?"

"—Because I want to get married, that's why!"

Frank gaped at him, burst out laughing. "You're kidding . . ."

"No, I'm not kidding."

"Well, I'd never have guessed it." Something strained and somber flickered again behind his eyes. "I guess you *can* keep a secret. Who's the lucky girl?"

Tip hesitated. No: to speak now would be to jinx things. He had to wait. God, he was getting as superstitious as Jophy! He said aloud: "You'll be the first to meet her, Frank, I promise you. If, as and when."

"Fair enough."

"Anyway, it's my right. I've earned a shot at the job."

"That's true."

"I can handle it, Frank. I know I can. I want the chance."

Delahant swung around in his chair, peering out at Faneuil Hall, Atlantic Avenue, the harbor traffic moving with dreamy persistence across the gray plate of water. His face, in profile to Tip, looked moody and troubled. "I've seen men given authority," he mused, his lips barely moving. "More than they can handle. I've seen what it's done to them, over the years. Racketing along, opinionated, self-righteous, minds blank as a washboard—finally they get to feel they're ruling by divine right. And all the time everybody else is hoping and praying they'll just get the hell out of the way and stop blocking traffic . . ."

Abruptly he swung around. "All right. You've got it. You'll move into Walter's office. See Madeleine about arrangements."

Tip got to his feet. "Thanks, Frank. You won't regret it."

"I'm going out on a big limb with George, the whole national headquarters. Don't saw it off, now."

"I won't. I guarantee it."

"And Tip . . ."

He turned at the door. Frank held one hand up, slender and admonitory. "Gently, Tip. Gently. Easy does it." He dropped his hand. "People are what you're working with. They're all that matter in the long run."

"I know that."

"I don't want to lose Maury over this. That clear? There are a lot of good men out there. Remember that."

"I will, Frank."

He was walking down the hall twenty minutes later when he heard the voices in Harry Littler's office, where the Boston crowd often congregated; a tense murmur, overridden by Maury Zimmerman's husky baritone:

"—*matter* with him? Has he lost *all* his marbles? Putting a snotnosed kid at the top!"

"Well," another voice—Ed Langevin's—countered, "you've got to admit, he's beaten the tar out of the rest of us . . ."

"And what's that got to do with running a successful sales organization? Jesus H. Christ, I had a drawing account with Doubleday, Page when he was filling sacks of sugar in some crummy Berkshire mill town! He isn't even dry behind the ears . . ."

Yes, he was young; but he'd learned a lot along the way. And one of the things he'd learned was that opposition was like a snowball: you let it roll downhill far enough and it could get so big it would roll right over you. He turned around and went back down the hall, walked into Littler's office and said, "Hello, boys."

The heads all turned. Langevin looked embarrassed, Web Bowers noncommittal, Littler mischievously amused, Zimmerman sullen and combative. Then Maury looked down, and turned his back on him. He was going to sulk now, he was going to infect half the force with his resentment and thwarted expectations—and then sulk himself right out of the game. Maury would quit over this, it was quite obvious; unless he could find a way to hold him . . .

"Hello, Tip," Ed Langevin said, and cleared his

187

throat. The rest were silent. They knew he'd heard them—at least the tail end of the conversation—they were waiting to see what he would do. Good; that was good.

He said: "Maury, I'd like to see you for a moment."

He turned away quickly then, so as not to give Zimmerman the chance to defy him right there, make an open issue of it in front of the force; led the way back down the hall to his new office and went around behind the desk. He left the door open on purpose: he wanted this exchange to be heard. He didn't ask Maury to sit down—he knew he'd refuse—and remained standing himself. To sit down would be too much; it was better this way, both of them on their feet.

Maury had clasped his hands and was watching him coldly. He was a tall man with a fleshy, rather handsome face. He dressed well, but not with Beau Frank's quiet elegance. Maury's shirts were high-key silk, his jackets flashy; he wore fawn-colored spats, and his fingernails were constantly manicured by the girl in the Parker House barber shop.

"Well, well—all moved in, I see." His lip was slack with scornful amusement. He was getting ready to tell this fresh kid where to get off, and then go on his flamboyant way; but first he wanted to hear what the new field manager had to say for himself—not that it would matter any. Tip pressed his knuckles against the desk top. Frank was correct: they were going to lose him, all right, if he didn't do something. He could tell Zim he rated the post on his sales record, he could maunder on till the cows came home about how fairly he intended to run the shop, and it wouldn't make one particle of difference. He had to think on his feet, he *had* to come up with something , fast—

Maury's hand went to his tie, an expensive silk foulard in bright diamond-shaped designs; thumb and middle finger cinched on the knot once, withdrew. Yes—that was it, that was the answer. Put it right on that basis.

"Maury," he said briskly, "Frank has made me regional sales manager for the New England territory."

Zimmerman's lip lifted still further in a sneer. "So I've heard. And let me tell you something, Ames—"

"No," Tip broke in on him flatly, "I'm going to tell *you* something first. Just one thing. In six months you're going to lead the entire sales force or I'll fire you."

Maury's eyes rolled up in angry amazement, his mouth dropped open. "You'll *what—?*"

"You heard me. You've got six months to sweep the field or I'll fire you. That's all."

Zimmerman started to say something more, something scathing—then his face became very smooth and hard.

"I see," he said. Slowly he nodded, his eyes riveted on Tip's. Then with easy deliberation he raised one hand, four fingers extended. "I'll remind you of this conversation in just *four* months. And that's all I have to say to *you*, schoolboy . . ."

"Fair enough, Maury. I hope you will. I really do."

Tip watched the salesman's broad back vanish through the door, sat down in the swivel chair and tilted it all the way back. His view of the harbor was more limited than Frank's, but that didn't matter a bit. Frank was brilliant, he had class, he'd read all the books, he'd mastered a lot of things he himself never would; but he didn't know all there was to know about applied psychology . . .

It had started to snow again, the first flakes large and lazy and tentative, the paw of a cat testing out the ground. The March air was raw and dense; east wind out of the Atlantic. Tip hailed a cab—a wild piece of extravagance, he laughed at himself as he climbed into the cold back seat—gave the driver the address and told him to pour it on. The cabbie, a bony-faced Irishman in a cloth cap, tilted his head back conspiratorially.

"What's the grand hurry, chief?"

"I'm going to propose to my girl, and I need speed!"

"—And you want me to get you there before you change your mind, is that it?"

Tip laughed, settling back. "Not me, pal. I've been planning this one for five years . . ."

The hospital looked grim in the late winter dusk. Public institutions were all alike—court houses, hospitals, jails. The humanity had been leeched out of them. Figures blew out of the metal doors like bursts of snow, long white skirts visible beneath their coats, crisp caps like little conical white badges in the gathering dusk. There was Jophy, there, walking with two other girls, arguing with angry animation over something. She looked thinner than when he'd last seen her back in September, her shoulders drooping under her cape. He could feel his heart surge toward her in one unreserved rush. She was so courageous, slaving away at this deadly job, emptying bed pans, changing dressings . . . And now she wouldn't have to contend with it any longer.

She'd seen him—her eyes widened, flashed in surprise. She broke away from the other two nurses swiftly and came up to him. There were hollows under her eyes; her face looked unnaturally pale. He watched her struggle through her fatigue to catch at her old vivacity.

"Tip! *What* are you doing in stodgy old Boston?"

"Waiting for you." It was no more than the truth. "I'm always waiting for you." Yes. In fire or in ice he'd be there—he'd always be there . . . She was looking back toward the group of girls she'd just left.

"Hard day?" he asked softly.

"*Hard—!* I've never been so furious in my life. They tried to force us to buy Liberty Bonds . . ."

"Who did?"

"Oh, these smug, self-righteous tyrants—haven't you run into them? They're everywhere you look. And one of them told us if we didn't start right now it could cost us our jobs."

"They can't do that . . ."

"Oh, can't they! And we can't *begin* to afford anything like that. Five dollars a week—it's hopeless, absolutely hopeless . . ." She threw out her hands, flinging a salt-rime of snow. "And I blew up, I had all I could take. I asked him if he was such a patriot why wasn't *he* in France, why wasn't *he* flying a plane over the German lines? He said, 'I have a heart murmur.' I told him, 'That's a lie—you've got to have a *heart* before you can have a murmur!' I said, 'How'd you like to be fishing off Georges Bank right now, and get shelled by a U-boat without warning? Liberty,' I told him, 'don't talk to *me* about liberty—you're the ones that are taking it away!' "

"Jophy . . ."

"Did you know they sank the *Rosa Santos* last week? and then fired on the dories? Frank Furtado was killed—he died before they could make a landfall . . ."

"Jo—"

"And anyway, they went to Miss Halloran, she's head nurse, and then to Dr. Townsend, and complained . . . I'm unpatriotic, did you know that?" she cried, caught halfway between laughter and tears. "Yes, un-American, a bad influence—because I haven't bought a lousy Liberty Bond I can't begin to pay for in the first place!"

"Jophy," he murmured, "Jophy . . ."

She shook her head, her eyes bright with tears. Her hair, coiled smooth in a figure eight behind the little white starched cap, was black as the night. "I'm sorry. I'm just on edge. God, I hate March. It isn't winter and it isn't spring . . ."

"Just three weeks to bluebirds," he said without thinking.

She stopped stock still and gazed at him, burst into

a fit of laughter. "Oh my God," she gasped. "Oh, Tip, you—are—"

"I'm what?"

Now, watching him, she swung her head slowly from side to side. ". . . I don't know," she answered in a small voice. "I don't know what you are."

"I'll tell you what I am," he proclaimed. "I'm the answer to an unpatriotic nurse's prayer . . . Tell them all to go to blazes!"

"Oh, sure."

"Tell them off, Jo. Waltz right out of there."

She glanced at him suddenly, that steady mirror-flash from under her brows like the beam from Turk's Head Light. "What's got into you?"

"My dear Miss Gaspa." He strummed his finger-nails archly against the lapel of his coat. "You are now looking at the new regional sales manager for New England."

"Oh, Tip! That's wonderful! Really and truly?"

"Really and truly."

"Oh, I'm so glad! Why on earth didn't you tell me, instead of letting me rant along like a perfect nut—?"

"I'm on my way, Jo. I can feel it—it's just the beginning." He turned and took her by the shoulders. "Jophy, *now* will you marry me? Will you?"

"Oh, Tip . . . She put a hand to her forehead. "Of all the times. Tonight's such a—"

"Honey, I came straight to *you* . . ."

"Did you?"

"Of course I did! You *know* you're my girl. You know you're all I've thought about, dreamed about, all these years . . . Everything I've *done* has been because of you—because I love you! Say yes, Jo. We can manage now—we'll have the money."

"But your mother—"

"I can carry it, I've figured it out. I can take care of you both now. I'll show you. Say you will, Jophy. Say ity . . ."

". . . I don't know."

She shook her head, not so much in denial as in confusion, the snow melting on her long navy cape like tears. For an instant he felt obscurely guilty, pressing her like this, tired and discouraged as she was; but he couldn't help himself. He had wanted her, ached to be with her on too many empty nights in too many strange towns. It had been so long, so everlastingly long—and now he'd put his foot on the first rung of the big, golden ladder . . .

"Let me think, Tip," she was saying, distraught and tense. "Let me think about it a little . . ."

He was filled with dread, as though his chest were flooded with ice water. It was impossible! Not after all their dreams—over far horizons to silken shores. Together. It was always going to be together . . .

"Think—! There's nothing to think *about* . . ."

It just wasn't possible. She couldn't be in any doubt—not now, not this triumphant March evening. He had to convince her, he had to! He'd never failed to persuade anyone of anything—and Jophy meant more to him than anybody ever would.

"—But you've got to Jo," he burst out. "You've got to marry me!"

She gave a low moan, a sound deep in her throat, half distress, half appeal.

"Why?" she groaned. "*Why* should I marry you—?"

"Because I want you so," he answered, as though it were a law of the universe. "I want you more than anything else in the world . . ."

She spun out of his grip so violently it shook him. "But me—!" she cried; and now the tears were streaking her pale face. "What about *me*—?"

"But that's just the point—it's *for* you," he declared, his voice deepening. "You'll be happier with me than anyone else—I'll make you happier. I know I will!" He had taken her by the shoulders again; he *had* to make her see this. "Anything you want in this world I'll get for you; that's a promise! There's nothing I can't do if you marry me, Jo . . . and you need me. You *know* I'm the man you need." He burned with his own fierce certainty.

A policeman was strolling toward them with the unhurried, almost majestic tread of the metropolitan cop. Tip looked up and stared at him.

"Everything all right, Miss?" the policeman asked pleasantly.

"What? Yes—I guess so," Jophy said; she sniffled once, gave a faint shivery laugh. "—He wants me to marry him," she burst out then in the old mischievous, defiant way, her eyes dancing in the snowlight. "Should I marry him, officer? What do you think?"

The policeman—he was a heavy man with a thick, homely face like melting wax—inspected Tip gravely. "Well," he said after a moment, "he looks presentable enough to me. A likely looking fella. Live wire."

"Yes," Jophy breathed; she was laughing now, laughing almost uncontrollably. "A live wire! You hit the nail right on the head . . ."

Smiling at her the officer raised his billy-club to his cap. "Good luck to you," he murmured, and moved off with the same deliberate, unhurried step.

"Thank you," Jophy called. She was still laughing.

"You see?" Tip pursued. "Even he says so. Oh Jo, the sky's the limit! Together we'll be unbeatable. Just name it and we'll do it. Oh Jophy, I do love you so . . ."

Her dark eyes watched him wondering, the snow crusting her lashes. She shook her head again, but not in disbelief.

"Oh Tip. Maybe we can. Maybe you're right."

"I know I'm right—I'm dead sure of it. I've never been so sure of anything! Marry me, Jo. Tell me right now."

She glanced around them once more, as if making a final, futile appeal to the raw sea air in off the Atlantic, the swirling snow.

"All right," she said quietly. "I'll marry you, Tip."

Her lips were warm and sweet soft; he fancied he

could feel her heart drumming through all their layers of clothing. He had never felt such bursting exaltation in all his young life. The job and the girl—he had the right job and the only girl—what more could any man want? He hugged her to him with all his might, laughed for sheer joy, feeling the snow cool and damp on his face.

"Tip," she was saying. "I just don't know. I don't know if I'm enough for you. I don't know if I'm sure what to do with you."

"You've done it!" he told her exuberantly. "You've just made me the happiest man in North America."

"I hope so," she murmured, and pressed her forehead hard against his shoulder. "I'll try. God knows I'm going to try . . ."

The wedding was in late May, in Boston. Jophy didn't want to be married in Turk's Head—Portuguese friends and neighbors would be hurt and resentful if the ceremony weren't held in St. Anthony's, she said wryly, and if it *were* it would be simply hypocritical on her part. They were going to be living in Boston; why not be married there? So they had a small, informal service in a chapel of Trinity Church. Jack Darcey had shipped overseas, but Frank Delahant came up from New York City to be best man, looking impeccably resplendent in a pin-stripe suit and a new Homburg, and Geraldine Marden, a nurse at the hospital and Jophy's best friend, stood up with her. Tip's mother was too ill to make the trip, and Serena Aldridge chose to remain in Washington on a prolonged visit; she had a handsome Georgian silver tea service sent them from Treffrey, Partridge. But Annabella Gaspa came up from the Cape, severe and grand in gray silk and a huge hat marvelous with feathers. Chapin, now a flying instructor at the same Texas airfield where he'd won his wings, sent a cool congratulatory wire.

After the ceremony Frank took them all to lunch at

the Parker House, along with Ed Langevin and Web Bowers from the Boston office. He ordered champagne and the party turned lively and sentimental. Frank was very taken with Jophy—everyone was. Tip, sitting across from her, watched the way the candlelight struck her heavy dark hair. It was twisted high and smooth, and held with a single great jade hairpin—one of Manuel Gaspa's treasures from the China Seas; Grama had given it to Jophy for a wedding present—lustrous under a pale green veil. She was wearing a dress of the same celadon shade—which surprised him, because she loved white.

"So *this* is the stunning creature you've kept all to yourself, Ames," Frank chided him. "I must say I find it uncommonly selfish."

"It's chicanery in restraint of trade," Web Bowers said.

"You didn't tell them about me?" Jophy turned to Tip. All day she had seemed strangely subdued.

He shook his head. "I was afraid you fellows would beat my time."

"Where's that old unbounded confidence?" Frank demanded.

"That's selling. This is different . . . My brother Chapin's the good-looking one. She'd have married him if he hadn't up and enlisted overnight."

"Oh no, I wouldn't!" Jophy said. He was shocked by the heat in her voice. "I can tell the difference between a salesman and a confidence man." For the first time she seemed to regain her old fire. "Giving himself airs because he went to Harvard and abroad, while Tip worked his heart out to support—"

"Now why don't I meet that kind?" Geraldine Marden interrupted. She was tall, with a long, angular face and pretty brown eyes. "All I ever run into are the ones whose wives don't understand them."

"I have no encumbrances," Web Bowers confided. He was already high on champagne, his guileless face beaming. "Not one."

"Except for a father who can't hold a job, and a sister in Revere who'd try the patience of a saint," Ed Langevin reminded him. "Not to mention a brother in France."

"Oh, well, yes, that." Web looked suddenly blank.

"The fortunate are not always so fortunate," Frank Delahant said in the silence. "Even John D. Rockefeller is carrying around with him troubles we know nothing about."

"I'll trade with him," Geraldine broke in. "My troubles for his, any time!"

"Are you sure of that?" Annabella Gaspa said. She smiled, but her voice was low; the wine had turned her somber. "Do not ever say it, menina minha—it might come true. Never think to exchange what you are. There is an old Portuguese saying—"

"Oh, no!" Jophy cried, and rolled her eyes.

"—that goes: 'Misfortunes always enter through a gate that has been left open for them.' Our troubles are our selves."

To Tip there would always be something portentous about that moment. Grama, proud and austere as some ancient priestess, watching a volatile, defiant Jophy; Frank with his fingers curled around the stem of his glass, that shadow of bottomless remorse flooding his fine, alert gaze; the others fascinated, a touch baffled. Our lives are set on this moment, like a chronometer, the thought came to him unbidden; all the cards are dealt, right here—and almost laughed out loud at such superstitious persuasion. Good God, he thought, I'm getting like Jophy—I've only just married her and I'm full of omens; perhaps it's catching . . .

"Well, here's to our troubles," Frank Delahant said, raising his glass, "May we evade them one by one—or failing that, never let them see the light of day! . . ."

Later they rode over to North Station and stood in a restless knot while the train hissed and clanked itself into readiness for the journey north.

"He's a good man, Josinha," Grama was saying.

"Grama, stop it. You'll spoil him!"

"No. He has a good heart, all the way through. Yankee or no Yankee." She smiled and embraced him, a bearhug that almost took his breath away. "Give to each other," she told them, her face infinitely stern. "Give fully, in love. There is nothing else in this slippery world that matters."

The conductor called then, that single word in raising inflection, and they mounted the iron steps. Jophy tossed her little bouquet of white freesias to Geraldine, who dropped it amid groans and laughter. And now the train was moving, sliding away north, they were moving with it as though drawn by its iron mass; and waving back, laughing, Tip saw with astonishment that Frank's eyes were glazed with tears.

The old mountain lodge stood on the very edge of the lake. It was nearly deserted except for an older couple on holiday and two spinster teachers from Springfield. Tip would have preferred to spend their honeymoon somewhere on the Cape, if not at Turk's Head, but Jophy wouldn't hear of it.

"I want to see your country—mountains, lakes. Fresh water, fresh land . . . And it's farther away from the war."

So he'd chosen the old inn on Lake Chocorua he knew about from his travels. The hemlocks were densely green, the lake was blue—so blue it almost hurt his eyes to look on it—sweeping north to the mountains, which stood like ancient guards in full armor, shutting out the world, the firm, the war.

And it was only the palest of backgrounds anyway, to the glorious presence of Jophy. She rushed into his life with all the force of one of her Line gales, a hurricane sea carrying away the rock wall of any Yankee properties and circumspections. She danced before him, sang to him snatches of song in her vibrant contralto, slipped her clothes from her shoulders and thighs and came to him with a tender ferocity that literally took his breath away. How had it happened? She was a goddess, mermaid, lover. Even in his lonely fantasies about her he had never imagined his lithe girl could prove to be such a woman. She would burst into soft, low cries of pleasure, her body answering that hastening, mysterious pulse as it arched to its own. Later she would fall sound asleep murmuring his name—and in a few short hours turn to him eagerly again, in a new storm of easy abandon. Ardent, wildly hungry for her, all of her, he was nonetheless startled at her sweet boldness, her natural sense of invention.

"My—God," he heard himself murmur once, in sheer delighted amazement, "where on earth did you learn that—?"

"I didn't. You don't learn things like this, you just *do* them, that's all . . . Oh Tip, I want to know everything, do everything! Let's dive deep—find all the pearls at the bottom of the sea." And she groaned as the waves of release crested and broke over her, shook her like a little sail in the south wind. "Yes, there, oh—*now!* Ah, lover, lover. Now come, I want you within me, darling, oh deep within me . . ."

Her long hair covered her throat, his belly, her arms gripped him with sure passion, her fine body sleek with sweat, like a mermaid who had drawn him with her—down, down into the very deeps of the green sea. For the first time in his life he felt actually bigger than life, masterful and rather grand. To bring this much joy, scatter it like liquid emeralds over your loved one—there was nothing like this in all the world . . . It was more than he could ever have imagined, even loving her as he had all those years; far, far more. That he could arouse this—! The thought sobered him even as it flattered.

They went walking through the woods, heavy with reawakened spring smells, the forest floor spongy with pine needles, sunlight filtering through the birch leaves. They watched a raccoon methodically washing some prize for her three cubs at the lake's edge, while beyond them loons vanished and reappeared in startling aqueous sleight-of-hand. He came alive to sensations he'd never even knew existed: the damp pressure of moss under bare feet, the clean rush of water over his body diving deep, the washed-gold flood of sunlight against his eyelids . . . above all the sweet, eager pressure of Jophy's hands stroking his face, his thighs, his genitals. They made love under the pines, the odor of moss and pitch and partridge berry deep in their nostrils, a chickadee singing its silly two-note refrain above their heads.

"This is crazy," he murmured. "Suppose someone came hiking along here."

"I know!" She shivered beneath him, her long thighs moving in tireless, gathering rhythm. Isn't it a delicious thought?"

Only one incident marred the idyll. The war did intrude, for all their resolutions—there was talk of it in the lounge, on the verandah; there were the Boston papers, a day late but black with headlines and the new terrible litany of the casualty lists.

"Thank God they made Chapin an instructor," Tip said, shoving the paper into his hip pocket. They were walking along the shore of the lake. "It means he won't be sent overseas, at least for a time."

"I don't know." Jophy was starting out at the fan of sunlight on the water. "It might be the best thing that ever happened to him."

Tip stared at her. "What do you mean by that?"

"I mean he'd have to meet it head-and-head. It'd be something he couldn't slide away from."

"But actually wishing he'd be under fire—that's a hell of a thing to say, Jo . . ."

"Well, isn't that what he's sending *other* men overseas to do?"

Tip turned and faced her. "—He's my brother," he said heavily. "You have no right to say something like that. Just because he's thoughtless, and—and selfish at times—"

"Yes, and—"

"And what?"

"Nothing. Nothing." Her eyes came up to his, level and hot with anger. "You don't know everything there is to know about everybody."

"Of course I don't, when did I ever say I did?" He shook his head. "But to hope someone'll be shot at and killed—"

"I never said that! I only said he's always evading things, I only said it might—"

She broke off, her eyes filled and she swung away. He came up to her then and slipped his arms around her.

"I'm sorry, Jo," he said. "I didn't mean it. I know you didn't say that . . . I'm all mixed up about this damned war myself."

"No reason you should be. You've got a mother to support. And now a wife."

"Yes—a glorious, ferocious Portagee wife. Forgive me?"

She turned in his arms, smiling ruefully. "It was a heartless thing to say—I don't know what got into me . . . Our first quarrel," she murmured.

"Now we're a regular old married couple."

"Oh no, we're not! Let's go for a swim, and then lie in bed and make fabulous love, hour after hour . . ."

She could never resist the impulsive, the unconventional. It was as if, swept on by the act itself, she needed to explore all the perimeters of the possible. One night he awoke and missed her; obeying some sure conviction he slipped on a robe and went down the hall, out the verandah along the worn path to the jetty—and there she was all right, in one of the canoes, gliding along under the hanging gold moon, erect as an island princess and as naked, her breasts white against the massed dark of the firs.

"Jo—!" he hissed at her. "What the devil are you up to?"

"Paddling," she replied in a clear, conversational tone that made his skin prickle. "It's lovely."

"Crazy . . ."

"Come out with me," she urged softly. "Take off that stupid bathrobe and come with me . . ."

He lunged for the canoe's prow; Jophy backwatered deftly, he almost lost his balance and fell in.

"I'll stay out here till daylight if you don't," she warned.

"—But I'm standing here on the *dock!*"

"I thought you'd always take a dare."

"You bet your tintype." He looked around once, shrugged out of the robe and whispered: "There! Now, come on . . ."

"No tricks now."

She swung the canoe in to the jetty and he climbed aboard, feeling hilarious and wild. They paddled out into the middle of the lake and made love as though it were the first time, Jophy astride him, their hunger sharpened by the canoe's fragile rocking, the sourceless night sounds, the water licking delicately against the fabric an inch from their ears. Tip found himself laughing.

"No wonder they called you wild," he said.

"Who said that?"

"I don't know."

"Yes you do, Tip Ames—now who called me that?"

"Shhhh . . ."

He laughed again, she pinched him, said in a different voice: "Well, they were right. Whoever it was. Only not in the way you think."

"I don't think anything."

Sobered now, she stared off across the water, supporting herself lightly on his shoulders. "Men think if a girl wants to *feel* things, everything, reach out for some of the gold rings as they come flashing by—they call her wild, and tell each other she's easy, she'll go to bed with anyone . . . It's not fair," she went on quietly, softer than the lap of water against the hull. "Why shouldn't a woman be free to do what a man does?"

"No reason," Tip answered, though he wasn't entirely sure he believed that.

"It's only to live. Fully, Tip. Really fully. Drink it all in! That's all . . ." Her voice suddenly broke with emotion. "Oh, Tip," she said, "remember me tonight, the way I am tonight, no matter what happens—no matter what comes our way! Always remember how it was here, tonight."

He drew her to him with a groan. "Jophy, oh *how* I love you!" he said, caressing her long, full thighs, the dark luxuriance of her mount. The moon turned her golden as he held her. He felt such a rush of love it made him dizzy. "Look, there's a moon wake behind us now. A moonglade . . . Oh Jo, you're this whole wide world to me. I'll never stop loving you. Never."

"Oh darling, I hope not." She trailed her hand in the silver-gold water behind them. "*Never* is such a long, long time . . ."

12

The snapshot showed a man standing beside an airplane's cockpit, lounging easily: Chapin Ames. Booted and blazoned, a dazzling white scarf around his neck. He was bareheaded, his hair smoothly combed, and there was a faint, speculative smile on his face, as if he were about to say something devastatingly amusing. Jophy flipped it over. On the back was scribbled: *The Hero poses beside his Caparisoned Steed.* Just the right touch and yet . . .

Smiling wryly she shook her head. There were other photographs: one of Chapin seated in the cockpit, helmeted this time, long white scarf still flowing, elbow nonchalantly resting on the cowling; another of him with three other men gathered by the propeller of a larger aircraft; and a final shot of a group of young men and girls lounging on a lawn under an umbrella-shaped tree. They were laughing, their heads thrown back, throats white in the sunlight, except for Chapin, who was on his feet, holding aloft a wine glass, a toast of some sort clearly; his expression perfectly serious. On the back it said *Fête champêtre in the provinces.* Holding the picture nearer—her eyes had been bothering her all morning, a curious, swimming, slipping-out-of-focus sensation—she studied it with care. He looked bigger than she remembered him, dominating the little group of officers and girls. Perhaps it was the uniform; and of course he was a captain and their

205

instructor, and they were student fliers, on their way to France . . . Looking at the faintly hawklike features, the broad, sensuous mouth, she felt the old, slow, visceral pull of desire. She tossed the snapshots on the bed and picked up the letter again, ran her eyes swiftly down the page.

I am still the ardent collector, if you must know; only now it is pupils. I put them through their paces high above the red Texas dust, hoping they won't freeze on the stick during that crucial first landing attempt and force me to wallop them on the head with a monkey wrench. (I did have to do that once—a rather depressing experience.)

I've fallen in love with flying. Not that I'm so tremendously good at it; just competent enough, with a feel for the craft, and a flair for imparting aerodynamic principles. You on the other hand would have made a marvelous flier: that just-this-side-of-reckless urge to the extremities of danger—furor volandi, you must call it, tempered with an awareness of just how much stress dragwires and struts will endure. The ship and the elements, so to speak. Is it an inherited characteristic? What a pity women can't share in war, I mean really take full hazardous part

The loosely penned lines had begun to ripple and run together again; she put the letter down and pressed her cupped hands carefully against her belly. Her head was aching and nausea had returned in a slow groundswell. She'd never thought it was going to be this bad. Morning sickness, of course; but for the past two days it had been much worse, and now this whirling, eddying sensation. She was sweating again, her blouse was soaked through; why was it so blasted hot? It was late September. The apartment was airless, pinched and low-ceilinged. But it was cheap, what they could afford. There was so much she ought to be doing: curtains to be lengthened, Tip's underwear needed mending, the kitchen floor needed a good scrubbing—and she couldn't do any of it, not right now; every time she bent over, this light-headed, floating sensation started up, and her stomach churned. On the Cape now the westerly would be blowing in from Blackfish Point, whistling at the screens, licking at the back of her neck like a cat's tongue . . .

Frowning, cross with herself, she picked up the letter again.

Win Murdoch came through a few months ago; and Tommy Vassall, whom you saw play so brilliantly against Yale. Impetuous princely Tommy—he was killed here last month. The official word was he got it during a training flight, which was *stretching the facts a touch—actually he walked right into a spinning propeller, which is not as hard to do as it sounds. Fortunately I was in the air at the time and did not have to view the results.*

I've met an extremely congenial chap named Harrodsen (Princeton, sorry to say; but a kindred spirit and the right sort). We've been hobnobbing after hours. As you can see from the enclosed, we've managed a social life of sorts, out here amid the mesquite and chaparral. The local belles are naturally enough in a perfect fever of expectation what with this heaven-sent invasion of Ivy League types to wait upon their every whim each sweltering weekend. The chance of a lifetime for them, and they are making the most of it. To date I have enjoyed three (veiled) proposals and seven (utterly unveiled) propositions. No. Just ragging. But it is a singular pavane we dance: we are of course captives of the war; and they are captives of geography and culture (or a distressing lack of it). And so we have worked out a modus vivendi (or is it a modus moriendi?) for the duration—which durates its merry way on and on. And on.

I was surprised at your marriage to Tip (or rather, his to you). I had never thought of you as grass widow to a drummer—even a crackerjack, five-alarm sales wizard like Tip (oh yes, I remember his vending prow-

ess all too well from our pre-salad days; he had as many sales angles as a hive has bees, and simply wouldn't take no for an answer until he'd closed the deal) . . . *Is that perchance what transpired in your case?*

She set the letter down again, feeling restless and aroused, and furious with herself for feeling aroused. "Nerve of him," she muttered half-aloud. Equating a proposal of marriage with a sales pitch. And then writing to her directly, not to her and Tip as a married couple, only to her. That was Chay and his fine Bostonian hand, all right: create a difficulty, a practically insoluble problem out of nothing. If she didn't show it to Tip, she'd be concealing something from him; if she did, he'd spot *her* name on the envelope, and the salutation—

"—Oh," she murmured, and gripped her head. It had started spinning again, an increasing dizziness that seemed *outside* her somehow, so that she could watch its course, like a compass needle aimlessly spinning—what Grampa used to say happened north of Bering Strait, near the Pole. A solitary puff of breeze sucked the curtain against the screen once, released it. The air was cool, but heat lay on her flesh like a foul hand; her throat was soaked in sweat. What was the matter with her?

She started to get up, retched dryly, swallowed, and began to knead her belly gingerly. Captives. She was one, too. Prisoner of the heat, her body, this dreary little apartment that wasn't in Cambridge but actually on the *fringes* of Cambridge, in Somerville. Chay was right, she could have been a flier, should have been one, cartwheeling and barrel-rolling high above the sea, doing loop-the-loops through the massed thunderheads . . . It was true, she did have more courage than Captain Ames; she could lose herself in a moment, a dream, Tip said she had the passion to dare things. Yes. Passion . . . And it had let to this: a swollen, fevered body in a squalid room in a strange city.

"Timing," she muttered aloud. Well, her timing had been all wrong. Tip had been overjoyed when she'd told him—as if he'd just received another promotion. He'd wanted to rush right out and celebrate. Her own fault, of course. She hated the condoms, the leathery, fleshless chafe of them, the cold absence of contact; their very color was like a dead cod's throat. French safes, Tip called them, when he referred to them at all; as though the term could make them more romantic, more intimate. Intimate . . . All these centuries—they could invent guns that fired a bullet every half-second, radios that sent signals 10,000 miles, planes that flew a hundred miles an hour, or more for all she knew; and they couldn't devise a sure, convenient method of contraception. But of course, as Grama would say, they didn't *want* to invent one: they needed more bodies, more blood, more fodder for the big guns of Europe. And Grampa—well, Grampa would have said that life is life . . .

What in God's name was she doing here? Cleaning house for a husband who was seldom home, carrying a child she hadn't yet wanted, standing in line for food she didn't want to eat? How had she let this happen to her? Had she swapped the institutional drudgery of floor nurse for the subtler drudgery of housekeeper and brood mare?

No, that wasn't fair. Tip wanted nothing on this earth more than to make her happy—she knew that; it was only that restless, burning optimism of his. He lived on the edge of a trip, a sale. One Saturday evening she'd come upon him packing the big Gladstone and whistling "Alexander's Ragtime Band" with ruffles and flourishes.

"But you don't leave till Monday!" she'd protested.

He'd laughed. "Guess I got sand in my shoes, honey. Just putting my ducks in a row. Lined up and ready to go."

The road. It was like a lure—his step was quicker, his movements crisper just before he left, as if he had a touch of fever. A compulsion already on him to practice his own particular magic, to keep his hand in; to take charge. That was his world out there, not hers . . . Did she *have* a world of her own any more?

"Skeets Brohammer's fallen off over in Hartford—got to build a fire under him. What's the matter with those guys? They've got the fattest territory in New England and they're barely pulling their weight, they're way under their quota."

"Does it matter? I mean, whether you sell more this month than last?"

He'd glanced at her in frank surprise. "Why of course it does, honey. That's the way the quota's set by the main office." He was fitting his collars neatly in their circular case so they wouldn't get crushed. "And now I've got you and the baby to plan for . . ."

"But *why* does the quota always have to be increased? Can't it just—well, run along the way it has?"

"Because that's the way it has to be, Jo. That's progress. That's what this country's all about. You can't sit still, marking time—you either grow or you shrink. That's business . . ."

"I see." But she didn't really. It seemed to her part of some diabolical conspiracy, sadistically inspired, the way the quota was raised. If it was 24 now, it must be 48 next month, 96 the next, a hundred and—well, a hundred and something the month after that: a timetable devised by madmen. She wanted to say, "But isn't there a breaking point somewhere? Surely everything isn't meant to expand *infinitely?*" But she said nothing. Doubtless he'd have had an answer for that one, too—he genuinely believed the sky was the limit, no horizon lay beyond landfall . . .

The phone was ringing. She had the outlandish sensation it had been ringing for some time, and the reverberations had only just reached her, in the manner

210

of light pulsing its lonely way through space. She
swung her feet to the floor, felt a sudden rush of vertigo and a sharp wire-borne dart of pain from her
skull to the bottom of her backbone. I really am sick,
she thought with quiet alarm; really coming down
with something. Hand to her mouth, fighting nausea,
she crept across the room and lifted the receiver off
the hook.

"Jophy?" Tip's voice, eager, expectant. To Tip the
telephone was always a kind of minor miracle, a phe-
nomenon far more radical than radio or moving pictures, whose magic must be celebrated with perpetual
jubilation.

"Hello, darling." Her own voice sounded muffled, as
if wrapped in gauze; she cleared her throat painfully.
"Where are you?"

"Springfield."

"How extravagant!"

"I'm winding things up. Business is deader than a
stillborn calf. This blasted epidemic has knocked everything on its ear. And everybody's all steamed up
about St. Mihiel, all they want to talk about is the
war."

"I know."

"I swear, people are going crazy. A woman tried to
stick a white feather in my lapel this morning. Would
you believe it? A turkey feather a foot long. Right on
the corner of State and Main."

"Oh, no . . ." Her voice kept fading, ringing its way
off into the air waves, beyond reach. "How awful.
What did you do?"

"I sidestepped her, tipped my hat and said, 'Sorry,
Madam, I'm in a hurry. Try to decorate someone else.'
Water off a duck's back."

She laughed, then—a laugh that turned into a fit of
coughing.

"Jophy. You all right? How you feeling, honey?"

"Well—not so good right now."

"I'm sorry. The morning sickness?"

"Uh-huh." The room was moving. Yes, distinctly moving, starting and stopping, rocking, a ship's cabin lifting and sinking on an easterly groundswell. She eased herself onto the stool by the phone. "I keep getting these dizzy spells—well, not quite dizzy, it's as though my head's trying to float away somewhere . . ."

A short silence. Then, more tensely: "Jo. You been out?"

"Sure, I've been out," she said irritably, "I've had to do errands—"

"Look now, you get back into bed, honey. Get back in bed."

"For God's sake, Tipton, I haven't got Spanish influenza!" And with this first mention of the word, the morose dread slipped over her heavily, chilling. "I've never been sick a day in my life."

"Drink a lot of water, squeeze some oranges, have you got some oranges?"

"We Portuguese are immune to contagious diseases—" She started coughing again, couldn't seem to stop. "Didn't you know that?"

"I mean it, Jo." His voice was tight with anxiety. "Don't you take any chances. This thing is going around like a cyclone. You get back into bed and rest. I'm catching the 2:19, I'll be there before you know it."

"Good. Good." Bent over, her eyes shut, she felt a sense of relief as solid as a hand at the small of her back.

"Go lie down, get some sleep if you can. Promise me, Jo."

"I—promise."

"Good girl. See you soon."

The connection clicked shut. He always did that, hung up before you could say goodbye. Live-wire. She smiled, wondering idly, Why didn't I tell him about Chapin's letter? She set the receiver back in its cradle. It fell to the table, then the floor, which was very

212

odd. Angered, reaching over for it she felt violently, savagely sick and barely made it to the bathroom, crouched over the bowl, finally sank to her knees, retching and gasping. She was bathed in sweat, it bubbled and boiled on her face. She rose wobbling to her feet and floated back to bed through a room that swayed malevolently, altering form in slow, rubbery distensions, and now pain shot swiftly into her neck and thighs, made her cry out. Influenza, then. And with the baby. Impossible, it was impossible! But she had caught it. Dizziness, nausea, pains in the back *an infectious disease which occurs in endemic outbreaks and can spread with great rapidity*. She'd done her homework like a dutiful nurse. *The cause is believed to be a virus. Symptoms: swift onset, fever and chills, and* something else and something else. Oh, Yes. *Rapid progressive obstruction of the respiratory tract.* The lungs.

Geraldine. Dear rough-and-ready Geraldine. She'd come over when she could get away, help her through this.

She swam to her feet—slipped sideways and down. The bed table went over, taking lamp and books and clock in a clattery jangle. She was on the floor, lying on her side on the floor, retching and groaning, with no idea how she had got there. A bell kept screaming shrilly, alarm, the clock's alarm. She reached out deftly and silenced it, but the clock glared back at her with its black eye-splotched face, watching her, getting ready to make a move. Ridiculous! But she nevertheless closed her eyes to remove herself from its obscene threat and the trick worked as she'd hoped it would. She had to get away. Away . . . They'd slipped the mooring, were making passage for the Offshore Grounds, dipping through water slick as oil, easing toward a tropic shore, a still channel where the jungle leaned and leaned, clutched the yards and braces, brushed her face, alive with shadows sheathed in crocodile scales. They were boarding, they were going to take over the ship. She struck again and again with the harpoon but the iron shank kept bending capriciously, curling on itself in mazy loops, and the creatures came on with silent, studied intent, watching her out of unwinking agate eyes—

Aloft. Must get aloft. In a terror beyond terror she ran to the foremast rigging and climbed to the top, the topgallant crosstrees, the skysail yard, the fore truck—and felt now the rush of clear air high above the jungle. North wind! The ship was moving now, they'd worked her free and were roaring north, the lee rail under green water, and now ahead rose icebergs, no open water, no true bearing she could give them below, and she was freezing, the spars rimed with frost, the sails like white iron; she beat her arms against her body, must keep the blood circulating, the blood!—But she couldn't hang on any longer, she was slipping, slipping, they were bearing her aft to her cabin . . . No, these were comforting arms, *dear*, anxious voices—Tip's, dear steady Tip. And he was peering down at her, his face tight with worry, straw hat tipped to the back of his head, he was saying, "All right, Jo honey, it's all right, I'm here. I'm right *here*, honey girl . . ."

"Get Geraldine." It was barely a whisper.

"Already called her. She's on her way."

Tip: good, resourceful live-wire, thinking-on-his-feet. She laughed—knew it wasn't a laugh at all.

" . . . Cold," she muttered; her teeth were chattering uncontrollably. "I know. Just hang on now, honey."

And there was Geraldine, right out of nowhere, her angular face calm and set, the way she looked when she was assisting.

"—I'll talk to Wally," she was saying, talking to someone else, "they'll find room, they'll *make* room if there isn't any, don't you worry about that . . ."

"It's flu. Flu, isn't it?" she forced her voice through the nausea, and Geraldine nodded once, mutely, and vanished.

This was bad. Very bad. With the baby. She would have to be careful, do whatever they said, no matter how silly. She was warmer, blessedly warmer, but now the pain licked out from the very base of her skull, she had never in all her life felt this sick. There was something she must tell Tip, something she'd hidden from him, what was it? Something very— stealthy. Yes, while the propellers were spinning lovely golden arcs in the early morning sun. Without effort she climbed into the cockpit and glanced back at Chapin who nodded once, his eyes narrowed to oriental slits behind the goggles. She gunned the engine fiercely, waved away the mechanics, and with a blast of frigid air in her face she was airborne, no reason she couldn't fly a plane, she knew it!—banking high over the harbor, looping, zooming down, and there was Newcombe's Marine Supply and the flake yard and there, riding at anchor proud as a caravel was the *Albatroz*—

But something had gone wrong; she was losing altitude, spinning crazily round and round, headed straight for the schooner in a furnace shriek of wind. She was going to crash. And turning she could see Chapin's white scarf streaming back like a lance pennant. He had tricked her into this!—he had tricked her, and she cursed him down to hell . . .

A room. Room, white and bare. The hush of surreptitious movement, tense emergencies. The blank comfort of a remembered atmosphere, and a face whose lower half was covered with a mask, deep brown eyes observing her closely.

"Doctor Halpert?" she heard herself say.

"No. My name is Ruggles."

"Oh." She felt guilty, as though caught doing something wrong. "I've had bad dreams," she said, to gain time.

"You certainly have." The mask moved away then. "Who is Chapin?"

"Chapin? Oh—a man . . ." She was flooded with

confusion and anger, she'd been saying God knew what. Talk about secrets! Patients in fever, under anaesthesia—

"Where is Tip?" she demanded. "Mr. Ames. My husband."

"He's gone now. He'll be back soon." The mask bent forward again; she felt a prick of pain in her arm, trivial and precise in the whirling, painful mass of her body.

"Fifty cc's vaccine," she said, hoping to impress him.

"Afraid not." The eyes above the mask shot up at her, shot away again. "Little late for that. This is something else."

"I see . . . I'm pregnant—twenty-three weeks, I don't know what—"

"Yes."

The voice was fading, floating off, and she strove to grip the lifeline of it with all her might.

"What will this do—how will this affect my baby?"

A hand on her forehead now, miraculously cool and smooth.

"You must rest. Just try to rest."

"No, you've got to tell me—"

But it was no use, they weren't listening to her, and the quaking cold came again, and then the pulsing jungle heat, and the pain. They had carried her up on deck, a kindly gesture though it was no cooler, and looking aft she could see there was no one at the helm; the sails backed and filled idly, the ship swung toward where the sea was furling into a bottomless black cone . . . Whirlpool, bad one. Must not slip into that, *must not!*— but its pull was too great, she'd fought all she could, there was nothing more to do, she was beaten. With a tearful, almost guilty acquiescence she finally felt herself let go, slip out and down . . .

* * *

"You gave us quite a scare, honey," he was saying, and now she could see how white his face was, the fatigue lines under his eyes. "Quite a scare." Tip. Tip's voice, clean and hopeful. He was so *alive*. He would always be so alive. It was something to put your hand in, your trust; all your hope and trust.

" . . . You all right?" she whispered.

"Sure."

"I was afraid," she said. "Afraid you'd caught the bug from me."

"Don't worry about that. You're looking at a real tough Berkshire Yankee. We're almost as indestructible as you Portagees."

She tried to smile, she wanted to say something impudent, even absurd, and no thought came. Not one. And now she had to say it, there was no way to evade it any longer.

"My—my baby?" she murmured.

His lips came together, his face looked still more drawn; he shook his head once. "We lost the baby," he said. "But it's all right, it's all right, Jo," he hurried along, and now there were tears in his eyes. "You're what matters, honey—you're all that matters."

Dear, steady Tip. But it wasn't true, she wasn't what mattered. She had been punished, then, for not wanting the child so soon, for feeling she'd been cheated; for her rash dreams . . . Closing her eyes she wept, tears she couldn't have checked with all the accumulated might of the world; wept and wept in perfect silence, and gave way again.

Voyages. Such long, terror-stricken voyages; and had they only led to this?—a bell jar where withered creatures stirred in a sterile, purposeless round? Her face, swimming in a hand mirror, stared back at her, haggard and distrustful, eyes alien. What a monstrous cheat! Had this been the way Grampa had felt returning from his voyages? Was this why he'd been so eager to go *back*, time after time, even knowing what he did?

But this was a wisdom she must hide, like the memory of some shameful act. Grama came up from the Cape bringing a great sheaf of yellow roses and bustled about, putting things in order; she answered her in monosyllables. Even when Tip got his Army induction notice she felt neither fear nor anger, only a deepening of her sense of desolation. News of more battles, at Cambrai, in the Meuse-Argonne, filled her with sullen disgust.

Time heals all things, Grama said one silvered autumn afternoon. But that wasn't true either, Grama didn't know—there were things all the time in the black universe couldn't heal. They discharged her and she came home, feeling tottery and petulant, hating a disorderly world that cared nothing at all for distant voyages . . . What did any of it matter? You tried to live generously, to reach out with high fervor, and here was where it led: to the dirty fragility of death. Everything led to pain and death and it didn't make a particle of difference whether you were honorable or servile or corrupt, you sank to mould anyway . . .

And this morning bells were clashing in three octaves, over and over—a silvery, boisterous carillon; and now factory whistles had joined in, and a siren in a nasal, ascending shriek. In the streets below there were individual cries, and the hum of excited voices.

"What on earth is all that about?" she asked.

"It's over," Grama said. She had been cleaning the apartment; her head bound in a red bandanna handkerchief knotted at the back, she looked like the voluptuous consort of some pirate. "The war is over. Now the *gentlemen* will sit down at the long table and carve up the melon again, to their flint hearts' content."

" . . . It doesn't matter," she heard herself say.

"Of course it matters. It means Tip won't have to go

to war, for one thing. That occur to you?" She laughed her hearty deep laugh. "Saved by the bells. Listen to them!" She cocked her head, enjoying the booming, clanging, discordant shivaree. "Just listen to that cats' concert!"

"Idiots," Jophy muttered.

Her grandmother pursed her lips. "You know what I think? I think this is a good time for you to get up and earn your keep."

Jophy watched her narrowly. "I feel weak as water."

"Well, you won't get any stronger lying there like the Queen of Sheba." She faced her granddaughter squarely, hands on her broad hips. "Come on now. On your feet. Tip'll be coming home from Camp Devens in a few days." She paused, said more quietly: "Josinha, you have a lot to be thankful for."

She felt her eyes fill at the memory. She murmured, "Grama, I lost my baby . . ."

Anabella Gaspa threw up her head. "Don't talk to me of losses. I lost my little Inez, with scarlet fever, only seven months old. My father at sea, my brother Antão killed by a whale, my wild, free, laughing Joey . . ." Her eyes rose to the window, flashing and dark. "And my own Manuel, man among men, glorious in his body, fierce and tender in his love—he'd leap down from the main chains to the wharf at Snow's his sea bag over his shoulder, like a curly-haired young god, and my very heart would rush out to him like a spring tide . . ." She broke off, her voice ringing under the chaotic wash of the bells; when she turned back her face was set and harsh. "Don't talk to *me* about losses! You have not scratched the surface of the word."

" . . . Then what is the sense in it?" Jophy burst out. "They go ahead and do what they want, anyway—the bankers and the politicians. Use us for their own ends, the way they always do. There'll be more wars, more dying. Why bother with anything at all . . .?"

Annabella Gaspa watched her a moment in silence. In a flat, almost toneless voice she said: "Because life is all that matters. That is why. Going on in life, taking joy in it. Fighting back. We always have to fight back. You poor, silly fool—haven't you learned anything? Because that is exactly what gives them the lie—your Grand Panjandrums." She drove her hand against her thigh once. "They *want* death, criança; they *stand* for death. Can't you see that? And every moment you insist on life, you make it that little bit harder for them to bend things their way . . . Don't make it easier for them, Josinha. They have enough of a following wind as it is."

Jophy looked down at her hands. "Who cares about the captains and the kings, anyway," she said sullenly. "I don't give a damn about them."

"Then care about those who love you and count on you."

"Why should I?"

"Because that is the cruise you've drawn."

Jophy raised her eyes to the older woman. She said pleadingly, "Grama, I almost died . . ."

"Deveras? Do you wish me to think you are something unique in the history of the human race? A hundred million men and women *almost* died this past year along, neta minha—millions of other poor devils did die, burned and bombed and starved and God knows what else . . . You want to be glad you didn't join *that* parade to the cemeteries. Tip, Geraldine, they've all been busting their gut for you—it's high time you faced up to a thing or two."

Abruptly she reached down and snapped back sheet and blankets with one vigorous flick of her hand. "Get up and get dressed, Josefina," she said. "Right now. I don't want to hear any more talk. We're going for a walk in that pleasant park near the college. It's a fine day for it. First day of peace." She stood over her granddaughter, fierce and unsmiling, implacable. "What would your Grampa say if he could see you—skulking below decks, shirking your watches? You're no mutineer—you don't even look like one. Up with you, now. Look lively! . . ."

II

THE PITCH

1

"Randy tells me you're from Boston, Captain Ames," Jennifer Harrodsen said from across the table. "I must say I *am* sorry to hear it."

"Why's that, Miss Harrodsen?" Chapin asked her.

"Because of old Lodge," Randolph Harrodsen said, buttering a slice of toast. "She hates Senator Lodge."

"Yes, I do—I certainly do!" Jennifer squirmed restlessly in her chair. She had a square little pug face with expressive hazel eyes; her hair was fine and very blond. "Trying to tear down everything President Wilson's over in Paris struggling to do—wants to hurl everything back to the Dark Ages." Her eyes darted around the table, back to Chapin. "I hope he's not a family friend."

"As a matter of fact he is," Chapin answered with a smile.

"Good! Then you can tell him for me he's a mean, vindictive old man."

"Jenny," her mother rebuked her.

"Last month you were furious with Wilson," Norris Harrodsen reminded his daughter. He had the same hazel eyes; they were twinkling, though his lips under the silver mustache were firm. "You said he was selling out the poor Croats, and the Chinese."

"Well, he did! Not that he could have made any difference . . ." She looked rather provocative when she pouted. "They've betrayed him. Clemenceau and the others."

Norris Harrodsen set down his copy of the *Times*. "Wilson is dogged by the failing of every sentimentalist: when he can't realize his dreams, he warps the facts to fit them."

"He did an awfully good job down at Princeton, Dad," Randy said.

"True enough. And that's where he should have stayed." Norris Harrodsen watched his son a moment. "Woodrow Wilson sees the world the way he wants it to be, not the way it is."

"Well, what's so criminal about that?" Jennifer wanted to now. "That's the trouble with you men— you always want things as they are . . . Well, *we're* going to set things up the way we want them to be!"

"Jenny," Corinne Harrodsen repeated placidly.

'Who's we?" Chapin asked.

"Just wait till the Suffrage Amendment is passed. Then you'll see things happen!"

"Have they attached a rider that will teach you to *use* that intelligence of yours?" her father said.

Chapin, sipping coffee, laughed with the others. It was pleasant sitting here in this elegant dining room of a handsome Fifth Avenue townhouse in Manhattan in the merry month of May, 1919; a delicious release from the relentless Texas wind, the dreary rituals of the mess, the coy avidity of the girls at the officers' club dances. He and Randy had got in the night before, sweaty and stiff from the interminable train ride. Now, wearing his A uniform, Chapin felt elated, unnaturally alert; he was ready for anything.

"What would you do," he asked Jenny, "if women got the vote, and they all voted for you, and you became President?"

"Oh-my-God," Randy groaned, *"don't* ask her that! You'll get the Grand Sermon . . ."

"Perfectly simple," Jenny said. "First, I'd nationalize all industry and transportation."

"Oh, then you—"

"The only intelligent answer is international socialism."

Randy said, "What Jenny would really like to be is Queen of the Wobblies."

"Very funny." She glared at her brother, and Chapin could see that for all her headlong bombast she was quite serious. She declared: "They are the vanguard of the future."

"Ah," Chapin said, "—then *you* were the one who sent out those package bombs with the Gimbels return address?"

"Don't think I wouldn't! That disgusting Mitchell Palmer—they're going to get him yet, you'll see!"

"Jenny, dear," her mother said.

"And how do you know they won't send you a bomb?" her father asked. "You're the enemy, too . . ."

"Oh, they know who their real enemies are!" She waggled one finger high above her head. "Don't include me in your doomed capitalist club— *I'm* not the one that's consumed with guilt neuroses . . ."

"But are you certain you're not the victim of a latent masochistic drive?" Chapin asked her, and the table broke into laughter again.

"Well, well . . ." Harrodsen glanced at his daughter, then at Chapin. "You're not a Freudian by any chance, are you, Ames?"

"No, sir. As far as I'm concerned, the more repression, the better."

"That's perfectly ridiculous—science has proved beyond question that all our troubles stem from repression of the libido."

"Jenny," her mother said sharply, "that is quite enough. You go too far."

"Nothing's changed," Randy told the table. "For twenty years the overriding question in this family has been: 'What are we going to do about Jenny?' And here we are. God help the man who marries you, Sissie."

227

"I have no intention of getting married." Her eyes rolled up at Chapin, slipped away. "Actually I've decided to become a devotee of free love."

"Jenny," Corinne Harrodsen exclaimed, "that will be all! You are impossible!"

"Bertrand Russell himself says—"

"I don't want to hear what he says!" To Chapin she said: "I hope you're not shocked. Jenny's always been overly impetuous, it's her way. Randy's right—I honestly don't know what we're going to do with her."

"Why, let her go on being impossible, of course," Norris Harrodsen said, and picked up his paper again.

An hour later Chapin rode downtown with Randy and his father in the chauffeur-driven Cadillac to the offices of Diehl, Harrodsen and over to the stock exchange where they watched the trading down on the floor, the cryptic symbols flowing mesmerically from the tapes. Symbols that meant fortunes. Everything was a symbol, viewed clearly and distantly: aviator's wings, a chauffeured limousine, an emerald brooch, WX 50.32 . . .

"Good volume," Norris Harrodsen observed to a thin, pale-faced associate named Saunders. It looked like pure chaos—men scurrying here and there, clustering around certain booths, clamoring at each other, frantically waving chits of paper, racing off somewhere else. But that was deceptive, Chapin knew. Here was where the power was centered: you could see it in the purposeful stride of the traders and floor brokers, feel it in the taut hum of voices, the occasional bursts of applause or roars of jubilation. Across the land all other activity—the rolling advance of combines over hot Kansas fields, rivet guns chattering against steel I-beams forty stories above the pavement, the dense scream of turbines, hops bubbling in great oak vats, oranges tumbling along conveyor belts —all that was only peripheral. This was the dynamo. This drove it all. You could feel it in the soles of your feet, hard under your heart: the dense thrum of power . . .

Reading was up. Baldwin Locomotive, Middle States Oil, General Motors, U.S. Steel . . . Harrodsen was explaining the symbols that ran with relentless progress under their fingers.

"Automotives leading the way. And the fundamentals." His face looked younger down here, his lips parted, hazel eyes snapping—he looked as though any minute he might break out in a cheer himself, join with the chaotic revelry down on the floor.

Boom, then. Postwar boom. Was that what it was? In ancient Rome the slave girls and ivory and cloth-of-gold flowed beneath the arches while the populace roared its approval and called for more. Now America had emerged triumphant and these were the new spoils of victory.

At the Union League Club the table cloths were white as samite and the waiters moved with the easy, measured tread of men who knew their masters had no need for haste. They brought Blue Point oysters and filet mignon, and Norris Harrodsen ordered two rounds of Bronx cocktails before, as he put it, the final Age of Barbarism descended on them all.

"It's definitely coming, then?" Chapin asked him. "Prohibition, on a national scale?"

"Cork goes into the bottle July first."

"Wild-eyed temperance biddies," Randy fumed. "Waited till we were in uniform and then ramroded it through." He emptied his glass with a little sigh of pleasure. He was solidly built, with a snub nose, like his sister's, and a pleasant, guileless expression. "Well, I'll tell you right now, *I'm* not going to stop drinking because of any stupid Wartime Prohibition Law."

"I'm sure you won't," his father observed dryly.

From far below came the blare of martial music punctuated by the visceral thud of a bass drum. Parade. Heads turned, conversations broke off; there was a steady movement of diners toward the windows. Carrying their drinks Chapin and the Harrodsens went over and watched.

A regiment was moving uptown in good order, the khaki thrusting with sharp, implacable purpose through the birdlike flutter of the crowds on the sidewalks, at the curbs.

"It's the Timber Wolves. Just back from France . . ."

Home from the wars. Scarves fluttered festively here and there, hats were waved, from some windows across the street confetti fell in fierce snowlike bursts. The band, sandwiched between companies, was playing "On the Mall." Chapin sipped at his drink, watching. It was a little like flying—there was that same beguiling sense of *distance,* of peering down omnisciently on the world's activities; the sense that one *could* spy into all those private lives if one chose, unseen; something remote and covert and forbidden —and therefore delicious beyond all comparison, he caught himself up with the ghost of a smile. Yes, that was it; you possessed them—all those unwitting thousands—because you possessed the power to invade their destinies . . . He found himself thinking of Jophy Gaspa—no, Ames!—wondered why. Ah, *a sense of the ship and the elements*—he'd written that because he knew it would appeal to her, arouse her sense of deprivation, envy; it had nothing whatever to do with what had appealed to him in flying. No wonder the ancients had invariably described the gods as swooping down, always swooping down on mortals—for combat, fornication, vengeance . . .

The parade below had passed on; the crowd stirred and moved aimlessly about, as self-conscious as children in an amateur theatrical. The diners drifted back to their tables, and the low hum of talk began again; talk of the attractiveness of shipping stocks, the latest warning by the Federal Trade Commission, the possibility of two-, even three-million-share days.

"See the conquering hero comes!" Norris Harrodsen

declaimed. " 'Sound the trumpet, beat the drums!' Now they've got to take off that uniform and come to grips with reality. You lads, too."

"Emerson said every hero becomes a bore at last," Chapin said.

"Well, he's right as rain . . . What do you plan to do with yourself, Ames? Now the Great Adventure is over."

Chapin wiped the corners of his mouth with his napkin. "I haven't decided, sir. Not finally . . . I imagine I'll go into business."

"Not up in Boston, I hope." Harrodsen cut at his steak surely; a vein in his forehead throbbed. "They're stuck back in the eighteenth century up there. Come on down here, Ames—here's where the excitement is."

Chapin laughed. "Yes, I can see that."

He had surprised himself with his answer—he'd had no intention of saying what he had. He'd thought rather idly—when he'd thought about it at all—that he would adopt the life of a Boston gentleman of half a century ago: mornings in the Athenaeum, meals at Somerset, evenings at theater or Symphony; faintly witty letters to the *Transcript* on some current topic, a leisurely monograph on some suitably idiosyncratic subject, annual jaunts to Europe, informed collecting —as much as his income would bear; and of course he stood to inherit Aunt Serena's modest fortune if, as and when . . .

But New York City had blown all that away like the blast of a plane's prop wash. It was so brash, so certain; fresh and gleaming in its rush toward power and notoriety and boundless wealth. Was it boundless? Everyone in this buzzing, majestic room seemed to think so . . .

After lunch Harrodsen went back to the office, and the two officers took a cab uptown: Randy to visit his fiancee, Chapin to pick up Jenny and take her for a walk; they were all to meet at the Waldorf at five.

The very air was metallic and bracing, festive. On

Fifth Avenue the great flags swirled and snapped in the light breeze, and the troops (there was another regiment parading, or perhaps it was the same column he'd watched earlier) poured under the jeweled arches while crowds gathered happily and waved greeting, and now and then more bits of paper rained down like flower petals. New York was like a big, boisterous family which had just come into a lot of money and was about to move into some newly erected mansion; the sense of expectation, of unrestrained holiday, persisted. He'd been to New York often, but its quick certainty, its opulence, had simply seemed nouveau; now he found the new atmosphere of freedom, of throwing off restraints, exciting. Skirts were five, six inches from the pavement, there were no veils anywhere, many of the girls were wearing rouge —Jenny's cheek, moving beside him on Lexington Avenue, was faintly touched with pink. After Boston's parsimony and frost and the brash vulgarities of Texas, Manhattan seemed like a huge, glorious jewel with a hundred glittering facets.

"It's fun," he said aloud. "It *is* the Greatest Show on Earth . . ."

"Yes. Isn't it a pity it's all going to be swept away?"

"What? Oh, by your invincible socialist utopia, you mean."

She laughed and tossed her head. "You'll see—the masses won't submit to senseless exploitation by finance capital any longer; they've had enough of—" Her voice trailed away in spite of herself, she was staring intently beyond him, frowning. "Goodness. What do you suppose is going on over there?"

Across the street there was a commotion. Servicemen—Chapin could see both Army and Navy uniforms—were crowding hard against a doorway; a sergeant was waving one fisted hand, shouting something.

"It sounds like a union meeting," Jenny was saying, "only they're in uniform . . ."

The center broke backward, was convulsed in a turmoil of blue and khaki. A gunner's mate roared something unintelligible, and the surge at the door began again—a many-armed beast, blind, flailing, insensate.

"They're trying to get into that building," Chapin said. "It's a meeting of some sort, and they're planning to break it up . . ."

On the edge of the melée an older man, smart in a gray suit and Homburg, was tapping at a soldier's sleeve, saying something to him, whether remonstrance or query Chapin couldn't tell. The soldier turned, shook him off angrily. The sergeant, two steps above, caught sight of the man and leaned down, red-faced and wrathful. Chapin saw him point, heard him shout: "Here's another one—lousy Bolshevik sons of bitches!" The gentleman's head snapped back from a blow, his hat flew off, and in another second the flurry closed around him.

Chapin gripped Jenny's wrist, said sharply: "You stay here!" and sprinted across the avenue between the cars and carriages. By the time he reached the far curb the man was down, on his hands and knees, and the sergeant and several other soldiers were kicking at him savagely, shouting with each kick. Chapin caught hold of the sergeant's shoulder and spun him around, seized the front of his tunic.

"Cut that out!" he roared. "Now *stop it—!*"

The sergeant glared back at him, his eyes wild and unfocused; his shoulder dropped, he started to swing —but the habit of rank was too great: the captain's bars, Chapin's threatening manner checked him. He stepped back, opened his mouth to yell something defiant.

"He's my uncle!" Chapin shouted hotly. "Touch him again and you'll draw the stockade! You hear me? My uncle!"

"Hey, now look here, Captain—"

"He's no more a Bolshevik than Black Jack Pershing! Now make way, God damn it, make way . . ."

The man was lying on his side, his knees drawn up, holding his belly. Blood was streaming from his nose and mouth in a thick bright sheen, matting his smooth silver hair, his mustache. He stared at Chapin without expression. Chapin lifted him to his feet. The man raised one hand to his head, expecting to be hit again; the blood was pulsing from a deep cut in his forehead. Every uniform was an enemy now. Chapin half-carried him to the curb and hailed a cab.

"Are you all right?" he said.

The man shook his head; his eyes were blinking stupidly, glazed. One sleeve was nearly torn away at the shoulder. He looked broken, a derelict; the transformation was frightening. Chapin eased him into the back seat of the cab, drew out his handkerchief and wiped away some of the blood, pressed deftly at the open wound on the temple.

"Where do you live, sir?"

". . . What?"

"I say, where do you live? You'd better go straight home. Get medical attention for that cut . . ."

"Thank you." The man nodded; his eyes were clearer now. "Those men . . ." His glance flickered away to where the small mob was surging against the doorway. "They actually—"

"I know. They're in an ugly mood. You're sure you're all right?"

"Yes. I want to thank you, Captain."

"Glad to be of help, sir."

"My name is Calkins, Avery Calkins." The hand he extended was trembling; Chapin took it.

"Chapin Ames."

Calkins smiled weakly. "We have the same initials. In reverse."

"So we do."

"I'm very grateful to you, Captain."

"Not at all, sir."

Holding the handkerchief to his head Calkins gave an address to the driver, and the cab moved off. Chapin nodded to him, crossed the avenue again. Jenny was standing exactly where he'd left her, her hands clasped in front of her, staring at him.

"He'll be all right," he explained. "He may need some stitches for that cut in his head."

"—They beat him," she breathed; she was shaking her head in childish bewilderment. "They were kicking him, there on the ground . . ."

"Yes, they're all awash in liquor and patriotism and now they've decided to hunt down some of your bomb-tossing confederates." He laughed; he felt a sudden need to talk, rattle on about anything at all. It was curious—he hadn't felt a touch of fear, even when the sergeant had started to swing at him. Of course it could have been that he felt protected by the uniform, the bars, the aviator's wings. But even so . . .

"His initials are the reverse of mine," he went on. "Isn't that strange? Says his name is Avery Calkins."

"Avery Calkins? Why, Daddy knows him," she said, and her eyes suddenly filled with tears.

"Does he really?"

"—It was terrible," she said, and her lips quivered now, her sturdy snub-nosed face crinkled up oddly. "Terrible what they did—*terrible* . . ."

He stared at her; he realized a great many things at once. She was not the fierce unreconstructed rebel she pretended to be, whose outrageous assertions her family affectionately indulged. No. It was the feigned recklessness of the deeply fearful. It took one thief to catch another. It was a pose she had consciously and carefully adopted, to offset that earnest little pug face, and to prepare the ground for the future—an eccentric, rebellious spirit too mettlesome to settle for humdrum matrimony, for motherhood and the social rounds. It was all a fraud. He had, after all, known the real thing in Jophy, who meant it to the very bottom of her hot, wild heart; who would live (and certainly die) by it. Jophy—fiery, unreckoning Jophy—now, incredibly, wife to a hard-driving, ripsnorting sales manager. She'd been sick with the flu, Aunt Serena had written; she'd almost died from it . . . Impossible: to think of Jophy *dead*—

Jenny was still watching him strangely; he saw she was trembling. She was in a kind of shock. He felt a strange, unfamiliar surge of compassion. That secret confraternity of the fearful, he thought.

He took her arm. "I believe we need something," he said with soft decision. "Something restorative."

She gave him a look of the most intense gratitude. He could feel her weight on his arm; her legs were unsteady.

"Oh, yes!" she breathed.

Five minutes later they were sitting in a dimly lighted room filled with bristling potted palms. Jenny was looking around her uncertainly; it was clear she'd never been in the twilight never-never land of the new lounges, as they were calling them. Chapin ordered tea, then slipped the waiter a bill and asked him for whiskey and water, a double, and told him not to mix it. In the ballroom the orchestra was playing the "Dardanella," and Jenny hummed the melody absently, staring hard at her square little hands. When the waiter brought their order, Chapin waited until he had served them and turned away, then surreptitiously emptied the shot into her cup.

"Do you mind?" he murmured. "I think you could use this."

She glanced at the tea cup, then at Chapin, with the same strained expression; she was feeling rather queasy.

"Yes," she said. "I could. I certainly could." Staring at the cup she sipped at it, cleared her throat; drank again and set it down.

"Famous first," she said with a trace of the old bravado. "I've—never had a drink of liquor in public before!"

Or anywhere else, perhaps, he thought. "Well,

cheer up," he said aloud. "We're starting a trend. In a couple of months they'll all be sneaking it."

"But it's the law of the land—"

"Dear Miss Harrodsen. Man *wants* to drink the product of fermented fruit or distilled grain—he's spent a million hours putting together the weirdest concoctions since the beginning of time. In point of fact, this asinine law will only make him want to drink more than ever."

"What a realist you are," she mused. She drank more of her laced tea. "I thought when I first saw you—you know, at the station with Randy—you were such a romantic person."

"Appearances are deceiving. No, my brother's the romantic soul."

"Is he? Tell me about him."

"Tip's a salesman—he sells dreams to people in place of reality, and so of course they eat it up. And so he's very successful . . . Well, perhaps I'm maligning him. They say he's very good at it. I wouldn't wonder."

"Is that what he wants to be?"

He nodded. "It's curious that you ask that—he's always wanted to be a saleman. Even when we were kids . . ." He thought idly, almost fondly, of a harsh, raw day steely with the threat of snow, the frozen ruts in a road, a burst carton of soap. No, it wouldn't do to talk about that. That was a world left behind . . . Long ago.

"And where do you stand, Captain?" she was asking, as if she'd read his thoughts on a slate. She'd recovered herself fully by now; her face was faintly flushed. "Are you with Wiggam and the influence of heredity? or with Watson and the grip of the environment?"

"Elementary, my dear Watson," he answered without hesitation. "You've just proved it yourself. Wiggam, that is."

"You're a curious sort of Bostonian, aren't you? As Bostonians go, I mean."

"There are Bostonians and Bostonians. Personally I've always tried to think of myself as the liberal sort. With conservative feelings."

She laughed with him. "Daddy likes you," she offered suddenly.

"Does he? I'm flattered."

"I could tell. He usually hates Bostonians. Says they have no flexibility, no sense of innovation."

"He's right. Most of them don't."

The orchestra had swung into the latest craze, "I'll Say She Does," and Jenny sang the refrain once, broke off with the exclamation: "What a vulgar song!"

He smiled at her over the smoke from his cigarette. "Maybe you just lack flexibility."

She laughed, wagging her head, and for a time they chatted about families and dances and women's suffrage. The liquor had made her garrulous, which she seemed to realize, but it also had given her, he could see, an easy confidence, and she was aware of that, too. The spring day slipped toward evening, the room began to fill. In the ballroom the dancers wheeled and glided, and women's laughter spiraled heedlessly above the music.

"There's a benefit Friday evening," Jenny was saying. *"Dear Brutus.* With grand old Gillette. For the Victory Loan—it's already oversold, I can't imagine what they need it for, now. Don't you like Barrie? I love the way he gets you involved, the—situations he creates . . . Wouldn't you like to see it?"

"Indeed I would. But I've got to be heading for home tomorrow. I haven't seen my Aunt Serena, any of my family actually, since I got into uniform."

"Oh, stay . . ." Her face had stiffened suddenly. "Just a few days more. Just till Saturday . . . I mean, you said yourself Boston's unpardonably dull."

"I did—it certainly is!" Laughing as he looked at her; she was staring back at him with a kind of frightened challenge. When she looked off toward the dancers her cheek had colored.

She was in love with him. It was clear as the rectangular panels of light above the mirrors. For a long moment he watched her over the cigarette's soft gray smoke: the little pug face, with its over-broad mouth, over-square jaw. The eyes, though, held that quick flash of spirit; and there was a nicety of mind, a delicacy quite appealingly vulnerable under the flip manner she affected. She would make a socially adroit, presentable wife; a very wealthy, helpful wife. A wife who would follow his lead—who would never make excessive demands; chance had let him catch her brave, fragile affectation and find a submissive nature, which would give way to him—

She was frightened: of growing old, a spinster, in glittering, glamorous Manhattan. He could see her in five years, in ten, the mouth tightening, the jaw setting still further, the eyes flattening in that time-killing round of social duties; she would never marry because the men would all be scared away—they wouldn't see that her radical stance was merely the protective device of an unsure heart. She was marked for solitude . . . He could free her from that with one word; and her gratitude would be boundless, would carry her—would it?—into the captive role he required. And he would be wealthy, if he played his cards correctly; wealthy not as Aunt Serena was, but as Norris Harrodsen was. Avenues . . .

She was silent now, as though she'd spoken her piece, revealed all of herself she could bear to; and now it was up to him. The orchestra was playing "Hindustan," and he started slightly with recollection of another band, other costumes . . . From a casual friendship forged at an air field, an even more casual visit en route home . . . could he really be thinking seriously about this? Maybe there was something to Jophy Gaspa's—Jophy *Ames's!*—obsession with signs and portents. Perhaps one *ought* to follow them, see where they led—

He ground out his cigarette, aware that he was leaving too long a silence between them, that with the passage of each second an obscure advantage was ebbing away. Well, what was so fantastic about it? Wasn't life, after all, a series of bargains? He had struck one with his aunt and had held up his end, in the main. This would be another, a different bargain—dramatically different in that *he* would set the patterns, dominate. If he chose.

Her eyes were on him now. With the old, arrogant sidelong glance, the barest trace of a smile he said:

"You've been eluding me, Miss Harrodsen. All this talk about Wilson and the Wobblies and Barrie—but what about *you?*"

"What is there to tell?"

"For instance, what about the men in your life?"

She colored again, faintly, but met his gaze. "Oh, there was Douglas Fairbanks, and then there was Francis X. Bushman, but I threw them both over. They weren't what I wanted."

"What *do* you want?"

"Oh—someone unpredictable and dangerous. That's why I was drawn to Jack Dempsey. Do you think he's dangerous?"

"Palpably."

"I turned him down, too. I may change my mind, though."

"Why's that?"

"Well you see, if we don't get along I can always get a divorce. And it'll be vastly more diverting to be a young divorcée than an old maid."

He laughed, still watching her from the corners of his eyes, liking her more than he had before, conscious of that light-headed sensation of hovering on the edge of a fateful decision. Still again, and almost against his will, he thought of Jophy, her hair long against a bare shoulder, coal-dark eyes flashing in

mischievous delight; but then a shadow behind her—
swaying in a searing dance of unbearable light—
drove the image away.

"Shall we dance?" he asked.

2

"I feel like a God damned Delmonico's waiter in this monkey suit," Web Bowers muttered; he kept wrenching his neck around against the hard white collar.

"Well, see you don't act like one," Tip warned him.

Jack Darcey laughed his high Irish laugh. "What's the matter, Web—you want to live forever?"

"So's your old man, Darcey."

"How about you, Bake? Another drop of happy poison?"

Bake Greenlaw shook his head. "No more for me."

They were milling around in the suite Tip had rented, twelve of them, feeling awkward and a bit nervous in their rented tuxedos, plucking at cummerbunds and lapels, swapping insults.

"Chief," Jack called to Tip, and shot his cuffs extravagantly. "How's about we make our entrance on a double-shuffle-buck-and-wing? little soft-shoe routine?"

"Go soak your head," Tip told him. The war had only made Jack more irrepressible. He'd served with distinction in the St. Mihiel and Meuse-Argonne drives, had risen to sergeant and been busted down to PFC twice for madcap forays in the brothels of Bar-le-Duc and Châlons. He had, as he said, talked his way into trouble and out of it again as many times as a caterpillar has legs, and emerged unscathed and unreformed. The war—that ridiculous, mismanaged carnival—had suited his mood perfectly; he'd walked into Tip's office on a clear, cold morning three months after the Armistice in a checked suit and a green hat with a pheasant feather in it and said: "Well, here I am—home again and stony-broke, Tip my boy. When do I start?" It was, incredibly, as though he'd never been away . . .

Smiling to himself now, moving quickly through his sales force, Tip stopped abruptly in front of Phelps.

"That tie, Clary—it's *blue!*"

"I know, Tip." Clarence Phelps had a round face and round blue eyes. He looked like a movie-palace usher and had already proved himself in the space of a year and a half to be a crack salesman. Now he looked crestfallen. "I'm sorry."

Clarence shifted his feet: "I didn't think it would show."

"Jesus Christ," Tip fumed. "Where are we going to dig up a black tie at this stage of the game?"

"I've got a spare," Maury Zimmerman said quickly. "I'll go get it." He was the only member of the force who had his own tuxedo, which was custom made and fitted him like a glove. He looked pityingly at Phelps. "What's the matter with you, Clary. Haven't you got any sense of class?"

Tip watched his big back vanish through the connecting door. Four months after their confrontation Maury had marched into Tip's office and stood in front of his desk fingers knotted in his belt.

"Hello, Maury," Tip had said innocently. "What's on your mind?"

"Remember that little conversation we had when you came in as manager?"

"Why, no—I can't remember every conversation I have with everybody."

Maury pointed a manicured finger at him. "I'll remind you, then. You told me I had six months to lead the force or you'd fire me. Remember that?"

"Why yes, as a matter of fact I do."

"Splendid. And I told *you* that I'd go out front in *four* months." He nodded grimly, his handsome face smooth. "Well, it might interest you to know I just stepped into first place this morning."

Tip watched him impassively. "Why, that's great news, Maury. You're not fired."

Zimmerman's head went back, he glared down at him—all at once burst out laughing; laughter that tailed off in a quizzical smile. "You're something, Ames," he said finally. "You're not as dumb as you look. Are you?"

"I wouldn't exactly put it that way, Maury."

"Well, *I* would . . . You wanted me to do just what I did, all along. Didn't you?"

Tip watched him carefully. "I didn't want to see you do something you might regret."

Hands on his hips, Maury nodded to himself. "You're one good jump ahead of everybody around here. How'd you learn to think so fast?"

"Desperation."

"I guess so. I guess we're going to have to call you Whizzer Ames."

"I'd much rather you called me Schoolboy, Maury," Tip answered; and both men burst into laughter.

That had done it. To everyone's amazement Zimmerman had turned into Tip's most ardent supporter. He would not allow a critical word against their boy manager; he backed him to the hilt in every new sales strategy, led the force consistently, and even took to wearing jackets and ties of a more subdued hue. Checking the seating plan now, Tip shook his head. Emotions never ceased to astonish him. They were like pendulums gone wild—always swinging through much greater arcs than you could foresee, for you or against you. It was human nature to rush to ex-

245

tremes; if he hadn't learned that, living with Jophy, he would never learn anything at all . . .

Maury was back from his room down the hall in less than a minute with a spare tie in one hand which he tossed to Phelps. "Here you go."

Clarence looked at it sadly and said: "Oh."

"What's the matter?"

"Well—it's the wrong kind."

"What do you mean, the wrong kind?—it's brand new . . ."

"I mean it's not—made up." He paused uncertainly, looking around at the others. "I don't know how to tie a bow tie. I never learned."

There were several snorts of laughter, and Jack Darcey barked: "Ten days piss-and-punk for *you*, lad . . ."

"It's perfectly simple," Zimmerman told him in a tone of martyred exasperation. "Drape it around your neck. That's it. Now take one end and fold it—"

"We haven't time for that," Tip cut him off. "Maury, stand behind him and tie it for him."

"I still don't see why we're wearing tuxedos anyhow," Clarence Phelps protested. "Nobody else is."

"That's just the point," Tip told him. "You'll see."

He called them all around the card table. "Now here's the set-up. Our table is at the far end of the ballroom, right below the speakers' dais. There will be place-names, but I want you to check this diagram and memorize now where you're sitting and who's next to you—I don't want a lot of aimless Alphonse-and-Gaston backing-and-filling when you get there. Style creates effect—remember that. We're going to do this with style. You've earned it. Let's make it count.

"I'll lead the parade. Maury, you follow me. They're going to ask you to speak on institutional sales. Remember, the limit is three minutes. They'll gavel you promptly if you run over.—Then I want Web and Jack and Skeets. Ed, I want you to bring up the rear, behind Clarence. I guess that's it."

There was a brief, tense silence, a little like the moment before a team's taking the field.

"Tip, it's five after seven," Ed Langevin said.

"I'll tell you when it's time to go down."

"But if we're late—"

"We won't be. You leave the worrying to me."

"How's about another throat blesser?" Jack offered.

"Nope," Tip said, and socked the cork in the bottle with the heel of his hand. "Two's the limit. You can get as pie-eyed as you want after it's over. But now we're going in on our own steam."

There was a rap on the door to the suite. Darcey opened it. A bellhop stood there, diminutive, eager in the wasp-waisted blue-and-gold tunic and brass buttons. Jack snapped to attention, brought up his arm in a quivering salute.

"Front-and-center, trooper!"

The boy started to salute in reply, checked the movement with a nervous grin, peered around Jack and said: "They're just going in now, Mr. Ames."

"Thanks, Billy." Tip slipped him a bill. "Good boy. Hold an elevator for us, now."

"Yes, sir. Thank you, sir."

"All right." Tip turned and faced the roomful of men, looked into each face: Web, brilliant at presentation but with a tendency to coast toward the end of the week; and Perry Millis, touchy and given to fits of pessimism, who forever needed praise; and Jack, whom he'd learned to sober up with an icy shower and three fingers of gin—who still sold better hung over than any three others; and Skeets Brohammer, whom he'd taught to organize his territory; and Bake Greenlaw, the Downeaster with the tenacity of a limpet but whose tart severity needed periodic unbending; and Maury, whose vanity was his great strength and his great weakness; and Ed, whose wife rode him mercilessly and who consequently needed bucking up on

247

Monday mornings; and little Sid Solotow, who'd started out in New Haven with a pushcart full of pots and pans at the age of ten, and whom he'd given poise and polish; and Tommy Bergeron, who oversold and whom he'd taught restraint; and young Clary, whom he'd taught everything. What was it Frank Delahant had told him that fateful wintry afternoon? "You've got to kick some and kiss others—and God help you if you mix up your formula . . ."

He'd driven them hard, very hard—it was the only way he knew; but he'd been fair enough. There had been a perfect uproar down here in New York when he'd informed them he would be splitting his commissions on sales when he worked with his men. Most sales managers simply traveled around and skimmed off the cream. He'd resented it bitterly when old Walter Dabney had done that to him, and he was damned if he was going to do it himself. George Maynard had called him in and started to give him the third degree about it.

"It's my understanding I have full authority with my regional sales force," he'd broken in. "*Is* that the case?"

"You do." Maynard watched him narrowly. "But you're setting a dangerous precedent."

"It's *my* commissions I'm halving—no one else is hurt. Why is it so dangerous?"

Maynard sighed and stared hard at a small stone polar bear on his desk. "Salesmen will come to regard it as policy—they'll resent returning to the customary practice."

Tip grinned at him. "You mean, after I'm gone? I plan to stick around for a while. And anyway, maybe they *should* resent it—that ever occur to you, George?"

Maynard locked his hands on the desk top. "You do have certain obligations to management, you know."

"That's right." Tip stuck out his lower lip. "But my

first responsibility is to my men—and don't you forget it."

Maynard nodded. "You've got your nerve, Ames."

"That's what they tell me."

It was funny—he'd done it out of a simple sense of justice; but nothing could have done more for morale. Working on straight commission as they were, it meant some income for his crew when they were in a slump; and it redoubled incentive all the way down the line. In some ways it may have been the difference . . .

They were still standing there—alert, aggressive, resourceful; all any field manager could want. Not a floater among them. Watching them he felt a sharp ache of affection different from anything he'd ever known before. For a heart beat or two it surprised him, shook him.

"All right," he repeated, a touch more harshly than he'd intended. "You're the best damned sales force in the whole U.S. of A. You've taken the rest of the country, going away, and you did it on confidence and ability and drive. On pure Moxie. I'm proud as hell of you. You're winners—and I want you to walk in there like winners. No shuffling or head-bobbing or glad-handing. Just walk in there with your chins up and sit down. As though you owned the place. All right, let's go."

The ballroom was big and bright and humming. Everyone was already seated; the speakers' dais was filled. Perfect! He gave one swift backward glance, and then led the procession, threading his way purposefully through the tables of salesmen. There were a few exclamations, then a falling-away of talk and laughter—and then, slowly, a rising rush of applause, capped by cheers and whistles. He found himself grinning in spite of all his good intentions and sat down quickly; his men fanned out neatly to left and right, seating themselves with care. Their black dinner jackets and white shirt fronts made a bold, dramatic contrast to the somber grays and duns throughout the hall. Theirs was the only table that was completely filled; every man had made his quota. The applause was general now, the ballroom rang with it. Clary Phelps was sitting grave as a judge, wanting to check his tie and not daring to, and across from him Maury was saying softly:

"Now do you see, Clary? Now do you get it?"

On the speakers' platform Beau Frank Delahant had risen, smiling that quick, charming smile.

"Well," he began. "I flattered myself that I had some surprises up my sleeve for you all tonight—but I see I've already been upstaged!" He nodded at the laughter, his eyes twinkling. "Effective salesmanship is seventy percent showmanship; making your point vivid, dramatic, unmistakable—some of you have heard me say that. And here it is, right before our eyes . . ." His gaze, playing over the ballroom, dropped quickly to Tip—the fond, indulgent glance. "I used to flatter myself that Tip Ames was a pupil of mine, but I guess I'd better get over the idea. I think we can all agree that the Schoolboy is the teacher here tonight. Let's hear it again for that amazing New England sales force and the irrepressible Tipton Ames!"

Tip looked around the table, meeting the other faces, while the applause beat over him like the surf at Turk's Head.

3

The ship looked huge—gleaming and sparkling like an immense tiered cake, frosted against the gloomy cavern of the pier; Tip was astonished at its sheer floodlit mass. Jophy was already hurrying ahead of him up the gangplank.

"Climb aboard!" she called to him, laughing. "Do you want to be left behind—?" She looked flushed and excited, as if eager to embark on a perilous voyage; it was the first time she'd been away since the birth of the new baby, whom she'd left with Grama after a lazy week in the sun. At the head of the gangplank, the assistant purser gave her a roguish salute and she laughed again, her lips parted. Impelled by the crowd, they passed through a corridor rich with the odors of polish and iodine and compressed air and entered the grand salon, where chefs in high fanciful caps presided over a Lucullan spread of patisserie and jellied wonders. The woodwork glowed, the brass winked in the lights. Stewards glided among the tables like messengers on the most grave and mysterious errands. On the bandstand the orchestra was playing "The Japanese Sandman."

"Dahhhling, pahhss me my lorgnette," Jophy drawled in her most extravagant posh accent. "Aren't there any nightingales' breasts ce soir? Ah, it's all so infinitely *dreary* here . . ." But her eyes were dancing and her hand trembled faintly when she caught his.

Tip laughed, knowing that heedless, madcap mood was on her. It was the ship, the sea . . .

They passed up a staircase, another—Jophy seemed to know her way by instinct—emerged on what he supposed was the top deck. The unique holiday sense of being suspended before an adventure prevailed, heightened by the night's soft pressure. There were gentlemen of Empire in blazers, carrying slim walking sticks, there were butter-and-egg men from Kansas City in double-breasted suits and polka-dot ties, there were diamond merchants—Jophy was absolutely certain they were diamond merchants—with short spade beards and paisley cravats; and everywhere there were women with bare shoulders and shining bobbed hair and the faces of ospreys or foxes; their laughter rang like glass shivering to pieces. In the floodlights their faces had turned to alabaster.

"—Let's stay on board," Jophy breathed. The night breeze came up the river, dense and fetid, almost tropical, and she stared out at the invisible night, her nostrils flaring. "Stow away—they wouldn't even know we were here . . . Like the man on Grampa's third cruise who hid in the steerage till the carpenter found him. A spoiled rich boy from Philadelphia—he was going to make his fortune in the mysterious East." She laughed again softly, gazing off at the darkness.

Tip watched her, feeling that slow surge of elation, of desire, her presence always brought him. Her recovery from illness and the loss of the first baby had been, characteristically, capricious and abrupt. For some months she had been subdued, ridden by fits of despondency. Waking early he would find her sitting by the window in her bathrobe, staring at the blank wall of the next house. Nothing he could contrive in the way of distraction seemed to lift her out of her profound dejection. Then one evening—he'd just got in from a protracted swing through Maine—she came running up to him with her old warmth and high spirits.

"Well," he said in surprise, "and how's my south wind girl?"

"Guess what?" she began. "I ran into Her Serena Highness today, at the Peabody Museum. Among the glass flowers!" She laughed—her old high, ringing laughter. "She's vexed with the world. She's miffed that Chapin's gone down to big, bad Manhattan to make his fame and fortune."

"That figures."

"It's disgraceful enough *your* ringing doorbells—though that's all right, of course, you hadn't any choice! But for Chapin it's spiritual treason. I told her she had nothing to worry about—the rewards weren't hedonistic enough for Chay; he'd get tired of stock-broking in a matter of months and rush back to something constructive, like collecting snuff boxes. That got a laugh out of her—though she didn't believe me, I could tell. She's already scheming how to lure him back to Merry Olde Beacon Hill. Afterward we had tea together, like two parfit gentil lay-dees. She's beginning to think I *might* do—might even be useful to her—with some judicious holy-stoning, of course." She laughed again, and threw her arms around him. "It was just what I needed. Oh Tip, hug me and hug me! God, I'm so lucky to be me—and not Serena Forbes Aldridge. To be the wife of Tip Ames, five-alarm fireball . . ."

Their love-making that night had caught up the joyful, unconstrained fervor of that first summer. His Jo was herself again, frolicsome and wild, green again with ardor. The birth of Joey that spring had put a golden crown on the year . . .

"Just sail away," Jo was saying now, pointing southward, "to Mombasa, or Tongatapu or Balikpapan. Where the coconut milk is sweet as honey, and the gods have emeralds for eyes . . . What's the matter, darling?"

253

"—I was just thinking how beautiful you are," he said.

"Were you? Perhaps I am," she considered. "I mean, why shouldn't I be?"

The door to the cabin was open—a babble of voices, breathless, as though its occupants were mortally afraid of being cast ashore before they could complete their latest bon mot. As they started to enter, a figure lurched out and collided against Jophy; his glass sloshed silver liquid in the air. Quick as light she darted sideways; the drink slopped wetly against the wall. Tip steadied the man. A soft affable face, almost infantile in its self-absorption, watery eyes solemn behind tortoise-rimmed glasses.

"—mensely sorry," he breathed, his gaze fastening with difficulty on Jophy.

"Quite all right," she answered laughing. "Never touched me!"

"—traordinarily sorry, really. Was just—just—" His eyes rolled around to Tip, bowled on somewhere else. He had already forgotten.

The cabin was larger than Tip had ever imagined a passenger cabin on a liner could be, even in first class. There were two cabins, in fact, a drawing room as well as a bedroom. Both were crowded and alive with a medley of raised voices. Nearly everyone held a glass.

"No prohibition here," Jophy murmured.

"I'll say."

The rooms split them up and swallowed them. A steward pressed on Tip a glass of champagne, someone welcomed him on board with violent warmth, someone else asked him if he knew where Blair Passey was. Over in one corner he saw his aunt talking with Corinne Harrodsen; he worked his way over to her and greeted her, said: "Where's mother?"

"Back at the hotel. She didn't feel up to something like this."

"Can't say I blame her."

Serena Aldridge frowned. "She's not well, you know."

"I know."

They stared at each other a moment.

"Well, Tipton." He could feel his aunt's intense blue eyes moving over him, testing, confirming something. She was the only person who never used his nickname; but then he'd never heard her use Chapin's either.

"Hasn't this been a glorious day?"

"I was telling your mother at dinner how marvelously well you've both turned out."

"In spite of everything, you mean."

She laughed once—that single high burst of amusement. "We all have our failings."

"No argument there . . ."

"You really were serious. Weren't you, Tipton?"

"About what, Aunt Serena?"

"About what you said. As a boy. About being able to sell anything."

He watched her evenly. "What I said was, I might be selling more than Shalimar Soap before I was through."

Her eyes dilated in that fierce beacon-flash that could always frighten and attract him. "You remembered that . . ."

"Not very likely to forget it."

"I suppose not. And do you remember what I said to that?"

"You said I could go way beyond that, if I wanted to."

"I meant it too." Pressing a hand against her thigh she sighed lightly. "Well, that's that.—And now you've both gone off and got married."

"And lived happily ever after—you've left out that part," he teased her.

"Ah—that remains to be seen. Doesn't it?" She laughed again, her glance flickering around the room, stopping on Jophy. Maybe his mother wasn't up to this sailing, but Aunt Serena was. She was wearing a dove

255

gray dress of crepe-de-Chine and a much lower neckline than she'd formerly displayed; a jet choker rode high on her proud, slender neck. Her hair—now a fine, blued silver—was still piled in a Gibson girl pompadour. She looked even younger than when Tip had seen her on the Cape the summer before, her face smoother, more alert. Money made you younger, among other things, and kept you that way; like an infusion. Vitamin $$$—the most potent of them all . . .

"Now tell me: what do you think of your new sister-in-law?"

"I like her very much, what little I've seen of her."

"I rather though you might find her—a bit drab."

He grinned, his lower lip protruding. "You mean, after Jophy? You're right—they're all drab, after Jo. But that's not the point—the real question is what *you* think of her, Aunt Serena."

She laughed soundlessly this time, her head back. "You're quick, Tipton! I'll have to give you that."

"Most people do."

He looked away restlessly, watching Jophy in an animated exchange with Norris Harrodsen and three younger men. Women always exerted a queer power over him at social functions; he seemed unable to terminate a conversation, no matter how trivial, and move on. He envied the way men like Frank Dela-hant graciously, deftly disengaged themselves. How did they do it? The men around Jophy exploded into laughter—she was obviously launched on one of her wilder tales, or maybe some impersonation, she was a marvelous mime—but her eyes kept lifting, searching beyond the tight little circle of her audience: a gaze strangely eager, fearful, almost desperate in its intensity. Following its scan Tip found his brother, oblivious and smiling, hemmed in by a covey of young women. In spite of himself he glanced back at Jo, but now her expression was matter-of-fact, distant, revealing nothing at all . . .

The wedding that afternoon had been held at St.

Thomas' on Fifth Avenue; a formal affair, quite grand. The very organ music had seemed hushed, as though a bit awed by the proceedings. An usher, a well-built young man with the assured, fatuous expression only three generations of funded wealth and the Ivy League can produce, nodded to them as they entered and inquired:

"Friends or family?"

"Family," Tip answered in a low, clear voice. "Brother and sister-in-law of the groom."

The usher's indifferent eyes roamed over him, edged with doubt, rested on Jophy with sudden pleasurable interest; he turned and led the way down the aisle to the second row. Aunt Serena and his mother were already there. His mother looked mousy and worn, her eyes quick with that submissive expression that always made him angry, and then immensely sad. She nodded to them with her apprehensive smile, but Serena Aldridge said clearly:

"Tipton, Josefina." Almost in spite of herself she added, "You're absolutely radiant, my dear."

"No more death's-door-pallor, you mean?" Jophy laughed softly, gazing straight at her.

The church filled with leisured purpose. Chapin and Randy Harrodsen entered from a paneled oak door on the right and stood together before the altar in their uniforms of charcoal cutaway and pearl waistcoat and gray trousers, as though it were the most natural thing in the world. Tip saw Chapin murmur something to Randy, who murmured something in turn, and glanced at his watch. Chay smiled—a brief, easy smile, nothing excessive or out of taste about it, perfectly in keeping with the ceremony; just easy good-humor under fire. His eyes met Tip's, registered greeting, slipped on. He looked handsomer than ever: the faintly hawklike features filled a bit, the full lips firmer. For the past two years he'd been working in New York, in Norris Harrodsen's firm; and now he was marrying the boss's daughter ("A rather homely, dumpy boss's daughter," as Jophy had pointed out dryly. "Make you wonder at all?" "Now don't be cynical," Tip had told her with a grin, "maybe he fell in love with her." "Uh-huh. Maybe.").

He shifted his feet. Curious—his sensitive, fastidious brother a Wall Street money-man. Had the war forced the change, made him restless? or was it simply the human condition—did having a certain amount of money make you want more, and then more after that? Chay had always been so contemptuous of the marketplace. "Oh, he's a *merchant*," he'd say with that languorous Harvard disdain that set Tip's teeth on edge; or with mocking levity: "A coster-monger, I believe!" Now here he was, all dolled up and a bit of a costermonger himself, though on a rather exalted level—

"You ought to be up there," Jophy was whispering in her sweet low contralto. "Standing up there with him."

"Best man? Well, he said he didn't want to hurt Randy's feelings."

"Ridiculous! *You're* his brother. You're *related,* for God's sake—"

"Only by blood. Money's thicker by far. Didn't you know that?"

To his surprise her eyes had flashed darkly at him. "Well, as a significant little matter of fact—"

She broke off. The bride was coming. The music had turned quietly martial, swelling powerfully. The bride was coming, to a gathering murmur of approbation and sentiment. Carefully Tip turned his head and watched Jenny Harrodsen pass on her father's arm, gliding easily and purposefully—as though all strolls, all guided tours, all dances had been rehearsals for this stately processional. Norris Harrodsen, slim and straight, was staring gravely at nothing; Jenny's eyes were fastened on Chapin—a look that seemed to gather up everything within herself and bear it to him. She is in love with him, Tip thought; completely and

258

utterly in love with him—no reservations, no conditions, nothing held back; all her eggs in one fragile basket—and the realization frightened him even as it excited him. A fellow voyager, he thought mawkishly, a comrade in arms. Glancing sharply at Chapin he could not tell from his brother's expression what he felt. There was warmth, a certain contained assurance and eagerness; beyond that nothing was apparent.

Father and daughter had reached the altar. The minister, gorgeous in his robes, with beautifully waved blond hair and a fleshy Bourbon face, was gazing at the couple with a smile of indulgent benediction. The maid of honor and bridesmaids in their matching ice-blue chiffon had deployed to left and right, the bridegroom had moved into position; the ceremony could begin.

Jenny looked even shorter in point d'esprit veil and heavy white satin brocade, with a train trailing behind her like the wake of a sturdy ship. Chapin looked taller in the long-tailed coat, the high collar. Sitting erectly, his arms crossed, Tip thought all at once of his father, the last time he'd seen him. The memory was dim—he could not remember what either of them had said—but his father's features were still clear: slim, handsome face, high temples, full lower lip under the down-sweeping mustache, the ardent restlessness in the eyes—Chapin's eyes, with their pale, milky rings on rings . . . Where was his father now? Peru, Horace Crowell had told him the last time he'd been back in Holcomb Falls; somewhere in Peru, he thought; in the mountains there, hunting for silver . . .

The minister was speaking now, in a voice so mellifluous, so artfully modulated, the words themselves were almost meaningless. Norris Harrodsen, impeccable and aloof, was still staring firmly at nothing—thinking perhaps of the sudden upswing of the market, American Telephone and Telegraph at 122, this astonishing surge in radio stock.

". . . Marry money, Tipton!" Horace Crowell's bony, elfish face, the harsh, dry cackle of laughter. "Marry money! That's how the world's fortunes have always been made—and kept . . ."

"But what about the *first* person," he'd asked, "the very first? *He* couldn't have married money."

"Oh—you mean the old Adam!" Horace had wagged his head, sardonic and gleeful. "Have no fear—*he* always had money: that's why they call him the old Adam . . ."

They said we were a democracy, but that wasn't true; people weren't equal. He'd learned that early enough. Society rose in a series of decreasing tiers, like that ancient tower—where had it been? in Miss Abbot's stereopticon—the rings narrowing to one small, lofty pinnacle. We had no royalty, no inherited titles. Money conferred *our* titles. Money, all-puissant, ran us. The Smart Money, we said; the Vested Money—our own special Almanach de Gotha, with its precise divisions and subdivisions. There was Old Money (the Harrodsens') and New Money (Tom Bush's ball-bearing plant over in New Haven). Yet it was more complicated, infinitely more subtle than that. Aunt Serena's Old Money was older (and therefore more prestigious) than Norris Harrodsen's, but Harrodsen had more *of* it, a lot more, and that acted as an equalizer: quality and quantity rose and sank in a fluctuating system of compensatory balances. "Society"—that was to say Old Money—instantly and instinctively despised New Money (which of course *it* had been decades or centuries earlier); but its disdain was ephemeral—give it a few years and the contemptible New Money became legitimized. You could see it all around you now—men who'd made a killing in moving pictures or cosmetics or oil were crowding into the pavilion, forcing their way; it was only a matter of time. What was it Grama Gaspa said? "There is no mountain so high a donkey loaded with gold cannot climb it." Fierce old Grama Gaspa—what a tonic she was—no, an antitoxin to the diamond-cool deceptions of this world . . .

Chapin had just spoken, his voice clear and incisive; Jenny kept glancing at him, as if to reassure herself that he was actually there, at the altar, in the flesh. She can't believe it, Tip thought suddenly; she simply can't believe in her fantastic good fortune—and his chest straitened in the old gripe of envy. Chapin had it all now—looks, education, background, and now the capital to launch his ventures . . . But I got the girl, Tip steadied; I got the girl even he wanted, the girl worth all the rest of them together—and his heart leaped like a colt in a meadow. He glanced sideways at Jophy. Her head was lowered, she was watching the service with a curious still intensity. While he watched, puzzled, something indescribably implacable and savage marked her features, then vanished as quickly; and in its place remained that rapt intensity, a shadow of boundless, unappeased longing . . .

It was over—he'd missed the exchange of rings. Chapin kissed Jenny, a quick, light kiss, neither perfunctory nor indulgent—then they were hurrying up the aisle, had vanished from sight while the organ burst into a tumult of peals and chords. Getting to his feet Tip saw that his mother was silently weeping; only his aunt's gaze was perfectly composed and serene . . .

"You're Chapin's brother."

Tip turned. He'd moved away from Serena, was easing his way toward Jenny now through the press at the sailing party when the man spoke; he was slender, almost fragile, with the face of an English aristocrat and fine amber eyes.

"Avery Calkins." He extended his hand, and Tip recognized him; he was head of the powerful Stock

261

Exchange firm of Calkins, Bliss, specialists in metals. "I spotted you at the wedding. There's a distinct resemblance."

"You flatter me," Tip laughed. "Chay's the good-looking one."

"Yes, he is, isn't he? Exceptional young man. Exceptional. Probably saved my life."

Tip started, said: "I beg your pardon?"

"Yes, indeed. First day he was back from the Army. Bunch of veterans, drunken rabble is what they were really." His eyes narrowed. "Turned on me like a pack of jackals, knocked me down, were actually kicking me! Chapin stood them off, the whole pack, and bundled me into a cab. Didn't he ever tell you about it?"

"No, he didn't."

"Mighty impressive performance. You must be proud of him."

"Well," Tip murmured. "Well, well . . ."

Jenny came up to them then, looking prettier and trimmer in a gray dress edged with pink, and cried: "Oh, I'm so glad you've met! Avery's a very special friend of ours. He brought us together, in a way . . ." Her little snub-nosed face was faintly flushed with excitement; she squeezed Tip's hand. "I'm so happy you could get away for the wedding and everything—you and Jophy!"

"Wouldn't have missed it for the world."

"What's your field, Ames?" Calkins asked.

"I'm in sales."

"Oh, come on, Tip—don't be so modest!" Jenny answered for him. "He's a sales manager for Alexander Hamilton Institute and he's brilliant—he's led the whole country for the past three years!"

"That so." Avery Calkins inclined his head a degree or two, and smiled; but his eyes were veiled with the expression Tip had learned instantly to recognize— the old disdain management held for sales; or, as Grama Gaspa might say, that capital held for labor. The two worlds . . .

"Jophy's just lovely," Jenny was saying, "I'm so glad to have got to know her at last."

"Yes," Calkins chimed in, "how'd you ever manage to win a stunning girl like that?"

"Superlative salesmanship," Tip answered, and they all laughed. Through the bobbing of heads and airy waving of hands Tip saw his brother move up to Jophy and murmur something, saw her turn with a sudden violent movement as though going on guard, lips parted, eyes alive with that fierce dark luster he knew. For one irrational instant Tip thought she was going to hit Chapin; then he saw her throw back her head and laugh, and raise her glass to her lips as though to toast him.

"—What a divine couple they make," Jenny was saying. "Look at them! Beautiful! They ought to be in pictures. Don't you think?"

"They certainly should," Calkins murmured, moving away.

"Maybe they will—I feel anything is possible tonight!" She blushed—she hadn't realized the implications in that remark until she'd said it. "Oh, it's so exciting!" she hurried on. "We're sailing at midnight. For Europe!"

"But you've been aboard."

"Oh, yes—but it was all wasted."

"Wasted!"

"Yes. Chay says I did the wrong scenes. Changing the guard at Buckingham Palace, the Paris opera, Versailles—Chay calls that the Dullard's Tour. He says it has nothing to with the *real* Europe, it's like the gesso masterpiece hidden by a contemporary poster. That kind of thing."

He grinned. "Good old Chay. What would we do without his esthetic sensibilities." He watched her eyes go wide with surprise, then harden defensively, and added: "Well, I think you saw the real Europe. I think Buckingham Palace is exactly the thing to see."

". . . You're sweet," she murmured after a moment. "You are . . . Chay told me you're a romantic."

"Did he?"

"He said you've found your true vocation—he says that's very rare, especially in a society like ours. He says you're the absolute epitome of the American Dream."

"Did he really?"

"Oh, yes!" Her sturdy little face was radiant. "Chapin's never wrong about things like that!"

He shook his head, looking into her eyes, said slowly and deliberately; "Chad knows a lot of things. But there are another lot of things he doesn't know anything whatever about."

"I don't believe you!"

"You should. I was there."

She looked directly at him now, with sudden importunate intensity—glanced off at Chapin, who was entertaining Jophy and several other young women; then peered down at her hands. She's afraid, Tip thought with a swift, heavy sense of affinity; deeply afraid—and she is willing to die before she shows it. We have more in common than I thought. Next to them a girl in a lemon-yellow dress with closely bobbed hair was saying with shivery feeling:

"—they're not telling us anything! Wally says not only were their bodies laid out side by side as if they were, you know, in bed together, but the Reverend Hall's body was *mutilated!*"

"What do you mean?" another girl asked her eagerly.

"They'd been removed, dummy. His *private parts*—" The Hall-Mills murder case. Of course.

Tip said to Jenny lamely: "I just mean—Chay isn't always right about everything. I know he *sounds* so positive, at times. Maybe that's only because he doesn't feel certain at all."

She nodded without conviction. "That's confusing, isn't it?"

"Yep. It is . . . *Ah, sweet mystery of life, at last I've found you,*" he sang softly, watching Chapin conclude an anecdote to a burst of feminine laughter and move off, as if on cue, working his way toward where they were standing.

"Yes," Jenny was saying. "It *is* a mystery. Isn't it?"

"No doubt about it."

"Mystery, mystery?" Chapin had reached them, had caught the word. His eyes slid from one to the other. "There *are* no mysteries. There are only the things we know and the things we don't yet know." Leaning forward he pressed his lips lightly to Jenny's brow, said: "Will you excuse us, love? There's something I need to show Tip." Slipping his hand under his brother's elbow he guided him out of the cabin and down the narrow corridor and out on deck, into a sudden rush of warm salt air, the light-glistered dark.

"That's better," Chapin said, and took a deep breath. "Awfully stuffy in there."

They moved to the rail. Ahead of them the Manhattan skyline winked and glittered; a new machicolated heavens low on the horizon, celebrating man's headlong ascendance. Chapin raised his arms to it in a grandiose, mocking embrace.

"Dear brother: one day all this will be yours—if I don't get it first . . .

Tip laughed. Chay wasn't high, he knew; he never drank much; yet a curious, tensed excitement seemed to be working in him.

"Greatest Show on Earth, isn't it?" he said genially. "Damn—I'm sorry to be leaving it, even for a month."

"I thought you loved Europe. You were furious when those mean old Hohenzollerns inconvenienced you . . ."

"Oh, I was—don't make any mistake about that. But it's a different kind of reality; a softer, weaker kind. This"—Chapin flicked a hand toward the geometric rain of lights—"is what's got hold of me now. The flurry, the rush—the big, roaring, hell-bent *adventure* of it. You know what I mean."

265

Tip nodded, watching his brother intently. Chapin seemed even more altered than he had at the wedding —as though a much harder, more aggressive shade had flowed into his epicene spirit. His face, in profile, looked sterner, more alert.

"You surprised me, Chay," he offered. "Going into business like that."

"Did I?"

"You always gave me the impression that it was too—too—"

"Too unspeakably vulgar?"

They laughed quietly, gazing down at the dock where the stevedores were still hurrying on board in a ragged line, absurdly dwarfed from this height, all back and shoulders, bent under huge burlap sacks.

"Yes," Chapin said, "I daresay I did. I was pretty obnoxious those days. The inevitable Cambridge product . . ." He sighed. "Fact is, something happened to me down there in Texas. Flying. The world looked so different from the air that I turned into something different myself. Everything began to look more real —and I wanted all of a sudden to be a part of it. Ride in the chariot myself. Up front." He turned and faced Tip. "You know what life is like? Really like? It's a great big parlor game of blind man's buff, only *everybody's* blindfolded, creeping around, stumbling and bumping into one another—and then this Lord High Umpire slips off your blindfold and you see everything—your playmates still foolishly groping their way around, and the way into the conservatory, and where the refreshments are, and everything else . . . I'm not laying claim to any superior insight; the Lord High Umpire just took off the blindfold, that's all."

Below them, faint and far-away, the band swung into "The Bells Are Ringing for Me and My Gal," and there was a burst of shrill cheering, like a triumphant horde assaulting some eastern citadel. High and ahead of them the office lights winked on and off.

Chapin said in a low, reminiscent tone: "You were

mad at me last time we stood looking out at the water—really good and mad. For a minute there I thought you were going to wallop me one. I deserved it, too, as I recall ... Now you've got the girl—and the whole New England territory, too; and not a single thing to get mad about."

"Well, I wouldn't go that far," Tip answered; but he laughed, liking his brother for the first time in many years.

"I would. I get around a good deal. I hear that you've burned up the track, Schoolboy."

Tip grinned. "When you call me that, smile."

"Yeah, they all use the term with affectionate respect. I've heard them. It's like the Babe, or the Little Corporal ... What a brilliant move that was, splitting commissions with your force. What a stroke!"

Tip glanced at him in surprise; Chapin *had* done his homework. "Where'd you hear that?"

"Oh, around and about. You've become a kind of minor-league legend." He clapped his hands abruptly, said: "Yep, you've done everything right, a cracker-jack crew that can beat anybody, absolutely anybody —and you're in the wrong boat on the wrong river."

Tip stared at him. "What do you mean by that?"

"Alec Ham. It hasn't any future for you, Tip. It's a one-shot. You sell your prospect and that's it, he's finished as a market, you can't go *back* to him. And it's a narrow market, too. There are woodchucks and hay-seeds ashamed to tell you they can't read, roughnecks making good money who wouldn't read your books if you paid them to ... That's what you don't see."

"Maybe so. And what's the happy solution?"

"Securities."

"You mean stocks and bonds? The market?"

"That's it." Chapin lighted a cigarette, blew smoke in a thin white plume toward the city lights. "I know what you're thinking: a bunch of pot-bellied pluto-crats slouched around the ticker at the Metropolitan

267

Club, chomping on cigars and sipping brandy, scheming up new ways to fleece the man in the street."

Tip grinned at him. "Grama Gaspa can't be all wrong."

"Nobody's all wrong," Chapin said with a trace of irritation, though he was smiling. "Sure—it happens. There *are* bloated plutocrats and they do chew on El Coronas and pluck the gullible. Now and then. My *point* is, things have changed. This isn't '93 any more, it isn't 1907. The man in the street is *in* the market —or he will be in the very near future, with both feet. *That's* where your woodchucks are heading—your nice little widows, too. Why should they grapple with double-entry bookkeeping when they can buy American Can or Anaconda and ride it all the way to the top?" He paused. "It's everybody's ball game, Tip. The market is wide open—and you can go *back* to those same customers time after time . . ."

Tip found himself staring hard at a silver-gray Rolls-Royce gliding majestically through the crowd down on the dock. "But my gang doesn't know anything about stocks . . ."

"Oh, hell—selling's the same game anywhere, isn't it, whether it's radios or cars or farming tools? Or soap. The same principles apply. Isn't that what you always said?"

Tip shook his head in slow wonder. "That's what I've always said." But Chapin was scowling down at his hands.

"Jesus, these sales types at the office. They've got a big-time broker complex, every last one of them. They've all gone to Princeton or Yale and they know which club you ought to belong to and who's a seven-goal prospect at Old Westbury, and they couldn't sell a jug of spring water to a Bedouin chief. They're order takers, Tip. Glorified spoiled clerks. They don't know a God damned thing about selling, about firing up a client, making a product or an idea seem indispensable—and they couldn't care less. I've watched them.

They sit around and fill each other's ash trays and wait for the phone to ring and gas along about just how good this fellow Bobby Jones really is with a putter—and the days fly by like wild geese going south . . ."

He turned and faced Tip again, said quietly, "My idea is to *pair* them: one of your sales crew with one of our Ivy League drones. Our man would initiate yours into the mysteries of the market, so-called, and set up the contacts and interviews; your boy would make the pitch, teach the club type how to sell. It's a sure-fire combination. What do you say?"

Tip thrust out his lip. "And you think," he said slowly, "I can just pick up my force and whisk 'em down here and point 'em in any direction you want. Just like a—like a bunch of wind-up toys."

"Oh, come on, Tip—this is no time for outworn sibling rivalry. Aren't we past all that? I'm talking about a plan that would make our fortunes."

"My crowd might not go for a deal like this."

"Ah, don't be a kidder. They'd lie down in front of the Twentieth Century Limited if you asked them to. Hell, you can talk a fish into flying, anyway—I know that. And they'll make more money than they've ever seen before. I guarantee it."

"If we did come in," Tip murmured, "before you could say Union Carbide my gang would take over. Leave your clubbies swinging on the garden gate. I'll tell you that."

"Of course they will! To the victor belong the commissions. We'll sweep the field—and *that's* the object of the game . . ."

His face, white in the smoky floodlight, was near Tip's; the eyes that Tip remembered, that curious soft shade of his father's, with those pale rings outside the pupils, like silver coronae; they glittered with assurance.

"You know, Chay, this is a very funny conversation."

"Isn't it, though?" His brother was smiling, but his eyes were still flat. "And very serious, too . . . Look, I'm no salesman—I don't have to tell you that. But I know what makes the wheels go round—the big ones and the little ones, too. Don't think I don't. I can spot the trends, the switches, new offerings, the rumors-under-the-rumors that spark the runs. I've learned how to read the tom-toms in that well-lighted jungle over there . . . And that's the way the country's going, Tip. Big roaring boom, all the way to the moon and back. The big boys want it, the country's ready for it, itching and aching to go. You can read it in the reports from the branch offices, the brokers' loans—the signs are unmistakable. And this is only the beginning. We're right on the leading edge of the biggest boom in the nation's history. Now's the time to get on board, while the express is getting up steam . . ."

Tip found himself following the inflections in his brother's voice—a habit he often fell into when he knew the direction a conversation had taken; it told him much more than the words themselves. Chapin had thought about this scheme for some time; why broach it now, on his very wedding night, just as he was leaving for his beloved Europe? . . . Why, if it were *my* wedding voyage, he thought with amused wonder, remembering the platform at North Station and Jophy's face rapt and glowing over the bursts of steam—why, my God, if anyone had even mentioned business to me at that moment I'd have clobbered him one. Well: each to his own . . . and he thought, for no reason he could see, of Antoinette Bouchard bending over his open palm in the parlor alcove, her face sad and lovely in the lamplight, and smiled in spite of himself.

No: Chapin had brought it up now because he wanted him to think about it for a while; read the papers, watch the market's heady climb, listen to the talk on the Street; Chapin wanted to give him time to sound out the sales force, call up the old magic to make it work. If he decided to. Chay had planned it this way. Yes. And there was more to it than that, too—Tip felt it deep in his belly, in the tips of his fingers. Chapin wanted him to hear this proposition here —right here at the rail of the most palatial of all the transatlantic liners—watching the easy parade of privilege and affluence that only the big money could command. *That* was the pitch, every bit as much as the deal itself . . .

"Well, let's not rush it," Chay was saying casually now, gazing at a woman farther down the rail with a striking, skull-like face and metallic hair that glinted like tarnished bronze coins in the vaporous light. "Give it some thought, turn it over a few times. I'll be back on the twenty-third. Let's get together then and see where we stand. I realize it's an unconventional idea. Most successful ideas are—I imagine you've already discovered that in your travels. If you're agreeable, I can set up a meeting and prepare the ground. And I believe we can talk Norris into the deal. He's a bit too rigid and old-school for my tastes, but he knows a highly lucrative idea when he sees one." He glanced sharply at the sales manager. "It's the answer, Tip. I'm convinced it's the answer. And I'd like to put it together with you and your people, if we can . . . But in any case, that's the way it's going to go. Whether you come in or not."

Abruptly he thrust himself away from the rail and said: "Let's get on back. We'll be sailing in fifteen minutes, and it'll take that long to pry the women away from each other." He clapped Tip on the shoulder. "Good hunting."

"Bon voyage," Tip answered, smiling at the curious salutation; it wasn't at all like Chay. He followed his brother's graceful, indolent movement through the midnight hilarity. Down in the salon the orchestra had begun to play "The Sheik of Araby," and he found himself whistling light cadences around the plaintive melody.

4

The meeting, six weeks later, was held in the conference room of Diehl, Harrodsen. There were only seven participants, and the long, beautifully polished conference table was designed to seat three times that many; but Tip knew why Norris Harrodsen had chosen it. The paneled wainscoting was walnut, the walls a cool, austere gray, the tall glass cabinets held row on row of Standard & Poor's and Moody's and other sets of market texts in red or black bindings, drawn up like antique infantry in line of battle. The very air, in marked contrast to the breezy bustle of the boardroom or the near frenzy of the wire rooms, had the portentous stillness of some great institutional library.

Harrodsen took the chair at the head of the table, and the others grouped themselves around him; only Chapin took a seat a little apart, as though to emphasize his position as sponsor, even mediator. Tip seated himself near the far end; it didn't matter to him where he sat—he was, after all, the outsider—and he wanted to be able to hold his listeners in the scan of his glance. Chapin, after a few light introductory remarks, turned the floor over to him and he spoke briefly and to the point—he knew Chapin had already outlined the plan in some detail—using these few moments to study his audience. Walter Diehl, the partner, sat on Harrodsen's right, a heavily built man with a square ruddy face and curly, rust-colored hair; on the Street he had the reputation for being impulsive and quick-tempered, given to violent enthusiasms and even more violent repudiations. Beside him sat Larry Bixby, the firm's sales manager, very tall, very handsome, stroke oar on Yale's undefeated 1912 eight, caught now between naked hope that the highly touted Schoolboy Ames could bail him out of the hole he was in, and sullen resentment that this hotshot upstart might euchre him out of his job.

On Harrodsen's left was Paul Saunders, the treasurer, thin, with a wan face and slender, tapering fingers. Tip didn't like his eyes; they were small and very cold. He was opposed to the whole scheme, Tip knew at a glance; he was going to be trouble. Beside him sat Randy Harrodsen, like Chapin in the research end; of course the old man was grooming his son for a partnership. His round, snub-nosed face was open, interested, persuaded neither one way nor the other. His father, at the head of the table, was studying Tip intently; there were intimations of vanity, of a certain testy good humor in the shrewd hazel eyes; but there was plenty of fiber there, too—Norris Harrodsen would make up his own mind, and the others would probably follow.

He concluded his presentation and sat quietly, watching Harrodsen, waiting.

"Highly unorthodox approach," Harrodsen said in that clipped, incisive manner. "Market's a very specialized field, Mr. Ames."

"That's true."

"I don't want to sound disparaging. But men have spent a lifetime mastering it. I trust you're aware of that."

"I realize that, sir. But it's been my experience that after a reasonable grounding in a given field, selling is a matter of principles—soundly and persuasively applied."

"You'll find it's a good deal more demanding than

fly-by-night correspondence courses, young fellow," Walter Diehl broke in. "Hell of a lot more hectic, too."

"My crowd is not in the habit of letting any grass grow under their feet. If you want action, I can promise you plenty of it."

"Well, we're not a lot of high-pressure drummers down here," Bixby offered in a defensive tone. "Banging doorbells, grabbing lapels. This isn't a bucket-shop operation, you know . . ."

Tip smiled. "My people have shucked off their bearskins for some time now. They know how to observe the proprieties. I don't have to remind you that Alexander Hamilton pays its sales far and away the highest commission rate in the country." He paused, said: "It was my understanding that you were interested in widening your market and increasing sales."

"We are," Norris Harrodsen answered. "We are indeed. Larry only meant that certain standards of conduct must be maintained."

"Of course."

"I believe you've initiated the interesting practice of splitting commissions with your force," Saunders observed; his voice was high and husky, as though he needed to clear his throat.

"That's correct."

"And would you continue that policy in the securities field?"

"I certainly would."

"We run a taut ship here, Ames."

Tip looked at him a moment. "Since it is *my* commission we're discussing, I fail to see how that would affect operating costs."

"I trust you could and would hold your force's expenses within proper limits."

"As well as any sales manager around," he said evenly. He decided he didn't like Saunders any more than Saunders liked him. The home office—which usually meant the treasurer—was invariably a trial, and this one would be particularly trying. "My men produce," he went on. "They've demonstrated that they're the best in the field, over a period of three years. I don't believe in muzzling the ox that treadeth out the corn. I *know* when a salesman has stepped over the line."

"A sales manager with a knowledge of *costs?*" Saunders said with a thin, skeptical smile.

"As a matter of fact I am just that." Saunders better find out right now who was going to run the sales force. "I would expect to have full authority over my crowd's drawing accounts just as I would expect to do my own hiring and firing."

"Tip's always been highly cost-conscious," Chapin interceded quickly. "Did you ever know a Berkshire Yankee who wasn't? Tip used to squeeze a nickel so hard he turned the Indian and the buffalo into a bloody minotaur!"

There were a few chuckles, the room palpably relaxed. Norris Harrodsen said, "By God, you might just pull it off. I think it's worth a try. Gentlemen?" He looked quickly around the table, encountered nods, smiles, a grunt of assent from Diehl; his gaze came back to Tip. "Now, what do you want, Mr. Ames?"

"Starting salary of $16,500."

Saunders gave a long, low whistle; Tip grinned at him. "You feel that's too much for a hard-working ox, Mr. Saunders?" Randy Harrodsen laughed and slapped the table. Tip took a slow, easy breath, said: "And a percentage of stock in the firm."

There was an instant's total silence, then a short, angry bark of exclamation from Diehl. Saunders was gaping at him in amazement, Bixby's face was frozen in alarm, so was Chapin's. Harrodsen's eyes had widened strangely, a little like Aunt Serena's.

"Out of the question!" Diehl snapped crossly. "You don't know what you're saying . . ."

"Stock, Mr. Ames?" Norris Harrodsen said. "What capital are you venturing to purchase it?"

"The proven record of the best sales force in the country."

"That is not capital, Mr. Ames." Harrodsen's lips were a thin bloodless line under the silver mustache. "Not remotely. I can't believe you're serious."

Ah. There it was. Still again. *There are those who pull at the seine in all weather, and those who sit in paneled rooms counting the gold.* He thought of Annabella Gaspa standing in the hallway in her oilskins, glowering at him. Oh yes. Capital called the turn, laid down the conditions, determined all deals, all courses of action. There they sat, very still now, their well-bred faces grave with disapproval, their eyes veiled with hostility. Chapin was gazing out the window, frowning, running his thumb lightly along the edge of his jaw . . . They all looked remarkably alike, now. He had assaulted their Ivy League exclusivity, violated the protective web of their sodality of privilege, or unwritten prohibition—above all, he had broken the Eleventh Commandment: Thou shalt not place labor on an equal footing with capital . . . He had reminded them of who they were, who he was.

Harrodsen said coolly: "At the end of six months or so, if things work out as anticipated, we might talk about an overridage on sales, possibly a title. Further than that, we are not prepared to go." His eyes glinted, there was not even the trace of a smile at the corners of his lips. The upstart drummer was being put in his place.

"Well, I'll have to think it over." He rose quickly. "I'll give you a decision the first of the week if that's satisfactory. Thank you for your time, gentlemen." He glanced at his brother, but Chapin was standing with the others, ranged beside them; facing him with the others. Chapin, who *had* capital and so would always have it, who was furious with him for snitching, for breaking the gentleman's code. The hell with him, he thought, shaking hands and turning away. Let them hear it once, anyway; do them good. Even if no one *could* do anything about it, cross that measureless, infuriating gulf . . .

It was easy enough to persuade the force to go along. They were hungry, they were restless; they'd seen their market drying up all around them; and they read the papers, they'd been watching GE and Atchison and Woolworth along with everyone else.

"And besides," as Jack Darcey said, "we've beaten out those lugs down in New York, out in Chicago, we've lapped the field—what'll we do for an encore?"

Only Maury Zimmerman showed reluctance. "I like Alec Ham. It's got class. Who else pays a thirty percent commission? Bond salesman—Jesus, they're the dumbest sons of bitches the world's ever seen, they don't even know how to find the can . . ."

"Then think how superior you'll feel, waltzing in there and taking it all away from them," Tip told him. "Think how you'll be raising the intellectual level of Wall Street."

The crowd laughed and Jack said: "You object to making more money, Zim? You're happy here in Bluenose Boston?"

Maury shrugged. "I owe Alec Ham a lot."

"You owe them flat feet and ulcers, that's what you *owe* them!"

"Simmer down, Jack," Tip said. "Of course you owe them a lot, Maury. We all do. But we did the job; the debt's paid, as far as I can see. And my brother's right—the vein's running thin. We've given it a good run; let's get into this new ballgame, show them what we can do."

In the end Maury agreed to go along—they all did; if the Schoolboy was for it, that was good enough for them. They were nothing if not loyal.

Down in New York Frank Delahant heard him out, smiled a fond, rueful smile, and wished him luck.

"You don't seem surprised," Tip said.

Delahant shook his head. "I figured something like

this was in the cards. I've been wondering how long we'd hold you. Well, I don't know but what you might be right—it certainly looks as though it's the thing to get into, these rip-roaring days . . ." He stood up and extended his hand. "I'll miss you, Tip. One hell of a lot. Let's keep in touch, now."

Jophy was something else again. She became quite still, her full lips thinned; she turned from the stove with a long fork in her hand.

"Securities," she echoed. "You mean the market? The stock market?"

"Well, sure, the best stocks are listed on the Exchange . . ."

"—But that's speculating!" she burst out. "With money, other people's money—"

"Now, hold on," he said patiently. "You're investing in the capital stock of a—"

"Gambling, you mean." She made a sharp gesture of distress, set a bowl of spinach in front of Joey, who was leaning back absurdly in his high chair. Tip hooked a thumb in his belt, watching her. So sold on the scheme had be become that it was inconceivable to him that she would take it this way; it shook him. He realized he should have brought it up later, with Joey asleep, the evening meal behind them, but he'd just come in, crackling with enthusiasm, he'd had to break the news bang, right off the bat . . .

"It's not gambling, Jo. We're talking about shares of stock in American business, honey. Why, that's shares in the country itself."

"Paper," she muttered with heavy scorn. "Worthless paper, floated around to snare the suckers."

"The *paper*," he said with a trace of exasperation, "is stock certificates, and they stand for cars and refrigerators and copper tubing, that's what they stand for . . ."

She paused in the midst of feeding Joey, who was shaking his head now, refusing the food, and looked at Tip with an expression he couldn't read.

279

"But you're a *salesman* . . ."

"I'll still be selling. It's just a different commodity, that's all."

"That's not true—you've been offering a kind of freedom, a way to set people *free* of the bankers and lawyers and money-men. Here you'll just be luring them into the whole, deadly system . . ."

"Jo, it isn't *deadly* and I'm not luring anybody anywhere! The public's *in* the market, right now, coming in by the thousands every day—that's the whole point. We may be on the rim of the biggest boom this country's ever seen; why shouldn't the man in the street share in it?"

"For heaven's sake, Tip, stop *selling* me," she exclaimed. "Damn it, I'm not a prospect, I'm not a sale you're making to fill the rotten quota! I'm your wife. Remember?"

Shocked, he fell silent, watched her unhappily as she bent away from him and said: "Come on, Joey. Eat your supper, now." But the boy was staring from one of them to the other, his large dark eyes—Jophy's eyes—huge with apprehension. She must have felt it too, because she passed her hand over his dense, curly hair absently. In a flat, low voice she said: "That sounds like him, all right."

"Sounds like who?"

"You said Diehl, Harrodsen, didn't you?" Her eyes burned up at him from under the dark winged brows. "It was Chapin's idea. Wasn't it?"

"Why yes, in point of fact it was. I was going to tell you, but you started climbing all over me . . ."

"I thought so," she said.

"He's convinced my force can learn the ropes in no time, and beat everyone out."

"I thought so," she repeated, and her jaw set. "Another one of his slick quarterdeck schemes—only *you're* the one who's got to lower for the whale . . ."

"What's the sense in that kind of talk?" he protested. "That's what I am—I'm a salesman, I go out and make the sales . . ."

She bit down on her lip. "You've already decided, then. Made up your mind."

"Yes," he answered, more sharply than he'd intended, "as a matter of fact, I have."

"Then what are we arguing about it for? What's the sense in my saying anything?"

"Honey, it's the chance of a lifetime . . ."

"—It's the *mistake* of a lifetime!" she said violently. "That's what it is!" Joey started to cry then, and she caught him up to soothe him, her hand stroking his narrow little back. She shook her head at Tip. "Don't you see it? Don't you see what he's up to?"

"Now look," he said, getting angry in spite of himself, "how in hell can you say that? You don't know anything about the business world, you've admitted you don't."

"I know enough to see when somebody's tricking you! He always uses people—"

"Now, listen here, Jo—"

"—he'll just use you till he's got all he wants, and then he'll drop you and move on! He's a *collector*, Tip —he'll always be one; he doesn't care about people, the way you and I do—he lives for *things*, to possess things . . ."

"*I* know that," he said. "What's the matter, Jo? Afraid I can't handle Chapin? Because I can. I always could." He paused, watching her closely. "Or is it something else, Jo? You're not by any chance the one who's afraid of him, are you?"

"Don't be ridiculous!" Her eyes flashed at him whitely. "Why in God's name should I be afraid of Chapin? He can't steer his own course. Why do you think he's gone down there to New York? He's decided he's going to *show* Serena . . . yes, and now you're going to *show* him; isn't that what it's really all about? Isn't it?"

She had passed into the little bedroom off the hallway and was settling Joey in his crib, her hands flying over the little blue-and-white flannel coverlet, while Tip stood in the doorway in his shirtsleeves, jacket still slung over one shoulder. Was that what it was all about? He didn't believe it—he was damned if he believed that. Joey had stopped crying, was hiccuping a series of low, subdued sobs, as though he'd sensed this grownup commotion was too momentous to contend with; but his eyes were still frightened.

"It's what they've always done," Jophy went on, her voice hot now, closing the bedroom door, brushing past him into the living room. "The robber barons, the Morgans and the Carnegies and the Harrimans, it's how they got rich, climbing up over the blood and bones of people like us. Why won't you ever see that? Captains of industry. *Captains* . . ." Her voice roughened, her lower lip went slack with scorn. "They profane the word."

He said: "Oh for God's sake, you sound like Grama! Next you'll start ranting about the land sharks and crimps—"

"Have you got a better word for them? Do you? . . . They're the enemy," she ground out. "The *enemy . . .*"

"—All right, then," he came back hotly, "then so am I!"

She looked at him as if he'd struck her, the marvelous long planes of her bright face shadowed; the jet-dark eyes that curved at their corners like some ancient queen's were suddenly bewildered. "What are you saying . . . ?"

"It's true!" He couldn't stop himself now if he'd wanted to. "Who do you think you married?—some Wobbly riding the rails, some bronzed son of the soil in a blue work shirt? Well, I did all that—yes, and plenty! I lugged hundred-pound sacks of flour for Horace Crowell, I shoveled stock into the beaters at the mill till my arms were ready to drop off . . . I used to lie in bed at night—after I'd done *my* studying—and pray. And do you know what for? that I wouldn't get sick. Yes! So I wouldn't get laid off, so there'd still be money coming in . . . You think it's something noble, something heroic, sweating at day labor? I'll tell you what it is—it's something to get away from as far and fast as you can. There isn't one God damned thing glorious about it. Not one!"

He broke off, flexing and flexing his right hand. There was a silence. He glanced at Jophy, glanced away again. Instead of the ferocious outburst he'd set himself for, she lowered herself into a chair and locked her hands in her lap, her head down. He was swept with remorse: here she was, still tired from moving into this new apartment and caring for Joey, she was three months pregnant—what in hell was the matter with him? He had no business pounding away at her like that . . . He moved up to her and held her head in his hands, pressed it against his thigh.

"I'm sorry, honey girl," he murmured. "I am. I didn't mean to blow off at you like that."

"It's all right. I didn't, either."

"It was only that you—you surprised me so."

"I know." She was weeping now, in perfect silence. He could count on one hand the number of times he'd seen her weeping, and it shook him hugely. He stood there, stroking her rich dark hair.

". . . I'll give it up if you want, Jo." He didn't think he could get the words out, but he did. "I mean it. If that's what you want. Hell, all I want is to make you happy—you know that."

He could feel her shake her head. "No. You've got to do—what you've got to do. I guess." She tried to laugh once, grew sober again. "It's only that it's Chay's kind of thing, it's not yours . . . I just think you'll come to hate it."

"Why should I hate it? It's what America's all about. It'll mean more money—we'll be able to have a real home of our own, go places and do things; you want that. We can sail out over those horizons—you know, to Samarkand, wherever . . . What's wrong with that?"

For answer she shook her head, but slowly this time, as though to clear it; her arm stole around his waist.

"What's the matter, Jo?"

". . . I'm afraid," she said simply. And now he could feel her whole body trembling.

"Afraid of what, honey girl?"

"I don't *know* what." And she gripped him as if she were drowning far out at sea. "That's why I'm afraid."

He held her as tenderly as he knew how, murmuring reassurances. They had each other, they had Joey, they were young; what was there to be afraid of? He would take care of them, fend for them, provide for them handsomely—there wasn't anything on this vast earth he couldn't do once he buckled down and put his mind to it; he knew it at the very bottom of his heart.

"Trust me, Jo," he said. "I can handle it. With bells. You'll see."

"I hope so," she said.

5

"All right, gentlemen." Norris Harrodsen extended the stained, battered crew hat like a chalice. "Choose your weapons!"

Skeets Brohammer reached in, plucked out a slip of paper. "It says 'brassie' . . ."

"Right. That'll be your club. That's the wrinkle this year. I'm calling it Russian Roulette Golf. The club you draw is the one you've got to use for all shots."

"—But that's crazy!" Skeets protested over the laughter. "I can't putt with a *brassie* . . ."

"Sure you can," Walter Diehl told him; his square face was already brick-red, though not from the sun. "You just think you can't. Drink up."

"What blesses one blesses all." Harrodsen smiled his frosty smile, his hazel eyes glinting. "Want to test your ingenuity. See how resourceful you really are." Chapin watched him move through the crowded locker room, passing the hat around. Norris had taken over the Hawkhurst Country Club on Dungeness Point for the firm's Grand Gymkhana and Frolic, as he was fond of calling it. It was an annual event, and he always put a lot of thought into it.

"At least it's better than last year, when he had us out there playing tennis with every God damned thing except a racket." That was Century Gifford, who had been football captain at Yale, and a three-letter man. "I drew a frying pan with a bent handle."

"And you still beat everybody," Chapin reminded him.

"No, he didn't—Tip beat him," Clarence Phelps said. He looked like a cartoon newsboy in the oversize plus fours, with the gold cap cocked on the back of his head. "Tip beat him with that sawed-off canoe paddle. Isn't that right, Tip?"

Chapin remembering now, eyed his brother who was fingering the mashie niblick he had drawn. Tip grinned and shook his head. "I don't know—I guess so."

"He'll do it again, too!" Jack Darcey emptied his glass with a flourish. "One more of these and I'll play with an Alpenstock."

"One more of those and the Alpenstock will play *you,*" Maury Zimmerman told him.

"Far side of brave, near side of reckless." Jack poured himself another three fingers. "That is—great—Scotch. Who's your bootlegger, Mr. Harrodsen? King George V?"

"Matter of fact I believe the man *has* done business with the Prince of Wales." The hat was empty now and Norris Harrodsen clapped it on his head and said: "All right. I've picked the last three holes—we don't want to be out there all day. We've got a lot on the program. How about the pot, Walter? Everybody in?"

"Everybody except Saunders," Web Bowers said, and there was general laughter among the sales force; the Treasurer was a notorious pinchpenny.

"How about a little side bet?" Jack Darcey called. "I've got fifty says Tip will take it all."

"You're crazy," Randy Harrodsen said. "Look what he drew!"

"I don't care if he drew a Siamese crutch—he'll still win."

"I'll take twenty of that," Walter Diehl said, and drank. "Century'll beat him."

"You're on." Jack glanced around the room. "Anyone else?"

"I'll take the balance," Chapin heard himself say. The locker room turned suddenly quiet. Both Randy and Larry Bixby were watching him with an odd, quizzical expression; Darcey opened his mouth to say something, closed it again.

Zimmerman said: "Bet against your own *brother?*" in a tight, incredulous tone.

"I never bet against a three-letter man," Chapin answered lightly.

"You'll regret it," Darcey said, and looked away.

"All right, boys," Norris broke in. "Drink up, now. We want to get started."

They straggled out onto the eighteenth hole brandishing glasses and clubs and bottles; and from the slate terrace around the pool the women watched them, shading their eyes.

"Norris is wearing that dreadful hat again," Corinne Harrodsen observed. "I've tried to throw it out twice but he won't part with it. Says it brings him luck."

"Boys will be boys," Jophy Ames said, looking down at her bare brown toes.

"Especially," Jenny Ames added, "when they're grown men."

"Oh, let them have their fun," Corinne smiled. "Does them good to frisk around, tell each other how wonderful they were in their salad days."

"It's better than one of those Chicago junkets," Eleanor Diehl said in her forbidding voice.

There was a short silence. Across the lush fairway they could see the men taking practice swings and calling back and forth in gusts of laughter.

"They're having such fun!" Suzy Diehl exclaimed. "They always do."

"Susan," her mother said, "pull up those straps! I don't want to have to tell you again."

"Oh, Mother—I'm just trying to get a smooth, even tan."

Eyes half closed, Jenny watched Suzy Diehl. She was a plump, pretty thing with her mother's pert good looks, her father's rust hair; it was bobbed square across her sturdy, low forehead, curled in charmingly at the corners of her mouth. She was seventeen. And ripe. Easing the straps over her round little shoulders again she was staring across the fairway.

"Mr. Ames is wonderful," she said impulsively. "—I could really take a tumble for him!"

"Susan!" Eleanor Diehl said sharply, though some of the wives laughed. "Is that the sort of thing you learn at Smith?" Then, as though her rebuke implied a belittling of the subject, she added judiciously: "Of course Chapin is a handsome man, very attractive."

"Oh, I mean *Tip* Ames!" the girl cried. "He's so *real*." And Jenny opened her eyes then and stared at her. The girl meant it, clearly. "He can make you laugh, too. Remember last year, when he did the crazy juggling act with those phony eggs? He's wonderful—he's got so much vitality! You know, pezzazz . . ."

"Yes," Jophy echoed dreamily. "He's got pezzazz, all right."

Turning her head Jenny covertly studied Jophy: the fine-cut cameo profile, the long, slender throat; that jet-black hair, still unbobbed, caught up simply with one amber pin, glossy-smooth and shining in the filmy August light. The fierce life in the dark, curving eyes. As if conscious of her scrutiny Jophy stirred, raised one brown knee, lowered it again. She'd borne two children and lost a third, but her body was as lithe and elegant as ever, and at the same time unmistakably voluptuous. She was wearing one of the new skin-tight bathing suits without a skirt, and her thighs—she'd just swum several laps with an effortless crawl, as though the water was truly her element—her thighs gleamed wet-gold, in a long, sensuous, slow-swelling curve from knee to pelvis . . .

Jenny flooded with envy so intense it made her

tremble. She closed her eyes with an effort of will. I'd
like her as a friend, she told herself; a real friend,
open and intimate. Closer than Nan Spear or Bunny
Ogden. Someone to talk to—honestly. If it were possible. But there was that current of something between
Jophy and Chapin—some invisible, mysterious, fine
wire that linked them. And for either of them to touch
it, they knew, would burn them both to a cinder . . .
Ridiculous. But there *was* something there, perhaps
neither as deep as desire nor as fierce as hatred,
something almost outside those things. She'd alluded
to it once, as casually as she knew how; and Chapin
had brushed it aside with that mocking tone he
always adopted to mask his most serious involvement.
Well; she'd find out about it one fine day. Isolate
it. She had—to coin a phrase—all the time in the
world . . .

"Lord, I wish those Walsh Committee hearings
would be over and done with," her mother was saying.
"All that nasty muck-raking—what good can it do beyond causing people to lose faith in their own government?"

Oh my God, Jenny thought, not that again, not all
that over and over again.

"She killed him," she declared flatly, flung her
upraised arm over her eyes.

There was a little flurry of astonishment and Barbara Gifford cried, as Jenny knew she would: "Florence *Harding*? Her own *husband*?"

"Think it's never been done before? President or no
President."

"Jenny," her mother said, "you are truly inexcus-
able."

"I try."

"But it was ptomaine poisoning," Betty Langevin
said earnestly, "the sea food—"

"Yes. Alaska crab," Eleanor Diehl concluded.

"Funny nobody else on board got it," Jenny pressed
on. "Only handsome, charming old Warren G. Look at

the facts; numero uno, there *wasn't* any Alaska crab on the steward's manifest at all. Segundo, he was recovering from pneumonia at the time, not ptomaine—or trying to . . ."

"But why," Blanche Saunders cried, as Jenny knew *she* would, "would she want to kill him?"

"To get him out of it," she answered matter-of-factly; she wasn't really enjoying this—not the way she used to, anyway—but it was infinitely better than lying here listening to them. And admiring Jophy's smooth brown legs. "He knew it was going to blow up in his face, he'd seen the handwriting by then. He couldn't believe they'd all betrayed him, he wanted to go. Maybe she figured if he checked out it might all disappear . . ."

"But then who poisoned *her*?" Jophy asked in the silence.

This set them off into even greater consternation. Eleanor Diehl said sharply: "Why, she's alive *right now*. What on earth are you talking about?"

"She's one very sick cookie," Jophy went on, unperturbed. "She's not long for this world."

"You mean—" Suzy Diehl gaped at her "—it's a gigantic conspiracy?"

"You bet your boots." Jophy was sitting up now. "Daugherty's behind it all. That funny-business 'suicide' of what's-his-name. Smith."

Barbara Gifford said, "But he shot himself. They said he shot himself. Out of remorse."

"Do you honestly think a man mortally afraid of firearms would go out and buy a gun and blow his head off with it? Oh, no—if you're going to do away with yourself you pick the most familiar way out, not the strangest."

She *is* really intelligent, Jenny thought; there was a time we could have been friends. Good friends, confiding. Most of my crowd are incapable of thinking through something like that. Usually we either behave like children, racing around the lawn playing at

Lancelot and Guinevere, and *really* waiting for Daddy to come roaring up the drive in the Pierce Arrow, scattering the gravel; or like some overindulged, sleek new breed of concubines—granted everything, absolutely everything, except freedom . . .

Frankly now she watched her sister-in-law. Jophy was sitting forward, the fine long legs straddling the deck chair, narrow high-arched feet hooked around the bottom. Her voice was quick, spinning wild tales about that arch-manipulator Daugherty's savage efforts to silence anyone who might say too much about the parade of strange deaths that had visited so many of the Marion Gang.

So she's thought about it, too, Jenny considered in great surprise, not listening to her. Strange . . . There she sat—stunningly beautiful, endowed with that unique, intangible power to captivate others—even Chapin; mother of an imaginative boy and a lively little girl, married to a man who adored her—she'd seen it in Tip's eyes a thousand times. Favorite of the gods . . . and yet there was that curious, almost desperate restlessness you could never quite place. Could she be lonely, too? What did she want? *What did she want—!* The things we revealed about ourselves on a lazy summer's day; the things! And for no reason at all Jenny felt tears swimming against her lids. Despite herself she felt a hot sense of kinship with this tempestuous girl. Ah, women were such fools—suffering in the dark, in silence; playacting, adapting, striving to recover what parched ground they could through dissembling, subterfuge, pretense: the brittle, thin weapons of the weak . . .

Europe had fleshed out the great shock of her own discovery: she hated all ships after that voyage. Their first night together had been so monstrously different from everything she'd longed for or wondered about, even vaguely feared. Nothing about her, she knew, could ever be the same. Ever. The great liner had rolled gently in the off-shore swells, counter-point to the sexual act itself. At first Chapin had been gentle, deft, just as she had imagined he would be; his touch infinitely more exciting than the tentative, guilt-burdened pleasures she had now and then allowed herself. Gripping his head, his fine, broad shoulders, she could feel herself awaken in a gathering rush of new, almost fearsome sensations. She struggled to free herself, to run with their coursing pressure—and then, magically, she had burst free: stars, white-hot stars burst over her, burning, as if stamped on her aroused flesh, until she was crying aloud—for what she did not know . . . and then she *did* know, with certainty— it was to feel her body made whole, star-borne—

"Oh my God, Chay, oh glorious, oh yes—!" until finally she half-opened her eyes—to find his face, in the faint glow from a porthole, peering coolly down at her. He was—he was *studying* her. Was he? She was conscious of a sharp twinge of uncertainty, beat it back. Well, that's all right, if he wants that, if it pleases him, I'm his and I want to be, to give him pleasure, let him, she told herself; but the shadow of uneasiness remained. That wasn't what love ought to be, love between two people. Was it? Willfully she shut her eyes tight again, crying out her great need . . .

He had left her then, to prepare himself perhaps, she wasn't sure; was back almost at once, running his tongue with feathery ardor over her breasts, her belly and thighs; he was—oh God!—entering her at last, a taut, straining pressure that hurt a little, as they said it might—then broke inward in easy release. Complete! She flung her legs high, arched her back. He was stroking within her, deep within her, the bands of tension shattered and she was sobbing her delight, over and over. She could hear herself as if from a distant corridor, but mingled now with other voices—a woman's laughter, and then a man's voice as if heard in some morning dream, loud, shockingly near: "—absolutely extraordinary!"—and forcing her eyes open she saw that the cabin door was flung wide to the companionway, its hard yellow light blazing in.

"Chapin, the door! The door is open—!"

"Yes," he answered. "So it is."

And she saw his head was raised, his eyes were riveted on the open doorway, glowing with unbounded gratification. The yellow light darkened; a shadow—a thin, white shadow—slipped out of sight, and the light from the corridor swept in again. Steward. Was it? A steward had just been standing there . . .

"—Chapin!" she cried, "for God's sake, close the door!"

"Not just yet," he said softly, between his teeth. "Not just yet, darling . . ."

He continued his motion, a whiplash rhythm that inflamed her, burning now, punishing—*punishing?*—and finally, cooled and tensed, she felt what must be his ejaculation, and still he was not spent, thrusting and withdrawing, holding her in a firm, imprisoning grip, as though he intended never to stop. She pleaded with him then, wept and struggled, begged him in mounting revulsion to release her, but it only seemed to increase his desire. Her head was whirling, all the stars were blotted out, forever; she felt feverish and sick, nothing she could say or do would ever matter— she was condemned to lie here, suffering this interminable plunging in her vitals, until the world ended; sobbing, gasping, she wondered if she had truly gone mad . . .

What was most deranging of all was Chapin's manner the following morning—his attitude of breezy good-humor, of pleasant attentiveness; as though nothing had happened. He was utterly unaffected by her furious sense of outrage, her icy anger; he joked and laughed during breakfast, pointing out various passengers and making up witty anecdotes about them. She stared at him in hollow bewilderment. But shock had rendered her taciturn. She could say nothing; there was nothing at all to say. And routine aboard ship made a scene impossible, anyway—table companions, the continual intrusion of stewards, the loungers on deck. But that night she refused him.

"What's the matter?" he asked her.

"I'm ill," she answered coldly.

"Just as you like," he murmured, and the light indifference in his voice upset her more than anything else.

Two worlds, then. Were there? The ever-so-proper social urbanity of the salon by day, this savage, humiliating nocturnal ritual. Sitting huddled in her streamer chair though the sun was warm, sipping bouillon, watching the great slate seas shouldering away eastward, listening vaguely to the shouts of the deck tennis players, her just-awakened body clamoring for this new arousal, she wrestled with the matter. That such sheer ecstasy should be manacled to this awful debasement—it was too cruel. Too cruel! An English couple had watched her with amused scorn when they'd gone down for lunch—she was sure of it; confronting their cabin steward was an agony. Were all men like this, essentially? Her mother had made a few allusions, very brief, very veiled, to their often uncontrollable desires . . . But his! No, they *weren't* all like this; she knew. Chapin had planned it, this demeaning act, the source of his pleasure had derived in some way from her very humiliation—and something more, there was something more she couldn't take hold of . . .

What a silly little fool she'd been. With raging fervor she wished she had sought out the maids, the cooks, the governesses who had passed through the Harrodsen household, even the street girls she'd glimpsed on lower Broadway, gathered to herself every scrap of information she could on sexual patterns, practices. It was all that mattered—the only, *only* thing that mattered!—and she had dutifully obeyed the unwritten law: mustn't ask, we don't talk about such things, well-bred young ladies do not concern

294

themselves—and here she was, as precious and ignorant as some Mandarin princess with bound feet. *Virgin*—what a travesty! . . .

Chapin had insisted they visit Paris first. Their
first evening in the City of Light he vanished; she
came back from a fitting at Worth's to find him gone.
No, the head concierge informed her impassively, his
eyes flickering over her face, monsieur had left no
messages. She sat on the edge of the watered-silk Ré-
camier divan and gazed at the trembling leaves of the
plane trees, the tinsel dance of lights around the
Étoile. This was what it would be like, then: Chapin
going his own way evenings—all evenings—and a
stately pavane as a proper married couple through
the daylight hours. She was caught in one of those
hideous dreams where one is falling an incalcul-
able distance, with time for all manner of boundless
dread . . .

"— I am not a whore!" she cried out at the soft brocade draperies, the diamond-mullioned windows—was
shocked at the intensity of her outburst. Just the
same, it was true: she had come with quite a dowry,
hadn't she? That ought to give her some equality in
her marriage. But that wasn't true. In spite of suffrage and all this talk of sexual emancipation, she
was still her husband's property—or if not his property, in an inferior position to him. She could not go her
own way, without devastating consequences; he could.
There was the inescapable, the immeasurable difference.

She heard voices out in the hotel corridor, a woman's shrill laughter, uncoiling bright as a sparkler.
She stirred, clasped her hands tightly in her lap.

But what, then? Run home, throw herself into her
parents' arms, confess all? Who would believe her?
She could see their covert glances. No, no, she'd imagined it—Jenny was always high-strung, overly nervous and imaginative, she was always rushing to extravagant, insupportable conclusions, she always

loved to shock . . . her own hard-mastered role mocked her now. Well-bred ladies were notoriously skittish on their wedding nights—everyone knew that. And Chapin wouldn't grant her a divorce, anyway; why should he? She was part and parcel of his grand design now—she realized it without question; he was a partner in her father's firm, he handled the money of his own family and college friends. She *was* his capital.

And what would she do if she left him? They hadn't equipped her to teach, or to type, or to *do* anything, but—

There was no use lying to herself. She loved him—that was at the core of it; shocked, mortified, enraged at his calculated, humiliating use of her, she still loved him. And now there was that new clamor of her body, the fresh memory of those stars of pure delight; to leave Chapin would be to forgo even the possibility of that for the rest of her life, sentence herself to abstinence, the empty ritual of good works—she could not do it, she couldn't—!

Round and round. She dozed off, for all her impotent raging, woke with a violent start when he came in.

"—where on earth have you *been?*" she cried.

"Oh, around and about." When he removed his hat she saw that his fine, silky hair was disheveled. Behind him the long windows were grayed with the dawn light.

"But I *worried,*" she protested, and went up to him.

"You shouldn't have." He held her at arm's length, firmly—and now she could smell brandy, and perfume—heavy, cloying perfume; he was reeking with it. She'd guessed where he'd been, what he'd been doing; but this acrid confirmation enraged her.

She cried: "Chapin, how *could* you—?"

"How could I what, darling?"

She watched him; a long, very long moment, through which complete awareness burned its way like a torch through steel. Whoever risked most became most vulnerable, and therefore suffered most: *there* was the deepest truth to life. To love was to abandon power; to withhold love was to assume it. There was pleasure in inflicting pain, and it was— was it?—deeper than granting pleasure. Chapin had the power, then: to hurt, to go his own way, to hurt again . . .

But she was her father's daughter—and she knew that, too. Very well. She had made a mistake: a crucial, immense mistake. In the disappointments of her adolescence she had created a façade to circumvent the demands of her peers; then she'd met Chapin and in her need had thrown that façade away, as one discards China dolls and miniature tea sets, and cast her lot with him. But that didn't have to be the end of it. No—she had worked up a role over nine years, good enough to fool everyone; she could work up another one ably enough; all it took was imagination and an iron discipline, and she possessed both in abundance. Only, having relinquished so much so quickly, it would take time; a certain amount of time.

Her eyes had filled with tears—tears of mortification, of simple rage; but tears were tears, they could mirror sorrow, contrition, acquiescence just as well. Couldn't they?

"—an idiot," she heard herself stammer, blinking rapidly, "it's my fault—I drove you there, didn't I? I see that now—I've failed you. Out of misplaced pride . . . " He was staring at her, a bit uncertainly. "It's my fault—ah, what a stupid little idiot I've been! Forgive me, Chay . . ." She touched his arm—and in spite of everything she felt, everything she was striving to accomplish, that hot interior flood of sensation had begun; it shook her a little. Timorously she repeated: "Forgive me, Chay. Can't you forgive me?"

She looked down; her hand on his arm was trembling. All at once he caught her to him with sudden fierce avidity, his hands tight over her buttocks, his phallus an iron rod against her belly. She was shaking violently.

"Maybe you *do* understand me, Jenny—maybe you do after all! What I need, the things I need . . . oh, you *are* a treasure!"

He had swept her up and carried her into the bedroom to the great Empire bed; he was tearing away her gown in a swift, silent frenzy. She helped him rip it away and fell back again, gave way utterly to every demand, every bestial excursion . . . But now a strange eye, as if from some distant, mindless star, watched coldly, dispassionately. She wanted to sob aloud her laughter. On the far side of the great mirror the counters were reversed: the slave became the master, the master the slave. The weapons of the weak were, after all, still weapons . . . She could wait.

"—Of course he'd been seeing her for years," Eleanor Diehl was saying now in her tight, vindictive voice. "She *claims* it's his child, and I imagine she's right."

"What's her name?" Blanche Saunders asked.

"Nan Britton. They've been meeting everywhere for years."

"Yes—even in a coat closet in the White House," Barbara Gifford exclaimed. "With his wife right there, upstairs!"

"You're not serious!"

"That's what they say . . ."

"Why not?" Jenny heard herself say aloud. "Maybe they could hear dear old Florence singing, 'Look for the Silver Lining,' and she could hear *them*—"

"Jenny!"

They were all staring at her, open-mouthed, shocked. Even Jophy was watching her with a thoughtful expression. Gazing back at her she laughed lazily, closed her eyes.

They were talking about Harding scandals out on the links too, though in a rather different vein. Chapin—he'd drawn a spoon but it didn't matter, he detested golf anyway—listened with amused detachment.

"They lost their God damned heads, is what they did," Walter Diehl was saying. He addressed his ball seriously, but hooked it into the rough under a stand of locust trees, and cursed feelingly. "Denby, the lawyers—the whole crowd. All they had to do w̄as stick to the story that the deal was for secret military appropriations, so no competitive bidding was necessary . . ."

Randy said: "But what about those cash payments of Harry Sinclair's?"

"Yeah, how about all those crisp new sponduliks?" Blazer Blaydon emitted his hooting crow of laughter, flailed at his ball, topped it badly and clucked in sudden disappointment. The Blazer was solidly built, with a smooth, cherubic face and knot of straw-colored hair that stood up on the very top of his head like a scalplock. A Yale man, he would have graduated with Century Gifford, but he'd been expelled when he'd failed to get a waitress from Mory's out of his rooms with the same ingenious dexterity he'd displayed in slipping her in.

"There was no need for those direct cash payments," Paul Saunders said. "They could simply have made deposits in Mexican banks, and then switched it over—"

He broke off, and the others also fell silent as Norris Harrodsen addressed his ball with a midiron and drove it beautifully down the fairway to the base of the green. There were murmurs of appreciation, and the talk sprang up again. Chapin smiled. God, the human animal's capacity for ritual was remarkable! Here they were, half-glued on Norris' clandestine Scotch, horsing around—and they stopped in midstride, knickered, visored statues, almost reverential, the moment someone's started to shoot. Consummate! Golf was going to become a national institution—it so perfectly met the American male's requirement for sport: a minimum of practice, pleasant bucolic surroundings, more or less private results (since only your own foursome knew your score), and above all a magnificent opportunity to get away from the women. A natural. Emerald-green links and plush country clubs were going to take over America like weeds.

"No, Harding's mistake was in letting things get out of hand," Norris said with that curt finality that always seemed to cap a given topic. He was only a stroke behind Gifford and Tip, walking up the fairway with his quick, short stride. "The man lacked judgment. Public mess like this only rocks the boat."

"Well, we've got a fellow there now who won't stand for any hanky-panky," Tip declared. "I guarantee it. Not while *he's* in the oval office."

"Fine," Chapin rejoined, "—only how will they know whether he's breathing or not?"

"Old Silent Cal," Norris said after the laughter. "Well, you won't *see* it, anyway. And that's what matters. Country doesn't want Walsh Committees. Country wants to get on with the game."

Maybe it does and maybe it doesn't, Chapin thought, watching Jack Darcey take a wild, larruping swing at his ball and slice it into a solitary oak tree near the road, to a chorus of ribald commiseration. *The game.* It was hard to say. Perhaps this wave of disclosures with their preposterous alibis and comical attempts at evasion would send the nation into an orgy of puritanical austerity, or even into one of its self-righteous hysterias. He thought of the mob of servicemen that soft spring afternoon of '19, and Avery Calkins staring up at him, dazed and bleeding. Calkins had wanted him to join his firm as a kind of personal aide-de-camp, but Chapin had recognized the pitfalls—it would have brought him in over more experienced men at a time when his ignorance of the Street would have been glaringly apparent. He had begged off on the grounds of his youth and incompetence, but he'd kept a sharp eye on the activities of Calkins, Bliss, who had a seat on the Exchange and who were now taking a strong position in automotive securities. He had more freedom of maneuver at Diehl, Harrodsen. He would call in his obligation with Calkins when the time was right.

Meanwhile it was hard to know which way the American cat would jump. Maybe it was a time to retrench, hedge one's bets. It wasn't what he'd felt in '19, walking up Fifth under the snapping flags, the arches, or in '21, coming back from Europe; but then of course they hadn't had a chief executive dead under extraordinary circumstances, or a Teapot Dome Affair, either. It was vital to read the signs. You felt the national pulse, anticipated trends correctly, and you made money; you failed to do that, and you fell back into the pack howling its way along in haphazard pursuit of the pace-setters—and of course by then it was too late. There was dour, prune-faced Coolidge at the helm, sipping on ice water—Jesus! *ice water*—in place of Harding's bourbon, munching on salted peanuts . . .

The irony of a north-of-Boston Yankee presiding over the destiny of the Republic! His type was never popular in America: people might respect him, but they didn't *like* him—all that sobriety and sanctimonious self-denial. Americans wanted their leaders to have the easy, common touch—by which they meant men who were no better than themselves; who played a little five-card stud with the boys now and then, who were often hung over Sunday morning before church—who might even keep a nifty little number with uncomplicated appetites in an apartment over on the far side of town . . .

"All right, Tip-O!" Jack Darcey was humming through his teeth. "Sink one for the Countess . . ."

"Who's the Countess?" Chapin asked.

Darcey gave his extravagant Irish wink; his hair was flame-red in the sun. "She's the smartest lady in the whole U.S. of A.—she knows what makes the world go round . . ."

"Or round-the-world, if you like that better," Skeets Brohammer added, and several of the salesmen laughed.

"All right, you guys, don't go telling tales out of school," Tip warned them lightly; he was taking some practice swings, peering at the flag.

"You ought to take pity on us home-office drones, Darcey," Chapin pursued. "Stuck down there in the canyons while you jokers are out making honey on the road."

Darcey watched him a moment, legs crossed, golf club at his hip; he was still grinning, but it was a very different kind of smile. "You know what Mr. Mason said to Marse Dixon, pal," he said in a tone that slipped along just this side of insult, and several others laughed. Chapin didn't like Darcey; there was something in the man's brash self-assurance that always made him uneasy.

The talk fell away again. Tip bent down; his whole body became charged, compressed like a delicate spring. He swung. The ball lofted higher and higher, a tiny white dot against the blue of the August sky, hung an instant at the top of its arc and dropped neatly in the center of the green. The group burst into a bedlam of catcalls and cheers.

"Bull luck!" Walter Diehl snorted. "Shot with it . . ."

Century Gifford cried: "Where in hell did you learn to shoot like that?"

Tip grinned at him, his lower lip protruding. "I didn't."

Skeets Brohammer was clapping his hands like a cheerleader: "And he did it! He did it!"

"He's up but he isn't down," Diehl said flatly, nodding. "Let's see him sink it with that potatoe hoe he's got." They trooped up the long slope, Darcey and Brohammer pushing the hand cart with the refreshments, Chapin bringing up the rear with Paul Saunders.

The new sales scheme had worked superbly, as Chapin had known it would. There had been some moments of friction at first. Darcey had got into a row with a quiet, inoffensive man named Phemister, and Tip had pinned his ears back; and Brad Elwell, the former varsity halfback and a classmate of Chapin's, had gone over Tip's head to Walter Diehl and complained that Web Bowers was high-pressuring his customers.

"What do you mean, *high-pressuring* them?" Tip had demanded.

"Why, he's barging right in off the street and trying to sell them, right off the—"

"Of course he's trying to sell them! That's his job. You prefer sitting around the office soaking up the sports pages?"

Elwell had cupped his big hands. "That doesn't happen to be the way we do things down here, Ames."

"No, I can see that—you feel it's more genteel to tell 'em you just happened to be passing through town and thought you'd drop in for a little chit-chat about Ty Cobb. The indirect approach. That it?"

Elwell's face set coldly, he rolled his shoulders inside his jacket. "You know, we don't seem to see eye to eye on this, Ames."

"You're right. We don't," Tip said. "You're fired."

"Now just a minute, big shot! My father happens to be a person of some consequence. Up in Boston. But you wouldn't know about that, would you?"

"Then you should by all means go work for him. Up in Boston. Clean out your desk. You're not working here any more."

There had been another, longer conference in Norris Harrodsen's office, but Tip was adamant, and the firing stood; Elwell left next day on the Merchants' Limited. And Tip had twice had words with Saunders, who'd tried to meddle in the drawing accounts, and who had once made a not-so-veiled reference to Zimmerman and Solotow as being "not quite our sort down here." Chapin had been in on that one, too.

Tip had become very still; his face, poker-expressionless, nonetheless turned hard and quite threatening; Chapin was suddenly aware of the ticking of the grandfather clock down the hall.

"You mean, because their blood hasn't that special shade of indigo?" He was grinning, but there wasn't a trace of amusement in his eyes. "Well, there is quality and there is quality." His glance shot over to Chapin, flickered away again. "For instance, I wouldn't say that coming over steerage from Strassbourg in 1868 is such big potatoes, would you? I mean, if you *want* to start parading pedigrees . . ."

Chapin glanced at Saunders in surprise—he expected the Treasurer to laugh in derision; but Saunders was gazing at his brother in angry consternation. How did he know that? Chapin wondered. Where the devil had he ever dug that out?

"Personally I don't give a hoot in hell about pedigrees," Tip's voice was icy with scorn. "I care about men. And I care about Maury and Sid. Plenty. If a man is decent and comes in with the sales, keeps his nose clean, I don't care if he's an Eskimo. But I can see you *do*. So I'll give you just one short piece of advice: you tend to your 'sort' and I'll tend to mine. You read me clearly?"

And that had been that. His force had taken over in no time, as Tip had predicted; they were burning up the track, they were already in fourth place, out of twenty-three regional offices. The old man was pleased. The market had recovered nicely from last year's recession, the rates on brokers' loans remained comfortably low. But it was hard to tell which way it would go now.

Gifford was shooting; he'd drawn a driver and consequently was well out ahead of everyone else. A natural athlete, he lined up his shot and swung effortlessly; the ball rose in low trajectory, heading straight for the flag, hit the lip of the green—and then kept bounding and bounding on across the close-cropped carpet and disappeared into the far rough.

"Too much follow," Diehl muttered.

"How could I stop it with this war club?" Century demanded, and laughed; but he was irritated. The talk was more subdued now. This was the last hole; Century had taken the 540-yard 16th, Tip the short, tricky 17th; this would decide it. They hurried up to the green, helping themselves to liquor and ice from the cart, and swapping advice on the lie of the balls. Gifford, back in the rough, stroked his ball with nice touch; it ran easily over the green, slowed and came to rest two feet short; a cinch hole-out, even with that great knob of a driver.

Tip, whose ball was lying about six feet away, knelt down and studied the green.

"Right to left, chief," Web Bowers murmured.

"No kibitzing," Diehl commanded. "He can see it."

"Just chip it in, daddy," the Blazer called. "Alley-oop! Like tiddlywinks . . ."

Tip bent over his ball, waggling the open-faced iron. All at once he turned around, hitting left-handed, and locked his hands; the heel of the club met the ball with a smart click, the ball rolled curving and curving and dropped into the cup, to a roar of delight, amazement, protest.

"And he did it!" Skeets and Jack were chanting, arms entwined in a Buck-and-Bubbles shuffle. "He did it again!"

"—He can't do that!" Century was saying hotly to Norris Harrodsen. "He can't shoot that way . . ."

"Why not?" Harrodsen gave his frosty laugh. "Perfectly permissible. I confined you to one club—I didn't say how you had to use it—face or heel or which end, for that matter. No, he's got you, Century."

After that there was a ragged five-inning softball

game, the field force against the home office, which the salesmen won, thanks to some wild and woolly base-running by Darcey and a clutch double by Zimmerman; and after that the Harrodsens, father and son, played a short exhibition polo match against two men from the Analysis Branch, over which a lot of money again changed hands. The wives had joined them by then, and everyone went swimming in the cove below the tennis courts. Chapin, standing at the water's edge and wearing a pair of violet-tinted sunglasses, watched all this female flesh, so startlingly exposed in the daring new suits—a beguiling frieze of shoulders and breasts and thighs. American women were flinging off everything now, it seemed—hats, gloves, stockings, petticoats, even brassieres—as if, overheated and restless, they sought a harsh, free wind. His gaze returned again and again to Jophy, marveling at that electric elegance and grace, the sheer unquenchable *promise* of her body. Inaudibly he sighed, thinking of other moments . . . She had glanced at him just then, as if she could read his gaze, before she whirled away and vanished under a rush of foam; he crossed his arms and studied his feet, white and bony in the clear shallows.

"Hello, down there!"

Chapin looked up. Blazer Blaydon was standing at the top of the float's twenty-foot tower. "I can out-dive anybody in this crowd!" he shouted down, cupping his hands. Even soaking wet, that kewpie-knot of hair stood straight up on the top of his head; his baby-blue gaze seemed both innocent and wicked. "Anybody! Who wants to bet?"

Maury Zimmerman shied a hand at him. "You're slozzled! Get off there before you break your fool neck . . ."

"Are you kidding?" The Blazer reeled backward in indignation. "I was a lifeguard at York Beach, I was a diving fool. I'm the best there is! Come on—who wants to try me?"

There was a chorus of derision and demurral, and then Chapin saw Jophy leap up on the float and call: "All right, Blazer! You're on . . ."

"Atta girl," Jack Darcey cried. In his old-style tank suit with short sleeves he looked like a wild Irish sailor who'd just jumped ship. "I've got a hundred on Jophy Ames. A happy green C-note!"

"Jo, you're crazy," Tip was hollering at her; for the first time that day he looked unhappy. "Jack, cut it out, now—don't egg her on—"

No one was paying any attention to him. The Blazer was capering around at the top of the tower and shouting at Jophy, who was climbing quickly toward him.

"A hundred happy simoleons," Darcey was waving his hands. "Who'll cover it?"

"Honey—look, you haven't done that in years . . ." Tip was pleading with her earnestly; Chapin could barely hear him over the uproar. "Jo! Listen to me!"

She had reached the top of the tower now. She made a face at Tip and stuck out her tongue. "Come on—it's nothing! It's like riding a bicycle—you never lose it . . ."

"The hell it is! Jo, you've—"

"—it's like swimming, dancing—and some *other things* . . ." She rolled her eyes and everyone roared. The whole crowd was standing in the shallow water now, chanting, waving, urging her on. Jophy, laughing, suddenly struck a winsome, teasing Atlantic City bathing-girl pose—knees together, chin resting on one hunched shoulder, wrist flipped insouciantly. Chapin found himself roaring and applauding with the others.

"You oughta be in pictures, baby!" Maury Zimmerman shouted.

But now, just as suddenly, Jophy held up one hand and moved back to the far edge of the tower. Feet together, arms at her sides, head slightly lowered, her body a slim golden arrow, she looked like a high priestess ready to undertake some momentous endeavor on which the fate of all her race depended. The shouts and laughter fell away; even Tip was silent. Chapin was conscious of the lap of water against the float's sides. For another beat Jophy held the position, three, four—then she strode forward proudly, and jackknifed into a perfect pike, somersaulted once, and entered the water in a neat, hushed *schloop* . . . and from the watchers there came a low moan of wonder; then everyone screamed and hooted wildly. And still nothing broke the water, which rippled away from her point of entry like the first ocean in time. The crowd stirred, there were murmurs of apprehension—and then Jophy's head burst into view on the far side of the float. She waved once, and everybody shouted in relief. Chapin became aware that his heart was beating powerfully.

"All right, Blazer," she called. "Top that one!"

"Ayyy?" He cocked his head comically, hand to his ear. "What's that ye sayyy?"

"Come on . . ."

"Uh—how's the water?"

"All right, get off the dime . . ."

"Move it or lose it, Blazer!"

They were all riding him now. Blazer extended both arms high above his head like a politician, turned and took his stance, strode forward immediately, a bouncy cherub, tucked himself into a ball and spun once, twice—and hit the water awkwardly, half-extended, trying to come out of it, raising a tremendous splash. He bobbed to the surface immediately and held there, treading water, then swam feebly over to the float. Chapin heard Jophy say: "You all right, Blazer?" He nodded, coughing water, but it was clear he was hurting; his whole left shoulder and side were reddened from the impact.

"What's the matter with you, Blaydon?" Century taunted him. "Let a girl beat you like that . . ."

The Blazer stared at Gifford a moment, then his

face broke into the old puckish grin. "Me and my great big mouth," he said.

"You just needed more height for that one," Jophy said.

"I needed another two drinks," he concluded. Holding his shoulder absently he stared at her. "You're a tough act to follow, all right! . . . You're crazy-wild. You know that?"

After the lobster-and-clam roast down on the beach they all showered and reappeared, ready for anything. The club's main ball room had been cleared and the band played and they danced with each other while the summer light faded to rose and purple streaks high over the Sound. Jenny, dancing now with Chapin, watched Suzy, in an outrageously short, fringed skirt and four-inch heels, swoop by with Tip, hear her ask him: "—do you have enough for me, too?" and heard Tip laugh, "Of course! I'm a human dynamo . . ."

"Little fool," Jenny murmured aloud.

"Which one, darling?

"The Diehl child. She actually thinks she's going to waltz off into the sunset with your brother."

"It's not impossible."

She drew back and stared up at him. "Don't be ridiculous—he'll never even *look* at another woman the rest of his natural life."

"*Un*natural, you might say.—You sound envious." His lips curled in the old bemused smile she had once found so charming. "Every ship's hull has a rotten timber somewhere."

"Every ship?" she caught him up with a smile. Chapin's choice of metaphor could now and then be quite revealing.

"Well—ship, tower, suit of armor. Everything has a chink. Our capacity for self-delusion is boundless. Bet on that, and you'll always win . . ."

Jenny was not really listening to him now, trying

to read the edge of something in his voice. On the little bandstand the saxophone and clarinet wound their plaintive melody an octave apart, and the vocalist, a pretty boy with no chin, sang in a soapy tenor:

> "—*I've cornered the market in dreams,*
> *Made a killing in moonbeams—*
> *Still, I'm overdrawn with you . . .*"

Chapin was running along in that mocking, deprecatory tone he was so fond of affecting, but he was preoccupied; he had been all weekend. Something was gnawing at him. She smiled to herself. She knew him better than he would ever guess; after all, for some years now he had been grappling with Studebaker and Allied Chemical and Houston Oil; whereas she had been able to devote all her waking energies to studying *him*. Their private (which was to say sexually perilous) life in the main followed his predilections: there were certain configurations (to use his word) she didn't at all care for, others she enjoyed a great deal—or had in time come to enjoy, which amounted to the same thing. It had to be; a week, a month, and she found herself driven by her own ungovernable, humiliating need. And so she had fallen in with every profligate scenario, each more precarious and dangerous than the last. Then, after one near-disaster when he had brought back to their hotel rooms a particularly violent street girl, Jenny had drawn the line: all excursions, however steamy, must be discreetly bounded; the places, the principals chosen with the utmost circumspection—or he would destroy them both.

Frightened at his own recklessness, a bit chastened, he agreed; and what exploits he'd dared back in New York he had managed with care; yet she was not deluded. She'd probed this dark current in him, charted it—this overmastering fascination with running on the razor edge of discovery, of outright shocking apprehension, that she feared in time could get out of hand. His appetites fed on themselves, devouring everything, demanding more, and still more—a fever of lust. She'd gone along, debasing herself, choking down her pride in everything she was; but nothing she could do was enough for him. It would never be enough.

On only one issue had she determined not to give in to him: she would give him no children. He had been alluding to the subject recently, playing with the idea more than with any immediate purpose, but the thought was there, and she knew it would intensify. She had led him to believe she was amenable if, as and when—but on this point her heart had set like flint. The price of his rapine of her body was that that body would bear him no offspring; his essential selfishness would render him sterile. She swore it . . .

She snapped back to the party. The band had just exploded into a frantic, wailing jazz tune, the couples around them began to bob and bounce.

"Saint Vitus time," Chapin said wryly, though he had shifted adroitly into a gliding one-step. "They tell me we're indebted to funerals in New Orleans for this caterwauling."

"I rather like it," she said.

"Well, everyone knows you're depraved."

"How true."

The floor was crowded now. The trumpeter, a jovial fat man with slicked-down hair and a pencil mustache, lowered his horn and sang with salacious glee:

> *"Down in Voodooland—*
> *Where the monkey-girls swing,*
> *They do the buck-and-wing!*
> *It's so ecstatic*
> *To go acrobatic,*
> *In hop-hazy, palm-lazy, jazz-crazy Voodoo-*
> *land—!"*

*   *   *

They were conscious of a small excited commotion near them. She saw Jophy then, the floor clearing away around her; she was dancing with Jack Darcey, the two of them in flashing, darting rhythm, elbows and knees pumping, hands flung skyward. Jophy was wearing one of the chemise dresses above the knees, lime green, with three long strands of crystal beads that flailed around her throat like holiday glitter as she danced; her head was back, her mouth parted in silent laughter. The dive that day seemed to have released something in her, something unreckoning and wild . . . She's enjoying this, Jenny thought, she loves it, she doesn't give a damn what happens next or whether she makes a fool of herself or not; and she was conscious of that quick, deep pang of pure envy she'd had that morning by the pool. It's the moment, she celebrates the moment. Completely . . .

You would have faced it down, wouldn't you? she almost said aloud, watching Jophy kicking high, her slim hips grinding in fun like a stripper's; and she felt a dart of hatred now, mixed with the corroding envy. You would have stopped him cold, you never would have permitted this destructive, humiliating—

"—That's it," Chapin was saying. She started, glanced at him almost fearfully. He'd stopped dancing, rapt in the scene before him, was gazing at Jophy, running two fingers along the side of his nose the way he did when he was really excited about something. "That's it."

"That's what?" she demanded.

'That's the way it's going to *go* . . . His voice had dropped, barely audible over the explosive blast of the horns; she had to strain to hear him. "The country. That's the way it's going to gò." He was still watching Jophy with that indrawn glaring intensity. Raising his free hand he pointed his finger like a gun barrel, aimed it straight at her splendid, gyrating tail. "One nonstop, sixteen-cylinder, barrelhouse, wild fling." He nodded tightly. "Yep. I'm sure of it."

"You sound just like Tip," she said.

He looked at her—really looked at her for the first time; a look that would have frightened her four years ago; now it only provoked her bitter amusement.

"But with a difference," he said evenly. "With a whole world of difference."

He withdrew his arm from her waist; but she wanted to keep him talking now—the more so as his sister-in-law, still shimmying madly, had prompted this.

"You amaze me, darling," she bantered. "You see a giddy flapper slap her bottom and cut the fool, letting off steam—and you project some kind of national mood?"

"Of course!" He smiled then. "The lengthened shadow of a woman," he said with mock sententiousness. "To bend a phrase."

"You think Jo is typical?"

"Yes—the way the lookout spots the unseen shore. Jophy's a spearhead, a catalyst; she heightens the drama. Look at her! She *acts*—when other people only wish they could."

Her eyes widened. "Why, Chay, I do believe you're becoming emotionally involved . . ."

"Why do you say that?" Did she only imagine his voice was flatter, more metallic? "No, Jophy's an irrepressible symbol. And I can read symbols better than anybody I know . . . Golf clubs, diving towers, whizzing strings of beads in a crazy dance—they all have their stories to forecast, chérie. *If* only you've got the key. The Champollion touch! . . ."

He'd slipped away again; abstracted, evading. Chapin's way. She hated him then, utterly. But she was not deluded: Jophy was no symbol—and certainly not to Chapin. Had she misread something fatally? Could Jophy in some obscure way be the reason for that ruinous obsession of his that sent him running in too close to the reef—was that possible?

Well. She would find out. In time. All that was needed was patience—and a certain guile . . .

Walking briskly up to Larry Bixby she asked him if he'd mind pouring her a drink from that cute little silver flask he had.

6

"They say Trimount's going absolutely through the roof," the tall blond woman in the electric-blue dress and blue beads was saying to Chapin. She was wearing the shortest bob in the room. Jophy had seen her the week before at the Giffords' lawn party, she'd forgotten her name. "They say Billy Durant's going to take it in hand. Is he, Chay?"

"Quien sabe?" Chapin gave her his bemused smile and raised his glass. "Who can read the mind of a man who's still boosting Prohibition eight long years after it's become a hilarious farce?"

"You're holding out on me," the blond chided. "You know it's going up and you won't tell me."

"What goes up must come down," Jophy said lightly. "Only faster!" There was some laughter, and the woman stared at her with immense irritation, which pleased her obscurely. "Well, don't blame me," she ran on, "blame gravity, or thermodynamics or something . . . Don't you know better than to believe *any-thing* he says?" she demanded. "Chapin's the original Pied Piper—only we're going to lose a lot more than just our kids. You'll see!"

Chapin was the only one not laughing. "Jophy doesn't believe in making money," he explained to the noisy group that had gathered around them. "Jophy's the last rebel. When the new millennium comes roaring in and we're all driving platinum cars with diamond wheels, old Jo'll be standing on a soap box in Herald Square, shouting: 'I *told* you so!' "

"Nonsense," she answered, "I'll be leading the assault on the Stock Exchange myself. Scaling ladders and all."

"But sweetie, who will you use for troops? Everybody's going to be rich—it's the American Century!"

Raising her glass she laughed with the others; but she'd caught the metallic glint in his eye. "Oh, the poor will always be around—otherwise it wouldn't be any fun for you. Would it? We all have to make sacrifices, Chay. Look at you: before, the girls all wanted to go to bed with you—now they want to pump you about the future of Trimount Mining . . ."

He bowed. "The burdens of command, lover."

She was glad now that she'd come to this extravagant housewarming at the new penthouse Chapin and Jenny had moved into overlooking Central Park. There were those who said the area was too volatile, too heterogeneous, that it lacked the solid dignity of the East 60s and 70s; even Jenny had been uneasy. Chapin had ridiculed the notion. "Today's vulgarians are tomorrow's trend-setters," he'd proclaimed. *"We* are the makers of manners, Kate. Who will lead better than we?"

The apartment *was* exciting—like being on the bridge of a luxury liner far out at sea, with the distant lights in the buildings across the Park for stars; the hurrying traffic below gave you the sense that you were in motion, drifting toward uncharted astral shores. The décor was stark and metallic—Art Deco, they were calling it—the walls bombarded the eye with huge Beardsley silhouettes and Paris affiches. Jophy decided she didn't like it. This strident welding of blued steel and white chrome and black lacquer struck her as hard and brittle, singularly bloodless. She missed the human warmth of old wood and bone and fired clay she'd known as a child; and there seemed to be entirely too many sharp, bright corners on the objects you encountered. But there was an unmistakable illusion of space, of airy movement she found appealing.

And the company was heady; it always was at Chapin's parties. There was pert, sultry Claudette Colbert, starring in *The Mulberry Bush*, and Robert Benchley, and the magnificent Geraldine Farrar; Jophy recognized the lawyer who had fought to gain a stay of execution for Sacco and Vanzetti, and a bespectacled young man someone told her was going to be the new George Gershwin . . .

"Chapin," Jophy teased, "you're going to come to a violent end—and it's your money that'll do you in!"

"How's that?" Randy Harrodsen wanted to know; he was already tight on Manhattans.

"He'll fall overboard from his yacht one fine day. He's a rotten sailor, you know—I taught him the little he knows about sailing. And he won't be able to let go his money-bags. They'll drag him down to Davy Jones's Locker . . ."

"Oh, you don't mean that!" the blonde—her name was Margo something—protested.

"I do. I certainly do! My grandmother says nothing makes better enemies than money . . ." She laughed wildly, and finished her drink; her second, or possibly her third. She felt reckless, on the razor edge of something. It was amazing; what Chay pompously called the Cultural Zeitgeist had caught up with her. She could utter anything outrageous that popped into her head now, and instead of the shocked disapproval of ten years ago everyone broke into gales of laughter, and hung on her every word. She had become like those girls in top hats and tights who came onstage with placards announcing vaudeville acts. Yes, that was it—she rather enjoyed the idea: bringing on the jugglers and the strippers and the clowns—

". . . *Money has no legs, but it runs.*"

317

The words were in Spanish; a man's voice, resonant and full, but subdued, as if he were speaking to himself, or perhaps trying to remember where and when he'd heard the adage.

She started, turned, replied in Portuguese: "True, Senhor—but who knows which direction?"

He was tall, with a deeply tanned, smooth face and black eyes under heavy brows. He was easily the handsomest man she had ever seen. Even in that first instant she had the distinct impression that she had seen him somewhere before.

"Well!" he said. His English was good, charmingly stilted. "A Portuguese lady!"

"At your service," she answered.

"Well," he repeated. His eyes flickered at her darkly. "We are compatriots, it seems."

"Not since the battle of Aljubarrota!"

He laughed then; he had perfect white teeth. This is what the conquistadors looked like, she thought; the fierce great ones, the fearless voyagers. Something caught once at her very vitals, released again.

"This legless money of yours, Senhor—have you given it all to Chapin to gamble with?" she taunted him.

When he smiled the two vertical lines ran deep into his cheeks. "No-no-no," he said, in the rapid-fire way Grampa used to speak. "My money is in land, in cattle, in diamonds, in beautiful automobiles."

"What fun!"

"Paper," he scoffed, indicating Chapin with his chin. "What good is wealth if you can't see it, use it, hold it in your right hand?"

"My sentiments exactly," she said. "Are you an international import-export wizard?"

"No-no-no." He seemed to find the question very amusing. "Why should I work with balance sheets? Why should I work at all?"

"You're one of these new international playboys, then."

"That's it," he agreed. *"Play-boy."* He gave the phrase a curious little twist. Chapin and the electric-blue blonde were both laughing, watching them, but for some reason it didn't annoy her.

"No . . ." she decided. She searched his face briefly; he had begun to find her attractive, she knew. The catch returned, in greater force. "You don't strike me as a playboy," she said finally. "Not at all."

"Oh—appearances." He shrugged. "I have my grandfather's face. He was a naval officer—very brave, very strict. He was the terror of the seas."

"—You're playing with me," she said, "you're a wicked tease and you deserve everything that happens to you!"

Just then a woman, passing close by, called: "Manolo! Good luck next week," and he nodded in thanks, his face all at once stern and very intent. And suddenly Jophy remembered him from the sports pages, the rotogravures.

"—You're Manuel Montoya," she said in a low voice. "The tennis player." Of course; he was here for Forest Hills.

"Your servant, Portuguese."

"She was entrapping you, Manolo," Chapin told him, "she was leading you on—she knew perfectly well who you were! It's one of the ways she secures an unfair advantage."

She shook her head; she had not taken her eyes from Montoya. "No. I didn't recognize you. I should have."

He blew out his cheeks comically and rolled his eyes. "Ah, fame . . ."

"Manuel—that was my grandfather's name," she said. "In his—when he was a young man he could throw a harpoon farther and straighter than anyone in the whale fishery."

"Really? So he followed the sea—like my people. *My* grandfather's name, too. Isn't that curious?"

"Yes."

"They call me Manolo here, and in England. In Spain they call me El Halcón."

"I know." The Asturian Hawk. The Falcon from Aviles. She remembered everything now—his austerity, his arrogance, his devastating overhead, his ferocity at the net; they were calling his semi-final loss to the great René Lacoste at Wimbledon that spring one of the matches of the decade.

"Don't let her corrupt you," Chapin was saying to Montoya. "She's a mutineer at heart."

"Oh, no!" And she felt her eyes grow hard. "*I* am not the mutineer . . ."

"Well—disruptive influence."

"This lovely lady?" Montoya said. "Why do you invite her, then?"

"I have to—she's my brother's wife."

"Oh. And what does he do?"

"He's a biff-bang, hell-for-leather sales manager. Of securities. He's rather like you, Manolo. Impetuous. Goes to the net before he looks."

Jophy said: "You could say—he throws the harpoons Chapin forges."

"I see." Montoya's eyes flickered back to her. "He is here?"

"No—he's on the road. He's always on the road. I'm a paper widow."

"Paper? You don't look like paper to me."

"Yes—the stock certificate paper." She was consumed with a nervousness that seemed to spring from her body's very core. "The paper we are all drowning in—this is the age of pretty, crinkly paper, suggestive paper. Haven't you seen the beautiful, half-naked ladies on the certificates, sprawled here and there, wrapped in sheets and sashes and scrolls? It's really quite significant, don't you think? This paper wedding of sex and money? A curious sort of fantasy—"

"Oh, we're all fantasists, Jo," Chapin broke in lightly. "This talk about our being crass and pragmatic—it's so much eyewash. Why, we're the greatest dreamers of all—we want nothing less than a new golden age when every Tom, Dick and Harry will own a mansion, two cars and three radio sets, with a tidy little $100,000, say, well invested—"

"Paper fortune," Jophy interrupted him.

"Yes, of course, paper—that's what makes it part of the dream. Don't you see? Look at Manolo, here—he's the supreme fantasist. He actually thinks he's going to beat Big Bill Tilden and those formidable Three Musketeers from France next week."

"I will beat them," Montoya said softly, and his eyes flickered again. Reaching back he tapped the grand piano's curved side with two fingers.

"Ah-ha!" Chapin watched him, delighted. "Do I detect a touch of superstition?"

"Of course." He was smiling again; Jophy had never seen such perfect teeth. "We are all superstitious. We Latins." His coal-black eyes rested on hers now, firmly. "We do it to remind ourselves."

"But Manolo darling, that's all medieval mumbo-jumbo," the blonde named Margo said archly. She had a hard, handsome Scandinavian face and flat gray eyes; Jophy realized she was interested in Montoya.

"I tap on wood to remind myself that the world is very big and ageless and cruel. And I am still a poor, naked animal with a club in my right hand."

"A very graceful club, though, of laced gut," Jophy added. It was gratifying, standing here with the two handsomest men in the room dueling over her (she knew that was what it was, there was never any mistaking that brisk shaking of combs-and-wattles, the arched neck and bristle of feathers) but it was dismaying, too. What on earth did she need to prove? that she was an attractive young woman, a woman of excitement and promise? Why did she think she needed this?

One of the Filipino servants was extending a tray of canapes; she shook her head decisively and said,

"No, thanks. I must be going now." And turned her back on Chapin.

Beside her Montoya nodded. "Yes. I must go, too. Early to bed and early to rise—"

"And that is the way the Falcon flies," she finished the rhyme, and they laughed together.

"May I drive you home?"

"Why—that's very kind of you, Senhor. If it won't inconvenience you."

"How could it?" He set down their drinks on one of the cold glass coffee tables. He was the only man in the room who hadn't been drinking—his glass of white wine was scarcely touched.

She found Jenny and tendered her regrets. Almost nobody did that any more—people wandered in and out of social gatherings these days as though they were railroad stations or department stores; but she refused to abandon the manners Grama had taught her.

"Not leaving . . . so early?"

"Well—the children. Actually, I'm dead for sleep."

"Of course. The death of each day's life." Jenny looked very grand, in a long black crêpe de chine gown with a diamond choker. She was very tight, Jophy could tell. "Manolo?" Her eyes darted to Jophy, back to Montoya. "What's this, what's this? Has this wicked mermaid lured you down to her coral caves?"

"I fervently hope so." Montoya smiled at her.

"What a romantic couple you make," Jenny said, holding their hands. But her cool hazel eyes were unsmiling. There was something about her lately that Jophy found deeply disconcerting—she'd been surprised to discover that she was even a little afraid of her. "Well, don't do anything premeditated. Will you? Rely on impulse." Leaning forward she embraced Montoya who responded a bit awkwardly. Everyone was embracing and kissing now, on the flimsiest of pretexts, or on no pretext at all. Warm and demonstrative herself, Jophy disliked the falseness: it

turned all greetings, all human contacts cheap somehow, stripped them of honesty.

The car, parked at the front door under the mar-
quee with its top down, was breath-taking: a long, angular hood, lowslung, its windshield tilted back rak-
ishly, all a-sparkle with silver knobs and spokes and
louvers—a glittering, gleaming jewel of a car. The
swan perched on its radiator cap like an elegant figurehead.

"It's glorious!" she cried. "What is it?"

"Hispano-Suiza. Do you like it?" He tipped the uni-
formed doorman and waved him away, not perempto-
rily, opened the door for Jophy himself.

"*Like* it—I adore it! Do you take it with you wherever you go?"

"Sometimes."

He moved around to the driver's side with a quick
grace. The starter whined in a nasal rhythm, then the
engine exploded into life, throbbing densely. She lay
back against the seat, her arms behind her head; she
felt encased in luxury and power. He drove swiftly
and surely, talking now in Spanish, now in English,
about tennis and the great Tilden, the complete, the
perfect player, and she listened, replying briefly now
and then. The lights swam above her; it was like gliding along the sea floor, with the streetlights and window displays like the phosphorescent streaks of great
silver fish flashing past.

At her apartment, a converted brownstone on 73rd
Street, he walked her to the door. She turned and
said: "Well—thank you. It was fun. Even if you did
trick me cruelly. You did, you know."

"I know."

He stood looking at her expectantly. Was that what
it was? She felt gauche, a bit apprehensive, and irritated with herself for feeling that way.

"Will you come and see me play?"

She nodded; it seemed very difficult to take her
eyes from his face. "Yes—if I can, I certainly will."

"Good. I'm going to win this time, you know. I am playing the best tennis of my life this season. I'll send you tickets."

"Oh, that's not necessary . . ." She felt more awkward than ever; her blood was surging like a tide rip.

"Of course it is. You won't know where to sit. You need to be at the center of the court, and fairly low. Besides, I am always at the net." He paused. "I like—"

"The close chance?"

"That's it!"

He laughed richly, his head back—and all at once she thought of her father bursting into the room, his furled-down sea boots flaring, the red woolen shirt smelling of brine, of fish scales and tar and dense male sweat, his big arms sweeping her up high in the air; his stubble tickled her cheek. *My Josinha! You been a good girl while I been gone?*

She shivered. "I really must go. Good night, Senhor Montoya."

"Portuguese." He was very near her. He was not laughing now; his eyes were fierce and tender both. His hand on her arm was very strong. "You may call me Manolo. If you like."

She tried to laugh. "I'd—rather call you El Halcón."

"That, too. If you like."

She had started to tremble uncontrollably, stepped back. "Now I must go. Boa noite, Senhor."

"Buenas noches, doña encantadora." He turned away—swung back suddenly and drew her to him and kissed her. She gasped, responded before she had even decided what to do. Lights rained crazily against her eyelids, whirled off in darkness—

With all the strength she possessed she broke away from him and stumbled up the stone steps, and half ran up the two flights of stairs, fumbling for her key; flung open the door and hurried through the cool, high-ceilinged rooms. Emmadella snapped off the radio and rose as she entered.

"Are they all right?" she breathed.

The tall black woman looked at her calmly. "Course they all right, Miz Ames. Sleeping like two angels."

"That's good, that's—fine . . ."

"Joey didn't want to go to bed right off. Lot of ridiculous excuses. Wanted an Eskimo Pie." Emmadella Haynes chuckled. "They all want Eskimo Pies nowadays. You ought to be stricter with him, Miz Ames, you ask me." Her soft steady eyes came to rest on Jophy's face. "Is everything all right, Ma'am?"

"Yes. Oh, yes."

"You look as if the devil himself been after you . . ."

"No. I'm fine." Her agitation was so great she felt it must glow on her body, like some luminous paint. "You go on home, now. And thank you." She pressed a five-dollar bill into her hand.

"Miz Ames, you don't need to do that. We already—"

"No—no, I kept you—later than I meant to. Much later. You go on home, now."

In the little bedroom Tessa was sleeping like an angel, as Emmadella had said: plump little body, placid face. When Jophy kissed her she smiled faintly, her brow untroubled. She knew what she knew. A sturdy, no-nonsense Yankee. How curious she should have borne her. An easy birth, too—almost casual; sitting there, eyes wide and serene, taking the measure of everything . . .

She moved quickly to Joey's room, where his thin, wiry body was stirring restlessly, contrasting moods chasing each other across his delicate features like shadows sweeping over the Lower Channel on a northwest day. She straightened the twisted sheet, put her hand on his forehead. He scowled, pipe-stem arms and legs contorted, almost as though he were rejecting her, as though he wanted to burrow deeper into his own fanciful world . . . Such a troubled child, given to outbursts of unfocused anger, unbraked hilarity—and always those flights of imagination that his drawings revealed—amazing animals with exfoliate horns and tails like jungle plants, creatures with bat wings and claws like sabers.

"Where do they come from?" she'd asked him once, studying them.

"They're here. All around us."

She'd looked up at him. "Well, you know, it's imagining. There aren't really such—"

"But I see them!" he'd told her. "I talk to them sometimes . . ."

And then one afternoon he'd torn them all up and stuffed them in the garbage.

"Now, why on earth did you do that, Joey?" she demanded.

"They were no good. I got rid of them."

"—But they were beautiful," she protested, "they were what you—"

"I hate them!" he'd shouted, and she was shaken by the ferocity in his voice. "I never want to look at them again!"

He would never tell her why he'd destroyed them. He kept on drawing, but now they were Roman legionaries, medieval knights in armor; the animals now were neatly rendered deer and steeds and hounds . . .

She withdrew her hand. "Be good, Joey," she whispered, with an intensity that dismayed her. "Try to be good . . ."

She turned off the lamp in the living room and stood there in the darkness, acutely conscious of every part of her body. Lights from the rear windows of other apartments bled through the curtains like distant fire.

"Oh Tip, come *home* . . ." she moaned softly, and gripped her arms. But he wasn't coming home for weeks. He was on the road more than ever now, with these new issues or whatever they were. Offerings, they called them—offerings! *Graspings,* more likely—she'd love to hear Grama on that one. And when he was home he was often irascible and tired. The more they sold, the more was demanded of them: it was a madman's game and there was no end to it. Why couldn't he see that?

They needed him, they all needed him, Joey especially. He'd taken the kids over to see the big parade up Broadway for Lindy, he'd taken Joey up to baseball games at the Polo Grounds, but he was away so much; and when he was home there were endless sales conferences. They'd had a bad quarrel last time over Joey's schooling—she wanted him to have the advantage of a private school education, and Tip had opposed it with a vehemence that had surprised her. That was how it started, anyway, but somehow it had turned into more than private schools or spending too much for a housekeeper and a car and the out-of-hand prices of everything, or even this raging bull market——*bull* market: God, she hated the very phrase!—that roared on and on and dominated every conversation . . .

She'd written him, timed her letter for his arrival at the Bangor House and told him she was sorry, it had been her fault for bringing up the subject that last evening; and he'd written back in the jagged, forward-racing hand of his that always made her smile, it was so like him, saying No, it was his fault, he'd had no business blowing off like that, it was only that he had so much on his mind these days; he loved her more than anything else in this crazy world, she knew that, didn't she? She was all that mattered to him, she and the kids . . . and turning the pages she had felt her eyes sting with tears.

Oh, what difference did it make whose *fault* it was!

Still standing motionless in the near darkness she pressed her hands to her Venus mount, hard, and bowed her head. The body. It pressed you so—begged and demanded, and finally threatened. Did he have this need rush over him like a tidal wave, seething, tearing at his very roots? On the road, all those lonely nights? He must—she knew him intimately enough: he was an intense man, a passionate man—

But for a man it was simpler. His sex hung out there in the world, thrust ahead of him like a ship's bowsprit, defined his direction. He could seize it, brandish it, release himself in minutes, if he chose. With a woman it was all buried deep within her, the most secretive and intimate of things; there could be nothing casual about it, nothing—no matter what they said, no matter how free and blithe and casual they claimed they were . . .

Everyone was sleeping around now, or talking about it if they weren't. Maureen Taylor had told her she'd gone off to Lake George with Art Black—and she'd found out later that Sue Black had gone off somewhere else with Jim Taylor, that same weekend. You could see the couples in the parked cars behind the country clubs, near roadhouses, at the edge of the fairways; the two heads, the hands groping, then the heads sinking out of sight. The new, unfettered age. She had come upon Chapin making love to Barbara Gifford in an upstairs bedroom at their country place at Glen Cove. She'd suppressed a cry of surprise but not the quick, indrawn gasp of air; what had shocked her was not the act itself but the fact that Chapin's eyes were wide open, fastened on her with an amused intensity—almost as though he'd been expecting her . . .

Chapin. He loved to discourse on sexual attitudes —it often seemed as though he was merely waiting for any opening gambit that would lead that way. He was always dissecting Victorian pruderies, bourgeois inhibitions. His eyes, pale in their concentric rings-on-rings, took on that curious, indrawn light, his fingers traced and retraced the fine line of his nose—

She shivered, thinking of all she knew and did not know about him, the old, inexorable tide that drew her to him; again she felt Manuel Montoya's arms around her, the pressure of his lips . . . But Montoya was hot, audacious, living in his body, risking defeat on a hundred green courts; Chapin never risked anything. Or *did* he, in some forbidden area she could only sense? Maybe he still had his own temptations —and she only resented the fact that she was no longer the temptress . . .

Why should it *matter* so? That sudden, terrible need, a wet conjoining of two bodies strained in mounting unison, cresting in that always fresh, always unimaginable burst of sheer floating rapture— why should it all be hedged about with such taboos, such deadly strictures? Why couldn't it be as pure and free as diving deep through blue-green waters—

She shook herself with a low moan and went quickly into the bathroom. Turning on the shower full force she flung off her clothes, and gasped as the icy spray struck her. Gripping the swan's neck of the shower with all her might she writhed under the water, her teeth clenched, her long hair streaming black against her neck and shoulders, unable to stand it another second, unwilling to let go.

7

"All right, Bake," Tip said. He threw the new Dodge in gear and pulled out on to the highway, fast. "Pick your toughest prospect. And let's go hit him."

Stiff as a poker beside him, Bake Greenlaw gave a wintry bark of laughter. "Hiram Colburn." He bit off the name.

"What are we waiting for?"

It was always the best attack. A salesman would invariably lead you straight to his most difficult prospect anyway. It was human nature: he was damned and determined to prove that the fellow *couldn't* be sold—and thereby justify his own failure. By bringing it up right off the bat you gained the psychological edge. This was especially true when a man was in a slump, and Bake had been having his troubles for the past month. The farmers were taking a bad beating here in Maine and every place else—along with the textile mills down in Haverhill and Lowell they seemed to be about the only ones who weren't wallowing in the national prosperity. A lot of them were in hock to the agricultural machinery corporations; prices had been skidding, the farm index had dropped to 131. Many of them were screaming for federal aid, which they had about as much chance of getting as a pair of wings. Their kids were taking off for the cities in droves.

"Hell, I wouldn't wish Hiram on anybody," Bake said. "Not even you."

"What's the matter, he got leprosy?"

"*Nobody* can sell him, Tip. He can't be sold."

Tip slapped the marbleized knob of the gearshift. "There's no man living who can't be sold, Bake my boy."

"Hiram Colburn can't be."

"And why's that?"

"Got everything he wants."

"Nobody's got everything he wants."

"Old Hiram does." Bake glared down the road as though there were hostile artillery at the end of it. "I wouldn't waste your time."

"Lawdy, how can you be such a hopeless pessimist?" Tip demanded. "Beautiful spring day like this."

"Probably snow before nightfall."

"That's the trouble with you Downeast sourballs— you're licked before you start. You beat yourselves, that's what you do."

Greenlaw hunched his neck inside his coat collar, his gimlet eyes half-closed behind the steel-rim spectacles. He seemed to be working himself up to some desperate expedient. He burst out: "I'm not a betting man, Tip—"

"Now *that* is God's truth."

"—but I'll bet you ten dollars you can't sell him."

Tip gazed at him in pop-eyed amazement. "You don't *mean* it, Bake! Stop! Withdraw that challenge before it's too late!"

"I mean what I say. *Ten—dollars.*"

Tip slewed the big car over on the left-hand shoulder of the road and back again. Bake looked around in alarm, gripping the dashboard.

"What's the matter?"

"The shock, Bake! . . . God, I *hate* to take money away from my own sales force. I do. Think he'll be home, bracing spring morning like this one?"

"Oh, yes. He'll be home." Bake grinned sourly down

the road again. "Sitting there just inside the barn door in that rocking chair, not a care in the world. Oh, he'll be there all right."

The roads were surfaced now, even way in hell-and-gone up here west of Skowhegan, on the route that curved all the way around from Dixfield to North Anson and that salesmen called the Horn. In the towns you saw far more automobiles than buggies; there were tractors in the fields, and the electric lines crimped in their festive little blue glass insulators followed the telephone poles northward. At the gas stations there were kids who knew how to clean a carburetor or turn a brake drum. Even with that battered old Tin Lizzie of his, Bake could cover ten times the territory Tip had struggled to open up back in '16. The April air, tart and damp, held the faintest odor of turned earth, the first brave verdure, At a barn entrance a man was working over a sack of seed corn, and Tip thought of the two farmers on the road to Cromwell, leaning on their pitchforks and staring at him and the girl tearing by in a churning, golden dusty cloud, roaring with laughter. What was her name? *Claudine*—that was her name. Where was she now, what was she doing? Damn, but life was cockeyed crazy, when you sat back and thought about it . . .

"Some change from the war days, isn't it?" he said aloud.

"Yes. And not all for the better, either." Greenlaw looked like a grim, black stork in his dark suit and hat. "Girls all running around in skirts up to their nates—"

"Their what? Their what?"

"Their nates. Their asses."

"Now I got you."

"Scrunched down in rumble seats smooching and petting half the night. Getting themselves knocked up and having to get married. And then buying on time, running into debt before they're even dry behind the ears."

"God Almighty, what a sourpuss. It's progress, Bake, progress!"

"I guess *so*."

The billboard blared at them out of a stand of pine: freckle-faced kid inside a 1920-model Marmon, his face long with disappointment; and the caption: *"Gee, Pop—they're all passing you! . . ."* And the Flying Red Horse of Socony for the clincher. He didn't like billboards—they ruined a pleasing stretch of woods or the sweep of a cleared field; but there was no getting around it, they drew. Look at those Burma Shave repeats. Advertising was working wonders—the figures were unbeatable. Even out here in the tall timber housewives knew all about Frigidaires and O-do-ro-no. And now with radio—! Why, the market was unlimited . . .

He scowled. Thinking about radio always made him think about Chapin; and thinking about Chapin made him uneasy. Diehl, Harrodsen had brought out Horizon Fund the previous fall, with the prestigious Stock Exchange firm of Calkins, Bliss sponsoring the issue. Chapin had put it all together. It had been an enormous success—they'd sold $46 million in twelve weeks—and now Horizon Corporation (which was really Horizon *Fund*, that is to say it contained the same personnel under a different corporate structure) was planning to issue Beaumont Fund, with an initial offering of three million shares, as the result of Chapin's urging. Chapin was very eloquent on the subject of investment trusts.

"What's it all about?" Tip had demanded over lunch with his brother at the Metropolitan Club. "What's the purpose of all these new issues?"

"There are several reasons."

"Such as."

"First, there's the little matter of supply and demand. The new offerings fill a need." Chapin examined his fingernails intently. "The fact is, the market appears to be running out of common stocks."

Tip stared at him. "running *out?*"

"That's it. There's the general feeling that stocks are getting overpriced because there aren't enough to go around. Blue chips are being taken out of the market."

"You mean," Tip said slowly, "people are hanging on the the high-class rails and industrials, salting them away."

"That's about it. So the new issues fill an urgent need."

"All right. But why all this leap-frog *pyramiding?* Why can't we simply make an issue and go out and sell it?"

Chapin locked his fingers together and leaned forward. "It's a matter of leverage."

"Leverage."

"That's the name of the game. The big, new game. Now: say your capitalization is $150 million, equal parts preferred, bonds and common. And let's say, easy figuring, your portfolio appreciates in value by 50 percent over the first six months. Your assets are now worth 2¼ million— but your bonds and preferred are *still* only worth their initial $100 million. So the 1¼ million profit lies in the value of the common stock—which means *it* has increased in asset value 150 percent. You follow me?"

"Yes. I follow you."

"Now—if that common is held by *another* trust exercising the same kind of leverage, the common in *that* trust becomes worth $337 million—or a profit of 670 percent from that original $50 million of common stock. Six-seven-oh. You still with me?"

"I think so." Tip nodded, said very slowly: "And then, if that second trust sponsors a *third* one . . ."

"Eureka, little brother." Chapin's eyes dilated, just the way Aunt Serena's did; he seemed to have taken on that mannerism of hers more and more. "Go straight to the head of the class. *That's* the magic of leverage. It's flawless, it's fantastic—it's the greatest invention since the wheel . . ."

He ran on, outlining other, more complex ramifications involving sponsoring firms' options, holding companies, bank participation and limited price concessions, and citing half a dozen dazzling examples of high-leverage operation. Central States Electric had soared from $6 million to $300 million, Founders Group had shot from an unbelievable $500 outlay to $80 million—and they were planning still newer offerings; they were certain they could rocket all the way to a billion dollars in two years . . .

"Of course," Tip murmured, after a short pause, "this greatest invention since the wheel—it can work just as fast in reverse."

"And what's going to cause that?"

"A bad break in the market. A panic."

"Oh, come on. *You're* not turning bearish on me, are you?"

"This market is too high, too volatile, Chay. It's out of line—you know that just as well as I do."

His brother made a ribbed vault of his fingers, peered at them.

"Nothing's going to happen."

"I see."

"It won't because they aren't going to let it happen."

"They?" Tip said with irritation. "Who's *they?"*

"Look, they've got it in hand. Jack Morgan and Whitney and Lamont over there on the Corner, old Warburg down the Street—do you think they're going to let this boat tip over too far? Ben Strong's a Morgan partner—and he's just lowered the discount rate for the Fed to three and a half . . . You've got to learn to read them, kid. They know what they want—and they know exactly how to achieve it. No fuss, no muss." He smiled the old supercilious smile. "You thing *this* is a strong market? Stick around another year or so, and you're really going to see something . . ."

Tip said nothing. His brother had changed. Where earlier Chapin had affected that air of easy deprecatory amusement—the Harvard manner, Tip always thought of it, with a mixture of irritation and envy—now he seemed more peremptory and brusque. He'd made fortunes for Aunt Serena and Gus Lawring, he'd made a pile for all his clients, and one for himself. Norris Harrodsen, who thought the world of him, had made him a partner; and so had old Calkins. Bankers and money managers sought him out at parties, divorcées hung on his arm. He owned a thirty-room estate out in Glen Cove, a thirty-eight-foot sloop with teakwood decking and five suits of sails, he owned a Rolls Silver Ghost and a Packard Boattail Speedster for Jenny to hack around in. To say nothing of those collections he doted on. He had it all, now—or almost all of it, anyway. Maybe he was right—maybe it *was* a New Era, as Raskob and Lawrence and those hotshot Ivy League professors were saying; maybe they *had* actually discovered a magic formula to keep this economy soaring on and on into the blue like some new kind of self-fueling rocket to the moon . . .

But somehow, somewhere, he didn't believe it. Now and then the old fears would wake him in the night, with a new foreboding; and he'd lie there, sweating, wondering why he couldn't quite buy his own sales pitch. What was the matter, what had gone wrong?

Hiram Colburn was exactly where Bake had said he'd be—sitting square in the middle of the doorway to his barn in a black Boston rocker. A solid block of a man, thumbs hooked in the bib straps of his overalls, old felt hat perched on the back of his head. Ira Belcher, over in Augusta, said he owned half the county.

They got out of the car and walked across the grass, spongy from the Easter thaw, across the churned, muddy area in front of the barn. The farmer watched them approach, still rocking gently. The house was nice—big, high-pitched slate roof, clapboard siding, well painted. Eight or ten head of Holstein, a small flock of barred-rock hens rooting and clucking under the forsythia. Nothing ostentatious, but solid, easy to keep turning over. At the edge of the fence a massive gray field horse shook his mane, rubbing his shoulder against a post.

Bake introduced them. The old man rose and shook hands, pushing up a worn Hitchcock chair, eased forward a small packing crate with one work shoe. "Sit down, gentlemen." His eyes were gray, and washed so pale they seemed colorless; but there was the faintest suggestion of a twinkle in their centers. "What can I do for you?"

"Bake here says you've been in the market, off and on," Tip said after a few desultory remarks about the weather and Silent Cal's decision not to run for another term.

"Yep. Have been. Not now, though."

"Why's that, may I ask?"

"Don't like it. Don't like the way they're doing things down there. That's why."

The man was a challenge, no doubt about it. Tip opened with providing for one's family; Colburn's wife had been dead nine years. How about the children, then? He had no children, no grandchildren either. Tip advanced the idea of invested income to keep pace with rising prices; Colburn said he had a tidy nest-egg in the bank over in Skowhegan—even had his headstone picked out for the family plot. How about travel—hadn't he ever had a hankering to see more of the world? He was sixty-eight, and he'd seen all he really wanted to; there were the same kind of plain and damn fools on the other side of the water there were over here. Tip kept reaching back farther and farther, racking his brains; there was simply nothing he could hang his hat on. The old codger was monarch of all he surveyed. It began to look as if Bake was right, after all.

"Mighty sorry to waste your time like this, Mr. Ames," Hiram Colburn said after a little pause. "I told Baker here the same thing a while back. Got more than enough for my needs. And there you are."

"I guess you're right, sir. Well, it's been a distinct pleasure to meet a man who's got everything he wants. Unusual thing, these days." He rose slowly; Bake was watching him now with barely concealed glee, his mouth prim. "I just wonder if you'd mind telling me something."

"Depends."

"You've been in and out of the market, investing, and you've done very well, Bake tells me. Better than most experts. And I just wondered if you'd mind telling me what system you use."

"System?"

"Well, yes—what rule of thumb. You've done so well over a long time it can't be just luck."

The farmer studied him, his eyes glinting faintly. "Tell you, son. I buy 'em when I dassn't."

"When you—?"

"That's right." Colburn switched his cud deftly. "When I'm scared to buy, I buy. Then when you slick city fellers come up here from New York City or Boston and tell me how everything's humming along so fine, going to usher in a new dawn of prosperity— why, then I sell to *you*. Simple as that." He rocked along, watching the salesmen.

Tip said quietly: "I'm a country boy, Mr. Colburn. I was raised in a Berkshire village myself."

"That so. Don't look much like one."

"Appearances can be deceiving, Mr. Colburn."

"True . . . How d'you plant beans?" he asked abruptly.

"Beans? Bush or pole?"

"Bush."

"Single seeds five to six inches apart, two inches deep. Tamp the earth gently, hill them as they grow."

Hiram Colburn grunted. "What do you do if your ax head's loose?"

"Put it in a vise and drive in a 1¼" wedge."

"What if it's still loose?"

"Soak it for seventy-two hours in a bucket of water—*after* you've greased the head to keep it from rusting."

Colburn chuckled and nodded. "You're a country boy, all right. Fooled me. So many folks running around pretending to be what they ain't, these days . . . Ames," he mused. "You related to those north-of-Boston hardware people?"

"No, I'm not."

"Used their shovels for years.— Well, I'm sorry to be taking up your time t' no purpose."

"Don't mention it."

"Fact is, there's not a thing I need on this earth. Not a thing I'd've done different. Barring a few chowderheaded indiscretions. Kind any kid's bound to make 'fore he's dry behind the ears . . ."

"Sure." Tip put his hand on the back of the chair. All his senses had come alert. *Indiscretions*. The word, coming like that out of nowhere, riveted his attention.

"You a college man, Mr. Colburn?"

"Nope." The farmer shook his head with a rueful grin. "Nothing like that. Read a lot evenings, is all. Don't take to these blatting radios. *Weather* forecasts—hell, any damn fool can step outside and sniff the air and look at the weathervane and tell what's on the way better than these oily-voiced donkeys with their fancy instruments . . ."

"That's exactly what my wife's grandmother says." He paused; Bake had already moved out into the yard, delighted, impatient to be gone. He said: "I detect a note of regret in your voice, Mr. Colburn. Do you sometimes wish you'd gone to college?"

The old man glanced at him, looked out at the raw

fields. "Yes. I'll allow as how I wish I'd been able to go over there to Orono, to the University. I'd have liked that."

"I would have, too."

"Well—little late for that now, I'd say." The farmer snorted. "For both of us."

"For us, yes. But there must be a lot of farm boys here in Franklin County who'd like to go. Why not give them the chance?"

Colburn stopped rocking. "Can I do that?"

"Sure you can. Set up a trust fund. For scholarships. Administer it any way you want to. It could even be in your name, if you'd like."

"Well, now. That's a thought." Hiram Colburn got slowly to his feet. "That's a real thought, Mr. Ames. You sure a body can do that on his own?"

"Dead sure, sir."

"Well say, now, that's something to turn over. Come on in the kitchen and let's talk about it a mite."

"Happy to, Mr. Colburn," Tip said. Bake's head sunk still deeper in his collar. Tip wanted to laugh, and couldn't.

"Now what's this fund you're hawking?" Colburn was saying. "Horizon Fund, is it?"

"That's right." The big gray horse shook his head, the massive neck arched proudly, and chafed his great shoulder against the worn wood. Tip watched it a moment. "I'm not recommending you invest in Horizon, though," he heard himself say suddenly.

The farmer stopped walking. "You're *not?*"

"No—I'd advise you to put your money in Westinghouse or GM preferred. Solid blue-chips." Bake was gawping at him now as if he'd gone completely out of his mind. "Or even some triple-A long-term municipals."

Colburn's smoke-gray eyes shot over to Greenlaw, back to Tip again. "But Baker here's been ranting and raving about this new Horizon Fund of yours. I thought you—"

"Sure, fine—but not for something like this. This is a long-range project. You want maximum security, minimum risk. You want to go conservative on this one."

Colburn was still staring at him. "You mean you—you've just shot half the morning talking me into this deal and you *don't* want me to put it in your fund?"

"That's right." Bake was gazing at the woods behind the farm as though he didn't want even to be associated with this conversation. "Grant Holden down in Waterville can handle it for you. Or your bank officer. I'll show you how to set it up."

The farmer gave him a long, piercing glance—uttered his first laugh of the day. "Well, if that don't beat the Dutch! If that don't beat the devil himself." He waved a big, broad hand. "Come on in and have a cup of coffee. I got to figure this out . . ."

Later, driving down the narrow blued ribbon of highway, Bake pounded the dashboard with his fist and said, "Jee-sus Cree-iminy Chee-rist! What in Tophet got *into* you?"

Tip said: "What's the matter, Bake?"

"Matter—! You're the first man ever to reach that old pinchgut, at the last possible second you manage to pull off a sale anybody in his right mind would say is totally impossible—and then you turn around and kill the deal . . . have you gone soft in the head? or what?"

"Just a whim, Bake. Just an idle whim."

"I guess so! You cost us a whopping commission, is what you did . . ."

Tip grinned at him. "You're not out anything, anyway—you yourself said he couldn't be sold. So it's just as if we never saw him. Right?"

"Great—jumping—Jehosaphat!" Bake fussed away down the road. "Anyway, you owe me a sawbuck."

"What!" Tip cried. "You owe me—I *sold* him . . ."

Greenlaw peered around at Tip, his jaw extended in

the lean, sardonic grin. "But you didn't, Ames. That's just it."

"But I *could* have—I just chose not to . . ."

"But you didn't. Won't wash. You owe me ten simoleons."

Tip laughed. "I might have known you can't beat a Maine man."

"Dang right."

. . . It's all wrong, he thought, watching a man moving a spruce log into the deep blue blur of the saw blade, the plume of sawdust spurting high; thinking of Hiram Colburn looking down at the barn floor, the slow rueful smile. It's all out of hand . . . That little stake he himself had been building up—he'd take it out of Horizon and put it in a savings bank. A bank in—well, maybe over in Providence, say, where he wouldn't be tempted to touch it for a long, long time.

8

"You look tired, Josinha," Annabella Gaspa said.

"Do I?"

"Yes. And thin. Too thin."

"Oh, that!" Jophy laughed into the sunlight. "But that's the style now—don't you want me to be in style?"

"Not especially." Annabella Gaspa watched her granddaughter thrust her legs back and forth in the sand. Such lovely long legs. Her own had been like that. Long ago. Very long ago. With a grunt she shifted her position painfully on the beach blanket; her hip was worse today—she'd broken it in a fall during a bad ice storm three years before, and it had never been right since. Well, that was what getting old meant: joints hurt, bones didn't mend well; the blood slowed . . .

Tessa, crouched over a sand castle, pointed a round arm at the harbor and cried: "See the sail boat!"

"Schooner," Annabella corrected her. "That's called a schooner."

"Scooter."

"No—*schooner*."

They watched the gray-hulled vessel ride up on its mooring, the sail climbing the mast like a great dun wing unfolding.

"And that's the mains'l," Annabella told her great-granddaughter.

Tessa looked at her—Tip's good, earnest face. *"May-zul?"*

"Mais ou menos." Annabella turned to Jophy: "You used to know them all. Every single vessel and rig. Remember?"

"I remember. Is that the *Cormorant?*"

"No. *Cormorant* was driven ashore off Peaked Hill Bars five years ago, pounded to pieces. Tom Rodrigues was drowned, two others . . . That's the old *Cape Girl*—Frank Rivard's rechristened her the *Leonora.*"

"Then—there are only four left?"

"Five. Louis Cardosa's still on the Banks."

"Only five! And there used to be so many . . ."

"Sixty sail." Annabella sighed, a heavy hissing sound through her teeth. "No, the refrigerated trawlers have got it all now. Out of Boston, Gloucester. Salt fish—who wants to soak salt fish any more when you can fry fillet of fresh haddock, straight from Georges Bank? They call it progress, Josinha!"

They were sitting on the narrow spit of beach that ran along the Lower Channel. The late September sun was still warm. Out on the sand bars Joey and several other children were playing on an old raft, one of those haphazard constructions; it barely floated on the slick plate of incoming tide.

"Come here, Tessa," Jophy said. "You don't want to get burned." She patted cocoa butter on the sturdy little shoulders. Her hand moved deftly, yet there was a touch of brusque impatience in the action.

"How is Tip?" Annabella asked her.

"Yes—speaking of progress! The same old ball-of-fire. You don't expect him ever to change, do you?" She threw the older woman a quick, enigmatic glance. "Honestly, sometimes I think he's stark, raving mad. He and Jack Darcey got caught in that flood up in Vermont last fall—the dam above Rutland was supposed to go out *any* minute, and there they were sitting around the hotel making bets about when the

346

great wall of water was going to sweep them all away. Ridiculous!"

Absently she watched Joey and the Rivard boy racing through the shallows, stamping the water into explosive silvered fans of spray. "So of course Tip looked up the local barber—he says barbers always know everything—and found out about this back road, and he organized a caravan of cars, all the salesmen there at the hotel. They stocked up on bootleg gin and tried to drive through it. Water was up to the crossarms on the telegraph poles in the low places, the bridges were awash, and one of the cars got swept away. Tip and Jack rigged a line—trust Tip to have a length of rope!—and they pulled the other idiot out of his car and almost drowned themselves in the process. Tip got home looking like a hobo. 'We made it!' he kept hollering. 'We made it out of there!' You'd have thought he'd discovered the sea passage to India. I was furious with him—I asked him what was the matter with him, risking their necks like that. And he gave me that eager look and said: 'Honey, you know I had to get back to you and the kids. How could I drown in *Vermont!*' "

She laughed, shaking her head, staring hard at the harbor, while Annabella watched her impassively.

"It's his work, Josefina," she said. "He has to push himself. That's how he is."

"Oh, I know. You don't have to tell *me* how he is!" She sifted sand swiftly through her fingers. "No—he wanted the excitement, the adventure. Breaking trail . . . That's supposed to be *my* role, anyway!" She peered seaward under her hand. "What are they up to, out there?"

In the shallows near the raft the children had surrounded something, their voices tense. One of them pounced and then straightened, holding the big horseshoe crab by its spike of a tail, the clumsy black shovel-body arched, pincers pawing feebly in the air.

"All right, Charlie!" Annabella called in her most admonitory voice, and they turned, staring back at her. "Don't you hurt that bully-bag, now! Put him down . . ."

The boy dropped the big crab with a splash and they raced away through the incoming tide, yelping and hooting. "Little devils," she murmured.

Jophy said petulantly, "Why are children so *cruel* . . ."

"People are cruel." For a moment Annabella watched Joey standing on the raft, his hair wild and black, tying a green-and-orange sweater to a bamboo pole for a pirate flag. "Do you see much of Chapin?" she asked.

"Oh, yes. Quite a lot. He's very grand these days— he and Jenny. He's just bought a plane."

"An aeroplane?" Annabella looked at her in amazement.

"Sure—he used to be a pilot, you remember. In the war."

"I remember." It was inconceivable to her that a man could actually buy an airplane for himself, like a hat or a lawn mower. "Strange, isn't it?"

"What?"

"That he never comes down here." She nodded toward the big, somber house on the bluff across the channel, the widow's walk rising above its screen of scrub-pines. "With his aunt always here every season."

"Oh, he's too busy making money. They're all making millions. Of course it's not *there*, you understand—you can't see it or hold it in your hand. But everyone's making it . . ."

"Does he still collect things?"

"Oh yes indeed! Only this month it's coins."

"Coins?"

"Very rare, very exotic coins. Greek drachmas, Spanish doubloons—very valuable coins. And ivory netsukes, too. He's become very fond of ivory."

"Has he.—And people. He still collects them, I suppose."

Jophy laughed. "He tries. He certainly tries!" She stared hard at the Bluffs from under her brows. "He surrounds himself with celebrities: opera singers, jazz composers, stunt fliers, moving picture directors—everyone who's en la corriente, that sort of thing . . ."

"—Spanish," Annabella said.

"What?"

"Spanish word. We say ao corrente."

"Oh. Yes—that's right."

"How is it you use a Spanish expression?" She looked directly at her granddaughter.

"Oh, that's Manolo—Manuel Montoya." Her eyes flashed at Annabella once, flickered away. "He's a great tennis champion, comes over for the big tournaments. He's part of Chapin's entourage. Well, not really. But he's there now and then." She gazed at the *Leonora,* swinging now on the swiftly rising tide, her lower course set—abruptly leapt to her feet. "I'm going for a walk, Grama—I'm tired of sitting. Keep an eye on my offspring, will you?"

"Of course, criança."

She watched Jophy move away with that lithe stride, her body slender in the tight jersey and shorts.

"Running from something," she muttered, not unkindly. She knew the signs. A heightened sharpness in the glance, a certain tremulous flexing of the long fingers, the too quick laughter. Coming back to the Cape on the spur of the moment, after the summer was over, jerking the children out of school. Something was wrong—that unusual irritation with Tip, the incessant running around . . .

Well, it was hard when the man was away. If any woman knew about that, she did. It could gnaw and gnaw at you, deep in your vitals; a consuming, mortifying, unquenchable need. All those months, those long years . . . She'd seen some women become defiantly wanton, others stony-eyed and dry as maguey leaf. The saddest—or were they the most passionate?—literally pined away, as the saying went, or turned viciously perverse, peddling scandal around town, slashing and rending in their misery . . .

Well. She had been lucky—more than lucky: blessed. She knew it. From that blustery April afternoon when she'd first seen Manuel standing in the whaleboat, the line tub in his hands, and he'd smiled at her—that sudden, radiant smile that could always make her heart turn right over on itself; and then his wind-burned face had, as instantly, grown darkly serious, and she'd known that he was to be her life. Even her own demanding body must always wait for the return of this man. Her bold, glorious Manny . . . The way he'd walk up Dock Street after a voyage, hat titled forward, harpooner's chockpin—the proud badge of his profession—wedged conspicuously in the lapel of his jacket; head high, his shoulders swinging as if he owned the very seas . . . and later in the soft night, his hand, his whole body moving with such tenderness. So male. Yet so tender. Setting her afire, and quenching that fire. "Jóia minha," he crooned to her—my jewel; and afterward she would lie with her head in that sweet hollow between his chest and shoulder, listening to him tell of fabled, sunny lands and strangely thrilling customs. "On Tuolatari, querida, any woman may sleep with any man she chooses, and no sin is ever thought of; the body is accepted as a joyous gift. And on Manokela not to share everything you have with your neighbor is held to be the greatest sin imaginable—and they are the happiest people in all the islands . . ." his voice running deep under the windborne clang of the bell buoy far out in the Lower Channel . . .

The plane roused her, a shuddering roar that shook her alert. Craning her neck irritably she saw it sliding down the sky, toylike and ridiculous with its bristling ruff of an engine and dangling wheels. She hated the sound of them. There was something wrong about soaring through the air with such a racket. They ought to glide soundlessly, like gulls, or the way sailing craft rode the sea. But everything had turned noisy nowadays, coughing fumes: autos and winches and boats and airplanes.

She sighed, and shifted her weight again. Her hip hurt deep in the joint, and the air seemed curiously cool. Joey was still playing on the raft with the other kids—she could see him doubled over, paddling furiously with one bare brown arm; beside her Tessa was patting lumps of wet sand on her castle and talking to herself.

And now Chapin Ames actually *owned* an airplane. Had walked in and bought one, like a new suit. That Chapin. How could two brothers be so different? Night and day. When she'd learned Tip had gone to work for him, it had been like a dart in her vitals.

"Mistake." She shouldn't have said it; she shouldn't have said anything, it was no business of hers. But she hadn't been able to suppress it. Tip had only given her that stubborn grin.

"Think so, Grama?"

She'd tried to pass it off with a laugh. "You watch out he doesn't take to the boats the first heavy weather, and leave you to founder!"

"Don't you worry," he said. "I can take care of myself."

So full of confidence! The Schoolboy, they called him; the famous Boy Manager of the securities field— and he *was* young; still so young.

The plane was gone, had dipped out of sight behind Cranham Headland. She looked up-channel to where the *Albatroz* had been moored; and thought again, as she had for eleven long years, of Chapin Ames. Joe Dutra the lobsterman, the one they called Touro, claimed to have seen Chapin driving very fast on the Old Burial Ground Road at two-thirty that terrible morning, heading for Barnstable.

"Barnstable! You sure of that?" she'd demanded.

She'd felt a foreboding then, like the first breath of an easterly. But later she'd learned that Chapin had gone into the Army, Jophy said he'd told her he'd enlisted. Joe Touro was notoriously unreliable—he drank too much wine, he was always telling wild tales. She'd thought no more about it until one afternoon, a full year after the fire, when Frank Cardosa had refloated the hull of the *Albatroz*. He had stood just inside the doorway, turning his cap over and over in his hands.

"I don't know whether it means anything, Annabella. It may be nothing at all. But I thought I'd better tell you."

She watched his face. "What is it?"

"We found this can."

"A can?"

"A two-gallon container. For gasoline. Down in the hold." He paused, twisting his cap. "There was a lot of junk down there. Blocks, grab-hooks, old iron . . . Of course it could have been for the winch. But it wasn't the type they use down at Newcombe's. And then it would have been forward, it wouldn't have been there near the companionway, aft."

"Then you think someone set her afire," she said quietly.

"Of course it might have been thrown down there earlier. By accident." His eyes fell away from hers again.

She burst out: "But who would do such a monstrous thing!—with my Manuel down there, asleep . . ." Staring at Frank's big hands twisting the visored cap, she was struck full in the face with the import of what he was afraid to voice. She heard herself gasp.

"—*You* think he—that Manny would actually set fire to . . . no, never!" she cried.

He was shaking his head fearfully. "I didn't say that, Annabella—"

"—he would die first, he would cut off his right hand with a knife!" she shouted; she advanced on

Frank Cardosa steadily, while he backed away, his hands extended, pleading. "And you his old shipmate! Tu és doido—deixa esta casa, sai de minha vista, já, já! . . ." Weeping, wild with rage she'd lost all her English and didn't care; she could have struck him dead where he stood. "Filho de uma porca! Get out!—don't you ever show your bastard's face to me again! . . ."

Later, rocking by the low fire she turned the thought over, as one might pick up a sack of guano. Her Manny, old and broken, dreaming discordant dreams; seeking death at last . . . *No.* He had remained a Catholic, he would have rejected suicide with his last breath; and anyway, he loved life too fiercely, the mysterious voyage of it, even its changeable, fleeting riches of sun and wind. Manny *was* life—he would never, never forsake it, whether on some treacherous reef of the mind or in momentary despair. It was not in him.

But what, then? Who would want to kill him, burn him to death like that? There were men he'd quarreled with over the years—but to coldbloodedly set him and his broken old ship afire, to carry a can of gasoline on board in the night—

It was then that she had thought of Joe Touro's remark about Chapin Ames; and a kind of certainty settled over her like a foul, black cloak. A strange gasoline can; Chapin racing up to Boston in the small hours—his absence from the carnival that evening; Josefina's tense preoccupation all that day. Bits and pieces. Yes, there was a connection, some kind of tortured, hideous connection . . .

But to want to kill a weary old man—why, in the name of God? *Why?*

But it was Chapin, somehow; she'd felt it in the cold deeps of her heart. By then of course he'd been far away, in Texas, in the Army. She had absolutely no proof, anyhow—she, who had always believed in proof, who had the most scathing contempt for blind accusations. And then Jophy had lost the baby and nearly died herself; and the other children had come, and the years had slipped away, stealthy as a Grand Banks fog . . .

"Évez, por fim," she said aloud. The airplane had decided her—it was a sign. A portent. She smiled at the childhood superstition. Well, why not? She had already waited too long as it was. If she was right . . . A man who would do something like that would destroy anyone, for any reason—there was that hollow look in his eyes that she remembered. Olhos homiziados, Manny used to call it: fugitive's eyes. Eyes without a compass point, fathomless and cold. Jophy and Tip— they were in danger; more than they knew.

Yes: she would warn her tonight, and if the girl laughed at her or got angry, so much the worse for her—at least she would have been warned . . .

The tide was coming rapidly now, licking at the sand not too far from her feet. The children's cries lifted her gaze to the harbor. Out on the makeshift raft the Cabral boy dived off, tipping it precariously; another child climbed back on, wriggling like a slick little salamander, and dove again. Joey was crouched near the broomstick mast, alone now, in a strangely awkward attitude that caught her attention. He called out to one of the children splashing about near him who ducked under water for answer. The others were all swimming toward shore. Kids.

"Joey!" she called hoarsely. The boy couldn't hear her; he was gazing around him apprehensively now. The raft was drifting off toward Cunningham's Wharf.

The devil. Now why hadn't Jophy taught him to swim this summer. Too busy. With theaters and cocktails and motor trips. What was the matter with them? Every child should get over his fear of the water—why, when Josinha was four years old she'd learned how. And dive—mother of God, the way that child loved to dive from high places!

"Joey," she called again, and waved her arm. "Come back, now—paddle it back . . ."

It was no use, he wasn't paying attention; and he probably couldn't manage it against the tide, anyway. With irritation she looked around. Jophy was nowhere to be seen; there was no one else on the strip of beach. No, of course not, why should there be? Summer was over. Bending down she drew off her shoes, got to her feet with a grunt. Her hip hurt her more than ever—she shouldn't have sat on the sand this long. Foolish. Scowling she hiked her skirts and petticoats up around her firm thighs and walked into the water, wincing—how could it be this cold? it was September, after all—and began to wade steadily out toward the raft. She roared at the other kids but they were all swimming away up-channel, their arms flailing like windmills. Joey was still calling out to them; he peered down into the water at the edge of the raft, drew back. Gazing wildly around him he caught sight of his grandmother.

"All right, Joey," she said. "Grama's coming . . ."

The raft kept drifting perversely away toward the channel. She felt out of breath. She stepped on something that hurt her foot, nearly lost her balance. The water felt heavy as syrup. She was too old for this sort of foolishness. She was up to her thighs now, her skirts billowing soddenly about her. The water still felt no warmer, and it angered her.

Joey was starting to cry, his lip trembling; his face was pinched and fearful.

"Grama," he shrilled, *"Grama—"*

"Jump," she called hoarsely. She was in water above her waist, she was shivering all over, shivering and shaking, she couldn't stop it. Joey started to step toward her, froze again in an odd little crouch.

"Jump!" she commanded. "Não tenhas medo! Don't be afraid, now . . ." She opened her arms wide. The sea was licking against her breasts, soaking her chemise and camisole. Maybe Jophy was right, women shouldn't wear so many undergarments. But she was not going to change at this stage of the game.

"Joey," she said firmly. Nothing was so bad in all this world as fear. Nothing. Someone was shouting at them from shore. She did not turn around, cried: "Salta, Joey! Come on—I'll catch you . . . *Jump*, now!"—half command, half entreaty. Held his eyes fast with hers.

He gazed at her in boundless apprehension— jumped without warning and rose immediately to her left, pawing at the water, panicky and wild, his eyes rolling white. She lunged to reach him, lost her footing and fell sideways, went under herself. Her hair swirled blackly in front of her, and then Joey's slippery small body, hands and feet churning in a silent rhythm; a dream dance. She shook her head in the bubbling white froth, caught him at last in her big arms; got her feet under her and lifted him above the water.

She said, coughing: "That's a boy, Joey—"

He was laughing now; clinging to her neck for dear life, his legs gripping her thigh. He was laughing at her, gasping.

"Oooh, Grama, you're—all full of sea water— Grama!"

"I know . . ."

Delighted with him, she laughed out loud herself, and hugged him to her in a spasm. She was shivering and shaking from head to foot, she was never, ever going to be warm again. They were hooting and hollering from shore now. Turning she saw Maria Alves screeching and waving her long scrawny arms like the hysterical fishwife she was, and Jophy running hard down the beach, her bare slim legs rising and falling, splashing into the water, hurrying toward them.

"See?" she said to Joey, wading wearily back with him, the water, her clothes dragging like mercury against her old body. "That wasn't so bad. Now, was it?"

"No!" he cried, and laughed again, his head back. For an instant, his black hair tousled, his eyes shining, like her own Joey. "I jumped, Grama!" And his reedy voice trembled with that bright catch of triumph, of fear surmounted that she knew was as rare as all the wealth of the Indies. "I—jumped right in!—from that raft!"

"Course you did. Nothing to it, now. Do not ever be afraid. You hear?

It came, then—a piercing, wire-borne pain that drove on through her chest, impaled her and bound her fast. Her breath was gone, her vision. What was wrong? She was on her knees, deep in the water again with no idea how she'd got there. *Joey,* she thought with dread. But he was gone. Where? Jophy had hold of her, was calling something to her but she couldn't hear it. There were only flashes of faces, voices, strips of light on water.

"—Oh," she groaned.

The pain doubled and redoubled, bound her chest and belly in iron hoops, in tight steel cable and crushed the very life out of her, the iron stake drove its way into her heart. She was lying on the sand now—was it? The sun high above her had no warmth, no comfort, and Jophy was crouched over her, her eyes full of fear. She was saying something urgently, begging her not to do something, but what it was she had no idea at all.

"Stá nada, criança," she said, or thought she said. "Just a little chest pain, cramp from the cold, that water is so *cold.*—Now teach them to swim, Josinha, for the love of God, I've got no business wading around in Turk's Head Harbor with my clothes on, at my age. You know that . . ."

But there was something else. Something she must be sure to tell the girl. What was it? Something she—but the pain was suddenly too great, far too great oh

357

my sweet Christ!—she could stand a good deal of pain, more than most but this—! She was moving, swaying and rolling along, at sea, on the *Albatroz*, of course, heading for the schooner race off Minot's Ledge. But the weather had turned foul, icy Arctic gale-force winds and they had *got* to draw this burning iron out of her heart . . .

Someone had hold of her hand. Manny, holding her. The lee rail was under, if she lost her hold now she'd be swept overboard, that was clear. And now she saw the huge sea rising, cresting, black as night; the last great wave that would swamp them all.

Manny! she screamed. *Save us—!* But he was gone. No one could hear her now.

9

They started out at Marty's speakeasy over in the West 50s steeped in red plush and bead curtains with butterfly pulls. Jack Darcey had got girls for all of them—Jack could always get girls, anywhere, any time; Tip could never persuade Jophy to go along on their revels these days—and they spilled over into three tables, sipping righteously from coffee cups, chewing on Kansas City cuts, making festive plans for the evening. Then they went on to the Emerald Room and danced to Paul Whiteman's Orchestra, and after that to the Café Montparnasse, where Jack tried rather forcefully to induce everyone present to join him in a toast to good old Al Smith, the next President of the good old U.S. of A.—an invitation several of thé club's celebrants just as forcefully declined. After profuse apologies all around they journeyed uptown to Henderson's Blue Rajah, where the Blazer decided to take over the drums from a very large and irate Negro named Pinky. The management had become a bit disenchanted with their patronage by then, the ensuing discussion was translated to the foyer and finally out into the street, where Tip was able to get it all straightened out through the discreet distribution of some high-denomination bills.

There was a little difficulty on the ride back downtown when Web Bowers, who was driving one of the cars, began to derive extraordinary enjoyment from aiming straight at oncoming vehicles and watching them swerve away into the curb. Tip, in the front seat with one girl between them and another on his lap, managed with exemplary dexterity to trade places with Web's companion, pin a hurt and resentful Web against the door with his shoulder, and more or less drive the car back to the hotel without hitting anything or getting pinched in the process.

There Jack had insisted that this happy few partake of a cup, just a simple stirrup cup, before retiring. This had appealed enormously to everyone, just the cat's pajamas; they wouldn't think of letting Tip go home—not this early, not after everything he'd done for them, by God: not on your tootsie roll! Tip pressed a twenty-dollar bill into the hand of his dancing partner and popped her into a taxi (he had the sense that he'd done nothing all night long but deal out bills like fluttery green playing cards) and shepherded the whole crowd up to the suite he'd engaged for the stars of his Diehl, Harrodsen sales force . . .

"—just one little number," the Blazer was hotly explaining to two of the girls; the altercation at the Blue Rajah was still troubling him. "Just a couple of choruses. That's all. I used to play drums in a band back in college. But no. Lousy son of a bitch wouldn't let me sit in. Nerve of the joker. I should have punched him right in the puss."

"Yes, you should have," one of the girls agreed.

"Oh, can it, Blaydon," Jack said to him. His face was white and drawn under the fiery red hair.

"The hell I will."

"All right then, don't can it," Jack bent over Clarence Phelps again. "How you doing, kid?"

"Fine." Clarence was sitting deep in one of the easy chairs with his hands hanging between his legs; he looked like a child who'd just learned he'd lost his father and mother in a train wreck. "I'm fine."

"How about Arlene? You like her, Clar? She start that old fire in the basement?"

"Sure, Jack. But—but suppose . . ."

"Suppose *what?* Speak up, kid. We've got a lot to iron out here, before bed time."

"You don't imagine I could, uh, catch anything. Do you?"

Jack collapsed in wild laughter. "Damn good chance!" Hands on hips he shouted in his old sergeant's voice: "She never tells you she's got it, soldier!"

"Were you in the Army, Jack?" Darcey's girl, a curvy blonde named Carol, asked him.

"Was I ever! You bet your gorgeous Armentière, baby . . ."

"Pipe down, Jack," Tip told him sharply. "You'll have the house detectives all over us."

"Hey—I'm sorry, chief. I am. I don't want to embarrass you. You know that. Don't you, Tip-O?"

"Go suck a duck's egg."

"Ooh," Carol rebuked him, and rolled her eyes. "That's naughty . . ."

Tip laughed in spite of himself, gazed wearily at the nervous, swaying tableau. Cigarette smoke stung his eyes. Well, it would do them good to blow off steam. God knows they'd be driving hard enough this next six to eight weeks. He refused another drink of what Jack swore was certifiable Gordon's gin, and rubbed his eyes. He was dog tired, he'd had too much to drink, he was chafed raw from the interminable wrangling over this new Greylock issue. The June break had scared him badly with its panic selling, the tidal wave of margin calls; the losses in the over-the-counter shares were terrifying. Here it comes, he'd thought, watching the ticker in Girney's office in Hartford, listening to the brokers and boardroom clerks screaming at each other, feeling a crazy mixture of relief and dread; now we're going to get it. But then, illogically, unbelievably, the market had gulped, hiccuped and started its run again, made up its losses in a matter of days and roared on; the volume was terrific.

"Didn't I tell you?" Chapin had scoffed at him. "What are you so jittery about? Hell's bells, I never thought *you'd* go weak in the knees."

"*Yes,* I was scared," he'd retorted sharply. "So would anybody be with any brains." This incessant equating of caution, of anxiety with cowardice enraged him. Everyone was doing it. Who the hell was Chapin to call him weak-kneed? He'd been out there on the line, pushing sales as hard as anyone . . .

"It was a periodic readjustment. They were shaking out some of the wildcatters, that's all."

"Wildcatters, hell! It's the *little* guy that's getting wiped out—the fellow out there in Des Moines with a nest egg . . ."

"That's his lookout." Chapin was smiling the old, superior smile. "Come on now, don't be naive, little brother. You've had your ear to the rails, you can spot the engine coming down the line. Hell, they're *all* begging for tips on new pools, hanging on the latest off-the-record pearl-of-market-wisdom from Cochran or Durant, and then clambering on board like kids racing for the gold fields in '49. You've heard them."

"So they're fair game. Is that it?"

"Tip, they *want* to play. It's the most exciting game of all, and they want to play it." Chapin pressed the tips of his slender fingers together and studied them. "You know, you've been out in that bustling marketplace for quite a while—but you simply don't understand human nature."

"Is that right."

"Don't you see, the deepest, bottom-most thrill is *not* in making money."

"It isn't—!"

"Of course not. The excitement springs from the knowledge that the dollar you've just put in your pocket is directly contingent on the default of a dollar in the pocket of the other fellow; if *he* didn't want it so

362

badly, it wouldn't have any charm for you. It's his loss that makes your gain so sweet. *That's* what spins the wheels of high finance."

". . . You are one cynical son of a bitch," Tip murmured softly.

Chapin laughed, gazed off toward the Narrows, the Statue of Liberty; a liner was coming in, alabaster and majestic, sooty tugs nuzzling at its great flanks. Chapin had the best office on the floor now, except for old Harrodsen. "That's such a harsh word, little brother. I'd so much rather you called me realistic—or even skeptical." His expression turned serious again; he looked older, harder in an instant. "They're not going to let it crash," he said in an utterly different voice. "The big boys. Can't you see that? They're in too deep, they're all in too deep. The banks are in to the hilt, gobbling up utilities, lending in the call market. It's solid—because they're going to *keep* it solid, keep it rolling. If you don't like the way I'm putting it, listen to Lamont, listen to old Kahn . . ."

And Chapin had been right again. He was always right. He'd taken a big position in metals, and metals were surging; he'd loaded up on Radio, and Radio was taking off to beat the band. There were people who said it could go to a thousand—and higher. Even the Senate committee, headed by crusty old men from the big farming states who were certainly no friends of Wall Street, had concluded the structure was fundamentally sound. Maybe it *was* a golden new era, maybe they had found some foolproof magic that would bring in the millennium on one grand, golden platter. It certainly looked that way . . .

And then Chapin had stunned him with the new fund. Greylock, he was naming it Greylock. An initial offering of 120 million, with a one-in-ten free option to brokers, certain concessions in price per share to shareholders, warrants for the purchase of common stock by the bond holders at a future date to stimulate sales. Calkins, Bliss again had agreed to sponsor the issue. Best of all, Tip would be first vice president, and with stock options—Chapin had persuaded Harrodsen.

Greylock would be their baby, his and Tip's. It would be an autonomous entity with its own books, its own corporate structure; they could hold it just as tightly as they wanted.

". . . Greylock?" Tip echoed softly.

"Why not? Our happy old Berkshire home—I rather thought you'd go for it. Has a nice ring, anyway." Chapin looked directly at him, the blue eyes flat, depthless. "Well: it's what you've always wanted, isn't it?"

"Yes." He nodded, feeling oddly torn in two. Capital. For the first time in his life he'd have a shot at capital . . . and yet it all rested on the shoulders of this careening Bull Market he'd begun to distrust so deeply. Was everything really like this?—did the thing you yearned for with all your heart become the very thing you most feared?

He hadn't told Jophy about Greylock Fund; it would only have brought on another row over stocks and speculation, prophecies about Diehl, Harrodsen, Chapin and the market—the whole system of American finance capital in which he'd cast his lot. He was guilty as hell about not telling her—it seemed like a kind of betrayal, but he couldn't help it; it meant too much to him, he couldn't take any further uproar and censure right now. Grama's death seemed to have cut through some final cable—Jophy had turned still more volatile, restless, at war with everything; especially with him. As though he were responsible for this stealthy frenzy that had invaded their lives.

"Oh, for God's sake, Tip," she'd cried, when he'd remonstrated with her about the alarming increase in their monthly bills, "why make such an eternal fuss about it? It's only money . . ."

"Yes, well, try going without it for a while," he'd retorted hotly, "and see how long it's *only* money! You'll find it's *absolutely* money, that's what you'll find.'

She'd faced him squarely, chin up, eyes burning. "Who do you think you're talking to? *I've* gone without money—"

"Not for quite a while, you haven't!"

"I see—you've suddenly decided I'm some kind of spoiled Southhampton rich bitch. Like Jenny, or that ice maiden Barbara Gifford . . ."

"I didn't say that—"

"But you thought it, though!" And she'd whirled away from him.

She was out most of the day and half the night, from what he could discover. She was always at Chapin's parties now, or dancing until dawn in some speakeasy or watching polo matches, for God's sake. Some foreign friend of Chapin's who played tournament tennis, they were always talking about him. When Tip came in from a trip Jo was invariably out, the only testimony to her presence a welter of notes to Emmadella, or Harriet the cleaning woman. Joey was away now at private school—he'd given way on that one, with raw misgivings. Only Tessa would be home, out in the kitchen prattling away at Emmadella. When he picked her up and hugged her to him she stared back at him coolly, a vaguely pleased but measuring glance that distressed him. His own face, his own eyes, gazing back. Where was their *family,* where was the—warm circle of love he'd dreamed of through five thousand empty nights on the road? When he and Jophy *were* together the air crackled with unresolved, unspoken conflicts. It was as if something was waiting to happen.

There was no way that he could see to get back to what they'd had before. When he'd tried to open things up between them, she'd either turned it aside with brittle indifference or lashed him for his involvement with Chapin and this runaway market that was bloating itself on the blood of a million unsuspecting victims. Precisely because she voiced his own fears, he was angrier at her than he should have been, and a month ago they'd had a violent quarrel about it; when he'd left early the following morning for Toronto she hadn't even kissed him goodbye . . .

He felt harassed, defeated. People ought to be happy now, shouldn't they? And he and Jo most of all. It was the big boom, the New Era, with everybody getting rich hand over fist, the lucky owners of cars and European villas and a glittering avalanche of gadgets and conveniences . . . and yet people *weren't* happy. Chapin and Jenny weren't happy, for all their yachts and penthouses and boxes at the opera—in fact there had been guarded rumors about a pretty sordid escapade in Munich that June involving a caberet performer and a street girl, that Chapin had apparently only just managed to smooth over. Walter and Eleanor Diehl certainly weren't happy—if they ever had been; nor Century and Barbara Gifford. Even Aunt Serena didn't seem happy, though she had all kinds of money now, and graced half a dozen museum and symphony boards up in Boston. Well, maybe old Harrodsen was happy—he seemed to be the only one Tip knew who was in his element. Everyone else struck him as tense, irascible, drinking too much; and waiting, waiting for something to happen—

He raised his head. Jack was pouring himself a drink. The Blazer was pounding his fist into his hand and snarling, "That Saunders. Paul the Pallid Puke Saunders. Nobody tells *me* I'm padding my account. Nobody!"

"Oh, dry up, Blazer," Jack told him.

"The hell I will."

"Have another drink and sober up."

"That puke." Blazer's face was a deep red. "It's that son of a bitch Ames."

"You watch your mouth, Blaydon," Jack said.

"All right, you two," Tip warned them.

Blaydon said to Jack: "I don't mean Tip, you

idiot—I mean that son of a bitching brother of his. He's got the Puke in his hip pocket. Siccing him on us all the time. I'm on to his game."

"What the hell are you talking about?" Jack demanded.

"You know. You know." Blaydon nodded owlishly, running his tongue over his lips. "Secretive bastard. I ought to wipe that shit-eating grin off his face."

Jack said: "You're talking about Tip's brother. You realize that?"

"Damned right I realize it. You think I'm talking about Clarence fucking Darrow? I know who I'm talking about."

"All right, that's enough," Tip said.

"I don't care whose brother he is, he's a prick with ears."

"Nobody," Jack said. "Nobody bad-mouths Tip around *me*, Blaydon."

"Well . . ." The Blazer peered at him with spiteful cunning. "Listen to the shining armor. You sucking for a medal, Darcey? A Croix de—"

Jack hit him then—three quick blows, his arms moving like pistons. The Blazer sat down on the floor, hard, his glass smashed against the wall. Then Tip got between them, his hand flat against Jack's chest, and said:

"All right, now! That's enough! Go on to bed, both of you . . ."

The phone began to ring.

"House ducks," Tip said. "That's all we need."

They half-carried the Blazer into the far bedroom and dropped him on one of the beds. His girl, an angular brunette with narrow Pawnee eyes, said: "What'll I do with him now?"

"Sing him a lullaby," Tip said. He went back to answer the phone; it stopped ringing as he reached for the receiver.

"Powie!" Carol was saying, her eyes shining. She

had her arms around Jack's neck. "Hey, did you ever paste him, daddy!"

"You bet."

"Come on to beddy-bye, daddy. Come *on,* now!"

"I'll get around to you, baby. Don't you worry. You go ahead." He spun her around deftly, patted her tail. "I'll be right in—Nobody bad-mouths you, old buddy," he said to Tip.

"Go soak your head." Either the law was already on the way up, or the management had decided to let matters simmer down.

"Hey, what are you doing, Tipperoo?"

"Going home."

"—Home?"

"You got it. And tomorrow I want you to apologize to Blazer."

"I will. I'll go right in there now and beg his humble pie."

"Tomorrow will do." He went into the bathroom. The floor tiles, a hexagonal shape and deep blue, moved when he looked at them. He soaked his head in the basin and combed his hair, hearing now a low commotion of voices outside. The law, after all. Christ. He opened the door and bumped right into Jack, who had one hand to his lips and was pointing frantically at the door to the suite with the other.

"Tip. I'm in a jam."

"What's the matter?"

There was a sharp rapping, and a woman's voice said: "Jack Darcey, you open up, now . . ."

"It's Hazel—!" Jack hissed at him.

"Hazel!"

"Shhhhh. She's right—out—there! In the hall . . ."

"Don't try to tell me you're asleep," Hazel Boyce was saying, "because I know you're not. Jack? Jack!"

"Better let her in," Tip murmured.

"But Carol's in *there* . . ." Darcey pointed wildly in the other direction.

Tip grinned at him. "Looks bad, all right."

"Tip, you've got to help me!"

"What do you want *me* to do? She's here, you can't—"

"Go on in—with Carol. Just for me, Tip. Just this once."

Tip stared at him—started to laugh. "Look, if you think I'm—"

"Tip, you've got to. She'll kill me, she finds I've got a girl in there—she will! You've never seen her when she's good and mad . . ."

"Jack, I know you're in there," Hazel was saying; she was knocking on the door again. "Now, you let me in!"

Tip whispered, "You want me to go in there—"

"Just—you know, make it look good. Come on—what difference does it make to you?—you're a *married man*, for Christ sake . . ."

"Darcey, you dizzy bastard." Shaking his head he walked quickly through the connecting door and closed it behind him softly. Carol was in bed, lying with her hands under her head, sound asleep; her clothes were flung all over the room. He could hear Hazel's voice more clearly now, and Jack's, earnestly remonstrating. He whipped off his jacket and flung it in a corner, kicked off his shoes and climbed into bed, pulling the sheet and coverlet up over them both. The girl stirred, murmured, "Wrap your troubles in dreams, daddy . . ." Her eyes flew open. "Why, you're not Jack!"

"That's true."

"I know you. You're Tip." She giggled; her hand reached out for him, struck his belt buckle and stopped. "You've got your clothes on!"

"Yep."

"But what for?"

"Well, that's how it hits me."

"Oh, God," she groaned. "One of *those* . . ."

The voices outside the door were very near now, Hazel's strident and harsh: "—Don't you kid *me*, Jack

Darcey. I know what you're up to—you're a rotten, two-timing son of a bitch, that's what *you* are!"

"Hazel, I swear, honey—"

"I'm going through that door—and if there's a girl, *any* girl, in that bed I'm going to shoot you. Right between the eyes. You think I won't? Do you?"

"Haze honey, now don't go in there."

"Why not? Why not—just answer me that, two-timer! *Let* me in there . . ."

"I can't."

"Why not?"

"—It's Tip. He's in there. With a girl."

"*Tip—!*" Her laughter was clattering and incredulous. "Tip *Ames*—? Don't even *try* to hand me that!"

"Haze, I mean it—"

"Of all the sneaky, underhanded dodges. Tip wouldn't even *look* at another girl besides Jophy, and you know it! You're lying to me, Jack Darcey—"

"I'm not, I swear I'm not. *Please* don't open that door, Haze—you want to get me fired? He'll never forgive me . . ."

"Forgive *you—?*" She laughed savagely. There was a thump and a low scuffling sound against the door, then it was flung open and light volleyed into the room. Tip had drawn the girl to him, pulling the covers up to his chin. Hazel glared at Tip, her mouth open; then her teeth came down on her lower lip and she shook her head solemnly back and forth.

"There, you see?" Jack was saying, outraged. "Now, see what you've done?"

"*. . . Tipton Ames,*" Hazel murmured; her head kept swinging back and forth like a wind-up toy running down. "I don't believe it."

"I'm sorry, Tip," Jack was saying in an aggrieved tone. "I'm sorry as all hell—I couldn't stop her."

"Get out of here," Tip said as crossly as he could manage. "Both of you. Can't you even respect someone's privacy?"

"I never would have believed it," Hazel repeated. "I

just never would have believed it." She threw him one last, piercing glare, turned and went back through the door, Jack hastily shutting it after her. Then the door to the suite closed, and there was silence. Jack had gone out with her, then; he was taking her back to their flat. Jolly Jack Darcey had wriggled his way out of another Houdini pickle . . .

He started. Carol had started to play with him—he'd come erect instantly, throbbing; her breast rolled against his chest, her lips feathered their way along his throat. With one swift, violent movement he flung himself out of the bed.

"What's the matter now?" the girl demanded.

"Game's over."

"What game?"

"Musical beds."

"Oh, come on . . ."

"Well, I'm not—in the mood."

She laughed a low, chuckling laugh. "Don't spoof a hoofer, daddy. You're in the mood, all right."

"Not really." He got into his shoes as fast as he could. If he got his shoes on he'd be okay, no problem.

"Jesus, what a circus." Carol sighed, and pounded the pillow with one small fist. "First Jack, then you . . . You guys always play like this?"

"Yeah, we're a weird crew."

He found his jacket and drew it on, pulled his tie out of a pocket.

"Where's Jack?" the girl said.

"I'll go get him." He had his hand on the knob when she said:

"Say, Tip: do me a little favor?"

"Anything, sweetheart."

"What's the word on Wright Aero?"

"The what on what?"

"Wright Aero. Are they running a pool in it? Meehan and the others? Is it a good buy at 67?"

He gazed at her, his jaw hanging.

"Well, is it?"

"Jesus Christ," he muttered. "Jesus H. Q. Christ."

"Well . . ." Propped on her elbows, her breasts lovely and white and round, she pouted at him, miffed, looking all at once very appealing. "Everybody's cleaning up—I don't see why I don't have as much right as everyone else . . . What's so darn funny?"

"Nothing, nothing . . ." He shook his head, convulsed with laughter. "You've got every right in this cockeyed world."

In the sitting room he grabbed his hat and hurried off down the long corridor toward the elevators.

"If that doesn't beat the Dutch," he said aloud. He fell into another fit of laughter and lurched into the wall, holding his hat over his face. He couldn't seem to stop laughing for the life of him.

10

The match was well underway by the time Tip got there; from outside the stands he could hear the taut, anticipatory silence and then the sharp burst of applause as a point was won. He wasn't even sure he could get a ticket, but a girl in a maroon linen jacket smiled at him in a well-bred way and assured him there were a few returned seats—it was only a quarter-final match. He hurried into the stadium—a tropic blaze of silk and linen and white flannels, the cool green patch of court—and moved along the high aisle, feeling guiltily pleased with himself: a kid out of school. He'd finished up early in Hartford and run up to the apartment straight from Grand Central to find Emmadella on her knees polishing the kitchen floor.

"Say—you don't have to do that," he protested.

"*Someone's* got to do it," she answered with the mock-defiance he loved. "You want me to *wish* it on the floor?"

"Well, but a scorcher like this one.— Where's the lady of the house?"

"Gone off again." She rolled her eyes heavenward in disapproval.

"Where away this time?"

"Forest Hills."

"Oh, the tennis matches."

"Whole caravan this time. Mr. Chapin, young Mr.

373

Harrodsen, whole gang of 'em. Dressed to the eye-teeth. That Latin Lover is playing again."

"Oh—Montoya."

"Mr. Valentino Barrymore. With his silver thunder chariot."

The idea had popped into his head right then. Why not? Hell, he'd never even seen a big-time tennis match, it was high time he did.

"I'm going to run out there," he said abruptly. "Surprise 'em." Without another thought he'd hopped in the Dodge and taken off, whistling "Yes Sir, That's My Baby" all the way across the bridge and out Queens Boulevard, drumming on the wheel. Damned if Chay was going to be the only one to play hooky on a weekday afternoon. He needed some release himself from the strain of the current sales drive, the grinding pressure of this wild bull market that broke, and surged, and staggered, and surged again . . .

The players were walking to the baselines now. Tip found his row, excusing himself as he sidled past the bared knees—he could never get over the shortness of hemlines; even with Jophy he would find himself staring at that beguiling insweep from the long curve of the calf above her lovely knees, with wonder How far *were* they going to climb? There had to be a limit somewhere. Like the damned market . . .

He recognized Tilden at once from the sports pages: the lean handsome head, the graceful, almost dilatory way he moved to the baseline and set himself. Montoya, standing deep in a crouch, swung his racket in a slow rhythm, as if it were a sword and he were feeling its heft. The champion served, his left arm flung high, the slim body arching, arching—then coiling on itself with the racket in a flashing, fluid arc, the ball a white blur across the net and wide to Montoya's backhand, kicking away viciously as the Spaniard lunged for it, lofted it weakly off to the left, out of court.

"*Fifteen—love* . . ." the umpire's voice droned after a perfunctory spatter of applause.

He looked around for Jophy, then—they must all be down there at courtside—found her with an ease that astonished him, in the first row on the opposite side of the court. They were in two tiers of seats, right at the barrier: Jophy, flanked by Chapin and Randy and a hard, handsome woman with metallic-blond hair he'd seen at some of Chapin's gatherings, and whose name he always forgot—he didn't much like her, either. Directly behind them sat Jenny with Bart Guild the trader and Suzy Diehl and Andy Rawless who'd been a flying ace in the war and who held the speed record from somewhere to somewhere, and who was trying to secure a listing on the Exchange for his airline. They made a colorful party. Jophy was wearing her flame-orange linen with two incredibly long strands of amber beads; they flashed golden in the hot sunlight. Most of the women were wearing big floppy leghorn hats or cotton crew hats, but she was bareheaded as usual. He found himself smiling, observing her: she was the loveliest woman in the whole section. Chapin murmured something to her just then and she nodded tightly without looking at him. She was watching the match intently, now and then shading her eyes with a magazine.

Tilden had just aced Montoya to win the game. The applause was light. It was a decorous crowd. You did not hoot and holler at tennis matches—you applauded, and perhaps murmured in genteel amusement or surprise. The chilly, subdued Anglophiliac manners of the rich. Or maybe it was only tennis. He thought of the stands at the Yale Bowl the year before, the crowd on its feet waving programs and banners, and Century Gifford, hatless and flushed, brandishing a flask as little Albie Booth broke into the clear like an orphan making off with a loaf of bread—and then turned and thumbed his nose at Army's hulking Chris Cagle while the stadium plunged in pandemonium; Jophy had shrieked something over and over, hugging him and Century and even Barbara, whom she dis-

375

liked . . . How would she ever manage to maintain the proper decorum at this strawberry social?

She had looked up in his direction now, but he knew she hadn't seen him. Her attitude had baffled him these past months. He would find her eyes on him, a measuring glance he couldn't read at all; as if she were trying to make up her mind about him, about something she'd always taken for granted. Things between them were strained. He'd wanted to speak to her, twice he'd been on the very edge of it, but there was a kind of prideful aloofness in her manner he couldn't seem to get past. Once he'd phoned her from Ste. Hélène—but then, chatting with her, hearing her voice with its note of guarded appraisal, his resolve had failed him. And once, earlier, she'd made an overture, he knew now that was what it had been—and he, his nerves scraped raw from a row with that tightwad Saunders over a drawing expense increase, had turned her aside snappishly. His fault, it had been his fault mostly; but she just couldn't comprehend how the pressure-cooker could rile you up, keep you on edge for days at a stretch. She'd never understand that . . .

Gazing down at her, watching the high plane of her cheek, her shining hair swept back from her forehead, its smooth, dark coil caught up with one enormous tortoise pin in that simple way she affected, he longed to sweep away the abrasions of the last frantic years. He pictured himself sauntering over to where they were, exclaiming: "Well! And fancy meeting *you* here!" and her eyes flashing up to greet him, her lips curving into that merry, heedless smile that was like the first joyful meeting on the planet earth . . . He started to get to his feet, decided he'd better wait till there was a break between sets.

On the court below they were exchanging shots with a fluid, easy grace, almost mesmeric. The power of their hitting was awesome. Then one ball fell shorter than the others; Montoya came up, drove it deep and raced for the net. Tilden hit low for the far side; Montoya with a tremendous diving lunge got his racket on the ball and angled it sharply crosscourt and away, ungettable. And the applause came again, stronger. Jophy was clapping, her hands held high. He could see her eyes shining from where he sat.

"Thirty—fifteen . . ."

The score, white against its black panels, surprised him. Montoya had won the first set, 6-2, Tilden had taken the next two, 6-4 and 7-5, and the Spaniard had come back to win the fourth, 6-3. Each had held service once in the fifth. All even. Could this intense, good-looking fellow actually beat the great Tilden, in the tournament Tilden virtually owned? It certainly looked possible; Montoya had upset Borotra the year before—Tip remembered Jo and the others talking about it excitedly at the club, where she had been taking lessons, and playing occasionally with Jenny.

Leaning forward, chin in his hands, he watched another booming exchange, feeling the mounting excitement in the stands. He'd always thought of tennis as a pleasant, easy-going affair for the leisured upper classes, like croquet or bowls; definitely not in the same category as football or baseball, which he'd played in high school when he'd been able to squeeze time for it, and which he loved.

But there was nothing easy-going about this match; not remotely. Montoya was serving now: a swifter, tauter tempo than Tilden's. He came in hard behind it. Tilden fed him a wickedly undercut ball that floated back tantalizingly low. Montoya volleyed it sharply crosscourt and Tilden, gliding to his right like an elegant panther, got to it and scooped it high. Montoya set himself, racket well back—leaped high, his whole body convulsed with the savage downward sweep of the racket. The ball slammed down into the service court and bounced far out of reach.

"What a shot!" he exclaimed aloud.

The spectator on his left, an old geezer with a

scimitar of a nose, shook his head in denial. He was wearing one of those floppy-brimmed hats Norris Harrodsen favored. "Routine," he said in a grating voice. "Lob was too short."

"I see." You should lob deep, then, make the angles longer, less acute. That made sense. For a time he watched Montoya exclusively, a trick Century had taught him at the Yale games at the Bowl. He'd met Montoya once at a lawn party at Chapin's fancy palace in Glen Cove, but the Spaniard had left early and he hadn't had a chance to talk to him. The man had great mobility; he seemed to be everywhere at once, rushing, changing direction, anticipating the return. But it was more than that—there was a kind of predatory ferocity in his movements, a dark intensity of purpose; no wonder they called him the Spanish Falcon. He seemed to hit the ball even harder than Tilden, and with more abandon—again and again his shots went on through for winners or were out of court. His strategy was clearly to seize the net, dominate the center, force the action whenever possible. The two adversaries made him think of bull and matador: Montoya charging hard, volleying and smashing, and Tilden parrying and evading with a dazzling array of chip shots, lobs, passing shots, dinks and slices; a very stylish toreador, affable and debonair, who could alter the style or pace at will. Once when a ferocious overhead glanced off Tilden's thigh and caromed into the stands, the champion whirled around as though sent spinning by the force of the smash, and thrust his racket out protectively, grinning. The crowd murmured in amusement, but Montoya only stared back at Tilden from under his brows; he was unsmiling.

But this time the bull seemed to be winning . . .

Chapin had just said something amusing. The entire group was convulsed with laughter, except for Jophy, who only gave him a nervous smile, her eyes still riveted on the court. Chapin was wearing a blue linen blazer and white flannels; he hadn't gone in to the office today, then. Tip decided he'd touch him up about that when the match was over. He enjoyed irritating Chapin these days—probably because everything Chapin did these days irritated him. Chapin had piled trust on trust until the whole structure resembled one of Tessa's Tinkertoy towers, rickety and swaying. Calkins, Bliss was a majority stockholder in Horizon, which held stock in Diehl, Harrodsen, who owned the stock of First Enterprise Bank (where Chapin was also a director), which was somehow tied into their own Greylock Corporation, which controlled the brand new Macomah Fund. A dizzying round. He couldn't hold it in his head any more—and neither could anyone else, as far as he could see. The only constant was this crazy business of leverage, which had now become astronomical, and frightening. What shook him most of all was his realization that the trusts owed their investors no accountability whatsoever—no disclosure of their corporate structures or the nature or balance of their holdings.

"The public hasn't the foggiest idea of what our portfolio is—they couldn't find out even if they wanted to," he'd protested hotly to Chapin. "It's wrong, it's just plain wrong! Jesus, no wonder they call them blind trading pools down on the Street . . ."

Chapin, as usual, had dismissed it all with a flip of his hand. "Caveat emptor, baby."

"I've forgotten the little Latin I had, Chay. But if it means *screw the customer,* I'm not all that impressed."

"Oh, come on—why the hearts-and-flowers! What do they know about the market—I mean *really* know? A great number of simpletons out there think Seaboard Air Line is an aviation stock with fabulous growth potential. But it doesn't matter—they hear 'Seaboard is hot,' and they come running, falling all over themselves in their haste to climb on board.

Don't you get it yet, Schoolboy? They don't *want* to know, they've *never* wanted to know—all they want is to double their money every six months, and never mind how . . ."

And it certainly seemed to be true. Nobody cared. A new fund hit the market, the drums beat and the bugles blew, and the public broke down the door in a clamorous hysteria to buy, buy, buy. That August the Goldman, Sachs crowd had topped Shenandoah with Blue Ridge, and sold seven million shares in six weeks—and the purchasers hadn't the slightest notion as to whether the original assets were in Swedish steel or Tasmanian wombats, and couldn't have cared less.

Chapin hadn't even been shaken by the sickening market break back in March; he'd been jubilant when Mitchell had openly defied the Federal Reserve Board and thrown National City's $20 million kitty into the breach, to free the call money squeeze.

"Didn't I tell you? They aren't going to let that money supply dry up."

"Well, he won't get away with it." he'd answered, angry over he didn't exactly know what. "The Fed will slap his ears back."

"Don't be ridiculous—Mitchell's giving the *Fed* the word. You still haven't learned to read the smoke signals . . ."

And Mitchell *had* got away with it. The Federal Reserve had sullenly backed down, and the market had taken off again, wilder than ever. Even that sudden, puzzling dive just a week ago—the Babson Break, they were calling it—hadn't bothered his brother in the slightest.

"That milksop with his forebodings and his silly goatee. He's a *theoretician,* trying to scare up a few headlines to bolster his ego. Sixty-to-eighty-point decline! What's he doing, sniffing cocaine?"

"I don't like it, I tell you—"

"You going to start that Panic of '07 drivel all over again? Listen to Lawrence, listen to Fisher. The market's strong as a horse, it's moving again, a broad advance—"

"No, it's not," he insisted. "They're off, Chay, they've been falling off for months. Look at Freeport Sulphur, Celanese—look at Pepsi or Studebaker, for Christ sake—they're depressed. All this talk about a sound, soaring market—it's a myth. You're not reading your own God damned charts! Check your indexes . . ."

Chapin's eyes had narrowed. "You're the one who's reading the charts wrong. You always do. The big boys are still leading the charge—and they'll pull everybody else right along with them. Stick with the headliners. Why, call loans have gone over six billion—they were over $130 million just last week—"

"Don't talk to me about call loans, I know all about call loans."

"But that's just it—don't you see what this means? It means buyers, massive support. They're still coming *into* the market, in force . . ."

He'd shut up, then; how could you argue with those figures? But there were other figures, and they made for nervous reading. All across the country plant inventories were staggering, mortgages were sky-high, credit purchases were out of hand—the whole nation seemed to be on one vast binge, snatching at trinkets, wallowing in bathtub gin, living on the cuff, without an instant's worry about what tomorrow might—just might—bring. Things simply could not keep on like this. Could they?

The heightened applause, stitched now with individual cries, snapped him back to the match again. Montoya had broken service, was leading 5-4. This time the hum and flutter of talk continued. The umpire, a dignified man with a fine head of gray hair, was requesting quiet, quiet please.

Montoya served, a blistering cannonball in the corner that pulled Tilden far out of court, and volleyed away the weak return.

"Fooled him," the heron-beaked man in the floppy hat remarked. "Figured he'd go down the line. Shame on you, William."

"—He's going to win," Tip said suddenly. "Montoya."

The Heron grinned at him maliciously. "Oh, no. This is Tilden's year. His last."

"But he's got him, he's—"

Tilden won the next exchange with a beautifully executed drop-shot that just cleared the net. Montoya took the next on a service winner that was all but an ace. Tilden, his handsome face showing the strain now, returned deep and low, and caught the Spaniard with a wicked passing shot that stayed just inside the line. The ball eluded one of the ball boys and rolled lazily across the service court while Montoya, streaming sweat, waited impatiently, glanced around the gallery, seeing nothing.

Tip followed his glance. Jophy was sitting very erectly with one hand pressed to her throat, her eyes fastened on Montoya with a hard, fearful intensity, as if all her life were gathered in this moment. Her lips were slightly parted, her right hand gripping the furled magazine. Her eyes flashed defiantly toward Tilden once, came back to his challenger, animate with hope, with naked, fearful longing.

She was in love with Montoya.

Jophy.

Sound fell away. The Heron was pointing out something in a rasping voice but he didn't hear it. He was conscious of the blood washing against his temples and the back of his eyes, distorting and dulling his vision. He looked away, looked again at Jophy. He couldn't not look at her. For one stark, frozen instant he had the thought that he'd just had a stroke, some coronary blow that had deprived him of all movement, all sensation. The ends of his fingers burned.

Maybe he was mistaken. Maybe he was imagining. No.

He was not imagining it. She had never looked at him that way. Never quite like that.

He made a low, animal sound far in his throat, tore his gaze away and drove it to the court, where Montoya leaped high for the descending lob, the racket flashed in a tremendous overhead that rocked down and away, unbeatable, and now the crowd roared above the applause.

"Advantage—Señor Montoya . . ."

"Well, well. Match point," the Heron said, grinning through yellowed teeth.

Montoya looked supremely confident—it was apparent even in the way he nodded to a ball boy for a service ball, fed it up the face of his racket and plucked it with his left hand. Tilden's face was impassive, worn.

Tip could not look across to the courtside seats.

Montoya served deep down the line. Tilden, expecting a ball to his backhand, lunged awkwardly, lofted it deep. Montoya hammered it hard crosscourt and Tilden, still struggling to get back in position, returned weakly. Montoya went down the line with a tremendous forehand; the champion, off-balance and desperate, lobbed high. Montoya, his face gleaming darkly in the sunlight, waited, waited—smashed crosscourt again and sprinted to the net. Tilden stooped and sliced softly, a ball that just cleared the net and sank leadenly at Montoya's ankles. The Spaniard, caught by surprise, chopped awkwardly at it; the ball hit the top of the tape, seemed to hang there for an instant—then fell back on Montoya's side. And now the crowd was on its feet and screaming, all decorum gone.

"Deuce," the umpire's voice came, barely audible in

383

the bedlam. "Ladies and gentlemen—please. *Please* may I have quiet . . ."

"There you go," the Heron was saying. "Touch of the master—*there's* your great shot, son. Ah, they talk about all these Frogs and Dagos. There's only one Tilden."

Jophy's face was white and drawn. Her eyes loomed large in her pale set face, desperate with apprehension. Tip could see her hand twisting and twisting the furled magazine.

Montoya faulted; his second serve was short and Tilden pounced on it for a winner. Montoya served well in the odd court but the champion returned deep, again the sliced shot into the backhand, tantalizing, deceptive, and put away the Spaniard's tentative return. It was five-all.

Jophy smashed the magazine with all her might against the railing.

"That's it!" the Heron crowed. "Now watch King William."

Tilden roared through his service with two aces. Montoya came back to lead 30-15, but the veteran caught him with a perfectly executed drop-shot in the service court, and then stroked a devastating winner past the diving Montoya. And after a furious baseline rally Montoya, charging the net, volleyed a topspin drive a foot beyond the baseline. And the crowd gave way, cheering.

"Game, set and match to Mr. Tilden . . ."

Jophy's head was bowed. Her hand was still gripping the railing. Chapin, smiling, stretching, said something to her. Her head snapped around. She was crying, the tears streaking her face like silver in the dusty September sunlight. She was clearly crying. She drew back her hand as if to hit him, said something—two words only, maybe three—something scornful and savage and insulting. Chapin's face went blank with shock. Then she had leaped to her feet and was moving up the crowded aisle, bumping blindly into people, her dress a darting orange flame in the crowd.

Montoya was sitting at courtside with a towel over his head, perfectly motionless, his hands hanging between his knees.

Away. Tip leaped to his feet, staggered, almost fell over the row of seats in front of him. He had to get out of here. Right now. He had to get away before they saw him.

"What's the matter, son? Had your money on the Dago?" The Heron cackled mirthlessly, his face sallow under the floppy brim. "Don't you know better than to bet against Big Bill?"

He hurried down the stone steps and along the tomblike corridors, slipping through the crowd. Where in hell was the parking lot? He felt sick— densely sick, his belly churning on itself. Men's room. He'd better find one.

A girl's voice said petulantly, "He tried *so* hard— it's not fair! . . ." The girl's black bangs looked as though they'd been painted on her forehead. Her companions laughed, and a fat man in a white linen suit said:

"You dizzy dishes—you're all ga-ga over him."

"I am!" the girl cried. "Those bedroom eyes! I'd go anywhere with him. Don't think I wouldn't!"

"Yeah, well, just you watch your step-ins, baby . . ."

Tip hurried away along another corridor, searching frantically about, wondering if he was going to be violently sick right there, in the middle of everything. He suddenly remembered Chapin in the Hawkhurst Country Club locker room saying the American male's greatest asset was that he didn't know what his wife was wearing 80 percent of the time, and *never* what she was thinking.

He turned another corner—and ran right into Frank Delahant. His old sales manager's face was flushed, his eyes alight with a certain suppressed eagerness, as though he were hurrying toward some wonderfully exciting good news. Both men stopped awkwardly, gazing at each other. Then Frank's hand shot out.

"Well—Tip! What a surprise! What brings you out to such an effete spectacle?"

"Oh—" Tip waved a hand vaguely, not knowing what he was going to say. "A friend. A few friends."

"Marvelous, wasn't it?" His gaze flickered once past Tip's shoulder. "I've been hearing all kinds of things about you."

"All of it good, I hope."

"I hear Greylock's burning up the track. Macomah, too."

"Can't complain." The parade of gaily colored dresses kept floating by them. "Zim told me you've gone with Lee, Higginson."

"Yes, they made me a very handsome offer—I couldn't resist it. Why should you fellows get all the gravy?" Again his glance shot past Tip; his face was still edged with that singular excitement. "How's Jophy?"

"She's fine. Fine. We've got two kids, you know."

"No!"

"A boy and a girl. Eight and—five. She's . . . they're, uh—"

Frank frowned suddenly, his fine eyes deepened. "You all right, Tip?"

"—Yes, sure." He was able to make himself grin. "All the excitement, I guess. The sun."

"Sure. Let's get together, have lunch soon."

"I'll call you. When I'm in town."

He swerved away, sick to his very guts, and hurried off, his eyes darting right and left warily, and saw the slender, good-looking boy dressed for tennis and holding two rackets in presses, watching him with almost surly intensity. He was waiting for Frank. Impulsively Tip nodded. The boy scowled back, his lips moving, still following Tip with his eyes as he moved away toward the cars. Tip was gripping his belly frankly now, thinking of Beau Frank, and the stove in Horace Crowell's store, and the platform at North Station; heartsick, doubly shaken, doubly saddened. Not knowing what to do with himself, now or ever.

11

Somewhere there was a dance floor like a checkerboard where girls in black satin tights and white top hats swung ebony canes and chanted a song Jophy hadn't heard called "Doin' the New Low Down"; and somewhere a frail brunette was draped on a piano and sang "What Wouldn't I Do For That Man," and Jophy smiled, liking her, feeling her electric intensity, the vulnerability in her voice, and wishing she were sitting up there beside her, singing too. And somewhere else the floor was bathed in looping blue-and-orange discs of light and a sinister-looking man in a cloth cap and matelot shirt spun a half-naked girl round and round, embraced her roughly and flung her tumbling away through the lurid spangles—which angered Jophy, though she knew perfectly well it was all an act. Apaches, Chapin informed her, Apache dancers; he seemed strangely excited, watching them. He said they were all the rage now in Marseilles, even in Madrid. She glanced at Manolo then but he was silent, staring at the dancers and not seeing them.

And later still there was a smoke-laden cave of a room where a fat, jovial black woman asked Central in a ringing contralto to give her Doctor Jazz. Behind her on the stand a jazz band thumped and wailed, and a young man with his hair parted neatly in the center, his cherubic face dead white, tilted high a gleaming horn and the melody spilled forth in bursts of pure hilarity, like pealing bells, like heralds in royal fanfare, and she knew she'd never heard anything played with such reckless abandon in all her life.

"Who is he?" she demanded, clapping her hands. "I've *got* to know."

"Beiderbecke," said Chapin, who always, distressingly, knew everything. "Bix Beiderbecke."

"Bix?" she cried, laughing. "What a wonderful, impossible name! Anyone named *Bix*—"

People came and went like vaudeville acts, like shadows. They were joined for a time by a German with a real monocle who Randy Harrodsen said had been a U-boat commander, and who would drink only from a bottle he carried with him, a dark bottle blown in the shape of a dancing bear. It tasted of oranges and cloves and made Jophy think of Bedouin tents and palm-edged isles. Bart Guild, with his beady trader's eyes, had left by then, and that was a blessing, and so had Jenny, and Randy, colossally blotto as usual, had wandered off into the night; but Suzy Diehl was still with them, flirting with Andy Rawless, who didn't look a bit as if he'd shot down eleven German planes and been shot down once himself; and of course the ubiquitous Margo Manwaring with her Viking face . . .

And now at their table was a thin, somber man who was wearing very dark glasses and who had a scar that ran from the corner of his mouth across his cheek to the lobe of his ear. He was escorting three girls, all dressed in mauve taffeta, like identical triplets, but who obviously weren't. Chapin introduced him to the company as Spider Danco.

"But why are you wearing those colored glasses?" Jophy asked him. His narrow head turned robotlike and regarded her; his hair looked as though he combed it with vaseline. "Because I like them," he said.

"But you can't possibly *see* anything," she pursued.

"Or can you? I can barely make out anything as it is . . ."

"Perhaps he doesn't *want* to see anything, querida," Manolo said, and emptied his glass again. He was smiling but his eyes were flat and shiny; she had never seen him drink before.

Danco grinned, which made the scar curve subtly, a living thing on his leathery dark face. "That's the ticket."

The big black woman sang:

> *"I could be a king, dear, uncrowned,*
> *Humble or poor, rich or renowned—*
> *There is nothing I couldn't do,*
> *If I had you . . ."*

Tip's song.

"How did you get that scar, Spider?" Jophy asked suddenly. Someone kicked her under the table—Chapin perhaps—and Margo Manwaring said:

"Don't you think that's in rather poor taste, Josephine?"

"My name is *Josefina*," she answered, smiling through her teeth. "You can call me that, or nothing at all."

"I'm sure Josephine didn't mean anything by it," Margo was saying relentlessly to Danco, ignoring her.

"Of course I did," she broke in. "I don't say *anything* unless I mean it."

The smile had left Danco's face; the table had turned oddly quiet, a round island in the clatter of laughter, the crash of the band. They were all afraid of this Spider Danco; even Chapin's face flickered warily at her in warning. And Danco's women—their eyes rolled whitely, their hands fluttered here and there—chattered furiously, trying to ignore her, too. All except Manolo: Manolo wasn't afraid of Danco either, she could tell.

"No, really, Spider," she said aloud. "How'd you get it?"

His thin blued lips barely opened. "I fell down a flight of stairs."

"Stairs."

"A very long flight."

"My grandfather had scars," she informed him. "Terrific scars, I wish you could've seen them, Spider. He had a scar that went from here to here"—she traced the line of her arm from wrist to shoulder impressively while they all watched her in fearful fascination—"and his leg, and his back, too."

"Jophy, love," Chapin broke in on her, "do we really need this anatomy lesson?"

She looked at him a moment with all the contempt she'd felt for him all afternoon, all evening. Why did he always echo her temptations?

"He called them his medals," she said to Rawless. "They didn't give out medals in the whaleboats, Andy."

"I'll bet not," he said, watching the table.

"I've got a scar, too," she told Danco. "When I fell out of the rigging on the old *Albatroz*. You remember the *Albatroz*, Chay."

"Yes."

"I could show you my scar if you're really interested, Spider. But not right here. Or perhaps I could at that. Why don't we all compare scars?"

"Jophy, darling," Chapin said.

"Some scars show, some don't show," Manolo said, smiling at her; but his gaze unnerved her a little.

"What a charming subject," Margo Manwaring said in her bored superior voice.

"At least it's real," Jophy said, and looked her full in the eye. "Scars are real—what gives us scars is real, too. What do you have that's real, Maggie?"

Margo looked sullen and apprehensive. "The name's Margo," she said.

Jophy smiled now, hating her, loving hating her,

wanting to inflict damage, insult. "That's right, it is. Isn't it?"

"I like you, sister," Spider said suddenly. "You got Moxie. I like that."

"Oh, yes," she said. "I've always had Moxie."

He asked her to dance with him and she did, liking the slinky, sinuous way he moved, his almost feline force. After that she danced with Andy, and then with Manolo; but being held by Manolo made her tremble too much, stripped away the mood in which she'd wrapped herself, and she was glad when they'd left the place and were driving nowhere in particular in a little three-car caravan, driving swiftly in the cool night. The wind tore at her forehead and eyes, hurt her pleasurably; she patted the velvet and crystal band that spanned her forehead. She sang "Who's Sorry Now?" and "I've Found a New Baby," enjoying the husky tremolo of her voice against the wind, forcing herself to think of nothing, and watched Manolo—the long straight line of his nose, the hawk's stare; the conquistador arrogance and great desire.

For three weeks now her very being had been immersed in him, steeped in him, an absorption so complete it seemed to her that her very chemistry must be altered. Out at the courts, watching him play, listening to him talk with other players, she embraced the purity of their vocation and their passion for it. There was no talk of money there; they were wealthy, most of them; they could master the game out of love. She felt free again there, purged of the hysteria that surrounded the stock market she hated so savagely . . . She could think only of Manuel Montoya, feel only his presence, hunger only for the touch of his hands. She had known this would happen—she knew no other way to love, to give of herself—but even so, the depth and intensity of her passion astonished her; much the way Manolo might watch films of himself in some hard-fought match . . .

But now his eyes had narrowed to slits, his lips had

hardened to one grim line, drawn down slightly at the corners. He was driving very fast, watching the road.

"—Say it," she offered, both as challenge and entreaty. "What you're thinking. Say it out loud."

"That I will see that ball for the rest of my life. That soft, dead ball, dropping at my ankles. I will play that ball a million million times, all hours of the day and night. And it will always fall back on my side of the net . . ." He struck the wheel with such sharp force she was afraid he'd broken it. "I had him, Portuguese! I *had* him, in my hand—!"

"I know," she said.

What a snare and a delusion everything was, what a cheat. You could strain every last fiber of body and spirit—and on the turn of a card it was undone, and all the craft and courage and resolution dammed up since the beginning of time availed you nothing. Life turned us inside out, one way or another. That was how the fates avenged themselves. Manolo, the king of serve-and-volley, was beaten by a puffball dink-shot. Chapin the raffiné esthete had become the shrewd merchant of the marketplace. Jenny, that most ingenuous of maidens, had turned into an enameled society bitch with curious appetites. Grama, who had more dignity and sense of her own worth than anyone, had died like a sodden castaway, her skirts rucked around her thighs, gasping for breath. Young open-faced Randy had become a drunk, evasive and vague. And Tip—

God. *Tip.*

She stared hard at the twisting road, the sweeping white cone of the headlights, blinking against the wind. Tip. And with a call girl, an out-and-out tramp. Too much. It was just too God damned much. Steady, constant, unswerving Tip. She would never have believed it if it hadn't been Hazel Boyce. As it was she'd laughed in Chapin's face, told him his love of mischief was getting out of hand.

"But she saw him! Ask *her*—don't lay it at my door!"

Trust Chapin. She couldn't remember how it got started. It had been at the club, with everyone irascible or silly or bored. Suzy Diehl had been kidding about Jack Darcey's sexual exploits, and then Chapin had put his oar in, and Hazel had lashed back at *him*, and then Suzy had said Tip always really kept the force on the straight and narrow; and that was when Chapin, his eyes gleaming, had said don't forget about Tip falling for the charms of that hot little hoofer named Carol—and when Jophy laughed at him, had referred her to Hazel, who suddenly looked scared, her eyes shifting.

"I mean, I didn't believe it myself, really . . ." Chapin was laughing by that time and Hazel had tried to carry it off, giggling nervously. "But there he *was!* Gee, I'm sorry, Jophy—if I've said anything . . ."

She had felt the heat in her face, the sudden pressure behind her eyes. *Tip,* she'd thought, with an unfamiliar sense of high walls crashing, caving in. Not really *Tip*—with some cheap little tart. Simply not possible. But she knew Hazel was telling the truth: you couldn't feign that rueful embarrassment.

"Well," she'd managed to say lightly, "you just never know, do you?"

"Oh come on, Jo," Chapin had taunted her. "What's a quick roll in the hay? Spice of life, to mint a fresh one . . ."

Tip. In the hay with a common slut. Not even a not-so-grand passion. Ah, there was no hawser that would not let go, no iron nerve that would not fail, given a certain provocation. It only needed the right moment . . . She would never believe that, never! But it seemed to be true—

She took another drink from Manolo's flask, the Scotch fiery in her belly; looked up to see a park with a fountain at its center, where black iron naiads, slick and naked and beautiful, sat astride leaping dolphins or poured from cornucopias. Jets of water arched around them in silvered curtains.

"Stop!" she cried.

"Whatever pleases you," Manolo said, and swerved to a halt with a low shriek of rubber.

And now nothing seemed more natural, more fated than to jump out and run across the worn stone, kick off her high-heeled sandals and dart through that fountain-fan of spray into the pool, and clumb up past the happy naiads to the top of the stone obelisk that stood in its center. Once there she balanced herself, arms extended, and looked down. The other two cars had come up, were swooping around the little park, milling in disorder.

"Come down!" they were calling, waving to her, their faces flat and white, looking up. Manolo was at the edge of the fountain, Chapin and Suzy standing by the Rolls. "Come down! You'll get all wet . . ." And this struck her as funny, very funny indeed because as they could see she'd already waded through the pool and the water had come up to her breasts. Deep enough. Or maybe it wasn't. But in that case it would be a challenge, something to find out about. Stooping briskly she undressed down to her silk step-ins because it seemed more suitable. They were still calling out to her, laughing and shouting advice, and it nettled her.

"What's the matter?" she demanded. "Why are you all so silly?" Chapin was still beside his car, a foolish stance with one foot on the running board. "What do you think you're doing—posing for a Rolls-Royce ad?" she taunted him. "Why are you always afraid of everything? Don't you see—the worst that can happen is you get killed! . . ."

She shut them out of her mind, peering down in the black water. There wasn't height enough for anything fancy. She would have to clear that figure reaching out toward the other one with the horn of plenty, drop between them. It would be tricky, a bit tricky. Well, that's what she was. A diver, uma intrépida mergul-hadora, Grampa had called her once, smiling at her from the corner of the wheelhouse. Oh, Grampa. So long ago . . .

She dove then, a quick swan, nice arch and fold—the slender black iron arm shot past her, very near. She hit the water, felt a violent shock against her hands and forearms that jarred her clear through. She grunted with the impact, broke out of the water. Her wrist hurt, and her shoulder. She waded clumsily through the oily water, stepped through the fountain jets—and saw the policeman talking to Manolo, gesticulating. She climbed over the stone lip of the pool. The cop was saying:

"—raise hell around here you've got another think coming, you'll see!" He was huge; his body strained in the shiny blue fabric, light glinted on his cap bill. Manolo said something to him and he turned away, turned back again. As she came toward them, her step-ins clinging wet to her breasts, her body, his eyes blazed at her, baleful and righteous.

"What's the matter with you—ain't you got no sense of *shame?*"

"Be careful what you say to me," she told him quietly.

His head went back, he shoved a thick finger in her face. "Don't you give *me* any lip, you naked, drunken slut!" he roared.

Manolo hit him, again, again, was all over him in a rush. The cop's hat flew off, he bounced against the Hispano's fender, rolled off it, and started plucking at his holster. *No.* No guns. In a swift, silent trance Jophy reached into the back seat and snatched up one of the rackets in its wooden press. Manolo hit the policeman again, spinning him almost entirely around. As he drew his revolver clear of the holster Jophy swung the racket and caught him flush on the side of the head. He dropped to his knees like a great blue dummy, then to his hands and knees. The gun went clattering away across the stone pavement. She had cried out, she didn't know what, something triumphant and savage. And then there was a fierce blare of light and a motorcycle came roaring at them. Another policeman. Manolo was standing over the fallen officer, looking down and cursing him in Spanish, and now Chapin had hold of her, was telling her something in a low, urgent tone, but she didn't care. She lowered the racket and wiped at her face absently with her free hand. She laughed, and then she began to shiver in the cool, night air. Her wrist was hurting badly now.

12

"And how is our impulsive high-diver?" Chapin inquired with a grin.

"Jophy's fine," Tip answered simply. His face expressionless and very flat, the way it got when he was most upset and determined not to show it. Chapin had always been able to read him like a primer. Only his finger tapping the immaculate line table cloth gave him away. "She's used to the cast—at least she pretends she is. Shoulder still hurts a lot—they had it strapped up like a strait jacket for a while. It's better now." Tip paused, said: "I'm surprised she could even pick up that racket."

"She swung it like the Babe himself!" Chapin had decided early on to angle the whole episode as a kind of Mack Sennett caper, complete with puffing fat cops and sexy girls soaking them with water bags. He derived a certain sharp pleasure whenever he discussed it with Tip. Of course it was nothing to the excitement he'd felt when he'd first broken the news to his brother early that morning four weeks before; but it was a distinct pleasure nonetheless.

"We're out of the woods," he said serenely. "I talked to Van again yesterday. There won't be any repercussions."

"Thank God for that." Tip looked down at his plate. "I'm very grateful to you, Chay."

Chapin permitted himself a smile. "It took some do-ing."

"I can imagine."

"Ah, well." He let his eyes rove around the sedate club dining room. "All's well that ends well. To coin a phrase."

It *had* been touch and go for a while. At the station house Chapin had been persuasive and forceful, but they would never have got it hushed up and off the books if old Schermerhorn hadn't been a close friend of Avery Calkins. Chapin had got on the phone imme-diately to Horace Van Diemen, the firm's legal coun-sel. Van had got to Schermerhorn, who had got back to the lieutenant on duty. It turned out that the mo-torcycle officer hadn't actually *seen* Jophy clout the first cop, who hadn't seen it either—he'd had no idea what hit him. After a number of intricate exchanges they'd been able to get the charges dropped.

Montoya's case had been more complicated—he had after all assaulted a peace officer and resisted arrest. But Chapin and Andy Rawless testified to the abusive and obscene language the cop had used; and the law had been a little afraid of Montoya—Chapin had read it quickly: he was an international sports celebrity, which along with Hollywood stardom is as close as Americans will ever come to recognizing royalty; and he had powerful friends at the Spanish Embassy in Washington. There was some even more delicate ma-neuvering; those charges, too, were dropped, and he sailed for home in five days.

The almost insoluble problem that night had been Jophy herself. She had been irrepressible, almost gleeful in her defiance.

"Go on, lock me up!" she'd kept saying. "That's where I belong, isn't it? With all the other Dagoes. Come on now, don't shrink from your duty—it's where you've wanted to put me all my life! Well, *isn't it—?*" her eyes flashing at them with savage scorn. Chapin knew she hadn't been nearly as tight as she'd pretended to be. In place of the morose despair that had gripped her after the match, she'd seemed actually elated, released in some wild way that filled him with awe even as it amused him . . .

"After all," he said now, "how many corporate wives can lay claim to braining the law with a tennis racket and walking away unscathed?"

But Tip did not smile in return—he threw him a quick, quizzical glance, looked around the room again. At a table near them two men got up and left hurriedly; over by one of the windows a banker named Elander was having a low, agitated conversation with two associates.

"We ought to be getting back," Tip said.

"What's your hurry? Fernand makes a delectable crême caramel. I had a hand in bringing him over from l'Aiglon Doré, you know."

"I don't like it, Chay."

"What on earth are you talking about? He's the most talented chef in New York—which means in this whole benighted country . . ."

"No, no, no," Tip answered crossly, and Chapin was conscious now of the strain in his eyes. "I meant the market."

"There you go again."

"You should see them over on the Treasury steps—they're standing there staring into space as if they've been pole-axed and haven't sense enough to keel over yet."

"It's just a little selling spree."

"No. It's more than that."

"Pull up your socks. They're shaking out some of the hot-shots, that's all." He smiled, twirling his stem glass neatly on the table cloth, wishing it were filled with Vosne Romanée. Well: it would be before too long. He felt powerful, expansive, utterly at ease. The general apprehension at the firm over the past several days amused him; there they were, getting themselves hot and bothered—all over again. What a waste of energy! It had been an eminently satisfactory month. The market had burst all bounds, empyrean now; their new Macomah had sold out, they were readying another issue for November 15th. He'd had an enticing passage-at-arms with three sumptuous black girls through the good offices of Spider Danco only the week before; and even though Jophy herself had been unrepentant, even contemptuous of his costly rescue efforts in her behalf, he knew his brother was finally and irretrievably in his debt. A certain balance had been redressed.

"I don't like sitting here," Tip was saying. "Not knowing what's going on."

Chapin sighed, and signaled to their waiter. "All right. If it'll make you any happier."

Out in the street the atmosphere *was* odd—people hurrying here and there, much quicker than the customary brisk pace, almost running, the footfalls sharp, unnaturally loud against the stone; like a city coming under siege. Men were standing in little clumps, as though huddling together for mutual protection. There was a curious sound over everything, not the easy hum of eager talk but something nearer the moan a person might utter at a moment of dread realized. At the entrance to their building a man flung against them violently, recoiled. Chapin recognized him as a broker with Stahl Brothers, Meeker.

"Manners, Wilson, manners," he chided lightly. The broker stared at him unseeing, bolted out into the street.

"What's got into everybody today? Have they all gone bonkers?"

"They're scared, Chay."

They got off the elevator and walked into chaos.

The boardroom was in an uproar. On the raised platform below the board the boys were scribbling and erasing and scribbling again in an indecipherable hash of smears. Chairs had been pushed this way and that, some of them had even been tipped over, and the crowd was milling densely, arguing and plucking at one another's clothing or staring at the board, the frantic clerks, or at the screen where numbers and symbols ran in a steady, jittering stream.

"Jesus," he heard Tip say. "Oh—my—Jesus . . ."

He was aware of Vera Gayne's voice even before he located her, crouched over Taylor, one of the wire operators. Vera Gaynes was a pert, pretty woman who had been a celebrated comedienne during the war, then had left the stage and gone into the market with a vengeance. For some years now she'd been the subject of much good-natured banter tinged with admiration: a woman who'd successfully invaded a man's world, a shrewd, bold speculator who lived extravagantly, followed her impulses, and got the same kick from playing the market that her men friends did.

Now her face was sweating and unlovely, distorted with anger, and she was shouting; "What do you mean, *you don't know*—*!* I'm telling you, I want the last on Paramount!" and Taylor, harassed and gaunt, was shaking his head at her saying nervously, "I'm sorry, Miss Gaynes, I just can't get *anything,* they're completely—" the rest of what he said swallowed up in a bedlam of shouts and curses and this hollow, disquieting moaning sound.

Bartells was staring at the board and shaking his head slowly back and forth. A trader named Moreland was pacing up and down, tearing what looked like an order form into pieces, tearing it and then tearing it again and talking to himself. Someone caught at his sleeve: Stearns, plastered as usual, eyes behind the tortoise-shell glasses glazed with fright.

"Have you got anything? heard anything? I saw you just come in—"

"Indeed I do," he answered. "I've just enjoyed an impeccably prepared repast."

Stearns gaped at him, gave a choked gasp of laughter and pushed away through the crowd.

Tip was saying: "American Can is off fourteen. And look at Studebaker—"

"Steel is holding," he replied smoothly. "Ninety-six, that's all right. There's your bellwether."

Walter Diehl came up to them and said, "I've been looking for you." His face was a dangerously deep red, almost purple, his eyes were snapping. "They've gone over to Morgan's. Just gone over."

"Who?"

"Mitchell, Wiggin, Prosser, Porter—the heavy artillery. They say they're going to build a floor under it."

"Of course they are." He'd never doubted it for a minute. He grinned at Diehl and his brother. "What's the matter with you characters?" he taunted them genially. "Here come the effing cavalry. Don't you remember last March? or June? Take a brace and a bromide."

"Old Stonewall Chay," Diehl said with a barking laugh. "Nerves of Damascus steel . . ."

"Bethlehem, please," he retorted. "Buy American, boys."

Diehl laughed again, and punched him on the arm. Tip's face was very flat and grave.

"This is worse than March," he said in a low voice. "Worse than last December. This is bad, Chay."

"All right, let's study the form, see how they're running." Calmly he watched the ticker, shutting out the babble of talk, Vera Gaynes's strident, angry voice. "Now, look—Allegheny's at 87.8, that's all right, they're holding. They're off but they're giving ground in good order. You'll see, the pool's probably already starting to—"

"—You're crazy!" Randy Harrodsen, who had come out of nowhere, was screaming at him. "*Fifty*-seven! It's *fifty*-seven . . ."

They stared at him.

"What the hell are you talking about?" Chapin demanded hotly. "It's right there—the last quotation."

"They're late, they're running three and a half

hours *behind* over there *right now* . . ." Randy's face looked puffed, he hadn't realized how puffy his face had become. Booze. Well, each to his vice. "Rick Deverell just told me over the phone—it's 57 and it's still skidding . . ."

Of course. That business of giving only the final digit. Three and a half hours late.

Then. Then they could all be like that, they could all be 30, 40 points lower than this. More. Perhaps more.

Chapin gazed at the ticker again, the clerks frantically writing, smearing, writing again, the figures an insane white scrawl, and the first edge of dread crept into his heart. The points meant nothing, then. They were always claiming figures didn't lie, but these did—if they were running that far behind, none of this meant anything. It could be worse than they thought, much worse. When in God's name were the bankers going to move, put a stop to this?

Someone was begging anyone within hearing for the very latest figure on Carbide, someone else was laughing hysterically; Stearns, the tears streaking his round face under the tortoise-shell glasses. Pomeroy, a big speculator in utilities, was snarling at the ticker, shaking his fist at it and cursing; cool, taciturn Allison Pomeroy. On the platform one of the boys was actually sobbing, erasing a Radio quotation clumsily with his sleeve; he was in himself, probably, had gone in heavy on 10-point margin.

Behind them a voice was saying, "Oh dear God, oh dear God," over and over. He turned and saw Paul Saunders wringing and wringing his hands, his eyes huge in his narrow, milk-white face.

"Pull yourself together, you pallid puke!" Chapin snapped at him savagely. "Or else go in the washroom and hide. I mean it!"

Tip was staring at him in surprise. He'd never used Tip's vulgar nickname for Saunders before; it had always been the exclusive property of the sales force, who hated the Treasurer to a man. Saunders was looking at him fearfully, his lips moving; then he backed away through the tormented crowd.

"Weak-kneed old woman . . ." He could have killed Saunders at that moment, instantly, easily, and the thought gave him an ugly thrill of pure pleasure. "Maybe he'll jump out of his window," he said, staring after him. "Like that fool Offrey over at Batchelder, Sprague. Did you hear about it? Idiot landed right on the roof of a taxi cruising around looking for a fare. Free ride uptown." He laughed harshly. Tip was still watching him in that steady, measuring way. "Well, what do you want me to do?" he demanded. "Hold the poor sod's hand?"

There was a small commotion at the boardroom entrance—they saw Norris Harrodsen come in, followed by the head of the Analysis section, a dour Scotsman named MacCrimmon, fending off a barrage of inquiries and recriminations. He said something to Diehl, signaled to Chapin and Tip; a barely perceptible jerk of his head. They hurried after him down the long corridor to his office, followed by Randy and Bixby and several others.

"Somebody close that door," Harrodsen ordered. It bumped shut, and the boardroom clamor faded. The room became quite still. "All right," he said, leaning forward on his desk, staring at them. His face was drawn, but his eyes were alive with excitement. "Now here's the word. Dick Whitney's just gone on the floor. He hit the steel crowd first, then fifteen or twenty other posts. Put in bids at each one for ten thousand shares at market."

There was an outburst of cheering. Walter Diehl and Randy were hugging each other, Bixby had flung a sheaf of papers high in the air.

"That happy Morgan cabbage!"

"Old J.P. to the rescue . . ."

Chapin declaimed: "Isn't Morgan on the ocean, just the same as on the land?" and the room roared.

Norris waved for quiet. "All right. Now we've taken a beating, but this is as far as it goes." His tone was a regimental commander's speaking to his staff. "Now we turn it around. I don't want to hear any more of this wailing and gnashing of teeth. Is that clear?" There was a low murmur of assent. "Now, there's a wicked backlog of orders out there and I want you to pitch in, double in brass until we can get things straightened out. All right; let's go out there and stop some of this crazy 'crash' talk . . ."

"Do you think it'll work?" Tip was saying. He was watching Walter Diehl, who was sitting down now, his face slick with sweat, his hands hanging limply.

"Of course it'll work." Chapin felt ebullient and powerful again, surging with confidence; the little tremor of apprehension was gone. "I told you they'd dig in, build support. But no, you were full of gloom and doom. You'll see it come back now."

"I'm not so sure."

"Relax—next thing you know they'll be breaking their shoulders trying to get through the door at the same time, and pick up the bargains."

"But what about the little guy? Out in Nebraska, someplace? He hasn't heard about your God damned bankers' pool. All *he's* got is a ticket that's four hours late and a flock of hot rumors. They've been having one hell of a blizzard out there—half the lines are down west of Ohio . . ."

"Where'd you hear that?"

"Over the radio. Where else? What good is this 'support' razzamatazz going to do him? He's cleaned out *now* . . ."

Chapin said: "Jesus God, Tipton, how'd you ever get to be such a bleeding heart?"

"I came by it naturally." Tip had stuck out his lip, looking more stubborn than ever. "Putting my ass in their place. You ought to try it some time."

"You don't think I do?"

"I *know* you don't. You never have . . . I *sold* those

people out there! I sold them in good faith. And God damn it, I've sold them a lousy bill of goods . . ."

Chapin sighed to cover his anger. "Don't you realize you can't change people?"

"I'm not trying to change anybody—"

"They *want* the thrill of danger, don't you see that? Hell, you ought to know—you're married to the biggest thrill-seeker of them all."

Tip's head came up, his eyes narrowed. "Is that a fact."

"And she's right, too—it's the most exciting game: driving as close to the rim as you can. It beats rum-running or robbing banks. Hell, it even beats tom-catting."

"Does it, now."

Tip was still facing him squarely with that flat, implacable expression. There was something faintly threatening about it, too, though Chapin couldn't say why; but this too was a pleasure, quite as much as anything else.

"Indeed it does. And I ought to know," he retorted with an edge of defiance. "Or haven't you read that one either?"

Tip made a sudden, impulsive movement, instantly checked—Chapin had the sense he was going to hit him. In his brother's eyes something anguished and fearful flickered once, and then faded.

He suspects me, Chapin thought. He actually thinks I've been screwing Jophy. Like Montoya. Yes. Of all the de-lovely ironies! He doesn't know where to turn, what to do . . . He would have roared with laughter if holding that discovery far inside himself had not conveyed an even deeper gratification.

"Yessiree, there's a broken heart for every light on Broadway, kid,' he said, and swung away to hide this almost sexual sense of excitement. "Let's go—they're going to be swamped out there . . ."

Tip plodded up the carpeted stairs, fishing absently

in his trousers pocket for his key; the second flight had never seemed so long. In the Stinsons' flat the radio was playing, two comedians' voices and then the bursts of audience laughter like water spattering on pavement. He let himself into the apartment quietly, but there was a light on in the living room as well as in the hallway, and Jophy came toward him quickly.

"Oh, darling, what a long day . . ."

" 'Home the sailor, home from the sea.' " He tried to say it jauntily, but it didn't come off; it just sounded stupid.

"Emmadella left supper," she said.

He followed her into the kitchenette and sat down. His senses were blurred and bruised, as though he'd been on the road nonstop for several months, or been wakened in a strange hotel. Jophy was spooning out chicken and rice. She had covered the slick white plaster of the cast cleverly with a sleeve of flesh-colored stocking, but it still looked barbarous. Women should never break bones and have to wear casts—it mocked their grace; and for Jo, of all women—

She set the plate before him and watched him steadily, her expression grave. He grinned at her and shook his head.

"Quite a day," he murmured. "Quite—a—day."

"I've been reading about it in the papers. Was it as bad as they say?"

"Worse. A whole lot worse. Worse than you can imagine." He rubbed his eyes, staring at the warmed-over food. "Thousands on thousands of people were wiped out today. Millions, for all I know. From here to Seattle."

"You mean, they lost *everything?*"

He nodded at her dumbly.

"But the stocks—they only went down in price, didn't they? Doesn't that just mean they're worth less than before?"

"It's the *margin,*" he said tiredly. He could never understand why she wouldn't grasp these things; her

409

mind was so keen. But she refused to, no matter how carefully he explained. It was perversity, a matter of attitude: we never comprehend the things we have contempt for, and this was truer of Jophy than most people. Grama's legacy.

"It was a chain reaction, Jo," he went on nevertheless. "The stocks fell out of bed, the brokers called for cash or collateral to cover the losses—"

"Oh yes, the margin."

"—and people didn't have it, so they had to realize on their holdings."

"Realize . . ."

"Sell out, *sell* their stocks, whatever they had . . ." His voice was rising, turning testy, and he forced it lower. *"And* that just dumped more stock on the market and forced prices still lower, and the brokers went on screaming for *more* margin—and so on, down the line . . ."

"I see." She pressed her teeth on her lower lip. "Then it'll just keep going down. Won't it?"

"No," he said doggedly. "It'll hold. It'll hold now. The bankers stepped in and held the line. Market even rallied a bit toward the end."

"But if people all over the country are having to hand back their stock to—"

"Jophy, they threw in a quarter of a billion dollars . . ."

"A *billion*—?" She was shocked now, frowning. "How could they possibly do that? I mean, *nobody* has that much money . . ."

"Oh, Morgan's got it. And Wiggin and the others—oh, yes. Lots and lots." He laughed grimly. "That's why they're bankers, Jo."

"Imagine, to be able to walk in and plunk down all that money on the counter."

"They know what they're doing," he hurried along. "They moved fast, put it where it would do the most good—with steel, the fundamentals. You could feel the mood change, you could see prices steady over the next two hours. It'll come back, they're not going to let things get out of hand . . ."

Christ, you sound just like Chapin, he told himself in disgust. Talking about *they,* and their omnipotent brilliance. The more he sought to reassure her about the merits of the bankers' pool, the more distrustful it made him. Would they really be able to hold the line? Now, sitting here exhausted, spouting these bracing platitudes, he knew he didn't believe it at all. Not a God damned word of it. He had sold them a bill of goods. He, Tip Ames. Who was one of them. If he closed his eyes he felt he could see them now, in town after town, in farm and city, where the trains and cars and buggies had taken him—all those faces, hollow-eyed, stunned, eaten away by panic and despair . . . Nothing was going to turn all that around. Nothing.

Jophy had sat down facing him, watching him unsurely. Tonight her very sympathy stung him. He wished she would roar at him with Grama's voice, about ice-eyed capitalists bloating themselves on the blood of the trusting working man . . . It struck him that for the first time in their lives she was seeing a piece of his world through his eyes.

"We won't know for days," he said quietly. "Maybe weeks. They're still trying to sort things out down there. Almost *thirteen million* shares traded. Do you have any idea what that means?"

"No," she shook her head.

"Neither do I. I was there watching it and I don't believe it. My God, it seems like only the other day they were whooping it up over the possiblility of a *five*-million-share day . . ."

"I guess," she said, "the real thing is always much worse than you can ever imagine."

"Maybe."

He didn't really believe that. What you imagined could be infinitely worse than what was happening right before your eyes. Chin in his fists he watched her face, the light on her cheekbone, the eyes where now there was a shadow; thinking again of that terrible afternoon, her face across the court pitiable in its naked desire, and Montoya's dark with purpose . . .

He had walked around in midtown Manhattan for hours afterward, unable to think clearly about anything; had finally wandered into a movie palace off Times Square, one of the new talkies, and watched the celluloid French baroness spurn the attentions of the American naval officer; staring at them and not seeing them, seeing instead Jophy weeping for Montoya—and then laughing with him, her high, heedless laughter, turning to him with that mirror-flash of eyes, reaching out to him, holding him—

He'd jumped to his feet and thrust his way out along the row, stood in the marble lobby with its central fountain and demure nymph, mopping at his face with his handkerchief. Why, I'm running away, he thought; from everything. I've never run away from anything in my life. Anger burned in him then. He had flung out of the theater and hailed a cab. He'd forgotten where he'd parked the car—he'd pick it up tomorrow; or maybe he wouldn't. The streets, the very passers-by looked altered, a familiar landscape revisited after long illness.

Well. He'd always been afraid it would happen. And now it had. She had turned from him. He had lost her. Where did you *go* from here? He was invaded by a sense of utter hollowness, of all things toppling, crashing . . .

She wasn't home; he knew she wouldn't be. He forced himself to read a chapter from *The Jungle Book* to Tessa, holding her in the crook of his arm, as if the warmth of her plump little body could actually warm his own. After that he sat by the window in the near dusk. If she left him, what would he do? What in God's name would he do? Jo lay at the center of his life—heartbeat and marrow; she always had, ever since that sun-washed moment on the deck of the *Al-*

batroz. If she had left him there'd be no point in anything, no point—

But she would leave him; he knew. How long had it been going on? What had it been—a year? two? No—that was impossible! But it had been. Should he—could he—pretend he knew nothing, that nothing had happened? No, he must have it out with her, slam it all into the open.

But then . . . then she *would* leave him, at once. Could he face that, could he stand it? Wasn't it better just to go along, pretend things hadn't changed?

But things had changed. Everything had changed.

It was all so unlike her. Dissembling, lying. It wasn't her way at all. But my God, it couldn't have sprung out of nowhere—

He'd fallen asleep finally, waked in white panic at the mad dangling bell of a fire engine racing down the avenue; and then, as if one bell had tripped off another, the phone call had come from Chapin at the police station . . .

He stirred now, looked up. Jophy was rinsing the dishes clumsily with one hand, to keep the cast out of water. She had realized he wasn't listening. Most people couldn't read his face, but Jo could. She always could. She knew what he was thinking, then. Did she? He watched the slender supple back, the nicely sculpted hips, so lithe, so tense with life; and for all his exhaustion his body ached with need, his heart turned over with sheer simple grief.

. . . If only I hadn't gone up there, he thought for the thousandth time; if only I hadn't been there, and seen her face. Then that whole crazy business with the fountain and the cops would have seemed like nothing more than a madcap prank, a night on the town that got out of hand. Not what it was.

She had reached high above her head with the good hand, putting a cup back on the cabinet shelf; her face, in profile, looked thinner, as though the past months had worn away her features subtly; there was a faint new tightness around her eyes. What had happened between her and Montoya?—what desperate entreaties and renunciations, what agonized resolves? He knew there had been all of that—with Jophy there would have had to be, and more. A lot more. She had never mentioned Montoya again. The action photo from the *Tribune* sports pages she had pinned to the kitchen bulletin board had vanished. She had thrust him out of her life with almost pagan violence—in a silent anguish he could only guess at. Montoya no longer existed for her, he knew . . . But now, neither did he. Maybe that was the cost.

The cost, at market.

The affair had changed her. She'd stopped running around, she no longer had anything to do with Chapin and Jenny and their crowd; she spent a lot of time with Tessa, worked on some madras draperies for the living room.

Her injured shoulder had precluded their sleeping together; or they'd used it as an excuse, which was nearer the truth. He didn't know what to do. Supposed to be ignorant of the affair, he didn't see how he could broach it without at the same time admitting he'd spied on her. That was certainly what it would look like: if he *had* gone up to the match, why hadn't he joined them after it was over?

—Though she'd wept for Montoya that afternoon; had gripped the green railing and wept, for all the world to see . . . Was she, this instant, wondering what Montoya was doing, what expression might be on his face? Did she long, this instant, simply to be with him, *in his presence*—did she feel for Montoya what he, Tip, had never stopped feeling for her one day of his life? It tore at him. And his grief bound him like a prisoner. How did you go forward from this? How could you ever go back, pick up the old, loving ways, make the past months cease to exist?

"You look so tired," she was saying, her voice low.

He shook his head. "I've got to be down there first

thing. Norris has called a board meeting for eight-thirty."

"No—not after a day like this . . ."

"Afraid so. That's what Jack Darcey says it was like in the line: just as you're falling over dead from shelling and strafing and no food, they come around asking you for the supreme effort."

"Yes—it *is* like a war, isn't it? Oh Tip . . . It's the first time I've ever heard you sound pessimistic."

She had passed behind him; her hand came to rest on his shoulder. Almost imperceptibly he started. He hadn't meant to—he was shocked at his response. But he couldn't help it. There had been too many days and nights since Forest Hills. He reached up for her hand, but it had been swiftly withdrawn.

"Maybe if you took a long, hot bath," she was saying in a flat, conversational tone.

"Good idea. If I don't fall asleep and drown in the process," he tried to joke.

Later he lay in the warm, still water, conscious of time's passing, dreading the next day, and the next, and the one after that; wondering how things could go so wrong. In the living room the ship's chronometer from the Gaspa house at Turk's Head struck its piercing glass-slivers of tone, pacing the night watches.

Maybe you couldn't ever get back to what you once had. Maybe that was what it was really all about, under the tinsel and bunting.

He looked at his hand in the water; lifted it out, steadied it. But he would never believe that. Even going down for the third time he would never believe it. Never.

13

By Sunday evening the entire staff was exhausted.
They had stayed up half the night Thursday, nearly
all night Friday and right on through the weekend,
wrestling with the tidal wave of stop-orders, margin
calls, bank drafts and sales records, and they hadn't
even begun to get out of the woods. People went away
for an hour or two, came back white-faced and grim
and flung themselves into the sea of paperwork again.
On Friday afternoon Miss Kendall had a fit of hysteria and someone had to take her home. Saturday
morning one of the clerks actually passed out on his
feet, hit his head so hard on the edge of the platform
Chapin was sure he'd suffered a concussion. But
someone brought him to, and after a time he put his
earphones on and went back to work again.

"—They've got to close the Exchange," Chapin remembered Walter Diehl saying at some point in a
hoarse, pleading voice, "They've *got* to, we can't go on
like this! Just three days, just *two*," and Norris answering tightly:

"And trip off a worse panic? Forget it."

"But another week of this, Norry—"

"What about the investors who're still solvent—you
thought about them? You freeze securities and what'll
they use for collateral? How'll they secure loans, keep
trading, bail themselves out? You want to start one of
those gutter markets out there, like the one we had in

'14, with everyone screaming for buyers and no takers anywhere? Use your head! Christ, all they've got to do is *whisper* they might be closing and the whole works'll collapse . . ."

On Monday it started in all over again, which was bad enough. But Tuesday was awful beyond imagining. From the moment the great gong sounded in the Exchange, huge blocks of stock were thrown into the market with torrential force. And now the leaders began to feel the pressure. Westinghouse dropped 26 points in the first two hours, Allied Chemical lost 28, GE 37½—even Steel, mighty Steel that had held the line all through Black Thursday, was off 14—

Rumors spread through the offices like brush fires. The Exchange was going to close for a full year; the Board of Governors had given up and were hiding in the cellar of the Exchange, watching prices through a periscope mounted in the center of the floor; in Chicago, gangsters, enraged at being sold out, were shooting up the Loop; Mayor Walker had appealed to Governor Roosevelt for the unrestricted use of the National Guard on Wall Street . . .

At eleven-thirty Chapin had gone over to the Exchange, hoping to find out something, anything solid and reassuring in this paperstorm of wild selling and wilder rumor; but it was even more unnerving watching the frenzy there at the very center, the aimless screaming and milling around. At one post a fist fight had broken out, two men trading blows while others tried ineffectually to separate them. Men he'd seen only weeks before nodding genially, signaling a purchase with one brief flick of an order pad, were now howling at one another like dogs, faces apoplectic and hair disheveled.

Genuinely frightened he half ran over to Calkins, Bliss, certain that this powerful Stock Exchange firm that had sponsored so many proud issues would be free of all this violence and hysteria—only to be met with the same boardroom pattern of frantic brokers and clerks and bewildered clients. Paper. It was all a sea of paper everywhere.

Avery Calkins was sitting at his desk, setting two spoons in precise alignment, handle-to-bowl, one above the other.

"Hello, Chay," he said, without looking up. "How's business?"

Chapin stared at him. "What's going on, Avery? What's happening?"

The trader smiled faintly, his eyes narrowed, still lining up the spoons. "Hard times."

"But—what are they *doing?* Whitney, Lamont, Mitchell, the big guns?"

"They just held a meeting. Which I dutifully attended."

"Well, what did they decide?"

Calkins hit the bowl of the first spoon smartly with his fist. The second spoon, porpelled upward, flashed once in the air spinning, clattered against a crystal highball glass and skittered across the desk top.

"Damn," Calkins said matter-of-factly. He sighed, stared out of the window. "The consensus was that it was not properly their function to maintain a specific level of prices. Or for that matter to protect any individual profit."

Chapin leaned over the desk, watching Calkins retrieve the errant spoon. "But they've *got* to . . .!"

"There was general agreement that there had been an excessive overcommitment on a falling market." He paused, sizing up the distance from the spoons to the highball glass. "Except for air holes, of course."

"You mean—"

"Yes, the block offerings that can't find any bid at all. That sort of thing. They reaffirmed their intention to plug those, wherever and whenever. Tommy Lamont was very explicit on that point."

Chapin struck the desk top with his hand, jarring the spoons' alignment. "But the price level—if they don't come in and support it now—"

"They can't, Chapin."

"Can't *what*—? Of course they can—they can do anything they want to do!"

"Not this time." Calkins brought his fist down again; the catapulted spoon missed the glass entirely and landed soundlessly on the carpeted floor. He made no comment, no move to retrieve it. "That $240 million—it was like trying to dam the Hudson out there with a couple of stone boats. It was swept away in hours."

"—But they can't—they've never let things simply—*crash* . . ." It was the first time he'd used the word seriously, it had just slipped out, and that frightened him more than anything else. *Craaaaaash.* "Even in '07 they stopped it—Morgan himself stepped in, they stopped it in one afternoon . . ."

"This seems to be a bit different." The old man's eyes rose to Chapin's with a weary sagacity, very cold, very steady. "What we have here is an irrational, overwhelming desire to sell. And sell. And sell again. They can't stem that, and they know it."

He bent over to pick up the spoon. Chapin watched him stupidly, hating him all at once, remembering now Calkins in September talking about getting out of Radio, reducing his holdings in Kennecott and Baldwin, maybe even taking himself out of the market entirely. Had he done that? Was he now sitting on a hefty cash reserve, waiting till this plummeting market had hit bottom to step in and pick up all the bargains?

" . . . So prices are to be allowed to fall," he got out bitterly. "No matter how fast or how far."

"Well. Seek their own level, as the saying goes."

"But there *is* no level," he burst out, "—how can you settle on what a stock is worth at a time like this, with all the fences down, with all the usual standards—"

He broke off, ran his fingers along the side of his nose. Calkins' expression hadn't altered a particle. He watched Chapin a moment, then turned his attention to the spoons again.

"I'm only telling you what I heard," he offered quietly.

"They don't mean it," Chapin said, more to himself than to the old man. "They've said that to discourage the stop-orders, raiding." He nodded, staring hard at Calkins. "That's it. They'll come in tomorrow and build a floor. They'll have to—they'll see they've got to, and that's what they'll do."

"They might," Calkins said still more softly. "But I wouldn't bet a great deal on it, Chapin."

There was no comfort back at the office, either. The torrent of selling had increased, if anything—five-and-ten-thousand-share chunks thrown in for whatever they would bring; a torrent surging, cresting savagely, the sell orders coming faster and heavier than any mere human beings could ever hope to handle them.

"It's the *volume*," he muttered. "Where's all this volume coming from?"

"Three guesses," Norris Harrodsen said grimly, banging down a phone.

"Thursday knocked out the little guy. Now it's our turn."

"Our turn?" he echoed.

"Yes. Ours. What the hell did you think?"

The boardroom was nearly empty now. Allison Pomeroy had stormed out of the offices on Monday, raging and cursing; Bartells and Trask had been cleaned out Friday, and so had Ritchey; the glamorous, adventuresome Vera Gaynes had wandered away in a daze, looking haggard and beaten. Stearns was still sitting there in the front row of chairs as though he had no other place to go, staring fearfully through his horn-rimmed spectacles at the stuttering, drifting ticker although he'd been sold out three days before. What did he expect to see? What could anyone expect to see now?

The ordered sequence of events vanished. People came and went, phones rang in a shivery jangle, brokers and traders shouted at each other, quarreled, traded insults, wandered away again. Chapin remembered an afternoon out on the Sound that summer, lounging over the tiller listening with bemused detachment to Andy Rawless reminiscing about the Argonne offensive, when all the pilots were flying support missions round the clock, and he'd actually lost all sense of what day it was, what week or year, and finally even whether it was evening or early morning . . . Now he himself was swept with the same viscous, dreamy, tormented sensation.

Jenny's voice over the phone. "You'll be home by seven-thirty, won't you, Chay? We've got Tina Cappelletti, and the Baylisses." She might have been calling from Saturn. He had no idea what he'd answered.

At some point there was Miss Lamprey—sturdy, imperturbable Jeanne Lamprey—screaming wildly at Norris Harrodsen, and then just as quickly collapsing into hysterical weeping, shaking her head desolately while Norris patted her soft round shoulder. There was Tip, looking stubborn and exasperated, saying, "Fine, swell—why don't you ring up that infallible *they* of yours and inform them they can't allow this to happen?" There was Walter Diehl crouched over his desk, slate eyes bloodshot, steadily pouring liquor from a square brown bottle into a paper cup. There was Jake Lynstrom staring into a green metal wastebasket crammed with paper and shaking his head dully.

"What are those?" Chapin had asked him.

Jake had looked up with a sick, hollow smile. "Orders."

"Orders?"

"Yeah. I—forgot them. I just forgot all about them."

Down, down, down. Everything tumbling. The investment trusts were plunging right out of sight. Mighty Blue Ridge down from 24 to 10 to 3, Greylock—his beloved Greylock!—falling from 58 to 37, to 29, to 22. There were no takers. Where in God's name were the big wheels, the titans? Even if Avery was right and they weren't going to throw in price supports, even if they *had* cold-bloodedly decided to abandon the market to its fate, why weren't they coming in now, *now* to scoop up all the basement bargains? What was the matter with them? He phoned Calkins six times and finally got through to him. No, there had been no change in the bankers' position; they *had* decided to keep the Exchange open, though . . .

And finally Saunders, his face white as old bone, a nervous tic clutching at his left eye, holding tremulous fingers over the phone's mouth and saying in a small, frightened voice:

"—that's the last of it, Norris. Our cash reserves. They're gone, they're all gone . . ." and Harrodsen, still impeccably groomed, turning and saying:

"All right. Tell him we're throwing in the blue chips. Steel, GM, Tel and Tel, the works."

Chapin couldn't believe he had heard him correctly. "But that's our solid base," he heard himself protesting. "Our last line of—"

"Do tell."

He clutched at Norris' shoulder, half-pulled him around. "But—we can't do that, we've got to hang on to that, Norris, we've got to!"

"Well, now . . ." Harrodsen straightened, shrugging off his hand, and Chapin was frightened by the look of intense loathing in his father-in-law's face. "Just what do you suggest? . . . We will hold the line," he said between his teeth. "We will *hold* it!"

"But that won't do it, that's crazy—in effect all we'll be doing is buying back our own stock, at depressed prices! We'll just be ruining *ourselves* . . ."

But now Harrodsen had gripped him by the coat lapel. "Now you listen to me, Chapin. It just so happens we have obligations to our stockholders, whether you want to honor them or not."

"But that won't solve it—we'll only be burying our- selves faster, wiping out what little chance we've got left—"

Harrodsen stepped back, his face wrathful in the sinking October light. "Very pretty," he said. "You've had a nice ride, and now you want to bail out. Is that it?"

"I'm trying—"

"You raked it in quickly enough when everything was happy days—now you want to run home with your own Easter egg. Is that it? Well, that's not the way the game is played."

"*Game!*" he almost shouted. "What do you mean, *game*—! It's life and death . . ."

"How true." The older man's eyes flickered with contempt. "Now you can take your lumps, right along with the rest of us."

Chapin gazed at the other faces in the room— Saunders, Tip, Bixby, Mal MacCrimmon. Their eyes were flat and accusatory, they were condemning him—Jesus, didn't they see that realizing on their blue chips would ruin them all for good and for ever?

"No!" he cried, and locked his hands together. "I'm opposed, I want it on record that I oppose any such unwarranted liquidation!"

Harrodsen threw back his head. "What do you want—a debate, a God damned congressional hear- ing? The whole forest's on fire, Chapin—can't you grasp that?" For another second he glared at his son- in-law, turned to the others. "We're wasting precious time. I am the head of this firm, and until I am re- moved I will decide on policy. Now get—"

Chapin grasped his shoulder again, but differently. "Please, Norris," he begged. "They'll plug it, they'll build a floor under us. They've got to! Just—hang on a little longer . . ."

"I'll tell you what your beloved *they* are doing," Tip said tightly, "—they're selling short. That's what *they* are doing right now."

"Where'd you hear that?"

"I just talked to Frank Delahant over at Lee, Hig. They've even given up plugging the air holes."

"They wouldn't do that—they couldn't . . ."

Harrodsen said: "Just what do you think those ten-thousand-share blocks are all about? They're bear raids. They're dumping everything they can overboard, before the ship goes down. Lamont's over there right now, trying to deny it all. That the support you had in mind?"

With this news the last fibers of his confidence gave way. The ripples of disquietude he'd felt on Thursday when the ticker had betrayed him now swelled to a millrace of fear. There was no salvage, then, no hope of recovery. They would all rocket right on down to rock bottom . . .

"All right," Norris was saying, "let's have this out. I want total unanimity, or I want to know why we *don't* have it. Somebody go get Walter, Jake, the rest of them."

"Walter's drunk, Norris," Tip said.

"I don't care if he's got the God damned bends. Take him down to the can if you have to, and sober him up. But get him!"

Tip nodded at Chapin. The two of them went down the hall and through Miss Hannegan's office, tapped on Diehl's door.

"Walter?" Chapin said. "Walter?"

There was no answer. Tip tried the knob. It was locked. They looked at each other mutely, thinking the same thing.

" . . . Yeah?" Walter Diehl's voice came just then. Chapin felt a surge of pure relief.

"Walter, Norris has called a meeting."

" . . . Go ahead. I don't care." An old man's voice, hoarse with phlegm. "All over anyway. *I* don't care . . ."

"Walter, open up," Tip said briskly. "Let's go, now."

" . . . Never forgive me. Never . . ." He was crying now, a thick sobbing that sounded almost as if he

425

were chuckling at some private joke. "My Suzy. My baby girl. I wanted—give her the whole wide, beautiful world . . ."

"He's pie-eyed," Tip said, "he's never coming out on his own." He turned to Miss Hannegan. "Elaine. Haven't you got a key?"

"He took it away from me a little while ago. Said he needed it."

"All right, who else has got one? Saunders? The janitor?"

The explosion stopped them dead. A savage coughing roar of an explosion. Chapin found himself staring at Elaine Hannegan's blank pale face in boundless fearful realization, piercing memory. Then Tip had whirled and flung himself at the door once, again, had reared back and kicked it open in an awful, splintering crash of wood, and plunged inside. Chapin followed him, conscious of the odor of gunpowder.

There was no one at the desk. The swivel chair had been kicked across the room, was facing the bookcases. No. There. Walter Diehl lay on the floor behind the desk, on his back, arms flung wide, the skin of his belly showing pastily through the twisted shirt. Blood was pulsing thickly from the side of his head. His face was gray, his eyelids fluttered; the entire body quivered, a dense shuddering quiver, as though unbearably cold. Unreal tableau. But of course it was. Real.

"My God," a voice behind him kept saying. "Oh—my—God . . ."

Tip was bent over Diehl, his head pressed to the man's chest. The gun—a black, long-barreled revolver—lay near the radiator. Someone pushed past Chapin: Norris, looking incredulous and shaken, his lips moving, then Elaine Hannegan, one hand to her hair, her eyes staring wide. Tip was already on the phone, was saying tersely:

"Connie? Get an ambulance, fast. What? *I* don't know what the number is—just *ring* the operator and *get* one. Now, step on it! . . ."

Someone was being sick. Saunders, gripping the back of a chair, was vomiting copiously, spattering on the rug. The Pallid Puke. Tip's name was prophetic, then. Chapin realized he was grinning idiotically, and covered his mouth with his hand. Elaine was kneeling beside Diehl now, patting at his head with a handkerchief that kept soaking red, soaking and dripping its way through her fingers. She was saying something to Diehl, over and over, but Chapin couldn't hear what she was saying.

All of a sudden he felt unsteady, he almost went to his knees, backed away toward the door. Diehl's face was gray now, a dark gray wax. Blood kept sliding through Elaine Hannegan's fingers, soaking the carpet. Away. He had to get away. From here.

"Good old stodgy Beantown by the bay," Chapin murmured. He was standing in the center of the great bow windows, looking off down Beacon Street toward the Public Garden. "I miss it, I must say."

"Do you really?" Serena Aldridge said. "I rather thought all those bright lights had ensnared you." She paused. "That and the Old World fleshpots."

He turned then and glanced at her sharply, looked away again. "Well. They're not glittering very brightly down there right now."

"No, I should imagine not."

"It's funny. I used to think that nothing unpleasant could ever happen to me here. In this house."

"Perhaps you were right."

"I used to feel time was like liquid, like gas or smoke, and this house had caught it somehow, captured it under a glass bell."

"Time isn't as easy to trap as all that."

He turned away from the window. "I'm sorry, Auntie. I'm not myself this evening. Walter Diehl shot himself. Tuesday. Right there in his office. I saw him. Right afterward."

She set down her stem glass of sherry. Ah, that was it, then.

"How perfectly awful for you," she said.

"I can't stop seeing him. Lying there on the carpet. His whole body was *shivering* so . . ." He shook his head as though to clear it. "One moment he was sitting there, on the other side of the door, crying, saying something about his daughter. Suzy. And the next he was—nothing. A shivering lump of flesh. Just—nothing . . ."

She'd known he was shaken from the moment he'd come in from the airport. What surprised her was the depth of his fear; she had not seen him as unstrung as this in a long while. Not in a very long while.

"Auntie, is that it? All there is to it? Just—quivering, rotting flesh? What do you think? Really."

Impassively she watched the handsome, slender face. "That's about it," she said.

"And you've thought that . . . for years?"

"Of course," she snapped, vexed with him. "Good heavens, Chapin, you've seen death before . . ."

His face closed then and hardened, his eyes fell away; he moved off across the room. She welcomed even that change of mood, though she hadn't meant to put it so flatly. She added: "All those flying accidents in Texas. Didn't you ever think about it then?"

He shook his head. "Not once. I don't know why."

—Because you were young, that's why, she thought—and had to forget another death; when one is young death is no more than a distant abstraction, something that happens to the very old, to others . . . For the first time in years she thought of Spencer Broome standing here in this still, stately room, very near where Chapin was now by the ribbon-backed Chippendale chairs, his eyes steady and ardent. He wanted her to marry him; he was perfectly serious about it, he was convinced she would say yes, she could see it in his face. She was fond enough of him, he could be such fun at cotillions, at skating parties on the reservoir in Brookline, or sailing out to Hurlestone Shoals . . . but to marry a *painter,* spend one's days in Venice or Rome in some damp pensione—no: it was out of the question.

She hadn't meant to smile—she knew now it had only been nervousness, the surprise of his proposal, the way his hair—he always wore it too long—looped down over his brows: the absolute incongruity of her becoming Mrs. Spencer Broome, living in a welter of half-daubed canvases and smeared rags and dirty wine glasses. But she *had* smiled. He'd been so shaken: his lips had trembled, his eyes had actually filled.

"Serena, I don't know what to say—I've always thought you cared for me—I was sure you felt real affection . . ."

And then, having smiled inadvertently, she'd been compelled to compound the felony by smiling at him broadly. It had been worse, much worse than if she'd laughed in his face or slapped him.

"Why, Spencer," she'd answered, "wherever did you come by *that* notion?"

Three days later he had gone off to fight against Spain. It was in this room, too, that Charlotte had burst in on her that other afternoon, her pretty face pale with alarm.

"Oh, Serena—Spencer's dead! Of fever. In Cuba . . ."

She shouldn't have said what she did then, either. It was Lottie's deep agitation, that heedless, affectionate way of hers that provoked her; it always could.

"He was determined to go," she'd said coldly.

"Oh—Serena . . ."

She had gone up to her room for the remainder of the evening. Later on Papa had tapped on her door and wished her goodnight in a hesitant voice. No one had ever mentioned Spencer Broome again; but Lottie had always known. Poor, guileless, emotional Lottie . . .

Chapin was wandering aimlessly around the room. She wanted to tell him to sit down, but she knew it was better to let him work his way around to what was eating him most. He had picked up one of the carved jades, was inspecting it intently.

"Lovely. T'ang, isn't it?"

"Yes. Ch'en Chou."

"Very elegant." His finger traced the intricately entwined figures of the panthers. "Are they coupling in love, or is it a struggle to the death?" he mused softly. "Hart to tell." He set the piece down with care on the Sheraton table, turned and looked at her directly.

"Auntie, I'm in a jam. A very bad jam."

"Oh?" She watched him from under her brows. "This latest *readjustment* in the market?"

He did not smile. "It's worse than that. It's a disaster." He paused. "We're in trouble, Auntie. We're all in big trouble."

"I thought as much. Your funds, too? Greylock and Macomah?"

He nodded, licked his lips. "It's fallen. Almost to nothing. All the trusts have plummeted right out of sight."

She said: "And you wanted me to put *all* my money into them."

"I know, I know." He ran his fingers along his nose. "I was wrong. I guess. I can't believe they'd betray us the way they have."

"What about Norris Harrodsen?"

"He's cleaned out. He threw in all the firm's assets, paper and cash—finally his own personal holdings, everything."

"Why did he do that?"

"He thought he was going to stem the tide. It was insane—he destroyed himself in one afternoon."

"And you didn't?"

"What? No, I hung on to some blue chips, my personal assets . . ." He said with sudden vehemence: "I tried to argue with him but he wouldn't listen, he was all pumped up with concepts of personal honor, corporate obligations to the stockholders. I tried to bring

430

him to his senses but he wasn't having any. Believe me, it's no time for altruism—it's a time for sauve qui peut, where's the fire exit. He's a damned fool . . ."

There was a pause. Serena said: "How is Jenny taking this?"

He shrugged. "Badly. Sullen, purse-mouthed stoicism. Sulks in her room, and then drives like Barney Oldfield all over Long Island."

"She's angry with you."

He laughed once. "You could say that. Oh, sure—I've turned overnight into an ogre who's betrayed the hand that fed him."

So Jenny would be of no further use to him—she probably had realized that by now. Had *he*? Would he leave her now, the better to pursue his own desires? Or was the habit of convention too strong for that? It would be interesting to see which way the cat jumped.

"I'm in a great deal of trouble, Auntie," he was saying now in some agitation. "Really and truly. I—I need your help."

She arched her back. "Of course you have other assets you can call on."

"What do you mean?"

"There's that airplane you bought last year, for one thing."

He shrugged. "Well, that, of course."

"And the yacht. And the fancy automobiles. And the summer place on the Sound."

He nodded tightly. "I suppose so. The market for them will be depressed, with so many people unloading now."

"And then there are your collections."

"My collections—!" He glared at her wildly—it was as though she had struck him. "But—those are *mine!* You can't expect me to part with *those* . . ."

What a maker and breaker of men money was! The books pictured it as an inert, lumpish mass, but she had always known better, ever since she'd accompanied Papa as a little girl into the First Federal Bank, into Maxim's, into Shepheard's Hotel in Cairo. Money could fly, it could run, it could strike with the force of a typhoon. Money was a vast, all-powerful djinn, exactly like the creature in the Arabian Nights. It put its huge hand under you and raised you above the clouds; it puffed out its dusky cheeks and blew once, and everything—everything!—was swept away . . . She knew that, too—that was precisely why she'd withheld most of her money from these trusts of Chapin's (to his great disgust), had left it in first-class rails and industrials or put it in real estate. The very first rule of human existence was that there is relatively little difference between a lot of money and a vast lot of money—but there is a whole spinning world of difference between a lot of money and no money at all.

Chapin didn't understand that rule, though she'd certainly tried to teach it to him over the years. There he stood, affronted and quite angry, cloaked in that brash impatience, that arrogance that had grown in him through the decade . . . Perhaps he needed a little chastising, a—a period of probation; a few hard knocks. He'd played the grand entrepreneur and social lion to his heart's content, he'd recklessly lost a good deal of her money and most of Gus Lawring's and God knew how many other people's. Why should he feel he could come running to her, get off scot free?

"—You're punishing me," he was saying hotly. "You're resentful of the enormous profits you've missed out on all these years, with your niggardly—"

"Don't go too far, Chapin," she broke in crisply.

"Well, it's true, isn't it? You've been hoping for a crash, to prove you were right! . . ."

She smiled. "You're losing your aplomb, Chapin. I assure you I haven't been hoping for any such thing. I'm merely suggesting that you ought to take your losses well. You certainly took your gains readily enough. Why should your *collections* be so sacrosanct?"

"—Because I built them over years, with loving care!"

He broke off, astonished at what he'd just said, the naked admission of it, and swung around and faced the windows again. In a more quiet voice he said: "They *matter* to me, Auntie—they matter a great deal. I don't see why I should have to give up everything . . ."

She picked up her glass and sipped at it, held the dry, smoky sherry in her mouth a moment before she swallowed it.

"What about Tipton?" she asked.

"Tip? Oh, *he's* all right." He laughed without amusement. "He went out next day and found himself another job."

"Another job!" she exclaimed. "You mean Harrodsen fired him? At a time like this?"

"Auntie, the firm is bankrupt, dead in the water— there is nothing to be fired *from,* there's nothing to sell; don't you understand?" He picked up the jade piece again, absently. "Jesus, you should have heard him. Everyone was sitting around in the boardroom looking at everyone else and Century said, 'What are you going to do, Tip?' and Tip said: 'I'm going out and get a job.' And Jake Lynstrom said, 'But there aren't any jobs—the Street is dead.' And Tip came right back at him: 'Of course there are jobs out there, don't be ridiculous! I've got a wife and two kids to support. I've got to have a job, and I'm going out and get one.' Which he promptly went out and did. Weeks, Barlow."

She uttered her sharp, single-note laugh, and shook her head. "That man is the limit!"

He stared at her. "What did you expect? Did you think he'd blow his brains out, too? Not the irrepressible Schoolboy." And now she could hear the edge of resentment in his voice. "Why should *he* ever worry? He's got his unshatterable illusions . . ."

"Is that what they are?"

433

"He'll always land on his feet, never fear."

"But he lost everything too, didn't he?"

"His stock is worthless, along with everyone else's."

Went right out and got himself a job. If there was one, he'd find it. Create it. She pressed her fist hard against her thigh. He was the limit! The limit! She was conscious of that clash of swords which his presence, even the mention of him, always aroused in her. She pushed her sherry glass carefully away from her with the tips of two fingers. Nevertheless, that put a different complexion on the matter. A very different complexion. Chapin—Chapin couldn't be allowed to founder if Tipton was still running on all six. The balance would have to be redressed somehow.

"She'll stay with him, then," she said aloud. "Josefina."

He threw her a quizzical glance. "I should think so—since she's stuck with two kids, and not a dime of her own."

Serena laughed again. "Oh, that won't stop her! She's far too bold for that. Something properly engages her passion, she'll be off and away, like one of her forebears—willing to sail right off the rim of the earth . . ."

He laughed for the first time; he seemed hugely pleased by the thought. "Do you really think so?"

"She's an adventuress, Chapin."

"No, she's not," he protested. "She's a—she's—I don't know what she is. But you certainly couldn't call her an adventuress."

"Oh, yes I can!" She laughed again, curiously elated with things. "You have absolutely no idea how lucky you are . . ."

He gazed back at her for a long moment, his eyes cold as slate, flat; an expression so unfathomable she could feel herself turn uncertain and apprehensive under it. Then he looked down and nodded.

"Perhaps you're right," he said. "Actually I haven't

434

laid eyes on her for months. I imagine she's lashing him properly, now the carnival's over."

"The carnival?"

"The *party*—the rip-roaring, five-alarm, go-to-hell fling. The whole country club picnic. Now she'll make him pay for the loss. That's what every American woman really wants, isn't it? To castrate us for life?"

"My, you *are* a cynical one," she murmured after a little.

"You've called me that often enough. It's true. I am. But at least I admit it, Auntie." Slowly he smiled. "That ought to score me some points, don't you think?"

Smiling in answer she nodded. The seven-foot grandfather clock out in the hall boomed the hour in its resonant, minor key.

"All right," she said briskly. "Let's get down to cases, shall we? How much will you need?"

14

"As near as I can figure it," Norris Harrodsen began. He stopped, stared dully at the far wall of his office, where a handsome old print of the port of New York was hanging. He began again. "As near as *anyone* can figure it . . . we owe about fifteen million dollars."

Tip, sitting across from him, made no answer. There seemed to be nothing to say. It was perfectly quiet; the offices and boardroom were deserted. The day, a Friday, was the first of a series of "special holidays" for the Stock Exchange that Whitney had proclaimed, ostensibly to allow firms to catch up on the sea of paperwork, but in reality to give the stunned, exhausted brokers, clerks and messengers some desperately needed rest. Harrodsen had sent home everyone but Elmer Taylor and a few girls in the mailroom. Tip had come over from his new office at Weeks, Barlow after a three-day swing through southern New England and found Harrodsen sitting there alone. Beyond the windows the late autumn sun sunk toward the Jersey shore through bands of slate and gold cloud; the wind moaned softly at the windows. Tip thought of Big Tom Flanagan punching the clock in the little gatehouse to Holcomb's Mill, buttoning his jacket collar against the wind and half-singing: *"Hear that north wind blow; where did your summer wages go?"*

"No, we're wiped out," Harrodsen said doggedly, as

if stating the fact would make it more acceptable. "We're all through. Done for." He drew his hand along the underedge of his mustache, an old man's gesture. He had aged fifteen years in the past two weeks. His hair, which had been such a rich, distinguished silver, now looked simply white and lifeless. The hazel eyes were wavering and uncertain; Tip remembered a long-ago afternoon and those same eyes, veiled with hostility, with disapproval. *"That is not capital, Mr. Ames. Not remotely. I can't believe you're serious."* Now Mr. Harrodsen had no capital—not remotely. Now we're equal, you and I, Tip told himself. But there was no pleasure whatever in the thought.

"—I never knew he had that gun," Harrodsen said suddenly, looking up. "Did you?"

"No," Tip said.

"He used to go shooting winters. In South Carolina. Never cared for shooting myself . . . I didn't think he had the courage for it."

"You think that took courage?"

"Of course it did. *I* couldn't do it. Could you?"

Tip looked at him. "I haven't any idea. It's never entered my mind." He watched the older man a moment, said: "How's Mrs. Diehl taking it?"

"Much better than I would have suspected." His eyes focused sharply, as though a new and disturbing thought had just occurred to him. "Well, Ellie was always down-to-earth. Her father was Reggie Barron, you know. Big commodities trader. Chicago. Back in the days when they shot first and found out who it was afterward. He used to team up with George Carruthers—'Close-the-Gates-of-Mercy' Carruthers, they used to call him. They took Armour to the cleaners one time. Lordy, what an old pirate he was . . ."

Tip let him run on. He was bone weary himself and on edge, but he knew Harrodsen needed to talk, reminisce about old friends and former days. Even buried ten feet underground an old watch has to go on ticking—

"It was Suzy who went all to pieces," Norris was saying. "Completely hysterical. Flew around smashing things, cut her hand badly. Absolutely refused to believe it. Hardy came over and gave her a shot and it didn't have any effect at all for ten minutes. Lay there shaking like a leaf, started accusing me, Paul, Chapin, everyone . . .

"Where is your brother, anyway?" he demanded sharply.

Tip stared at him. "Why, I don't know, Norris. Gone home, I suppose. Or he's over there with Calkins."

"That's about the size of it." Norris nodded angrily, wrenching his neck in his collar. "Old Avery's in clover. Took himself out in August. Trust Chapin to switch his flag to the vessel that's still afloat." His voice rose hoarsely. "He's angry with me. At the board meeting Wednesday he accused me of selling him out—did you know that? *He* accused *me* of betraying him . . .!"

"He's wrong," Tip said quietly. "You did the right thing. You were trying to protect the stockholders."

"Yes. Well. Maybe I'll pick up a few points. In heaven. Or wherever. They bailed out over at Stahl Brothers, you know. Let the fund go down the chute, clung to the holdings." He rubbed his eyes. "Mason Frye is up on charges already, I heard. Obligating clients' unearned assets on margin." He snorted. "They start that game and they'll have to indict the whole Street . . .

"Well, they will if they want to. Ever noticed how nobody even *thinks* of putting up a stoplight at a bad intersection until there's one big smash, with cars and bodies all over the road? Now we'll have the commissions, the charges and investigations. Hell, they'll be over here any day now."

"You?" Tip said. "If they investigate you they'd better look into everybody."

"Ah, but I've gone under, son. It's a lot more fun shooting at a sitting target than a moving one. Country *wants* vengeance, villains. Someone to blame. And here we are: the big bad bogeymen of Wall Street. What a field day there's going to be."

"I can't believe they'd do that," Tip murmured.

"Can't you? Just wait a bit." Harrodsen threw himself back in the chair. "Blame," he muttered tonelessly. "I still say it was England did us in. That crook Hatry, all those unauthorized issues, forged certificates. And Ben Strong giving in to Norman, lowering the rate, back in '27. That's when it started to get out of hand, I'll tell you that . . ."

No, Tip thought heavily, listening to Harrodsen rambling along about Britain's return to an overvalued pound, and Montagu Norman's appeal for easier money, easier credit; no. It was the margin, that God damned gambler's ten percent margin. That and Chapin's crazy leverage, which went just as sensationally in reverse once it got going. It wasn't the beleaguered pound sterling or the federal discount rate or some slippery counterjumper like Hatry. The whole machine got out of hand. Like one of Chapin's parties. Like Jo and that cop. You had to pay your way, pay the piper some time, and nobody wanted to. We got what we deserved, he thought, all his Yankee probity outraged and smarting—and immediately after that: Sure, but does *everyone* deserve it?

He stirred restlessly, troubled, and Norris, distracted as he was, caught it. "Well, the hell with all that. How do you like it over at Weeks?"

"All right. It's a different operation. They're a lot more—deliberate, cautious."

"Maybe that's what we need. More caution. They let you bring your force over with you?"

"Four men."

"I see. Some difficult choices for you, then."

"You bet there were."

"Going to be a lot of good men out of work soon. If they aren't already. Lot of good men."

"It'll come back, Norris," Tip said. "It's got to. You'll be back on top again."

440

Harrodsen shook his head. "I wish I could believe that. I'm too old, Tipton." Norris always called him by his full name, but he'd never resented it as he did with Aunt Serena. "You can start over again. You and Chapin. You're young enough to bounce back. I'm too old. Old men lack resilience. They lack—nerve . . ."

"Well, *you* don't."

"You can fake it perhaps, for a while, but it's always there. The sense of disaster. You hesitate when you should move, you find yourself saying *no*—or *I'm not sure,* which is even worse—when you ought to say *yes.*" He smiled for the first time, a weary, naked smile. "You'll see."

"I don't believe it," Tip said stubbornly. "You've got nerve enough for twenty."

"Thank you, Tipton. Thanks for saying that." Harrodsen got to his feet, gave a little stagger and righted himself. "Been sitting too long." His eyes flared irritably at Tip, who stood up and said:

"You need a rest, Norris."

"Yes. I do." He moved toward the door. "I'm going home for a spell. Take it easy. Few holes of golf, do some puttering around in the garden, maybe rake a few leaves. I haven't raked any leaves since—Jesus, since I came to work in the Street." At the door he turned and faced Tip. "I put my money on the wrong horse. You're the one I should have backed, Tipton."

"Me?" Tip said, startled. "I'm no money-man, Norris. Hell, I'm just a salesman."

"You've got what matters. I didn't like you, first time we met. You struck me as a bit of an upstart. Over-reaching yourself. But I was wrong: you're the real thing. You know how to take it. And you can deliver." He clapped his hand once on the sales manager's shoulder. "Good luck to you, son."

Tip watched Harrodsen walk away down the hall, the trim figure faintly stoop-shouldered; he heard the outer door click closed. Then he went into his old office and sat at his desk, looking at nothing, listening

441

to the quick hum of time. The sun had dropped behind the cloud bank—heavy, dirty ridges of cloud promising sleet and snow. The wind rattled one of the window frames harshly now. There was the feeling, high here above the town, of being on the bridge of a ship—a condemned ship whose crew had taken to the boats. He thought of the old *Albatroz,* and a smoky, sun-shot morning long ago . . . but then at least there had been the smells and textures of human emotion, human struggle. Here there was nothing but bare walls and expended paper.

He didn't know how long he'd last with Weeks, Barlow; they didn't look in too good shape themselves. Henry Weeks had been glad to get him—he'd tried to lure him away from D, H back in '27—but the whole operation felt tentative and shaky. He'd been able to bring Jack and Blazer and Web and Skeets over with him, at least for now. Maury had surprised him; he'd said he'd had enough of the market—he'd gone in heavy in automotives and taken a bad beating—and wanted to go back with Alec Ham. Bake was through with selling, he said—he'd gone to work in his father's general store back home in Kingfield. He'd felt worse about Sid and Clarence, having to tell them; maybe if business picked up he could take them on. Only it didn't look one hell of a lot as though business was going to pick up for quite a while.

He'd better give Jophy a ring, let her know he was coming home for dinner. He dreaded going home: she'd never understand this. Worth $60 million one day, in hock $15 million the next. Well, have to tighten the old belt now, the clubs, the extras. Cards started running against you, you cut your losses or you went to the cleaners. The car would hold up, he could reach his territory by driving. And there was that little nest egg he'd stashed away in the Providence National to tide them over if things got tighter. His hole card. This was going to be a long haul, no matter what Hoover and Livermore and some of the hot-dogs were saying.

As he reached for the phone it started to ring. He picked it up and said: "Diehl, Harrodsen."

A voice said sharply: "Who's this? Who's this?"

"Who is calling?"

"—Tip? That you?" Chapin's voice, unmistakably.

"Yeah, it's me."

"Thank God—I've been calling all over trying to reach you! Thank God you're there. Tip, they're on their way over . . ."

"Who's on their way?"

"The examiners, the Exchange people! Harvey Branch just tipped me off—I'm out here on the Island. They're after the Macomah records."

"Macomah? Why do they want to look into Macomah?"

"It's the bankruptcy matter—with D,H the issuing firm they'll shut down Greylock, Horizon, all of them . . ."

"All right, if they've got to check out Macomah, what's so—"

"No, it isn't *all right!* The underwriting was set up on an exchange of stock with Horizon—they'll invalidate them both, don't you see that?"

"No, I don't see it, I don't see it at all." He looked at the palm of his free hand, said: "Just what the hell did you pull with Macomah, Chay?"

"Tip, there isn't time to go into this, believe me! It's purely technical, a matter of financing—I'll go into it all later. Right now you've got to get those Macomah records out of there!"

"You what?—you want me to *what*—?"

"Just get them out of there—the *blue* files, the entire *blue* files, they hold everything on Macomah."

Tip said: "You're asking me to remove all trace of the existence of an issue—"

"They'll take it away from us. Tip, it's ours! *Our fund . . .*"

443

"Do you realize what you're *saying?* That's embezzlement, corporate evasion, that's a—"

"Oh my God, if you're going to start in on ethics—"

"You bet I am! It's wrong, Chay. Just plain wrong . . ."

"*Wrong*—!" There was a faraway crash of something dropped on the floor, glass shattering. "Jesus H. Christ, is it any more wrong than Ben Smith's pools on Anaconda, or Wiggin selling his own bank short, or those flim-flam Peruvian bonds of Mitchell's? Haven't you learned anything at *all*—?"

"That doesn't make it any more right, and you know it! I say we'd better take our medicine along with the rest of them."

"Medicine—! Why should *we* go down because D,H has had it? What sense does that make?"

"Chapin, what are we fighting about? It's cleaned out anyway. Macomah. It's a shell . . ."

"Of course," Chapin shouted, "of course it is, but it's *our* shell! If you get those records out of there we can preserve Macomah's corporate identity for another day, don't you see that? Tip, it's our only chance to come back—!"

There was a cigarette burn on the corner of his desk that looked like a mashed brown slug; it seemed to move minutely while he stared at it.

"No, Chay," he said heavily. "It's no good. It's wrong, and that's all there is to it. It won't wash and it won't wear."

Chapin cursed, cursed again, said tightly: "I might have known, I might have expected as much. God damn it all, I saved Jophy's bacon for *you*, when they had her booked and printed and were all set to throw away the bloody key! I saved your marriage and your family—I didn't bother about moral niceties that night! I used every means that came to hand—yes, and some that didn't, too . . ."

Jophy.

He was sweating, his hands were sweating, his skin

444

crawling, his throat had gone dry. Jo, in jail. The kids. Well. What could—

"Do you wish *I'd* gone into a lot of soul-searching that night, decided it was all morally indefensible, washed my hands? Do you? . . . But no, of course, it's only cynical, immoral old Chay, *he'll* pull it out if he's got to subvert every fucking judge on Long Island! *He* doesn't have to be Simon pure, he's always been corrupt anyway . . . Tip, I'm begging you! Get those files out of there—give us one, last chance to come back, put it together again! Please . . ."

He realized he was standing up, at his desk, his thighs pressed against the wood. Chapin's voice clashed in his ear. He felt as if the office had been tilted in some irreparable way and he was about to fall the length of it. Then it passed, and his sight cleared.

"—All right," he said. "All right."

He hung up while Chapin was still talking and walked quickly down the hall to his brother's office. Yes, it was there, just as Chay had said—a series of blue folders and clasp envelopes: certificates of incorporation and participation, corporate minutes, amendments, correspondence. A dream in a great wad of paper. It was too much to fit in his briefcase. He stood there a moment, conscious of two girls talking with Elmer down in the mail room—crossed to Chapin's closet and flung open the door. His eyes fell on a handsome new British Gladstone, all dark red leather and shiny straps and buckles; the kind of bag he had never permitted himself to buy. It held all the records with ease. At the doorway he paused, listening, moved quietly down the hall and out through the boardroom to the elevators. The indicator started, stopped, then began its slow clock-hand upward sweep; from somewhere deep in the shaft there came a faint ringing, like a bell entombed. The light in the hallway seemed unnaturally bright.

The elevator doors opened. Empty. The operator, a nervous, eager boy said: "Afternoon, Mr. Ames."

"Hello, Tommy."

"On the road again, sir?"

"No rest for the weary."

He had started down the main foyer when he saw the cab at the curb; the two men coming toward the doors. Two men. The closed, matter-of-fact faces, the bulging black briefcases. Too late. Just too late. No faltering now! They were talking, looking at each other, they hadn't seen him. He wheeled to the left and entered the barber shop. Frank Morelli was there alone at one of the sinks, stirring thick lather in a gilded mug; he nodded, his leathery face cracking in a bright smile, one gold tooth glinted. A customer lay corpselike under a mound of steaming white towels. Without hesitation Tip dropped the suitcase into the big canvas laundry hamper, flipped a sheet over it, caught up another sheet from an empty chair and slid into it, flung the sheet over himself, and nodded sharply to Morelli. The barber, his face expressionless now, stepped up to him and began to lather his face briskly.

There was a step in the doorway. Frank's voice said: "There'll be a short wait, sir—my other two men are off today."

"No, it's all right.—Tipton Ames? Aren't you Tipton Ames?"

Tip opened his eyes and turned. A fat man with quick, snapping eyes. A man he'd seen somewhere.

"That's right."

"I thought I recognized you—I saw you just sitting down. I'm Harry Small."

Tip extended his hand. "Oh, yes. Of course. How are you?"

"I heard you speak last spring out in Cleveland. I'm with the Exchange—we've come over to examine the Diehl, Harrodsen books in the bankruptcy proceedings. And of course the affiliated firms . . . Terrible thing, isn't it?"

"Yes, it is." Three of them. Small must have been paying off the taxi. He had seen the suitcase, then. Or had he? Probably not—the glass was higher than a man's chest, he'd have seen only faces, heads. Well. Have to chance it, brass it out. Frank Morelli was stropping a blade now, *whssst-thttt, whsst-thttt,* in deft, rapid strokes.

"Mr. Ames, I hate to trouble you, but would you mind coming upstairs? Just to help familiarize us with the set-up?"

"Certainly.—Never mind, Frank. I'll be down shortly."

"Yes, sir." Morelli carefully wiped the lather from his face and tossed the apron into the laundry basket. Tip got up and passed a bill into the barber's hand, said:

"You'll take care of me later. Won't you?"

The dark, lined face was utterly impassive. "You can count on me, Mr. Ames."

"Good." He shook himself loose in his jacket and followed the examiner out into the corridor.

Standing by the neatly laid, unused fireplace with its birch logs and brass-tipped andirons, Jophy watched her husband. He was moving the palm of one hand lightly over the back of the other, something he did when he was very upset about something. She knew his news was going to be bad, she'd prepared herself for it for three days, but watching his face now she wasn't so sure she was prepared for it after all. Outside, blue under the streetlamps, a fine, chill rain was falling.

"It's less than half what I was making with D,H, Jo," he was saying. "And no stock options, no overridage. And to tell you the truth, I'm not sure how long this job will last. The market's still falling."

"You mean, that stock you had—"

"It's worthless. Diehl, Harrodsen's in bankruptcy, Jo. Full liquidation."

"I see."

"Jo . . ." He threw a hand out, as though scattering something. "We're going to have to give this up."

"I see."

Arms folded, she looked around the room. She'd been proud of this apartment; the big, high-ceilinged rooms with their classical fretwork molding, the black marble of the hearth, the parqueted floors . . . It had seemed to symbolize their first giant step to the world of elegance and taste. She had got exactly the right soft shade of gray in the walls, the right note of warmth in the draperies. It had none of the flamboyant extravagance of Chapin's penthouse. It was her style, her way, but it had grace.

Now it would vanish, in a sentence. It wasn't theirs any more, it never had been; it was a—a stage set, on loan to those who could afford it. It was a faithless courtesan, who gave herself to any ascendant warlord . . .

"What about the lease?" she asked. "Doesn't it run till April?"

"We can break it. Forfeit the deposit. No problem there." But his voice held a note she'd never heard in it before: a fearful, suppliant note. She glanced at him sharply. He was gazing at her with a kind of dogged appeal that moved her even as it angered her. She knew what was coming next.

"Jo, we're going to have to cut back hard. Really hard. Till this thing blows over . . ." He paused, added: "We'll have to take Joey out of Choate."

"Oh, no . . ."

"Honey, I just can't afford it now."

"I see," she repeated. You never wanted it, she thought resentfully, studying the pattern of winged lions in the Persian rug. You never wanted him to go to private school and now you've got the perfect excuse to yank him out and shove him in some dreary public school where they couldn't begin to care about his special talents . . . Then she felt ashamed for thinking that. After all, Tip had agreed to Choate. She ought to be fair—she ought to *try* to be fair, anyway.

"Then you think we're in for heavy weather," she said aloud.

"Yes, I do. Very heavy. We've got to get out, Jo."

"All right. We can find something cheaper."

"No, I meant out of the city."

"Oh." She nodded, not in agreement. "You mean, really get out."

"You can always make out better in the country. We'd have no rent. Food's cheaper, clothes, everything. People know each other, help each other out. You remember."

"It'd mean kicking the Santoses out of Grama's house—I'd hate to do that, Tip."

"I thought we might go back to Holcomb Falls. Live with Mother."

"I see." She bit her lip, and walked around the room. She liked Charlotte Ames well enough; but living with her, day in and day out, listening to that weary, defeated voice . . . Well, she was ill. God knows she'd had a hard time of it, even with the money Tip sent her every month. Damn it all, Jo, be *fair!* she told herself crossly.

But the mention of Holcomb Falls made everything suddenly real in a different way; she sat down, her hands between her knees. Now, half listening to Tip, she realized that for all her forebodings she had never believed it would crash; not really. Panics, disasters, instant poverty happened in other times, other countries; not theirs . . .

Tip was running on about what they ought to do. He'd paid off the mortgage on his mother's house, it was free and clear. He could cover his territory with the car, he'd actually be nearer northern New England and Boston. The kids would live it up there, with open fields to play in, clean mountain air to breathe. On and on he rambled in the buoyant tone, expanding hopefully as he sold himself on the prospect, while she bowed her head in mounting resentment. Stop trying to sell me! she wanted to shout at him. Look—we're broke, the roof has fallen in, I'm perfectly willing to give up everything we have and do the best I can to make a go of it—but for the love of God don't insult me by expecting me to buy the high adventure of it all—!

He'd switched back to business now: Richard Whitney's efforts to steady the market, the new set-up at Weeks, Barlow. She tried to listen, she knew she ought to be grasping this, but she couldn't. Bred to tangibles—rope and canvas, wind and water, the vivid cohesiveness of things seen and felt, she simply refused to take hold of what he was saying: words like *arbitrage* and *security affiliates* and *consortium* veered away from the net of her mind like strange, menacing fish, slipped away into subaqueous murk. She would still be clumsily wrestling with one term while several others followed—whereupon she would sweep them out of her mind and try to begin all over again. What did it matter, anyway? What mattered was that the stock market she'd hated and feared all these years—that royally caparisoned, satin-skinned beast everyone petted and cosseted and rode on so blindly —had turned on them all without warning, flung them off and raked them with one terrible claw . . . Grama would've understood it clearly enough, she thought bitterly, Grama would have cut through this nonsense with one stroke; she would've been ready for this moment all along . . .

"I need a drink," she broke in, getting swiftly to her feet. "A good, stiff drink. How about you?"

"Why yes," he said in surprise. "I could use one."

On her way out of the room she took his soggy raincoat from a chair arm—stopped abruptly and peered at it, examined the label.

"Why, it's Chapin's," she said, turning. "Chapin's raincoat . . ."

"That's right. It started raining out there and he loaned me his."

"Out where?"

"His place. I had to go out to the Island."

"Really?" She stared at him. "What for?"

His eyes dropped. "Oh, just—some business."

"Business. Of course." She stood there facing him in intense agitation, said suddenly: "What about Chapin? Is *he* retrenching? Is *he* going back to live with Mother, too?"

"Honey, that's—"

"Oh no, of course not—*he'll* be living with Aunt Serena. With noble, rich-as-Croesus Aunt Serena."

"Jophy, he's cleaned out, too—he's in the same boat we all are . . ."

"Ah, but with a difference! Oh my, what a difference!"

She couldn't help it. She simply couldn't help it. She'd told herself that he didn't need any recrimination, what was done was done, the ship was aground, all that mattered now was to salvage what they could—she'd told herself all that and more, but his defense of Chapin, coming on that dismissive, condescending "Oh, just some business," was more than she could stand this mean November night. Why in God's name should men make all the crucial decisions, choose the hazardous passages? Women were expected to share readily enough in the dangers of abandoning ship, the burdens of salvage—why should they never be shown the charts, know where in hell the ship was headed?

And how in God's name could he stand up for Chapin, even now? when he knew Chapin would wriggle out of this the way he always had, leaving some poor, trusting fool stuck with the lease? Why couldn't Tip ever see this—why did he always come running every time his brother whistled? The fool, the fool—! Hadn't he learned *anything* yet?

"I'll bet brother Chapin doesn't give up that glass-and-chrome monstrosity over on the Park, or the Renaissance castle at Glen Cove, either—you'll see!"

"Jophy, the stock in both trusts—"

"Damn the stock, and the trusts and the bankruptcies and everything else! Don't you see it doesn't make a bit of difference? *He'll* never be heading back for the tall timber—oh no, not Chapin! Because Avery Calkins is right there to bail him out, grease the skids, float the loans. Right? Am I right?"

"Jo, you're—"

"It's all smooth sailing—that sterling old-boy network is standing by, ready and able to look out for its own . . ."

Her voice had got away from her but she didn't care —this one time she was going to have it out, and to hell with it. She had to make him see this if it was the last thing she ever did.

"Because they never lose—not really. They *know* it'll all come right in the end. Wiggin goes to Mitchell who goes to Whitney who goes to Morgan, and everybody's happy. We're good, straight fellows—you can tell just by looking at our well-fed faces, our Savile Row and Brooks Brothers suits. We went to the same schools and joined the same clubs, we married the same *under*dressed, *under*sexed women, we sail in the same regattas and some of us even keep the same high-breasted, wheedling girls over in the West Forties—and that *proves* we're the right sort—!"

"Jo—"

"By God, Grama was right, they do stand for death and disaster—only it's everyone *else's* death and disaster, not theirs! Oh no, they're too good for that, it's people like us who go down. You mark my words, Chapin will come out of this richer than he ever was —maybe they arranged this whole bloody smash just to impoverish the rest of the country, so their own

wealth—their own crème de la crème—will look all
the crèmier! What's his phrase? 'Shaking the wildcatters out of the trees?' You've heard him! Sure, the
only *real* gratification comes from knowing the other
son of a bitch has lost the very same dollar—"

"God damn it, Jo!"

She stopped then and looked at him, saw he was
glaring at her miserably, his face contorted. The tears
were hanging full in his eyes, streaking his cheeks.

"Jo," he said softly, and swallowed. "Jo, I'm sorry,
believe me, I'm sorry to let you down like this. I
wouldn't have had it happen for the world. I swear it
. . . I know you were against it all along—" he broke
off, cleared his throat painfully "—you're right about
every last bit of it, everything you say . . . only I can't
hear any more about it tonight. I just can't. I've had a
bad—a very rough day, rougher than you'll ever
know. And I can't take a lot of pounding right now. I
can't, Jo. Please . . ."

She had never seen him weep before. A silent, con-
strained weeping, holding himself rigidly, as though
he were ashamed of it, the weakness it implied—of
showing it even to his wife. Her Yankee.

"What is it?" she whispered, staring. "What's the
matter, Tip?"

He shook his head doggedly, his eyes shut. "It's all
right. It's all right. I'll snap out of it. I just need a little time, that's all. Just a little—"

She ran to him then in a sudden awkward run; he
flung his arms around her wildly, almost threw them
both to the floor.

"Oh, Jo," he cried softly, and she could feel his body
shake. "I feel so rotten. So very rotten. Oh Jo. Hold
me. Just hold me . . ."

And still he didn't break down and cry. Her Yankee. Instantly shamed, contrite, she held him, murmuring words that didn't matter, crooning to him in
tones that did. Who cared about Chapin, or the old-
boy network, or whose stinking fault it was? He was

her husband, he was in misery, he needed her and said so—that was all that mattered now.

Healing. There had to be healing. Nothing more or less than that.

"Come on to bed," she whispered. "Come to bed, now. I want you to hold me, too . . ."

III

THE CLINCHER

1

The snow lay even and deep, so white it was almost blue, glittering in the late afternoon sun; beyond it the woods were black and still, climbing back to Mount Macomah. Standing at the sink with her hand on the brass handle of the pump, Jophy watched the deer approach across the clearing in their tentative, stiltlike gait, looking at Joey, out beyond the woodpile in the plaid mackinaw Tip had got him for Christmas, holding an apple in his hand, high. A yearling came forward several steps and paused again. Jophy could see the boy's lips moving, the steam bursting cloudlike in the still air. His hair flowed over his head in a tousled black shock; he would never wear a cap.

"Boy from Horace's is late with the delivery today," Charlotte Ames said in her soft, spent voice.

Jophy made no reply. Joey and the yearling were only about eight or ten feet apart now. He hadn't moved a muscle; she was amused at his patience—he was usually so restless, so volatile. Something in the way they stood there facing each other, Joey with his hand extended, the deer balanced delicately on its fragile sticks of legs, its eyes oval and huge, made her throat constrict on itself.

"The deer are back again," she murmured. "They're so *bold* . . ."

"Hungry, I expect," her mother-in-law said, and sighed. "Like everybody else."

457

"The winters last so long up here."

"Indeed they do."

"On the Cape the snow never lasts more than a week or so—sometimes not even that."

"What was the longest winter you ever saw, Grandma?" Tessa was sitting at the kitchen table making an elephant out of clay.

"Well, let's see." Charlotte rested her head against the carved back of the rocker. "I remember once we went for a sleigh ride in May."

"In May—!"

"Yes. The lilacs were in bloom—I remember the snow bending down the blossoms." Her gaunt face relaxed in a fond smile; she looked all at once younger, carefree. "We kept pushing each other off the sleigh into the snow, and then getting up and pushing each other off again. Everyone was laughing—we had such fun . . ."

Snow in summer, Jophy thought, looking out at the field again. As snow in summer, and as rain in harvest, so—something—is not seemly for a fool. *What* wasn't seemly?

The yearling had bounded away, spooked by something, its scut swaying whitely. Joey threw the apple then; it landed in a little bomb-burst of snow near the deer's feet. One of the does pranced up and reared, her hooves flashing daintily, and drove the yearling off. Reaching down she began to eat the apple, her mouth working comically, like a mule's. In the long, blued shadows at the edge of the clearing the buck, his antlers like a fanciful crown, still had not moved.

"Too crafty for your own good that time," Jophy said aloud. "Did yourself right out of a snack, big boy."

"Who's that, Mother?" Tessa said.

"The buck. He's stayed there in the woods."

"Oh, they always hang back," Charlotte explained. "Push the does out ahead of them, to see if the coast is clear."

"Why do they do that, Grandma?"

"It's the state of nature. They're more valuable than the does."

"Why are they more valuable?"

"Bucks make the rules, I guess," Charlotte said shortly, and Jophy was surprised at the bitterness in her voice. After all these years. Still, there were things you never got over. You could cover them in layers of ashes, layers of time, and in a second's disclosure there they would be, glowing white-hot coals . . .

Joey was in front of the shed now, splitting wood. The light cruiser's ax went high in the air, his slender body arched like a bow, feet spread wide; the ax flashed in the low winter sun like a mirror tilted, and the halved pieces of wood spilled off the block. His lips were moving again, and Jophy knew he was dreaming, spinning some Camelot fantasy. On guard, traitorous Sir Mordred. Curiously, he'd come to love it up here in the Berkshire wilds. He'd hated it at Choate —he'd confessed that to her one night; the other boys had bullied him, he'd been desperately lonely, counting the days till vacation. She'd felt saddened listening to him, and guilty—she should have spent more time with him, those earlier years . . .

As though her thoughts had reached him he turned and saw her in the window; raised the ax over his head and shook it like a gisarme. She nodded, smiling; watched Tessa methodically patting the blue clay into different shapes. What a comfort the children had been this past year and a half. Your children were such an arresting series of anomalies: yourself extended—and yet not yourself at all. Joey was a loner, as she had been, hiking through the woods, skating off by himself at Fanchett's Pond; yet he was introspective in ways she could never be. He still drew compulsively—Spanish grandees with cold, haughty features, Barbary pirates dueling ferociously over coffers of jewels. She'd managed to buy him a sketchbox with a set of oil paints, and he dabbled in it now and then;

459

but what he really loved was simply to draw: to stroke the image into reality, limning and shading . . .

For Tessa there were no air-built castles. Her sturdy little Yankee soul saw things exactly as they were: life was what you could see, mold into honest, concrete shapes and figures. Yet there was little of Tip's boundless effervescence; she was more guarded and reflective; even as a baby she had thought something out before she moved. But there was a thread—as slender and elusive as the scarlet strand in the old hawser on the *Albatroz*—of Grampa's merry extravagance . . .

The wind whipped the snow into a hundred toy cyclones, rimed the scaly black trunks of the maples. Time had altered so. In New York City whole years had swept by like chips in a bore; here, held in the grip of the seasons—the flame-shower of fall foliage, the burnished shield of ice, the stealthy, glorious onrush of green, time slowed; one was conscious of each day's measured passing.

They had made leaving New York into a kind of adventure. Tip had loaded the Dodge to the gunwales —suitcases held by collapsible metal frames on the running boards, trunks lashed to the roof. The kids lay on their bellies on layers of cartons and bedding and stared ahead through the windshield, keeping tally of cars with rumble seats or white horses. Jophy had packed a picnic basket and they ate in the car, singing "There Is a Tavern in the Town" and "Blow the Man Down," roaring the choruses and spilling crumbs and orange peelings all over the upholstery. North of Danbury they got a flat but Tip repaired it himself with a cold patch, and outside Canaan it rained, but they went on singing anyway; the holiday mood, the sense of voyage, persisted. The car was a conestoga wagon, a Banks pinkie, a catamaran bearing them to new lands, new beginnings. Running north toward the mountains, Jophy hugged the children's round heads to her, kissed Tip on the ear, and made a fervid resolution to throw off all the guilt and resentment that had clutched her so tightly over the past two months; she would become a resourceful, loving wife and mother, a real support to Tip, who had his old verve and excitement back again.

Charlotte Ames, ailing badly now and subdued, had welcomed them warmly. Neighbors in Holcomb Falls stopped them on the street, grabbed Tip's hand; everybody seemed to remember him with affection. They wanted to know what he thought about the Crash, if the country was going off the gold standard, if there was any federal help on the way for farmers.

"So *you're* that Portagee girl Tip was so moonstruck over," Horace Crowell said, peering at her through his steel-rimmed spectacles with shrewd, sardonic glee. "No small wonder. Married above your looks, Tipton."

"Don't I know it, Horace," Tip answered; he smiled his old sweet smile, and took her hand.

New beginnings . . . Tip had fixed the old furnace and pointed up the foundation; in the spring they planted a vegetable garden, and Jophy put up small mountains of tomatoes and beans in a welter of steaming kettles and mason jars. She helped the children with their homework through the long, still evenings; she even taught herself how to cane chairs. As Tip was fond of saying, they weren't licked—not by a long shot. Standing at the sink she would feel his arms steal around her waist and move gently up over her breasts, the way they'd used to do, and with a little gasp she would turn and press him to her . . .

They'd got it back—a lot of it, nearly all of it: the old sweet sea-surge of passion and release that to her was the very pulse of life. They'd never spoken about Montoya or any of the rest of it, but she didn't care. What did it matter that her defection had been all-consuming and Tip's a casual roll in the hay? By what convoluted logic would she dare to condemn him? His straying was certainly less reprehensible than hers;

461

its very sexual triviality hadn't blurred the intensity of his feeling for her, as her affair with Manolo had done . . . Now, bound in a regimen of hard work, those years in New York seemed like an exotic dream, something that had happened to someone she knew. She looked back on those nights and afternoons the way a reformed gambler might reflect on days of headlong prodigality. They were not for her any more; this was another ship, on a vastly different voyage, and she was at the helm.

The second winter was a different story. That fall Holcomb's Mill laid off thirty of its people, then forty more, running on reduced shifts—finally shut down altogether, keeping only a skeleton force; several men were working without wages, simply to hold on to their jobs. Russell's dry goods store folded up, an empty glass-fronted cavern between the bank and Birchall's Drugs. Weeks, Barlow went under, but Tip landed another job with Wetherell Brothers, at a reduced salary. This time he couldn't bring any of the old sales force with him. His unflagging optimism had begun to wear on her. Things weren't getting better; they were getting steadily, inexorably worse. Men were selling apples on street corners in the cities. Over six million people were out of work. The government was doing nothing about it at all; President Hoover told a delegation of clergymen there was no need for a public works program, the depression was over. The market fell again, and still again. Every time you opened the paper Richard Whitney, the man Tip said had single-handedly stopped the worst of the panic on Black Thursday, was defending the Stock Exchange, calling on American business to reform itself. Jophy didn't like him; there was something in his superior self-righteousness she didn't trust, and she said so.

Tip had grinned at her. "Now, how can you say that? You don't know anything about him. He comes of very good family—his brother's a Morgan partner."

"Which proves just what?"

"Oh Jo, come on. He's one of the pillars down there. You can't blame him for everything . . ."

"Yes, I can," she said, laughing. "I can if I want to!" Turning serious again she declared: "He's one of those mush-mouth Groton horrors. Feels he's too good for the rest of the world, the rules don't apply to him. You know the type. Come on, admit it!"

"Grama rides again!"

Yes, that was probably true. She missed Grama terribly—her caustic wit, her boundless strength; the sense of her sustaining presence, there in the world. Now there was only a void, a scrim of memories. Charlotte Ames, increasingly ill with dropsy, was petulant and bitter. This winter was colder, laden with more snow than its predecessor. Macomah Mountain bulked higher, more forbidding than before . . .

"Fire's getting low, Jophy," Charlotte was saying.

Leaning forward she rapped smartly with her wedding ring on the glass. Joey turned, shaken out of his Camelot dreams. She pointed to the woodpile, and he nodded and socked the ax into the block. Looking up then she saw the Model T coming down the road, its top covered with snow like a cap of icing. To her surprise it swung into the driveway, a broken chain clanking, flailing snow like a stern-wheeler.

"Now who's that?" Charlotte said.

"I don't know."

A figure got out, muffled in a red scarf and coonskin cap, unhooked the catches and flung up one of the hood panels and bent over, fussing with the engine; and Jophy could see steam hovering around his head in a white cloud.

"He seems to be having car trouble, whoever he is."

She blinked. A snowball had just struck the fender, spattering white fragments. The traveler skittered to the other side of the car, slipping and staggering.

Kneeling by the wheel he made a snowball and threw it at the woodpile. Joey was nowhere to be seen.

"What *is* going on out there?"

Another snowball struck the windshield. The man sneaked around to the rear of the flivver, slipped on the slick grooves in the driveway and went into a series of pinwheeling gyrations. His coonskin cap fell off and now Jophy saw the slicked-down red hair.

"Why, it's Jack! It's Jack Darcey . . ."

Joey rose up on the far side of the woodpile, the snowball hit the radiator cap and shattered. Jack laughed—whirled around, wound up like Walter Johnson and pelted the Ford himself. He waved at Joey and shouted something, and they both started making snowballs as fast as they could and firing them at the flivver, pasting the hood, the headlights, the windshield.

"That fool!" Jophy cried. She was laughing helplessly, shaking her head. Jack made a big, sweeping motion with his arm and they rushed the car, flinging snow in all directions, pounding on the fenders, jumping up and down on the front bumper, hooting and howling. Steam was still issuing feebly from somewhere inside the engine.

Still laughing, Jophy threw open the storm door and shouted: "Jack Darcey, you stop that foolishness and come in here!"

"Baby!" He sank to his knees in the snow, head waggling, arms flung crazily skyward. "I can't—go on . . . Where's the cognac, the calvados? Where's Rin Tin Tin with his little wooden cask?"

"You idiot! Come in and get warm." Jack clapped the coonskin cap on Joey's head and swung the boy up in his arms. As he came toward the door, Jophy saw his left cheek was puffed and discolored.

"What are you doing out here in the frozen sticks?" she asked him.

He set Joey down and embraced her, shook his coat free of snow. "The fact is, they called me in down at

464

GHQ, they said, 'You *must* get through to Jophy Ames. With the serum. Dead or alive. She's got cabin fever.' And here I am. Dead."

"Jack, you perfect fool." She felt a fierce, unreasoning elation, listening to his blather, laughing, helping him off with his coat. His suit was starting to shine at the shoulders and knees, his shirt collar was frayed. His face looked narrower, the skin drawn more tightly over his nose and cheeks. She smelled liquor on his breath, sharp under the peppermint.

"I was over in Pittsfield trying to scare up a little business," he went on, "I'm with Fanning now. And then I remembered where you were, and off I flew. There's no business in Pittsfield, anyway. No business anywhere.— Tessie, sweetheart!"

He warmly greeted Charlotte Ames, whom he'd met during the Alec Ham days, and took Tessa on his lap. He gave Joey a big league baseball which he swore Lou Gehrig had hit foul off George Earnshaw, he gave Tessa a yellow metal wind-up bug that scooted along the table waving its antennae and waggling its wings.

"What's his name?" Tessa demanded.

"Name? Oh, his name's Herbert."

"Why, Uncle Jack?"

"Because he's always running around in circles flapping his wings, getting nowhere. Doing nothing. You know how it is, sweetie-girl."

Charlotte said defensively: "I think President Hoover's doing everything he can, given the awful state things are in."

"Maybe so, Mrs. Ames. I wish he'd make payment on our bonus certificates, I'll tell you that. Lot of the boys are getting awfully mad about that—1945's a pretty long time to wait. He's going to have a new Coxey's Army on his hands if he doesn't look out."

"I remember Coxey," Charlotte nodded. "Didn't come to anything. Only a handful of them showed up. They arrested them for trespassing on the White House lawn."

"Might be different this time."

"Well, this calls for a celebration," Jophy broke in. "You look half-frozen, Jack. I'll bet you could use a drink."

His green eyes rolled around to her significantly. "Why, I do feel a tad rheumy." Unseen by Charlotte, his lips mimed: *I dreamed you'd never, never ask . . .*

He stoutly refused a second drink, accepted with alacrity Jophy's invitation to dinner. He told the kids a funny story about two hoodlums who broke into a filling station one night to find that the owner had installed a pet python behind the counter as a watchdog; putting Tessa to bed he entertained her hugely with a song called "Minnie the Moocher," complete with gestures. He had another drink at Jophy's insistence, and after Charlotte retired he helped Jophy with the dishes, wiping the plates with elaborate care. He wanted to hear all about Tip, he wanted to bring her up to date on the old crowd, Skeets and Blazer, Clarence and Bake. Most of them were working—if you wanted to call it that. Skeets was selling insurance out of Pawtucket; Maury was back with Alec Ham, but he said the old pezzazz had gone out of it, people were too busy trying to meet the grocery bills to get very excited about correspondence courses; hell, there wasn't enough business around to study *for* . . .

But mostly he wanted to talk about Tip.

"—Christ Almighty, how he used to needle me! 'Look at you: you're six feet tall and I'm not, you're a good-looking son of a bitch and I'm not, you won a medal in France and I never got out of Camp Devens, you've got the Irish gift of gab—you ought to be ashamed of yourself, letting me beat you out like this!' Yeah! And I'd go roaring out of there with the sparks coming out of my ears, I was going to beat him if it killed me. But I never could . . ."

He was seized with a fit of laughter, patting at his face with the dishcloth.

"I ever tell you about the time I got into the Donnybrook with that stuffed-shirt Phemister? God, how Tip-O read me off. 'What do you want—a medal or an aspirin? You think you're one of those fat-assed babies at the Metropolitan Opera with three chins and a mustache Chapin's always drooling over? You're here to learn about securities, in case you've forgotten it. Don't you try and pull that prima donna act with me—!' He gives you holy hell one minute, and the next he's got you believing you're the hottest ball-of-fire to come waltzing down the pike, there's nothing on *earth* you can't do! I tell you, he's some punkin . . . when we walked into the Waldorf ballroom that evening, the year we beat them all out, all the rest of the country—when we walked in there in our tuxes and they all began to clap . . . I want to tell you, it was a moment you'll never forget, never feel like that again if you—if you live to be—"

He broke off. She turned and saw he wasn't laughing any more, he was weeping, his face white and strained, his eyes squeezed shut. She put her hand, soapy with dish water, on his sleeve.

"Jack—" she said.

He seized her with a desperation that made her gasp, released her as fiercely and sat down, squeezing his hands between his knees.

"Ah Christ," he moaned, his voice hoarse and low, "ah Christ, it's all gone to hell, what are you going to do when the bottom's fallen right out of everything? It's no use, no use . . ." He rocked back and forth tightly, his eyes still shut, while she watched him, feeling angry and helpless and shaken. "It's no use, Jo," he repeated. "I'm not like Tip—I can't go along believing things are going to get better. Keep going out there driving and driving, pushing for the sale. Maybe if he was still there, building a fire under my tail . . . But this way, I can't cut it. It's been too long, Jo! Too long . . ." He looked up at her imploringly. "I've got nothing to keep going on, I'm busted, Jo . . ."

"Everybody's broke, Jack," she said softly.

He shook his head. "Not the way I mean. I've got no home, no kids, nothing. God, how I envy you . . . Hazel left me," he said abruptly.

"Oh, no . . ."

"Yeah. Walked out on me. Just like that."

"Oh, Jack—I'm *so* sorry . . ."

"Called me a no-good dead-beat. Yeah. Told me she was sick of my running around, playing her for a sucker . . . I told her there hasn't been any of that for two years, now. More . . . But she didn't believe me." He wiped his mouth with the back of his hand. "I know I'm no holy monk. I never pretended to be. It's the way I am. But to run out on me now, when everything's coming all apart—"

Standing there beside him Jophy was ashamed to feel a certain elation (All right! Now you know what a woman feels. Why should it be only men who're free to break away, sail out whenever they're damned good and ready?) which in another moment had ebbed away into sympathy. Why should she of all people fall into the old, vindictive female role—waiting till the man was vulnerable, to strike?

"I can't believe she'd walk out on you for good, Jack. It was a quarrel—everyone has those. Why don't you see her, soon as you can . . . Hazel loves you, Jack."

"No." He broke down completely then, his shoulders shaking. "No. She's through with me."

"You've had some good years together. She loves you, she won't walk out on you now . . ."

Why am I lying like this? she wondered. I haven't the faintest idea what I'm talking about . . . She'd disliked Hazel a good deal the few times she'd seen her—the girl had struck her as brash and hoyden and not very bright. Or did she only feel that way because of Hazel's embarrassed admission about Tip and that hoofer? And what difference did it make now, anyway? I *will* not lie to myself, she thought fiercely, shaking her head; I'm damned if I'm going to turn into some vengeful, puritanical bitch, whipping others out of my own disappointments.

She put her hand on Jack's shoulder. "It doesn't matter," she said. "Everyone falls off course somewhere along the line. Any woman knows that, Jack. If she's honest. Hazel knows that—she'll understand if you talk to her."

"You're different—you and Tip."

"No, we're not. We're no different from anybody else. I—made a mistake. A big one. And look at Tip, that night at the Montclair with that Carol. You've got to put it behind you, that's all. There are other things, more important things . . ."

He looked up at her, then. "Carol?" he said. "Carol Stacey? That was a gag—there wasn't anything to that." His mouth quirked at the corner. "She was with *me* that night—Hazel came up to the suite hollering blue murder and I talked him into jumping into bed with Carol, to take me off the hook. He never even took his clothes off." His eyes held her own. "That's all there was to that. Honest, Jo—that's all it was . . ."

"I believe you," she said.

She wanted to laugh—instead tears stung her eyelids. Perfect, perfect! Constant Tip, loyal to the end—no sacrifice too great for the force, loyalty from top to bottom. She might have known . . . For a single instant she was furious, then she very nearly burst into hysterical laughter. Menin Jesu'! And here was Jack, near breaking, still trying to protect Tip's honor . . . But he'd forgotten about it already.

". . . All that lousy mess over in France," he was saying, in a hollow singsong. "Forges Brook, Montfaucon. All that misery in the mud . . . And yet I wasn't afraid, Jo. I mean, not panicky scared. I did fine. Too young and dumb to be scared." He gazed blankly at the stove, which was ticking now, cooling down. "Now I am. Scared all the way through . . . Who'd have believed this could happen? They said it was a whole new era, they all said that. I've always kept on driving, made my quota . . ." He looked up at her, his green eyes dark with loss. "I can't make it, Jo. I just can't make it any more . . . !"

She held him firmly, held his head against her hip, swaying gently while he gave way to another fit of weeping, clutching at her as though she were the last solid thing on earth, while the ship's chronometer struck the start of the midwatch.

"Jack," she said at last. "Jack, you need a good night's sleep. Try to get some sleep, now."

He drew away then, blew his nose hard. "Jo, can you put me up for the night? Just for tonight? I haven't got the dough for a hotel room."

"Of course, Jack. Of course we can." She went over and shook down the ashes in the kitchen stove briskly. "You'll feel better in the morning, you'll see."

He stood up and hitched at his trousers. "Right," he said.

Jenny's illness had come as a complete surprise. At first Chapin thought she was feigning it, or that it was a psychic reaction to her father's bankruptcy and heart attack, or Randy's prolonged convalescence at McLean's—some bizarre sympathetic pattern: the violent dizzy spells, the nausea. But Rasmussen diagnosed it promptly as Meunière's Syndrome, an imbalance in the fluid of the inner ear; medication might alleviate the condition, but the only remedy was immobility, and a great deal of patience.

Her confinement went on for months. Without warning she would be prostrated: the most infinitesimal movement of her head would bring on waves of vertigo, and the pain. Imprisoned in its mailed grip she would moan softly, her eyes narrowed with suffering; a small animal in a trap. This was no act, no act at all—Chapin knew that. She was in such pain; she was so nobly, pitifully brave . . . Sitting one winter afternoon at the edge of her bed reading to her, holding her damp little hand in his, he'd felt without warning that stealthy pressure against his heart, the old sweet need awakened, the iron door swinging open again—and then the boundless anguish . . . *Jenny!* After all these contentious years. Pug-faced, homely Jenny, with her overlarge hazel eyes and mettlesome, outrageous pronouncements, her all-too-transparent subterfuges! What in God's name had happened to him? This was—this was preposterous—

He'd left her in panicky dismay and walked for hours through Central Park, watching the officious nannies with their well-dressed, shrieking charges, the broken young men in shabby coats and cracked shoes huddled silent on the benches, nursing their hopelessness and hunger, hugging it close to their bellies like some loathsome disease; feeling a curious, strained kinship with them, a dark sympathy. There were so many kinds of fear abroad in the winter of 1932 . . . Later that evening he'd gone alone to the opera to hear Pinza sing *Don Giovanni;* that past master of intrigue and seduction had never failed to fire his fantasies—his very unregenerate defiance in the face of the Commendatore's icy grip had served Chapin as a paradigm ever since school days; now, all his senses inflamed after the devastating moment with Jenny, he heard the "Deh, vieni alla finestra" with different ears: he'd been wrong, irreparably wrong— all those webs of lechery and defilement spun by Giovanni were essentially innocent, nothing more or less than a romantic quest for the perfect woman, from whose lips and thighs he could draw the sweetness and glory of all women . . .

Sitting in the cavernous dark he caught himself thinking fiercely, desperately, of Jophy, remembering her coal-dark eyes shining with amusement or blazing in fury, the slow, sensuous curve of her lips, the warm copper glow of her skin, like frosted grapes in sunlight, the way her hair fell in a single, thick glossy braid nearly to her magnificent tail, or loose and dark as night, a mantle against her throat; remembering the rolling pearl of her laughter, the swift, supple flow of her body—the high fire at the heart of her, that unreckoning, soaring force, the profound *mystery* she embodied; and leaning forward, watching the incorrigible Don strumming on his mandolin, that glorious baritone reverberant in his very being, Chapin knew as never before that her wild grace, her quicksilver vitality were what he wanted, would be all he would ever want, for the rest of his life. He had once had her in the palm of his hand —but he'd drawn back, afraid. Fool. He'd let his rivalry with Tip distract him, turn him from what he'd really wanted all along. Tip. Tip's wife. What a fool—!

It had been absolutely essential then that he sail for Europe. It was purposeless, extravagant—he couldn't begin to delude himself or anyone else that any investment possibilities existed in a Germany with its economy reeling from the total collapse of the Austrian Credit Anstalt and ministries succeeding one another from month to frantic month. He only knew that he *had* to go—he needed it the way a famished street urchin might need to gorge himself at some lavish and forbidden table . . .

He had come out of the Crash pretty well, all things considered. He'd escaped the utter débacle at Diehl, Harrodsen; Avery Calkins had taken him in at a much reduced salary and with stock options. Tip had done his job deftly and well: no trace of Macomah Fund had turned up anywhere in the old firm's records; and its brief existence had precluded an annual report or any other disclosures. There had been rumors and intimations, but he was prepared for those. The man named Small had come to him at Bliss, Calkins and made some rather veiled and hesitant queries which Chapin had been able to dispel; Avery had come to his aid, too—as a Stock Exchange governor he was beyond reproach. The examiners, harried and shaken by a hundred greater corporate convolutions and falls from grace, had pressed no further; they'd accepted Horizon and Greylock as the whole story.

And so the cadre of Macomah Fund reposed in an oversize safety deposit box at the National City Bank, with its tidy corporate structure and its paper capitalization of three million dollars, waiting for a favorable wind, a shift in the tide. It was merely a question of time. There would be more stringent regulation of issues, probably—a sizable faction on the Street was already screaming for reform—but that could all be dealt with in due course. For now, the market would continue to fall—he saw it with the same cool clarity with which he'd divined the onset of the wild Bull Market back in '24. On various occasions he'd allied himself with Joe Kennedy or Jesse Livermore or other notorious bears and had made a lot of money selling short as stock prices continued their deadly downward glide. He'd had the capital for the initial ventures: Aunt Serena had bailed him out handsomely—the $350,000 she had stubbornly withheld from his trust ventures was liquid gold now. It had let him keep the penthouse on Central Park West, the box at the opera, the cooks and maids. She had laid down only one condition that gusty October night: he *must* sell his collections.

"—But that's ridiculous!" He'd stared at her in angry consternation. "You say you're willing to help me—why should I need to sell them?"

"Because those are my terms."

"But what's the sense in *forcing* me to give them up? That doesn't make any sense at all . . ."

"Nevertheless." And she'd smiled her wintry smile. "That is the choice: your collections, or the money."

"Why?" he'd raged. "Just give me three good reasons why!"

"I just happen to think it'll be good for you."

"Good for me. Yankee discipline, renunciation—the sick satisfaction of giving up what one loves most. Is that it?"

"Has it ever occurred to you that you've had things entirely too much your own way for too many years, Chapin?"

"—But that's my right!" he burst out. "I've always had them—that's what you brought me up for . . ."

"Ah. That's the initial fallacy right there, you see." Her smile at this moment was utterly infuriating. "Then you shouldn't have jeopardized your position. Should you? One has to pay for everything in this world."

"Don't be ridiculous—!"

"Oh, yes. For this so much, for that so much more. That is the only law in this world, Chapin. The only inviolate one. It's high time you learned it."

"You're such a ruthless Yankee trader," he said after a pause.

"How true. But I know the game—the *real* game —and the rules it runs on. A lot better than you, my dear, for all your operatic soirées, for all your little foreign frolics."

He'd turned away, sullen and furious. She was playing with him, punishing him, paying him back for the years he'd escaped her recently, hadn't needed her; for flaunting his financial success, even for his bawdy diversions, which she had somehow—God alone knows how—got wind of. It was simply another, more painfully intimate move in the perpetual bargain struck between them that bitter November night twenty years before. The surrender of his collections was the price of his deliverance. She would not relent on this, no matter what arguments he advanced, no matter how much he raged or threatened or pled. He knew.

And so he'd got rid of them all—the ancient gold coins, the lovely ivory and jade figurines, and finally the little inlaid boxes, his first love—sold them off with the harsh haste of real pain. He knew he'd have to make a clean sweep of it; she would never be fooled if he withheld anything. It had been infinitely harder to do than even he would have believed: he felt bereft, stripped naked in a way he'd never known before. Compared to his collections the loss of the Glen Cove estate, the yacht and the fancy cars was a trivial matter. It was no consolation at all that his father-in-law had also lost the great, secluded place at Cold Spring Harbor and moved to a cramped apartment in Little Neck, where he sat huddled in a wing chair doing crossword puzzles or staring at the fire in the grate . . .

It was no consolation either that Tip was now selling bonds for Arthur Wetherell. The night he'd brought the Macomah records out to Glen Cove Tip had demanded to know the details surrounding the financing of the fund, and they'd had a long, bitter exchange.

"What the devil does it matter?" he protested. "Why all the hair-splitting? Everybody was pyramiding, everybody was pledging unrealized—"

"It matters to me." Tip's face had been pale and hard, his lower lip thrust out sharply. *"That's* what matters. I'm not like you—I've got to believe in what I'm selling. I've got to know it's sound, it's put together fair and square."

"Well, of course, that was predicated on a—"

"It was predicated on the whole crazy structure going up and up forever, on nobody ever asking questions—that's what it was predicated on." Tip had picked up one of the blue folders and slapped it down on the sturdy table. "All right. We're square, Chapin. The debt is paid." And he'd turned and walked out of the room.

Only of course it wasn't paid. That was the trouble with people like Tip—they always saw things in blacks and whites, in neat parcels; and they were hardly ever that. The action had bound Tip to him for life, an indenture tighter than any blood or legal obligation could ever be . . . And it had only happened because of Jophy; Tip never would have done it otherwise—not in a million years . . .

He thought of Jophy now, up in Holcomb Falls, pinned in that icy valley, peering out through the frost-glazed panes of glass. She'd certainly had her comeuppance, as Serena would say: reduced to a hand-to-mouth existence in a broken mill town on the Housatonic. The very life, ironically, that he had escaped. Destiny . . . There was a certain wry satisfaction there—and yet at the same time something in him was outraged. She was too fine-spun, too animate and adventurous for such a fate—it was like burying a priceless emerald in a casket of costume trash. And she had the boy, too—that lively, sensitive, eager boy; the boy he wanted, that he now feared Jenny would never give him. A son he could shape to his own grand designs, rear with discerning artifice—

And so he had fled to Germany, hurried off to Munich and its shamelessly dissolute brothels to forget them all . . . Munich accommodated him—as it always had. Leaving Elfreda's establishment one early spring night he felt pleasantly light-bodied, emptied of all the burdensome rivalries and resentments of home. The air was surprisingly cool, with a rising wind. He liked the pervasive throbbing in his genitals these bouts at Elfreda's engendered. Her slanted eyes held a bold ferocity that made him think of Kirghiz chieftains, tents flapping in a whirling dust, deeds of swift, sexual savagery; a Mongol horsewoman with hard brown thighs, companion in bold experiments and extravagances from which she derived the same grotesque excitement he did. He paid her (and her eager associates) handsomely, in dollar pourboires that were little fortunes against the disastrously deflated Reichsmark.

His footsteps rang in the late stillness. He liked the crooked streets, the narrow housefronts with their slate roofs and heavy oak doors; the massive, battlemented aspect of the city. The Communists had gained substantially in the recent elections, and so had this posturing visionary Hitler with his ludicrous

Roman salute and black-shirted followers. Well, Thyssen and the Krupps would contain him; they called the tune and they would control both left and right, encouraging here, checking there—what ultimately emerged would be what the Junkers and the industrialists wanted, and that alone. The problem, of course, was whether some kind of Anglo-American consortium could be induced to shore up the tottering economy here, and what guarantees could be—

He heard the steps then, directly behind him. He whirled—felt a sharp, stinging sensation on the side of his head. Then he was down. On the pavement. It kept tilting subtly away from him. He tried to speak, could not. His mind would not work. A face—wolfish and savage and utterly cold—swam close to his; he could see it more clearly now. A face without mercy. He struggled feebly, saw the broad, stubby blade of the trench knife, very bright, very near.

"Don't move, American. Or you die. I've been watching you. For a long time. Waiting for this moment." The voice progressed, cultured and toneless, as though this were some lecture hall for the insane. "We are going to do away with you. All of you. Filthy Americans with your filthy dollars, who come to play, to dance on our misery, to use our women for your amusements . . . All that is over. Finished. We will bring a new Germany soon. Very soon. A new world order where your kind will have no place. No place at all."

"Look," he gasped, "take my money, I have—"

"Be still!" The weight of him increased, the blade now pressed against the flesh of his face. "Money," the voice resumed tonelessly. "You Americans think money will solve anything, buy anything, corrupt anything . . . We will take your kind and gut you, burn you, stamp you out like the vermin you are . . . *We will not be despised!*"

The man's eyes blazed at him, his breath hot against Chapin's lids. "Now you go home, degenerate

American. Go home and don't come back here again. Ever! Or you will die. I promise you.

"And now, because the memories of Americans are so short—oh yes! I know how short they are . . ."

The blade moved, Chapin felt the prick of the point, felt it zig-zag along his cheek. He gasped through his teeth.

"Here is a message. From the coming Third Reich. Something to prod your memory. You understand?"

The pressure on him was lifted, the face was gone; footsteps spattered away in stillness. He staggered to his feet. His heart was beating wildly, he was shivering uncontrollably, shivering and shaking. He could feel blood moving on his cheek.

"Help—!" he cried. "Hilfe! Hilfe mir . . . !"

Nothing moved anywhere. Nothing stirred. The high, warped roofs, the massive stone housefronts faced him coldly. He reached for a handkerchief, realizing that his wallet was still there in his breast pocket. Pressing his handkerchief to his face he began running heavily toward the hotel, and safety.

2

In June Wetherell Brothers called Tip in and told him they had to let him go. After five weeks he landed a job with Waldheim, Simons selling bonds, or trying to. Business was rotten, and it kept getting worse. They said Washington was like a funeral parlor—the optimistic side; the other side was like a morgue. Everybody was paralyzed, waiting for something to happen, for business to get better. The Reconstruction Finance Corporation didn't seem to be doing any good—"a fancy soup kitchen for big business" was the crack you heard everywhere. The Hoover Administration, dying by inches, kept muttering about the Villainous Bears of Wall Street, who were undermining the market and destroying any chance for an upturn; and threatening full-scale investigations.

Chapin scoffed at all this as so much political eyewash—Tip ran into him on the Street. "Those cretins! *Short sale*—it's nothing but a sale for future delivery. It presupposes a later purchase, right? Hell, you can argue that it creates a reservoir of buying power that actually works to shore up the market, stabilize it." He'd had plastic surgery done on the scar he'd got in a taxi collision over in Germany, but parts of that curious zig-zag cross on his cheek still showed. "Anyway, it's all academic—you can't outlaw short selling. It's been tried half a dozen times in two hundred years and it's never worked. But you can't expect those fiduciary clowns down there to understand anything as mundane as that." He said there'd been no further repercussions on Macomah Fund; the Exchange had called off the watchdogs. Tip gathered it had a good deal to do with Calkins' fine Italian hand. Chapin wanted to see which way the cat would jump before making any decisions to revive it, though; there was a lot of talk about new federally imposed regulations and the licensing of all securities.

That winter was brutal—it was as if the elements had waited for just this moment, when human resources were at their lowest ebb, to strike. Blizzards and sleet storms swept in off the lakes in blinding white waves, blanketed the towns and choked the roads. Creeping into Ste. Hélène one bitter afternoon the old Dodge finally broke down. A surly mechanic informed him that the water pump was shot; it would take two days to locate one, and he wanted the money in advance. Tip ordered mulligatawny soup and a cup of coffee in the diner on Main Street. At the cash register he counted his money: he had exactly $1.37.

He stood outside the diner a moment; then turned abruptly and plodded through the fresh fall of snow toward the lake, thinking of Jack Darcey, his green eyes sparkling gleefully, crying, "Spring! When the iron in the air puts the lead in your pencil. Tell me you'll relent tonight, Tip-O. Won't you relent?" God alone knew where Jack was; he'd been working for some novelties outfit the last he'd heard.

The house looked a ghostly gray against the mantle of snow thrown over the lake. The Georgian portico was neatly painted, the walks shoveled and strewn with rock salt. A LaSalle was parked at the curb, and beyond it a long, black Packard, its engine idling and the driver snoozing behind the wheel, his hat barely visible. Smiling faintly, Tip knocked once, then three times, then once more. After a moment the section of molding in the upper panel slid back.

"Jethro?" he asked.

"Whom do I have the pleasure of addressing?" the voice boomed richly.

"Jethro!" Tip said in relief. "I'm Tipton Ames. From the early days with Alec Ham, and later with Diehl, Harrodsen . . ."

"Ah, yes. Mr. Ames."

The bolt shot back, the door swung in. It was Jethro all right, huge and majestic as ever, mahogany face heavier, wiry cap of hair gray now. "Fall of '27, wasn't it?"

"Yes, that's right—the flood. I was afraid you might not recognize me."

"I usually manage to recognize everybody, Mr. Ames. Though I'm a bit slower than I was." He stepped to one side while Tip removed his overshoes. "A hard winter, isn't it?"

"Indeed it is. Is the Countess in?"

"Yes." The bouncer extended one massive arm grandly. "If you would care to pass on through the second parlor. She's in her study."

"Thank you, Jethro."

The decor was unchanged: the same fringed lampshades, the same wine-red velour draperies, the same stiff-backed Victorian couches. The only addition seemed to be a Stromberg-Carlson cabinet radio with cloth panels, which was playing "Whistling in the Dark." Two girls in evening gowns were sitting at a round table playing double Canfield with silent intensity. One of them rose with a bright, eager smile, but he raised a hand, demurring, and went on through the rear parlor. Antoinette Bouchard was seated at her little fruitwood escritoire, making entries in a bound ledger. She looked up.

"May I help you?"

"Madame Bouchard," he said. "It's Tip Ames."

"Of course! Mr. Ames. Quel plaisir!" She rose and came toward him quickly. She looked thinner, her hair a darker blond, in the same fine, feathery halo around her face; she still wore the single strand of pearls close against her throat. Her face was suddenly pretty when she smiled. "How fitting that you should find me here, doing my lessons."

He took her hand. "Countess, you've cheated time."

"Flatteur! No one cheats time. Least of all a woman. Come and sit down.—Jethro, would you bring us some coffee?"

She drew him down beside her on the watered-silk loveseat and said: "And does your wife still understand you?"

He laughed and shook his head. "Yes—she does. Too well, maybe."

"Many wives do. That is one of the reasons I am here."

"But only one of many, Countess."

She laughed now. "Quick as ever! It is good to know that certain things remain the same."

"I was thinking the same thing about you. Continuity—it's a rare item these days . . . I didn't know whether I'd still find you here."

"And why not?" She gave him her charming, impudent grin. "We are both salesmen, are we not? Only the commodities differ. And mine is always in demand—in good times and bad." Jethro entered with the coffee on a silver tray, and the Countess poured from a delicate silver pot with a swanlike spout. Why, it's as elegant as Aunt Serena's, he thought with pleasure; good for her . . .

"Oh, I've had my ups and downs, like everyone else. though my real trials will commence now, perhaps. Times of adversity invariably arouse pangs of remorse in the human heart, and then cries for reform. Have you ever noticed that?"

Tip recited: *"When the devil was sick, the devil a saint would be; when the devil was well—the devil a saint was he!"*

482

Antoinette clapped her hands, delighted. "Oui, c'est ça, exactement! Ah, you Yankees—you have a verse for everything! I must remember that."

He tried to smile gallantly. "For your memoirs, maybe."

"Hélas! I have no literary ambitions. A shame, isn't it? What an extraordinary chronicle I could relate."

"Married men would have to take their beds and walk."

"Pardon?"

"Old blues song, Countess. About Memphis town."

"Ah yes, Memphis. My southern competitors. Eh bien, it's just as well that I continue to maintain discretion."

"It's the better part of valor."

"True. This is not a time for valor. Is it?" Her eyes rose to his over the cup's rim. "Well. And are you still selling the stocks that the other stocks gave birth to?" she asked him slyly, but without malice.

"No—I'm selling bonds now. Utilities, long-term municipals."

"I see. And how is business?"

"Picking up. Starting to move again, it's just a question of time before things turn around, and we . . . it's a . . ."

He faltered, ran down. Who in hell do I think I'm fooling? he thought, watching those alert brown eyes darting over his worn suit, the frayed cuffs. Here, sitting with this valiant woman, he could admit things were bad—couldn't he?—it was somehow insulting to her *not* to admit that.

"It's rotten," he heard himself say heavily. "Business. It's terrible—and I don't see what's going to make it get any better for a long, long while . . . I'm glad I couldn't sell you any of the trust stock," he added.

"I, too!" She smiled a sad, wise smile. "But you see, you were working at cross-purposes: those first courses you sold me so masterfully warned me against your later wares. You were simply too good a salesman!"

"Maybe so . . . Countess," he drew a deep breath, "I'm here on false pretenses."

She stared at him. "Comment cela? I doubt that very much."

"I am, though. Countess, I don't have the money for a hotel room, and my car is on the Fritz. Can you put me up for the night?"

"Any port in a storm, hein?"

He knew he was coloring; he bit his lip. "Madame, you know me better than that. I have an important prospect tomorrow morning at ten. I've got to make that sale—and I've got to look presentable when I go in there."

Her face became serious and smooth. "I didn't mean to joke, Mr. Ames. This is a poor time for jokes. Of course I can let you have a room."

"I'll repay you as soon as I can. I promise you."

"Don't worry about that . . . You may find the furnishings a trifle—bizarre, but you can manage, I trust."

"Thank you—I'm very grateful to you."

"Nonsense! Your courses were such a help to me—they made me rich, you know. I am simply returning the favor. That would only be fair, after refusing to buy your trusts-out-of-trusts."

". . . But what *did* you invest in?" he couldn't help asking, watching her stir her cup. "Everything's come crashing . . ."

"Almost everything, true. Well, when you came by to sell me your certificates, when you told me everything was *'fundamentally sound'* "—she dropped her voice, like his—"I said to myself; 'Those paper documents?—they look entirely too pretentious, too imposing to be real.' I have a horror of façades. Perhaps because I must live one myself—but that is a different matter. Au fond, I do not pretend to be anything other than what I am. I do not lie to myself about it.

"No, I said to myself, after all the chutes des bourses, after all the banqueroutes and screaming and barricades, what remains? Paper can turn to ashes, gold can be stolen, curios pass out of vogue. But what is still there, indestructible, is the land. *That* is what is 'fundamentally sound' . . . Alors," she concluded briskly, "I bought real estate, here in Ste. Hélène, in Burlington, along the lake. Thanks to your courses, Mr. Ames, I became my own real estate agent, my own appraiser, my own trusted financial adviser."

She laughed her light, trilling laugh, turned serious again. "Is there anything else I can do for you?"

He shook his head. "The room is a life-saver."

"As you wish." A moment longer she gazed at him as though making up her mind about something. "That first time you came—you were so full of hope. Such hope and promise! Do you remember?"

"Yes."

She said softly: "And do you still believe in those rainbow skies of progress?"

He looked down. "I try to . . . It all went wrong. Too much greed, not enough responsibility, something. It got out of hand—" He looked up again. "I still believe in people, though. I'll always believe in us . . ."

"I know. We are both honest salesmen, you and I. We have to believe." Impulsively she squeezed his hand, released it and rose. "I'll speak to Jethro about a room for you."

He sat there holding the empty coffee cup, thinking of that long ago evening and the Countess bent over gazing at the palm of his hand . . .

It was two days before he found the hundred-dollar bill fastened with a small gold safety pin to the change pocket of his overcoat, along with a note that said: *Consider this a gift if you can, or a loan if you must. ("Unsecured," as the steel-eyed banquiers would say!) There are altogether too few men like you in this unsteady world. Bonne chance, A.*

He refolded the note very carefully and inserted it in his wallet, right behind his driver's license and his membership card in the Bankers Club.

Charlotte Ames died in March. Chapin and Jenny drove Aunt Serena out from Boston in a brand new Buick. Chapin and Jenny were deeply tanned from a vacation in Jamaica, though Jenny seemed abstracted and remote, biting continually at the inside of her cheek. Both women wore furs, Serena a beautifully cut mink coat with a matching hat. She was in excellent spirits—younger and more vigorous than ever. She brought expensive presents for the children: a Windsor-Newton watercolor set for Joey, a beaver muff for Tessa. Jophy, worn down from the weeks of nursing his mother, was tense and on edge.

The ceremony was an agony. The ladies of the Eastern Star hovered over the bier, chanting some monotonous litany. Ralph Tackett, the minister, had a severe cold, and snuffled his way through the service. At the cemetery one of the straps broke and the casket spilled crazily into the pit, setting off a chorus of shocked cries. Standing in the chill, damp air, staring sightlessly at the scarves of old snow, the ice-rimed puddles, remembering his strained and harried childhood, the unremitting pressure of his father's dereliction, Tip felt wild with grief, overborne, provoked beyond his strength. Tackett droned maddeningly on and on. Oh, shut up! Tip wanted to shout, just shut your mouth and let her be! Just—let her rest, now. Can't you even do that?

Tears kept blurring his vision, lying cold on his face. All that effort, all that skimping and sacrifice—and for what? A narrow, gray box sunk deep in eight feet of half-frozen ground. There was no sense in it! No sense in it at all . . . From across the trench his

486

brother's eyes met his and flickered away; his face had that resentful, uncertain expression Tip had hated so when they were kids. He doesn't like it either, Tip thought with grim satisfaction; remembering things. That scar on his face, here in the cold, made an odd little cruciform outline that showed palely against the Caribbean tan.

Later Chapin admired Joey's drawings extravagantly: the boy had an unusual, a really extraordinary talent—he ought to have individual instruction; Serena enthusiastically agreed. Jophy replied that she'd been well aware of that for some time, and her eyes flashed at them hotly. There was an awkward little silence after that, and then Chapin glanced at Tip and said:

"I wish Dad could have been here."

"Trust Lyman Ames!" Serena remarked. "He was never around when you needed him."

Chapin looked grieved. "That's hardly fair, Auntie. Nobody's known where to contact him for years."

"I shouldn't think so."

Even then they'd have got through it all right if only Chapin hadn't taken him aside as they were leaving and offered to help defray the funeral expenses.

"I guess not," Tip said shortly.

"Really? Are you sure?"

"Yes. I'm sure."

"I know you've been having your troubles."

"Is that right."

"I know it's a strain, these days. I wish you'd let me—I'd be more than happy to—"

"No!" He didn't mean to say it so sharply, but he'd had enough. "No," he repeated. "I took care of her when she was alive, I'll take care of her now she's dead."

Chapin looked sullen and hurt; his breath was white on the late winter air. "I'm sorry you feel that way, Tipton. After all, I was her son, too . . ."

487

"The hell you were! You never were!"

He fell silent. Jophy, hurrying over to them, had heard him; her eyes flared at him, wide with reproach.

"Tip! What a thing to say . . ."

"That's how it is." He looked away, to the gaunt, gray mass of Mount Macomah, blinking rapidly. He was angry with himself for saying that; but he couldn't help it. Not today. Serena was calling to them from the car and he swung around to face his brother again. Jophy was walking stiffly away.

"That's a hard thing to say, Tipton. Really very hard."

"What do you want—egg in your beer?" He didn't know why he said that either, only that he had to. Don't expect charity from me, big brother, he thought hotly, staring; I'm flat broke—I can't afford it.

"Come along, Chapin!" Serena called. "It's getting late . . ."

Chapin kicked at a piece of dirty ice. "Well, I'm sorry," he said.

"Sure." Tip watched him walk quickly off toward the little group clustered around the Buick.

The summer of '32 was worst of all, worse than anything he could have imagined in his most panicky sleepless hours. The Federal Home Loan Bank was ushered in to hymns of praise, but nobody believed it would do any good; the small farmer and homeowner didn't seem to be any better off; nobody did. In April came the European speculators' attack on the dollar and the Marthe Hanau scandal; there was talk that the country would be forced off the gold standard, and the rumor of a million-dollar bear raid on the Exchange—and the market, which seemed to have sunk as low as it could possibly go, went into still another sickening plunge; a bottom below bottom.

Right after Labor Day, Waldheim fired him, and he couldn't get a job anywhere. On the road he took to living at the Y, whose occupants each morning bent over the communal washbasins, eyeing each other with surly speculation, shaving in silence. For meals he sought out the cheapest diners and hash houses, washed his own socks and underwear. In Providence, running down a lead, he finally gave in and with a sense of shame drew $1,000 out of the savings account he'd set aside there, sent half of it home and kept the rest.

The political campaign that fall enraged him: Roosevelt joking with reporters in his hearty, patronizing Groton voice, tilting that damned cigarette holder skyward to the tune of "Happy Days Are Here Again"—as though there were any happy days around for *anyone* but his Union League Club set; and that purse-mouthed prig Hoover, with his columns of statistics and his China money, saying nobody was starving, when all around you men—not bums either, but decent men down on their luck—crouched in the doorways of dead factories, crammed cardboard in their shoes and newspapers under their jackets and bitterly proffered apples or pencils or nothing at all, simply walked on and on through the cities in a purposeless, haunted round . . . It was "Brother, Can You Spare a Dime," all right; how much did they think men would take? One night he thought he saw a face he recognized—and to his horror discovered he'd already turned away in instinctive aversion. In deepening desperation he contacted the William Street firms, the bucket shops—he even called Lee, Higginson, and was coolly informed that Frank Delahant had not been associated with the firm for some time.

Two weeks later he went down to the Bankers Club and turned in his membership card, told them to withdraw his name. It was the hardest thing he'd had to do yet—it seemed to symbolize his whole dizzying descent down the ladder. The high, stately rooms looked subtly alien now, even menacing; he was on the outside again, peering in . . . He was sitting in the lounge for the last time, trying to get up the gumption to leave, wondering what to do, thinking fondly of the old crowd and the Alec Ham days, when a voice crowed:

"Well, chop off my pins and call me shorty!"

It was Blazer Blaydon, cherubic face beaming, blue eyes wide with surprise.

"What you been doing with yourself, Tipper?"

"Chasing around," he answered. "How about you? Web told me you're selling cars."

"No, I got out of that. Detroit and the dealers skim off all the gravy. Nobody's buying cars now, anyway." He clapped his fat pink hands. "No, I'm with Oneida Container."

"Who the hell are they?"

"Don't knock 'em, young fella." Blaydon dropped one eyelid and clucked; his kewpie-knot of hair stood straight up on the top of his head. "Waxed containers—they're the coming thing. Going to put the glass bottle right in the old ashcan."

"That a fact."

"Skipper, did you ever know me to kid the product? It's the slickest idea since the wheel."

"Where have I heard that before."

"They're cheap, light, disposable, sanitary, they stack like a dream. Cross my heart! The orders are coming in like Niagara." All steamed up now, he leaned forward, belly straining against his Harris tweed jacket. "Say, it's a break my running into you like this. We're building up the sales force, need to take on three or four men. You got any ideas about anybody I could contact?"

Tip looked straight at him and grinned. "Yeah. Something tells me I've got a cracker-jack candidate for you."

"Who? You mean—" The Blazer blinked, his cherub's face went blank. "You mean, *you'd* be interested . . .?" He frowned. "Well, look, they can't match what you've been making, they're not—"

"Try me . . . I'm sick of selling bonds. Market's dead, brokers are lying around with their feet in the air. There's no kick in it any more. I want something with romance in it . . ."

"Now you're talking! We'll burn up the track, Tipper . . ."

Tip said: "You hiring and firing?"

"Hell, yes. What you think I've been gassing about? They gave me a blank check, they want to open up the whole northeast. I'm their fair-haired boy out there. What's funny?"

"Nothing, Blazer, nothing." It seemed fantastic to him that he could be working for Roscoe Miles Blaydon. "Hell, let's give it a whirl."

"Bo-dee-oh-doh, daddy!" the Blazer hunched his shoulders. "Let's get out of this mausoleum and wet our whistles. With me to make the pitch, and you coming in for the close—zowie! It'll be like old times . . ."

Tip ran up the marble steps of the Yale Club, went straight to the desk and said: "Is Roscoe Blaydon registered?"

The steward, some Iowa Rotarian's idea of a British butler, replete with high collar and overlong upper lip, stared back at him a moment.

"May I inquire who it is that wishes to see him?"

"*I'm* the one who wishes to see him. Tipton Ames —I'm a business associate of his."

The steward peered remotely at some list tacked to the cage. "Yes. He is registered. Would you like me to ring him?"

"I've rung him twenty times since nine o'clock," Tip said crossly. "Is he in his room?"

The steward's eyes flickered at him once. "We think so."

"You think so." Tip leaned over the counter, said impatiently: "Give me the key to his room."

"Sir?"

"You've got a spare key, haven't you? Let me have it."

"Oh, we couldn't do that, sir."

"All right, then—you come up with me and open up, if you don't trust me."

"Oh, we couldn't do that. We never open the rooms of members."

"You're going to this time. It's extremely important I see him at once. Do I make myself clear?"

"You must understand our—"

"You're going to let me into his room or I will let myself in—my way. You won't like that at all."

The steward looked distressed at this, and began to open and close a series of small drawers. "I must tell you, it is club policy—"

"He may be dead up there," Tip pursued menacingly. "Mr. Blaydon's a Bones man. You don't want a dead Bones man on your hands, do you?"

Mention of Skull and Bones alarmed the steward still further. He fussed with some keys on a large ring and came out from behind the counter. "This is highly irregular . . ."

"That's perfectly all right—Mr. Blaydon is highly irregular himself. He won't mind at all."

The room was a magpie's nest of old newspapers and empty glasses. A torn blue pillow with a block Y lay on the floor by the fireplace, and there was part of a letter in huge, looping handwriting and apparently signed with a lipsticked kiss, badly smeared. The Blazer was lying on the bed in his underdrawers, his face sunk so deep in the pillow that for an instant Tip wondered if he *was* dead from suffocation. He plucked Blaydon's head up from the pillow by the twisted scalplock.

"Blazer," he hissed. "God damn it—Blazer!" The cherub face hung there puffy and white, mouth drawn down petulantly; the eyelids never once quivered. Out cold. He dropped the head into the pillow again.

The steward was saying stiffly: "You can see for yourself—"

"I certainly can," he broke in. "You can leave us now."

The steward hesitated, unsure, hands at his sides, opening and closing them in the approved butler fashion. "If there should be anything we—"

"There's nothing God Himself can do. I'll take it from here."

The door closed discreetly. Tip rolled Blaydon over and slapped him briskly, twice. His face gave a faint unhappy tremor, and he raised one shaking hand fearfully to his head.

"Where am I?" he groaned.

"You're in the bag, sonny. That's where you are." Tip went into the bathroom, jammed the plug in the bottom of the tub and turned on the cold faucet full force.

"And how were all the festive old grads?" he inquired grimly. "A rah-rah good time was had by all, mmmh?"

"Oh, God," Blaydon moaned. "Someone shoot me . . ."

"That's a damned fine idea." Tip heaved him over his shoulder in a fireman's carry into the bathroom. "And I'd love to oblige you, but unfortunately there's this little deal over in Brooklyn, and I need your——sterling—presence!" Crouching he dumped him into the tub.

"—Oh!" Blazer cried. His eyes flew open wide, he began floundering in the water, gasping, "Oh, oh, oh . . . !" while Tip held him down, watching him.

"Afterward I'll be more than happy to shoot you. But right now we're going over to see your old Yalie Buddy Morantz—"

"Let me up, Tip—"

"No."

"Let me up. I'm dying—"

"There's always hope."

"I'm okay. I'm okay. I'm sober as a—as a—"

"The hell you are. But you're going to be. I guarantee it."

Half an hour later he'd got him dressed and shaved and poured into a cab bound for Brooklyn. The Blazer, with four cups of steaming black coffee under his belt, puffing on his tenth cigarette, was wound up like a top, telling Tip what a comical bastard Walt Morantz had been back at New Haven, the capers he could pull, what a barrel of laughs . . .

Still tight as a tick, Tip thought morosely, staring out at the dead factories, the empty streets littered with garbage and old newspapers, a thin man in a pinstripe suit moving with that aimless, somnambulistic stride that meant only one thing. He shivered inside his old topcoat. Another winter coming. Still another. Hoover out, Roosevelt in. One of Chapin's Groton-Harvard clubmen. Maybe Roosevelt was different. He doubted it; but it was possible. Anyway, the country wanted a change, *any* kind of change. Anything was better than this drifting, stunned paralysis . . .

"Just what the hell *is* mocha milk, anyway?" he demanded.

Blaydon blinked at him. "Mocha milk? You know what mocha milk is, Tip, it's a coffee-chocolate blend, a choice blend of the finest Brazilian—"

"Spare me. You ever tasted it?"

"Why no, can't say that I have. It's a new taste sensation."

"I'll bet."

"I wouldn't jazz you. Remember Coca-Cola, remember how they laughed at it? The gags about sniffing coke? Eskimo Pies. They all laughed at Christopher Columbus, you remember that. Mocha milk's a revolutionary idea in kids' drinks, grownups' too, it's going to sweep the country, give it half a chance. Old Walt's hot for the containers. What we want to stress is the labor angle—no bottles to wash, no deposit-and-return—"

494

"Save it for the fight."

"I'm serious. That and the waste problem, here in Brooklyn."

The plant looked tired, stalled on dead center. There were water-stained crates stacked near one of the entrances, unopened, and everywhere there was an odor like burned licorice. Two men were sitting in the inner office, silent and still. Tip had the impression they'd been having an argument over something. The plant manager, a lanky towhead named Wendom, shook hands with them. Morantz, behind the desk, raised one hand briefly and then locked it with the other across his ample belly. His eyes were frozen behind rectangular slits of flesh.

"Walt!" the Blazer waved at him. "Long time no see, baby! You get up to the Bowl? Great game, great game . . ."

"Seddown, boys," Morantz said. His eyes seemed locked on Blaydon.

"Right with you, Doc!" The Blazer, still hopped up to the eyebrows, opened allegro with a few winsome allusions to their salad days at New Haven. Morantz, motionless, made no reply. Without missing a beat Blaydon shifted gears, launched into blithe predictions of a dramatic upturn with the new administration (whatever you felt personally about Fearless Frank he was *our sort*) and from there to the glowing future of cardboard containers—their fantastic superiority over glass bottles in a cost-conscious era: light, disposable, and let's not forget the advertising angle —four flat sides and a top to push the product, a natural! The Blazer's baby-blue eyes were snapping with enthusiasm, his head pumping in emphasis. He had the display out now, was deftly flipping through its pages . . . And all the while that comical bastard from those madcap days at New Haven hadn't moved a muscle, hadn't even blinked; his little button eyes remained frozen on Blaydon in that glazed, narrow stare—

Why, *he's* pie-eyed, too, Tip realized suddenly, with a start. He's totally and utterly glued. Jesus H. Q. Christ. His glance met Wendom's; the plant manager rolled his eyes toward the ceiling. Tip nodded and the two of them rose and went toward the door.

"Let those two drunks commune with each other," he muttered. "Show me around the plant."

As they left the room the Blazer was still crouched over, selling up a storm.

That was November. Three weeks later, wandering aimlessly through an insanely glittering, raucous Woolworth's, looking for something cheap he could bring home to the kids for Christmas, moving through the chaotic islands of G-men badges and Mickey Mouse watches, bumped by other shoppers, he found himself listening to a voice—a voice he'd recognized before he'd realized it:

"—because it's so *easy* to use, so quick and easy, you simply insert Mister Juicer in your orange, like this, twist once, and presto!—in less time than it takes to tell you about it—"

Incredulous, fearful, he peered through the heads of a score of mildly interested women and saw Frank Delahant, holding the small orange impaled by an odd-shaped red metal gadget. His face was thinner and more drawn, as though some of the flesh had been flayed away over the past three years, and his hair was thinning, but he was still smiling that well-bred, charming smile.

"—then simply *squeeze* your orange, like this, and voilà!—a glass of tropic sunshine ready to drink. No more slicing and squeezing, ladies, no more sawing away at sections or straining pulp, just a simple twist of the wrist and leave the rest to Mister Juicer! Try some, Madam, see if that isn't as fine a glass—"

Shaken and frightened, Tip started to turn away, but Frank had already spotted him—his face stiffened, then his mouth quivered into a sour, defiant smile. Sick at heart, hands thrust deep in his overcoat pockets, Tip hurried out of the store. He was two blocks away before he remembered that he hadn't got anything for the children.

3

He pulled into Holcomb Falls just after noon, a year to the day after his mother's death, feeling duped and angry and apprehensive. The mill looked abandoned through the bare trees—a sacked fortress; a few bulbs glowed palely from the skylights over the beaters. For the past ten miles the car had been making an ominous rumble in the left rear wheel; it sounded as though a bearing was gone. He ran slowly down Church Street, recalling the houses—Myricks', Lefevres', Gilmans'—where he'd cranked the shivery bell-pulls, the Shalimar samples tucked under his arm. He wondered if he could sell those people now. Now there wasn't money for chipped beef or shoes, let alone oil of palm straight from the Spice Islands. Maybe he'd be back to that too, before long—a bell-banging drummer like Web Bowers, who was working for Fuller Brush. Well, he could if he had to. Selling was all he knew; and he was still one of the best. He knew he was . . .

The house looked shabby; it needed a coat of paint, the cellar bulkhead doors ought to be replaced. Maybe he could get to it this spring, with a spell of dry weather. He couldn't get used to the idea of his mother not being there; her worn smile, the spicy odor of apple turnovers. He let himself in the back door.

"Home is the hunter," he called in the old ritual.

He could see through the dining room to where

Jophy was sitting by one of the kitchen windows, gazing out, her face in sharp profile. Her head turned as though she'd been asleep; then she rose and came toward him, and they embraced.

"You caught me," she said, and blew her nose. "You said Wednesday or Thursday."

"Well, I had a change in plans . . . Honey, you've got a bad cold."

"All the usual March megrims. Can't seem to shake it off."

"Where are the kids?"

"Gone skating, over at Fanchett's." She pushed vaguely at her hair, which looked uncombed. She was wearing her old brown knitted suit and a baggy chain-knit sweater that was unraveling at the hem. There were dark circles under her eyes and her nose was swollen.

He said: "It seems awfully cold in here, Jo."

"I've been keeping the thermostat down. To save."

"But you ought to be warm enough . . ."

"Well." She made a quick, dismissive gesture. "We're two months behind with Lefevre's."

"But he'll carry us, Jo—he knows I'm good for it . . ." He felt irritated, out of sorts with everything. Jophy looked so bedraggled—of course she hadn't known he was coming home, and with this head cold—

"I was listening to the inauguration." She was blowing her nose again. "He sounds so hopeful, so —full of beans! Roosevelt. Do you think he can really do something?"

"—He's done plenty already," he answered sharply, unable to stop himself. "He just closed the banks this morning. All of them."

"Really? For how long?"

"Four days, they say. But it could be a lot longer than that."

"But then—how will things get done? people get paid?"

"That's a good question."

She set the tea kettle on the stove with a clatter and said: "How about us? Have we enough money to last it out?"

"I don't know." He sat down in his father's old chair, his elbows on his knees. "Bank manager over in Buffalo said sure, sure, go ahead and make deposit, nothing to worry about. I went over to the window—and all of a sudden I thought: What in hell does *he* know about it? What's so bloody infallible about him? I told the clerk I wanted it in cash, I'd worry about my balance later. Damned good thing, too. Hell, I wouldn't have got home. Anyway, we can ride it out for a while."

"But how could he *do* that? Roosevelt?"

"He's President. He can do anything. I guess. Well, they had to do something, there's been an epidemic of bank failures out in the Middle West, Michigan, Ohio. It's just to get things straightened out."

"What things?" she said irritably. "I don't understand it. Why did those banks fail?"

"Well, people got panicky and started a run. And the banks couldn't meet their obligations."

"But why couldn't they? Why didn't they have the money the people had put there?"

He sighed. "It's a matter of credit. They were overextended—they got involved in holding-company procedures, security affiliates. That kind of thing."

"Talk plain English to me, Tip. I'm not one of your wise-apple customers with his feet up on the desk. They gambled with the depositors' money: is that it?"

"It's more complicated than that. But yes, their investments were unsound, or their structuring . . ."

"But then why close *all* the banks?—Oh, I see," she ran on tightlipped, answering herself, "I get it, the other banks were in it too, they're just bigger—"

"Not necessarily—"

"—or they loaned the crooked ones the money and now they haven't got it either, and the gambling banks are pulling them down, too! I get it. It's a chain reaction, just like the Crash—"

"No, it isn't like the Crash!" he snapped at her. Discussions about finance with Jophy always irritated him—her views were remarkably like those of a Hearst cartoonist: lurid oversimplifications, complete with hero and villain, and just enough truth in them to make any rational explanations utterly futile; and now he was sore and on edge with worry. "If their credit balances are good, their reserves are solid, they ought to come through all right. Why do you always have to make a five-alarm disaster out of everything? *Everybody* isn't an Ivar Kreuger. We'll just have to hope, that's all. It'll straighten itself out . . ."

"Hope?" Her head came up, she set down the cups. "What do you mean? Hope for what?"

He shook his head, nettled, scowling. "Nothing, it's nothing." But his growing anxiety, those seven words, had betrayed him. She was looking straight at him now, her face flat with perplexity.

"Tip, this is no time for mysteries. What do we *just have to hope* about?"

He sighed inaudibly. "I put some money in a bank over in Providence. Back in '27, when things were rolling along. It was just on a hunch."

"You mean savings? A savings account?"

"That's right. It was just for a rainy day. A sheet to windward, as Grama used to say."

"And it's closed now. Of course, along with all the others . . . But why didn't you get it out?" she pursued. "If you knew there were failures in Michigan—"

"It didn't seem necessary, Jo," he answered. Fear had always made him testy. He swallowed, forced his voice lower. "It's a national bank, it's solid. There didn't seem to be any need for that. I called Chapin from Buffalo—"

"Chapin!"

"Yes, of course, why not? I wanted to check with someone. He's got his ear to the ground on things like

502

this. Calkins is on the Exchange Board of Governors . . ."

"And Chapin assured you everything was going to be just jake."

"No, but he said he thought it was unlikely they'd close."

"I see. And you believed him. As usual."

"Jesus Christ, Jophy, you've got to believe *somebody!* He told me Lamont had personally appealed to Roosevelt not to do it—give the national psychology time to regain confidence, with the new administration. To ease us through the crisis. Hell, it's just a question of confidence . . ."

She walked slowly over to the window above the sink and stood looking out, watching the long sweep of snow and ice, the ghostly gray mass of Macomah Mountain.

"Confidence," she murmured tonelessly. Then: "How much money was it?"

He hesitated. "Just under five."

"You mean four. Four *what?* Hundred or thousand?"

"Four thousand . . . Look, it may be all right, Jo. They may pull through okay, they probably will. It's only a four-day holiday."

Holiday! Santa Virgem, what a word for it."

"Well, a moratorium. To check out the books."

Still staring at the long field, the escarpment of woods, she said quietly, "You're saying we had —money, all this time. And we never used it."

"Well," he said uneasily, "I had to hit the till twice, the past two years. I didn't want to— I didn't want to have to touch it at all; things could still get worse, and we might need it even more, you know. It was for an emergency . . ."

"*Jesus—!*" The heel of her hand struck the bread board on the counter, so hard it split. She whirled on him, her eyes blazing. "All these years! Wrestling with that cranky beast of a furnace, nursing your mother, skimping on food and clothes and shoes and every God damned thing else, doing the laundry by hand, turning your collars nights—and all this time *you* had money squirreled away in a . . . No! It's too much! It's too damned much!"

"Jo, I told you, it was for—"

"*This* is an emergency!" she shouted. "What in Christ's name do you think this is—we've been *living* in an emergency for the past three and a half years! . . . And most of all, why didn't you tell me about it? *Why*—?"

"But . . ." He was shaken by the force of her fury, the glare in her eyes. She's sick, he thought with alarm, she's got fever, this terrible winter's got to her. He said: "But I've always handled the money . . ."

"Oh my, haven't you! You dole out the money each month, sometimes more, sometimes less, sometimes nothing at all. And I'm expected to make a go of it, no matter what. *You* chart the course, not I . . ."

"But that's my department . . ."

"And why should that be? Give me three reasons —give me one! You haven't made such a roaring success of it, lately. No, you've always made the decisions —to leave Alec Ham, to join forces with Chapin, to race around New England like a mad animal selling those trust issues while he sat back and raked in the money . . ."

"Jo," he pleaded, "what's the sense in bringing all that up now?"

"—Because I never have, that's why! Isn't that a good enough reason? Did you ever stop to consider, just once, what might be going through *my* mind? Did it ever occur to you that *I* might like to know about the existence of four thousand lousy dollars while I was hanging up the wash in five above zero?"

"I told you, it was a—"

"No, it never did, did it? Because money calls the tune. Because *you* make the money—when you do, I mean—and that means you control it all. You do what you want, and the rest of us can think what we want."

"Jophy, that's not—"

"Maybe *I* would have wanted to put it into emeralds, or champagne, maybe I'd have wanted to put it under a loose board in the floor! Something female and silly. Only we'd still have it right now, if we'd done that. Wouldn't we?"

"I couldn't foresee they'd shut down the God damn works!" he cried. "I was saving it for the children. Be reasonable, Jo . . ."

"I'm sick of being reasonable! I'm sick of ice and snow, and that mountain out there—and what I'm *really* sick of is that mackerel-mouth old bitch over in Boston running our lives!"

He stared at her. *"Serena—?"*

"Who in the hell did you think?"

"She's not running our lives, she doesn't even—"

"Isn't she? Isn't she? Then just why do you think you've driven yourself like a madman for twenty years, if it isn't to prove to her that you're better than Chapin—that she made the wrong choice?"

"Jophy, that's ridiculous!"

"You *are* better than Chapin, you don't have to prove it, you never did—but you'll never believe it. No—she turned it all rotten between you from the beginning, but you'll never see it and neither will Chapin—"

"You don't know what you're talking about!"

"Oh, don't I! I've watched the three of you for years . . . Well, I'm sick of it, I'm sick of your damn competition. I've had it! I've had it to my very guts . . ." She moved toward him, her breast heaving, her eyes snapping in darkest rage while he stared at her, angry and fearful and confused. *"What I think matters,* Tip. Yes! What I care about matters, big salary or no big salary. Whether you want to admit it or not!"

He began, "If you would listen to me for one minute—"

"No! There's nothing to hear." Her eyes filled with tears and she shook them clear. "I'm going to the Cape, Tipton, and I'm taking the children—we're going to see something besides frozen ponds and frozen mountains and frozen Yankee faces. I'm going tomorrow."

"Jo," he stammered, "you don't mean that . . ."

"Oh, yes." She was weeping now, openly and thickly, struggling to clear her throat, but her face was set. "I do. By Jesus and the Virgin Mary, I mean it!"

He had got to his feet—he didn't know how. He had that awful sense of the room being upended, he had to clutch at the table for support. He took her by the shoulder, and she flung him off.

"Don't—!" she cried softly. "I'm going, Tip. That's it!"

"Jo, please don't. Please don't leave like this." Everything was opening away under his feet. "Jo, I know it's been lonely for you, these years. I know it's been hard, pinching pennies. But Jo, I'll make it up to you . . ."

"Oh God, it's not the damned money! Can't you see that—?"

"If only you'd said—"

"I shouldn't have *had* to say it! No one should have to . . ."

"Please. Can't we talk this out—"

"No. No more talk. It's no good. I'm going down tomorrow. And that's an end of it." She walked quickly out of the room and he heard her feet thudding on the stairs.

He sat down in the chair again as though he'd been bludgeoned into it, breathing heavily. In all his life he'd never felt so whipped. How had it gone so wrong—so horribly wrong? That ace-in-the-hole account he'd stashed away in Providence, to be there in case some real crisis came up, to *protect* them—and it had led to this . . . He knew she meant it, beyond any qualification or condition; she would not change her mind, she would die first. That pitiless, unforgiving Portuguese ferocity—he'd always feared in his heart's pit that it might one day be turned against him, and now it was. Now it was.

But Christ almighty, anyone could make a mistake; anyone! Working your guts out, giving them the best when you were making it; trying to see, to plan ahead—

The back door bumped and banged, he heard voices calling: "It's Daddy!" "Dad's home!" and the kids burst into the room, tracking snow, the pompoms on their caps bouncing crazily, skate blades flashing in the room like swords; they flung themselves on him, their cheeks cold and smooth, their fingers clutched at his neck.

Joey said: "Dad! I got As this month—all As and one B . . ."

"That's great, son. Just great."

Tessa had climbed into his lap, was gripping his tie. "I skated all the way across Fanchett's, Daddy. We played crack-the-whip and Jimmy Gilman tore the whole bottom out of his pants—!" She was laughing, burrowing her head into his shoulder; but now Joey was frowning at him unsurely.

"Dad. . . ? What's the matter?"

He'd have given anything he owned to have kept the tears back at that moment; anything. He couldn't help it—they kept spilling over his lids and running down his face, while Tessa looked up too, her merry little brigand's face troubled.

"Why are you crying? Daddy?"

"Nothing, nothing . . ." He shook his head, crushing her against him, feeling more misery than he'd ever known. "It's just—because I'm so happy to see you both again. That's all . . ."

Upstairs he could hear Jophy moving around quickly, the sound of a sticky bureau drawer slammed closed.

"Darling, would you have any objection to telling

507

me just what you thought you were trying to prove to-night?" Chapin's face, reflected in the blued mirror of Jenny's vanity, was smiling, but his eyes were not.

"Why nothing, really," she answered coolly. "Perhaps if some of your friends weren't quite so hide-bound, nothing would have happened at all."

"Hidebound." He touched his fingertips together lightly and studied them; he was sitting on the edge of her chaise lounge.

She said: "Heinz Krasnodar happens to be a distinguished novelist."

"He's a pompous baboon. And a boor."

She twisted around on the satin banquette and faced him directly. "What did you do with him, by the way?"

"I politely escorted him to the door and put him out for the night. Like a house cat. And told Benson not to let him in if he tried to gain reentry."

She laughed without enjoyment. "*That* was a cultivated solution!"

"I thought so. Given the circumstances." He paused. "I declare, poor old Randy was right: you still want to be Queen of the effing Wobblies."

"Don't be tiresome," she said crossly, and turned back to the mirror. "Are they all so afraid to hear one dissenting voice? these power-broker pals of yours?"

"The man is a roaring Communist."

"You haven't the faintest idea whether he is or not. Everybody who disagrees with Wall Street's quaint world-view these days is a Communist. Or worse."

He leaned forward on the chaise, peering at her intently. It was curious the way a reflected face always looked altered, even faintly menacing—as though some alien spirit had invested a familiar form.

"It just so happens," he said in the soft, lanquid tone that masked his moments of deepest anger, "that our lives are indissolubly tied to these contemptible 'power-broker pals' of mine. For better or worse. What they think of me determines what they will entrust me with, what privileged knowledge they will impart."

"That isn't knowledge, that's glorified gossip."

She knew she shouldn't have invited Krasnodar tonight—the man was pugnacious and strident, bound to cause trouble; but she'd been in a rebellious mood all winter long. She was sick of entertaining the brightest new SEC assistant, the dullest old Stock Exchange governor, the latest foreign correspondent just back from Nanking . . . She wanted to embarrass Chapin, that was at the bottom of it; but she was fed to the teeth with him—his shameless pursuit of the money barons when the country was in unrelieved misery revolted her. She thought of her father sitting in the rattan lawn chair with the blanket over his knees, the dulled misgiving in his eyes, and her heart hardened still further.

"You know," she offered, "I don't really find this terribly profitable, Chay. It's been a long evening, and I'm rather tired. Why don't we just drop it?"

"Because I don't want to *just drop it*," he said.

She looked away and went on working on her face, hating its puggish cast, the over-wide jaw. Her neck had thickened and creased over the past few years, and her mouth—her mouth had tightened curiously, as though she were gripping between her teeth some invisible object; perhaps a bone. And there was something else that disturbed her, some indefinable *hollowness* in her eyes that hadn't been there before . . . or did she imagine it? What a depressing cheat time was. She'd begun to put on weight badly; she'd tried dieting but every time she did that pain high in her stomach got worse. Chapin was never bothered by thickening or creasing or anything else, she thought with savage resentment; he got in his tennis in the summer and squash in the winter, he drank less than ever, in spite of the fact that good liquor was now available on every hand . . .

In silence she picked up another jar and unscrewed

509

its enamel top. Her head ached, and that swollen, burning sensation had started again, high under her rib cage. She would have to stop drinking. Soon.

"I think," Chapin was saying, "that from now on we'd better confer about the guest list."

"Diversity," she answered. "A lively mix—isn't that what you've always wanted?"

"I'm afraid my tastes aren't all that catholic, sweets. The old melting pot *can* get too rich, you know."

"What an exquisitely fascist thought. The Nazis would adore it."

He moved so suddenly then that she gasped—it was as if she had burned him with a hot wire. He paused directly above her, one hand extended, very near her eye.

"Enough," he said flatly. "You've had your little joke this evening, and that's the end of it. Do you understand? Now here is Lesson One for your political primer: there will be no looting in the palace, no sudden overthrow of the capitalist exploiters—of which you are a conspicuous example, by the way." He had himself in hand again, his voice resumed its easy, lanquid pace. "*I* have seen the future—and *this* is the way it works: the dear old U.S. of A. is going to go right along the way it's been going since 1786 or whenever, with the privileged doing as they please —and the lesser breeds longing with all their famished little hearts to become top dogs themselves, any way they can; just as dear old Karl Marx predicted they would. The real trouble with these Soviet demagogues is that they never really read him very carefully." He straightened, still gazing at her. "From now on you will be more circumspect about the people you invite to our evenings, my dear. Do we understand each other?"

"Circumspect!" She laughed flatly. "What a curious word to use, Chapin—you of all people. With *your*—exploits on two continents—"

"I've stopped them."

"You've what?"

"I've put an end to them."

She studied him covertly. He was capable of anything. But she had learned to read him very, very well over the years. There was that tell-tale flicker of thwarted indulgence in his eyes. She decided he was telling the truth; for once. Or if he hadn't given them up, he intended to. But why?

"A new leaf," he said in the old musing tone. He was standing directly behind her now. "A different life, to go with a different age." He stood looking at her face in the mirror—a remote, disturbingly enigmatic glance; bending over he ran his hands over her neck and throat, over her breasts.

"I want to go to bed with you," he murmured.

"For Christ's sake, Chapin!" she exclaimed. "You go from right-wing diatribes to seduction rather abruptly, don't you think?"

She had stiffened minutely at his touch, though he seemed unaware of it. She said coldly: "And to just what do I owe this?" Because he had shown no sexual interest in her at all, ever since that last trip to Munich. His hands caressing her breasts made her realize how much she'd cooled since the early years of their marriage. She could not understand what he was up to, and it troubled her.

His lips were soft and warm against her ear. He said slowly and distinctly: "I want a son."

"—You're joking!"

She twisted around, using the gesture, her shocked amusement, to free herself. "What on *earth* has got into you?" Here it was—the moment she had feared for so long; the moment she had known would happen.

"I'm quite serious."

Searching his face she saw he was—as she had always known he would be; but she stood her ground.

"I can't imagine why," she said. "In the first place, I'm sick . . ."

"No, you're not. You haven't had an attack for months, now. You're perfectly capable of bearing children."

She forced herself to smile. "How eminently Victorian of you, Chapin."

"I *am* a Victorian. Prude and snob and libertine, all rolled into one."

"How true. But it's a little late for all this, isn't it?" she asked somberly.

"Not really. I wanted children years ago, you'll remember—you weren't terribly enthusiastic."

"Then why press me now?"

"I told you. A new leaf . . . I want a son, Jenny. Terribly."

He ran his fingers along the side of his nose. His face, usually so sleek and impermeable, looked all at once tremulous and uncertain, and this enraged her beyond measure.

"Look now," she said hotly, "you set the pattern for our lives. Such as it was. And I went along with it. All of it."

"Why," he began, "I thought you were in agreement, I thought you enjoyed—"

"You can stop being hypocritical, at least that—you *knew* I hated it, every minute of it! Animal . . . no, no decent *animal*—it sickened me!"

He looked actually quite shocked. "You mean—all this time, you were really—"

"You can't *conceive* how I detested it—every last she-ape in your disgusting menagerie—and myself for being one, too—worse, because *they* at least needed the money . . . and I despised you most of all—yes! For standing there over us, cracking your swollen red whip . . ."

She listened to herself in frightened, furious amazement. She had no idea why she was throwing away the image she'd constructed with such disciplined subterfuge and calculation, the iron performance of twelve miserable years—smashing it in an instant like some priceless Dresden figurine. But she could not stop herself. The defeats she'd suffered these past years, the reawakened scorn for the irresponsible class that had destroyed her father, drove her headlong. It was a fierce, unholy joy to be telling him this—that was suddenly all that mattered.

"Then why did you go along with it?" he was saying in dismay.

She felt such overwhelming rage she thought she would choke on it; her sight was actually blurred. She nearly bit her lip through. His sullen bewilderment was worse than any physical despoilment.

"—Because I made the catastropic mistake of falling in love with you!" she cried. "Which you perfectly well know . . ."

"Then give me a son." He caught her at the shoulders.

She made a low sound of animal fury, animal need. "No, I tell you, *no—!*"

His grip on her increased; his eyes—so pale and hollow at the points of the pupils—swept very near hers.

"Perhaps we'll see," he said with soft ferocity. "Perhaps we'll see about that."

She stopped struggling. She felt revolted and aroused at the same time; but the sensation was distant, like a solitary bell tolling across desert spaces. Her shoulders hurt where he gripped them.

"I will never give you a child, Chapin," she said in a low, hard voice. "Ever. No matter what you do."

He released her then and moved away and sat down on the edge of the chaise.

"Then . . . I want a divorce."

She caught her breath. "Why, on earth?"

"I want to be free."

"Free—!" She had doubled over in crazy laughter, half-hysterical with the volcanic release of what she

had held to herself all these desolate years. "Free! You sick, besotted fool—you're no more *free* than some dope addict in a Bellevue ward. Look at you! Dancing attendance on Auntie Serena, with her providential chest of gold pieces—only *really* hating her for saving your hide. Patronizing your brother every chance you get—only *really* envying him, hating his very guts. Bantering with Jophy—and all the time dreaming of her golden thighs, wanting to thrust your way into that glorious body of hers . . ."

His head went back, he was glaring at her; his face was chalk white. "You know, you're mad—you're actually demented . . ."

"*I'm* mad—!" She laughed through her clenched teeth. "You think I'm some kind of moroon, that I haven't seen it? Don't insult me! The way you've watched her all these years. Do you think I have to read twenty chapters of Freud to figure that out? You can't beat him as a man, you know you never will, so you'll beat him by fucking his wife. Elementary! You think you can match her sexually, don't you? You idiot! She's the *real* thing—she's what you've only tried to fake, with your disgusting pig-wallowing fantasies! She'd laugh in your face . . . Free! Why, you're locked into that royal family battle till you die—you're the perfect *slave* of slaves . . ."

"*That's enough!*" He was shuddering, she thought for an instant he was going to do some sudden, violent thing. Then in another few seconds he had himself in hand.

"This is not a game," he said tightly. "I mean it."

"It's not? So many things *have* been, over the years. There was Lizette, and Loretta and Gwen up in Harlem, and Elfreda over in Munich . . . You can't blame me if I—"

"*No more games.*"

She sobered then, still shocked at her outburst, fell silent herself. Chapin's eyes were immensely flat and cold in their slate, concentric rings-on-rings, unwa-

vering; a malevolent, pitiless look, all the more menacing for its very speculative distance. It was a look
she had never seen on his face before—not in the af-
termaths of any of their most violent tableaux, not in
any of their bitter quarrels, not even the night she
had accused him of willfully ruining her father. She
had gone too far. When she'd touched him on his rivalry with Tip, his obsession with Jophy—

She had lived with fear of one kind or another for a
long time now, but this was a fear below those other
fears. In spite of herself she shivered inwardly. There
was danger here, now. Great danger. She knew it
without question.

She would have to be very careful. Now.

She dropped her eyes, turned her back on him and
picked up a lemonstick from the top of the vanity. It
took every last ounce of her self-control, but she did
not drop it, and her nails did not chatter against the
lacquered surface.

"I don't know about you, darling," she said airily,
"but I'm absolutely bushed. I've got to get some
sleep." Her voice was steadier than she would ever
have believed, and that pleased her. "I'll think about
it long and seriously, all day tomorrow. That's a
promise. But I really do think this discussion has
gone about as far as it can go."

He made no reply. She knew his eyes were still on
hers, in the mirror. Inclining her head, breathing
with deep, stealthy care, she bent her attention on
her cuticles, working industriously. After what
seemed a long time she glanced up, to find he was no
longer sitting there. He had left. Rising she went
quickly to her door and locked it soundlessly. It was
the first time she had ever done that. Then she sat on
the bed with her knees drawn up, gripping them
hard, staring at nothing.

There were certain things she could do. There were
many things she could do, in fact . . . but she was not
brave enough. It would take exceptional courage to go

on with him now, day after day. And she lacked that kind of courage. Maybe Jophy could meet it head on, match him stroke for stroke; she could not. She knew it.

God help them, she thought. Tip and Jophy. God help both of them. They don't know what they're in for.

She would clear out tomorrow morning: take only what she could carry easily; clean out her accounts, what was properly hers, go out to the Island and stay with her father and mother. Until she decided what to do. She'd tell them she was redecorating the apartment, something like that to allay talk. Until she figured out what to do.

The important thing was to get out of here. Right away.

4

There was something wrong about the place—something strained and out of key; Tip could feel it in the soles of his feet. Maybe it was the mercury-painted globes flashing on top of their concrete pillars lining the circular driveway; maybe it was the classical statuary, overlarge nude figures posed amid eerily sculpted boxwood hedging. A gnarled old man snicked savagely at the edges of one of the boxwoods with a big pair of shears, now and then throwing glowering looks in Tip's direction. The building itself was a maze of turrets and cupolas and gables, as if the architect had pasted them on as he went along. An enormous black touring car thrust its grille out of the doors of a miniature Cape Cod cottage that was apparently the garage.

"Well," Tip said, half aloud. "Here goes nothing."

He rang, and heard strange chimes like falsetto bells clashing away deep inside the house. No one came to the door. He peered at the old gardener, who threw him a glance of terrible menace and went on snipping at the shrubbery. It wasn't quite what he'd expected, from the phone call. But then, nothing was quite what you expected, these days.

The door opened so abruptly he blinked. A man with sleepy purple eyes and a face like a Sioux chieftain, wearing an overtight double-breasted suit, was staring at him.

"Tip Ames," he offered. "With Rademacher Corporation. I called about an hour ago."

"Oh, yeah. Sure." The purple eyes covered the driveway behind him. "Come ahead." Inside Tip paused, waiting for this butler or whatever he was to lead the way, but the man only gestured with one big blunt hand. "On your right, there."

Tip went down the hall and entered a darkened room crammed with sofas and chairs upholstered in a violent shade of yellow. The curtains were drawn; all the lamps were lighted. In the far corner a thin, sallow-faced man in a silk dressing gown of the same yellow hue and wearing sunglasses was standing in front of a cage and saying something to a green-and-orange cockatoo rocking back and forth on a swing.

"Mr. Danco?" Tip said.

"Check." The man turned away from the cage, and Tip saw a long scar running across his left cheek; his hair looked as if it had been painted with lacquer. "My friends call me Spider," he said, coming forward. "I guess I'll have to change that, though. Hey, Louis?"

Tip, glancing behind him, saw the Sioux chief had silently taken up a position by the doorway.

"Yeah, got to be some changes made," Spider Danco observed. "Like the song says. New times coming. Know what I mean?"

"*And how!*" the parrot squawked with such violence that Tip started.

"Park it, Ames." Danco pointed to a chair and sat down in one of the egg-yolk couches. "Louis, pour the man a stiff one." He smiled, the scar moving stealthily with his lips. "Punctuality. I like that. Politeness of kings. Know what I mean?"

"*He gassed!*" the parrot shouted, swinging violently.

"Shut up, Roxy," Danco said without irritation. "I like the deal, Ames. I did a little checking and I like the set-up. It's tailormade."

"*Can it, Jack!*" Roxy said.

"Now what's the story on delivery?"

"The Queens warehouse is our main storage center," Tip said. "We can make shipments within the week—would it be here, in New Haven?"

"Check." Danco touched his varnished black hair as if to confirm its condition. "Know what's going to be the biggest thing in America?"

"Pussy!" the parrot shrieked, and behind Tip the bodyguard chuckled.

"Beer," Danco continued, oblivious. "That's right. Now, people like you, me—we like a shot of Scotch maybe, a tall gin—"

"He's squiffed, and how!"

"—but the average jomoke out there is going to drink brew. Glass after glass. It's cheap, it's filling, he gets a little buzz on . . . It's drinking—and yet not drinking. You follow me? Women, too. All that's needed is some high-class, hoity-toity advertising and they'll lap it up. It's going to be big, big business. What do you think?"

"Sarsparilla!"

"You could be running a sales force, Mr. Danco."

"Nah. I got the bankroll. I'll let *you* do the selling."

Tip smiled slowly. "That's the way the system works, all right."

"Dry up, buster!" Roxy called.

"Check. Listen, I want to shoot fifty grand."

Tip stared at him, brought his lips together. "Fifty thousand. Well, that's great news, Mr. Danco. Great. Now, how would you like to arrange the financing?"

Danco grinned—a lean, humorless grin. "What's the matter, Ames? You don't think my credit's good?"

"And how, sonny!"

"Not at all. But an order like this—a check for this amount—"

Spider raised a thin, bony hand. "No problem. I never write checks. They only make trouble. Louis." The henchman moved somewhere behind Tip and set a large new canvas bag on the cocktail table. "Be my guest."

Tip opened it and began to take out stacks on stacks of bills—twenties, tens, even hundreds; even gold certificates. Jesus Christ, he thought. Jesus H. Christ. What am I getting myself into?

"It's exact?" he asked.

Danco looked at his nails. "I like that: you want to check it out. Go ahead and count it. I got plenty of time."

He counted it with care, thinking rapidly, wondering what to do, while the parrot bounced back and forth in its cage, calling abuse, trying to rattle him. Its scraggly orange crest kept reminding him eerily of Blazer. But Blazer was far away now, in Spartanburg or Rocky Mount, selling a soft drink called Nehi . . .

"That's quite a bird," he said when he'd finished counting. "He's got an amazing vocabulary." The parrot glared at him glassily, refused to comment.

"Yeah. Arnie Tambkin gave him to me. Token of friendship. Know what I mean? Two weeks later they starched him like a shirt . . . Hey, Roxy," he called. "Hey, mitt the crowd!" The bird remained silent, snapping its head about. "He's a—what do you call it? A talonsman. He brings back the wild days. All I got to do is hear him and they come flooding back." His head sank forward on his chest. "Ah, the kick's gone out of it. That snotty gimp Roosevelt and his Repeal. I'll go along, sure, but it'll just be playing out the string. I ain't kidding myself."

"Get off the dime!" Roxy jeered.

Tip wrote out a receipt and signed it. Watching Louis put the money back in the satchel he said suddenly: "May I make a call, Mr. Danco?"

"Sure. Who to?"

"Police station. Right here in town."

Danco's face turned very narrow and hard. The gunsel's hand stopped with a packet of bills, moved again.

Tip said quickly, "I just want a cop to escort me down to the bank, that's all."

The scar curved snakily again. "You scared, Ames?"

"You're damned right I'm scared," he answered, "—there's guys out there who'd part my hair for just a piece of this . . ."

Danco nodded. "You're scared smart, Ames. I like that. Well, Louis here can run you downtown. No problem."

He didn't even hesitate—he had never thought so fast. He said: "That's nice of you to offer, Mr. Danco. But look at it this way: if anything should happen to me—or the money—think how it would look. Embarrassing all around. Why not let the law assume the responsibility?"

Spider Danco laughed out loud for the first time. "Call the station, Louis.—How you like selling beer barrels, Ames?"

"Not one hell of a lot, to tell you the truth."

"How long you been pushing them?"

"Six months.'"

"What'd you do before that?"

"Securities—investment trusts, bonds. Some other things."

"I like you, Ames. I like the way you operate. If you ever need a job, come around and we'll talk."

"You know, I just might take you up on that."

"Yeah, everything's changing." Danco stretched, his forearms oddly fragile and white inside the yellow silk sleeves. "Well, no more headaches. Sweating out drops off Morgan Point, driving all night. I'm going to miss that action . . . You in France?"

Tip shook his head. "I never got out of Camp Devens."

"Who you jazzing!" the parrot barked.

"Yeah, I'll get fat," Danco murmured morosely. "Wear spats, make noises about running for the state legislature." His fingers gently traced the long scar across his face. "Maybe I ought to get this removed, ah? Improve my image. Your brother had that scar of his worked over, didn't he?"

"You know Chapin?" Tip said in surprise.

"I know a lot of people. Here, there and everywhere. Queer-looking nick, wasn't it?"

"Accidents will happen."

Danco smiled slowly. "That wasn't no accident, pal. A shiv did that. *Zzzzt-zzzt.*" The sound came through his teeth; his hand, holding an imaginary knife, moved twice—quick, jerky movements. "Somebody wanted to leave a mark on him. Take it from an old pro."

"So's your old man!" the parrot squawked.

"Shut up, Roxy. You're interrupting me."

"Who you think you are—Moon Mullins?"

"Yeah, I met your wife once. Through him."

"My wife," Tip said.

"Yeah. Back in the wild and woolly days—'27, '28. We were on the town. Harlem and all around. She's got a lot of Moxie."

"And how!"

"How is she, anyway?"

Tip set down his glass. "I wouldn't know," he said flatly. "We—haven't been living together for some time, now."

"—You're kidding!" Danco's mouth dropped open, the whites of his eyes were palely visible behind the dark lenses. "You trying to tell me you let a gorgeous, feisty broad like that get away?"

Tip was on his feet, shaking, half dizzy with rage. He shouted: "How'd you like to mind your own fucking business—!"

Louis, standing in the doorway again, moved toward him swiftly, his sleepy purple eyes wide now. Tip stepped behind the chairs where there was more room, and brought up his hands. The parrot had started to scream something unintelligible and Danco's voice cut through it, incisive and high:

"Louis, *no!*"

The gunsel stopped. Danco, still sitting on the couch, had one hand raised, palm out. Tip said tightly:

"Keep your lousy money. I don't have to take this."

"Keep your shirt on, pal. You'll live a lot longer." The mobster grinned his slow, bitter grin. "A compliment—I said it as a compliment. She's a fantastic dame. The real thing. You're too touchy, Ames."

"Maybe so," he answered lamely. He was sweating under his arms and his throat was hoarse. Louis had moved away to the front windows.

"Don't get me wrong, pal. I was just sorry to hear about it. That's all."

"Well." Tip moved the toe of his shoe over the rich floss of the rug. "I'm sorry, too."

"Here's your protection," Louis said from the window.

Tip picked up the canvas satchel and said: "Thanks for the business, Mr. Danco. I'll be in touch with you tomorrow."

"I know you will." The Spider shook his head. "You're either the craziest guy I've ever run into—or the nerviest. I can't make up my mind which."

"Maybe it's both."

Danco laughed again. "I meant what I said, Ames. Look me up, we'll have a little talk."

"Thanks. I may at that."

"Put the cover on me!" Roxy screeched. The bird was still cackling maniacally as he stepped through the front door toward the waiting policeman.

The teller was very uneasy about the money. When he saw the gold certificates he became visibly nervous and hurried off to consult with an assistant manager, who broke off what he was doing and conferred with the manager, a fussy man with square, rimless glasses and a very small mustache.

"This is very irregular, Mr.—"

"Ames. Tipton Ames."

523

"Very irregular. I'm afraid we'll require a fee—"

"What fee? There's no need for a fee, this is a simple transaction."

"Why all this specie?"

"It's cash—my client wants me to make payment in cash, that's all. What's wrong with that?"

The manager's eyes narrowed behind the spectacles, he kept fingering the gold bills as if they were something unclean. "I don't like it."

"I don't care whether you like it or not. This is genuine legal tender—"

"I'm sure I don't have to tell you that current possession of gold certificates is prohibited, a direct violation of federal statute."

"All right, fine—my client is surrendering them in a legitimate investment. My God, you ought to rejoice that somebody's still able to hold on to gold certificates these days!"

But the bank manager only stared back at him coldly, fussing with the bills, arranging and rearranging them. "I don't like it, Mr. Ames. I'm afraid we cannot accept them—it's a patent illegality."

Only then, balked and furious, watching their closed, forbidding faces, feeling this windfall commission slipping out of his grasp, did he remember that Jake Lynstrom, the old Diehl, Harrodsen broker, was right down the street with the corporate attorneys Hewlitt, Deming & Bryce.

"All right," he said, and swept the money back into the satchel. "I can see you doubting Thomases require further assurance. I'll be back shortly."

"Just a moment," the manager said sharply. "Where are you going with those?"

"Oh no! If you won't accept this as legal tender it doesn't exist for you, buddy. You can't have it both ways."

"I must ask you—"

"This money is in my possession—you have not accepted it. Are you challenging my right to it?" The three men paused, looking baffled. "Thank you, gentlemen."

He walked quickly down the street, climbed the stairs to the Hewlitt offices. Yes, the girl said, Mr. Lynstrom was free. He walked into the office, dumped the contents of the satchel on Lynstrom's desk and said: "Hello, Jake. How's tricks?"

Lynstrom gazed at the money, at Tip, at the money again—leaped to his feet and half-ran to the door, closed and locked it, swung his back against it.

"Tip, where in God's name did you get that?" His good Swedish face was blank with horror. "What kind of trouble are you in?"

Tip said grimly: "I've had enough. We just knocked over Merchant's National. Me and Spider Danco."

"Who? Spider who?" Jake licked his lips. "Jesus, Tip, things aren't *that* bad . . . Why'd you do it?"

Tip sat down and laughed until the tears came, while Lynstrom still gazed at him in bewilderment. "Well," he said after a moment, "We'll probably be doing that next. If the damn banks have any moolah left *in* them, which is doubtful . . . No, this is a customer's investment in Rademacher Tunnage. Believe it or not."

"You gave me a scare, Tip." Jake was fanning out the currency with his big, splayed fingers. "Gold certificates," he said with awe. "Jesus."

"Yeah. That's the problem."

". . . Is it hot?"

"Beats me. I don't know and I don't care. It's money, isn't it? More than I've seen since October, 1929. All I know is, the commission's going to feed my family for another couple of months."

Lynstrom was smiling at him mournfully now. "You're still out there selling."

"Hope springs eternal."

". . . I couldn't do it."

"You're not a salesman, Jake." He leaned forward. "Just vouch for me, will you? Those timid souls up the street seem to think I just lifted this out from under Henry Morgenthau's nose."

He was leaving the Hewlitt offices around five that afternoon with the transaction approved and his commission safe, when a voice called softly:

"Mr. Ames? Tip?"

He turned. It was Suzy Diehl. That curly, rust-colored hair was still in a short bob, her pert round face still strangely youthful and eager.

"Suzy!" He felt a sudden deep rush of affection, memory—he had embraced her before he'd even realized it; her arms came around him, she kissed him full on the mouth. Then they both stepped back and looked at each other. In the softer tailoring and longer hemline of the Thirties her neat little figure looked fuller, more womanly.

"Well, long time no see, baby . . ."

"As the song says."

They laughed together.

"As the songs says. You look wonderful."

"Flattery, sir, will get you absolutely anywhere!"

"You're . . . here?" he gestured.

"Secretary to Mr. Hewlitt. Jake got me the job."

"How's your mother?"

"Formidable as ever. Living with Aunt Cynthia out in Erie. Poor Aunt Cynthia!"

"Poor Aunt Cynthia."

"Oh, it's so good to see you again. You're like a—like a tank of pure oxygen. I mean it! New Haven may be near New York—but New York it ain't, daddy . . ."

Gazing at her, laughing, moved by her vivacity, remembering the field day with its crazy roulette golf, the dance, the whole bright promise of it, he said:

"Come on out with me and have a drink. Can you?"

"I'd love to!" she cried softly. "And just think—now it's legal . . ."

They had martinis in a bar on Whalley Avenue.

When he suggested dinner she said she wouldn't hear of it, she'd rustle up something if he could stand her cooking. They went up to her apartment, a cramped room with a wildly unmade Murphy bed and a kitchenette you had to back out of. Clothes were strewn everywhere and she ran around snatching them up and stuffing them in the closet, her high heels clicking on the worn floor.

"You can see I wasn't expecting anybody! Alas, the poor working girl . . ."

She set up a card table and pan-fried hamburgers, and her little Philco radio played a soft medley of dance tunes while they talked about the old crowd. Larry Bixby had gone to jail for using clients' securities to pay off his debts; Paul the Pallid Puke Saunders was teaching business management at Columbia; Century Gifford was coaching a high school football team in Connecticut somewhere; Barbara had left him and taken the kids.

"Oh, and Jack Darcey—I ran into him at a party last summer. He's with this novelties outfit, he had dozens of wacky gadgets all over him—there was this mouse that kept crawling up his lapel, and a pistol where the barrel went limp. He had on a bow tie, and all of a sudden it would light up like a Christmas tree!" She laughed and then frowned. "It's not very funny. Is it."

We're like a college class, Tip thought. A class who never got to graduate, just broke up instead.

"How's Jophy? And the kids?"

"I don't see very much of them . . . We've split up. Sort of. She's moved back to her family's house, on the Cape. With the kids."

"Oh, Tip . . ." Instinctively she put her hand on his. "I *am* sorry."

"Forget it." Angry with himself for saying anything about Jo, he withdrew his hand gently and patted hers. "I'll get over it. Or I won't. Or something."

She gazed at him for a long moment, her pretty little round face grave, almost sad. "I was always so in awe of her," she said dreamily. "Everyone was."

"Yes."

"She's so beautiful, so—so full of fire. Real fire! So unpredictable—you never knew what she might do next. Remember that spectacular dive from the tower?"

"I was thinking of that, too."

"She was—it was as if she was challenging the whole world in that instant: she was perfectly willing to die—actually *die*—if she failed! That crazy night at the fountain—" She broke off, her eyes slanted toward Tip fearfully once.

"I know," he said.

"Me and my overgrown mouth."

"It's all right. I've known about it for a long time."

He stared into his empty coffee cup. That summer the sheer heartsick need to see Jophy and the children had become so great he'd driven from Rochester to Turk's Head in a night and a day, had hurried under the bleached whale's rib with no idea at all as to what kind of reception he'd get. Jophy, very beautiful and brown in a sleeveless striped top and denim skirt, seemed pleased to see him; she'd come running out to him, kissed him warmly—then to his deep disappointment had broken away out of his arms to show him what she'd done with the house. She'd painted the wainscoting herself in that distinctive Cape Cod blue that was neither cerulean nor cobalt nor teal but a captivating mixture of all three. She'd replanted the garden and relaid the blackfish walkway, papered and sanded until the cool, shadowed house shone like old bronze.

She had also got herself involved in local affairs. "Oh no, not politics—*economics!*" she'd corrected him, laughing, her teeth gleaming white against her tan. "That's far more important! But I don't have to tell *you* that, do I?" She'd founded an organization called the Sea Anchor, some kind of community fund for the

528

families of out-of-work fishermen; she seemed to be trying to get the men to join together. They paid her something now and then; she'd made her grandfather's old chart room into an office, and people kept coming by for advice—lobstermen, trawler crewmen; she heard them out and talked to them in a lively mixture of Portuguese and English. The Fish Exchange was at the root of their misery, the real enemy. Tip got most of it.

"Look—the corporation owns your vessels. If the catch is poor, it writes off that loss against *your* shares and expenses; if the catch is big, it sells *to itself* at a low price—then marks up the price to the retailers. Don't you see what they're doing? They're shorting you at the wharf—and then bleeding the customer white at the market. Pois bem, you've got to fight them! Band together, gain strength in your numbers."

"But if we don't catch fish—"

"If you don't catch fish, who else will? Who, even today, is eager to lead the life of a fisherman? If you join together and hold out for a better, a decent price, they'll have to give it to you. But you've got to pull together—share alike, help the ones who're foundering, stand *fast*. And write to Washington, all of you! Demand a congressional board of inquiry, a government investigation of the Exchange and its thieving ways . . . *Then* you'll see them sing a different tune. Garanto-lhe!"

One dragger crewman called her Senhora Gaspa and she didn't correct him. Tip knew it was because of Grama, but it pained him. After a bold initial curiosity, the townspeople accepted his presence readily enough. He was a salesman, from the great, hostile world beyond the Cape. If they had second thoughts about his prolonged absence they kept them to themselves.

"Well," he remarked during a lull in the proceedings, "the spirit of Grama Gaspa still walks Cape waters!"

"Don't be blasphemous." She laughed, turned sober again. "I'm not Grama—I never will be. But you've got to do what you can . . . There's a lot of skullduggery going on down here, Tip."

"Who's that? Grama's land sharks again?"

"You bet. Speculators moving in, outfits with funny names: Dune Vistas, Inc. Bayberry Shores, Ltd. God knows who they really are. Offering more money than these people have ever seen, buying up choice waterfront in big chunks, cheap."

"What do they have in mind?"

"Rumors say resort complexes, motels, marinas. Long-range plans . . . While men are going hungry." She smiled, but her eyes glinted. "If they're planning to turn my Cape into a Coney Island midway, they'd better think twice!"

The children were wildly excited at seeing him again. Joey looked less reedy and unsure; he'd become a crack sailor and was secretly very proud of it. Tessa sat on Tip's lap and prattled away happily about boatbuilding and other goings-on around the harbor. For Saturday Jophy had already planned an all-day picnic on the Back Beach with Tony and Inez Cardosa, whom Tip remembered from high school days, and their children. The weather was perfect—a fine sea running, the sky a faultless, fathomless blue. Above the surf snow-white terns wheeled and dove like aerial toys, and a hundred yards offshore porpoises rolled their slick ebony backs in echelon, in tandem, while the kids danced up and down, pointing at them. They played one-o'-cat with an old tennis ball and a barrel stave until the grownups ran out of steam, and after that they went in swimming and Jophy plunged through the breakers like a porpoise herself, all sleek and shining, showing the children how to time the surf's rhythms, when to fight, when to yield, her voice piercing and wild on the sea wind. Watching her, Tip's throat ached with sadness.

Later he and Tony built a fire in the apex of two bleached balks of timber, and Jophy made sea-clam chowder in a big agate kettle, sizzling salt pork and onions and clams and potatoes and finally adding the milk in a proudly simple ritual, stirring it with a long wooden spoon, while the dense, pungent odor cloaked them all, and the kids capered and shouted with impatience. Lying there propped on his elbows in the warm sand, watching Jo's lovely face intent on her work, her black hair whipping wildly around her face and throat, looking like the first woman on the pristine shore of a just-born world, Tip felt his love must burn through to her, beckoning wildly like a beacon, or some crazy semaphore; that his very heart would burst with his desire . . . The great beach swept away for miles on miles; on the etched line of the horizon a freighter lay frozen under its tiny canopy of smoke. Soothed by the measured spank and seethe of surf, holding Tessa's sweaty, salt-rimed head, he felt all at once at peace, his irascibility and frustration dissolved in the clean salt air—all the anxieties and desperate expedients of the past terrible five years utterly dispersed in that glorious northwest sky . . .

But the next day was sullen with low-racing ragged clouds and rain. The procession of suplicants began again, capped by a querulous woman with a long, involved story about a son who'd been hurt by a carelessly dropped block on one of the wharves; and Tip could feel his resentment build in the gray light. Jophy, forceful and partisan, struck him as deeply altered. She seemed able to go her own way, she seemed strangely happy . . . She didn't need him: that was what it was. The thought frightened and angered him.

". . . You didn't have to take a *job*, Jo," he couldn't keep from saying later that afternoon. "I've always provided for you—for us . . ."

"That's true. It isn't a job, of course; and it doesn't pay much, anyway. That isn't the point. I *want* to work, Tip. It's good to work—to do something useful. Why shouldn't I?"

"But the kids . . ." he began.

"They're happier down here, much happier. Can't you see that? It's just part-time. I'm with them after school, in the evenings . . ." She watched him a minute, thoughtfully. "Don't put up silly reasons, Tip."

"They're not silly."

"That's not fair to either of us . . . Your pride is hurt. Isn't that what's at the bottom of it?"

"No, it's not that at all." But it *was* that, or mostly that, anyway; and admitting it to himself made him cross. "Pride," he burst out, "—damn it, Jo, nobody on *earth* has more pride than you do . . ."

She became quite still; her eyes were dark as jet. "That's true," she said. "I meant false pride. Look, it's not taking anything away from you—I couldn't if I wanted to. You're you. You always will be. I only want to reach out a bit, become whatever I can—or try to, anyway. Don't begrudge me that, Tip."

"—But what about *us?*" he cried. "What's to happen with us—?"

"I don't know." Her voice was low, reflective, without heat, as though she was searching for the answer and not at all certain she would find it. "I have to make a life *out of* myself, Tip. My kind of life. One with some purpose, some real—well, meaning."

"But you had that," he protested.

"No, I didn't. You may have thought I did, but I didn't." She smiled at him sadly, gently—a smile that made him smart with bewilderment and chagrin. "I'm not staying on the course you plotted for me, and you're hurt. And I'm sorry for that, darling. I am, I swear it. But it's something I've got to do—it's like breathing for me now." Her face, near his, looked unutterably beautiful in the topaz glow of the converted whale oil lamp; mysterious and elusive and alive. He thought of them years ago in this same room, heads together, pouring over the great charts, murmuring aloud: *Submerged coral heads reported. Dangerous passage. Unexplored.*

"Don't press me, Tip," she entreated him. "I'm not *excluding* you. Or the kids. But I am being me again, and maybe—with a little fresh wind in my sails—that means more for everyone. I don't know. I need time. To think about things, to do things. Give me time . . ."

The clack of dishes brought him back to the pinched kitchenette and Suzy Diehl. She was putting plates away now, in a cabinet beside the sink. Leaning against the door jamb he watched her moment, said:

"Somebody told me you got married to that flyer. Rawless."

"I did." She wrinkled her pretty little nose. "It didn't take. As they say. Andy's the moving-on type. Maybe it was the war: Dawn patrol against the Red Baron tomorrow at six ack-emma, boys, let's live to-night! . . . Well, it was my fault, too. He was right there, he seemed so heroic, and I was all apart—couldn't get hold of myself after Daddy died. Everything seemed a bad joke . . . It was like the absolute end of the world then, wasn't it?"

"Something like that . . . I'm sorry," he said.

"Don't be. It was my own stupidity. I wasn't in love with him and I knew it, down deep." She came up to him then, said simply: "Who I was in love with was you."

"You weren't in love with me—" he protested, "—you just had a schoolgirl—"

"No. I was. I am." She shook her head wonderingly. "You've always been so sure of yourself—who you are, where you're going. I've always wanted you. I used to believe if I thought that hard enough, really concentrated on it, you'd catch the electricity—like psychic arrows or something. I guess I still believe that . . . I want you now, Tip."

He gazed at her in silence. There was something compelling in the way she stood there in front of him; something exigent and appealing in her very humility. After all the hopeless rejections of the last years it seemed preposterous that he could be the object of such intense devotion. She had moved closer to him; or perhaps he had moved. He didn't know. The radio was playing "Yesterdays," and the melody, haunting and sad, seemed somehow to merge with the moment.

> Then gay youth was mine, truth was mine,
> Joyous, free and flaming life, forsooth, was mine . . .
>
> Sad am I, glad am I—
> For today I'm dreaming of yesterdays . . .

He didn't know. All he knew was that the rending hollow of losing Jophy, the knowledge that she didn't need him any more, was too much to be borne. He put his arms around Suzy; she gave a deep, even sigh and came against him with soft force.

Her body was white and plump and small-breasted; not like Jophy's at all. Almost a little girl's body; the image chilled him briefly—then he thrust it away. Unlike Jophy she was expectant and still, saying nothing, murmuring nothing. She was both adept and awkward, as though she were trying to relearn a forgotten lesson—where Jophy had been as natural, as alive and various, as the sea. He was tender and skillful, arousing this soft, alien body, and Suzy strove and strove with him, rocking and flexing in tense, labored rhythms. But there was no magic in it, no surging, fierce sunburst and release; it was too frantically urgent. All wrong. It was simply—that his heart wasn't in it. Not remotely.

After a time he came; he couldn't help that either, he couldn't delay matters any longer. "I'm sorry," he whispered lamely.

"It's all right."

"I guess—I'm just tired, or something."

She made no reply, and then he realized she was weeping.

"Oh, Suze," he murmured. "I *am* sorry . . ."

"It's all right . . . Oh, if only it could all have been different," she said in a lost little voice. "If only things could have stayed the way they were. Just the way they were . . ."

"I know."

He tried to comfort her, though he knew there wasn't anything he could say. After a while she fell asleep, and he lay wide awake with one arm around her and one behind his head, watching the car lights glide across the ceiling, furiously chagrined with himself for failing this troubled girl, putting still more strain on her sense of insecurity—for having succumbed to his own loneliness and grief and gone to bed with her in the first place; fighting off thoughts of futility and despair, worrying whether Rademacher could keep going now that the big beer manufacturers had turned legit and begun to soak up the market for hops and malt and barrels, wondering what in God's sweet name he'd be selling next year if business kept slidding off; thinking fondly of Jack Darcey, and sadly of Beau Frank Delahant, and then bitterly of Chapin, flying out to Denver to look over some silver mine, down in the Carolinas shooting quail with Avery Calkins; wondering why it was that adversity fell hardest not on the greedy and irresponsible but on the considerate, the generous; wondering how it had all gone so wrong, what had led to so dark a turning of his dreams, the blighting of that green desire . . . and then, his eyes smarting with tears, thinking inevitably, achingly, of Jophy and the children; wondering what she was doing right now, if maybe—just for a fleeting moment—her thoughts might have turned toward him . . .

5

"Well," Serena Aldridge said, "—my two irrepressible nephews!" Smiling at them both she put a hand on each of theirs. "It's so good of you to give me this little party, let me have you all to myself."

"You know there's never been a woman in our lives quite like you, Auntie," Chapin said.

"Rascal." She laughed, pleased with herself, with the day, and looked around the restaurant with a finely critical eye. She was wearing a well-cut suit and blouse, ashes-of-roses they called it, with a small amethyst pin at her throat. Serena had nothing but scorn for the dowdiness of Boston women of her class, and Tip liked her for that.

"Dear old Locke's," she was saying now, nodding to a party seated near them. "It never changes. When I was a little girl I once had lunch here with your grandfather and Oliver Wendell Holmes."

"That old fraud," Chapin said.

"Chapin, you do go too far, you know."

"You're right. He wasn't a fraud, he was a satyriasist."

Serena gave her short, high laugh. "Good thing nobody knows what that word means any more."

"Chapin does, though," Tip offered easily. "And that's all that really matters."

"Chapin used to take me here in his college days.

Of course he took his favorite girls here a good deal more often. The presentable ones, I mean."

"I only went *out* with presentable girls." His pale eyes slid over Tip's, slid away again, while Tip watched him impassively. Why was it Chapin didn't look a day older than he had in '29—in '22, for that matter? His features were a bit sharper, the vertical crease between his brows a touch deeper; and that curious scar had vanished utterly, thanks to the expensive expertise of an old classmate over at Peter Bent Brigham. It was as though he'd discovered some nefarious way to preserve himself indefinitely, outside of time, like those insects trapped in amber; like Locke-Ober itself. The venerable restaurant, with its slabs of rare roast beef, its boiled scrod and corps of grave waiters, its atmosphere of portly Brahmin affluence, looked exactly as it had before the war.

"You've eaten here, haven't you, Tipton?" Serena wanted to know.

"Oh, yes. Though not in some time."

"Tip feels it's too staid, too *vested*," Chapin said.

"Not at all." He smiled. "It's been a little too rich for my blood these past few years, that's all."

"What a vulgar phrase, little brother."

"Apt, though."

"Down-to-earth Tipton," Serena marveled. "Were two brothers ever so different as you two!"

Tip smiled at her. "We've traveled very different roads."

"Not as different as all that, really."

"Oh, yes. Different as night and day."

She looked at him very directly. "You don't believe blood is thicker than water, then?"

"Oh, yes, Aunt Serena. But it's an awful lot thinner than fire."

It was curious; there was a tensed, awkward instant—a starting, like the flaw in a motion picture. His brother and aunt exchanged a hooded glance, a flicker of something piercing and precarious. Then Serena smiled and clasped her hands and said, "And how are Josefina and the children?"

"They're fine," he answered. What was the sense in lying about it? She knew, just as she knew Jenny had left Chapin and was—incredibly—working for some federal theater project in Chicago. Turk's Head was a small town. "Jophy's very busy these days."

"I know—she testified at the committee hearings over the Fish Exchange. I heard her." His aunt's eyes rested on his speculatively. "She was very good. Very—persuasive."

"I'm told she led the charge," Chapin broke in. "To the barricades, comrades!"

"That's right," Tip retorted. "And now they're up on five counts of collusion and price-fixing."

"Oh, come, Schoolboy." It was the old amused, indolent tone. "You're not actually buying all that poppycock about intentionally defrauding the public, are you?"

He stared calmly at his brother. "Let's say it got out of hand, Chay. Like the market."

"Well, *that's* all over now!" Chapin laughed and brandished his napkin. "Joe Kennedy's standing over us with his terrible snicker-snee. I'll tell you what *I* think: I think we ought to sic Jophy-girl on him. She'd have him running back to Hollywood and the arms of Gloria Swanson."

"Chapin, that is rank gossip," Serena chided him, though she smiled.

"You're right—there's a new one, isn't there?"

His aunt ignored him, turned to Tip: "She reminded me so of her grandmother—had the whole courtroom in an uproar half a dozen times. Only of course she's far more subtle. Just when everyone's all relaxed and laughing, having a good time, she drives the knife home. Don't tell me blood isn't thicker than water! She's a regular stormy petrel, that one."

539

"Say rather, a charming champion of the oppressed." Tip summoned up his best grin.

She laughed. "Still a dash of the old tabasco, I see!"

"Nobody's said anything about putting me in mothballs, Aunt."

"I guess not." Her eyes dilated in the old way, glinting; that unmistakable edge of steel. "I guess not."

She turned to Chapin then, and the two of them talked about Symphony, and the Museum of Fine Arts, where Serena was a trustee.

There were so many things that never needed to be said, Tip thought morosely; the unspoken pitches. A dealer in words, in commitments and convictions, he had always distrusted the tacit, the blandly implied. Chapin had invited him up here to Boston for a reason, had invited Serena to join them at this culinary bastion of the old guard for a reason; and now this leisurely chatter about Koussevitsky and Impressionist painting. Uh-huh. He had put on his best Tripler pinstripe, such as it was, and taken the train—the day coach, not the extra-fare Merchants' Limited—from Grand Central, but he wasn't buffaloed. It was another stage set. Chay was setting it, the better to remind him of that same old capital he controlled, the power that was his to wield. The acid fact was that he'd be walking around in a barrel today without Serena's money; why not admit it?

But of course no one ever did. It was part of the unspoken pitch. Their wives had left them both—for different reasons and with very different results—but that was never discussed, either.

Well. He had come through the fire, he was still on his feet. Shakily maybe, but still afloat. He could sit here with the palm of his hand on the clean linen table cloth, and look interested, and bide his time. After the last seven years he could wait out the God damned Sphinx of Giza herself—in fact, he could probably fire a couple of riddles at the old girl that would scare the holy hell out of her . . .

Later they walked Serena up to Tremont Street and put her into a cab, and then walked on through the sparkling fall weather, past the Parker House where Beau Frank Delahant had taken Tip and Jophy for that confident, convivial luncheon after their wedding. So long ago . . . He shut the memory out of his mind, turned to Chapin, who seemed to be in a mood of supressed excitement.

"I think we're out of the woods," he was saying. He had taken to carrying a tightly furled umbrella, swinging it airily ahead of him, though there certainly wasn't going to be any need for one today. "We're back on the high road again."

"That's a refreshing thought." Tell it to the poor bastards crouched on those benches back there on the Common, Tip thought grimly; tell it to the guys making thirty-seven cents an hour in the beater rooms at Holcomb's Mill—the ones lucky enough to *have* jobs there, that is—or the drummers working Aroostook County on straight commission and a drawing account that wouldn't keep a chicken alive . . . Aloud he said:

"You feel your Harvard buddy Roosevelt has things nicely in hand, then."

Chapin smiled at him. "Not at all. In point of fact I think he's managed things very badly. His timing was right, that's all. It's a question of the public's mood. He'll beat that idiot Landon next month because people want to think he's on top of it. They want to believe things are coming back, so they will . . . But it's got nothing to do with that, really. War's coming."

"War?" Tip glanced at him.

"Bet your bottom dollar. Reoccupation of the Rhineland was the opening gun. And now Franco's making his move in Spain. Europe's at war right now—they just don't know it."

"Why, the League's threatened sanctions if they try anything more . . ."

"The League is dead. The Ethiopian fiasco finished

it off. Ciano's in Berlin right now, setting up a German-Italian alliance. We'll be at war in two years, three." Chapin's face, caught in the flat, hard light, looked astonishingly stern and vengeful. "He wants to humiliate us, destroy us. Hitler. England, and then us . . . They're beasts, the lot of them. Hitler's reversed Circe's formula—he's taken the menagerie of pigs and wolves and jackals and turned them into things that look like men. Actually like men."

Tip turned and studied his brother's face ". . . But you were always an isolationist," he said slowly.

"I'm not gabbling about ideologies. I'm just telling you the inevitable drift of things. That's what's going to happen—and that's what'll bring the old economy back with a roar. Nothing whips up the wheels of industry like a good, spanking war."

Tip shook his head. "The country won't go overseas to fight again. People won't stand for it."

"Of course they will. They'll do precisely what the powers that be want them to do—pressure or manipulate them into doing. They always have."

"—Damn it, Chapin, don't you *ever* believe people are capable of making up their own minds?" Tip burst out. "That they can swim against the tide?"

But Chapin only smiled. "Yes. Sure. Of course. All those long, white bones you see lying along the shore at low tide. That's them."

Tip fell silent, gazing up at the Old State House with its gilded lion and unicorn flanking the bold escutcheon, thinking of that hazy August afternoon he'd tramped these streets for the first time, a wide-eyed kid in a blue serge suit two sizes too small for him, gazing at the clerks and bankers, dreaming dreams of glory. His life had been on the cusp of irreversible change and he hadn't known it: in two days he would be walking along the Upper Channel at Turk's Head, would spot that solitary mast above the roofs and trees . . .

Chapin had opened new offices on Congress Street

the year before: sedate, faintly gloomy rooms with lots of paneling and glass cabinets and fine old prints, very Bostonian. Stage sets. He took him around and introduced him to some of the staff. Most of the faces were new, but Chapin had brought Elmer Taylor over from the New York office to head up the wire section, and Mal MacCrimmon for research; and surprise of surprises, there was Bradford Elwell—whom he'd fired back at Diehl, Harrodsen in that row over Web Bowers' high-pressuring of the Ivy League old boys— in charge of sales.

"Well, Ames." He rose slowly, leaned across his desk even more deliberately, slowly extending one of his big, broad hands. "It's been quite a while "

Tip shook it, said: "Hello, Elwell."

"I haven't heard much about you lately." Elwell's eyes glinted. "You still selling?"

"Oh, yes. I'm still selling."

"Who you with now?"

"Drennan Brothers."

Elwell pretended to frown. "I don't believe I know them."

"No reason you should. It's a highly specialized field—aluminum fittings." He glanced at his brother, who was gazing away out of the window, smiling. "You're heading up sales for Chapin?"

"That's it."

"Business rolling in?"

"Can't complain." Elwell shifted his big shoulders inside his jacket. "Well, business is slow. But it's picking up. You know how it is."

"Sure."

They chatted a few minutes longer, or pretended to, and then Chapin led Tip into his own office, stopping on the way in to say, "No calls, Miss Herrick—for any reason." Chapin always addressed his secretaries formally. He closed the door and they sat down, on opposite sides of the handsome rosewood desk their grandfather had used.

"Well," Chapin laughed softly, his eyes resting on Tip's face; he was swinging to and fro in his chair. "Here we are."

"So to speak."

"I suppose you're wondering why I dragged you up here to pompous old Boston."

"It crossed my mind."

"The inimitable Schoolboy . . ." Chapin shook his head, smiling broadly now, tapping the tips of his fingers together; that pulse of suppressed excitement was still working in him. He spun a slim gold pencil in the air, said suddenly: "Well, we're ready."

"Ready for what?"

"Ready to roll, kid. The skids are greased, the chocks are pulled. Tom Holliman has given us virtual assurance of SEC approval and registration, the works." The pale eyes dilated, unblinking. "It's time to resurrect Macomah Fund."

"How'd you manage that?"

"Don't ask!" Chapin laughed, threw open his hands. "Just accept the fact that it's in the satchel. I've been talking to Avery all week. We can be cleared and in the market in ninety days." He leaned forward intently. "Now how about you? Can you put together one of those hell-for-leather, go-for-glory sales forces you're so famous for?"

"That's pretty short notice, Chay."

"For the incomparable Schoolboy? Look, we're counting on you."

"Is that right."

"Absolutely. I'd like to bring you in on this, if things work out that way."

Tip watched his brother for a long moment. "All right." he said. "You've got it."

"That's the spirit that opened up the West. Now let me show you what I've got planned." He caught up a sheaf of papers. "We'll set up an initial offering—"

"*No.*"

The word came out more harshly than he'd intended; but maybe that was just as well. Chapin had stopped in mid-career, his mouth ajar, the sheets still in his hand, waving above the desk.

"What's the matter?"

"No." he repeated. "You let *me* show *you* what we're going to do." He drew a quick breath and said: "We're going to reorganize Macomah as a mutual fund."

Chapin was staring at him, exasperated. "What? You mean, like Bay Colony?"

"Don't knock BCT. They've never skipped a dividend, right through the past seven years."

"That stodgy bunch of old women—they've been doddering along for—"

"This would be with a difference. We'd offer ten funds: four in commons, four in bonds, two in preferred—a nice spread of options ranging from absolutely safe to moderately speculative portfolios."

Chapin was smiling that supercilious Harvard smile; he beat back his anger.

"Mutuals. You can't be serious, Tipton. Who in hell wants mutuals?"

"The American customer. He may not know it yet, but that's *just* what he wants. He's been burned, Chay—he's gun-shy, he's got to be lured back into the securities market. He wants safety now, and competence, expertise. And that's what we'll give him: a nice, broad, two-hunderd-stock spectrum, and a crack research staff that stays up late nights, studying the form sheets. We sell confidence—in management, in across-the-board balance."

"That's ridiculous—I defy anybody to make a killing with a set-up like that."

"Nobody'll make a killing, Chay."

"You're telling me!"

"But nobody'll wind up on the floor with his brains spattered all over the carpet, either. Like Walter Diehl. That should have a certain appeal for you."

545

The vexed, impatient look had crept into his brother's face now, as he'd known it would; the corners of his mouth had drawn down. He said coldly: "And would you mind telling me just how you arrive at this brilliant conclusion?"

"Yes. I'll tell you how, Chay." He'd been waiting for this moment for a long, long time. "Applied research. On the pavements. I haven't been cruising around on somebody else's money—strolling through the Prado with a lorgnette or sitting around sipping Chivas Regal with the old boys at the Somerset Club. I've been ringing doorbells from Machias to Sandusky, stretching a buck into four meals at Hays Bickfords and Automats, pressing my pants under the mattress. I've been in touch with the man in the street, Chapin. In fact you could say I've *been* the man in the street. For seven lean years. With bells.

"So I know what he thinks, Chay—this everyday joker you've got such contempt for. And what he feels. He wants to invest—not much, he hasn't got very much right now—but a little. And you can talk him into it. If you're good. And if you've got something to sell, something you can put real confidence in. He'd like to make a little money out of the God damned economy, if he can. But he knows he isn't going to be an instant billionaire any more—and he sure as hell doesn't want to get taken to the cleaners because Mike Meehan and Sell 'Em Ben Smith and some of the boys have decided this is the week to give Hudson Motors a whirl. He's had enough of that. He wants an *investment*— not a rigged Reno crap game . . ."

"This is the most asinine piece of—"

"No. You let me talk for a while. You've been gassing away for fifteen years and I've kept my mouth shut. Now I'm going to talk, and you're going to listen. We're going to go mutuals because they're reasonably safe, they're balanced, they're *fair*, and they're what the little investor wants. And there are

546

millions and millions of him—which is something else you big-deal hot-shots never think about very much."

He set his hands on his hips, turned his neck in his collar. "Serena's dead right, Chay. I'm not the least bit like you. I've got to feel I'm doing the right thing. It's not an amusing anecdote over the Limoges coffee cups we're talking about. It's people—flesh-and-blood people, and what happens to them . . . Remember what Norris said that afternoon? About responsibility, obligations? Well, they're there, we have them—whether you ever choose to admit it or not."

Chapin's face had set, harder and harder; his pupils were pale as agate at their centers, deadly pale. They looked strangely remote, and menacing. Actually quite menacing. But it didn't matter. He'd waited all his harried, topsy-turvy life for this instant. And he was ready.

"Are you quite through?" Chapin was saying.

"For the time."

"You know, you seem to have got things turned around, little brother. Macomah is my baby—I got the underwriting, I secured the capital, I've set up the SEC clearance now. You were sales—you *sold* the fund. You happen to remember that?"

"Oh yes, I remember. But this time it's going to be different. We tried your way, remember? This time we're going to do it my way."

Chapin's jaw flexed once, again. Tip had never seen an expression remotely like this on his brother's face before.

"That's too bad . . . I was hoping we could bring you in with us on this deal."

"Oh, you are, Chapin," he said quietly. "You're going to."

"—Just who the hell do you think you are!"

"The very best you could get. The best sales manager in the country."

"Don't hand me that—what have you been doing? Selling milk containers, beer barrels. You think I haven't kept tabs on you? *Beer barrels,* for God's sake..."

"That doesn't alter it. I'm still the best. And you know it."

"You stupid, misguided son of a bitch!—You still haven't learned anything, have you?"

"Oh, yes. A lot."

"You're still as arrogant and dumb as ever. I've half a mind to tell you to pick up your hat and take yourself out of this office before I have you thrown out..."

"I wouldn't do that, Chay."

"Why? What'll you do if I did?"

Tip leaned forward; he'd kept his voice steady and low, but now it began to tremble. "The first thing I'll do is beat your teeth in. And the next thing I'll do is go to the SEC and tell them all about Macomah, and Greylock, and Horizon. Everything. Chapter and verse."

Chapin's face altered suddenly—there was that tremulous, sullen uncertainty he remembered from long ago, in the frozen road above the falls.

"Why should they believe you? I've got all the records."

"No. Not all of them. I had copies made of some, before I took the train out to Glen Cove that evening. And there's a barber still around who'll corroborate a few things, too."

"A *barber—?*"

"That's right. Oh, you might get your legal batteries lined up wheel-to-wheel and control the investigation technically; but you wouldn't be *left* with anything. The publicity alone would pull you down—you can figure that out. It would all come out, one way or another."

Chapin's mouth was working strangely; he looked half crazy, gripping the edge of the desk with both hands. "Why, you God damned stupid fool—you'll go to jail right along with me! You think you'll get immunity? They'll burn you first! You won't even be selling safety-pins when they get through . . ."

"That's right," he said.

"What do you mean—*that's right!* Have you gone clean out of your head—?"

"You think I care about immunity?" He'd come to his feet. He was leaning over the desk; he could hear his voice shaking with rage. "Why, you poor bastard—you're the one who hasn't learned shit, all these years! Let it come. I'm perfectly willing. I'm broke anyway, I've lost Jophy I couldn't *begin* to care less what they do to me . . . I sold my very soul for you that afternoon!—and it didn't mean any more to you than one of your nights at the fucking opera! Anything they do to me would be a favor . . . What I *do* know is you're not going to take Macomah and use it to pull off any more of your lousy thimble-rigging crap again. You got that?"

". . . You're bluffing," Chapin stammered. "You wouldn't do it—not really do it . . ."

"Then try me!" he cried, and slapped the phone off the desk; it hit the floor with a hollow clatter. "Go on! . . . You want to wind up like your father, do you? Running out on everybody?"

"Don't you bring up our father to me!"

"Hits too close to home, does it? Think about it . . ."

Chapin looked down, staring at the phone. "It's envy," he muttered, "you're jealous of me, of everything I've had, you've always wanted to be in my shoes—"

"Brother, I wouldn't be you for all the gold lying at the bottom of the seven seas. And don't you ever forget it."

"Too good for me, of course. Infinitely superior in every way. Oh, it's marvelous!" Chapin gave a savage laugh. "I see you're not too noble to resort to blackmail . . ."

"No, this isn't blackmail. It's simple justice. Blackmail's more in your line. Isn't it? You can call it anything you want to. But this is the way it's going to be. Make no mistake." He locked eyes with his brother for another moment, then sat down and shoved his hands deep in his trouser pockets. "Don't throw temper tantrums with me, Chapin. It won't work. Now I'll give *you* a basic rule of economics. When an enterprise is in jeopardy, whoever has least to lose has the most power. I've got nothing to lose. And you have a great deal. That's one of the troubles with being top dog . . . You relax and face the music, now."

He made himself sit perfectly still for two minutes, three, five; perfectly still; watching his brother's handsome, drawn face, the flow of contrasting emotions flicker across it—apprehension to vindictiveness to hatred, and finally abating to sullen acquiescence.

". . . All right," Chapin said flatly. "That's it, then." He gave a wry smile. "I don't seem to have much choice, do I?"

"No, you don't." He lighted a cigarette and relaxed then, threw one leg over the other. "Don't worry, Chay. It'll go all the way. I guarantee it. I'll put together the hottest sales force the industry's ever seen. I've done it before—twice—and I can do it again. We'll sweep the field—even MIT, even Wellington, the giants. I can feel it in my bones. The timing's right. We'll make a bundle—and it'll be an honest bundle this time. You'll see . . . One thing." He snapped his thumb back toward the other offices. "I want that stuffed-shirt Crimson gridiron hero Elwell out of there by tomorrow morning."

"Tip, I know you hate his guts—but he's brought in some very solid accounts."

"I don't care if he's brought in King Farouk and the Aga Khan in a platinum Rolls-Royce. I'm going to want salesmen, not ships' figureheads. Tell you what, though. I'm willing to forgo the intoxicating satisfaction of firing him for the second time—I'll let you do that. Now let's talk about who might head up Research and Analysis."

Chapin kept rolling the gold pencil back and forth on the desk top. "What'll I do about Avery?"

Tip grinned for the first time that day. "Perfectly simple: convince him that mutuals are the wave of the future—you've *always* known about the future, Chay. Remember? Tell him we'll even let him come in with us, if he's good . . ."

6

"What do you suppose happened?" Chapin murmured.

"Three terrific gales back-to-back, out of the northwest," Jophy answered, peering down. "Broke down the sea wall, the breakwater there—see, over there? —and the surf did the rest."

The two of them were lying prone on the bow of Chapin's new sloop, gazing down through the clear water. The wind had shifted to the southwest, as Jophy knew it would, then had fallen away and left them becalmed far out in the bay. The sea was glassy smooth, disturbed only by a slick, undulant swell that lifted and sank, lifted and sank—a motion deeply sexual in its rhythm. Below them in the shallows seaweed of the deepest green hues swayed like the unbound hair of drowned nymphs. Bits of wall glided past, the oval of a cellar, now a spooky black eye socket, brick fragments like dulled coral, and then the barnacled, cylindrical base of the old lighthouse itself. Atlantis, right here on the bottom of Cape Cod Bay.

"Eerie, isn't it?" Chapin said, echoing her thoughts; his chin rested on the backs of his hands. "Did they get away?"

"Oh, sure. They had plenty of warning. Everyone got off except old George Hinshaw, the lighthouse keeper. He refused to go."

"Why, for pete sake?"

She turned her head; their eyes were only inches apart. "It was his responsibility. To care for the light." She looked away again. "He's down there, somewhere."

"The idiot," Chapin muttered.

"I knew you'd say that."

"But what was to be gained?"

"Nothing. Except the satisfaction of knowing he'd kept the light going till the end . . . Don't be such a grubby Yankee!" she taunted him.

"This George Hinshaw was a Yankee."

"Yep—the right kind, though."

They laughed, eyeing each other a moment, gazed down into the sea. Jophy wondered idly why she'd let herself in for this. The occasion was a sailing lesson on this new acquisition Chapin had christened *Turandot.*

"The ice princess!" she'd exclaimed when she'd first seen the name painted on the boat's transom, several weeks earlier. "What a choice!"

He smiled at her. "Ah, but I know the answers to all her riddles."

"Don't be ridiculous!" she jeered at him. "You'll capsize her first time out. Or run her aground on Blackfish Point and sit there all day waiting for the tide to float her off, with the whole town laughing at you."

"Then you'll have to instruct me on the fine points," he told her. "You promised. Remember?"

He looked uncommonly handsome in white ducks and polo shirt, his face tanned, his eyes narrowed in the fierce, flat light. Gazing at him she felt the old surge toward him, that tidal pull in the deepest reaches of her body. She looked at the sloop again, followed the sheer of the slick blue hull, the dainty, proud line of the bow, the rake of the tall slender mast. Mia mãe, what a beauty! With a good, smart, twenty-knot breeze—

"I've no time for such foolishness," she declared.

"What? From the daughter of the legendary Joseph

Gaspa, King of the Grand Banks fleet? Where's all that wild, singing, seafaring blood?"

"It's—congealed."

"I don't believe it . . . Just a quick tutorial. For old times' sake," he entreated. "Do you *want* to see me ignominiously beaten by some young slip of a girl in a leaky old catboat?"

She'd laughed and turned away; but he persisted. He'd kept sending her pictures of terrible wrecks cut out of magazines—the *Wanderer* on the rocks at Cuttyhunk, the *Celestina* breaking up on the Outer Bars, the *Carrie Knowles,* the *Essex,* the *Portland,* the *Carib Queen*—each adorned with facetious comments: "All for want of one intrepid Portuguese maiden," "See what you made me do?" "I *said* 'right rudder' and I *meant* 'right rudder,' you idiot—" One afternoon he'd left a piece of splintered planking under the whale ribs with the letters *TURAN* barely legible; and finally, laughing, she'd given in and made a date with him; and here they were now, becalmed, hovering over ghostly Hurlestone Shoals . . .

Chapin had moved in with his aunt since Jenny had left him: he stayed at the Bluffs weekends if the weather was fair, driving down late Friday night and returning to Boston early Monday morning. Macomah Fund (or funds actually, there seemed to be several different ones) had done brilliantly over the past two years; it had gone over $30 million that spring and was still growing by leaps and bounds. Tip had come down for the Fourth of July weekend that summer, bubbling with enthusiasm, his eyes snapping; she hadn't seen him so wound up in years. He'd put together another crackerjack sales force—he'd even managed to round up some of the old crowd. Maury Zimmerman was brilliant, just brilliant, he was leading the pack again. He'd tracked down Jack Darcey, on his uppers, and got *him* straightened out and rolling. Clarence Phelps was going great guns, so was little Sid Solotow. They'd just qualified in the Midwest

—Chicago all the way to San Antonio—they were leading everyone in sales; it was like old times . . .

"Wonderful," she'd marveled. "I'm proud of you, Tip. How do you manage to cover all that country?"

"Just get on my horse and go; and keep those bags packed. Don Forst, a dealer out in Cincinnati, told me he heard Maury talking with this fellow with Incorporated named Redmond about a swing he and I'd made through Ohio and Indiana. Redmond said, 'Jesus. What do you do when you get tired?' and Maury came back at him: 'You stop working for Tip Ames!' I tell you, he's a hummer."

"What about the Blazer?"

He'd shrugged sadly. "No dice."

"What do you mean?"

"He's out of it. He's in a sanitarium down in Maryland."

"You mean—"

"He's an alcoholic, Jo. He's in bad shape. They can't do anything for him. Liver is gone."

"Oh." It seemed impossible somehow, remembering Blaydon bounding around on the diving tower, his pixie's face beaming down on them, to think of him lying in some darkened room, sweating through his pajamas, or screaming, or staring blankly at a wall . . . Well, there were always casualties, she'd learned that well and early. And yet to think of Blazer—

Tip was talking about some research wizard Chapin had lured away from Keystone. The drought was over, the money was rolling in again. Tip had rented an apartment out in Back Bay, a large, light place with long windows that overlooked the Fens; though he wasn't in it much, truth to tell.

"I wish you'd use it, Jo. Whenever you want to."

She'd thanked him. "I almost never go up to Boston."

"Well. In case you do. It's better than putting up at some hotel." Then he said, as though he couldn't help it: "Come home, Jo. Please."

"I *am* home."

"You know what I mean. Honey, I need you . . . I've made it all the way back—for us. Oh Jo, I love you. You know I'll never change—don't you feel anything for me?"

"Of course I do." She'd watched his good, steady brown eyes, the intense yearning in his face. She loved him, she would always love him; yet that compass needle that had guided her through these past few years refused to waver. There were things she wouldn't have come upon any other way; and there were more things still she needed to discover.

"I won't lie to you, Tip," she'd said softly. "I never have . . . I'm not ready." Yet, looking at the hurt, the entreaty in his eyes, her heart failed a little. "Maybe soon," she'd murmured. "Maybe some time soon. I don't know . . ."

She came alert. Below her now, in a little swirling forest of seaweed, something glinted. Something bright and oddly shaped.

"I've got to see what that is," she said, and jumped to her feet.

"What?"

"I'm going down there and take a look."

Chapin sat up. "Jophy-girl, we're in fifteen, twenty feet of water. Maybe more."

"And so?"

"We're miles away from shore. What if you get a cramp, or something?"

"Oh, what if you get bubonic plague and die in convulsions tomorrow noon!" she cried. "Does that mean you should spend the rest of your life in a blasted bell jar?"

He laughed, and said: "Look—*I* can't go down there and rescue you . . ."

"I know better than that!"

She perched on the rail—barefoot, her skin gleaming gold-brown against the white swim suit, taking several slow, very deep breaths—and dove straight down, the water sluicing cool as wine against her sun-heated flesh; stroking hard when her momentum was lost. It was deeper than she'd thought. She'd lost her bearings, moved north against the slow current. Her ears clicked sharply, she felt a dull pressure against her sinuses. Full fathom five. Then she caught sight of the object, kicked near, plucked at a lock of sea-weed and drew herself down. A school of herring veered away in a ribbonlike, flickering surge, and a crab scuttled backward, scooping sand. She caught up the object. A table knife, the blade broken crookedly. Of course! Luck of the Portuguese. Her head hurt now. She let the knife fall. Doubling over she pushed hard against the bottom and shot upward toward the silvery, swaying light, the sloop's hull like a dark beast looming. She broke surface and gasped happily for air. Chapin was leaning out over the rail, looking troubled.

"Stop—*worrying!*" she called.

"What was it?"

"Knife from some poor soul's kitchen."

He lifted her back on board. "You looked wonderful. Slinking around . . . I thought for a second you were going to stay down there."

"I just might, some time."

"Like Undine."

"No—not like Undine. If she couldn't keep that simple-minded Huldbrand from walking out on her, that was her fault."

She lay down. Her heart was still beating densely, and there was that pleasant tingling in the tips of her fingers, at her nerve ends, that always came after swimming.

"You don't think she should have given him that fatal kiss, then."

"Oh, that! All kisses are fatal."

He laughed and lay down beside her and they stared vacantly up at the smoky southwest sky streaked with mare's tails, and talked idly about a fisherman's benefit Jophy was running at the Cape Playhouse, and the astonishing growth of Macomah Fund.

"All that money," she murmured. "What are you going to do with it?"

"Oh, one thing and another."

"Don't be so *secretive!* I won't tell on you."

"Well . . . there's a perfectly dazzling Degas, of a dancer bent over tying one of her—"

"Collecting again!" she scoffed. "How dreary . . . *I* want to sail around the world. I still want to go ashore at Socotra, and Makassar, and Rangoon. I want to see elephants hauling teak logs, and pearl divers in lost, exotic lagoons . . ."

"Jophy, you're magnificent. You're the only person in the world with runaway nostalgia for places you've never seen."

"And I want to ride the surf at Kawailoa, and make a landfall at—"

"Too late, sweetheart."

"What?"

"Too late. There's going to be a war. In weeks."

She peered at him, shading her eyes.

"Hitler's holding maneuvers on the Czech frontier right now, the French just started full mobilization. Don't you read the happy tabloids?"

"I don't believe it. Not *war . . .*"

"Don't, then. But it's on the way. Read the signs. It's about over in Spain, Franco's forced a crossing of the Ebro—"

He broke off abruptly, peering hard at his nails. "I'm sorry," he said. "I forgot."

"It's all right." She closed her eyes again. She had come upon it in the papers that winter, purely by accident, the terse three-inch column tucked in at the bottom of an AP dispatch almost as an afterthought, with its tiny sub-head: *Net Star Slain. Manuel Montoya, the international tennis champion, was killed in the fierce fighting around Teruel, Loyalist forces an-*

nounced yesterday. Montoya, known as the Asturian Falcon, reached the semi-finals at Wimbledon on three occasions and once nearly upset "Big Bill" Tilden at Forest Hills. He had been serving as a captain of infantry, and was leading a counterattack against Insurgent positions when—

She had been flooded with black, vengeful rage, and then immense sorrow, to think of that sheer beauty, that intense, fiery grace smashed into bloody pulp, flung into a pit with a hundred other corpses. She hadn't looked at the papers since.

"Going to be the biggest war ever," Chapin was saying now. "Whole world on fire from pole to pole."

"Stop it, Chay!" She glared up at him, at the bright, steely sky. "How can you talk about it like that?"

"What do you want me to do? Recognize the realities, Jo. It's coming—and a good thing, too . . . They're beasts," he said with such sudden low savagery that she raised herself on her elbows and stared at him. His face was rock hard, his eyes narrowed to slits. "Butchering swine. We're going to have to slaughter every last one of them—man, woman and child. And plow their cities in salt."

"Chapin!" she cried. "You're sounding just like *them* . . . A lot of us screamed about Hitler years ago, and you never said a word."

"We will wipe them off the face of the earth. As thought they had never been."

"Chapin, you don't have a son! . . ."

He shook his head, as if he'd just been slapped awake. "You're right," he sighed. "You're right. I take it all back . . . God, how I envy you."

"He's a good boy," she said.

"He's more than that, he's extraordinary. Thank heaven he took after you and not our practical Tip."

"Oh, I don't know."

"Of course you know. All that imagination, that talent—where do you think it came from? . . . Where're you going to send him?"

"Harvard. If his grades are good enough. He's always drawing, when he ought to be studying. Tip isn't very keen on the idea, of course."

"That's because of me," Chapin said. "The old rock of sundering. I'd be glad to see what I could do, you know."

"I'm not sure that's such a good idea. Joey would rather make it on his own. Or not at all."

"But why should he be deprived of the opportunities Cambridge offers because of some romantic foolery? Surely you've no objection to an old grad's putting in a helping word?"

"I'll think about it . . . Don't feel obliged to see *everything* in life as a bargain, Chay," she said after a moment.

"Bargain?"

"You know what I mean."

"Yes. I know," he said, to her mild surprise. He fell back on the fine teak planking, his eyes closed against the light. "It's a bad habit, really. I got into it early in life."

"I know."

"As the twig is bent. To coin a phrase." He laughed listlessly, fell silent for a time. A tiny puff of breeze, the leading edge of the southerly, blew over their bodies, fluttered the mainsail once, and fell away. "Dear irrepressible Tip," he said in a curious, reflective singsong. "How I envy him, really."

"You do! I thought you looked down on him."

"Not at all. I only try to. No, Tip is better than I am, a better man. He always was. Does that surprise you, my saying that?"

"Yes."

"I used to hate him for that. Myself, too. Maybe I still do. Because I went to live with Serena and he didn't. He had the courage to stay there with Mother. And I didn't. The thing was, I *wanted* all that so—fine clothes and prep school and travels. The lovely things. But part of me hated myself for having them, all the time . . ." She could feel his body twist and shift near her, as though he were wrenching out of some demonic grip. "I can't imagine why I'm telling you all this. I've never talked like this to anyone."

"You need to," she murmured.

"Need to! Do I?"

"Everyone does."

He shook his head. "No, I've always felt I could talk to you this way. Only you . . . I made a big mistake with you. You never forgave me. Not quite. Did you?"

"No."

"I was just unsure then. Of myself."

She was acutely conscious of the sun on her breasts and thighs, that wine-tingling in the tips of her fingers, the very surface of her skin, and the pressure of his nearness, his insistent masculine presence.

"It's his *gullibility* I can't stand," he burst out. "Tip's. Look at him—still whistling "There's a Rainbow 'Round My Shoulder.' Still roaring all over the country, fourteen-hour days, sales meetings, hitting the dealers. Never letting up, as if his life depended on it."

"It does."

"Or he believes it does, anyway—which I suppose amounts to the same thing. All right, fine. But he *still* doesn't understand how it all works. He doesn't! He just—believes in it. He doesn't see where it's leading. He doesn't even seem to care . . ."

"It's the chase," she said. Piqued by this astonishing rush of disclosure from Chapin, she understood for an instant there on the sloop's deck that the whaler and the salesman were alike. It was the chase that mattered, far more than the commission or the oil. Both gave their hearts to it. That part of it was pure. The harpooner could lose his life if he failed; the salesman lost his livelihood. Only the owner evaded the purity of personal risk. His capital made him invulnerable—he had only green cash to lose. Nothing human.

"All that drive," Chapin was saying, his voice caught between awe and disdain. "All that fantastic energy, expended like Niagara Falls . . . and it's all for nothing. He just doesn't see that."

"But things are different now, aren't they?"

He shook his head. "Only the counters are different. The game itself is exactly, inexorably, the same. Individual excellence *doesn't* matter, virtue *isn't* its own reward. There is no contract a battery of high-priced lawyers can't circumvent, no firm so powerful it can't be brought down or bought out. Hard work alone doesn't 'win through' to anything but betrayal and unjust deserts. *That* is the only unalterable law."

She said: "You underrate him. Maybe he sees it and just goes his own way, anyhow."

"No. Even if he sees it with his eyes he doesn't believe it in his heart."

She bit her lip. "Tip's the original American. He *is*. Caught up in the pure, naked challenge of it."

"Worse—he's the ultimate innocent."

"Yes. That's what you can't forgive him for. Perhaps *I* can't, either. But I respect him for it."

He had stirred again; he was staring at her. "Yes, and you're one, too," he told her. "Another bloody innocent."

"No, I'm not," she answered quickly. "Not like him. Not at all."

"You're a pair of anachronisms—clinging to a world that never existed."

"Yes, it did," she protested, "it did exist! Once."

"What do you mean—some ragtag Johnny Appleseed, tramping through the forest primeval, wandering around in circles because he's forgotten to bring a compass along? Or Thoreau, sitting on a stump in the rain moping about the Athenians, swiping an apple pie off Mother's kitchen windowsill when nobody's looking? Don't be a kidder! Those glamorous Portuguese explorers you used to rhapsodize about—who do you think outfitted *their* ships and press-ganged the

563

crews? Cold-blooded financiers who wanted a 500 percent return on the original investment, that's who!"

"You're getting carried away."

"You bet!" He laughed, but he hurried on. "And your swashbuckling bravos wanted it, too—they were after the gold and the silks and spices, and they didn't care how they got them, either—looting and raping and butchering their way across the seven seas. There's your pure love of discovery! . . . Except for the out-and-out nuts, man has always hunted down something of value. No motive is pure. And don't give me that you're-so-cynical blather, either. *Everybody* wants something. Chapin Ames's Law. Even you, sweetheart."

"And what do I want?"

"To get the best of Serena."

She sat up with a jerk. "Serena Aldridge? That's ridiculous!"

"Is it?" He was smiling now.

"I couldn't care less about anything she thinks. That arrogant old dragon—she made you rivals, tempted you both in different ways: you to leave, and Tip to stay—just to show her she didn't make him leave . . ."

"You see?" He sounded gleeful. "You still resent her, you want to square accounts."

"The devil I do."

"It runs right back to your grandmother, and *her* grandmother, for all I know. It's the age-old racial war. It's never over."

"*Now* who's defending inherited attitudes?"

He laughed again. "I know, I know. Why should I be consistent? Nobody else is. You know what she said the other night? She told me I ought to patch things up with Jenny."

"Not really."

"Isn't that priceless? God, the convictions of the despotic are amazing. She has absolutely *no* idea what passed between us." He paused, said in a lower voice:

"She wouldn't give me a child. Jenny. Did you know that?"

‌ "No. I wondered about it."

"We married too early," he said abruptly. "You did, too."

Lying back again she considered this. Was age the problem? No, age had very little to do with it.

"We always choose the wrong partner—first," he was saying in a remote, musing tone. "Why do you suppose that is?"

"I don't know. Ignorance, maybe. When we do. Innocence." That sensual stirring had come again, the groundswell tremor she remembered; she found it suddenly hard to lie still.

"No, it runs deeper than that. Every partner's wrong, ultimately—that's at the core of it. Marriages aren't made in heaven, or hell either—it's a patent absurdity for two complex, constantly changing human beings to cohabit for half a century."

"Grama used to say marriage ought to be terribly hard to get into and extremely easy to get out of. Rather than the way it is now."

"Too simplistic. Like all Grama's maxims. Pungent, but fallacious. Don't you see? That would only make marriage all the more desirable—the idiots would walk barefoot through fire to reach it, and bind themselves for life." He was propped up on his elbows now, staring sightlessly at the distant, smoky headland of Manaquoit. "No, sexual pairings should be one enormous, overcrowded bazaar—like the thieves' market at the Porta Portese in Rome. You pick up an intriguing little piece of marble fretwork at one booth, stroll along and swap it for a fragment of Etruscan vase, trade that a little farther on for the hilt of a short sword . . . Jenny's the girl Tip should have married," he said abruptly.

"Tip and Jenny! Oh, you've never really known him. You're wrong."

"Why not? They're essentially simple natures—they

deal in tangibles, they distrust complexities, nuances. They'd have answered something deep in each other . . . And"—his eyes came to rest on her—"then I should have married you."

She smiled. "Don't be ridiculous. We'd have been fighting like cats and dogs in a matter of weeks."

"No. We're alike in certain ways. We're both drawn to beautiful things. Moments of grace."

She looked hard at him then, remembering, and said: "I have to give everything, Chay. Nothing held back."

His eyes wavered, came back to hers. "I could have learned that. I still can."

She shook her head vehemently. "You won't risk anything."

"Of course I will—I have."

"That's not the kind I mean. You *want* to get caught."

He gazed at her in great surprise; then his face darkened against the white sky. "That's preposterous."

"I don't want to make you angry. But it's true, and you know it."

His eyes were wide with wonder. "You're not afraid of anything. Are you?"

"Sure, I am. I'm afraid of a lot of things."

"No—not really. Not far deep down inside you. At the very roots of everything . . . You wouldn't even be afraid if I were to toss you overboard and sail away and leave you out here in the middle of Cape Cod Bay."

Her eyes seemed to have locked themselves oddly with his; her heart was beating thunderously, but it was not in fear. "I'd be awfully cross with you, though."

He laughed softly as if to himself; his fingers moved with infinite delicacy along the edge of her cheek, her throat. *"Everything they said of her is true,"* he murmured.

"What's that?"

"Old Chinese poem. Very old. Very apt—the man must have been thinking of you. Secret, mysterious, elusive . . . better than her legend. There *are* people who are grander than the rest of us. You're one of them."

He was very near her. His hand seemed to have set off a chain of tiny electrical sensations all over her body.

"Be careful now," she said faintly, almost pleading. "Don't—tempt me . . ."

"Yes, that's it!" he murmured in a kind of exultant triumph. "Temptation—we can't resist it, either of us. That's our bond . . ."

She tried to think about this, could not. She was trembling minutely in every part of her, aware of that stealthy, rushing clamor deep in her belly. Was that true? Was that the obverse of the spinning gold coin of her need, that consuming hunger to press beyond the last horizon? To dare all was to be tempted by all, to risk—

His hand rested at the edge of her breast now, softly insistent; it was exquisitely intolerable. A moment longer she gazed at him blindly—then his body was hard and lean and long against her. She came almost instantly, a long pent-up burst that racked and claimed her. His phallus was long, his stroking shockingly, marvelously deep; a prolonged invasion that spitted and spun her wildly, while wave after wave spilled over her, raced foaming through her. Distantly she heard herself call aloud to the sun blazing on her eyelids; the gently rising southerly swept her cries away toward the open sea.

"—I knew it!" he exulted at one point, "oh, I knew it—! You can fly as far as I can."

"Oh, yes," she whispered between her teeth. "And farther than that . . ."

"All the others were just play-acting, child's games—"

He was inconceivably tireless, he was inventive and bold, and she felt herself rise to meet him, extravagance and invention and nuance, two racing hulls tacking in the wildest of gales . . . Later they fell apart and lay spent and stunned, rolling with the easy movement of the boat; the awakened breeze laved her body, lifted her hair, lying long and dark around her. In a slow trance Jophy got to her feet and moved aft.

"Here's our southerly," she said, suddenly cold with memory. Hauling in the mainsheet she brought the sloop into the wind. "And we didn't even have to whistle for it."

"I'm going out to the Coast next week," he said. His body looked slimmer naked, curiously vulnerable. "Come out with me." She shook her head. "Why not?"

She shook her head again. She had the wheel now. *Turandot* picked up her head and heeled over a little, gaining way.

"Don't expect all kinds of things of me, Chay," she said abruptly.

"But I do." He was sitting up, his arms locked over his knees. "I'm right to."

"I'm a very passionate woman—"

"You certainly are. You're glorious! You're what I've always wanted, what I've always needed—I mean that."

"—but that doesn't mean I'm going to drop everything. Or anything."

"But you're what I've longed for. You are!"

"Well. I have obligations, responsibilities. I do love Tip, you know. Whatever I may decide to do about it. However it may seem. I just don't know . . . I don't intend to toss between the two of you like a cork." She ran her eyes expertly over the sleek white swell of the mainsail, looked at her brother-in-law again, very directly. "Life is not a collection, Chay," she told him with mock severity. "You know something? You're a lot more attractive since you had to get rid of yours."

"Oh, but I've started new ones," he said with that boyish sideways flicker of his eyes, and she laughed, easing the wheel.

"Chay, you're incorrigible!"

"We all are," he answered. His face had turned hard again, the openness gone as suddenly as it had come. "That's what makes the game so fascinating . . . Isn't it?"

7

Everyone was depressed by the stream of shocking bulletins out of France. All week they'd been coming in, as unthinkable as the pavement opening up right down Michigan Boulevard, or the lake erupting in lava. A radio voice, smoothly modulated but a bit tense, was drifting in even now from the outer office, saying something about armored columns, the German High Command.

"Marion," Percy Warren called without rancor from his desk. "Turn that thing down, will you?"

"I'm sorry, Mr. Warren," the girl answered, and the voice vanished.

"I'm running a brokerage office, not the corner saloon," he added to no one in particular; though it was after five o'clock. Perry Warren liked to hold open house in his office after the exchanges had closed. Tip and Maury Zimmerman were there, along with Sonny Keller, area salesman for Jay, Laughton, and Tim Landry, who was with Scudder, Stevens. Don Peterson, one of Warren's own brokers, was half-sitting on one of the radiators, chain-smoking.

"What's the matter with those people, anyway?" Warren said. He'd served in France with the Rainbow Division in '18. "Folding up like that. Hell, they held on for four years last time."

"The British are wading out into the Channel," Maury said. "No weapons, no equipment, nothing. Je-

571

sus, they're picking them up in launches and sailboats."

"They're through," Peterson said, and brushed cigarette ashes from his knees.

Tip asked him: "You heard anything on Paris?"

"It's just a matter of time, place is wide open."

"The Germans decide to cross the Channel, boys," Percy Warren said, "and we are going to be in one high old sling, I'll tell you that."

"I declare, it's getting time to switch," Sonny Keller observed. "Start selling for Krupp and I. G. Farben." He laughed his slyly genial laugh. "How's your German, Ames?"

Tip scowled at him. He'd never liked Sonny Keller—there was something malign behind his comical poses, his repertoire of over-elaborate jokes, his pretended camaraderie. But a lot of the brokers seemed to like him.

"Now we're in for it," Maury said soberly. "Now we're going to have to fight. Maybe we should have made a stand a long time ago."

Keller grinned at him. "Hell, that's easy for you to say."

"It isn't easy for anybody to say."

"Yes, well—let's say it's easier for some than for others. You know?"

Maury looked at him a moment. He'd held his weight down but his face had betrayed him—his features had thickened and melted as if under heat. He looked like a Bourbon princeling who's been passed over for the succession.

"Because I'm a Jew, Keller," he said in a sharp, clear voice. "That what you mean?"

"You said it, I didn't." And Sonny flashed his sly grin. "Getting nervous, Zimmy?"

Maury started to reply but Tip cut him off. "If that's a joke, I don't get the punch line, Sonny, *Is* it supposed to be one of your funny jokes?"

Keller shrugged once. "Could be, Schoolboy."

"I've never found you funny at all, Keller. In fact, I find you offensive. You know that?" He looked coldly at Keller, hoping the other man would make something of it.

"The hell with this European war talk." Percy Warren flung himself back in his chair. "Who likes Cleveland in the American, this season?"

Harold Browne from Vance, Sanders leaned in at the door and said hello. His eyes met Tip's and flickered once. There was some general banter and then Browne said:

"Perc, how about calling a sales meeting for me tomorrow?"

Warren's expression changed, the talk fell away. "Sorry, Hal."

"Why not?"

"I never call sales meetings for visiting firemen."

"Yes, you do—you called one yesterday for Ames, here."

"I did not."

Browne jerked a thumb toward the outer office. "You certainly did, you had a—"

"I put a notice on the bulletin board that Tip Ames was going to be here at eight-thirty on Tuesday morning. And the boys came in. To a man." He paused, his gray eyes level, cool, a touch amused. "When they all come in for you, I'll put a notice up on the board for you."

Browne scowled at them and left in a huff, muttering to himself. Maury snorted once, and Warren glanced at Tip and nodded. "Nothing more than the truth." He looked around the room. "You know, there's a lot of prima donnas cruising around these days, think the world owes them a living."

"Yeah, and you never know where they'll turn up, either," Keller added.

Tip glanced at Maury, who had busied himself with a cigarette, his eyes averted. Tip knew he was broke—and he'd made as much money as any mutual

573

fund salesman in the country. He'd sponsored half a dozen refugee families from Germany, relatives and friends of relatives; he'd adopted a lovely orphaned girl named Lisa and was putting her through Wisconsin. Unlike all the others he'd never married—and here he was with more family to support than any of them. He dressed soberly now, slate or dun suits with subdued foulard ties. He was suffering from a duodenal ulcer and had quit drinking, but he couldn't get off cigarettes. Remembering their first meeting, Tip felt a slow rush of affection. They were still here, a world war and a crash and a depression later; they'd been to the wars, and then some . . .

"No, they caught the kid the next day," Peterson was saying now to Tim Landry. "He confessed to the whole thing."

"A sailor?"

"That's right. Signalman from off the *Oklahoma.* Said Frank lured him up there under false pretenses. Tried to get him drunk."

"What good does it do to rake that up?" Maury said crossly. "Lousy reporters—they'd sell out their own mothers for a story. Why can't they leave a man alone?"

Warren said, "Sells papers, unfortunately."

"Well, he was the best."

"Was, is right!" Sonny Keller said with a laugh.

"He was better than you'll ever be," Maury came back at him, "if you live to be a thousand."

"That's your opinion."

"That's no opinion, that's a fact," Percy Warren told him shortly. "Christ, Beau Frank Delahant forgot more than glorified shoe clerks like you will ever know."

Tip looked up quickly. "Frank Delahant? What about him?"

"He's dead," Peterson said. "They found him in a hotel room in San Diego. Stabbed to death."

"—Frank *Delahant* . . .?"

"Kid killed him with a hunting knife. And then robbed him."

"Wasn't a hell of a lot to rob, the way I heard it," Keller said with his falsely genial laugh. "Hell, you know what it was."

"Frank Delahant?" He was on his feet now, staring at them all; he could feel the heat in his face. "I don't believe it. It's somebody else . . ."

They watched him in the silence. Percy Warren said gently: "Kid had Frank's watch on him, Tip."

"Oh." He looked down at his hand. "Where's he been? What's he been doing?"

"They said he was working as a short order cook at the time."

"What's all the hearts-and-flowers about?" Sonny wanted to know. "You play around like that, you get burned. Hell, he's been asking for it for years."

Tip turned and faced him directly. "Some day someone is going to punch you right in your big mouth, Keller. And close it for some time. You know that?"

"Now listen, Ames—"

"One more word," Tip said in a very low voice, almost a whisper. *"Say it—!"*

"Boys," Warren was murmuring. "Boys . . ."

Sonny laughed then, and shrugged. "Jesus squeeze-us, everybody's touchy around here today!"

"That's right, Keller," Tip answered. "I'm touchy today. And I will be tomorrow. You can take your filthy notions and shove them up your ass." He felt sick to his very vitals; his head was hammering. He nodded to Warren and Peterson and walked out of the office. Maury said:

"Wait, Tip, I'm coming." At the door he swung back and said distinctly: "And if you get past Tip, Sonny —which I very much doubt—then you can go a few with me. Have a lovely weekend."

La Salle Street was hot and gusty, and contained far too many people. He couldn't seem to get enough air into his lungs.

"I'm sorry about Frank," Maury said. "Damn, I'm sorry. I thought you knew."

"No. I didn't."

"It happened four, five days ago."

"I've tried to locate him for a couple of years. I even tried to—"

PARIS FALLS!!! the headlines blared at the corner. People snatched at copies, tossed coins and turned away, already reading. The world loomed ahead like an unhelmed battleship—grim, huge, out of control. The Germans marching into Paris, British Tommies wading in good order out to the crazy, makeshift flotilla under the Stukas and Heinkels, and Beau Frank Delahant dead in a cheap San Diego hotel room—Frank, who had turned selling into an art, given it depth and distinction, who had been so generous, taught him—taught them all—so much; opened the world to them. Ah, Frank . . .

"Now they'll start rounding them up," Maury was saying with heavy savagery, glaring at the headlines, the June light bombarding them from the tall buildings. "Women, kids—old men who've pored over the Talmud all their lives, and never harmed a fly . . ."

Tip stopped in the street and gazed at him slackly. "God, Maury—how did we *get* here? How did we let it all happen?"

Zimmerman smiled an old, weary smile. "We've always been here, Tip. Only now they've pulled the curtains back. That's all."

That fall the fund hit $80 million and they passed Loomis, Sayles and Scudder, in spite of the recession. In spite of the war in Europe. War fed business, as Chapin was fond of saying. They qualified in California, and Tip sent Maury to head up the office out there, and moved Jimmy Danton and Clarence to the Midwest. There was plenty of money for everything now, plenty for everybody. Chapin bought a sprawling Spanish villa in Palm Beach with two tennis courts and a huge swimming pool. And he refurbished the Bluffs. He was spending more and more time down there summers. Joey had gone to Harvard and was starting his sophomore year. Tip wanted to send Tessa to Cambridge or Dana Hall, but to everyone's surprise she refused; she wanted to stay on at the Cape, and go on to the University of Connecticut. She had turned into her father's girl, sturdy, plain-faced, with a quick, ready smile and a sunny disposition.

Late that winter Tip picked up Jophy and Joey's girl, a good-looking, rather intense brunette named Beth Bryson, who was also a fine arts major, and drove them over to Cambridge to see Joey swim against Yale. It was strange, sitting there in the close, unnatural heat, following the taut, premonitory silence with the swimmers crouching on their marks; the crash of the gun and then the thunderous seethe of trashed water and the booming cavern-echo of young voices bouncing off the tiled roof. The Yale team, unbeaten, looked big and competent and relaxed. Staring at the block Y's, Tip thought of old football games down at the Bowl, of Century Gifford waving his crushed hat in a frenzy, and the Blazer in a mountainous coonskin coat, tilting a silver flask toward the frosty sky. So long ago . . . His mind kept skittering away, snatching at goofy scraps of memory.

The meet was lost by the time Joey's event, the quarter mile, came up. Standing on the mark in the skin-tight silk suit, wringing his arms from shoulder to wrist in that peculiar way swimmers always did, Joey looked almost fragile beside his Yale counterpart, a tall blond man with huge shoulders named Harcourt. After the first few laps Joey was well behind the other three, swimming effortlessly, his arms dropping out and down in a graceful, gliding rhythm.

"He's fallen off the pace," he couldn't help saying.

"He always swims his own race," Jophy answered. "He can keep it up all day and all night. You'll see."

"He swims even better than you do, Jo."

"Blood will tell!" she cried softly, and winked at him. "Water's our element, don't you know."

After the tenth lap Joey began to inch his way up, gaining at each turn; he passed his team mate and the other Yale man. Tip could see him pulling harder now, stroking faster. Team mates were capering along the pool's edge now, flailing towels, urging him on. He kept gaining, his face strained with effort, until he came out of the last turn almost even with Harcourt, and the racket in the stands was overpowering. Then the big man pulled ahead for good, his hand flipping one of the lowered pennants, and the cavern roar died away.

"Almost!" Tip shouted. He was surprised to find he was on his feet and sat down hurriedly, shaking his head. "He almost had him! What a shame . . ."

Jophy was watching him ruefully. "What does it matter? He did his best—he swam beautifully. He's only a sophomore, Tipton . . ."

"Sure. Of course." But somehow he couldn't control his disappointment, gazing down at Joey and the others hanging on the lane floats, their arms around one another's shoulders, sluicing their heads in the green water; an easy camaraderie. College men. A world he would never know.

Afterward he invited several members of the team and their girls to the Ritz Roof to hear Tommy Dorsey. After a drink or two the alien, fusty sensation began to recede. Dorsey, suave and bespectacled, he remembered from the Jean Goldkette jazz band at the old Greystone in Detroit, and several of the tunes were familiar—"Who" and "Chicago" and "There'll Be Some Changes Made," but set to a more pronounced beat, a slower, swinging rhythm. He had the feeling of things coming around again. Jophy felt it, too—she was in rare high spirits as they danced to "East of the Sun." A round-faced kid named Bunny Berigan played a rich, darting trumpet solo, a slender boy named Frank Sinatra movingly sang the lyrics. Jophy danced then with Joey, gliding with that lithe, sensuous grace that would always stir Tip to the farthest reaches of his heart. He could never quite believe this tall, uncommonly handsome young man out there dancing with his wife was the same over-thin, nervous little boy who had sat on his lap listening to him read about Mowgli and Gray Brother . . . When the band broke into a fast number and the other boys discovered Jophy could do the Lindy—jitterbugging, they called it now—better than their own dates, they all wanted to dance with her.

At some point there was a vigorous discussion about *The Maltese Falcon*.

"Humphrey Bogart," Jophy told them airily. "Why, I knew the man he's imitating. Spider Danco."

"You knew Spider *Danco?*" they demanded, amazed.

"I certainly did. I danced with him."

"—I don't believe it!" Joey taunted her.

"He felt your mother had Moxie," Tip heard himself say suddenly.

Her eyes flashed at him, very wide. "That's right, he did. Where'd you ever hear that?"

"You knew him too, Dad?"

"In a way. I once handled a sort of transaction for him."

This set the kids off—they'd been reading Scott Fitzgerald and they wanted to hear all about the wild Twenties, bathtub gin and Harlem and madcap frolics on the lawns of lush Long Island estates. Tip found himself telling them about the time Jack Darcey rented the Chrysler phaeton and took off with a luscious blonde named Lulu for Atlantic City, only Lulu got so sunburned on the drive down he couldn't get near her all weekend long; and a Diehl, Harrodsen field day when Chapin had taken several of them up in the plane and the Blazer, squashed as ever, had decided he needed to relieve himself and had opened one of the cabin doors and was about to step out, high over

Long Island Sound, when they'd grabbed him . . .
We're history, he thought wryly, watching the kids'
excited, eager faces. Hell, what we *were* was a bunch
of God damned fools—

Tip paid the tab for the younger generation and
drove Jophy through the chill March night, talking
about the kids, and the war, and Turk's Head, and everything except what he was thinking about, until
she turned to him in surprise and said:

"We're not going out Commonwealth Avenue . . ."

"No." He glanced at her. "I'm damned if I'm going
to drop you off at some stupid hotel. You can stay at
the apartment perfectly well."

"Tip—"

"Hush. I'm holding you captive. Like Spider
Danco."

She smiled out at the night. "Abducted. At last."

"We only abduct the young and beautiful," he said.

He showed her the apartment with a certain pride.
They stood side by side at the long French doors looking out over the Fens, and after a moment he embraced her with the old firm tenderness; but the shadow of pained uncertainty in her eyes stopped him.

"Tip—we can't just go back to things. Just like
that."

"I can," he said. "I can, Jo."

"I know." She looked so overpoweringly beautiful to
him at that moment he wouldn't have been surprised
if his heart had stopped, right then and there. "I'm
sorry," she said. "I mean it."

"I'm just happy having you here," he said, and he
held her hands the way he used to. "In the room
here."

Her eyes glistened suddenly. "You're an awfully
good man, Tipton Ames. The best. You always were."

"I don't know about that."

"Well, I do."

"But I do know I'll always love you, Jo. I can't help
it."

She turned away in real distress, and sighed. "Oh, Tip," she murmured, "sometimes you make me wish I were somebody else . . ."

He gazed at her slim, straight back, the shimmering dark of her hair, so smooth in the figure eight. The hair he longed to loosen, to let free, as he'd used to do. It didn't matter how long he had to wait for her to turn around; there was nothing else in his life he wanted.

"Well, I don't want you to be anyone else, Jo," he said. "Ever."

When Hitler invaded Russia that June Tip knew that cynical brother of his was right: it was going to turn into another all-out world war, with no holds barred. East as well as West. Business picked up from the previous year's doldrums, the factories and mills began to hum again. He felt pressed and apprehensive and drove all the harder in his work to keep from thinking too long and too much about it. He'd just have to keep things turning over, he told himself.

Pearl Harbor caught him in Louisville, at the Maxwell House, lying on the bed in his room reading a magazine. He was angry, and then numb, and then very worried. He phoned Jophy, and then Joe, but neither of them was home. Chapin was there at the Beacon Street mansion, though, and vengefully jubilant.

"And high time! Velly honolable Mikado did us a great big favor. This'll put an end to all the royal pussyfooting, with a bang."

"God damn it, Chapin!" he shouted.

"What's the matter? It was inevitable, you know that just as well as I do, it's *been* inevitable from the moment that moronic little paperhanger—"

"You don't have to dance a bloody jig about it!" He hung up on him and went out to a movie.

Ten days later he'd barely got in the door when Joey phoned him from college and said he wanted to see him right away. He caught a cab over to Cambridge. His son was looking moody and casual in a crew-neck sweater and loafers. His room mate, a solemn, matter-of-fact boy named McComb, greeted Tip respectfully and then departed for the library.

"Well—how about a drink, Dad?"

He shot a glance at the boy. "Yes, I believe I would like one."

Joey took two glasses out of a handsome walnut liquor cabinet Chapin had given him for his birthday the year before, threw up one of the windows and leaned out on the ledge.

"One of the dubious advantages of winter in Cambridge—the ice keeps almost indefinitely." He popped several cubes into the glasses and poured liquor over them with slow care.

"Not in training?" Tip said in surprise.

"Oh—that. No. I'm not." The boy grinned and shrugged his shoulders, and Tip felt his heart sink. "Well, call it one for the road . . ."

Joey was standing by the fireplace, snapping a thumbnail against his teeth. Tip watched him soberly. He could never overcome the curious mix of emotions he always felt, visiting him here at college. There was the venerable ease he envied, and a youthful companionship he actually hungered for, and at the same time that parochial stuffiness that always made him think of Elwell and aspects of Chapin, which he despised; and there was something else too, something he could never quite put his finger on: a certain self-indulgent, profligate manner that stung his sense of rightness, of earning one's own way. Well, maybe that was too harsh. The fact was, he hadn't ever—

"Dad, I'm going into the Navy," Joey said suddenly.

"I see." It was what he had feared, then. He saw the boy in blues, skipping smartly up a ship's ladder, wigwagging signal flags, and then stripped to the waist in some cramped, smoky space, cradling a huge shell

582

in his arms . . . thought, my God—*Jo;* drove the image away and sipped his drink.

"Why the hurry?" he asked casually.

"We're *in* it, Dad. It's here . . ."

"It'll be here for quite a while."

"That's no answer . . ."

"You graduate next year."

"Next year!" the boy's eyes flashed with that exasperated outrage that made him think again of Jophy. "The Japs could be in St. Louis by next year!"

"I rather doubt that."

"You rather doubted Hitler was going to overrun Europe, as I remember. You felt—"

"Nobody's perfect." He made himself grin, and Joey ducked his head and said:

"I'm sorry, Dad. I can't stay on here, pretending to study, going through the motions. *Delacroix,* for Christ's sake . . ."

"You'd be more valuable with a diploma, you know."

"As a fancy-pants officer, you mean." His lip curled. "I don't see it that way."

"The living's a lot easier. Believe me. I have reason to know."

Again the defiant mirror-flash of eyes. "I'm not looking for an easy way."

Tip set down the glass, and leaned forward. "I can see you've thought about this. Look, why don't we talk about it. Why don't you stay with it, just till the end of term. That's only—what? Six or seven—"

"I can't, Dad." The boy looked at him squarely. "The thing is—I've already enlisted."

Of course. I should have known, he thought, fighting down half a dozen angry responses, physically swallowing them, thinking Jesus, that impulsive, crazy, Portuguese thing, just like his mother; thinking with real pain of Jophy. She will blame me for this, he told himself like a condemned man standing

583

up for sentencing; for some insane reason she'll see this as my doing and she won't forgive me for it.

"Well. If it's done, it's done, I guess. Have you talked to your mother?" The boy shook his head, silent. "She'll be very upset, Joe. She's set her heart on your graduating."

"I can't help that," he said harshly, "—I've got my own life to live. You had your war, and you didn't handle it very well, either. And now we've got ours . . ." Then he jammed his hands deep in his trouser pockets and looked down at his loafers. "I was hoping you might put in a good word for me."

Tip studied him for a moment. "All right. If you want. But you're going to have to tell her yourself first. You want to be a man, then you go ahead and *be* one."

Joey smiled. "I figured you'd say something like that."

"Good. that saves us an argument . . . I wish you'd at least discussed this with me," he permitted himself.

"What difference would it make? Everybody's going . . ."

"No, everybody *isn't* going. A lot of boys your age are—"

"Uncle Chapin's going."

"What?" He'd turned suddenly, splashed some of his drink over his hand and sleeve. "When did you hear that?"

"The other day."

"He was over here? at school?"

"Yeah. He's going in next month, soon as he winds some things up. He tried to talk me into signing up for that Air Corps Reserve program—using his influence with the high brass. Special duty. You know." He gave his mother's impudent, dazzling smile. "I told him to get lost—the sea's where my roots are. *He* was cross with me, too."

Tip wiped at his sleeve with his handkerchief, thinking, God damn him to hell! In war, except for the professionals, the young men went. Older men had other fish to fry. The fact that Chapin had approached Joey, that the boy knew this about his brother and he didn't, infuriated him out of all proportion.

"I'm sorry, Dad—I thought you knew."

"Well. I didn't." He stood up abruptly, feeling cross, feeling beleaguered. Out of it. As usual. "When do you report?"

"They said next Monday."

Jesus. Three days before Christmas.

"All right," he said. "You're going and that's it. Now go down and see your mother right away. Putting it off won't make it any easier. I'll back you up, but you've got to do this one on your own. You'd better start packing. I'll help you move your junk out over the weekend."

"Okay. Thanks, Dad . . . I'm sorry."

He turned. The boy was troubled now, he could see it. He'd gone over to Boston on a wave of fine, patriotic ardor—and now for the first time he was thinking about boot camp, and dark, hostile headlands, the lightning flashes of great guns . . . He wished suddenly with all his heart he'd managed to get closer to him. He'd tried—he really had tried—but it hadn't been easy. There'd been the break with Jophy, and there was that over-sensitive, withdrawn side to the boy he'd never been able to overcome. Now here they were, standing on the edge of something momentous, maybe something irrevocable . . .

"It's all right, Joey," he said softly. "I'm right there behind you. It's all right."

The boy stared at him a few seconds longer—a strangely hollow, importunate gaze—then threw his arms around him and hugged him hard.

"Dad . . ." Joey's voice was low and hoarse.

"You'll do all right, son." He let him go then, and cleared his throat. "I'll call you tomorrow."

He walked down the entry stairs, past a raucous chorus of swing bands and shouts and news announcers, and his sight kept blurring with tears.

Chapin's attitude the following day was infuriating, as he'd known it would be.

"That's right," he admitted. "They've told me my services are urgently needed." He anticipated Tip's rejoinder with a wry smile. "Of course it's pure bushwa. Though I must confess it's a touch flattering. After all these years."

"You think they'll let you fly a plane over Berlin."

"Why, not at all—it'll only be a dreary desk job somewhere. But they also serve, who only sit at desks and send the wrong matériel to the wrong theater at the wrong time." His brother's use of the word *theater*, the facetious glint in his eye, angered Tip all over again.

"And so you've decided you *are* indispensable to victory."

"I wouldn't put it quite that grandiloquently." Tip could see he was serious now. "But yes. It's my duty to go. It's the duty of any—"

"It's your *duty* to sit right here in this unglamorous old office and manage Macomah's portfolio—not take off on another one of your carefree overseas junkets."

"I can assure you I don't look on it as any kind of carefree junket, little brother. It's going to be a big, long, dirty job, and we're going to do it to perfection. Only *this* time we're not going to run home and sashay up Broadway and forget all about it. This time we're going to dismantle the plant and run it to *our* advantage."

"When this one's over," Tip said heavily, "there won't be enough of anything left around to make tin cups."

"Of course there will. There always is. We'll *really* be running the store next time. You'll see."

"And meanwhile Macomah can go to hell in a basket."

"Oh, come on, Tip. You can handle it. You and Mac and George."

He stuck out his lip. "I'm only sales, remember?"

"Now don't start that—you know it's not true. It's yours just as much as mine." He ran his fingers along his nose. "God Almighty, don't you start in on me. I'm going to have enough trouble with Serena as it is."

"I hope so. I hope she reams your irresponsible ass," Tip told him. "She's the one who knows how to do it."

Chapin grinned ruefully. "Isn't she, though," he said. "Isn't she just."

But Tip refused the disarming overture; he was too harassed and apprehensive for any of that. He turned at the door. "Some day I hope you'll decide to grow up, Chay. I really do."

He didn't have to call Jophy; she called him, and she was wild.

"What, just *what,* were you thinking of?"

"Look, Jo, the boy—"

"Yes, that's just it, he's a boy, a boy . . .!" He could feel the rage in her voice, the blank terror; he could hear her breathing in the earpiece.

"He's old enough to make—"

"Why in God's name didn't you talk him out of it? You can talk anybody into and out of anything, when you want to . . ."

"Jophy, I told you, he'd *already enlisted* . . ."

"But you could have stopped it, got it revoked, done something—if you weren't always racing around the God damned country, talking people into buying stocks—"

"It's my work, Jo."

"Do you think that matters now? Do you think that has any meaning at all, with Joey going off to *war*—?"

"As a matter of fact," he broke in, resentful, hurt at the palpable injustice of her assault, "my sophisticat-

587

ed flyboy brother seems to have caused it as much as anyone."

"What? What do you mean?" He told her. "Of course," she said between her teeth, "the dear old fraternity of males—heroes all, wielding clubs and roaring at each other, egging each other on—God, how I hate it!"

"Jo, listen a—"

"We ought to band together and slaughter all of you some fine patriotic night, like those women on that damned Greek island—"

"Jo—"

"No! No more talk. I'm sick to my very guts! My very guts, Tipton. I'll talk to you later. Or maybe I won't. I don't know."

She hung up on him then. He sat there staring at the phone for ten full minutes, not thinking about anything at all. After that he poured himself a drink, a stiff one, and pretended to read *H. M. Pulham, Esquire* till almost two; and then lay wide awake with his hands behind his head, worrying about Joey, but forcing himself to consider the travel schedules of his sales force, and which of the younger men he'd lose right away, and whether the government might even freeze private investment altogether . . . Finally he fell asleep, to dream fitfully of fanciful Jules Verne ships colliding in an inky sea, and fires on grim, barbaric shores.

8

"Did you see it, Colonel?" Weinstein was saying in his soft, high-pitched voice. "Where the road starts to turn, just before the river . . .?"

Chapin peered hard at the photo spread over the light-table, the blued, lacily etched rectangles that meant schools and churches and civilian dwellings—checked on a short section of highway just a shade different from the rest: neater and smoother.

"Ah," he murmured, smiling. "That Teutonic genius for perfection! It always betrays them, sooner or later . . . Yes, I see it. Good work, Benny." He turned to the Intelligence officer. "You're sure, now?"

"Yes, sir. It's part of Schwiegerfabriken, no question about the—"

"Good," Chapin cut him off. "Now let's get back up there before they start pot-shotting each other with forty-fives."

The argument was still going hot and heavy—hurrying up the stairs Chapin could hear their voices clearly over the chatter of the teleprinter in the ops room and the incessant coughing rumble of motors being tuned at the far side of the field. He knocked smartly once, and he and Weinstein entered Brigadier General Steyer's office.

"Three reasons!" Colonel Curns was shouting, waving his big gloves at the operations map, where a thick black circle had been traced on the acetate over the town of Hexenkirchen, deep in the province of Bavaria. "Give me three good reasons. Give me one!" He was still wearing coveralls and flying boots; his broad, handsome face was brick red.

Steyer said: "I won't pretend I like it, Bucky."

"Like it—! It's straight out of the shit house, that's what it is . . . A two-bit burg with no military value at all! Have they lost *all* their marbles, up there? Or is this their idea of a gag?"

"It's no gag," Major General Thornton said in his dry, nearly inflectionless voice. "All Studs said was that the directive came down from the top." He paused, said significantly: "The *very* top."

Steyer shook his head doggedly. "I can't believe Studs would approve anything like this."

"He hasn't any choice, Tom." Thornton ran one hand gently back and forth over his thigh, staring at the Academy ring on the third finger, and sighed. "The word is that it's a reprisal. In return for Coventry."

"Tit for tat!" Curns burst out savagely. "And so for that they order a run right into the heart of dear old Krautland, 250 fucking miles beyond fighter cover—no!"

"Bucky, no purpose is served—"

"Why don't they just set up a couple of twin-fifties and cut us down, right out there on the line?" Curns slammed his gloves down on Steyer's desk and took another savage drink from the tumbler of whisky standing next to a small wood-and-fabric model of an ancient De Haviland biplane. The glass was nearly empty but Chapin knew he wasn't drunk. Nobody in all the Army Air Corps—which was saying a great deal—could hold his liquor like Bucky Curns, and probably no one ever would. "It'd be one hell of a lot quicker—and think of the gas and ammo they'd save . . ."

"All right, Bucky," Steyer said then. "Simmer down, now. That's it."

Yet there was an undercurrent of affectionate reluctance in the reprimand. Bucky finished his drink and stared out of the window, where the roaring of the engines went on without cease. The two generals exchanged a glance and Steyer went over to his desk. All the world was an old-school tie, Chapin thought, half-irritted, half-amused, imagining Jophy in this room now: her dark eyes lighting on the campaign ribbons and decorations, the service rings, the stern and self-important faces—glittering with high scorn; how she would lash them!

This tie was Army aviation, born in the Flanders squadrons and stateside flying fields of World War I, and nurtured through the starveling years when its embattled pilots limped along in rickety Ryans and Curtisses and died like flies the awful winter the government made them fly the U.S. mail. They had claimed Chapin for one of their number and, flattered, he had kept and increased his contacts, watched the crucifixion of that empestuous heretic Billy Mitchell, the struggle for appropriations. After the Rhineland reoccupation he'd got into the fracas actively, applying pressure through old friends of Avery Calkin in Washington, even testifying at one of the interminable hearings . . . which was why he was here now with a colonel's eagles on his shoulders in this drab gray room with its map curtains and performance boards, carefully watching Bullet Bob Thornton, down from London for the day with his disquieting news, helping himself now to coffee from a huge aluminum urn some enterprising soul had smuggled over in a flight of replacement Flying Fortresses eight months before . . .

"All right, Ames," Steyer was saying to him, "let's do a run-through."

"Yes, sir." Chapin always knew when his chief was particularly angry or upset because he used his last name. Stepping up to the desk he read from the clipboard: "Fifteen Minor Repair guaranteed by 1400 hours, eleven from Major Repair by 2300. Thirty-four

Replacement Craft arriving stations by 1630—they can be listed on tomorrow's board."

"Battle damage from yesterday?"

"Eleven—they're included in the Major Repair figure." He paused. "There were eighteen Category E."

The general swore. "What about crew strength?"

"That still remains a problem, sir. Fourteen returning from leave and/or convalescence, thirty-three promised from Replacement—but not until tomorrow or Wednesday."

"Weather?"

"Knaust says it will hold CAVU through Wednesdy at least. Shall I send him in, sir?"

"No, no. That's the least of our problems."

"You bet!" Curns whirled around from the window again, glaring at Thornton. "What's weather, with a happy turkey shoot like this one, eh?"

Thornton stood up and deftly pulled down his blouse. "All right, Bucky," he said patiently, "you've had your little scene. Now let's get on with it. I've got to run over to—"

"Not me," Curns said tightly. "Not this time! I signed up to fight the frigging Luftwaffe, not to blow a lot of kids and women apart. I've had it!"

"Then you won't need to lead this mission, Colonel." Thornton's voice was like ice now.

"That's right. He won't." Steyer was staring at Thornton, his worn, lined face stony. "Because there isn't going to be one."

"Now *listen,* Tom—"

Steyer snatched up the teleprint order from his desk. "It just so happens it reads 'subject to divisional commanders' discretion.' "

"Tom, that's subject to *weather,* that's understood . . ."

"Not to me, it isn't." Steyer said in hard, steady voice: "You can get back to Studs and let him know exactly how we feel about their fucking vengeance mission."

"Tom, I've explained twice before that Studs has no control—"

"Or you can go back to DC and cry on the Old Man's shoulder, for all I care. Secure a postponement—at least that. If you can't—or won't—" and his voice cracked with fatigue "—then I cannot accept the responsibility, General."

Everyone in the room stiffened—even Bucky Curns's mouth dropped open. It was the field commander's final, irrevocable protest: no issue could go farther than that. Thornton stared at him in cold amazement.

"You're willing to go to the mat on this?" he almost whispered.

"You bet I am! Look at these." With the heel of his fist he struck the chalked-up figures on the losses board. "Look at them! We can't *take* any more—least of all in a lunatic spite raid like this one. And I won't. And that's the name of the game." Thornton's eyes narrowed to white slivers of light. "Now, you listen to me," he began hotly, "a directive has been handed down—"

"And they can stick it!"

There was a short silence. One of the engines out on the line was running very rough, skipping and fading; and the fliers listened to it absently, clinging to its harsh, tangible claim: something not working right, something to fix with wrenches, with gauges and windings. Chapin watched the others out of the corners of his eyes, caught in the old interior laughter, laced now with caution.

They saw what they wanted to see, not what was there. Emotional bias always grounded them. Thornton was beguiled by advancement—his own and that of an Omnipotent Air Army that would one day dominate the other branches with its limitless thunder. Steyer was distracted by losses, his face haggard from that never-ending flow of eager, laughing young men so soon to be burned to charred lumps or crushed in grotesque steel skeletons or bobbing soddenly in the icy Channel chop. All he could see was that grim parade—he could barely face it any more. He was willing to risk a board of inquiry over this—even a court martial and dismissal from the service. Like Tip; it was what Tip would have done. Another fool, ready to die for principle. And Bucky Curns had the combat flier's contempt for administrative fol de rol, global strategies; he wanted to get the hell out there and kill Germans, ram one right down the Reichs Chancery chimney—touch off the biggest cannon-cracker of this great big nonstop Glorious Fourth.

How very like the business world the war was, really. Chapin had been struck with the similarities ever since he'd been assigned to logistics in a training command back at Selleck Field. Management, research, accounting, personnel, overhead, cost pricing, production—all had their precise application to the world of Mars. Not to mention advertising. Oh, yes. The fact was, precision bombing was a farce: they had not put a dent in the Third Reich's war production, even with the mammoth raids against the fighter plants in August. They had reduced a number of towns and parts of cities to rubble, and torn up a lot of beet fields; German ingenuity in dispersing and reorganizing their factories after the raids—even the moderately successful ones—had neutralized their effect.

All of which they knew, these three hell's angels trying to stare one another down. They were every bit as familiar as Chapin with the padded claims, the doctored strike photos, the jiggled statistics. But they refused to look at them coolly, accept them for exactly what they were—a time-serving device to raise morale, arouse the patriotic fervor of civilian audiences in stateside movie houses, swell the eternal glory of military aviation. They saw what they wanted to see. Everyone did.

Aloud now he said to Steyer: "May I make a suggestion, General?"

The Division Commander frowned at him. "We've covered everything we can operationally, Chapin."

"It concerns the projected mission, sir. Major Weinstein has discovered something quite interesting." He paused. "There *is* a war plant in Hexenkirchen, and we know definitely that it produces mortar tubes."

All three men were staring at him in irritation. Curns said: "Hot dog. What's that got to do with the price of egg foo yong?"

"That makes it a legitimate target, Bucky."

"Fourth Priority, probably," Steyer said.

"True, sir. But, since there seems to be so much controversy surrounding this mission, why couldn't we angle it as a major effort in behalf of ground forces, in support of the forthcoming invasion? A little interservice cooperation, effectively publicized, wouldn't do us any harm right now, especially after that unfortunate flap during the Salerno landings. We might even work up a special presentation for the press, if the strike photos turned out to be dramatic enough: I could get Winninger's people to give us some blow-ups mounted on four-by-six panels, before-and-after shots framed on flat white board, with red-and-khaki lettering to emphasize our support of the infantry . . . you know, call it 'One for GI Joe'—something along that line."

"What a crock!" Curns exploded hotly. "Jesus, you are one conniving, calculating bastard, Ames . . ."

"Shut up, Bucky," Thornton said, but without heat; he was snapping his fingernails rapidly against one another. "That's a very creative solution, Colonel." He turned to Steyer. "It has its merits, Tom."

"But our *losses*," Steyer protested, his mouth working, "—they're already prohibitive . . ."

"We could close out the month with two or three milk runs over France, General," Chapin interjected smoothly. "Hit the Lorient sub pens, a few Third Category targets in the Pas de Calais area. That way we could average down our monthly losses and maintain our sortie and bomb tonnage levels—and at the same time score points by honoring what's clearly a high-level directive."

Again there was a silence. The shot-up engine was running more smoothly now, settling down into a rich, throaty drone. Thronton was watching him steadily—for a second or two Chapin thought he detected the shadow of a smile at the corners of the thin, bloodless lips. "Most ingenious," he murmured. "I'd say we're indebted to you for such exemplary research."

"Thank you, sir. In all truth the discovery—and the intelligence spadework—was Major Weinstein's. I merely saw some of the possibilities."

He broke off there; to press beyond that might invite a reprimand, or at the least set off another wrangle. Thornton peered again at the West Point ring, then cocked his head and said: "Well, Tom: what do you think?"

Steyer ducked his head in his broad shoulders; he was visibly torn between resentment to his own chief of staff's siding against him, and gratitude at being handed a way out. He fussed irritably with some papers on his desk, and then Chapin saw him make up his mind.

"All right," he said tersely. "What have you got on this bloody mortar-tube workshop?"

"I'll let Weinstein fill you in on that, if I may," Chapin answered. He turned to the Intelligence man with an easy smile. "Ben?"

Listening to Weinstein reading from the material in the big red target folder, Chapin felt the dry laughter well up in him again. Bucky Curns was glaring at him and he grinned benevolently in reply. They also serve, he thought, who only connive and calculate . . .

She came wide awake with the telephone's first, fierce scream, thinking *Joey, it's about Joey*—caught at it in the dark and knocked it off its cradle, snatched it up and said: "Yes?"

"Josinha?" Manny Furtado's voice, low and hoarse; she felt a rush of indescribable relief. "I'm down at Cunningham's. We've got trouble. Big trouble. Sub hit a tanker off Salcombe Bars, Frank Cardosa's just brought them in, everybody he could find out there. They're in bad sape. Doc Glover wants you down here, fast."

"Be right there."

She was on her feet at once—she always slept naked except in the dead of winter—pulled on jeans and shirt and sneakers, caught her hair up in a twist with a tortoise-shell clasp, picked up the Navy battle lantern from the hall table, plucked her windbreaker off a peg and was out the door in less than a minute. Her watch said 1:55.

The station wagon was parked in the driveway, looking slick with two new coats of spar varnish on the wood and the big red crosses painted on the side panels forward of the rear wheels. She let in the clutch and ran down Crown Street toward the harbor, feeling light-headed and alert, wanting a cigarette.

"Submarines," she muttered crossly. "Inventions of the devil." She realized she sounded just like Grama, but hearing her own voice steadied her. Wisps of fog lay low in the street. It was eerie driving without headlights, but she could probably have done it blindfolded. The night was gray-black, the locust trees swaying darker against the sky. The town looked spooky without streetlights; no lamps were visible behind the heavy black-out curtains. She knew people were up—fishing families were always stirring at ungodly hours. At Dock Street a car passed her moving fast, its painted-over black-out lights glowing like the lidded evil eyes of a sea monster.

At Cunningham's Wharf someone waved her on through. The ambulance was there, next to Shed Number One, with the town patrol car, and people were milling around at the rear of the ambulance. She ran in beside it, the car's tires clunking hollowly on the wharf planking, got out and followed someone through the heavy canvas curtains, the cutting shed door.

Inside, the sudden blast of light was shocking. Stunned, blinking hard, she looked around, trying to anchor herself in the tense, barbarous clamor of many voices. She saw two men laid out on the cutting boards, with people bent over them; others were lying along the outboard wall in a row. At first she thought they were Negroes, some black crew from a South American ship; then she saw a face, a naked arm upraised, and the odor drove deep into her head—oil and scorched fabric and something sickly, sweetly bad she remembered from her nursing days: the smell of badly burned flesh.

She went quickly over to the first group. Doc Glover, his white hair sticking straight up on his head, was saying, "God alone knows what else is wrong in there. I don't know why he's still breathing.—All right," to Art Atwood who drove the ambulance, "you better take him first, and the belly case. Get going, now. Make all the time you can." Several men eased the long, oil-coated body on to a stretcher and Glover pointed and called in the tart, peppery voice: "All right—that big fellow with the leg, there. Come on, now. Quick but careful." He looked around then, and saw Jophy. He was wearing his pajama top, pale blue with red piping, the collar turned up on one side; the cuffs were brighter red with blood.

"Good girl," he said. "Help me, here."

She gazed at the huge furrow of torn flesh and thickly pulsing blood, the slick, blue-white splinters and ridges of bone; set her teeth and picked up the pieces of lath and set them in place while Glover worked.

"There. That'll have to do" He handed her a Flit gun. "Hit his arm. there. Paraffin solution. Maybe it'll hold down the infection till they can get to it over in Hyannis. Just a light coat, now. We can't afford to waste it."

Charlie Simpson, just starting to set up private practice in town, had stepped back from his working area farther down the board, his face strained. "Verney, look," he said; he dropped his hands. "I can't cope with anything like this . . ."

"Course not," Glover answered. "It's just stop-gap, that's all."

"But we can't *move* him—"

"What do you suggest we do—let him go out on us right here?" Then, more gently: "Come on, son. We'll do what we can—it'll have to be good enough. Just make sure it's on that pressure point."

Helen Duarte came in then, looking angry and efficient; Jophy, wiping her hands on her jeans, smiled at her gratefully. Glover was saying, "Jophy, take these two. Right now. Wally will drive you. And stay with them, check on that tourniquet. You got a watch?"

"Yes."

Jimmy Vieira said, "How we going to move him, Doc? No stretcher."

Vernon Glover looked around wrathfully. "Jesus, didn't they leave that stretcher here—?

"No, Doc. They must have put it—"

"Then, *make* one!" he snapped. "Take down a door. Quick. Use your *head*, boy! It's not a hat rack . . ."

She knelt between the two men on the floor of the wagon while Wally Snow drove. The tourniquet case was bald, with a broad, tough face and flat, gray-blue eyes. He hadn't made a sound when they transferred him to the car. Now he stared up at her speculatively and said, his voice thick with morphine:

"What's a high-class lady like you doing in a job like this?"

She smiled. "I'm no lady, I'm your nurse."

"Don't hand me that." He turned his head toward

599

the thin boy with terrible burns on his arms and chest.

"Hey, Morales."

"Yeah, Barney?"

"Hey, you seen Hennessy?"

"No."

"He was standing right beside me when we got it. Just outside the galley . . . The lights went out so fast! I tried to get to him. I could hear him holler. Where I thought he was. You didn't see him in the water?" Morales made no reply. "You think they might have picked him up?"

"—I don't know, I don't *know!*" Morales cried suddenly, his voice ringing over the motor.

"Hush, now," she said, and the big man muttered: "Take it easy, kid."

". . . I did all I could, I tried my best—"

She put her hand on his forehead, stroked hs hair soothingly, but it was as if the outburst had released a flood of anguish.

"I lost him," he cried more softly. "I couldn't help it. Bobby Walsh, he couldn't move his legs at all, I was holding him. And I couldn't hold him any longer—my hands, I didn't have the strength! . . . and I let him go. I couldn't help it, ah, I couldn't . . ."

"It's all right," Jophy murmured, stroking his head. "It's all right now."

"No, it's not all right! It'll never be all right. Never again." And the boy began to weep helplessly, his face turned away.

"Take it easy, Jimmy," the big man said. "Put it out of your mind. Jesus, you Spics."

"I'm a Spic," Jophy said; her voice was tremulous, too high.

His flat, prize-fighter's eyes swung up to hers. "You, Ma'am? You're no Spic."

"Yes, I am. Portuguese. So don't you knock us, Barney."

"Go on . . ." He grinned at her slackly, not believing

600

her; his voice sounded very faint now. "A high-class number like you."

"It's true," she said. "My father was a Grand Banks captain. My grandfather was a harpooner. He sailed all over—I bet he sailed to more places than you have. Islands you never—"

His free hand gripped hers then, so hard she gasped.

"Tell about it," he muttered, staring up at her. "Tell—me."

"Manuel Gaspa was his name. He came from Fayal. You know Fayal? In the Azores?"

"Ponta—Delgada," he got the words out.

"He swam out to a whaleship at fifteen, worked his way up from cabin boy to first harpooner." The big hand tightened its grip and she talked faster, leaning down. "They always picked him to go ashore first. On unexplored islands. You know, to see what—" She sheered away in midsentence. "On one island the people were cannibals—they only found out afterward, after they'd sailed away . . ."

"Ah, shit. I'm going," he whispered; his eyes flared. "I'm going out."

"No, Barney. No! Hang on, now—it's just a little farther, just a little bit farther, now . . ."

"How—abou' women."

"The women?—the women are beautiful, they wear chains of flowers in their hair, around their necks, hibiscus and bougainvillea. Their breasts are always free, uncovered, and they wear lava-lavas, open at the side—if a woman wants a certain man she brings him her clan totem and hangs it around his neck and they go off together, for as long as they choose—listen to me, Barney! Look at me! . . ."

She raced on, saying she scarcely knew what, her hand hurting now, hurting quite badly, though his grip was weaker, while the pine woods swept by and the bay lay black as ink beyond the dunes. She remembered to release the tourniquet and set it again, talking incessantly, insanely, knowing only that she must keep his flat gray eyes fixed on hers, hold him fast, keep him from slipping away . . .

"Think we'll get there in time?" Wally whispered once from the driver's seat. "Think we'll make it, Jophy?"

"Shut up!" she hissed at him. "Shut up and drive the God damned car! . . ."

They were waiting for them at the emergency entrance with whole blood and morphine, and rushed him into surgery. She and Wally drove back fast and made another run with two burn cases, not as serious, to learn that Barney—his last name was Diedrick, they told Jophy—had died.

They returned to Turk's Head in hot, brash daylight, to find Doc Glover treating the last of the survivors for superficial cuts. Antoine Rivard's boat had come in with two more seamen, both dead in their life jackets. Jophy helped clean up and then drove home, feeling wobbly and tense, trying not to think of anything at all; unable to get the smell of burned flesh out of the front of her head.

When she saw the gray Buick parked in front of the gate she gave a low sharp cry. Tip was standing on the walk under the whale's ribs, in his shirtsleeves, thumbs hooked in his trouser pockets. It was funny—for a man as active as Tip she so often remembered him waiting for her; just waiting, and then coming toward her with that open, eager expression on his face.

"Tipton!" she said brightly, moving up the walk. "What brings you here?"

"Oh—I was in Providence, making some calls," his eyes had not once left hers, "and I thought I'd run over. Just—see how you are. How are you, honey?"

"Me? I'm fine. Why wouldn't I be? I'm just—"

And to her great surprise she burst into tears, her hand to her head—ran against him and clutched him to her with all her might.

"Oh, Tip," she said. "Oh, Tip. The boys . . . Out on those ships, helpless in the water—can't defend—"

"I know, honey," he was saying. "I just heard."

"Oh Tip, I'm so afraid! Joey's out there, way out there, he's going to be killed, he'll be killed—"

"No, now Jo, now honey. He's going to be all right—we're building the best Navy in the whole world. He'll be all right, honey, let it go, now . . ."

She stopped talking then, sobbed hard and dryly, buried her face against his shirt, smelling the starched cotton, the old familiar odor of him, letting him hold her, rocking gently. So comforting! He was so reassuring. He was there, he was always *there,* when you most needed him, no matter what, solid and unshakable—it was the most important thing on earth, wasn't it? Worth more than anything else. Anything.

"Oh, Tip. Just hold me close. Just hold me close, now. Oh, I am so *glad* you're here . . ."

The landing craft swayed and slewed on the light swell; the tropic sun danced on the water, played over it in lazy streaks and whorls of light. Mac Kleeman, the coxwain, bare-armed and looking even more massive than he was in the puffy blue kapok life jacket and helmet, eased the big horizontal wheel and cut the throttle, holding them in the idling circle of LCVPs. He winked once at Joey Ames, who winked back and looked away. Below them in the well marines were huddled densely, hunch-backed and conspiratorial in their packs and camouflaged helmets, bristling with weapons. Joey could see two men playing a game—the quick ryhthmic pump of hands and then the show of fingers: odds and evens. Behind them more men were climbing down the nets along the side of the *Arcturus* and dropping into the waiting boats like shaggy young birds kicked out of their nest. The pulsing thunder of the bombardment was heavier now; the battle wagons standing off to the south flashed salvo after salvo, and smoke billowed and boiled in soot towers over the island.

"Can't see a thing," Jimmy Pellegrini, the motor-mac, said from the engine box, craning his head, his face cadaverous under the helmet. "Where's the sleepy lagoon?"

"There's nothing sleepy in there, Pelly," Kleeman told him. "What you looking for—sexy broads waltzing around strumming ukuleles, handing out palm wine? Forget it. There's nothing on that rock but palm trees and lizards . . ."

"There are natives there," Joey said suddenly. "My great-grandfather went ashore. Right here."

"Your great-grandfather—!" Kleeman snorted. "Who you shitting, Ames?"

"He *did*—he was a whaler . . ." He'd held it to himself ever since they'd learned they were going to assault Manokela the second day out of Pearl, marveling at the strangeness of it, wishing absurdly he could phone his mother and tell her. Now, bound in the holding pattern, waiting for the word, it suddenly seemed tremendously important to share it with the other two members of the landing boat's crew. "They went everywhere, those days—half the islands hadn't even been *discovered* then. They used to go ashore for water, trade for fresh food."

"Little happy R&R, too, maybe," Mac said, grinning his slow, indulgent grin. "Some of that delicious South Sea island poon tang."

They all laughed, a little nervously, gazing shoreward, and Joey said: "Sure—why not? My mother used to tell me some of his stories. They used to come out to the ship in outriggers with bowls of fruit, beautiiful chains of flowers—"

He broke off. Jensen was snapping signal flags briskly from the command boat; he finished with a tight, circular motion, and the lead LCVP broke out of the circle and headed in toward the destroyer that had taken station at the Line of Departure.

604

"Here we go," Kleeman said. "Let's do it right." He tapped Joey once on the shoulder. "Watch the coral heads, kid."

"Right, Mac." He ran forward easily along the narrow gunwale and took up his boat hook's position on the grating near the ramp. The island was completely obscured now, except for that gaunt, purple twinned peak at its center. Another destroyer was moving in close, pumping five-inch shells low into the beach, and bits of trees and debris whirled lazily in the air and then sank back into the boiling flash-shot smoke. Off to the east the low gauze line of a rain squall ran toward them, incongruous in the dancing sunlight, and a flight of planes floated toward the island, silent in the mounting roar of shellfire, fat as bees.

Crouching by the ramp's leading edge, he felt faintly out of breath, and dizzy, but the sensation was not unpleasant; he was wrapped in a certain prideful exhilaration. They had trained for this moment at Coronado Beach, and again at Kawailoa Point, had run through the drill over and over, in pounding surf and flat, glassy calm, roared at by bull horns and reamed out by the boat commander; and now they were as ready as they would ever be.

The boats had fanned out in line now, rocking and sliding, guiding on the destroyer. *"Take your marks."* There was the same quivering, barely contained impatience he remembered, crouched low on the mark, toes gripping the cool tiles, the still, glassy look of the pool stretching away toward the diving boards. Now here he was, like Grampa Gaspa, poised in the bow of a small boat—holding a boat hook instead of a harpoon, though. Funny . . . Mother would be in the garden now, she'd started a victory garden, everyone had; meat was rationed, so were sugar and rubber and gas, Dad had had to quit driving and he couldn't fly either because he didn't have any priority; he was hopping trains and buses like the old days; running for seats, holding babies for weary young mothers following their husbands to camp . . . The home front. Business booming. everybody loaded with dough, ex-waitresses dragging down $3.75 an hour in the aircraft plants, and Dotty Lamour handing out kisses at war bond rallies, solemn old Glenn Miller a major—a frigging *major!*—leading an Air Force swing band, blaring out "Chattanooga Choo Choo" at the bomber bases while the gunners and bombardiers swung the soft-skinned English girls in a tight-stepping Lindy Hop and the crowd roared.

Uncle Chay had been very funny about it in his last letter. All the comforts of home, he'd put it. Well, that *was* where all the steak and eggs and gas were going—they sure as hell weren't coming out here. Chapin had sent a picture some months before, a glossy shot of him and two generals, immaculate and confident in pinks and visored garrison caps, shaking hands with two fliers in jackets and heavy boots, their faces grimed with powder and sweat. Looking at it he'd had a momentary twinge of regret: he could be a pilot right now, flying one of those big birds high over Europe, streaming vapor trails; only then he wouldn't have this harsh, wine-and-iodine smell of the sea deep in his throat, the magical heave and —

The signal flags fluttering from the DD's yardarm snapped down and away like a magician's palm trick. EXECUTE FIRST WAVE. The diesels roared thickly, the boat surged under his feet. The shore began to draw nearer subtly—there was the wharf, and what looked like a building with silver thatching; then it grew dark, and the squall swept over them with shocking silver force, soaked and chilled him, and blotted out the shore. He glanced aft, watching the marines bent over protecting their weapons. There was no grabassing now, no talk. One man was sick, vomiting an enormous undigested mass of ham and eggs against the boat's side. Joey spotted Kempner, a corporal from Falmouth he'd got to know on the run out from Pearl and once played chess with; he grinned and nodded, but Kempner's eyes stared back at him without expression.

The rain quit, stopped as abruptly as it had come. The shore was near now, quite near. The shelling had lifted, and the smoke broke away into sifting skeins and smears. Sunlight returned in a hot, fierce rush and turned the exposed bits of beach into flickering jade and ivory patterns. Near him the marine platoon sergeant, a tall man with a handlebar mustache and narrow hawk's eyes, was staring at the cockpit. Kleeman, bulking over the wheel, nodded to him and the sergeant roared: "Lock and load! Now lock and load!" and slipped a shiny black magazine into his submachine gun by feel. The faces under the helmet rims all looked strange; all stamped with the same remote rigidity.

A shadow passed by to port. Coral head. Joey snatched up the boat hook and rose up behind the high lip of the ramp. Something skittered toward him along the surface of the water like tiny flying fish, glinting. Startled, realizing all at once what it was, he glared ahead at the smashed tangle of shattered palm trees and cascao and jungle, the roiling yellow dust studded with winking points of light, the curving red wire of tracers. With an effort he tore his eyes away from the silver skittering and saw the shadow looming, like a huge misshapen skull cloaked in seaweed, gave the hand signal for left rudder and felt the boat obey. They slipped past. Something clanged against the ramp near his head and sang away in space, and he ducked involuntarily and said: "Jesus—!"

He was conscious of nothing but the bottom, shoaling rapidly now, the shapes and shadows rushing toward them. A great plume of water rose on their right, towering, and fell back, drenching him. He could hear gunfire now—a fire-cracker popping that swelled into a mountainous coughing roar. Twelve, fifteen feet now, maybe less. Another coral head, ridged like a whale's back looming. He signaled left again. The boat kept heading for it. He signaled again frantically—whirled around in dismay to see Kleeman slumped forward over the wheel, one huge bare arm reaching out and down, clutching at something. There was a cry, and at the same instant they hit with a shock that slammed his helmeted head against the ramp, half-stunned him. Below him marines were tumbling and sprawling into one another in a welter of curses and cries, faint in the uproar.

Hung up. They were hung up. Kleeman hadn't moved. Where the hell was Pelly? He threw down the hook and raced aft along the gunwale, dropped into the cockpit and started to lift Mac away from the wheel, wrestling with the great inert weight of him, shouting, *"Pelly—!"* and at the same moment saw the motor-mac sprawled on the engine box, holding one arm and gazing up at him in blank fright. Jesus. Had to get off. Get off this bastard! Get in to the beach, unload. Nothing else mattered. Nothing.

With one big heave he yanked Kleeman off the wheel and let him down to the grating, felt the blood welling up through the life jacket; straightened up and spun the wheel, threw the clutch into reverse, and ran her up to 2800. The boat shuddered and shook, without moving. No dice. But she was rocking a little, he could feel it in his feet. Hung up on her port side. The rest of the wave was in now, unloading, he could see them on both flanks. All the marines were facing him now. The platoon sergeant had his hand on the ramp catch, was looking at him, questioning.

"No!" he screamed. "You want to drown—? Move to starboard!" They stared at him. *"Right!"* he roared at them, his voice cracking, waving his arm. "All—move—*right!*"

Another towering geyser, and spray swept over them like blown spume. The marines were crowding hard against the starboard gunwale now. He opened her up, full throttle and spun his rudder back again.

"Watch your revs!" Pelly was crying. "You'll burn her up . . ."

"Fuck that!" He eased the wheel over gently. There was a sickly groaning sound along her keel and skeg, and all at once she was free in the water, rocking. He threw in the clutch again and spun the wheel hard. They eased by, bumping the coral, and in a few seconds he felt her chafe lightly forward, the feel he knew.

"Down ramp!" he yelled, gesturing. The sergeant nodded and released the catch, and flat, hard light volleyed into the well. The sergeant had shouted something, and then they were in the shallow water, splashing and wading. One man dropped in a hole, rifle held high, free hand flailing, before some caught him under the shoulders and swung him free. As in a fragment of a dream Joey saw the clumsy raft and Grama easing toward him, her clothes floating high around her, calling to him hoarsely, her face stern and undeniable: *"Salta, Zezinho! Don't be afraid, now . . ."* Then the last marines were gone, moving away up the beach, running hard. One man lay quiet in the shallows, his legs churning feebly.

He ran forward again and began to crank up the ramp in an agony of desperation. The wounded marine had turned in the slick plate of water, was motioning to him with one hand, calling to him; he could see his mouth working in the uproar of small arms fire. He started to run out on the ramp, forced himself to stop. No. Must make room for second wave. *Must* be clear for them. So many coming. He looked away from the wounded man, secured the ramp and went aft, retracted easily, turning, saw the second wave was nearly on him, coming in good order, rocking and dipping. He picked a hole and slipped out through their wash, reached deep water and put the clutch in neutral, huddled over Kleeman.

"Mac," he said tightly. "Mac . . ."

The big man's eyes rolled up at him, all whites. Blood had soaked the jacket through, was sliding thickly on the steel, dripping in long greasy skeins and loops through the grating. At the base of his chest the kapok was blown apart in crimson tufts and tatters. Pelly was still holding his arm hard against his body, his face white and sick with sweat.

"He's bleeding, Joe—you got to stop the bleeding . . ."

"No good! I can't. We've got to get him out there."

He ran for the ship, full throttle, weaving his way through command craft and LCIs and destroyers, the sun sparkling innocently on the morning sea, mocking everything, the roar and thump of gunfire, the smashed palms, the blood. At the *Arctucus* two men dropped down with the litter and they lashed Mac into it while Joey held the boat carefully in place.

"That you, Ames?" Lieutenant Getchell, the assistant boat commander, was calling down to him.

"Yes, sir."

"Your boat seaworthy?"

"Yes, sir."

"No rudder or propeller damage?"

"No, sir. She's answering well."

"Can you form up for fifth wave?"

"I—yes, sir."

Getchell watched him a moment longer. "You're sure, now?"

"Yes, sir—just give me somebody for motor-mac and boat hook. I can handle it."

"Good boy. I'll get you some help."

But now, watching Mac swinging gently far up and away above him, and Pelly riding a cargo net, he felt his eyes fill, and fill again. His hand on the wheel was shaking. He put his head down so they couldn't see him, and looked off toward the beachhead again. He felt unutterably weary, and shaky, bursting with he didn't know what; very near to something.

I did it, he told himself grimly, fighting down his tears, shivering. I did it. Anyway. Grampa Gaspa would be proud of me. He would.

9

The Ozymandias Club was on Half Moon Street, off Green Park. Before the war it had been a fashionable gambling club, but the younger gamblers were now in Burma or Italy or making vast sums of money producing munitions, and the older ones had retired to their country estates and given up gambling for the duration; and so the club had been taken over by a very different clientele. It was a charmingly dilapidated pile with a great curving stairway and badly worn wine-colored carpeting—the kind of threadbare elegance that outdid even Brahmin Boston's shabby dignity. Chapin was delighted with it. The more intellectual high brass came here, as well as certain hungry young economists out of Oxford or Yale or Chicago, and big-time journalists and other movers-and-shakers. The waiters could have been batmen for the Duke of Wellington, and perhaps had been, and there was a talented, epicene young man with a drooping forelock who played Noel Coward tunes and occasionally sang lyrics of his own rather saucy invention in a brittle, bored voice.

Chapin knew from the moment he'd first come here that it was his kind of place. The war was out there, of course, in France and Italy and right here in London (the Germans had stepped up their bombing raids in recent months); but in the Ozymandias Club the war was not the all-engulfing cataclysm it was to the lesser breeds, but a rather unpleasant hiatus, a prelude to the unfolding of momentous new forces. The talk here was not over whether the gas and ammunition ought to go to Montgomery or Patton or if there should be a diversionary landing in the Balkans, but the gleaming new postwar world that would emerge after the echoes of the final gunshot had died away—and the shape it would take.

Any number could play. Lorenzo McCallum, one of the key planners of the Normandy landings, was often there, and C. V. Headley from the British War Ministry, and a poet-diplomat named Levasseur who was said to be the real force behind de Gaulle. Chapin had been surprised to run into Margo Manwaring, who was heading up some hush-hush mission with the OWI; her table was always the liveliest—she drew controversy around her like a gleaming steel magnet. Chapin, a scarcely tasted drink in his hand, would listen to them all, stirred with a rare excitement. *These* were the people who would remake the world after Armageddon, not the Churchills or the Roosevelts —for the simple reason that they wrote the reports and recommendations those harried giants would read too quickly and act upon. The musty, smoke-webbed air in the Ozymandias Club was heavy with power.

"It is —priceless!" Laszlo Tzechenyi was saying tonight with his nervous laugh. "It is the first time in recorded history that a military strategy has become the perfect instrument of sound political theory." He was a swarthy man with the eyes of a betrayed mesiah. High up on some British propaganda branch, he was often given to fantastic postulations. "Our carpet bombing will transform Bismarck's industrial Moloch into a wasteland—which is precisely what should be done. A bucolic buffer-zone, no longer a menace to Europe or the world. I salute you, Colonel Hines!"

"Ames," Chapin murmured, and Margo, looking

614

handsome and martial in her blue uniform and her gleaming gold helmet of hair, laughed.

"Absurd," Jamey Culloden retorted. He was a scholarly, sour man with a bony face—a Lincoln without a sense of humor—and black, wiry hair. He was on loan from the Administration, where he'd been one of FDR's top economic advisers. "It will not happen."

"It is happening right now!"

"It will never happen because it cannot be allowed to happen." Culloden squinted dourly at Tzechenyi. "You want to dismantle the most efficient industrial complex the modern world has ever known? A manifest absurdity. No, what *will* happen is that Europe will go Communist to a man—and *you* people are doing it." He jabbed a blunt, dirty-nailed finger at Chapin. "You're wiping out the middle class far more effectively than the run-away inflation of the Twenties ever did."

From behind them in the Palace Gardens the air raid sirens began their soaring clamor, and east of the city gunfire returned a rhythmic *bump-ump-ump-ump*.

"Oh, not again," Margo said, and rolled her eyes. "Don't those idiots *ever* take the night off?"

"Rest assured," Chapin said to Culloden, "the vast majority of our bombs are falling on the poor. We're wiping out the proletariat at a far faster rate."

Jamey scowled in fine Scottish disapproval. "Be as facetious as you like. We'll find a social and economic vacuum when we get in there comparable to the devastation of the Thirty Years' War. There will *be* no stability. Europe will become one huge Soviet satellite, and we'll be left trying to woo South America."

"Precious little fear of that, I daresay." This was Broughley, who'd been a Labor MP and now did something immensely mysterious for MI-6. "After two centuries of militarism—*and* authoritarian conditioning —fascism in one form or another will continue to be the order of the day. Different trappings, but the same inexorable direction." His clear blue eyes rested on Chapin, twinkling. "You chaps too, perhaps."

The sirens had quit. Anti-aircraft batteries opened up nearer and nearer, like some cleverly staged heightening of effect, and above it now the pulsing drone of the planes. Tit for tat. Chapin felt himself smile; that breath-caught excitement had begun again, a fusing of the argument and the approaching raid—a curious intoxication that actually made him want to jig around the room, scream insults and obscenities at these assured, imperturbable souls, shock them half to death.

"No," he said aloud. "We will stay this time."

"Nonsense!" Tzechenyi glared at him with his liquid, holy eyes. "You will throw away all your winnings, like the paranoid gamblers you are . . ."

They could hear the thump of bombs now, and nearer batteries began firing suddenly, defined and harsh.

"No," Chapin repeated, "we will stay. We'll garrison Western Europe for a generation, perhaps indefinitely. Our satellite, not Uncle Joe's."

"Preposterous!"

"And the irony of it is that Hitler will have succeeded where Teddy Roosevelt and all the other American Century hucksters failed."

The bombers were overhead now in a deepening thunder, and there came another rush of explosions. Much nearer.

"Now we play German roulette," Margo said, and finished her drink in a gulp. Her cold hard eyes met Chapin's, and they laughed in unison. Margo was like him in so many ways. They'd gone to bed together several times over the past weeks and enjoyed themselves hugely; there was a lazy voracity in her that complemented his own thwarted hunger for violence. There were times when they understood each other perfectly . . .

Now he found himself staring at the wine-red blackout curtains, which trembled and rippled with concussion. I broke off too soon, he thought, with that visceral tug which comes with sudden revelation. I should have taken the idea further. The American Army will stay this time. Yes. And it will be forced to stay on and on—if only because a rebuilt German industrial plant will be even more enticing to the Russians . . . What was that tired British line about Yanks? Overpaid, overfed, oversexed, and over here. Right! A huge, perpetual occupation force—whose members would want to put all that accumulated overseas pay to work, keep pace with the inevitable inflation . . . What a vast market for mutual funds!

The idea caught him totally then. Why, there'd even be a built-in system for sales and marketing; field grade officers first, who would sell or tell their associates, put pressure on the lower ranks; in time they'd even reach the leading lights of the local population and turn them, too, into investors. A perfect chain of selling and control! Excited, he fought to clear his head in the mounting racket of bombs. Of course a lot of European countries had regulations prohibiting the licensing and sale of American securities, but that could be got around, everything in this world could be got around in time, given shrewd legal planning—he'd get Horace Van Diemen to look into that; and in any event the garrisons themselves would certainly be considered *American* soil . . . That was it! He'd have the jump on all the others. While they hemmed and hawed about reconversion and fought over the first rush of postwar manufacturing, he'd be using the whole damn U.S. Army to sell mutuals—a virtual captive audience, tailor-made for exploitation. Macomah would cover the world, like that old Sherwin-Williams paint ad, dripping its rain of—

There came now, over the deafening uproar of explosions and gunfire, a thin, high whistle that swelled to a fierce, descending shriek. His eyes met Margo's again—a glance not so much of fear but of a terribly heightened awareness. Then he kicked back his chair and plunged under the table.

The detonation was immense—followed by the brittle icicle sounds of shattering glass. The room heaved like a ship's deck uplifted, fell away again. The lights went out. Someone screamed—a man's voice, definitely—and the rumbling crepitation bowled on through the night, fading, mingling with the thunder of other bombs falling. The lights came on again, flickering and pale.

Chapin got to his feet. All sights, all sounds seemed curiously far away, inconsequential. His ears were ringing, and he'd bumped his head somehow, above one eye. Tzechenyi was leaning toward him over the table like an outraged apostle, screaming, "—can't you get those *bombers,* Hines!" And he felt himself smile strangely. Broughley was dusting off his sleeves with an air of fussy irritation, his face brick red. Culloden was nowhere to be seen. Across the table Margo was still sitting tightly, smiling at him in bright defiance; she still had her empty glass in her hand. He laughed then—a completely nervous inhalation of air. For a bad moment he was afraid he wouldn't be able to stop. Then he could, and he knew he was all right.

A British major was sitting on the floor several feet away, holding a napkin to his neck, the white linen staining a brighter red than the General Staff tabs on his collar. For the first time in years Chapin thought of Walter Diehl lying dead under the big desk, and Miss Hannegan cradling his head, trying to stop the gush of blood.

He walked carefully around the table. "Let's go on," he said to Margo as coolly as he could manage. "This place has outlived its usefulness this evening."

Outside the night was alive with fires. Three doors down, a building had been shorn away, open rooms like a third-rate designer's stage set, above a great pile of rubble where the Air Raid Rescue teams struggled in the fitful glare to release someone. They were moving with unhurried, deft precision: director and actors blocking the scene. The air was foul with cordite and old plaster and burning.

"I certainly hope that fool Monty gets across the Rhine and into Germany," Margo was saying. "That one was entirely too close."

"Wasn't it." Her arm beneath his hand seemed perfectly steady. "Well, there'll be more to worry about than bombing raids if what Brookhouse was telling me is—"

He stopped abruptly, almost pulling Margo off-balance. Directly in front of him lay an American sailor's hat, startlingly white, with its sides curled down in a particularly salty way; sitting all by itself in a puddle of water and pulverized glass that glittered like diamond dust in the glow of the fires.

"What on earth's the matter?" Margo demanded.

"Sailor's hat," he said.

"I can see it."

"My nephew's in the Navy."

"Oh. That boy of Josephine's?"

"Yes. In the Pacific."

"Dear high-wire Jophy," Margo said, and her laughter uncoiled flatly in the raucous London night. "Just how *is* she, these days?"

". . . She's gone back to Tip," he said suddenly. "Back living with him again."

"Tip! But why? What's he got for her? Or has he changed?"

"No. He hasn't changed."

He'd been amazed when Jophy had written him about it; amazed and deeply angered, as if his pet Degas had been stolen by a second-story man. It made no sense, no sense at all! It had been the boy—the boy and the war. War drew families back together, tightened the bonds; he'd seen it. Only Jophy had never seemed to need rot like that: she was beyond obvious conventions, common ties . . .

But the boy *was* special. Out there in the islands now, running leathernecks in to the beaches, under fire. My son. He should have been my son—

"God, how she'd love all this!" Margo flung her free hand out to embrace the gutted buildings, the hurrying figures, the leaping, savage light of the fires. "Wouldn't she adore it?"

"No. She'd hate it. Every minute of it."

Margo glanced at him sharply. "But she was the great one for all that crazy high-diving. Helling around, picking fights with gangsters . . ."

"That's—that's something else entirely. It's not the same," he finished coldly. "She's not like us . . . She cares."

Still watching him she laughed. "Well—still a certain craving there, is it? Do I read you, Chay?"

He said nothing; averted his eyes from the sailor's hat, so white lying there on the stone.

The train racketed along, jolting wildly on the untended roadbed. What would the railroads do without a war every twenty years to bail them out? Tip smiled faintly, watching the river unreeling its pearl-and-umber plate in the early spring sunshine, the trees in first leaf rushing low along its banks. Like old times, he thought; riding the locals through the snug little towns, watching the cars and trucks at the level crossings. The stale, musty odor of coal dust and sweat and ancient plush clung to the air around him like bars; he started to sneeze and stifled it deftly by rubbing his forefinger back and forth under his nose.

Beside him Jack Darcey was asleep. Robbed of the piercing, testing flicker of the green eyes, his face looked drawn and pasty, the vertical lines plowing his long cheek. The once fiery red hair had turned sandy and mottled, and retreated to a narrow scalp-lock high on his temples. Leaving Pittsfield he'd been talking to a soldier in the seat across the aisle, but an argument had arisen over the merits of artillery in combat, and the soldier had got angry and stomped off to the toilet and then buried himself in a copy of *Life*. Jack was always quarreling with people now—a gnawing irascibility he either couldn't or didn't want to check; he seemed to have some deep-seated need to scourge himself and everyone else within reach. Even the triumphant conclusion to the war in Europe hadn't cheered him up any. He'd antagonized Alan Lothrop down in Hartford and blown a big sale, and after that he'd got in a shouting match with imperturbable Henry Gray in Montpelier over nothing at all. Tip had read him off royally, told him he'd have to quit drinking or he'd fire him. Shocked and hurt, Jack had gone on the wagon that winter, but it hadn't made much difference. Tip didn't know what to do with him. He'd have to find some way to straighten him out—he'd never carried a salesman before and he wasn't going to start now. Not even a man he cared for—not even Jack.

He sighed and picked up the magazine with the sheet of stationery from the Highland Inn on top.

It's really a handsome house, he wrote in the jerky, forward-slanting hand the family had always kidded him about ("chicken-track hieroglyphic," Tessa called it), now rendered even more indecipherable by the jarring rhythm of the train. *Not in the class of your Grandaunt Serena's palace, of course, but it's got a pretty little entrance with boric or laconic columns or whatever you call 'em, and a portico like a small Greek temple (I'll let you fill in the architectural terminology). The BIG news is that Mother loved it on sight. I was afraid to show it to her really, you know how she is about first impressions, she either loves something to a passion or takes a death-hate to it for the rest of time. But I could tell the way she walked around the rooms—her eyes had that shine to them. You know. Of course it needs work. But it was a steal at the price.*

What do you think of that? A house on Beacon Hill!!! Your room is on the fourth floor, with your own sitting room and bath. There's even a partial view of the river. Can't wait till you see it. It's something I've dreamed about for 40 years. Well, almost. And now we've got it.

Movement in the far scan of his vision disturbed him. He looked up, saw the big bomber descending, headed for Westover Field, sinking gently through the pearl gray air. Watching the sunlight flashing on the gun blisters, the sleek aluminum fuselage, he thought of the kids inside who'd soon be over Japan, crouching at those guns, and bit hard at a hangnail.

He had a sense of guilt about this war that he'd never felt with the first one. The fact that it had brought Jophy back to him only deepened the crazy irony of it. Now and then he'd have the sense that he'd taken unfair advantage of her again (as he had that snowy March night when he'd proposed to her) —distraught, her jeans smeared with men's blood, trembling with exhaustion, a prey to dread. If it hadn't been for the war—this immeasurable agony that had killed or maimed so many millions and put their own son in jeopardy—would she have gripped him hard to her, crying his name? He honestly didn't know—he was just quietly, abidingly grateful; he accepted and returned her love, held it close, like some priceless gem that might be taken from him at any moment. Bad things could bring good, then, he'd find himself thinking in some sweat-soaked bus depot in Georgia, sharing a bench with two paratroopers and a miserably pregnant girl; maybe there *was* a mysterious rhyme and reason, after all . . .

That's great, your making coxwain, he wrote still more rapidly, *now you're captain of your own boat. Mother was so pleased. A boathandler, like his Grampa, she said. Blood will tell, she said, as though you couldn't guess, eh? Well, it's been a long, hard haul, son, and no one can imagine all you've been going through out there, but it's going to be over soon, now that Germany's quit the Japs will see the writing*

622

on the wall and throw in the sponge. Always the incurable optimist, I know, I can hear you saying it, but what the hell, that's better than always looking on the dark side. Which is always dark enough. Hey, it's going to be one great day when we're all together in one

"Spring*field*, Spring*field*!" Fat Freddy Hanlon the conductor called, hurrying down the aisle; he winked at Tip, who winked back and slid the letter into his brief case. Jack Darcey came awake with a start and jumped to his feet, reached up to the rack for his bag and then lowered his arm, rubbing it vigorously.

"Gone to sleep again. Pins and needles." He reached up with the other arm and swung the heavy Gladstone down to the aisle, went into a sharp fit of coughing.

"You ought to quit smoking," Tip told him.

"You ought to quit criticizing." Jack shrugged himself loose in his rumpled clothes. "All ashore that's going ashore. God, I wish I had a dime for every train I've ridden in. I'd be a trillionaire."

Union Station looked more forlorn than ever; battered, dirty depot at the raggedy end of a war. The last cab pulled out, jammed with four occupants sharing the ride; there were no others. They stood around a few moments and Tip said, "What the hell, let's walk it. Nice spring afternoon like this. You game?"

Beside him Jack seemed to hesitate. He coughed again harshly; his face was slick with sweat.

"You all right?" Tip said.

"Course I'm all right. Never better." He caught up his bag and stepped out smartly. "All I need is seven shots of red-eye and I can lick my weight in leprechauns . . . Just horsing around," he said, glaring at Tip. "You know me, Al."

"Yeah, I know you, all right."

The papers were full of the surrender. Tip grabbed up a *Republican* and examined the German generals sitting at the table, looking bald and disheveled and diffident, a far cry from the visor-shaded, rock-hard

623

faces he remembered from the fall of France, or the first months of the invasion of Russia. He thought of that afternoon in Chicago, with the Paris headlines, and Maury's face sullen and wrathful. Now they'd found those awful camps, terrible beyond any reckoning, the bodies stacked like ragtag cordwood, the empty shoes of children, and hollow-faced skeletons who gazed out at the camera in stunned apathy; men and women they'd stripped of all dignity, or tortured out of life itself. Human beings. The newsreels had shocked him profoundly—more than anything else in his life. It was a death-fantasy below savagery, below vengeance, even below the primeval slime—for this had been designed by a cold, utterly cruel intelligence . . . Maybe Chapin was right, after all, and human history wasn't any more than a reptilian grapple for power: the imposing of will, the inflicting of pain, on the weak and vulnerable. Maybe that's all it was . . . but he would never believe it.

"How the mighty have fallen," he said aloud now, looking at the photos.

"What we should have done last time," Jack muttered. "Gone on in there and taken the place apart, plank by plank. Should have—" He fell silent suddenly.

"Too bad Franklin D. couldn't have been around for it," Tip said.

"Roosevelt! You hated his guts."

"Yeah, I thought he was a stuffed-shirt and a tyrant. But I wish he could have seen this." The thought saddened him obscurely and he jammed the newspaper into the side pocket of his jacket, walking rapidly uphill now, trying to think about the next day.

"What you got lined up for tomorrow, Jackson? You want to hit Andy Phillips first thing?"

Jack wasn't beside him. He turned. Darcey had stopped stock still, was staring at him—a stark, glassy look, white in its intensity.

"Jack," he said softly, "you know, you don't look—"

Darcey made a funny sound deep in his throat and lurched forward, then doubled over and fell full length on the sidewalk, his bag spilling off into the gutter. Tip bent over him swiftly, wrenched open his tie and collar. Jack's eyes opened, closed again, again opened; his face was dead white now, sweat was pouring over it. He started feebly to move his legs, kept trying to gather them under him.

Tip said: "Don't move, Jack. You're going to be all right."

"I—"

"Don't move, now. I'll get you a ride."

"What's the matter?" A voice behind him; a passer-by bending down.

"He's sick." Tip looked off down the street, saw the bulky blue serge figure approaching. "Hey!" He waved. "Get an ambulance!" Jack was trying to get to his feet again—a clumsy, somnambulistic movement —and Tip held him firmly by the shoulder. "Stay quiet, Jack. *You've got to stay still.*" The cop was running to the call box on the corner.

Jack gripped his chest with his hand. He was on his back now, his head on the dirty concrete, looking up into the sunlight. "Can't—get my—breath," he said, straining.

"Take it easy, now." Tip pulled off his jacket and wadded it up and eased it under Jack's head while Darcey's bright green eyes watched him.

"Told you—shouldn't have got—off the booze," he gasped. But his lips wouldn't turn up in even the ghost of a smile.

"Very funny. You'll be okay now."

People had gathered around, six or seven; they were talking, making suggestions but Tip didn't hear any of them. The cop had completed his call and was hurrying over to them.

"No wonder—they—wouldn't take me. This time. Huh?"

"Don't talk, Jack," he said, watching his friend's face, the agonized effort to breathe, feeling deeply afraid. "Just rest."

"Ah, Tip-O. What's—matter? Hate—let you down like this . . ."

"Don't be ridiculous. Just relax, now."

"Went—far's I could go. Too many trains . . . Can't —cut it—any more."

"Jack—"

His thin, straining body contorted in a single violent lurch, and he fell limply back. Tip, holding him, wiping his sweaty face, knew long before the ambulance got there that he was dead.

IV

THE CLOSE

1

The snow fell almost reluctantly, as though it knew it was meant to be only the gentlest of benisons. In the glimmer of the hooded black-iron streetlamps it glittered like blown crystals, then shaded off whitely in the darkness. The fine brick façades with their classic white portals looked as if they had been there forever; the candles ranged in their elegant long windows flickered and gleamed: a stately peace. From down on Mount Vernon Street there came the sound of caroling, and another group, fainter, was singing somewhere over on Pinckney. Sightseers strolling, pausing to admire a particularly beautiful arrangement of candles and wreaths or tiny stained-glass nativity, were amiable, quietly celebratory—it seemed to Tip that people were more congenial than they had ever been on this first, joyful Christmas Eve after the war.

The band trooped up the stone steps of Spencer Bewlett's lordly façade on Louisburg Square and ranged themselves with care, and Tip, standing below in the crowd with Tessa and Joey, could hear the murmurs around him: "—Bellringers . . . it's the *bell*-ringers . . ." Serena, a white gossamer cashmere scarf over her head, said something and the rest of the band raised their brass hand bells alertly, gripping the stout leather straps, awaiting her direction: Jophy, and Meg Hutchings, and Arthur Speares, who taught musical composition over at Harvard, and two women whose names Tip had already forgotten; and Chapin, with the bigger brass bells. Serena nodded once, and the old melody burst on the frosty still air, piercing and pure, utterly unlike any other sound; a glorious, festive pealing.

> " . . . *peace on earth, and mercy mild—*
> *God and sinner reconciled . . ."*

The applause was restrained, as though the dense crowd of listeners was almost afraid to intrude on its ethereal purity.

Tessa said: "Doesn't Mother look fabulous?"

"Yes, she does." Tip smiled softly. Kids threw that word around these days without caring what it meant, but that *was* exactly how she looked—her hair gleaming like moon jet in the snow, her eyes expectant and merry. He knew she was enjoying herself hugely.

"If there's a bell ringing somewhere, Mother'll be in on it," Joey said, and the three of them laughed together.

They played three more carols. Jophy apparently made a mistake in "Joy to the World," though Tip hadn't caught it, because she made a face and rolled her eyes, and Serena smiled at her. They'd only had five rehearsals with the full band, which struck him as miraculous, the way they had to time their strokes with that one quick flip of the leather straps. The applause was heavier now. Spenser Bewlett came out, impeccable in evening jacket and pearl studs, and thanked them, asked them in for a spot of cheer.

"Oh, we can't, Bew," Serena told him, laughing. "We've three more places to ring, and then we're having open house ourselves—I've got my tribe all together for the first time since Pearl Harbor . . ."

They rang across the Square at the Storrells', and ended up on Mt. Vernon Street at the magnificent Bulfinch mansion of Marcia Hurlbutt, the formidable grande dame of the Hill—climax to the time honored ritual Serena and Abigail Crownley and Meg Hutchings had started thirty-eight years before; and the crowd followed them eagerly, swelling, drawn by the bells' shivery resonance. They concluded as always with "Adeste Fideles," and the crowd burst into song with the final chorus. The applause and cheers were tumultuous now. Serena blew kisses to them, and Tip saw Chapin hug Jophy and then raise the big, gleaming brass bells high above his head.

After that they plodded back through the silent snow to Beacon Street, where the first guests had already begun to drift in. The crystal chandeliers in Serena's great double living room were lighted, and firelight from the two black marble hearths fickered along the dove walls. The long refectory table held Narragansett oysters on the half shell, and a mound of Beluga caviar glistening in a cut-glass bowl; there was a huge rib roast, and a Virginia ham studded neatly with cloves, there were candied yams in orange cups and hors d'oeuvres cut into fanciful shapes, a rich black plum pudding and dainty little chess tarts. Serena's silver—George III, was it?—shone against heavy white damask. At the other end of the living room the massive marble-topped table held eighteen-year-old brandy, Bernkastler Riesling Chapin had brought back from Germany, and the traditional Joseph Peabody punch, fuscous and potent in the great Lowetoft bowl. The tree, perfectly symmetrical and so tall it nearly reached the fourteen-foot ceiling, glowed and glittered; candles burned on its boughs among the fine old ornaments. Holly, ranged on the mantles, gleamed the dark warm green of Christmas.

"You've pulled out all the stops, Aunt," Tip told her.

"And why not?" She'd got herself up grandly for the occasion, in a long deep burgundy velvet gown with a high neck; her hair, now pure white, was piled high and close to her head, and the great Aldridge emerald sparkled and glittered at her throat. "You're a stormy, heterogeneous crew—but you're the only one I've got!"

"But are we really worthy of all this?" he couldn't help teasing her. *"Beluga* caviar! . . ."

"The fatted calf." She gave her single high burst of a laugh. "Après tout, all the prodigals are back under my wing."

"Not to mention those of us who stayed home and minded the store."

She looked at him. "You sound a bit envious, Tipton."

"I am. A little. I wish Mother were here for this evening."

Serena's eyes tightened. "Yes. Lottie loved these celebrations almost as much as I do."

"True," he answered. "But in a different way."

Their eyes met, clashed once like blades, and broke away. "How perceptive you are at times, Tipton." He said nothing and she went on, "May I ask you something?"

"Your wish is my command, Aunt."

"No, seriously. Would you keep an eye on things? Who's coming and going? This is Thompson's first year at this. I'm afraid he won't be as firm as he ought to be. I miss Hynes so." Her mouth drew down. "We had trouble last year. Some rowdies got in at the Martineaus' and they had to call Officer Callahan, and at Spencer Bewlett's some things were actually stolen."

"Oh, but Chapin'll protect us. Won't he?"

"Now be serious. It isn't the way it used to be on the Hill."

"Nothing is," he said.

"People knew their place then, knew where they weren't wanted." She looked up at the Copley portrait of Great-Grandfather Joshua.

He smiled very faintly. "They've had a taste of grandeur, Serena. They've been plucked out of slums and cornfields. We've taught them how to build ships, ferry planes all over the world . . . even how to die in strange places. Now they feel important—they feel there's no place they can't go, nowhere they're not wanted."

"Well, I don't like it!" she laughed. Jophy and Joey came up to them then, holding glasses of punch, and Serena put her arm around Jophy and said: "What do you think of my new bellringer? Didn't she do wonderfully?"

Jophy threw back her head; her hair was wound in a high coronet. She was still excited from the ringing. She was tall and regal in the long crimson silk dress which crossed over her breasts and one shoulder; her arms were bare. She wore no jewelry except the pearl earrings Tip had given her for her birthday the year before.

"A little shaky here and there," she laughed.

"Oh, but the rest of us have been at it for years and years, dear. Meg played with the first bellringers this country ever had—the old Philomela." Serena turned to Joey: "What's this I hear about you going abroad? Haven't you had enough of foreign shores?"

He gave her his mother's radiant smile. "Paris, Auntie, Paris! Uncle Chapin's going to let me have his apartment in Montparnasse."

Tip was conscious of a stab of irritation. "You can have your own place, you know," he said.

Jophy was watching him with a thoughtful frown.

"But it's a real atelier, Dad," Joey was saying, "with a fabulous skylight and a linen shade you can raise and lower like a sail—and a view of the Luxembourg Gardens . . ."

"You're going to let him go, Josefina?" Serena asked.

Jophy turned to her in amazement. "I? *I* tell Joey what he should or shouldn't do? He's a man, he's been to war . . ." Her eyes flashed at Serena, a look he couldn't entirely fathom. "He knows what he wants to do with himself."

"Well, of course," his grandaunt said, a touch cautiously. "Though there are the graduate degrees. They could come in handy in the—"

"No more *school!*" Joey's face was animate with comic outrage, a merry defiance so like his mother's at that moment that Tip blinked. "Now I've got to paint, just go off somewhere and *paint*—!" Some of his friends had come in and he broke away then, calling softly, "No more gray old theories, Auntie—'green alone life's golden tree!' "

"Exactly like his Ma*ma*," Serena laughed, accenting the last syllable, "the same headlong spirit . . . He's certainly your son, Josefina!"

"He's his own man," she answered. "He will go his own way."

The guests were arriving in force now, and the two women went forward to greet them while Tip sipped gingerly at the heady rum punch and watched them, marveling. Serena's recent interest in Jophy mystified him. True, Abigail Crownley's death had left a vacancy in the Mt. Vernon Bellringers band, but why should Serena have picked Jo, after nearly twenty-five years of not-so-veiled intimations that she "wouldn't quite do" in her haughty Brahmin world? Maybe it was time; maybe it was merely another instance of Tipton's Law: New Money (his, with the meteoric rise of a renascent Macomah Fund) winning the gracious (if grudging) acceptance of Old. In all truth his aunt's overtures to Jophy had only begun after he'd bought the house three blocks away on Chestnut Street. His resources could never hope to equal Serena's (and therefore Chapin's); and Jophy remained— God be praised!—an unregenerate Portuguese; yet that natural elegance and vivacity, her sheer unconventional charm, provided ballast enough to offset any social bias—and he *was* Chapin's brother, for all their divergent lives and hot hostilities . . . And just possibly, too (though this thought he knew might be the effect of the punch, the propitiatory tenor of this hallowed evening and the war's end)—just possibly his aunt's action was simply old age seeking the animal comfort of family solidarity: bygones could indeed become bygones as the shadows lengthened. Anyway, it was nice to think so . . .

The rooms were quite full now. There were contemporaries of his aunt's in trailing ancient Worth gowns, and velvet neckbands and powdered faces; middle-aged friends of Chapin's in tuxedos and maroon cummerbunds; classmates of Joey's, several still in uniform, their girls in gay woolen dresses with very high heels, looking flushed and happy from the cold. From across the room Tessa caught his eye, promptly disengaged herself from a group of young people and came over to him, said:

"Merry Christmas Eve, Dad! And a buffalo nickel for *your* thoughts . . ."

She had turned into a lovely, self-possessed young women, her earnest practicality leavened with a quiet merriment; she had come up to Boston often during the war and stayed at the apartment, and the two of them had had some fun times. Together they watched Chapin bantering with Joey while Jophy laughed at them both and Serena, her fine eyes narrowed, smiled and nodded approval.

"Well—there they all are!" Tessa wrinkled her short straight nose and stuck out her lower lip, the way he always had; and they winked at each other and laughed, as if at a very old joke, both of them thinking about the rest of the family—that quartet that was so much more clever and imaginative than they were. Tip hugged her to him once, let her go. His Tessa. She was popular enough, there were lots of boys hanging around, he'd noticed that—but unlike Joey she wanted to take her time, threading her own way through the long labyrinth. Like Tip she was drawn to tangibles—what could be held in the hand and fashioned—to the earth itself; flowers and trees and all growing things. Summers she worked for a local horticulturist, studied botany and landscape gardening in college, and spent hours at the Arboretum. She designed and built gardens in restful arrangements of fern and trillium and laurel, rocks and water; wanted to make little green corners here and there, she said . . .

A season of endings, new beginnings. Tip chatted for a while with Gus Lawring, fatter and quite bald, who had apparently forgiven his brother over the years for the loss of his considerable fortune—a loss that in any case the providential death of an immensely wealthy uncle nicely remedied. He let Lawring talk, and watched Joey joking with his new girl, an ebullient, sexy little brunette he'd met at college that fall. In spite of his high spirits Joey seemed steadier and more withdrawn, as though the war had taught him things he didn't want anyone to know he knew. All those islands, those hell-shot landings . . .

He'd come home one windy night in October, had walked in with that easy, rolling swagger of the sailor, his coxswain's crows riding high on his sleeves, as if stepping into a swell-front pile on Beacon Hill were the most natural thing in the world. The new house hadn't seemed to mean very much to him—his reaction had hurt Tip at the time, though he'd brushed it aside in his joyful relief to have him home. The boy had accepted a huge Scotch and kept them up all night long, talking of atolls and monsoons and tropic sunrises while Jophy sat still as marble and listened, her lips parted and her eyes dark with memory, that old, smoldering fascination . . . Just before morning he'd given his mother a tiny, beautifully carved outrigger made from some exotic wood, and a rare shell he'd picked up on Manokela. The next morning he'd hung his uniform at the back of his closet and never put it on again.

Chapin on the other hand had worn his for some time after he'd returned. It facilitated matters greatly, he said. He had urgent business in Washington, he was always flying somewhere—there seemed to be a C-47 or a bomber available to him every time he snapped his fingers. He was constantly on the phone to Bonn or Darmstadt, he was full of plans and schemes he didn't want to talk about just yet, though Tip had a pretty good idea of what was in the wind. Chapin's attitude seemed more cavalier than ever. The war hadn't changed him at all; it had only confirmed him more deeply in his cool appraisal of the working of this world . . . War didn't change anybody, it seemed: it only accentuated attitudes already held.

Tip sighed. In his own naiveté he'd expected to return to pre-war rhythms, but he was wrong. Everything would change now: Joey off to Europe and some kind of bohemian life, Jophy increasingly involved in her battles with those suspect real estate speculators down at Turk's Head—and now and then with Serena's bustling Boston scene. And his own business world would change mightily too, he could feel it— there was that inexorable groundswell toward huge, impersonal forces, international combinations . . .

As though to personalize the transformation, Bradford Elwell was now standing in front of him—the square, self-important face, smiling in guarded bonhomie. From beyond the windows came the sound of caroling.

"Well—Tipton Ames." He extended his hand and Tip took it. Why not? Peace on earth, goodwill toward men. "Chay tells me you've bought a place over on Chestnut."

"That's right."

"The old Liversey home." He nodded, as though confirming something significant, looked off around the crowded, convivial room. "Glorious evening, isn't it?"

"Yes. It's been a long time coming."

"That your boy over there, talking to young Storrell?"

"Yes, that's Joe."

"My boy Tom was in the Navy, too. Gunnery officer on a tin can." His cold little eyes rolled around to Tip's. "Let's have lunch at the club some day soon."

"Fine—let's do that." By *the club* Elwell of course meant the Somerset, or perhaps the Union, neither of which Tip had been asked to join, and probably never would be, given the Bostonian pattern of things. Chapin had never offered to sponsor him, and Tip would cheerfully have put his hand in a blowtorch before he would broach the subject; it was another of the games they played . . . He scowled at himself in irritation. Why should it matter so much? What did matter was that Macomah was flying high, one of the three leading mutuals in the country—and Brad Elwell, that erstwhile Crimson gridiron stalwart, was vegetating in his father's one-horse brokerage office on Federal Street. Perhaps it was an olive branch of sorts: why not take it? This was certainly no night to rake up—

He became conscious of a small commotion at the hall entrance, and turned his head. A man stepped into the room, his overcoat hanging open and a yellow woolen scarf flung back over one shoulder. Then in the next second Thompson appeared, ineffectual and flustered, plucking at the man's elbow and speaking inconsistently. Tip threaded his way deftly through the crowd to hear Thompson saying, "I'm sorry, sir—I *must* ask you to leave . . ."

"Nonsense, nonsense!" the intruder was saying, pulling away. "Miss Aldridge will see *me*—no fear of that!"

"May I help you?" Tip said crisply.

The man's eyes fastened on him then. "Why yes, you can—you certainly can . . ." Tip guessed he was about his aunt's age, but he looked much older; a slender, worn face that you would have called handsome if it weren't for the supercilious curl at the corners of his mouth, the disdainful impatience in the

638

pale blue eyes. The coat was old and worn, his shirt frayed, his hair overlong and damp with melted snow. He was not drunk. Tip felt he'd seen him somewhere, maybe on the road.

"I'm looking for Miss Serena Aldridge," the old gentleman said, his tone both imperious and deferential. He smiled in a resentful but assured attempt to exert charm, revealing discolored teeth. "This *is* her home, isn't it?"

"Yes, it is. Who—"

"For old times sake—just a brief visit in the spirit of the Yuletide season . . . Serena!" he called, looking past Tip then, gesturing with a bony hand. "I say, Serena!"

She had turned, squinting at him—then her face broke into the strangest mélange of astonishment and fear and anger.

"Lyman!" she exclaimed softly, and came forward. And at the same instant Tip recognized his father. "Well . . . What a—what a *surprise* . . ."

Serena put out her hand but he ignored it and embraced her, held her a full moment while the guests gave way around them, watching the scene with indulgent, faintly mystified expressions. And now, tense with emotion, Tip looked across the room and saw Chapin's face frozen in the old, pained, tremulous uncertainty—then his brother had forced his way rudely through the press and flung his arms around the old man.

"*Dad,*" he was saying, his voice oddly muffled, his mouth working, "oh Dad, I'm so—so glad . . . I've had people looking for you, trying to find you for years. How wonderful!"

Tip averted his gaze, saw Serena watching him; he could tell what she was thinking. The rest of the room was a discordant blur. Before he could move she had taken his arm and drawn him toward Lyman Ames and was saying, "And here is Tipton! He's here, with

639

his whole family," and his father was looking at him beseechingly now, murmuring, "Well, Tipton, Tipton," his worn, furrowed face actually streaked with tears, and holding out his hands.

"My boy," his father said. "How are you . . ."

"Hello, Father."

He could not take the proferred hand. He tried to, and he could not. He felt tears welling up in his own eyes, and it enraged him. He saw only his mother then, bent over her sewing under the lamp, hanging out washing in the bitter Berkshire wind, talking to Luther Finch in that frightened, self-effacing way; all those years on years of clerking and peddling and counting change on the kitchen table after supper, that blind tunnel of worry and naked fear—and his heart hardened inside him like green wood in fire. And now to drop in like this on Christmas Eve, all smiles and tears and Christian forgiveness—no! They could hug and slobber over each other all they wanted, but he would not. He would not! There *were* things that were unforgivable in this world, and this was one of them, by Jesus Christ, it was!

"—Tip," Chapin was saying in an unhappy, importunate whisper, "Tip, it's Dad, it's *Dad*! . . ."

He shook his head, turned on his heel and started back through the living room, bumping into people and not caring. Someone had hold of his arm. Jophy, her eyes huge, her lovely face long with reproach.

"Tip, it's your *father*, you can't mean to walk away—"

""You don't know anything about this," he told her flatly. "Stay out of this."

Her eyes flared at him hotly, but he was angry now, he was angrier than she would ever know.

"Your father!" she was saying in a low, intense voice, "after all these years—"

"Let me alone," he said, and she dropped her arm and stepped back. He went on down the stairs, got his

640

coat and hat and went out into the street, his heart pounding savagely. It had stopped snowing; here and there cold, tiny stars glinted through the overcast. The carolers were gathered down near Charles Street now, their voices dreamy and innocent on the still air.

2

On Beacon Street the trees were coming into full leaf, sliding shadows in lacy, sun-dappled patterns over the old brick sidewalks, which were smooth as glass, and about as treacherous. Strolling downhill, Chapin gazed at the Common rolling away beyond the high wrought-iron fence, where figures lay sprawled under the warm sun, reading newspapers or peering at the traffic speeding along Charles Street. Another merry month of May, at the satisfactory conclusion of another world war. Sublimely at ease, ticking off the year's achievements like a string of prayer beads, Chapin began to hum the triumphant "Gloria all'E-gitto" chorus from *Aida,* smiling to himself; turned up Spruce Street.

There was no place he felt more secure than on these narrow, steep streets with their classic porticoes and stately façades: the Hill, fount and matrix of the men who had hammered the fledgling republic into being, stamped indelibly its direction. The many-talented Adamses had lived there, and the blunt (not to say rude) Cabots, and the high-and-mighty Lowells (to whom Aunt Serena was related), and crusty old Henry Cabot Lodge (to whom he himself had once owed a very great deal), and the Phillipses and the Channings, and King John Hancock, who had once put down George Washington himself. It was such an illustrious roll call! Those incredible Jameses had lived there for a time, and Julia Ward Howe and Edwin Booth; Longfellow had been married here: Louisa May Alcott had written her sentimental tales, William Prescott his thundering histories. Poor, tortured Poe had (typically) misbehaved at some very proper entertainment and been ushered out (just as typically)—forever . . .

Boston. He loved it all: the absurd, anomalous patterns—where the richer you are, the more threadbare your clothing; where you walked over the Hill to your place of business in the foulest weather (you took cabs only if you were irreparably crippled or at death's very door); where you attended Symphony as if it were church, and church as if it were a meeting of the state legislature; where your final club and war record were infinitely more important than your bank account or advanced degrees could ever be; in which nothing was ever expressly stated but everything was always known.

Boston. And now his brother had bought himself a home on this brick-and-granite citadel of frosty privilege and cantankerous self-denial. He could imagine the comments at the Somerset or the Athenaeum. "Ames?" "*What* Ames? What's his background?" "You know—Serena Aldridge's nephew. The other one." "Oh—*Chapin's* brother. Well . . . " And then that fractional tip of the head that signified assent, partial assent, anyway (he was, after all, related to the right sort)—but combined nonetheless with a certain misgiving (there *were* some curious individuals coming on to the Hill these days; well—the war, the general roiling-up of things) . . .

Of course a lot of the Old Guard had already been captivated by Jophy. Whenever she entered any room you saw the heads turn—you could feel the balance of things shifting. Chapin smiled. There was nothing, absolutely nothing the rock-ribbed Puritan delighted in so much as forbidden dalliance, thoughts of wanton venery; he had watched their eyes pause, then stop on her glowing, animate face, that arrestingly sensual body, with the particular glint of high fancy he so well understood . . . She could travel far, even here, if she played her cards right. Nothing on this arrant globe succeeded like casuality. The slightest incident could initiate a pattern; patterns distended and sustained created tradition. Q.E.D. Who was to say that Josefina Gaspa might not herself become in thirty years or so a Beacon Hill matron in her own right, leading the Mt. Vernon Bellringers, taking her season seat at Symphony, presiding over the Horticultural Society? Serena in any event seemed to think it possible—to his great surprise Serena had made her peace with Jophy, after all those years of not-very-disguised references to adventuresses and stormy petrels and trouble-makers.

A season of changes . . . Best of all was having found his father again. It was the ultimate satisfaction, such an unlooked-for comfort! He had sat for hours by his hospital bed at Peter Bent Brigham (his father had been confined for several weeks after the holidays with a severe case of pleurisy; he was quite ill) and after that in the spacious apartment Chapin had got for him in one of the remodeled brownstones out on Commonwealth Avenue, listening delightedly to the old man's tales of hazard on four continents. There had been a tin mine in Bolivia, but governmental interference and the perfidy of an associate had ruined the deal. He'd had some luck with a pineapple plantation in Madagascar, and a typhoon had come along and swept him clean of everything but a suitcase. After that there had been ill-fated ventures in niccolite and cocoa beans, and a final, Homeric effort to recoup his fortunes in a wolfram enterprise deep in the wilds of Borneo; he'd got out of Padangtikar on a rickety copra schooner with a handful of Dutch engineers, just hours ahead of the invading Japanese—this time without even the suitcase—and spent the rest of the war in Melbourne.

And now Lyman Ames was home—or near it, anyway; he'd come from a little town on the Housatonic—excited and proud of his eldest son's achievements. He wanted to hear all about Diehl, Harrodsen, and Macomah Fund; his worn, slender face had lighted up at Chapin's accounts of the new overseas expansion. Only once during those months had he asked, rather diffidently, about Tip. Chapin, still smarting from that painful scene on Christmas Eve, had brushed it aside: Tip was on the road most of the time, he was under a lot of pressure; he'd come around in time. The old man had looked deeply shaken.

"I didn't think he'd feel that way about me. That unrelenting." The jaundice-stained eyes had filled. "I know I've given him reason enough."

"No, you haven't, Dad . . . "

"Leaving you boys like that, wandering the globe, chasing rainbows . . . I wanted to come back in triumph," he said with sudden hoarse vehemence, leaning forward, "turn it all to happy account, don't you see? And all I did was leave you both to fate's tender mercies . . . "

"It doesn't matter, it's nothing, Dad," Chapin protested. "You're home now, *that's* all that matters . . . " And holding his father's hand in both of his, gazing at the pale gray eyes, conscience-stricken now, he had felt that stealthy pressure low against his heart, the iron door swinging open in the old anguished need —and realized that for the first time in his life he didn't care; that in fact he welcomed it, with open arms.

"It'll be all right." He gripped the bony, spotted hand; his own eyes stung with unfamiliar tears. "You'll see. Don't you worry about it, now. I'll work it out—I'll make it all come right . . . "

It had been a highly emotional spring. He and Tip had had no end of arguments over Macomah's new overseas operation. Tip didn't like the use of the mili-

646

tary as what he sarcastically called in-house sales representatives, and the basic disagreement had come to a head over Chapin's choice to run European distribution and licensing, an ex-brigadier named Allison whom Chapin had served with, who had degrees from Harvard and Wharton and spoke several languages fluently.

"I don't care if he speaks Urdu and has fifty Phi Beta Kappa keys—he doesn't know mutuals and he doesn't know selling. He'll make a mess of it . . . I don't like the whole set-up. Preying on a captive clientele—"

"Tip, it's a very different kettle of fish over there —it needs a highly specialized approach . . . "

"There's only one approach to selling, and that's been the same since Jacob talked Esau out of his birthright."

Chapin had laughed. "Aren't you forgetting Eve and the serpent?" Tip had made no reply. "Look, give him six months, see what he can do."

"No. I can't see it."

"Tip, I've more or less given him assurance that he'll get a shot at it . . . "

Tip glared at him. "You had no right to do that. Sales is my prerogative, and you know it! What the hell are you trying to pull?"

"I *told* you, it's going to take someone who knows how things work over there. It's not your province . . . "

The wrangle went on for another half hour. For the first time Tip had walked out on him in a huff, dissociating himself entirely from Macomah Europe. Things between them were still cool. That spring Tip had turned increasingly difficult, as though their father's return had touched off some dark reservoir of resentment. He was short with staff and particularly querulous with the research people, maintaining that they were getting much too speculative for current market conditions. He'd even had words with Serena over Harry Truman, whom curiously he liked, claiming he had what it took, he'd make a fine President in time. He was vigorously supporting Jophy in her forlorn battle to block the new marina and resort complex in Turk's Head Harbor. God alone knew what a ruckus there'd be if any of them discovered who was *really* behind that project. Chapin smiled thinly, remembering Jophy rising to speak at Barnstable Courthouse, her voice modulating from softly impassioned plea to the most biting sarcasm, the court roaring with laughter; so like her Grama Annabella. And Serena sitting there smiling her tight, secretive smile. Everything's come full circle, he thought; everything. Except that May of '19 I hadn't the faintest idea about what I wanted to do with myself; now, this May, I do know—with a vengeance.

Softly, majestically, he sang the King's aria to Radames: *"Now ask of me whatever you most desire. I swear, by my own and the sacred gods, that nothing shall be denied you this day . . . !"*

Henrietta Pincher, pixilated in tricorn hat and high-button black shoes, coming toward him; she glanced at him, startled—then gave a sharp, wintry bark of laughter. He smiled charmingly and tipped his hat to her as she passed; sauntered on down Chestnut Street until he reached the perfectly proportioned arched portal with its delicate fanlight and leaded sidepanes. A diminutive townhouse, but elegant. Tip could have done a lot worse.

Full circle. In point of fact there was only one fly in the aromatic ointment; and he was going to use all his persuasive skills to see what he could do about that right now . . .

He mounted the three steps of white Chelmsford granite and pulled briskly on the wrought-iron key, heard the shivery jangle far inside the house. Tip himself opened the door, in his shirtsleeves. Typical. They'd refused to hire full-time servants. A massive Swedish woman came to clean and cook and that was all. Tip still drove his own car, stacked his own firewood the New Hampshire woodcutters hurled contemptuously into the narrow cellar. He still refused to get a decent tailor or buy his suits at Brooks—he claimed the latter could make even Jack Dempsey look like a broken old man.

The brothers confronted each other a moment in silence. Then Chapin said: "Standards, Tipton, standards! Where is your jacket? The Proprietors will take a dim view of this."

Tip grinned at him. "You playing hooky today, too? Come on in."

"I *thought* you'd be back a day early." He hung his hat on one of the porcelain-capped knobs in the vestibule and followed his brother up the stairs.

"I got things wound up sooner than I thought."

"And how is the Golden West?"

"Not so golden. Young Parker didn't work out—I fired him. He's a floater. Maury's ulcer's very bad. He's in hospital, just had surgery—they seem to have taken most of his stomach out, from what I can gather. He was feeling pretty low."

"You going to replace him?"

Tip turned at the doorway and stared at him. "No, I'm not going to replace him. Maury with no stomach at all is still worth any five of your Harvard Buzz School jerks."

"Such lèse-majesté, little brother."

"Nope, just the truth. Want a drink?"

"Why, yes—don't mind if I do."

The living room was lightened by the triple window, and pleasantly appointed: warm woods—walnut and mahogany and rosewood—and watered silk and velvet in shades of that celadon green Jophy favored. Her taste and textures. Still, there were none of her family mementos—no shells or masks or spears; she'd kept them at the Cape house. Interesting.

"Jophy gone down the Cape?"

Tip handed him a glass. "No, she's still here. She's

up at the State House, wheedling documents out of the clerks—stockpiling ammunition, she calls it."

Chapin laughed. "Dear old Jophy-girl . . . But the windmills are so big, and there are so many of them."

"Well. Those windmills better look out—they're going to get their vanes clipped."

"Conceivable." Chapin leaned back on the couch. "Progress, my boy. Que voulez-vous dire? That's what people want now: a big, splashy yacht basin, with all the trimmings. For hundreds of little boats roaring around. And that's the way it's going to go."

"That isn't the way Jo sees it. I don't either. Not to mention the fishermen . . . They're wrecking the harbor with that stupid dredging, is what they're doing."

"Do you think so?"

"I hear there's a lot of strange money behind it." Tip sat on the arm of the chair facing Chapin, swinging one foot restlessly. "I hear Arnie Koltisiak has bought into the marina complex. Spider Danco's crowd. What do you know about that, Chay?"

"Danco? Where'd you hear that?"

"Harvey Williams, down in Taunton."

That followed. Amazing—Tip always knew more than you thought he did. He'd have to be more careful; they all would. He shrugged, said: "Nothing much. Rumors. Personally I doubt it. People are always uncovering a nefarious conspiracy every time something's controversial. They said the same thing over the Old Harbor ruckus here in town—you remember. Even eagle-eyed Serena was wrong about that one—she was sure it was some Sicilian gangster ploy to run a gambling hall right down there on T Wharf." He snorted. "I wish to hell your charming wife would give it all up and help Serena with the annual Garden Club crise de nerfs."

"She wound up over that again?"

"The customary frenzy. The wistaria is looking tired, and she's in a tizzy over the English ivy—I thought she was going to order me to fly over to Canterbury for a replacement." He paused, sipped at his drink. "Also, she's planning a small party for Dad. His birthday's on the twenty-second, you know."

"I know." Tip looked away at the fireplace."

"Just the immediate family, a few close friends . . . She hopes you'll come, Tip. So do I."

Tip twisted his neck inside his collar, though it was unbuttoned. "Now why bring that up? You know how I feel about it."

"Serena's disappointed over your attitude. All these months. Family matter like this."

Tip looked at him then. "What you mean is, *you're* disappointed. Why don't you say what you mean?"

Chapin smiled his mournful, contrite smile. Admissions were often far more effective than denials; he'd learned that long ago.

"All right, then—yes, I won't pretend I'm not unhappy about it . . . You make it very awkward, Tip."

"Awkward." His brother had stuck out his lower lip in that stubborn way he hated. He sighed inaudibly, contained himself; said:

"Look, I know how you feel . . . "

"No, you don't. You haven't got the faintest idea how I feel about this."

"After all, he's your father, too . . . "

"That's a matter of opinion."

"All right, then," Chapin offered with mild exasperation, "I *don't* know how you feel. I took the easy way out. I sold out and went to live a life of grandeur and cosseted ease with Serena. Is that what you want me to say?"

"You don't need to say anything."

"I admit it, if it's any consolation. And *you* chose to stay on with Mother in Holcomb Falls, and years of penury and hard labor. Don't look at me like that —I'm not being facetious . . . But what does it matter now? Tip, he's a sick old man, whose life is just about over."

"Chay, it isn't a question of—"

"What would it cost you?—just to show up for the occasion, say a few civil words, make him feel a little less lonely? He's made some mistakes. Bad ones. Is that so unique? Hells bells, haven't you made any mistakes yourself, along the road?"

Tip looked at him coldly, unblinking. "You know I have, Chapin."

"All right, then . . . Look, I don't blame you for Christmas Eve. I knocked galley-west myself, we all were. I defended you that night with Serena, with all of them—I even calmed Jophy down after you told her off and stormed out of there. Ask *her* if you don't believe me. I had a damned good idea of what you must be feeling. But what the hell—he's dying, Tip. He's dying. Let it go—can't you? If not for me, if not for Serena, then for Mother. She never stopped loving him—you know that. Let it go, Tip. I'm begging you . . . "

Tip was staring hard at the rug, gripping his glass in both hands, tightly. "All right," he said with an effort. "For Mother's sake I'll do it. Tell Serena I'll be there."

"Thanks so much, Tip." He smiled at his brother, nodding; he hadn't realized how much this concession would mean to him. He felt a warm suffusion deep around his heart. "I'm immensely grateful, I really am. I knew you'd relent. Tip, he's so weary and worn out. And he's done so many things! It's amazing how much he knows about the world, about out-of-the-way places—markets, raw materials, government regulations. He's devoted a lifetime to mastering all these things, and now he hasn't any outlet. It's such a waste. You ought to hear his stories on bureaucratic chicanery in Spain, investment possibilities in South America—it's incredible, what he's retained. I don't see why he couldn't even make a contribution to the firm. In a small way, of course. And for the short time he has left."

Tip's head came up, he set down his glass. *"Macomah . . . ."*

"It's just an idea. Something to play around with. A small office of his own, in R & A maybe, under Mac. Just something to give him back his dignity."

"Dignity—!" His brother had come to his feet now, hands stiff at his sides, his face hard again. "Don't talk to *me* about dignity! He gave up his dignity, long ago—and other people paid for it. In blood . . . "

"Tip, it'd be just a token, a—"

"No!" Tip chopped at the air sharply once, with the edge of his hand. "No—not Macomah. Look, I'm willing to help support him—God knows I took on *his* responsibilities long enough. The ones he threw over. But take him into the fund—*no*. And that's my last word on it."

"But why? What would it cost you?"

"More than you'll ever know."

"It's not like you not to be generous, Tip."

"Generous—!"

"Yes, you've always been so generous."

"Big and easy, you mean . . . " Tip swung away, spun around again, one arm outthrust, his face contorted. "God damn it, Chapin, can't you ever let up? Aren't you ever satisfied?" He chopped at the air again. "Now quit trying to manipulate me. *He does not come into Macomah.* That's it!"

He moved across the room toward the big window, and there was a silence. The leaves soughed lazily outside; across the back courtyard someone was faltering through a Czerny exercise on the piano. In place of the warm elation of a moment ago, Chapin felt a sullen, mounting anger. All right, then, he thought, watching his brother's square, tense back. The break was bound to come, sooner or later—maybe it was better this way. Face it out now.

"You make it very difficult, Schoolboy."

"Difficult."

"Yes—stop echoing me!" he exclaimed in sudden irritation, suppressed it with an effort. "Do you want out, Tipton?"

His brother turned then and stared at him. "Out?"

"That's right. I'm willing to buy you out, if you want it that way."

"What the hell's this all about—who said anything about my wanting out?" Tip's face was blank with perplexity—then set with a sudden cool awareness. "I see . . . You'd force a fight, over this."

"You're unhappy with Macomah International, anyway," Chapin said easily. "Your heart isn't in it any more—you've been fighting the job all spring. Wrangling over portfolio, new issues. Hell, you're through with Macomah—you just won't admit it."

"I see . . . You've got it all figured out." Tip laughed once, tightly; then his lips came together. "I think not, Chapin."

He was standing very still over by the window. Now he came forward. His face had turned harder than Chapin had ever seen it—harder even than the afternoon of the mutual funds row; those small triangular points at the corners of his mouth were very pronounced. Chapin, outwardly impassive, thought of the frozen, rutted road above the falls and a burst carton of soap—drove the image away ruthlessly.

"Now you listen to me, Chapin," Tip was saying in a flat, level voice. "And you listen hard and well. Yes, I'm unhappy with your European operations. I don't like these rotten sales training programs you've set up at the Army bases, I don't like pressuring the GIs this way, and most of all I don't like this latest dodge with the Swiss banks—the foreign scrip certificates."

"It's a perfectly legitimate means of converting—"

"I've done my homework. I know perfectly well what you're up to. It's speculative, it's unsound, you're already getting overextended and top-heavy, the way you did in '28, and it's going to come back and haunt you, too—just the way it did before. And I don't like it one single bit . . . But if you think I'm going to pick up my marbles in a huff and go home, leave you the whole lash-up over a stupid, personal issue like this, you'd better shop around for another set of brains. I'm staying. Macomah is mine every bit as much as yours, pal. In fact, it's mine more than yours. I built Macomah; you didn't."

"That's absurd!" Chapin burst out, amazed and angry. "Who do you think set up SEC clearance, who put the research staff together, who arranged blue sky all the way down the line? And just who had the capital to begin with?"

But Tip was smiling at him now; a cool, hard smile that infuriated him. "You know something, Chay? You've never made a dollar by yourself. All right—so you can project, and analyze, and huddle with your legal jackals and dope out ways to slide around the rules and regulations. But you've never gone out and *done* it. Sold the commodity, made the dough. I've had to do that. I'm the one who thought of converting Macomah to mutuals—and I had to ram the whole idea down your protesting throat ten years ago. *You* wanted to go back to radio pools and bear raids and leverage and all those wonderful people who gave us Black Thursday. Remember? It was my idea, and my timing, and it was right *then*, that moment—not some God damned abstract theory for some nebulous future . . .

"And you want to know why?" And now the smile had vanished utterly. "Because I've always had to make the correct move right off the bat, gauge the look in the other man's eye and play it from there. I've *had* to know, right then—because my daily bread, and Mother's and Jophy's and the kids', was on the line. I know it from the inside out, club man. Because I pounded the pavements year in, year out, put cardboard in my shoes and slept in two-bit hotels and ate in hash joints, counting my change before I ordered —and then I went out and hit the customers again at nine the next morning. Your capital . . . I made your fucking capital *work*, and you know it!"

655

Chapin demanded tightly: "And that Horatio Alger odyssey's given you some divine insight, has it?"

"Oh, nothing as grand as all that. What it does is give a man a certain competence. A certain self-reliance. You know? . . . Someone's always done it for you, Chapin. That's the truth of the matter. Serena started you off in style; Jenny handed you the chips to get you into the big game, and old Calkins bought you a front row seat; Serena bailed you out when you were going under, along with the rest of us; and I rebuilt Macomah for you—into something solid and worthwhile, something you could have been proud of . . . Only you weren't because you're always after something else, you always have been, something bigger and shinier and more slippery—because if it doesn't have that little element of danger, the risk of exposure, it just doesn't appeal to you. Does it?"

"—You don't know what you're talking about!" He leaped to his feet and moved over to the mantel, his back to his brother. He felt an overmastering rage—he wanted to lay about him in a frenzy. Just who was this drummer brother of his to tell him *any-thing* about himself or business or any damned thing else—! Enough! He didn't have to listen to this, and he wouldn't, he—

"Oh yes, I do," Tip continued implacably; it was as though, after the months of stiff altercations and sullen silences, he couldn't stop now he'd started. "I know one hell of a lot more about you than you think I do. I learned to read you a long, long time ago . . . Don't talk to *me* about buying me out of Macomah! You couldn't buy me out with all the gold bullion your sainted father has been *dreaming* about for the past fifty years . . . And if you try to force me out, you're going to be in for the fight of your life—I guarantee it. And you're not up to that, Chapin. I'll tell you why you're not. Because you've never had to get out there with the rest of the world and scrabble for it, sit on a strange bed and hold your fear right there

656

in the palm of your hand, like a—like a filthy toad, and look at it, nights. You've never really been up against it—life, or death either. Just the way you've never watched a man die . . . "

"What—!"

"You hung around the plant. You sent them out to get blown to pieces all right, but *you* stayed in your comfy office back at the airfield and made your clever little projections."

"You stupid fool," Chapin shouted, "I was in the streets when the bombs were falling—*you* were the one back home, goggling at the newsreels! . . . "

But Tip only smiled at him, again, nodding—a faint, mocking smile that strung him to insupportable fury. "That isn't the same thing. Is it? You know, Jophy's right about you: you're incapable of feeling anything—you walk around in a shiny, plastic bag, and other people are a collection—a collection you can't own . . . ."

"*Jophy—!*" He heard himself cry with harsh, raging laughter, out of control now, hardly aware of what he was saying. "What do you know about what Jophy thinks, or feels either? *I'm* the one she's always loved —not you. I won her!" He struck his chest savagely. "Oh, yes! I'm the one she *gave* herself to—"

"—*You?*" Tip's mouth had formed the word, the word itself was inaudible; his face had gone white as milk.

"Of course!" He raced on, gripped in an unbraked frenzy to cripple, to destroy, "—all that time after she left you—who do you think she was with? You poor fool . . . she was never yours, never!"

"I don't believe it—"

"Ask her, then. Go on and ask her! I can see you've never summoned up enough courage for that . . . "

His brother's face had flushed a deep red now, his eyes uncommonly wide and clear against the rush of blood. " . . . You rotten, no-good son of a bitch," he whispered hoarsely. "You bastard—"

657

His hands came up then, he came forward quickly, with a funny moan far in his throat. Chapin, raging and fearful, dodged to his left, swung at him and missed. His head snapped back with a sound like a popped shingle, he was spinning around—he'd crashed into something hard. Table edge. Crouched on his hands and knees his eyes lighted on the brass-handled poker in the stand by the hearth. He would get to that poker and then we'd see. Yes. He weaved to his feet, snatched the poker out of the stand and whirled around, his left arm out, fending—to see Tip staring blankly past him, his hands at his sides again. Involuntarily he turned. Jophy was standing in the doorway.

"What in God's name is going on here?" she said; her voice seemed absurdly light and conversational, though it was edged with dismay. "What's the matter with you two!"

"Reality!" Chapin shouted. He flung the poker back at the hearth, where it clattered on the stone. If he hadn't been able to speak at that instant he felt his lungs would burst. His head was ringing strangely. "We're finding out who can face it, and who can't—that's what we're doing . . . !"

Her eyes kept flickering from one to the other fearfully—it was as if she already knew the quarrel was over her.

" . . . He says you love him," Tip said then in a low, tremulous voice. "Is that true?"

She made a sharp, distressful gesture. "Tip, for the love of God!"

"Is it true?" he repeated.

"Tip, you *know* I've—"

"He says you've—been with him. Have you? Slept with him?"

There was a terrible, tense pause, while Jophy glanced wrathfully, almost vengefully, at Chapin, and for three heartbeats he thought, She'll deny it—what woman wouldn't? I've gone too far, she'll deny it and I'll be left swinging on the garden gate. I've lost it all.

Then her eyes came back to Tip's and held there, fully.

"Yes," she said.

Tip started to speak, nodded once instead and headed for the door, his face set.

She said: "Tip—wait . . . " As he passed her she put a hand on his arm. "You don't understand, it was a—"

"I don't need to wait," he broke in on her.

"Won't you even let me speak? Try to explain? Won't you—"

"There's nothing to explain." His face was dead white, the brown eyes clouded. "I understand all I need to."

"Please wait," she entreated.

"I've always waited. I've waited for you too many times. Far too many." He looked at her with dogged implacable force. "You talk to *him*," he said, indicating Chapin with a contemptuous toss of his head. "I won't be back."

He shrugged off her hand and left the room quickly. She started after him and then stopped where she was, looking off after him down the stairs, her hand still reaching out. They could hear his heels clack on the downstairs hall, and then the front door closed with a heavy thump, and the silence returned.

Jophy wheeled and looked at Chapin—a look flooded with so many contradictory emotions he could not for the life of him tell what she would say or do. He had never seen her totally vulnerable before. He only knew, with a certain instinctive elation, that it meant a vacuum which must be instantly filled.

He went over to her and said gently: "Jo."

She caught her breath, as if she wanted to laugh, and couldn't; then in great agitation: "What did you *tell* him—!"

But he cut her off. "Nothing more or less than the truth."

"The truth! *You*—? Just how can—"

"That we were lovers. What's fabricated about that? Are you going to deny it? We were—*we are* . . . "

She made a despairing gesture with one hand. "Chay—one crazy, thoughtless moment, out there in the bay . . . "

"Now who's evading?" He caught the hand and held it in his. "Oh, come on, admit it, Jo. You've always wanted me, more than anyone. You can't feign something like that. Or ignore it, either—don't try to tell me you can."

He put his hands on her lovely, sloping shoulders. He knew without question that it was the most important thing he would ever do—more momentous than going to Boston with Serena, or Wall Street or Macomah or even his Degas collection. *Providential*, the word rang in his consciousness. First Dad, here at home again. And now Jophy, swinging unhelmed, a royal prize. The two people who had pressed deepest against the stone of his heart. Why not? Great Circle, come full. The last barrier had been cleared—in a way he could never have foreseen. The fortunes of love and war . . . "

"I've got to talk to him," she was saying tensely, biting her lip.

"It won't make any difference. He's given up—he won't change his mind. Can't you see that?"

"I've got to talk to him," she repeated, like a prayer.

"There are things you can't recover from, Jo. Moments no relationship can come back from. Believe me, I know—it was for Jenny and me. I know you can't see it now, but it's true."

"Let me go, Chapin," she pleaded. "I've got to think . . ."

"There's nothing to think *about*—it's happened, it's done." He could feel her wavering under his hands; she had never looked so desirable. "You said on the boat that day you weren't ever going to be a cork bobbing between Tip and me—and I honored that, though

660

I wanted you every night and every morning . . . Now that's over, Jo. He's gone. And you *know* what there is between us. What's always been between us. You can deny it all you want to—turn from it out of pride, or distrust it, or just plain put it out of your mind, the way you did all during the war. But it's there, just the same. It'll always be there. I can feel it, I can see it in you eyes . . . "

She looked at him then, with a searching, fearful intensity. "Yes," she said. "I've always wanted you, Chapin. My body has always wanted you. I can't help that, I never will. But there's more to me than my body, and there's a great deal more at stake—"

"But there's nothing to hold you now," he insisted. "I tell you, he's not going to change his mind on this. That's the way he's made. You know that. The kids are grown up, your life's your own—what is there to hold you?"

He touched her cheek with his lips, the line of her jaw. She was trembling, but he could feel one final hawser somewhere deep within her refusing to let go.

"We'll get married," he urged; and then more lightly, "It's the only way I'll ever get free sailing lessons."

But she had left him again, he could tell.

"I need to think, Chay," she said sadly.

"No, you don't. Just act. That's always been your way. Just—act . . . "

"I need to think, Chay," she repeated.

3

There had been a few changes. The neat picket fencing had given way to an untrimmed privet hedge. The blackfish vertebrae had rotted away with time, and in their place Jophy had laid worn, ruddy ballast brick in a pleasing herringbone pattern. But the whale's ribs were still there; they looked rather larger than Serena remembered them. She passed under their slender shadow with a strange little tremor. The windows were open to the somnolent July heat, and now she could hear music, a record of a woman's voice soaring—Bidú Sayáo singing the "caro nome." Serena smiled grimly and turned to inspect the garden. The beds looked more luxuriant than she'd remembered: sea lavender and heather and rugosa; hollyhock, lemon verbena; a handsome Chinese dogwood edged the wall. Curiously, here on the far side of the harbor, the growl of the dredger and the tractor-clatter of bulldozers were much louder, more oppressive.

The soprano's voice faded, sweet, credulous. "E fin l'ultimo sospir, caro nome, tuo sarà . . ." Innocent, trusting Gilda, enraptured, had declared her undying love for the dissolute Duke of Mantua. Serena stepped up to the screen door, raised her cane like a baton and knocked smartly with its chased silver head.

"Come in!" Jophy's voice, musical and light, almost an echo of the aria.

Squinting in the cool, soft gloom, Serena could

make her out standing by the phonograph, the record in her hands. She was dressed in sleeveless blouse and denim skirt and sandals; her hair, caught back, flowed long and rich over her shoulders. For just a second or two she looked like the young, eager girl who had once turned that exquisite inlaid box of Chapin's this way and that, studying it with such solemn intensity. Then she turned and saw her visitor and the illusion shattered.

"Oh—*Serena* . . ." Surprised, she came forward in that quick, lithe way, as though about to break into a run, or launch herself into one of her fancy high-dives. "How long have you been there?"

"Not long."

"I had the phonograph going and didn't hear you."

"I was listening." Serena nodded toward the stack of records. "She's no Galli-Curci, but she's lovely. Good pure color, nice legato line. But will she last?"

"Will anything?" Jophy shot a glance at her, that mirror-flash of the jet-dark eyes. "She's singing gloriously *now*—isn't that the important thing? Come in, come in. Will you have a glass of wine?"

"Why yes, thanks, I believe I will." She would not make that mistake again. The room was just as she'd remembered: the stiff horsechair sofa, rather ratty now, the heavy, high-backed chairs with woven antimacassars, the tall glass cabinet with its trophies and scrimshaw; even the engraving of the *Amelia Snow* still hung on the wall between the seaward windows. It was—almost unnerving . . .

"Well," Jophy was holding the two stem glasses with the pale amber wine, "what brings you over to the wrong side of the tracks?"

She laughed easily. "Just a chat, dear. I haven't seen very much of you lately."

"No—I've been fighting *that!*" She tossed her head, fisherman-style, toward the windows, the racket of harbor construction, muffled now inside the house. "That rotten crook Crozier. Holding town meeting in

664

a damn gale to make sure half the town couldn't get there—and then all those slimy lies about gaining increased shore acreage from the dredging. *Shore* acreage! That stinking muck—it's worse than a guano factory. Don't you get the smell over on the Bluffs?"

"Now and then."

"I'll bet you do. Perhaps," she grinned mishievously, "you've come to join the cause. Have you?"

"Oh, I'm far too old for such pastimes, my dear."

"Nonsense—Grama was up there at Barnstable stealing their wind the summer she died . . ."

"Senhora Gaspa was a great rarity," Serena answered. "I lack her—fiber."

"We all do." Jophy smiled. "But we can emulate it, perhaps."

"But after all, why fight the inevitable?" She sipped at the smoky, full Madeira. "Fishing is dead as an industry—you know that yourself. They'll have to adjust, concentrate on tourists."

Jophy's face became very grave and intent. "You wouldn't say that if you were still running out there in a trawler trying to scratch out a living, Serena. And anyway, it's not that simple. You *know* what this will do to the town. They're trying to turn it into a watch-charm Atlantic City—a midway of bars and hamburger joints and all the rest of it. Give them their way for two years and Turk's Head won't bear any resemblance to the honest village we've known."

"Nothing ever does."

"That's no reason to give way . . ."

Serena let her rant along about the hideous pastel-colored motels lining the Hollow, the new pollution in the Lower Channel from the marina, Koltisak and his Buzzards Bay hoodlums; watching over the rim of her wine glass the animate face framed in that gleaming black hair, remembering Annabella Gaspa's voice that faraway afternoon. *"No. She is beautiful. There is an ocean of difference."* Even now, studying her coolly, weighing stratagems, she had to grant that: Jophy had held her beauty— that deep clarity of eye, the vibrant copper glow of her skin; and there was that sense of expectant promise. It was miraculous, in a way . . .

"You're not listening to a word I'm saying." Jophy was gazing at her steadily, the corners of her mouth on the edge of a smile. Quietly she said: "What's on your mind, Serena?"

She laughed again, to cover her surprise. All right, then. The frontal approach. "My mind *was* wandering, yes. It's one of the privileges of age. I was thinking of the first time I saw you. Over at the Bluffs. You and Chapin were looking at each other. I remember I thought, Could two beautiful young people ever be so different! I certainly hope they don't become interested in each other . . ."

Jophy was still smiling faintly, but her eyes had taken on that particular shine. "And perhaps you still feel that way, Serena?"

So she knew, then—or had guessed. Well, that was to be expected. After all, the girl was no fool.

"Chapin's been talking to you," Jophy said.

"Yes. In point of fact he has . . . He tells me he's finally made up his mind to marry you. In the early autumn."

"I'm not sure I'd put it exactly that way— I was more under the impression I'd finally made up my mind to marry *him* . . ."

"As you wish. Once you've divested yourself of— other ties, I gather. What about Tipton, may I ask?"

"Tip?"

"Yes—how does he feel about it?"

Jophy tucked her lower lip between her teeth. "I don't see that that concerns you, Serena."

"What concerns either of my nephews concerns me."

"Ah—the bond of blood. Of course. But maybe there are bonds stronger than blood. Do you think that could be possible?"

The glint of derisive amusement in her eyes was unmistakable. Why, she's laughing at me! Serena told herself with sudden sharp indignation; she will regret that. As if to accent the moment the ship's chronometer struck its taut, two-stroke message, delicate and ephemeral against the distant flatulent grinding of the bulldozers. With an effort Serena arched her back and composed herself. Calmly, now; calmly. Thirty years ago she had sat on this hard black couch confronting the Portuguese Lawyer; now here she was facing the granddaughter—the Portuguese Adventuress. This perpetual, maddening threat to the ordered world she'd striven to create.

But this time she had more formidable weapons.

"It seems to me to be a matter of taste," she led in again, judiciously. "And of course responsibility. When the emotions are involved people invariably forget that—they rush into relationships, whose—consequences they refuse to foresee."

"Consequences."

"Yes—consequences," she pressed on, a bit sharply. "Have you thought about how the Hill would react to this?"

"Yes. I've thought about it."

"And the prospect doesn't trouble you."

"I've never lived to satisfy others."

"You won't be happy together, you know," Serena offered suddenly.

"Really? And why is that?"

"You're simply too different."

"They say opposites attract."

"A myth, my dear girl." She smiled now, realizing the girl was drawing her out; she was quite content to run that way. "The fact remains, you're just not his kind of person."

"True enough. I am my own kind."

"You see things simply, starkly, romantically—no shadows, no qualifications. You're a partisan spirit."

"So they tell me." That edge of mocking amusement

667

kept reminding her of someone. The father. Of course. All those years ago. She placed her hands on her thighs firmly, repressed her rising anger. Gently, now. She could afford this light baiting easily enough; yet the younger woman's attitude—of holding key cards, of being securely at the helm—nettled her.

"Perhaps it's a mistake. Is that any reason to shrink from it?"

"Well, you're certainly casual enough!" Serena couldn't keep from exclaiming.

"I'm not casual. Not casual at all. I've been thinking about it for months now. Even longer, perhaps."

"You'll remember that your first—involvement with Chapin had some very unpleasant consequences."

Jophy's head came up then; she stared at her gravely. "He told you about that . . ."

"I can't recall whether he did or not. I believe I deduced it from what happened later."

"Nothing happened later. Not then, anyway."

"Oh, yes. A great deal happened. I *do* know all about that, you see."

The girl was frowning at her, mystified. Good. It would increase her own leverage, so to speak. Before she had decided which card to play next, Jophy had jumped in with both feet:

"Oh, come off it, Serena! Let's stop this pussy-footing around. Are you trying to dissuade me from marrying Chapin?"

"Of course I am."

"But why?"

"Frankly, I'm afraid for you both."

"No, I mean *really* why?"

"You don't know Chapin. You may think you do, but you don't. Marriage with him would be a disaster. For you both."

"Well, that's plain enough." Jophy looked down at her hands. "Have you made your rather predictable views known to him?"

"Of course."

"And what was his reaction?"

"He is determined to go ahead with it. Even knowing everything he does." She paused. "It's in your hands, Josefina. That is why I'm here."

"So I see." When Jophy looked up again her eyes held that warm, mischievous sparkle. "Well, I guess it's a risk we'll simply have to take. I do know him quite well, Serena. Maybe better than you think."

All right, then.

"Ah, do you. Then of course you know that Chapin is behind the marina, the entire Hurlestone Sands project? It's *his* money—and his influence—that's behind this whole Buzzards Bay group you've just been raging about?"

The girl was staring hard at her now, shocked and angry. Didn't know it. Of course. How could she? Chapin always moved so carefully . . .

"That isn't true—I don't believe it."

"I'm afraid you'd better." She reached into her purse, lifted out an envelope and passed it over. "Here is a letter from Chapin to the irrepressible Mr. Koltisiak. If you want evidence—I imagined you would."

Jophy's eyes were hurrying along the lines; she set the letter down slowly. "He would have told me—something like this . . ."

Serena permitted herself a single soft chuckle. This was already turning out to be a satisfaction. "Chapin tells very, very few people about his really grand designs. He's always been like that. Haven't you noticed?"

"But why?" Jophy said uncertainly. "It's everything he loathes. Surely he doesn't want to destroy the Cape, the harbor? It makes no sense!"

"My dear, God Himself long ago gave up trying to figure out why Chapin does the things he does. He has his own reasons."

Jophy raised her glass and drank. Her hand was still perfectly steady, her composure superb. Even

669

hating her as she did, fearing her, determined as she was to thwart this last dangerous scheme of hers, Serena had to admire her poise.

"Well, then I guess I'll have to find a way to dissuade him, won't I?" Jophy said with a pained little smile.

"It won't work," she answered crisply. "It goes deeper than any influence you might have on him. Much, much deeper."

The girl's eyes turned still darker, steady and opaque; that vertical line reappeared in the center of her forehead. She's trying to figure it out, Serena thought with sudden fierce excitement, she's struggling to fathom it, and she can't. She doesn't know where to look. Or she's refusing to look.

"Isn't it enough that you've ruined one brother, without destroying the other one as well?" she said then with quick, hard vehemence.

"Destroy—!" Jophy shook herself alert at that, angry now, her eyes flashing. "We'd better not talk about who's done the destroying in this family." She leaped to her feet then—that lithe, disturbing animal grace. "You know, I don't think there's any sense in prolonging this, Serena. You've had your say, your afternoon's amusement—now why don't you go on back across the channel and we'll forget this ever happened. All right?"

Serena sat perfectly still, refusing to rise, one fist gripping the angular head of the cane. Oh no, my pretty maid. You don't get off that lightly! Not on your life.

"You're quite sure you won't reconsider?" she asked softly.

"Who are you to tell me what I will or won't do—!"

"Absolutely sure?" Her voice had dropped nearly to a whisper. It seemed difficult to breathe, yet the sensation was exquisitely constricting. "Think it over very, very carefully, Josefina."

"Are you actually *threatening* me?" The younger

woman made that brusque, demurring gesture of her grandmother's, but fiercer. "It so happens I've never been impressed with your advice—your perpetual meddling in other people's lives . . ." She ran a hand through her hair, flung it back, her rage mounting. "If there ever *was* a chance I might change my mind, it's over now. Yes, I'm going to marry Chapin—and you can go straight to hell! . . . You know, you're rotten," she said finally. "Really rotten. Evil. Worse than I thought. Nothing fazes you."

"We'd better not discuss what fazes people, my girl."

"You're right. I've done some thoughtless things, some bad things. I know it. But you—you're the *real* corrupter. You knew how to tempt us all, corrupt us all from the start. Your kind always knows how to do that—"

"Don't you try to lecture me!" Serena snapped at her, glad of the release now, rejoicing that it was out in the open at last, all swords drawn. *"You've* never known how to manage anything—neither your life nor anyone else's. You romantic souls! Oh, blood-and-thunder, yes, wild postures and wilder speeches . . . I have a piece of advice for you, my dear. I suggest that in future you confine yourself to your sea shells and protest meetings, and leave the real world to those who know how to cope with it—"

"Shut up! Now shut up!" Jophy was weeping now, in spite of an immense effort not to; she was shaking her head wildly as if to will the tears away. Serena had never seen her weep before. "All you know is how to degrade people, bring them down to your sick level. You think I haven't read you, years ago? You set those boys against each other from the beginning—you ruined Chapin by making him over in your own rotten image, you half-destroyed Tip by forcing him to hold his own against you, devote his life to proving you wrong! What a satisfaction it's been, hasn't it? Yes, and you've half-destroyed me, too, tempting me—into fighting you . . . You scheming, contempt-ible bitch—!"

She whirled and flung her glass at the *Amelia Snow*. It hit the wall below the picture with a terrific smash, like a gun shot; crystal fragments flew around the room. Serena, who had started violently, forced herself again to sit perfectly still, her eyes fixed on the Portuguese woman who was crying openly now, her slender body shaking with grief and rage.

"You win anyway, don't you—no matter how hard we try. Hold the line for dear old cod-faced Boston, drive back the lesser breeds . . . Now get out!" Her voice was 'hoarse and unsteady, thick with weeping. "Get out of here before I lose hold of myself and give you what you deserve! But make no mistake about it, I *will* marry Chay now."

"I see. " Serena had not moved. She pressed her hand hard against her thigh. "Very well, then," she said, her voice trembling a little in spite of her great effort to hold it level, "before you hurl yourself once more into holy matrimony, you had better know that Chapin killed your grandfather."

Jophy stopped stock-still. Her face went stark white—then blood began to wash into it in waves, like a tide seeping. Then drained white again. Her eyes were huge.

"Oh yes." Serena nodded. "It was Chapin who set fire to that old schooner. Burned old Gaspa to death. The night of the carnival."

Now the girl's face darkened thickly, as Annabella's had that other afternoon, like hammered bronze. But this time Serena felt no fear at all.

"—*That's not true*," Jophy gasped, her hand at her mouth.

"Oh yes. It is. I was with him, right afterward."

"He—couldn't have, he—" Her eyes were searching wildly around the room as though for some consoling object. But no whaler's trinket or South Sea talisman would make this go away. Ever. Yes: she was shaken.

Utterly and irrevocably shaken. Shattered. Nothing would ever be the same for her again. It had been worth it, then—the admission, the tremendous risk it meant . . .

". . . How—do you know this?" Jophy was asking fearfully, almost suppliant.

"I was there, my dear. I rescued him. He'd gone all to pieces, of course. Eyebrows scorched, clothes burned. I still have his sneakers—they weren't as easy to dispose of as his sweater and slacks—I didn't think it was a good idea for them to turn up on the town dump, people are always picking it over at odd hours, you know. Still, I can show them to you—if you need proof for this, too." It was difficult to stop herself now. "And then I whisked him up to Boston that night; and into the Army. Fortunately Tipton was with you and didn't come back till much later, or the fat *would* have been in the fire. To coin a phrase. Tipton had his suspicions—he's always more perceptive than any of us give him credit for—but oddly enough, it was you who allayed them: something Chapin had said to you at the ball the night before, about becoming a pilot. So we skirted that reef. Quite fortuitous."

She forced herself to stop talking then. Gripping the cane stoutly she rose, took one last, lingering glance at that beautiful, anguished face—turned now to stone before her, to cold silent stone. And then she moved away, went out through the hall. Sunlight, flat and fierce, half-blinded her; the screen door shut behind her with a bang. She strode quickly along the walk, jabbing the point of the cane against the bricks.

"And that is that," she said tightly, aloud. It had taken her thirty years, but she'd done it. The heavy equipment grinding away across the harbor rank like a distant battle.

With a sudden swift movement Serena Aldridge raised the cane and shook it once above her head. Before her the bleached whale's ribs glinted like a barbaric, triumphal arch.

4

The shells were where they had always been, on the second shelf: the golden cowrie from Moapora, and the court volute from Mindanao, and the great conch from Anguilla Cay her father had plugged and learned to blow when he was a doryman. On the shelf below were ceremonial masks, and the carved paddle, and the shark-tooth sword from Manokela, and the amulet from Tuolatari Grampa said the bravest of the warriors wore when they paddled out to fight the great sharks beyond the reef. On impulse Jophy slipped its finely woven thong around her neck so that the amulet lay deep between her breasts.

Then her hand resumed its passage over the familiar objects, caressing wood and bone and shell, remembering the fierce, leaping joy these things had first stirred in her, the tumult of daring they'd called up in her young heart. The brass compass on its lanyard, the ivory fids and needles, the white oak chock pin, the harpooner's badge of distinction. Holding it in her palm she could hear behind her Manuel Gaspa's rough, deep voice. *"It is the world of duty and trust, criança. To mutiny is to destroy that world, and throw everything back to the beginning, with one savage's hand raised against another. That is why it is the mortal sin. That is why it is always punishable by death."*

Her hand moved on softly, searching—closed on the

ivory haft of the knife. Slowly she drew it out of its worn dark sheath, her eyes fixed on the bright blade.

"Never unsheathe a knife unless you intend to use it, Josinha."

Sim, Grampa. Sim.

She held it tightly for a moment, then reaching back slid it diagonally through the belt of her jeans at the small of her back, so that the steel pommel pressed against her right ribs; closed the cabinet doors and snapped the lock on the front door and left the house. She could feel the corners of the ballast brick through the soles of her espadrilles. The night was warm and very dark; off to the southwest the stars were blotted out in a vast, blank curve, and the branches of the locusts were seething in the rising wind. It would storm in a few hours; maybe sooner.

She walked quickly down Crown Street, through the darker tunnel beneath the trees. The heat was oppressive; the very air seemed thick with the approaching storm. Across the channel she could see the glow from the marina, the mock-festive web of strung lights over the new slips. The stench of dredged harbor muck spilled out on the Point hung heavy in the air.

"Bastards," she said under her breath.

Someone was coming toward her; a woman. Agnes Dutra, on her way home from working in the kitchen of the Vista del Mar restaurant. Vista del Mar. Jesus, Mary and Joseph.

"Josinha."

"Agnes."

"Going to storm."

"Yes."

Now someone had seen her. Well. It didn't matter. Or perhaps it did, there was no telling.

On Dock Street, by the Upper Channel, she paused. Against her will she glanced at the spot where the *Albatroz* had been—looked away savagely. Now even Brewster's Wharf was gone. There was a pizza parlor where the sailmaker's loft had been, a noisy, smelly place patronized mainly by teenagers; she could see several figures slumped in front of the rainbow panels of slot machines, swaying. She stepped through the brash flare of light and into the shadows.

The old footbridge over the channel had been replaced by a blacktopped roadway the width of a car. She walked over it, peering down at the inky water, then left the road and moved up through the pine grove. Over here the wind was stronger, hissing its fine sea-roar in the gnarled branches. Her eyes were accustomed to the darkness now. Walking with more care she skirted the Simpsons' old saltbox, the low, ranch-style summer place of the Lovells'; Charlie Simpson's dog, an old Labrador, barked once, belatedly, then fell silent. The sky off toward Manomet Headland flickered.

When she reached the Bluffs she stopped and studied the windows. The main floor was dark, as she'd expected. There was a dim, low light in Chapin's bedroom on the northeast corner of the second floor. He'd called her early that evening, when he'd got down from Boston, wanting to see her, and she'd told him she wasn't up to it; concerned—or perhaps alerted by something in her voice—he'd wanted to come over, but she'd said no and had broken off the call abruptly. There was only one way she wanted to face him now. Yes. Only one. In the dark. Like another night. Maybe he only told the truth in the dark, in the night —when he was surprised. Shocked into it.

The truth.

Well, he was there now. Right up there. Reading late. Burning the midnight oil, you might say—making plans. Oh yes! Making plans . . . to lie and cheat and betray, to—

Louise's bedroom was dark. The cook always spent Friday nights with her sister in Harwich Port, and that was a blessing. At the far west corner, the big bedroom was dark, too. Serena was asleep there, dreaming her satisfied dreams. Yes, well, we'll see about that.

Here, in front of the great house, her pulse had begun to throb a little, but that was all. She slipped through the break in the high barberry hedge, the tiny thorns pricking her shoulders through the light jersey, and crossed the lawn, the hog cranberry springy and dense underfoot. From off toward Sagamore there came a low rumble of thunder, like naval gunfire, and the breeze died, sprang up again. Once on the long verandah she saw that the glass door was closed, and when she tried it she found it was locked. Trust Chapin. She cursed under her breath and stood there indecisively, her hand on the knob. She had been so certain there would only be the screen door with the catch on. Bloody Yankees! Lock up your very souls . . .

Very well, then. The back door. The Portuguese entrance. She went down the steps, slipped around to the rear. The apartment over the garage where Thompson lived was dark. He might have driven to one of the bars over in Yarmouth, but he also might be right up there, asleep or awake. If he heard or saw her, if he even thought he heard something—

Here only the screen door was hooked. She drew the knife and ran the blade along the edge of the wood, and the screening curled away soundlessly. She replaced the knife, unhooked the door. Sweat was sliding down her sides. The thunder rumble was nearer, more prolonged, and there was another dull flare of lightning. She gasped and looked back, but she was out of sight of the garage now. And again the darkness was total.

She passed cautiously through the pantry to the dining room and into the long living room, skirting the camelback couch and the grand piano. Light from the marina poured in the great windows and blared against the interior wall, where the glass on Chapin's Winslow Homer watercolors flashed like shields. For a moment she peered through the window, hearing over the rising barrel-tumble of the storm snatches of dance-band music and a medley of voices singing. That filthy marina, with its fiberglas powercruisers from Cape May and King's Point, nestled in side by side. Amateurs and drones. One big happy nautical cocktail party with all their radios blaring . . . Not one of them could sail. *His* marina, *his* filthy creation—

Her foot struck something with a low thump. She nearly fell to her knees, righted herself and paused, trembling now; bent over and felt the little needle-point footstool where it had never been before, in front of the cabinet. What was it doing there? Lightning flashed violently again, invested every object in the room with a blue sheen. She thought she heard a sound of movement on the main stairway and crouched utterly motionless, the blood pounding in her head now, thinking of Grampa and the Kanakas, that plan he had to hide below decks, waiting for them to come wandering through, hunting for trinkets; waiting, waiting in the close dark. *"The steel is always surer, criança. And it is silent."*

There was a small beacon-flash from below Blackfish Point, swinging here and there like a finger pointing. Searchlight. Vessel coming in, hunting for the buoy. The thunder boomed and echoed sullenly, the light kept playing over the harbor water, flickering. She was frozen in time, her thoughts swirling, surging forward and back, forward and back . . . Stand fast! she told herself fiercely. What is the matter with you! You're here, now. Here in this house. Now go on up those stairs and face him, tear away that mask of easy evasion, *force* him to speak; find out if there is any reason on this earth or under it that could—

There was a click behind her. The room blazed shockingly into light. She whirled around with a gasp. Chapin was standing by the dining room door in a beige silk robe, his face stiff with tension, his eyes narrowed. He was holding a shiny black foreign-looking pistol in one hand. His eyes dilated in immense surprise—then he relaxed with a snort of relief.

"Well—Jophy-girl! For God's sake! *What* are you up to?"

She said: "Breaking and entering."

He laughed softly, pointed above their heads. "Serena's here, you know."

"I know."

"Nevertheless, I'm glad you've come, darling. Like a thief in the night." Lowering the pistol he came toward her.

"Don't touch me!" she said suddenly.

"What?"

She averted her eyes—she didn't want him to see what was in them. Not yet. "Put that thing away," she said irritably.

He paused now, uncertain. "What's the matter?"

She watched him shove the pistol into the pocket of his robe. And now a gun, she thought. Trust him. Trust Chapin. A German pistol, that's what it was, something he'd picked up during the war. From someone else's battle. Well: we all had our curios, our souvenirs . . . She had only drawn in her breath when he'd surprised her. She'd made no other sound. She wondered if he'd seen the haft of the knife before she'd turned.

"Well," he said again. He was off-balance, intrigued and troubled at the same time. Sensing something, perhaps. Perhaps not. "Sorry if I frightened you—I had no idea you might be paying me a mad nocturnal visit. It's necessary to be a bit—circumspect, these days."

"Yes. I can imagine." Her voice was steady, even matter-of-fact, though her mouth was bone dry. Now, face to face with him under the lamp light, she felt cold, implacable. Quite ready.

"I can well imagine," she repeated. "Running

around with Arnie Koltisiak, all your gangster friends."

"Koltisiak?" His eyebrows rose. "He's no friend of mine . . ."

"*Associate,* then. Is that more palatable? Vicious swine."

He threw her the quick, sidelong glance. "Wherever did you hear that?"

"Here and there."

"Well, don't believe everything you hear, love."

"I never do. Only the things that are true."

He stared at her then—an amused, irritated expression. "Well, *you're* certainly in a festive mood!"

"No."

"The fiery, dramatic Josefina Gaspa," he proclaimed, as though he were presenting her at some grand function. "Avenger of the downtrodden . . . How Grama would have blessed you!"

"Yes, she would."

He moved off across the room, his back to her. "I believe I'll have a little nightcap. Care to join me?"

"Why not."

She watched him busy himself with his Great-Uncle Jeremiah's cut-glass decanter and two pony glasses.

"How'd you get in, by the way?" he asked casually.

"Walked in."

"Really? Curious. And I try to be so careful." He kept studying her—that covert glance out of the corners of his eyes—as though he knew something was wrong, all off-center and wrong, but he couldn't fit the pieces together. Angry at having been caught by him this way—how could he have moved so silently!—she felt irresolute again, overborne. Mistake. Standing around like this, while the minutes ticked away . . .

He came over to her again. She took the glass of brandy in her left hand and eased away from him.

"To a new life," he said, raising his glass, watching her.

"To a clean slate." The brandy licked hot at her throat and burned soundly in her vitals; living coals. There was a broad shutter-flash of lightning, and a savage crack of thunder that bowled off in a long, tumultuous cannonade.

"Wow—that was close," Chapin said. "Looks as if we're in for it tonight."

"Oh, yes. We're in for it."

At the same moment her eyes met the painting of the *Turandot,* heeled over, under full sail, on the wall above the record player; and all her rage came back in full force. A sign, she thought fiercely. Good. If one was needed.

"Isn't it curious," she said.

"What's curious, darling?" He'd moved uneasily over by the big leather wing chair.

"All these years you've talked about Grama, and my father Joseph, and even Frank Furtado . . . but never once have you mentioned my grandfather. Manuel. Manuel Gaspa. Don't you think that's strange, Chapin?"

She detected something—a flicker of misgiving, of sullen apprehensive surprise, something—she wasn't sure.

"Really? What an odd thing to say."

"Do you think so?"

He'd looked away now, at the harbor. "Oh, I think you're mistaken. I distinctly remember I—"

"No," she said, with such cool force it checked him. "Never once, in all these years. In fact you've never once alluded to the carnival—the one with Konomaku."

"The what?"

"Of course not—you missed it, didn't you? You decided not to go, at the last minute. Left Tip and me to go alone with Grama. Or the fire," she went on implacably, "—you've never once mentioned that, either. You know, the fire that destroyed the *Albatroz.* When

682

my grandfather was burned to death. Burned alive. To death. You remember *that* . . ."

His eyes had darkened now—had darkened around their pale rings, had dilated the way Serena's always did. His voice was brusque, rather edgy.

"Of course I remember it. I'd gone into the Army. You probably don't—"

"Oh yes, that same night. Very late that very same night . . . Was it a long drive, Chapin?" she said in her softest voice. "That narrow, twisting old road up to Boston? It's impossible to get the smell of burned flesh out of your head for days. I know. Not to mention the cries of a crippled old man, burning to death before your eyes . . ."

He was shaking his head at her now in flushed, angry disbelief, shaking and shaking his head. "Are you crazy—? Where in God's name did all this come from?"

"Or did you kill him first, Chapin? while he was sleeping? And then set the fire?"

"Jophy, of all the insane—"

"I *know,* Chapin." She eased a step nearer to him, holding the empty glass in her left hand, watching him very intently. "No more theatrics. No more denials. I know all about it."

". . . Serena," he said with weary, hollow chagrin. "Serena told you this." And then suddenly: "And of course you believed her."

"Yes. I believe her. And now *you've* just told me, too . . . Only *why?*" she said, and took another step nearer; she had not once taken her eyes from his face. There was a terrific clap of thunder high overhead, and a great bolt of lightning scribbled its mad calligraphy over the town. She raised her voice above the storm. "I need to know why, Chapin. Was it because he had so much courage—because he would risk everything, and had suffered so because of it? Was he a conscience to you? to your cowardice? your hatred for life? Was that why you had to kill him?"

His eyes had turned very flat and cold now, unwavering, the pupils starkly ringed with white; a look speculative and distant and utterly malevolent. She had never seen quite that expression before, on any human face—even in her savage rage she realized with a still, small shock what had produced that depthless terror in Jenny, what had finally broken her. It could have frightened *her* here, now, seeing it—it *would* have. Any other time. Any other night than this.

"Ah," she murmured in confirmation, and put her right hand on her hip. She was near enough now.

He was shaking his handsome head at her, but differently; the old bemused, supercilious smile again. "You could not *begin* to prove the remotest fraction of all that," he told her coldly. "You will break yourself if you try to make a case, I can assure you."

"Com toda a certeza."

In all her life nothing could have enraged her half so deeply as that reply: nothing! Impassioned denials, black remorse, a fever-flood of excuse and extenuation, even disconsolate rage—she had been prepared for any or all of these . . . But not this icy, malignant arrogance. She had never known such fury. Behind the squall struck in a hard slam of wind, and a wall of rain lashed the verandah and drummed against the screens. Chapin's face, the beautiful great room, darkened subtly, blurring.

All right. All right, then!

He had started to say something further, something insulting and threatful, but she heard none of it. With one swift, convulsive movement she flung the glass in his face, plucked the knife out of her belt and stepped forward and drove it up into his belly with all her might.

For an instant she thought she had missed. There was no sense of impact. Then with a high, sucking groan he doubled over and came against her, clutching at himself. She staggered backward, withdrew the knife in a dreamy, darkened red haze and swung again, hit something hard that jarred her to the shoulder, realized dimly it must be his arm, the bone of his forearm. Something hit her, hard, spun her half around, and at the same instant she heard a flat report like compressed air released, muffled in the booming uproar of the storm. The gun, she thought with a curious detached clarity, it has some kind of silencer on it, how clever of Chapin, he always thinks of everything. His face, lower than hers now, was white and strained, his eyes distended, his mouth gaped wide as if he might vomit or scream; but no sound came out of it as he struggled with her, dragging her down. Wrenching free she struck at him again, sobbing with the effort, and the gun went off once more —that empty, pneumatic *thoong* sound; then he'd dropped it and clasped his guts to him in both hands, had slid to the chair arm, to the floor, sitting awkwardly with one leg extended, the beautiful champagne of the robe staining richly, seeping.

She drew back, saw the gun lying near the chair leg, kicked it away across the floor in a spasm. Only then did she feel the leaden burning deep in her arm below the shoulder, realized she had been shot—and turning saw her own blood soaking the sleeve. She touched the wound gingerly, looked back at Chapin. He was still slumped against the chair, staring up at her—a look of boundless, stunned surprise.

"—Estuprador de mãe," she said, panting and dizzy. She bent over him, right in his face. "That is for killing my grandfather. And for making Tip ashamed of his work, his life. For destroying our love. And for fouling my fishing town . . ." His eyes still clung to hers, in glazed awful stupefaction. "Filho de puta. *Listen* to me! Yes—and for lying, lying, lying, turning every good thing on this earth dirty"—and now her eyes filled—"for twisting my love into something dirty, too—cheapening everything . . . Do you hear me?" she panted savagely.

His eyes narrowed—they wavered to the knife blade, darted over to the telephone on the little Florentine table by the wall. He made a faint, slow heave of his body, and then sank back with a low groan. His thighs, his groin were soaked thickly now, the fine old oriental rug around him.

"Of course!" she invited him, with cold raging scorn. "Go phone them —your lawyers and gangsters and your powerful old-school friends in Washington. Have them get you out of *this* . . . Go on, try!"

He understood now. He knew. His eyes, clearer and quite bright, came back to her; his lips curved in the echo of a sad, bitter smile.

"—Accident," he gasped out. His tongue seemed to have swollen too big for him to speak around it. "Didn't—know there—in cabin . . .!"

"What? *What?*" She crouched lower. "Mentes! You're lying—!"

He shook his head. "Only meant—burn boat. *Your* boat. *Yours.* Didn't . . ."

His words were lost in another rolling peal of thunder, the rain lashing against the windows; or perhaps he hadn't said anything more. She felt sick all at once, sank to an arm of the chair, still gripping the knife, holding her hurt arm tight against her body.

"I don't believe you!" she cried.

"Swear it. *True.*"

"*You*—swear!" She was sick with consternation, still raging with it. "Then why didn't you admit it? tell me—or anyone, anyone at all—!"

"—Too late," he breathed; he shook his head still again, but not in arrogance or denial. "All—too late . . ."

Then he went over, still clutching at his belly, and lay with his face pressed against the carpet, his mouth gaped wide.

Yes. It was all too late. The rain was falling in torrents, rumbling on the verandah roof and spattering from the downspouts. She had to get up. Slowly she got down on her hands and knees, bent her face low to Chapin's. It was pale as quartz; his eyelids kept lowering and then snapping open as though he knew he had to keep them open at all cost.

"No more games, Chapin," she told him solemnly. "No more lies, no more using people . . . There's an old Portuguese saying, Chapin. Can you hear me? 'When the game is over, the king and the pawn go into the same box.' Sim. The game is over, now."

To her surprise he nodded, staring hard at the rug. She got to her feet, staggered and righted herself, feeling sick again, very sick to her stomach and dizzy, as though the gale's electricity had set her inner compass spinning. She walked unsteadily over to the telephone table, looked at the phone cord, at Chapin again. No. He would never reach it now; she knew. And what difference did it make, anyway? It was finished. It was all over.

She set her grandfather's sheath knife down on the table beside the telephone. It was slick with blood, her fingers and knuckles were sticky with it, and while she stared down at the ivory handle blood dripped on the table and the floor from her elbow. There was no difference between her blood and Chapin's, and the thought depressed her deeply. Her arm hurt her more now, a hollow, grating pain. The thunder bumped and thumped sullenly, muttering, going off to the eastward, out to sea. She looked around the room with slow, dogged intensity. One of those fancy Abercrombie bush jackets Chapin affected was flung over the back of the couch and she took and wound it carefully about her arm; looked around her once more.

A voice, very faint and far away over the rain, calling. Serena; was it? Calling from upstairs? Go on

—call, Serena. Call for him. Cry for help! He is never going to come running any more.

Then she wasn't sure she'd heard anything at all. Holding her injured arm close she eased open the front door and went down the verandah steps into the lashing rain.

5

Tip swung the old pre-war Buick into the circular drive and braked hard to a stop, the big car skidding a little on the wet sand, killed the engine and ran up the verandah steps and flung open the screen door. The front door was standing open. Serena was sitting in her nightgown in the big Windsor rocker, her hair bound in the gauze net she always wore to bed, her head tilted forward primly, her back arched; perfectly still. Caught in the low light from the stand lamp she looked like an old portrait in profile, serene and self-contained.

Jesus Christ, he thought crossly. Tired and on edge from the wild two-hour drive down from Boston through the storm, prey to all kinds of eerie conjecture after her phone call (she had waked him out of a sound sleep, her voice cracked and shrill with hysteria, screaming that Chapin was hurt, terribly hurt, he must come at once, *at once!*—and abruptly hung up on him; he'd called back and got no answer), he was furious with her. Chapin had made a few allusions recently to what he called her "dotty fugues"—something Tip himself had doubted; but it certainly looked as if his brother was right.

"Now, Serena," he began, "now just what's—"

Then, stepping into the room, his eyes quickly adjusting to the near point, the light, he saw the body on the floor beside the leather chair. Chapin. Serena had turned toward him, her eyes huge in her white pinched face.

"Tipton," she was saying in a small, frightened voice, a voice he'd never heard her use. "Oh, Tipton, you came . . ."

He knelt down. Chapin was lying on his side, his head resting on one of the couch pillows—it had obviously been put there by Serena—a great moon of blood beneath him, bright against the faded reds and blues of the carpet. Tip felt for a pulse, glancing here and there distractedly, fighting the whole outlandish moment, its sheer shocking unreality—spotted the gun lying under the lowboy against the far wall and thought discordantly of Walter Diehl sprawled under his desk, the clamor of voices, the screams. But for *Chapin*—

No pulse. He looked down again, saw now the cheek's slick waxen pallor, the staring glazed eye, the open mouth.

"Why, he's *dead* . . ." he murmured in consternation. My God. Chay . . . dead. Serena was bent toward him, her face pinched in that importunate, timorous gaze; one hand, raised from her lap, shook in the air. "What happened?"

"You've got to help him, Tipton. Please help him . . ."

"He's dead," he repeated stupidly. She's in shock, he thought; been sitting there like that for two hours. Jesus. He said: "I'll have to call Chief Atwood."

"No—don't. Don't call. No police."

He stared at her blankly. "Why? What's the matter? Why didn't you get Thompson?"

"I sent him away. Told him you were coming." Her eyes flickered once with the old cunning. "He didn't see anything—I stopped him at the door." Her lips started quivering again. "You've got to help me, Tipton. Help us all."

"—But what *happened?*" he cried.

". . . She did it." Her voice was savage and querulous both, on the point of breaking. She drew breath

690

noisily, as if there wasn't either air or time enough for all she had to say.

"She?"

"I tried to tell him. I tried!" She wagged her old head vengefully. "He wouldn't listen."

"She?" he repeated. His aunt's eyes were still fastened on his in that vengeful, terrified glare. Suddenly she pointed a quivering, skinny arm toward the telephone table.

"There. There. Go on! See for yourself."

He followed her gesture, saw nothing; leaped to his feet and ran across the room—saw now the bone-handled knife streaked with blood, recognized it at once. A great cold fear sank through him. He started to pick it up, snatched his hand back.

"—*Jophy?*" he whispered.

"I tried to warn him and he wouldn't listen to me. He knew better." Her eyes were shut tightly now, her head was wagging about eerily. "He never would when it mattered most. Except once. Once he did."

"Where is she?" he cried, knowing the question was absurd even as he said it. "Where did she go?"

"*I* don't know. Care, either." She disclaimed any further knowledge with a single abhorrent shudder, pressed and pressed her hands against her bony thighs.

"Did you see her? here?"

"No—no. The storm—it was thundering and lightning so, I thought I heard voices, something . . . and then I thought I must have dreamed it, I've had such awful dreams, Tipton, *awful*—and then after a while, I couldn't get back to sleep and I came downstairs, the light was on, and there he was—on the floor . . ." She broke down, then, weeping fitfully, her head bobbing toylike. "Oh, Tipton, he was my life—ah, he was my whole life, you know that!—I only wanted what was best for him, what would make him happy. Surely you can see that . . ."

He had been staring at the knife, wanting to pulverize it, fling it into the sea, wish it out of existence; now he turned around slowly. Suddenly he knew a great deal.

"What have you done?" he said. "Serena!" He went up to her and took her by the shoulders. *"What did you say to her?"*

She looked up at him then, her mouth pursed and working—a terror-stricken, broken old woman, fantastic in the antiquated nightgown and hair net. The change was terrifying.

"Tell me!" he damanded.

". . . I told her," she stammered, "—about Chapin."

"Told her what about Chapin?"

"About the fire."

"Fire?" he echoed—all at once remembering now, remembering everything, catching it all up: that tense, troublesome morning at breakfast here, Serena's curious solicitude. *"What a tragic thing. What are they saying caused it?"* Her eyes so blue and level and measuring. *"You're not close, you two. Chapin rarely confides in others."* Everything that had nagged and nudged at him—Chapin's seclusion on the day of the carnival, his absence that evening, that astonishing departure for the Army and Serena's ignorance about where he was being sent—Serena, who always knew about addresses and time tables and destinations down to the last dotted I. *What are they saying caused it?* It seemed to him now, watching his aunt's panicky, distraught face, that he'd always known, and had simply allowed himself to forget.

Then he was guilty, too.

"So he did set the fire." He needed to say it aloud. "On purpose. And killed old Captain Gaspa. And you got him out of it. Helped him skip out. The way you've always done. So he never had to face anything, the consequences of anything. And now you had to tell her about it . . . What's the *matter* with you!" he shouted frantically. "What in Christ's name did you think you were trying to do . . .?"

"Now, don't be angry with me, Tipton—I couldn't stand that." She wiped at her eyes, sniffling hoarsely. "I couldn't let it happen," she said. "You can see that. I was willing to put up with her, even encourage her a little, here and there—you know, when you moved on to the Hill. I was willing to make my peace with her, even though it meant—"

"Serena, if you think—"

"But not with Chapin!" she exclaimed, and her eyes dilated fiercely, the old cat's glare; she reached out to him with one wildly shaking claw. "I couldn't let her work her will with him, ruin him the way she ruined you. I couldn't!"

He said nothing, listened to her in dulled, implacable despair. Jo. Jo.

"Vicious little trouble-maker—I warned him, I begged him, all but got down on my knees to him . . . and he only smiled at me! It was what *he* wanted. And now see—!" And she broke down again, her hand to her mouth.

"Yes," he said grimly. "I see, all right."

"My Chapin—ah, I devoted my whole *life* to him, you know that, ah God, dear, dear Chapin." She paused, staring. "But I never thought anything like this . . ."

"But she loved him," he murmured. "They were together—for years . . ."

"No. Never! Oh, he may have seen her once or twice: no more than that. No—she got round him, tricked him just the way she tricked you!"

He took his hands from her shoulders and moved away, feeling utterly helpless and desolate. "She never tricked anyone in her life. She's not like you, Serena. Not remotely like you. She never was." His voice was shaking. "No, you had to manage everything, as usual. *Arrange* things . . . You old fool," he said with the deep, hard frustration of a lifetime. "You poor, witless, meddling old fool. Now you've really done it."

"Tipton, I tried—"

"Yes. Didn't you, though. You've never learned anything—not the simplest God damned *human* thing. You judge everyone—everyone!—by your own warped, starved, pussy-footing standards, you can't *begin* to comprehend what a person like Jophy can feel, what she's capable of. You sit back there behind your money and your phony pretensions and you think that's what life is all about."

"Tipton, please don't attack me, I can't—"

"You've never understood anything, have you? A life-and-death commitment to anything. That open-hearted, surging—" He broke off, bound in anguish, very near tears himself. "No, you never have. For you it's all a nice, neat parlor-game—laced with just enough intrigue to keep it moderately exciting. And of course the filthy rotten capital. No wonder you had such a grip on him."

"Please, ah *please*, Tipton—"

"Jo is right. We wrecked ourselves fighting you, fighting each other because of you. Used ourselves up on it. All three of us."

He knelt down again and touched Chapin's cold smooth forehead, his cheek—a tender, helpless gesture; pressed the lid down over the glazed, glaring eye. He felt more affection for his brother at this terrible moment than he had in forty years, and the realization was unbearable.

"What a waste," he murmured, and his eyes filled. What a sorry waste . . . Old betrayals. What did they matter now?

"You've got to help, Tipton," Serena was saying to him again—a plaintive, croaking litany that maddened him. "You're always the one who knows what to do, dear. You always make it right."

"There's no way to make this right, Serena. No way at all."

He wandered around the room again, paused behind the big couch, trying to think, to force his mind away from this hideous, unreal tableau, grip the possibilities. He ought to call the police, he knew. He looked at the knife across the room. I could hide it, he thought insanely, desperately. If Thompson didn't see any of it, didn't see her leave. Hide it, get it back to Casa Gaspa and swear Serena to secrecy—God knows she ought to be good enough at that, keeping secrets; she didn't actually *see* her . . .

Crazy, crazy. There would be fingerprints everywhere, Jophy wouldn't have cared about that; someone could have seen her coming or going. What the hell was the matter with him! His thoughts kept grouping and then scattering like a flock of disoriented birds. There was no way to take hold of this . . . Why, he groaned aloud, why this once, just this once, did I let my own passion take over, my own pride. Year after year, loving her and waiting for her, being there when she needed me, or even if she didn't—why did I have to turn away that one moment, refuse even to listen to her? Drive her toward this. After a lifetime of feeling her in the very marrow of my bones, why should I have—

There was a dark spot on the back of the couch beside his hand; another. Bloodstains. He had seen them, had sensed what they were before his mind had registered the fact. He swung around and peered at Chapin lying there so still ten feet away—crossed quickly to the telephone stand again. Yes, drops on the floor there. More of them. Of course they could be from the knife, it wasn't—

He got down and picked up the Luger although he knew he shouldn't do so, caught the sharp powder smell. He didn't know how to pull back the receiver or eject the clip, but he knew it had been fired. Chapin, with the gun. Then the shock hit him, and a taut, panicky dread.

"Oh Jesus," he muttered. "Oh—my—Jesus . . . Serena, you're sure you didn't see her?" His aunt stared at him timidly, uncomprehending. He half ran to the door.

"Tipton, where are you going?"

"I've got to find her," he breathed.

"Oh please—you can't leave me here. Alone . . ."

"I've got to—I'll be back soon. Go upstairs. Go back upstairs."

"Tipton!"

He snapped on the porch light and ran outside. The verandah floor was slick with water, nothing else was visible. No blood. He stood there in the warm, wet wind, his heart leaping with fear. Hyannis Hospital. But she wouldn't have driven there. Think! Or Doc Glover's, she worked with him during the war. But if she went there . . .

How bad was it? Jesus God, *how bad was it?* Oh Jo—

He threw himself behind the wheel and roared around the drive, heading for Casa Gaspa.

6

The tide had turned. It was on the ebb now. The wind had fallen with the storm's passing; there was only an intermittent flicker low on the horizon, off to the northeast. Jophy walked along the shore of the Lower Channel, swaying a little on her feet. Now and then rain fell in light, haphazard patterns. She herself was on fire, all of her on fire, trembling, still fighting nausea; but her head was clear. The wounded arm didn't hurt so much now; though she was fearfully thirsty.

After a time she stopped and stared at the waves rushing in almost playfully, tumbling, sliding gray-light fans at her ankles: the old, sibilant, mesmeric rhythm that, along with her grandmother's voice, was the first sound she remembered. Out in the channel the bell buoy dipped its emerald cone, tolling an erratic one-note threnody. West-southwest she could make out a single light hanging low on the horizon. Out there lay Hurlestone Shoals, where they had drifted in a crystalline trance over the broken walls and swaying manes of seaweed, and Chapin had leaned over her, his eyes pale as star sapphires, and said—

Don't think of that.

She was shivering again, a quaking tremor that spun out from her body's core; shivering and consumed in fire. Don't think of it. Think of—think of Joey in Paris now, in shimmering Paris, in his own digs on the Rue Henry Barbusse (Chapin's had been "too rich for my Portagee blood"—she'd laughed aloud reading it, Tip's old line); he'd be in a blue work shirt and sailor's dungarees, black hair tousled, a red-tipped brush between his teeth, a smear of viridian on his forehead, filling a huge canvas with enviable isles, storm-lashed seas, night battles on barbaric coasts . . . sweet, fiery Joey, who used to race along the Back Beach towing that waggling old kite, with Tessa tagging behind . . . Tessa, and her gardens. She would always find a green spot, or make one. She'd be all right, in time. Tessa. Steady as Tip. Tip's girl. Tip—

No. No more of that.

She unwrapped the bush jacket gingerly from her arm, her eyes averted; drew the jersey with clumsy haste over her head with one hand, stepped out of her jeans and underclothes, and kicked off her espadrilles. She was shivering uncontrollably now, though the wind was warm.

You are a Gaspa. Manuel and Annabella Gaspa's grandchild. Come on, then.

The sea was cool, pleasantly cool—icy and fiery both; like dipping hot iron in a barrel of spring water. Why was that? It was almost midsummer. She waded forward, nearly fell, the water absurdly heavy against her thighs, then dropped forward and down, crying out with the pain as she moved the arm; rose and started stroking her way seaward in an easy, lazy crawl. The arm didn't hurt quite so much swimming, though it was stiff and leaden, throwing her off-rhythm; she felt so weak it made her angry. After a while she stopped to get her breath, treading water and squinting up into the night sky. There were no stars, but she didn't need them, she never lost her sense of direction. Over there, west by north, was Manomer Headland, its ocher cliffs the first far shore she'd ever seen, and two compass points north of it, Minot's Ledge . . .

Her father. Lost at sea. Or was it found? Grama

weeping and raging, inconsolable, and Grampa holding her to him with his great scarred arm.

"Assassinos! Porcos carniceiros! Ah, meu único filho . . . Bloodsucking Yankees—they will kill us all!"

Ah, Grama.

A tiny yellow light was sliding along to the northeast; trap boat going out, Tom Rodrigues, maybe. She started swimming again, harder, aiming for the bell buoy, grunting with the effort. The arm hurt her more now, a sickly grating sensation that fed the nausea.

—Think of past times, early morning with the sun sliding its diamond shawl over the harbor, the great net on Cunningham's Wharf swinging high above the cutting sheds, raining silver, and the dory coming in from the mooring, her father deep in the stern, the oarsmen pulling in a quick, lifting rhythm like her own now, the oars sounding their hollow, gourdlike *ratta-thunk, ratta-thunk* against the thole pins, and the gulls wheeling overhead . . . "My Josinha—! You been a good girl while I been gone?" Smelling of salt and sweat and tar, the wine-deep odor of the fishery . . .

—Another day, mysterious with fog, on the still deck of the *Sea Eagle*.

"Grampa, what's that plug for? in the bottom of the dory?"

"To let the sea water out, when it's nested after the day's catch."

"But what's that loop of line on the bottom of the plug?"

"That's to hang on to criança. When she's capsized. Your father spent seven hours on a dory's bottom, hanging on to that grommet. There is a reason for everything aboard ship, Josinha . . ."

A reason for everything.

The buoy was quite near now, heaving its iron cage into the sky, clanging shrilly whenever she turned her head to breathe. Tired. Very tired now. Keep swimming. For an instant she wanted to stop and look back toward shore and fought down the impulse fiercely, flooding her mind with memory.

. . . The *Albatroz*, battered and proud at Brewster's Wharf, and she was playing "Hester Banning," her favorite game; she'd bound her breasts in a canvas bodice to hide her sex from the rest of the crew, gone aloft to reef or furl in all weather and never once shown her fear; she was going to scour the whole watery world of the Pacific until she caught up with the man who had betrayed her, and then she would—

Yes. That.

Well.

But he said it was an accident.

An accident, he didn't mean to, didn't know Grampa was there. He swore that to me, dying.

How could that be? *How could it—!*

Yet it was so. She knew it with a terrible certainty that clutched her in a remorse so strong she felt she could smell it in the tossing seas around her. She took a big swallow of water and brought up coughing, wagging her head crossly, sobbing her laughter at her fear; talking to herself now.

Can't swim any more. Can't. *You will.* No time to stop now. The current was pulling her eastward. Of course. Beyond the buoy the chop was heavier, and the swell had begun, lifting her powerfully. She switched to breast stroke now, kicking hard, her arms barely keeping her head above water. The bullet wound burned like ice drawn over her flesh, draining away all her strength. She gritted her teeth. Once you go on the whale, Grampa said, there must be no turning back. Ever. "The sea is our country," he said. "We belong to the sea." Rogue whales and stove boats and long nights adrift, terrors by night and day . . . Oh, Grampa. If I hadn't left the ball with Chapin. If I hadn't given in to that pull toward him—

Don't think of that. Don't!

Why not? Why not, now, here? Face it, Josefina. Face all of it.

So. The *Albatroz* that first morning, playing at "Hester Banning"—and there he was, grinning at me; and my hat falling off. Just as if he'd seen a magic trick. Dear Tip. Dearest Tip. All of us lost at sea, o pecado mortal.

The sea kept surging toward her, drawing her on. In the corner of her eye she caught a final glare of lightning, blue and unearthly: St. Elmo's fire. Ghosts of drowned men, Grampa said; a sign of death coming for others. He said the ancient giant turtles were the souls of ships' officers come back to life. O pecado eterno . . .

She couldn't swim much farther, she knew it. The sea looked harder now, more metallic, heaving steely lights, and the sky had lightened subtly. First light. It would be morning soon.

And she—what had she done? Betrayed them all, somehow. How could that be? She who loved them so, loved life so. Only wanted to set her own course. Yet her passion had undone her, undone them. Had it? And now she had robbed Chapin of life, too. What right had she?

"Não faças caso, Josinha: a fé é que nos salve, e não o pau da barca." Grampa nodding, his lips curving sadly under mustaches. It is faith that saves us, and not the ship's planking.

No. For her there was only trust. Trust between heart and heart. One golden hawser that must not slip, no matter what, or everything foundered. What Tip always had; like Grampa. Tip. Best of all. You cared—cared about people. Grama knew.

Tip. Beloved of all . . . Tip, forgive me.

The buoy was far astern now, faint as an echo, the dream of a bell tolling. "All—gone!"—the sailor's cry from aloft when he had loosed sail. The dark surge of waves was everything, lifting and sinking. Mighty. A tumbling wilderness of wind and water. The pain had dulled, her legs had lost all feeling now. Too late, as Chapin had said. She was going soon, she knew it. Let it come. She would choose her own passage the way she always had.

Eastward the horizon lightened swiftly, bathed the oncoming combers in a dull, nacreous sheen. Wings of the morning. "A dying whale always turns his head to the sun, criança." Though I dwell in the uttermost parts of the sea, in great waters, the sea in ships, for those in peril. Ah Tip, forgive. Lead me not into temptation. But deliver from. Deliver me. All—gone!

Tip.

Oh, take me now.

The last sound she heard was a distant bell.

He found the espadrille first. And then the rest of her things. There was no question. He knew as surely as if he, not Chapin, had taken the knife. He stood there on the shore, holding the narrow rope sole in his hand, weeping, staring at the empty night sea.

Jo. Oh my God, Jo. Why couldn't you wait, why couldn't you *wait* for me. I would have made it right somehow. You knew I'd come . . . It was as if he could hear her laughter: It's you who've waited too often for me, Tip. Not this time. This was mine, to do alone . . .

He sank down to the wet sand and wept as only a New England Yankee weeps, holding it hard inside him, choking it back, half-blinded, his shoulders shaking.

I wanted to bring you every golden thing. But I was wrong. You wanted only sea and sun, the green rush of every moment. We think we evade our derelictions, but we never do: something far down inside us wants to pay off the debt. Paid in full . . . You were not like the rest of us. Our rivalries, our bargains were so cheap beside you—meager and hollow. Forgive us our debts. As we forgive—

Oh Jo. I betrayed you, we all did. We measured you by the wrong soundings.

Home now. You're home free.

He sat there weeping in silence until the sky was edged with gray off toward the east; then he got to his feet with a low moan. He must take care of things. There was no one else to do it. He would have to get up and go on.

Nearly morning now. He left the channel as the light broke over the bluff. But he turned back once when the breeze awakened, fretted the sea, touched his hair.

South wind.

COMING IN OCTOBER

AN INDECENT OBSESSION

The National Bestseller by

Colleen McCullough

Author of THE THORN BIRDS

This dramatic novel unfolds on a remote Pacific Island in an Australian military hospital. World War II is just over, but not for nurse Honour Langtry, who runs Ward X—the ward for soldiers with "invisible" wounds, those whose souls have been scorched and blackened by jungle warfare. Honour's job is to help put them back together again while maintaining her own emotional distance. But when a new and unexpected patient arrives, Honour's caring for him turns to love, and the ward's hidden frustrations, secret passions, and subtle jealousies come to the surface—pulling them all toward a shocking spectacle of violence.

"Leaves one's pulse racing a little faster...Miss McCullough is a natural storyteller."
— *The New York Times*

"An intelligent tale of love and human responsibility."
— *Chicago Sun Times*

"A stunner."
— *Library Journal*

AVON Paperback

60376-4/$3.95

Ind. Obs 7-82